PRAISE FOR

hula girls

"This novel is an emotional journey with great storytelling and a satisfying ending. It can inspire readers to contemplate gender roles and conflicts arising from World War II that have left an impact on our world today."

—*The US Review of Books (Recommended)*

"Though it covers only three decades, this story has the feel of a saga and is as satisfying as one. A wonderful evocation of a time and place and a woman's indomitable spirit."

—*Kirkus Reviews*

"This is an immersive novel that examines how one reconciles with the past, while providing insight into American women's changing roles in the mid-twentieth century."

—*BlueInk Review (Starred Review)*

"*Hula Girls* is a gritty historical novel in which a woman becomes a widow and experiences gradual flourishing."

—*Foreword Clarion Review*

also by eric b. miller

Little Known Stories: Prose in Format

hula girls

A Novel

eric b. miller

MILBROWN PRESS
Denver

Cover illustrations: Emily Shirron, Unsplash (*front*); Maarten van den Heuvel, Unsplash (*back*). Author photo by Larry J. Cohen.

Published by Milbrown Press
An imprint of JBM Publishing Company
1265 South Columbine Street
Denver, CO 80210
(303) 503-1739

Printed in the United States of America

ISBN: 978-0-9906893-3-1 (paperback)
ISBN: 978-0-9906893-7-9 (ebook)
ISBN: 978-0-9906893-9-3 (hardcover)

Publisher's Cataloging-In-Publication Data

Names: Miller, Eric B., 1948– author.
Title: Hula girls : a novel / Eric B. Miller.
Description: Denver, CO : Milbrown Press, [2021]
Identifiers: ISBN 9780990689331 (paperback) | ISBN 9780990689393 (hardcover) | ISBN 9780990689379 (ebook)
Subjects: LCSH: Navy spouses—Hawaii—20th century—Fiction. | Mothers—United States—20th century—Fiction. | World War, 1939–1945—Hawaii—Fiction. | Man-woman relationships—Fiction. | Sacrifice—Fiction. | LCGFT: Domestic fiction.
Classification: LCC PS3613.I5361 H85 2021 (print) | LCC PS3613.I5361 (ebook) | DDC 813/.6—dc23

Cover and page design by Pratt Brothers Composition

To my mother Erica and my wife Lisa,
who would recognize little of themselves
in this, but Claudia Wyler didn't just
come out of nowhere.

CONTENTS

ACKNOWLEDGMENTS

I would like to thank Tom Locke for a monumental editing job, Dan and Jim Pratt of Pratt Brothers Composition for their good taste in design and text, and Tracy Jones for last minute saves in proofreading.

I extend my apologies to *Woman's Home Companion* for putting words in the mouth of a fine extinct publication, and to the State of Hawaii for liberties taken with topography.

I am most indebted to my true and stalwart brother Jeff. Without his administrative energy and creative input, *Hula Girls* never would have gone anywhere.

AUTHOR'S NOTE

Hula Girls is based on a true story I made up.

ebm 2021

PART ONE

"Are You Making Your House a Home,
or Spending Your Nights Alone?"

—PENELOPE J. TWIGDEN. *WOMAN'S HOME COMPANION*, NOVEMBER 1941

CHAPTER ONE

There were pretty palm trees swaying in the wind. There were red flowers and yellow flowers and lavender flowers, white blossoms in the hedges and tangles of green vines growing over anything that wasn't nailed down. There were high white clouds and black ones thick with rain, soaring from the endless horizon of blue-and-turquoise ocean, and from time to time over the grassy bluff at the end of the backyard, antennas and turrets of gray navy ships went by, heading out to sea. It was too beautiful for words. She could write that to Mom and Dad, leaving out the ships. "It's too beautiful for words!!" She did not think she had said it before, at least not in those words.

After the breakfast dishes, Claudia Wyler sat down at the kitchen table with her coffee and her first Chesterfield and leafed through *The Newlywed Cookbook* and wondered what Jack might like for dinner. She already knew about tonight, but looking through the book was the way you got ideas. Mom was right about that. She was right about all kinds of things. She was right about the blue blazer. There wasn't enough room to bring many of her clothes on the boat, but Mom made her take the blue blazer because she said there was no such thing as a blonde without a blue blazer. Claudia liked the padding in the shoulders. She had to stand up straight in the vonrensberger, and it gave her self-confidence when she went into town. One or two sailors always whistled at her if she went by the navy yard. You can get a lot of self-confidence from your clothes. Everything in *The Newlywed Cookbook* looked delicious. She was getting so many ideas she couldn't remember them all.

When Claudia finished her coffee and two more Chesterfields, it was time to wash the sheets again. She wheeled the washer out of the back room into the kitchen. She screwed the brass coupling of the stiff black hose to the hooked end of the faucet in the sink and turned it on. Then she settled down with her elbows on the rim of the tub to watch it fill up with hot water. She could have gone to get the electric wringer out of the back room, but that would only save time, and there were too many hours in the day left to fill up. Jack told her it wasn't all going to be clear sailing and breeze astern. Sometimes you just ride at anchor. So she was going to learn patience. It was the Order of the Day.

Jack couldn't teach her how to be a navy wife. She was on her own for that, and she would have to teach herself. There were things like patience and being alone most of the time. Patience was watching the washtub fill up so slowly and not getting annoyed. Looking at water for a long time was good for learning patience, and she sure was in the right place for looking at water.

There was nothing but ocean all around, stretching out forever to the horizon. When she turned to let the little cat in through the screen door, she could see high jungle green going up the mountains out in front of the house across the little macadam road, and ragged rain clouds hung up in them like dirty cotton candy. It was very far from Connecticut, where it was the day before Thanksgiving, just like it was here—although maybe not. The paper said President Roosevelt just changed it to the week before. But it didn't really matter. Everybody in the navy was going to go to work anyway.

There might be snow by now in Connecticut with Christmas coming, and Claudia felt again how far away she was from home. There were strange plants here with big green leaves and it never got cold. People going by on the road out front, walking down to Honolulu, were always in short pants and bare feet. It was mostly the native people. There were only natives and navy men, and lots of pineapples. Trucks full of pineapples, big dirty farm trucks one after the other, whenever she came out of the hairdressers in town, throwing all that dust in the air.

Claudia noticed that she had begun to pull strands of her hair and twirl them between her fingers when she sat at the table with her Chesterfields and 7Up. It wasn't really anything to do with her hair. She loved her hair. She loved being a natural blonde. You could tell when a girl wasn't. It was her crowning glory, just like they said in the ads. She was thinking of letting it get long like Veronica Lake—but then people would be disappointed to see it was only you and not Veronica Lake, and why would you want your husband thinking about Veronica Lake all the time?

Claudia took the box of Rinso out of the cupboard under the sink and measured a cup and poured it into the tub, and when the water was all the way up, she went to the bedroom to get the sheets. One thing at a time. She unplugged the toaster and plugged in the washer and watched the agitator jerk back and forth. It was fascinating to watch. Thirty minutes to wash, then fifteen minutes to rinse, and when the pump would not drain any more water, she took the hose out of the sink and let it go into a bucket on the floor. The little cat was sitting in the open door of the lower cupboard.

"Do you want to watch the wringer now, little cat?"

"Sure," she replied to herself. "Heave to and on to the wringer!" It was the part she liked best. Claudia put the electric wringer over the tub and plugged it in. She snapped the big black knob to ON, and the rollers whirred into each other like there was nothing it couldn't flatten, flat as a pancake. Sometimes she jammed it on the sheets. It took practice to feed them in right. It could grab too much and blow a fuse trying to flatten big things like sheets or Jack's canvas deck shoes. Claudia was learning to treat the wringer just like people. You have to watch your fingers.

Jack did not like a laundry line in the yard, so she put it up and took it down every day. She unfurled the sheets in the steady wind off the ocean and pinned them tight. The waves broke way out, and all that thundering too far away to hear came down to nothing but little laps down at the beach. The wind was the only thing that made noise, roaring through the palms and brush and vines. She held her dress down as she went back to the house, even though the cars in the neighborhood were gone. It was only the girls at home, but when you were married, it wasn't like school. You had a man, and you wanted your privacy. Each girl in the little white houses along the road had a man. One kind or another. Jack was the best. He was tall, dark, and handsome, and she was blonde and beautiful, and more than a few times people said they looked like the couple in the Ipana ad with the great-looking teeth.

It was only nine-thirty. Claudia oiled the frying pan and put it away. She took the dishes out of the new drain board Jack had brought home. She would not have spent the money on it, even though it was only a quarter, but Jack said that was what money was for, to get things she would not have bought herself. He was so considerate, even after a year of being married. Then she took out the dust mop and ran it under the bed so Jack would not see dust when he did his push-ups tonight, and then she did the other bedroom and the hallway that ran down the middle of the house, and then around the rugs in the living room and dining room. She got out the sweeper and did the rugs, and before she knew it, she was done.

It was that way with everything in such a little house with only two people. The dusting, the cleaning, the wash, the cooking. Before you knew it, you were done, sitting at the kitchen table again, having another Chesterfield, tracing with one finger the shapes on the tabletop. They were like a photograph of marble, or like looking at marble in water through a glass-bottomed boat. It was called Formica. It was the latest thing. She wondered what the latest thing was doing in a place like this. It was in the house when they moved in. You could clean up even the worst mess in a jiffy. It was pleasant to look at and mesmerizing if you looked at it too long. Then she noticed herself twirling strands of her hair again.

Thank goodness they had Chesterfields and 7Up in Hawaii. She had been silly to worry. The navy had everything from America. Jack said if he were assigned to Timbuktu then Timbuktu would have Chesterfields and 7Up because the United States Navy was so great. They even had Kotex pads for the active young navy wives, so she could put tennis and the rumba back on her okay list on those "difficult days." Jack said in a year or two they could move into a bigger house on the other end of the island, and everything Jack said came true.

Jack only went on one cruise before he got the desk job, and that counted as his year in the fleet because his dad had connections in the War Department. He left the day after they got to Hawaii, only ten days after they were married in Connecticut. She was so upset. She imagined him on night watch, going overboard and disappearing into the dark waves, but then she went down to the navy yard to see him off and saw how big the ships were, like looking up fourteen floors to their room at the Astor on their one-night honeymoon. She cried anyway. Jack said he would be back before you know it, and he was, in only a month, but it seemed a little longer than before you know it.

He had been out to some islands and back. It was secret. Not top secret or most secret, just secret. There were different kinds of secret. Jack said there were going to be things he could not tell her because he was in Naval Intelligence. She was so proud of him and how responsible he was, even though he was only twenty-four and nobody would expect it of him. The navy probably did, and Jack was all navy, so no mystery to that.

Claudia was glad he wasn't one of those men you had to push. He loved the navy so much. She had only pushed about getting married, and sometimes she wondered if she was going to be sorry for it someday because he still acted like a college boy, the way he looked at girls. She noticed that Jack never looked at blondes. He was probably the only man in the world who didn't, and just her luck, he was the one she talked into marrying her.

Claudia planned her New England boiled dinner for tonight. She always thought New England boiled dinner was god-awful, but now it reminded her of home, and she had a brisket of beef in the icebox ready to make sail for the dinner table. She cut up her potatoes and carrots and cabbage wedges and put them in a bowl. She could wipe the beef and put it in the pot about one o'clock and put the vegetables in when Jack came home. He could get out of his uniform, relax, and have his gin and tonic.

It was almost eleven. Claudia started looking out the window for Mary Ann's car. She tried not to look too often because every time she looked out, Mary Ann's little boy, Edgar Lee, saw her and popped up in the window with Petey the puppy beside him and they had such sad faces being locked in the house with Mrs. Bigalow all morning while Mary Ann was down in Honolulu doing the bookkeeping in a filling station. She always smelled of gasoline when she came home. Her husband, Bill, smelled of gasoline too. He was in a supply depot for the ships. He was only a spec-something, whatever they call it, after fifteen years in the navy. Bill and Mary Ann were never going to get out of the little white houses. You had to come out of Annapolis or you wouldn't get anywhere in the navy. Bill had to salute Jack and Jack had to return it, so they avoided each other.

Mary Ann was cautious around her at first. Claudia thought Mary Ann might be afraid she could tell Jack to demote Bill or transfer him and Jack could probably do it, but now they were just regular girls with each other. Girls had to stick together. It was understood between them that nothing they said was to get back to their husbands, although Claudia did not quite trust it and tried not to say anything personal about Jack.

Claudia envied Mary Ann in one thing. She would love to go to town every day to work in an office and have friends. But right from the start, Jack said navy wives did not work. Then he always had to clarify that it was officers' wives who didn't work because he knew Claudia would bring up Mary Ann. Once in a while he said flat out he would not let his wife work. Claudia understood, but she thought there would be more point to it if there were a baby on the way. Jack did not seem too interested in that. She wondered what she could do differently. Nights were always the same. Jack liked to read the paper with his gin and tonic. Then he had the radio shows he put on during dinner so he would not be bothered by her asking him how his day was. His days were always fine.

Claudia did not want to feel sorry for herself. That was one of the warning signs *Woman's Home Companion* told you to look for. It meant trouble ahead. She went to clean the bathroom and by the time she was finished, Mary Ann was home and she went over for coffee.

Mary Ann was a dear, but she was such a mess. It was a shame because she wasn't a bad-looking girl at all. She was only in her mid-thirties, but she had let herself go. She was short and pudgy. Not the young pudgy—the middle age pudgy where your arms get flabby. And her bosoms were too big. There was nothing she could do about that, but the least she could do was find a brassiere with better lift. The new Lastex yarn could give her a flawless fit and the youthful, separated uplift that smart moderns want in their lingerie, along with corrective support. But it was no use trying to explain that to Mary Ann.

Her best asset was a cute face, and when you come down to it, the face is everything, isn't it? Mary Ann had a cute little nose and plump cheeks and rosy skin, which was a blessing because there isn't much you can do with foundation in a humid climate. Thank goodness for Pond's four-step beauty ritual, which gives you petal-smooth skin. Mary Ann never said a word about her weight either. That was very unusual. She was always eating something whenever Claudia came over.

"Do you want any cottage cheese?"

"No, thank you. Coffee is fine."

"Anything new?"

"I heard your telephone ring," said Claudia. "Two times."

Mary Ann went to the back door.

"Stay in the yard, Edgar Lee," she called. "We'll go to the beach later."

She came back and sat at the kitchen table across from Claudia with a dish of cottage cheese with pineapple slices on top.

"Want to go to the beach later?"

"Sure. What time?"

"How about right after lunch. Then I can make Edgar Lee lie down for a nap."

"Okay, fine."

"I wonder who called."

"I wish I'd get a call."

"You only get calls when you're gone, honey. Do you think I ever get a call in the afternoon? No siree."

"So tell me the latest on Bob and Susie."

"Oh that. Okay. Let's see. Oh, I didn't tell you this. Big development. Susie said Bob's wife came around to her apartment Sunday morning, and she took off her shoe and threw it through the window and kept shouting, 'I know you're in there, Bob.'"

"Oh, not really."

"Oh, yeah. Susie said she had to call the police. Bob got out the back window before they got there, and he sprained his ankle jumping down."

"She's such a fool," said Claudia.

"Who?"

"Susie—who do you think?"

"I'm not taking sides."

"Well, of course not. She's your friend."

"Not that much. I mean, I talk to her. She calls when I'm in the middle of my receivables, and it's hard to do numbers when she's going on and on, and Mr. Sterrin doesn't like the phone tied up either. The only reason I even pay attention is I know you'll want to hear details."

"Well, I just think it's interesting, don't you? It's like a story in *Woman's Home Companion*. Sometimes I'll read one and think about it all day. I wonder what I would do if my husband had an affair or if I found out my mother-in-law thought I was a tramp. It's really fun to read stories like that because they really make you think."

Mary Ann laughed. "Not like the real thing makes you think, let me tell you."

Claudia put her hand up to her mouth in surprise. "Oh no, Mary Ann. You had the real thing? Which one?"

"Let's say I've been around long enough to have them all."

"Did Bill have affairs—Oh, I'm sorry. I don't mean to be nosy."

"That's okay. Let me have one of your Chesterfields."

"Oh sure. That means a good story, doesn't it?"

"Not much, sweetie. It weren't no big passion."

"But it was an affair, wasn't it?"

Mary Ann lit one for Claudia too and took a big inhale.

"It was more like fooling around. We were about your age, twenty-three, twenty-four?"

"Twenty-three."

"Yeah okay, about like that. Ten years ago we were like you and Jack. He fell for this dumb blonde."

Claudia looked down at the ashtray between them, and Mary Ann caught herself right away. Claudia knew she had a good heart and would not hurt her feelings on purpose.

"It's just an expression. You know."

Claudia could not help but smile. People were always surprised at how intelligent she was, and she always took it as a compliment to her hair. Sometimes she felt like doing something different with it, but she didn't want to ask Mary Ann. Mary Ann would tell her what to do without thinking twice, without due consideration for important factors like bone structure, and she'd have to go along just to be polite.

"So what happened?"

"Well, like I said, it wasn't any great passion. He just wanted to fuck somebody else for a change."

Back at home by herself, Claudia had a cheese sandwich for lunch and a 7Up. It was such a disagreeable word. It always disturbed her, and Mary Ann said it almost every day. She realized after a while that she was on edge with Mary Ann half the time just waiting for it. Mary Ann was a little coarse. Jack did not always have to explain the difference between officers and enlisted men. Claudia could see it for herself, and she realized at the first mixer for officers' wives that in the navy, you were what your husband was. It shouldn't be any surprise for bad words to come out of Mary Ann. She probably got it from Bill.

It was just like Mrs. Bigalow, the neighbor on the other side. She put Claudia on edge as much as Mary Ann. She was so sweet otherwise, but she said a bad word when she had something to say about colored people. Her husband was a civilian engineer, and he came to Hawaii in the '30s to work on the harbor. They would probably stay in the little white houses too, long after she and Jack moved up the ladder. Then she could start all over with new neighbors. Jack said the houses higher on the ladder were not so close to each other, and she would not have to get to know anyone who made her uncomfortable.

Claudia put on her suit and looked out the window for Mary Ann. Then she put on her blue robe and took her Chesterfields and the lighter Jack gave her and a bottle of 7Up and a towel and walked down to the beach beside Mary Ann, with Edgar Lee and Petey running ahead. She put her hair in a ponytail with a rubber band and lay down on her towel. It was glorious weather again, like always. They came to the beach almost every day, and Claudia turned over every ten minutes while they were there to make sure she tanned evenly. Her legs were so golden that she didn't need nylons, but she wore them anyway when she went to town or went out with Jack because she liked wearing a girdle, and anyway, bare legs are indecent. She had a nineteen-inch waist and she liked a tight pantie-girdle or a good all-in-one. It wasn't easy, but she found some girdles in Honolulu that looked no bigger than rumpled socks when you held them up.

Mary Ann was a different story, all around, starting with her hair. Obviously, she had given up on it ages ago. She said it was naturally curly, and then the sea air made it worse, and there was nothing she could do about it. Claudia tried to explain how she could add body and luster to it with eggs. There were other ways to spotlight the beauty in your hair, but Mary Ann said she didn't really care, so it stayed the way it was, as dull as brown could be, curly, but going in all directions at the same time. Claudia also suggested that Mary Ann might want to get the kind of bathing suit that had the little skirt around the bottom, but Mary Ann did not care about her heavy thighs or what else showed. It was no use. There was nothing subtle or discreet about Mary Anne's body. It was just a broad expanse of brush, prairie, and rolling hills that civilization had passed by.

And if you ever doubted the value of wearing a good stout brassiere under your nightgown at night, Mary Ann was a good example of what could happen if you didn't. Claudia tried to tell her that once or twice, and about wearing panties at night because she read in a magazine strictly for girls about that sagging too.

"Don't wait for the danger signs, Mary Ann," she said.

"What danger signs?"

"They're in *Modern Girl* magazine. There are twelve of them."

"I don't get *Modern Girl*," said Mary Ann. "I'll take my chances."

But to tell the truth, Claudia did not know what she would do if she had Mary Ann's negative thinking, which was the biggest beauty challenge of them all when it came to self-improving Mary Ann. She would probably stay in the house. She wouldn't be caught dead letting herself go. It was a slippery slope, but she knew she was different. It always brought to her mind Mammy trying to get Scarlet O'Hara into her corset in the movie. She knew she could get her figure back too if she had a baby. She would be determined, and even if the Yankees captured all the little white houses and she had to eat dirty carrots out of a field to keep from starving, she would never neglect her figure.

Mary Ann watched Edgar Lee and Petey play in the shallows. She hummed "Bewitched, Bothered and Bewildered" over and over and only seemed to know the line "I'm wild again, beguiled again." Claudia sunned. She always thought about so many things when her eyes were closed. She should shave her legs before Jack got home. Maybe he would be in a good mood tonight. She had to get the meat boiling right away so it could simmer for three hours. She had to get the laundry line down. She had to iron the sheets and make the bed and mop the kitchen floor and press Jack's trousers for tomorrow and iron one of the shirts she washed for him yesterday. Why did they call their navy shirts blouses? Nobody knew. That's the navy for you. Jack always said it just like that. "That's the navy for you."

CHAPTER TWO

Claudia could not sleep that night and got out of bed at two o'clock. Jack was sound asleep. She found her brassiere and panties and nightgown at the bottom of the bed and pulled them out without waking him up. She put them on again and took her bathrobe off the back of the door and tiptoed out. She sat in the dark at the kitchen table with her Chesterfields. She did not know what to think. When Jack didn't want her, she felt blue, and when he did, she felt bad afterward. She guessed she was admitting something for the first time. She wondered what it was. It was facing reality, that's what it was. *Woman's Home Companion* said that was good for you.

Claudia went outside to the backyard, to the way back and over the grassy bluff down to the beach, where the sand looked so white in the dark. It was almost windless for a change and she could hear the waves break way out. The ocean was black except for the white lines of surf, and the sky was black with a million billion stars. Sometimes there were ships out there, steady little lights, but tonight all the boats were in bed, and it was just black.

She took off her robe and brassiere and panties and just dropped them behind her and walked into the dark water. If there were snoopy people around at that time of the morning, she didn't care. She wanted to be naked outside. God knows what came in close to shore at night, but she was thinking about Jack and got out to her chest before she woke up and realized there was nothing out there but scary dark and stars. Panic seized her. She turned around and barely kept herself from thrashing back to shore as fast as she could, yanking her last foot from the water as if there were shark jaws right at her heels. Then, safe on shore with the sand still warm from daytime, it struck her as funny that she was subject to such primal fears of predators in the water and the big black universe. Facing reality was nothing compared to that.

Claudia dried herself with her robe, and with the breeze picking up, her hair was almost dry by the time she got to the house. It was only four o'clock in the morning. She left the door open, and by starlight she found Jack's shoes, the Kiwi shoe polish, the brush, and a clean rag. It was important for Jack to have polished shoes. She did all his spit shines the way he taught her. It was lovely and warm on the porch steps. There was hardly any reason to have doors or windows on the houses here. Claudia arranged the polish, brush, and rag beside her on the step. Then, cradling Jack's shoes in her arms, she fondly beheld the hard, black footwear of the man to whom she had dedicated her life, her husband, Jack, Lieutenant Jack Wyler, United States Navy. She worked with humility, brushing and polishing Lieutenant Jack Wyler's shoes until she could see the stars in the shine off their toes.

The next thing she knew, Jack was shouting goddamnit far away in the house, in the bedroom, and then he was picking her up off the porch, and it was daytime.

"I fell asleep," she said.

"What are you doing out here? I'm late."

"I'm sorry, Jack. I got up to shine your shoes and I was going to stay up to wake you at five."

"Oh, Jesus. Thanks. It's six thirty."

"I'm sorry."

"It's all right. Never mind. I've got to get going. Go hook up the hose for me. I have to shave in two minutes."

Jack went off to the bathroom, and Claudia got up and looked at her hair in the little mirror over the sink. He wouldn't notice it wasn't brushed, and he sure wasn't going to stick around to see how silky it could be with the boar-bristle brush that brings out the natural oils and leaves your hair lustrous and full-bodied. She shook it out and put it behind her ears with a headband and went out and around the side of the house. The garden hose lay coiled up on the little cement patio under the kitchen window. She slid back the long, heavy kitchen window and flopped the end of the hose inside. When she got back inside to the sink, she realized she had put the wrong end of the hose through the window and had to go outside again to switch ends. She screwed it onto the kitchen faucet and turned on the hot water so he'd be all ready to go.

"I need the hot water," he shouted.

She quickly turned it off. "Sorry."

"What?"

"I'm sorry," she called out. "I was getting your shower ready." Claudia heard the running water go off in the bathroom.

"What?"

"I said I was getting the water warm for your shower. Sorry."

"Oh, Jesus, honey, I'm shaving. I can't talk now."

The water in the bathroom went back on, and Jack shouted that he couldn't hear her over the running water, and every time she said something, he had to turn it off and stop shaving to hear her, and he didn't have time to fool around like that.

Claudia got the bread out of the breadbox. She made him a cream cheese and jelly sandwich and wrapped it in waxed paper. Jack came out of the bathroom with shaving cream behind his ears and a towel around his middle and hopped gingerly over the gravel outside the door to get around to the patio.

"Okay," he said.

Claudia turned on the water at the sink and waited. The towel came down and Jack held the hose over his head and looked up into the water.

"A little more hot."

Claudia opened up the hot side a little.

"Okay. Right there."

Claudia watched him when he turned the other way. He dropped the hose and began to soap up. He was such a good-looking man. Mary Ann would be able to see him taking his shower if she climbed up on her roof. Mrs. Bigalow probably couldn't make the climb and was over forty, so she probably wasn't interested. Jack turned around with the hose over his head and started rinsing off with his face up to the water and his eyes closed. He was peeing too at the same time. Men didn't have to concentrate on anything.

Claudia snuck looks at him every morning when he showered. She pretended to be busy in the kitchen. There was always a moment when he turned toward the house with his eyes shut, stretching up with the water spraying into his face, when she could see all of him naked, with the water running down the black hair on his chest and all down his front. The splendor of it took her breath away, and she felt a funny constriction in her groin and a little grab deep down. She liked the little grab feeling very much. It was a very private thing. Maybe it was only her. She never came across it in *Woman's Home Companion*. She liked it as much as her coffee in the morning and the first puff of her Chesterfield. Just that little grab. She only wished it had more to do with real life, where it never happened.

Jack came racing back in the house with his towel around him, and now it was her stomach's turn to grab. When he was in a rush, it made her stomach hurt. It was hard to take a morning like this and then be alone all day. He came out of the bedroom pulling up his trousers and putting the parts of his uniform together.

"I need my gum and the car keys. Where did you put my shoes?"

"They're right here, Jack."

He went back to tie his tie in the mirror. He wasn't going to have trouble with it today because she had pressed all of the black navy ones using a piece of cardboard inside. It took an hour to cut the cardboard to exactly the inside dimensions of Jack's ties, but it was worth it. Whoever discovered cardboard was really a genius. Claudia put Jack's attaché on the kitchen table. Car keys and gum on top with the sandwich.

"But I don't want Juicy Fruit," he called.

"That's all I can find."

"Did you look in the desk drawer?"

"There's only Juicy Fruit in there."

"Check the car."

Claudia ran out to the car and looked all through it. It was a new 1941 Roadmaster coupe. Jack was nuts about it. He had to have a nice car in Hawaii, so his father sent it by boat. Once a week he had an enlisted man at the navy yard wash and wax it, so it always looked good. Claudia liked the Roadmaster, too, but Jack sometimes went overboard about it. Jack came out the door with his jacket and attaché, and Claudia moved quickly out of the way as he swung into the driver's seat.

"No Spearmint?"

"No, I'm sorry, Jack."

"Don't worry about it. I'll pick up some. Watch the door. Love you, bye." He rolled down the window and started backing up.

"Did you get your cream cheese and jelly?"

"I'll pick up something," he called back. "Love you, bye."

Then he was gone, and Claudia felt lonely right away. There was a little rivulet of water coming around the side of the house, and she rushed in to turn off the kitchen faucet. There wouldn't be any more hot water for an hour. She unscrewed the garden hose and went out to coil it up.

Claudia ate Jack's cream cheese and jelly sandwich. It was right on top of his attaché. He just didn't want it, but he was too considerate to say so and pretended to forget. When they were married longer, he would probably just tell her the truth. She smiled to herself, imagining a time when Jack would be completely honest with her. But she wasn't completely honest with him either. She did not tell him how lonely she was in their house. It was so small, and she missed going upstairs to go to bed like you did in a real house. And she only brought up once in a while that she wanted to go to town, like he did, and have a job.

Claudia pushed in all the drawers of Jack's bureau that he left out and put the hangers back in the closet. He left things in a mess when he was in a hurry. She pulled the sheets off the bed. She knew the bathroom would be a mess too. Jack said their bathroom was the same size as the ones on submarines. There was only a sink and a toilet, and you could use both at the same time. He had not flushed the toilet.

Claudia looked at the water in the bowl and knelt down under the sink beside the toilet. The water was a delicate light yellow. It was almost the color of her hair. She put her arms lovingly around the edge of the toilet on the cool porcelain and rested her chin on her hands and thought it was almost the same color as their wedding rings too. She felt so close to him.

She looked into the water until it became mesmerizing. She wanted to put her face and her yellow hair into his light-yellow water and drown for love of him in their tiny bathroom.

She knew she was a hopeless romantic, but she had to pull herself together and get some work done. It wasn't just girls. There were men who were hopeless romantics too, famous ones. She sat down to pee and looked down between her thighs.

"Our two pees mingled be—" she said. She was thinking of John Donne and his poem about fleas. Then she thanked God for Jack and flushed.

Claudia looked out the window at the ocean when she did the dishes. It was the same every day, and she could say that with authority now because they had been here a year. She recorded the readings of her outdoor thermometer. Last Christmas was 78 degrees. On Jack's birthday it was 82. Everyone said it was so nice. Claudia sat at the kitchen table and wrote to her mother every other day. Today she ended with "The weather is nice. No sign of a baby yet. I'll let you know!!!"

It was Thursday, and *Life* Magazine would be coming in the mail. Every Thursday Claudia had her lunch with *Life* magazine. It was the best part of the whole week, and then there was only one more day until she had Jack to herself for two whole days. She got the sheets out on the line early, and then she did another load of darks. She had waited too long to do the darks on purpose because she wanted to test Jack, and now she knew she had failed her own test.

Mrs. Bigalow taught her how to darn socks. It took her forever to learn and it hurt because she couldn't get the hang of using a thimble. But she did it. She darned a sock of Jack's. A month went by, and the pair with the darned one kept moving to the back of the line in Jack's sock drawer. The darning job came out lumpy, but she didn't think it was that bad. So she set up a secret test and let Jack run out of all his black socks until he got to the darned one and its mate, and this morning he had gone into the hamper and taken out a dirty pair instead. The darned one was on the floor, and its mate was in the drawer. It looked like he had thrown the darned one across the room. Claudia wasn't going to cry over it. She was just going to put both of them together in the trashcan behind the house and make sure he never ran out of black socks again. It must have been very upsetting for him to go into the hamper of dirty clothes. He did not expect much from her, and the least she could do was keep him in clean socks that weren't lumpy.

Claudia liked sprinkling and ironing. She filled up the old 7Up bottle with water and put the cork sprinkler in the top and sprinkled Jack's shirt. Mary Ann's car came in while she was ironing, and she heard Petey and Edgar Lee bound out of the house a moment after the sound of the car door. Mary Ann called out over the bushes.

"Want some coffee?"

"I'm ironing," she called back.

"Beach at one?"

"Okay. See you there."

"Get your *Life*?"

"Not yet. I'll bring it."

Claudia said oh damn to herself. If it was windy at the beach, Mary Ann would tear the pages. Why couldn't she get her own *Life*? She was in town every day. It only cost a dime. Then she felt bad for Mary Ann because her parents were both dead. Dad gave her a subscription every year for Christmas. He started the year she went off to Sweet Briar. Everyone liked *Life*. She treated each magazine as if Dad had given it to her himself, and she hated to see Mary Ann treat her *Life* as if it were one of the common magazines at the hairdressers that you tear recipes out of and no one cares two hoots.

Claudia was pushing the heavy wooden ironing board back in the little closet when she heard the wicker mail basket creak. She peeked out the window and saw the mailman go around Mary Ann's house, and then she went out to get the mail. *Life* was there and a letter from Jack's mother. It was addressed to Lieutenant and Mrs. Jack Wyler, so technically she could open it, but she never opened anything with Jack's name on it. Those were Standing Orders. She took her magazine to the kitchen table and made her cheese sandwich and got a 7Up out of the icebox. She looked at "Speaking of Pictures" first. She did not want to look at "The Week's Events" because it would just be about the war and they always had pictures of dead people. Now it would be frozen dead people in Russia. She saved "*Life* Goes To A Party" for Friday. By next Thursday she would get around to reading everything, but on the first day she liked to treat herself. You can't eat worms all the time.

She came to a picture of Claire Trevor with that gorgeous blonde hair. Claudia had seen her in *Dead End* and then *Stagecoach* back in America.

Why was she always playing prostitutes? She must have gotten herself stuck. Claudia didn't care for the little poof in front. It was easy to see that Claire Trevor wasn't doing the best she could with her hair, but it probably wasn't her fault. It could have been the studio stylists didn't have the right eye for her bone structure. While she was thinking it over, Claudia had an impulsive idea. She took the scissors out of the drawer under the kitchen table and went into the bathroom and looked at herself carefully in the mirror. It wasn't really impulsive. She had thought of it before, but now she had the self-confidence to do it. It made her really encouraged about herself.

Mary Ann and Edgar Lee and Petey were already on the beach when Claudia came down. Claudia pretended to be normal and spread out her towel and sat down on it. She said hello to Mary Ann, who sat up and squinted at her. Of course she noticed right away.

"Bangs?"

Claudia tossed her hair and turned to show Mary Ann a profile. "I just thought I'd see how it looks."

"Well, you sure got guts."

"It'll grow back."

"Not by Saturday night it won't."

"Oh my gosh, the party."

"You forgot about that? Gee, Claudia. Sometimes I wonder about you. I remembered, and I'm not even invited."

"Oh no, Mary Ann. What'll I do?"

"It's fine. Don't worry about it."

"Jack doesn't know. He'll kill me."

"You just did it, huh?"

"I saw a picture of Claire Trevor—"

"Oh, you got your *Life?*"

Claudia carefully turned her blue robe over and pulled the big magazine out of the side pocket. The self-confidence she'd had in her bangs was out the window. What a stupid thing to do.

"Let me see."

"Well, it isn't like Claire Trevor exactly," said Claudia.

Mary Ann flipped the pages and Claudia pointed out the picture.

"That isn't bangs. That's a poof."

"I know, but it reminded me of bangs. What am I going to do, Mary Ann?"

"Well, you have to stick with the bangs now. Why did you cut them so short?"

"I wanted it to be a change."

Claudia felt the tears beginning to rise, and she tried to be mature. She could tell Mary Ann was trying not to laugh. She didn't have to go to a party with officers' wives.

"There's nothing wrong with the bangs," Mary Ann said sympathetically. "You just have to figure out what to do with the rest of your hair. Don't worry about it."

"They'll know I did it myself."

"Don't worry about them, Claudia. Those dames are just like you and me."

"Oh no they're not, Mary Ann. Only the old ones are halfway nice because their husbands are admirals and commanders and high up. The younger ones are all snobby like sharks, and I'm supposed to be friends with them. They're stuck up and mean and they look for things to pick on."

"Well, if you ask me, you know what they need?"

"No, what?"

"All they need is a good fuck. Say that right to their faces if they bother you." Mary Ann laughed, and Claudia lowered her eyes.

"I don't think that would do me any good," she said. Claudia thought that would be the end of it, but Mary Ann took it the wrong way and leaned over and grabbed her arm.

"Take it from me, sister," she said. "A good fuck would do you a world of good too."

Claudia tried to manage a little titter. Mary Ann said she was only kidding and touched her on the shoulder, and then Claudia lay down on her front to sun with her head turned away, and Mary Ann settled down to look at *Life*. Claudia thought it was better not to say anything when Mary Ann used that word. This time she said it twice. Now Claudia had to think of something to do about her bangs, but she drifted off to sleep. She did not know what was the matter with her. Mary Ann had to wake her up at quarter after two.

Claudia hurried to get the sheets off the line and ironed and back on the bed. She was going to have spaghetti and meatballs and a salad cold plate with tuna that Jack liked, but she had not made the meatballs yet, and she was out of waxed paper, and she hadn't had her bath. It wasn't really a bath, but she called it that. She did what Jack did with the garden hose on the patio. It wasn't really a patio either. It was just a three-foot square patch of cement under the kitchen window where she crouched down naked and put the hose over herself. Jack wasn't afraid of anyone seeing him naked. He said they would just get what they deserved. He didn't understand that it was different with girls. You could not afford to be that way. If men saw you, they would get aroused, and that was just asking for trouble.

Claudia soaped up as quickly as possible and rinsed off and hurried back into the house in her robe. By the time Jack pulled into the drive with the Roadmaster, she was in her pretty blue sundress, frying her meatballs. He was happy to see her and kissed her after he put down his attaché, but the first thing he noticed was her bangs.

"What did you do to your hair?"

"I just wanted to see, Jack. Don't be mad."

"I'm not mad," he said. He put his hand up to her bangs and flicked them with his fingers. "It's just that the party is Saturday night."

"I know. I forgot about it."

"How could you forget? This party could be important to my career."

"I wasn't thinking."

"That's what everyone will be saying, all right."

Jack stood off and looked at her. He was very calm. He looked down and considered the problem and ran his hand through his dark hair. Claudia knew he would come up with something. She knew he would. She could count on Jack.

"You go fix me a drink," he said. "Let me make a call." Jack went into the hall where the telephone table was, and Claudia heard him give a number to the operator right off the top of his head. She put her head into the hallway, and Jack looked up and held his hand over the receiver. "Girl at the office," he said.

Claudia went to the kitchen cabinet and took out the bottle of gin. She got a tall glass and then a 7Up and Jack's tonic out of the icebox. She waited a moment before she started pouring. Jack didn't even say hello. The first thing he said was, "Who does your hair?" Then he laughed. Then it was quiet while the girl at the office talked.

"Listen, Annette," he said. "I've got kind of a crazy problem here."

Claudia did not want to hear any more, so she poured the gin and tonic and her 7Up and then she took the lid off the steamy spaghetti pot and stirred it around with the wooden spoon, humming a song. Jack came out of the hallway.

"We're going to town," he said.

"Right now?"

"Right now. We're getting your hair fixed."

Claudia was so relieved. Jack was masterful, he really was. Claudia put her arms around him and kissed him. "Oh, Jack, I'll never do anything like this again."

"You keep saying that."

"This was the last time, really and truly."

"Well, let's get going."

Claudia turned off the stove and put the cover on the pan and got out another lid to cover her meatballs. Jack had to put his tie back on and take his hat because he could not appear in town half out of uniform.

"We'll need some of that money."

"How much?"

"Oh, maybe fifty," he said.

That was a lot, but Claudia went to her dresser in the bedroom and took out five tens from the envelope in her pantie drawer. The last money from her parents was getting low, but she knew Jack had his reasons. Before long they were backing out of the little driveway in the Roadmaster with the flowery bushes scraping along the sides of the car. Jack said she ought to trim the bushes back sometime, and Claudia thought it would be a good thing to do tomorrow, until Jack reminded her not to take any chances with her hands before the party Saturday night.

When they got on the macadam, the Roadmaster picked up and seemed to fly down the road with the jungle on one side and the ocean on the other. As they swooped in and out of curves, she could see Diamond Head in the last bit of sunshine. It was just glorious to feel the wind and look out over the sea and be with Jack and have the evening so lovely and soft.

"It's like an adventure," she said. "Like when you drove me to Annapolis, remember?"

Jack smiled and said he remembered. Claudia turned to him on the seat and put her hand on his shoulder. It was just like it was then, as if they had gone back in time.

"But now we're on a mission," he said.

"We're going to rescue my hair, and it will be top secret." She kissed him on the cheek and lit a Chesterfield for him and they went on down the side of the mountain to Honolulu.

CHAPTER THREE

The streets were very quiet. Tourists were having dinner in the hotels and restaurants, and only a few shops were still open. Jack drove down to the Grand Hawaiian and took a side street just before it. He went on a few blocks, looking at the street signs and turned off on another little street. Halfway down the next block, he pulled over to the curb behind a big black car and parked. It was a hairdresser shop with a sign that read "Mr. Anthony."

"Looks like the place," said Jack.

A gentleman in a tailored striped suit got out of the big black car and met them at the door. "You must be Lieutenant Wyler, and you must be Mrs. Wyler with the unfortunate problem."

The two men shook hands, and Claudia smiled. Mr. Anthony took her hand and brought it to his lips, kissing it lightly. Then he fished around in his pockets for the keys and let them in. A little pair of bells tinkled in the dark. They waited while he went through a side door to flip a row of switches that brought a flood of light into the room. It was like Christmas morning.

"What a beautiful salon," said Claudia.

"It's nice, isn't it?" said Mr. Anthony.

There was a row of dryers on one side and a row of shiny, pink porcelain sinks on the other, and there were large mirrors lining the wall over the sinks. Mr. Anthony led Claudia to the superbly upholstered barber chairs in front of the sinks, seated her like a maître d', and swiveled her around to the mirrors.

"What are we going to do?" he asked himself, surveying the damage. "What *are* we going to do?"

Jack said, "I was thinking of something like Ann Sheridan."

"Ah, good choice," said Mr. Anthony. He drew up her bangs with one hand and moved some around to the side with the other. "You mean like this."

"Yes, that's about right."

Mr. Anthony looked critically at Claudia's hair and spread it out in back. "I think we can do it. Lovely hair, perfectly lovely hair," he said, "but we'll have to shorten it up, set a good wave, and give it the full treatment."

"That's fine," said Jack. "Take it away."

Jack sat down in one of the waiting-area chairs and picked up a magazine. He crossed his legs and looked at his watch. Mr. Anthony brushed Claudia's hair out, then combed carefully, following the contours of her head, explaining it was important for a good cut. Claudia smiled gamely into the mirror and tried not to flinch.

He had a little mustache, and there was plenty of cologne in the air. She thought it was Acqua di Parma. That would be right for him. He looked like a gangster—or like a movie gangster anyway. He had thin, slicked, black hair and narrow eyes. He could have just walked off the set of *Gun Moll* or *Syndicate Fugitive*. If he wasn't a gangster, you'd have to wonder about his wife letting him out of the house looking like that.

"We're going to shampoo first," Mr. Anthony said. He tilted the chair back with a foot lever and slid out the headrest and got the water running in the sink. He took off his jacket and hung it on a hook, and then unbuttoned and turned up the cuffs of his shirtsleeves. It was nothing like the regular hairdresser chair. It was so versatile. Mr. Anthony maneuvered it with foot levers and pumps so that it went out almost horizontal, bringing the headrest over the sink in complete comfort.

"Let's get started, shall we?" He lifted her head and let her hair fall, and then as she closed her eyes, he smoothed it back and ran the water spray over her forehead through the hairline. The water rushed by her ears, and she only heard Jack ask Mr. Anthony how long he would be. She heard Jack say see you soon, honey. She kept her eyes closed and only lifted one of her hands to wave goodbye to Jack because she had already been so much trouble and she knew Mr. Anthony would not want her moving around in the chair.

The little pair of bells tinkled on the door as Jack left. He must have had important things to do. Then there was only the soothing sound of the running water through her hair, the flowery scents of the shampoo, Mr. Anthony humming, and the chair, which was so comfortable she began to drift off to sleep. She did, in fact, fall asleep, and what woke her up was a light touch under her sundress, on the inside of her bare thigh. Instantly her heart quickened. She kept her eyes closed and tried to take a breath again without a gasp. She hoped that it was an accident and Mr. Anthony was concentrating so hard on shampooing that he had not noticed where his hand was. If it was the worst thing, she hoped he would be satisfied with a quick touch and pull it away. But she felt the hand go higher up her thigh.

She kept pretending to be asleep, but she had to swallow. She felt burning hot and knew she was perspiring, and her heart was beating so hard. The hand went higher up. She was so stiff with shock and horror that she could not feel the position of her legs anymore and hoped to God she had left them together at the top when she fell asleep, but she could feel Mr. Anthony's hand moving without any resistance, and then the awful sinking feeling hit her that the hand was at her panties.

She tightened her eyes closed. What are you supposed do with impolite people? It was like the boy who came down from Kenyon at Joanne's party, who licked around the whole top of the cake right in front of everybody and then handed out pieces on plates with his tongue marks all over them. The only one who didn't eat the cake was that girl—what's her name—the one who married the blacksmith. He was really bright, he was out of Princeton, but he wanted to be a blacksmith, and his parents were mad about that but they liked Betsy so much—that was her name—Betsy. They met at the polo club where he did the horseshoes. He had good taste in people shoes, too. Those two-tone wingtip Roblee Dress Ups he wore were fabulous, and so were the Florsheim Majors. They got married and lived in the woods in Tennessee, and she heard Betsy had a baby and was deliriously happy, and you can't beat that, you can't touch it with a ten foot pole. And now she's getting her hair done and it will look great at this party that was so important for Jack's career—

Claudia smelled herself for a moment in the warm running water rinsing through her hair, and she opened her eyes as if she had just awakened. Mr. Anthony dried his hands and cut a hundred little snips in different places while her hair was still wet and set it with rollers and curlers, placing each one very precisely in the right place. His eyes remained on her hair and he continued humming the same song. She made up her mind that he was just a different hairdresser she was trying. She had decided to get a permanent and look like Ann Sheridan. It was going to turn out just like she wanted, and she would have no reason to regret it.

Claudia felt safe under the dryer, but she kept her eyes wide open and flipped the pages of a magazine while Mr. Anthony busied himself over at the pink sinks. Jack would be back any minute. She only had to keep her eyes open. If she had kept her eyes open, none of this would have happened. If she had not cut her hair, it would not have happened. People think they can cut their own hair, but they can't. It started with the picture of Claire Trevor. It started with being vain about her hair. But she could not be faulted for that. She had always been vain about her hair. It wasn't the worst thing in the world. There were worse things than being vain about your hair, for heaven's sake.

Claudia was so relieved to see Jack. Mr. Anthony deftly removed the curlers and brushed out her hair. Then he stood her up out of the chair and turned her around for Jack to consider the transformation. Claudia felt better right away, seeing Jack so pleased with the results. That's why they came, after all.

"You can go out to the car, Claudia," Jack said. "I'll help Mr. Anthony close up."

"No need for that," he said. "It's just the lights."

"Claudia, go on—"

Mr. Anthony pressed a hairnet into her hand as he smiled and said goodbye. "You make sure you wear this on the ride home. The wind and night air is no good for your hair."

Claudia went out to the car and got in. There was a large, flat box on the back seat and a new hatbox beside it and a shoebox. She just wanted to get home. The lights in the shop went out, and Jack came out the door and got behind the wheel. As they drove off he said, "Well, that was a pleasant surprise."

Claudia did not say anything. She did not want to guess how much it cost, and Jack finally told her that Annette was taking care of it.

"Who's Annette?"

"The girl at the office. We got you a terrific dress for the party. We got you a swell hat too and new shoes. Annette has great taste in clothes, believe me. You'll look terrific. I didn't want you coming in any of the dresses you have. They all look kind of beat, you know."

"But the stores are all closed."

"Annette made some calls, and they let us in after hours. That's the navy for you."

Claudia looked out the window and smoked three Chesterfields one after another on the long, curvy road along the mountain going home. Usually it was a one-Chesterfield ride. When Jack asked her why she was so quiet, she said she was very tired and hungry. She was thrilled about the dress and said she would look at it tomorrow. It was ten o'clock when they got home. Claudia pulled herself together and got out of the car.

"I'll get your dinner ready," she said.

"Oh, never mind. Annette and I picked up something."

Claudia turned to him in exasperation. "Jack, you have to eat nutritious meals, not just something you pick up."

"We did."

"How can you just pick up the four basic food groups, Jack?"

"We had dinner."

"Well what did you have? What do you call dinner?"

"I had shrimp cocktail, a steak, baked potato, some kind of soufflé they had, some peas, salad, you know. Oh, rolls. I can't remember everything. Annette had crab cakes and French onion soup and some kind of thing they do with roast beef and something else I don't know what they call it. I guess that covers your food groups."

"Well, where in the world was this?"

"The Grand Hawaiian. We weren't there very long because we really wanted to get you something perfect for the party, and Annette thought that was going to take some time with us guessing your size."

Claudia knew Jack had gone to a lot of trouble for her. All because she did something foolish. He had to call the girl at the office—Annette—and she arranged a free salon appointment at night and made calls to get them into stores after hours. She probably had to try on dresses for him too. So naturally, the least he could do was take her out to dinner. Annette. That was her name.

"I'm just going to bed," Jack said. At the bedroom door, he turned around as he was taking off his tie and said, "You better get something to eat so you'll be fit for duty tomorrow, First Mate Wyler."

Claudia walked around the kitchen wondering what to do. She ate part of a cold meatball. She dumped the sodden spaghetti in the bushes across the road, but she ate a few forkfuls of tuna out of the tomato she had carved out for Jack's salad plate. She was going to cover it all with waxed paper and have it for lunch tomorrow, but then she remembered she was out of waxed paper, so she went back and put all of it in the bushes. She sat down at the kitchen table with the half empty 7Up she had been drinking before they went to town. She had another Chesterfield and waited for Jack to fall asleep.

At all quiet, Claudia went around to the side of the house and slid the kitchen window back enough to get the hose through. She went back inside to hook it up and turn on the water. She crept quietly into the bathroom to get her robe and towel and was soon squatting naked in the dark on the cool cement patch under the kitchen window. She held the hose over her shoulders and let it flow over her until the water got too hot.

She did another stupid thing. She had turned on only the hot faucet, and she didn't feel like tramping back inside all wet to turn on the cold. She soaped herself while the hose ran on the ground, sending up steam that she could see against the starlight, and then she took the hose again and sprayed it lightly over her upper body. It wasn't so bad. Then she put the hose on her belly and it suddenly started to feel so good as the hot water channeled down between her legs. She moved the hose farther down and put it right up to where she split into her peach halves and the burning water suddenly made her double over with the most excruciating pleasure she had ever felt.

"Oh, God." She clamped down hard on her mouth and only little squeaks got out.

It was a fantastic discovery. She braced her back against the house and pressed her heels into the cement and put the hose back where it had been, letting the steaming water send her into a turn-your-insides-out ecstasy, and then suddenly there was only an awful fire alarm pain and a horrifying awareness that she had gone too far and done something bad to herself.

Claudia dropped the hose on the ground and stood up slowly, hardly able to put on her robe and walk bowlegged into the house. She turned off the water and flipped the end of the hose out the window. The effort of trying to slide the window closed made blood pound in her groin and she just left it. She dried herself and sat with her robe open on the toilet seat. She turned on the light to look at herself. Spreading the fleshy halves apart carefully with her fingers, she saw that it was all flaming red in there. Oh ye gods, she had burned herself. She really did it this time. There was the jar of Vaseline in the medicine cabinet behind the mirror. She spread a fingerful of it on and then washed her hands and turned out the light. She went into the dark bedroom to her bureau to get out a new brassiere and clean panties and slipped her nightgown over her head. Then she got in bed beside Jack. What a terrible day it had been. Now she had burned herself badly, and she could not help thinking that if she had not tried to cut her hair and had gone to her regular hairdresser, none of this would have happened. She could have gotten her nails done at the same time, and maybe she would have overheard something more about Bob and Susie.

CHAPTER FOUR

In the morning it was still bad, but before she did anything else, Claudia brushed her hair. She brushed only fifty strokes this time and was so glad the permanent worked out so well and looked like something Ann Sheridan might try on for size if she was in a good mood. She didn't know Jack liked Ann Sheridan so much. The Oomph Girl. He didn't miss a beat—he suggested Ann Sheridan right off the top of his head. *Woman's Home Companion* said a girl should be vigilant and take note of such things. No husband wants to be unfaithful. It is so often the fault of the wife, a self-centered wife who fails to see the warning signs. But now that she knew, Claudia thought perhaps she could do something to fashion herself after Ann Sheridan. She would have to know more about her likes and dislikes. She was pretty sure Ann Sheridan was one of those Hollywood sweater girls, but she thought she had seen a picture of her in a tennis dress, and if she was athletic, well there wasn't much she could do about that. Claudia was sure that if she looked through her old *Life* magazines, there would be a story on her. A photo essay. There would be a photo of Ann Sheridan starting her day, waking up in bed, drinking her orange juice, and having a smoke. That was another reason to always wear a brassiere under your nightgown, in case *Life* took you by surprise.

She woke Jack at five thirty, put the coffee on, and went to take a look at herself. She was startled to see her belly had a big red patch, like a sunburn, and then her heart almost stopped when she gingerly parted the hair away and saw how burned she was between her legs. Oh no. It was horrifying to look at. It looked like raw meat inside, oozing, cherry red, raw meat. She put more Vaseline all over the red parts and shuddered.

"Jack," she called, "you'd better get up."

He didn't make a sound. She came out of the bathroom and looked in. He was still asleep. He was lying on his back and he only had the sheet over him and his thing was standing up in the middle. It always made her think of the playing cards Laura Lamb brought home from junior year abroad in Paris. None of the girls could tell what the pictures were supposed to be, especially the ones that looked like parts of an elephant. When Laura said it was a man's thing, they all shrieked and covered their eyes and laughed all over the place, and then everybody wanted to look at the cards again. The housemother knew something was up and searched all the rooms on the floor when they were at chapel convocation. The cards were never seen again.

Claudia learned everything from Jack. She knew he wasn't necessarily dreaming of American Oomph Girls. It was always that way in the morning.

"Jack, honey—it's getting late."

He opened his eyes, glanced at the clock on the night table, and quickly turned on his side. He did not like her looking at him like that.

"It's almost six," she said.

Claudia set his place at the table and got out the frying pan and his eggs. Jack shaved and came out with his towel around him and went outside. He put the end of the hose through the window, and Claudia hooked it up and adjusted the water for him. She had just turned away from the sink when he called her.

"What are these doing out here?"

She looked out to see Jack standing naked and dripping on the cement patch, holding up her panties from last night.

"They were out here in the mud. And why is it so wet out here?"

"I don't know," she said.

"You can't leave your damn underwear out where everyone can see them."

Then he shook his head in disbelief and hung them over the kitchen windowsill. Claudia took them into the bedroom and rolled them up with her blue sundress under the bed.

She stayed to make Jack his breakfast and have coffee and a Chesterfield together. Then she said her tummy hurt and she had to go lie down.

"Oh, Claudia," he said. "Before I forget. I want to pick up a pair of sunglasses today. Do you have any more of that money?"

"A little bit. How much do you need?"

"Five."

"For sunglasses?"

"They're a new kind with special lenses. They're good for your eyes."

"What about the ones I got you?"

"They're fine, but all the best navy men are wearing the new ones. You have to fit in. They notice when you go against the grain, and they don't like how it sets a bad example for the enlisted men."

Claudia hated to see the money go so fast, but Jack always knew what he had to do to move up in the world. She took five dollars out of the envelope in her pantie drawer and brought it into the kitchen.

"Thanks," he said. "Hope you feel better tonight,"

He had to go, and he drank the last bit of his coffee standing up. At least he always kissed her on the way out.

"Love you, bye," he said.

Claudia wanted him to kiss her more and hold her and come back to bed with her. She just couldn't face it anymore, being alone all day. By Friday she was always at the end of her rope. As far as Jack knew, she only had a morning and a night. He didn't know she had to live all the empty space in between by herself. She came alive when Jack came home and died when he left. She knew she had to snap out of it. She knew she had to try to think of it as part of her training to be a navy wife, the tough part when you get your sea legs or it's man overboard.

Claudia lay down on the bed and listened to Jack drive off in the Roadmaster. She always thought about so many things. You can't get away from it when you're alone. Except for that, she and Jack were getting somewhere now. He was more considerate, and she was beginning to understand how men are, that they did not intend to be hurtful. Men have standards, especially navy men. They expected a lot from their wives. If a girl could not measure up, well, then naturally she'd get hurt sometimes.

She didn't know what Jack did with the money. He must get paid every month. She thought he might be putting it away in a secret bank account to pay her father back. Jack's father was in jail for fraud. Not just jail, it was the federal penitentiary. He talked Daddy into investing their life savings in some currency scheme that went down the drain. So Jack's father was in jail and Daddy was back working at Towers & Henderson. Barb couldn't go to college and went to work at Woolworth's in New Haven, and Harry turned eighteen and joined the army. Mom still talked to Jack's mom on the phone behind Daddy's back. They expected there were going to be grandchildren. Women conspired together all the time like that. It was a wonder they couldn't do more with their husbands.

Jack's father was a pip. He said the money was just plain gone. Then he bought Jack the Roadmaster and shipped it to Hawaii and went to jail. The car came all the way across the country by train and by steamer from San Francisco. That must have cost something, not counting how much the car was. Jack said it was custom built. Jack never said anything about what had happened, but Claudia knew he was sorry about it and knew he would pay Daddy back. Jack said you could never be a naval officer if you didn't have high moral standards.

Claudia lay in bed all morning. The little cat came in and jumped up on the bed and curled up beside her. Claudia wondered what she was going to do. She thought the burn would be better by now but it still hurt and throbbed down there. She couldn't go to a doctor. What would she say? It would only make Jack look bad. She got up when she heard Mary Ann's car come in because she knew she would be calling over. She waited by the side window of the kitchen.

"Want some coffee?" Mary Ann called.

Claudia opened the window and put her head out. "Girl troubles today."

"Oh, sorry," said Mary Ann. "Got everything you need? I can go to town—"

"No thanks, I'm okay." Claudia could see Mary Ann's head over the bushes.

"Just let me know."

"Okay. See you later."

They waved to each other, and Claudia shut the window. She forgot to ask Mary Ann last night about waxed paper. What did people do before waxed paper? It would be interesting to have a time machine to go back and see. But now she had to get practical. She did not want to irritate the problem by doing laundry. She could do that tomorrow, and it would be better anyway because Jack might need something washed for the party. The only things she really had to do were the breakfast dishes and put something together for dinner. She still had the hot dogs. She looked in *The Newlywed Cookbook* and found a wonderful thing to do. It was called Coney Island Hot Dogs. You cut the hot dogs halfway through and put melted cheese in them. Whoever thought of that?

Claudia went out to the little garden she had started and picked pole beans. She could make mashed potatoes too, and there was still a can of fruit cocktail. Fruit cocktail could pep up any meal. She had seen that somewhere, and it really was true. The pole beans did well here, but she did not have much luck with anything else. It was so strange that inside the wire fence the garden was a catastrophe. Jack said the volcanic soil was supposed to be good for plants, but it looked like civilized plants like carrots and tomatoes did not like it. Just outside the fence, the uncivilized plants grew like crazy. She did not know the names for any of them. They all had flowers, and they were absurdly large purple and luscious pink things she was almost embarrassed to look at, hanging their sex parts out like that, which was exactly what it was if you knew anything about biology. It just didn't seem like a good enough excuse to do that out of doors.

Claudia remembered her panties and her sundress. She put the basket of beans on the step and went in to get them and a bottle of rubbing alcohol. In the middle of the garden, she started digging a hole, and then she started thinking about it again—it was only last night. A shudder went over her, head to toe. It wasn't just unpleasant. It made her think. Could Mr. Anthony claim that technically he had possessed her? Would that give him any rights? What if Mr. Anthony took Jack to court for half ownership of the Roadmaster? Jack would fight for the Roadmaster. It could go to the Supreme Court. How embarrassing.

Claudia put the dress and panties in the hole and poured alcohol over them. She jumped when the flame caught from her lighter, and she watched them burn down to ashes and then covered over the hole. She wasn't going to think about it anymore. Out of sight, out of mind.

Claudia went in and got her dinner things ready. She cut up her three last potatoes and plopped them in a pot with water and washed up the beans. Then she made her cheese sandwich for lunch and got out her 7Up and *Life* magazine. Her burn did not hurt so much. The Vaseline felt icky, but it seemed to be helping. "Speaking of Pictures" was funny. "Letters to the Editor" was snappy. "Movie of the Week" and "*Life* Goes to a Party" were her favorites. She reached for her Chesterfields, looked out the window at the palm fronds blowing around, then back to her *Life*, then back into thought.

The soonest Jack would want to do it would be Sunday afternoon, when he took his nap. Two days. She would probably be better in two days. She certainly hoped so. He was not very gentle, but she couldn't blame him for that. Jack needed a strong wife to stand by him. The first year was the shakedown cruise. A navy wife was unlike any other kind of girl. She had to be able to take it, and Jack had to test her strength if they were to be shipmates.

Claudia always dreamed of Jack when she lay down in the afternoon, how he looked at cotillion in his dress whites, how he removed his hat and put it under his arm and introduced himself in a deep voice. "Cadet Midshipman Jack Wyler," as if he were reporting for duty. He was so dreamy, she almost died. The other boys were from Randolph-Macon and W&L and a few from UVA with pocket flasks who got disorderly.

Jack wasn't like that at all. She thought he was just trying to impress her by telling her he was career navy, but it turned out he really was and didn't care if he impressed her or not. He used words like secure this and secure that. He said he was angling for a Pacific Fleet assignment and told her about beautiful islands he had heard about that were not on any maps. She looked away while he was talking and imagined them shipwrecked on a desert island, hardly knowing each other. He in tatters of his dress whites, and she in tatters of her lovely gown.

In the powder room, Twinkie said she shouldn't let a boy kiss her on the first date just on principle, so she wasn't going to, but then someone else came in—Claudia couldn't remember her name, the one with red hair who was so innocent it made you want to say a dirty word and wake her up—which made it all the more surprising when she said that if a boy as cute as Jack came all the way from Annapolis and didn't get at least a kiss, he would never come back. He could go to Mary Baldwin and get enough kisses to sink his boat any day of the week.

That was enough to convince Claudia. They ducked the chaperones and were in the Green Room alone in the dark. The soft spring night breeze came through the open windows, stirring the curtains, with the orchestra far away playing *I've Got a Feeling I'm Falling*. She pretended to look as if a great emotion were overcoming her when she looked into his eyes, knowing it would make him hold her in his arms and kiss her, and she knew if he did that he would want all of her to marry, and she knew she wanted to marry him, right from the start, when he first stood in front of her in his dress whites and she almost died.

Claudia got up at five o'clock and started the beans and potatoes boiling. She had not considered how many boiling pots she was going to need and had to put the hot dogs in with the beans. It was getting time to change when she remembered the dress they brought home. Jack started picking out her clothes after he realized she didn't have a single thing he liked. He brought home everything from dresses to lingerie and had her put them on to see what he liked. What other husband would take on so many extra duties to keep his wife looking her best? Jack was one in a million.

She went and got the box and opened it in the kitchen, almost gasping out loud when she held it up. It was a silk gown in a slender dance sheath with motifs of island flowers rising from the bottom hemline toward the midriff like an erupting volcano of pistils, stamen, petals, and leaves in all their colors on a red background. Claudia never had a red dress, let alone a full-length gown that knocks your eyes out. Jack was one in a million all right.

Claudia got out of her sundress and put it on right away. She felt stunning, and rushing to the bathroom mirror to make sure, she saw instantly that she was. Stunning. The neckline plunged from high, built-up shoulders into the shallows of her small breasts like a daredevil cliff diver risking everything. Oh dear, what could she wear under it? The hat was dramatic understatement, a tiny white-and-gray rain cloud to the flowers of the dress, with tear brim and veil trim. The shoes were impossible four-inch spike heels. How was she going to walk in these? They were like stilts.

The Roadmaster pulled into the driveway. Claudia got up on her heels and posed herself at the open kitchen door so he would see her as he got out of the car. He was flabbergasted. He came up on the porch and looked her up and down.

"Gosh, you look terrific, honey."

"I don't know if I can walk in these shoes, Jack."

"Oh, you'll do fine."

"Jack, you can fall down in these."

"I'll hold you up," he said. He put his attaché down and put his arms around her. She was right up to his height in the high heels. He must have had a drink or two. She smelled Jack Daniel's. The ads in *Life* said it was charcoal mellowed and aged in barrels for ten years, but how did you know that for sure? They probably rushed it after Prohibition got taken off.

"This is different, isn't it?" He held her tightly and raised her up higher, right off her feet. She could tell he was getting ideas, and she knew what was going to happen if she didn't do something fast. You couldn't stop a man after he got past a certain point of excitation because they lost control over their urges and couldn't help themselves. He would see her all red, and she would have to explain how she burned herself. She needed the two days till Sunday. She arched her back and pushed away from him.

"Oh Jack, guess what?" she said. "We're having hot dogs."

But that didn't stop him. He had his arms around her thighs, and she was completely off the ground. Her high heels fell to the floor, and he got his hand between her legs from behind and grabbed her hard, right through the silk dress. She almost screamed, and tears burst from her eyes.

"Jack, the dress," she cried. "You'll ruin the dress."

He let her down right away.

"It's all right. The dress is fine."

"No, it isn't, just look." Claudia could not stop crying and showed him the faint creases on the sides.

"You can't even see it," he said. "And it's silk. It won't stay that way. It's not worth crying over."

"It's such a beautiful dress. I love it so much. Oh, Jack."

Jack took her in his arms and held her head against his chest.

"You don't have to cry about it."

"I can't help it, Jack. It's such a beautiful dress."

"You can hang it up, and by tomorrow it'll be fine. Go take it off, and we'll have dinner."

Claudia picked up her sundress and escaped into the bedroom to change, and when she came out, Jack was peering into the pots on the stove.

"We really are having hot dogs, I guess."

"Not just regular hot dogs though."

"Then what?"

"I don't want to spoil the surprise."

Jack looked annoyed. He was getting into a bad mood. She had not caught him soon enough and he was sexually frustrated. It was in *Woman's Home Companion*, so she knew it was true. A bad mood was stage one of the four stages of sexual frustration. He raised his hands in exasperation.

"What can you do different with a hot dog? You just cook it and put it in a bun."

"Oh, no," said Claudia.

"You don't have any buns, do you?"

"Oh, Jack, I'm sorry."

"Well, I better get going." He sighed heavily and started for the door. "Didn't even take my tie off—"

"We don't have to have buns, Jack, we can use bread."

"It's not the same thing. You can't have a hot dog without a bun. Jesus Christ, I get so sick of driving back and forth."

"Please, Jack," she called.

Jack got in the car and started backing out of the driveway.

"Jack, please."

"Just get the rest ready. Don't worry, I'm fine. Love you, bye."

He waved and smiled, and then he was off. He was never mad at her for very long. She was so lucky to have him. She watched the Roadmaster back out of the drive, and she felt so lonely again. The sun was going down. She had not wanted to mention that as long as he was at the market, she was out of waxed paper. It was bad enough about the hot dog buns.

Claudia slipped her panties down and looked at herself again. That really hurt. Oh God, that hurt. It was still about the same, but it was just red, and she thought it might be better by tomorrow if she could keep Jack's mitts off.

Claudia mashed up her potatoes carefully because Jack did not like to find lumps, but he didn't like it too creamy either. The baked beans were ready, and she let them sit. Two starches weren't the best nutrition, but it was supposed to be a treat. So was the fruit cocktail. She opened the can and spooned it into a glass bowl and put it in the icebox to chill. Then she sat down at the table with a 7Up and a Chesterfield and looked at the Formica.

CHAPTER FIVE

An hour went by. No buns. No Jack. It only took twenty minutes to get to town. Claudia turned on the lights because it was getting darker, and after another hour went by, she turned on the porch light. She suddenly remembered the cheese and got out her smallest saucepan, warmed it on the burner, and sliced off the last thin slivers of the cheddar and was happy to see it was melting nicely without separating into oils. It was harder than *The Newlywed Cookbook* made it out to be because the first hot dog curled up when she cut down the side of it. They all did. She tried to put the cheese in but when she released the hot dog, it curled up on one side and splayed out and the cheese went all over the plate. She heard the Roadmaster pull in, but she was just then working on another hot dog and could not get up. Then his big navy shoes came up the porch steps, and the screen door banged.

"Sorry it took so long," he said.

"What happened? I was so worried, Jack."

"I bumped into Annette at the market. What's that?"

Claudia looked up at Jack. She was trying to hold down a hot dog and her fingers were covered with melted cheese. She couldn't do it. It was a mess.

"It's Coney Island hot dogs, Jack."

Jack started laughing.

"Don't laugh, Jack. It's hard to do."

"I'm sorry," he said. He kissed her on the top of her head. "It just looks like a disaster area. What's that stuff?"

"Melted cheese."

"Well, it's all yours. Don't worry about me. I picked up something."

"Don't you want a hot dog?"

"No thanks. I forgot the buns anyway. What's in here?"

He was at the stove, picking up the lids and looking in. Claudia gave up on Coney Island hot dogs. They didn't tell you it was hard to do. They never tell you that. She cut up the hot dogs and put the little pieces into the saucepan with the melted cheese.

"Your beans and mashed potatoes."

Jack went to the icebox and looked in. "To tell the truth, I'm not hungry. Maybe just a little something. Is this fruit cocktail for me?

"Yes, Jack."

"That's just the thing."

He came to the table and started eating out of the bowl with the large serving spoon. It was going to be for both of them, but how was he to know that? She was the one who was supposed to be in charge of the galley, and she couldn't even do that. Then he suddenly jumped up and turned on the radio.

"*Swing Hour* coming up."

"You bumped into Annette?"

His eyes were intent on the radio dial. "Good thing I did. She gave me this list she made up for you." He took a sheath of typed pages folded together out of his side pocket and held it out behind him without turning around. The radio was warming up and *Swing Hour* was coming in with only a little bit of fuzz tonight.

"These are all the wives coming to the party tomorrow night. See on the left side? Annette put down the husband's rank. She thought you could memorize the list, and then you'd know who you were talking to. I thought it was damn nice of her."

Claudia looked down the list. "I don't know which rank is which, Jack."

"I'll explain it to you later. Annette told me it's Artie Shaw at the Hotel Pennsylvania tonight. I don't want to miss it."

"What's Lt. JG?"

"Lieutenant Junior Grade.

"That's less than you, isn't it?"

"I'll tell you all the ranks later." He turned up the volume to make the point and then set it back a little so he could read the paper. "Clear the decks, clear the decks," he said, clapping his hands and reaching for the attaché case and the *Honolulu Daily* inside.

That meant the table. Claudia whisked the dishes out from under the newspaper as he spread it out and moved the lazy Susan to one side so the paper could lay flat. Claudia brought him his coffee and set out a fresh pack of Chesterfields.

Claudia ate all four hot dogs. She turned each piece in the cheese and ate every bit. She even turned away to lick the cheese out of the bottom of the saucepan. Then she ate the whole pot of mashed potatoes. She wasn't sure about the beans, but she was suddenly taken by a desire to eat them with a lot of pepper. She ground the pepper mill over the pot so long that Jack briefly looked up from his paper with a puzzled expression. Beans down the hatch. Stomach—this is the bridge. Secure the beans.

Claudia sat down across from Jack and looked at the list. How could she memorize all this? She knew admiral was at the top and ensign was at the bottom, but there weren't any ensigns. Lieutenants were at the bottom and, because it was alphabetical, Jack Wyler was the last one. There was an asterisk by his name and the girl at the office—Annette—had written, "Nowhere to go but up" and "The sky's the limit!!!!"

Claudia did not particularly like another girl being so familiar with her husband, but Jack was irresistible, and she knew it was bound to happen. All the girls at school knew he was a catch. Well, she was the one who caught him. She should check to be sure Jack had his wedding ring on when he left every morning. But she knew a wedding ring was like waving a red flag in front of a bull for some girls. She got to the end of the fourth page and didn't remember anything and noticed she was twirling strands of her hair again. She was going to have to clear her mind and concentrate.

Jack tapped his finger on his coffee cup, and she quickly got up to get him more coffee. He depended on her so much. He would not have done very well with the kind of girl who put her needs ahead of his and didn't lift a finger to help him advance in his career. There were girls who shopped all day and could not get a good nutritious meal on the table when their husbands came home, and girls who only cared about how they looked, and then the girls who didn't care how they looked and took their husbands for granted. They got what they deserved more often than not.

Claudia started at the top of the first page again, sitting across from Jack at the table. It was very cozy in the little house sometimes. She felt like she was reading the newspaper too, and they were like a couple in one of those cartoons in the *New Yorker* with their papers held up between them. Pass the butter. Is that you, Mrs. Peabody?

Jack knew all the songs Artie Shaw played and hummed along as he looked over the paper. After that it was going to be *Mr. District Attorney* for an hour. Claudia could never follow who was who. She could go through half the show mixed up because some of them were complicated. Jack did not read his paper during *Mr. District Attorney*. He sat with his elbows on the table, looking at his cigarette. He always figured them out. The navy was going to send him to law school. Jack had big plans, and Claudia knew she had her job cut out for her.

Last year she had taken The Housewife's Pledge in *Woman's Home Companion*. It could not have been timed better because they had just arrived in Hawaii and moved into the little white house. Among other things, Claudia had promised to do her man proud by looking her best at all times, to do clever things with leftovers, to make the most out of every dollar, to do something about those dirty window frames, to check over her kitchen utensils, to put a light coat of wax on her venetian blinds, and to plan her perennial borders now, while the nurseries had a good stock. It was made up for girls in America, so not everything applied, but Claudia knew what they were getting at, and whenever she remembered about perennials, she went out front with a big flat shovel and whacked the damn flowers back into the jungle a few feet.

Claudia poured Jack a little more coffee and went to the bedroom because the same old Vitalis commercial came on and *Mr. District Attorney* was not far behind. She lay on the bed and looked at the long list again. There had to be a better way. Flash cards! Claudia went back to the kitchen. Jack hated being interrupted during his *Mr. District Attorney* show, but it couldn't wait.

"Excuse me, Jack," she said. "Can I use some of your note cards?"

He said sure without looking up from the table, where he was hunched over his coffee and cigarette like the prosecutor looking over a brief while the girl with the trembling voice begged him not to send her brother to fry in the chair. That was how the girls talked. Claudia always believed the girl was sincere and her brother was innocent, and Jack always had to explain it to her later. She always felt so duped and stupid. The girls on *Mr. District Attorney* were always trying to get away with something, and a lot of men got the wool pulled over their eyes, but not Jack.

Claudia went into the drawer of the desk and got out Jack's gray metal box with the file cards. She took an inch thick of them and settled on the bed to copy down each lady's name and husband's rank on a card. She shuffled them and lay down on her side with the cards propped up on the pillow and began turning them over one by one. Before long she was sound asleep. When she woke up, *Forum of the Air* was on. Theodore Granik had someone with a British accent talking about the Nazis, and he was pronouncing Nazis as if the word had three z's. London was getting it like nobody's business now, according to *Life*'s "The Week's Events."

There was so much to be thankful for. Claudia was thankful for Jack. She was also thankful that she was beautiful. It wasn't as superficial as it sounded. She had struggled with self-confidence for many years as a girl. It seemed impossible that a girl could be beautiful and still be insecure. She knew she was insecure and had no self-confidence, so inversely, how could she be beautiful, even if people were telling her so? When other beautiful girls slipped up and revealed the same insecurities, it was like a revelation.

It wasn't superficial at all. It was part of what you really were. Jack had to think a moment when she asked him an important question. After considering it, Jack said that the problem with still loving her if her face was burned in a terrible accident was that her face was truly a part of her and she would not really be herself without it. Claudia felt much better then because that's how she felt about Jack.

"They're talking about Hawaii," Jack shouted from the kitchen.

Claudia rushed in, but all she caught was that some government person said the Japanese were not happy about something.

"The navy base here and the British in Singapore," said Jack. "Shhh."

Then an American commentator asked someone a question, and a man with an upstate-New York accent said, "Well, Albert, considered across all categories, I'd say the Pacific Fleet is not even at 1939 levels."

Then the commentator said, "That was Lieutenant-Commander Robert Rodgers, right here in Honolulu."

"That's him," said Jack. "He's in my office. Bobby Rodgers. He'll be at the party. I want you to meet him."

"Oh, Jack. You know someone on the radio!"

Claudia was thrilled to have some news to put in her letter home. It wasn't very often you knew someone on the radio.

"Damn nice guy," said Jack. "He's on the selection board, so if you want us to go places, you better run up the colors for me."

"I thought you were doing so well, Jack."

"It doesn't hurt to know people. I'm getting tired of waiting for a war. How are you doing with the list?"

"Okay. I think it's going to be a long night though. I put all the names on cards."

Claudia went back to the bedroom and sat on the bed looking at her cards one by one. Jack was moving around in the kitchen. He was probably looking in the icebox for Jell-O and a brownie. In a minute he would be calling her because there weren't any. She goofed again. Reef dead ahead. Hard to starboard, reverse all engines. Jack called her out to the kitchen.

"Why can't you remember to make Jell-O?" he asked. "There must be ten packages in the cupboard. You just keep buying more, but I never see Jell-O in the icebox."

"There are so many different flavors, Jack. I only got the last two packages because we didn't have strawberry or lemon."

"But I only like raspberry. You know I only like raspberry. So why do we need any of the other ones?"

"I thought you might like another flavor sometime."

"Claudia, come over here and sit down."

Claudia sat down across from him. He took out a Chesterfield for himself and one for her, and then he bent over to light them both at the same time, the way he did that first night at cotillion, sitting at the little round table with the white tablecloth and the rose. Love was all around. Not this time.

"Claudia, you're not being logical. Listen to me now. You would only make one pan of Jell-O at any one time, right?"

"Right."

"And you know I only like raspberry, right?"

"All right."

"So if you only have one pan of Jell-O to make, and I only like raspberry, why would you make a pan of Jell-O in any flavor but raspberry?"

"I don't know, Jack."

Claudia could see the influence of *Mr. District Attorney*, and she resented the advantage it gave Jack. Logic was just so tedious. But she had common sense, didn't she, and it wouldn't be the first time it beat out logic.

"I thought you might like to try something different."

"Not if it's something I don't like," he said.

"How do you know you won't like it?"

"This is ridiculous. You just want to argue. I've had a tough week, you know. There was your hair and then the hot dog buns. It's getting too much to take."

"I don't want to argue, Jack."

"Then why are you turning the Jell-O back on me? It doesn't matter if I might like another flavor. I might. I'm sure I might. I might like all the other flavors. But that's only speculation and is completely irrelevant. The only relevant facts are these: number one, that you know I like raspberry, and number two, you only make one pan at a time. Even if you made a pan every day, would you ever make one that I wouldn't like?"

Claudia lowered her eyes. "Of course not, Jack."

"Do you understand me now?"

"Yes, Jack, I'm sorry."

"Well, we can forget about it then." He smiled.

Claudia knew he was smiling, and she looked up into his serene gray eyes. He was so strong. She wondered how she could ever help him with his career. That was her job. It was only the house and the chores, but he was letting her do them so she could believe she was helping him. He knew she needed the self-confidence.

"Let's see your cards."

Claudia went and got the cards and put them down on the table in front of him.

"Oh Jesus," he said.

"What?" Her heart went through the floor.

"You got these out of the gray box?"

"I thought you said I could."

"Not the ones in the box, the ones in the package. These are my code cards. Look. Up in each corner there's a little square with a number and a symbol down in the other corner. Didn't you see those?"

"Oh, Jack, I'm so sorry." She could tell he was positively livid.

He got up and turned off the radio. "I'm going to bed."

"Jack, I'm sorry."

"It's twelve thirty-five. I need eight hours. Be sure I'm up by eight forty. Can you do that?

"Yes, Jack."

"You'll have to copy the cards over, and they better be right. Mistakes don't go in the navy, you know."

He turned around at the door of the bedroom. He still looked exasperated. "I wish you didn't have to do that. I really do," he said. "You waste so much time doing things over. I don't know how you can live like that, I honestly don't."

Claudia stayed up until three in the morning, copying the little boxes with numbers and symbols onto the new cards and trying to memorize her party cards. Then she brushed her teeth and put more Vaseline on her burn and went to bed. She wasn't so worried about it now. It was still sore, but it seemed to be getting better, and if they came home late from the party and he left her alone on Sunday, it would give her another week to get better and make the right kind of Jell-O.

CHAPTER SIX

Claudia woke up without the alarm at five thirty. She went to the bathroom and looked at her hair. It was still okay. She put on her robe and puffy pink slippers and went to the kitchen to plug in the percolator and plopped herself down at the table. She put her head down on her arms and listened to the percolator go blup, blurp. The Baby Ben on the counter ticked away, and she opened one eye every so often to check the time.

The coffee and a Chesterfield helped, but she always felt terrible when she didn't get enough sleep. The darkness under the eyes wouldn't start for another day, so she would still look good for the party. She thought the burn felt less raw, and that was a big relief. She could never go to a doctor with something like that. Even a girl doctor. Especially a girl doctor. When she was completely healed, she would try it again to see if it worked with warm water, but for now she had to lay low.

Claudia got Jack out of bed at eight exactly. At breakfast she showed him his new code cards, and he looked them over and put them in the right order. Then she took them back to the gray box. She said she was sorry again.

"I wish you didn't have to say that so much," he said. "It's like you just aren't thinking half the time."

"I don't know what's wrong with me lately." She tried to say it humorously.

"The trouble is," he said, "you can't even do the little things right, and then something as important as this party tonight comes along."

"Do you think I've never been to a party before, Jack?"

"What are you doing with the toast?"

"Oh gosh."

Claudia jumped up and flipped the wings on the toaster. There was a little burned part on the toasting side but not too bad. Jack turned around in his chair.

"Well don't turn them over now," he said. "If they're burned on one side, it isn't going to fix them by burning the other. Then you're wasting electricity too. Just throw them in the bushes. Jesus, we're feeding half the wildlife on the island."

"I'll eat them," she said.

"Darling, that's how you get stomach cancer, eating burned food. Just put them out for the birds. We don't want to beat the world record for how fast a couple can die of stomach cancer."

She had to laugh.

"Come here," he said. He pulled her over and sat her on his lap and put his arms around her. "I don't know why I love you."

"But you do, don't you?"

He looked at her with a frown, as if she was really and truly hopeless, and let her go. "Well that's what I just said, isn't it? Jesus Christ."

Claudia puttered around the stove and hid the tears that were coming to her eyes. When she thought of the things she said and the way she constantly provoked Jack, she couldn't blame him at all for being cross. Why did she always have to ruin everything when he was being so sweet?

Claudia made bologna-and-cheese sandwiches and filled two empty 7Up bottles with milk, and they drove up to the north shore that morning. She loved driving along the coast and then through the farm country where you couldn't tell you were anywhere near an ocean, and then back along the shore again. She liked being with Jack so much, and it was such fun in the Roadmaster with the top down. The only time they talked was right at the start, when she went into the glove compartment, and he wouldn't let her use his new sunglasses. It sounded like he was only kidding at first, but he got mad when she took them out anyway and tried them on, so she put them back.

"Now don't pout."

"I'm not pouting."

"Better put your scarf on."

"Oh, that's right. My hair." Claudia looked in the side mirror and put her scarf over her hair and tied it in back.

"I'm sorry I lost my temper," he said.

"That's all right, Jack."

"I don't want you to scratch the lenses or lose them out the window."

"I wouldn't do that."

"How do you know? Can you say that with absolute certainty?"

"I guess not."

"Well?" Jack turned towards her and took his hands off the wheel for a second, hunching his shoulders up like Jack Benny asking a rhetorical question, but Claudia could tell he was annoyed. Then she could not leave well enough alone and had to make a stupid suggestion.

"Why don't you wear your good ones, and I'll wear the ones you have on?"

"Claudia, the good ones are my navy ones, and these are my civilian ones, and right now I need them for driving."

"That's silly, Jack. You bought the good ones yourself. They aren't navy ones."

"They're for official navy use only, whether I bought them or not. That's the trouble these days. I see it all the time at the yard, but I thought it was only the enlisted men. I'll give you an example. You know those copper awnings that Bill put over all the windows on their house?"

"I think they're pretty," said Claudia. "Mary Ann says Bill is handy with tools."

"Well, he obviously cut them out of sheet copper, and where do you think that came from? The navy yard, of course."

"I never thought about it."

"It isn't right, is it?"

"Well no—"

"It's no different from the sunglasses. Official use only."

"But my eyes hurt, Jack."

"You can just close them. I'm driving. I can't close my eyes. So I get the sunglasses. Think of it like this: There is only one pair of sunglasses in the car, got it?"

"All right, Jack." Claudia leaned out the window with her head back and her eyes closed. Jack liked to see what the Roadmaster could do, but he took the curves so well, you hardly knew you were going fast. The wind rushed around her ears, but she caught "Chattanooga Choo Choo" on the radio and they both shouted "Track twenty-nine!" right on cue. That made her very happy. It showed how meant for each other they really were. "I'll Never Smile Again" came on, and she moved over on the seat close to Jack.

Claudia closed her eyes dreamily. She was just asking for it, arguing about the sunglasses. It wasn't worth fighting over. Last month's *Woman's Home Companion* had a feature called "Walking Away from a Fight," and it was so true to life. Her life anyway. It said you shouldn't worry about wearing out too many pairs of shoes walking away from fights.

It was fun going to the north shore, but Jack pulled the Roadmaster off before they got to where all the people were and parked under some palm trees. He stood up in the seat and looked around and said it was a good place, so Claudia got the picnic basket out of the back seat and their towels and the beach blanket and her new book, *The Heart Is a Lonely Hunter,* and followed Jack out onto the sand. Jack looked all around again, picked a good spot, and helped spread out the blanket. He sat down and took off his shirt and wristwatch.

"I want to look good for tonight, but I don't want to get burned, so you're going to have to let me know every time ten minutes go by. Can you do that?"

"Sure, Jack. I'm just going to be reading."

"Just don't fall asleep, okay?" Without another word he wiggled out of his suit and lay down with nothing on but the jock strap thing.

"Jack—"

"Nobody's going to see. Just read your book and watch the time. Let me use your towel, will you? You can have these now." He tossed her the sunglasses and lay back with both towels under his head. After a little while he turned his face toward her and said, "You know what?"

"What?"

"I think you forgot something," he said.

"I don't know, what?"

"You should have shaved your legs and underarms before we left. Now you're going to have to do it just before the party, and you aren't so good with the razor, are you?"

"Oh darn it, Jack. You're right."

"I don't think you're ever going to learn." Jack turned away and closed his eyes again. "It's wearing me out having to tell you everything."

Claudia moved the picnic basket around to prop up her book. She ended up on her elbows, lying the other way so the sun wasn't reflecting off the white pages, and she could not help looking over because Jack had his eyes closed and her face was closer than it had ever been to his private parts. She wished he didn't have the jock strap thing on and she could get a good look at it.

Mary Ann was so vulgar sometimes, but she could be a good source of information. One time, before she said the bad word again, Mary Ann alluded to girls who put it in their mouths and sucked on it. Nice girls, not just the girls she knew. She said men liked it. It was a wonder they weren't afraid a girl might bite. Jack would be so surprised if she slipped off the jock thing while he was asleep and did that. She wondered what he would do. He might slap her across the face.

What was wrong with her? She was supposed to be devoting her time and energy to helping him advance in his career, not sucking on his thing.

"What time is it?"

"Oh, Jack, I'm sorry."

He kept his eyes closed and pointed at the wristwatch beside his head.

"I don't remember when you started," said Claudia.

"Oh swell." He turned on his side and looked at the watch. "Okay, we'll start over at quarter after. Jesus, you're hard to beat, Claudia."

Everything else went fine. They drove back and got home with plenty of time. Jack took a short nap while Claudia ironed his dress shirt and got out his dress whites and put a fresh coat of white on his shoes and made them a light dinner. He looked funny at it because it was only a cold plate with saltines and Campbell's Cream of Mushroom Soup and toast slices she cut into fingers, just to be fancy.

"I guess you didn't go to too much trouble for this," he said.

"Well, Jack, I thought you didn't want a big meal before the party. This is perfectly nutritious but not too filling."

"It's aggravating. How are you supposed to eat it?"

"You take a saltine like this, and you put a slice of cheese on it, then a pickle slice, and then a slice of tomato on top. Then you pop it in." Claudia did one for him, explaining it again as she constructed it, and put the sample saltine with its complement into his mouth. "Do you like it?"

Jack made a face and said, "Too much trouble, and we're getting behind. I'll get to the soup, and you can make up the crackers for me."

Claudia made up the saltines for him and arranged them in a circle around the plate. It was supposed to be for both of them, but Jack ate them all, almost as fast as she could put them together, and before she knew it, the whole cold plate was gone as well as all the cream of mushroom soup.

Claudia hooked up the hose and Jack went out to take his shower on the little cement patch patio. While she was waiting to turn off the water, she ate a couple of pieces of bread. Then she got out the safety razor and the little mirror and went out to shave her legs and underarms and take her shower under the hose. Jack had not kissed her all day. Not even once, and now he was expecting her to be so good at this party.

CHAPTER SEVEN

They drove through Honolulu and a little way up into the country to the Admiral Harris estate. There was a high iron fence along the road for a quarter mile before Jack turned the Roadmaster through the gates and into the driveway. Claudia had been there once before, when Jack first reported for duty. They'd had fifteen minutes with the Admiral and his wife in the library. At least there were going to be other people tonight. Claudia was so proud of the Roadmaster on occasions like this. They parked on the grass beside the other cars, and it was easy to see who was going places in the navy.

It was just getting dark, and there was a Hawaiian man going around lighting tall bamboo torches lining the marble steps from the lawn to the terrace. The large Georgian house was lit up on three floors, and there were French doors that extended the length of the terrace, open with light curtains moving in the breeze. It was such a lovely night. At the top of the steps, Claudia turned around to look at the view that seemed to be entrancing everyone. Spreading out below were the lights coming on in Honolulu and the navy yard, with the ships lit up and the dark ocean beyond.

There were a lot of people on the terrace, and she looked around to get the lay of the land. The navy men were in dress whites. Jack whispered that the ones in the short, black frock coats with the old-fashioned stand-up collars were diplomatic corps people.

"This will be us before you know it," said Jack as he looked around the grounds. "Everybody moves up with a war. It's a good way to get rid of the old guard."

It seemed to Claudia more likely that a war would get rid of the young guards. The old guards would be playing golf, but Jack was laughing to himself at what he had just said, and she did not want to start anything now. She could tell he was warming up for the party.

Claudia took his arm, and they went through the French doors and into the crowd moving between the open downstairs rooms. Jack said he was looking for someone. There was a string quartet playing Mozart in the dining room, where a buffet was set up, with the lights of a large chandelier twinkling off the silver and cut glass on a very long white tablecloth. Someone in a room off to the side was playing a piano and singing "I Like

New York in June, How About You?," but you could hardly hear either one over the people talking and laughing.

"Don't you think we'd better find Admiral Harris?" said Claudia.

"That's what we're doing, but we need someone on the inside track to run the introduction. Captain Locarno's a buddy of mine."

"I thought you couldn't be buddies with a captain."

"I let him use the Roadmaster to go into town."

There was a narrowing in the hallway where the presence of a powder room had eddied a flotsam of ladies. Jack stalled, but Claudia recognized it immediately as her call to duty. The USS Wyler, in danger of coming to grief in congested waters, takes on a pilot. Too-wee goes the bosun's whistle. Claudia Wyler on the bridge. Set the topgallants. She took Jack's hand and steered him right through the channel as the group parted for Claudia's sleek and stunning red gown. She felt all eyes upon her and then all eyes upon Jack. Sometimes that's all you need to get your self-confidence back.

They ended up by the banister of the grand staircase in the main hall and took up a position where Jack could lean casually against it and watch who came in.

"Make conversation," he said.

"Okay," she said. "Why can't I drive the Roadmaster? I didn't think you let anyone drive the Roadmaster—that's what you said, but now I find out this Captain Locomotive—"

"Locarno. Locarno. Oh God, Claudia. Don't goof up on that one. It's only once a week. His girlfriend likes the car."

"But his name was on the list, so he has a wife."

"That's why we're buddies."

A waiter walked by with an empty tray, and Jack asked for a Tom Collins and a daiquiri, and soon they were standing with their drinks. Claudia didn't know why she bothered to learn all those names. They weren't meeting anybody.

"There he is," said Jack. "Short, blond fellow."

It was time to make the catch, and Claudia did her best to glide behind Jack across the black-and-white marble floor in the four-inch heels. Claudia could see right away that Mrs. Locarno knew about the other woman. She was probably no more than forty, but she looked much older, even in a lavender gown that should have done wonders for her. Her eyes had lines under them, and her hair was styled but lifeless. She offered her hand and a tired, polite smile as Jack made introductions.

Captain Locarno was the usual. Just some man—short, with receding blond hair, and maybe forty-five. He was very trim and packed nicely into the dress whites. Not bad looking at all, but nothing compared to Jack, with those steely gray eyes of his, luxurious brown hair so full of body, but light as a feather when you touched it, and a square jaw and chin that Dick Tracy would have if he were real, and such an intelligent brow. What was there to notice about anybody else?

"It's very nice to meet you," he said. "We should have more of these affairs for the wives."

He did not let go of her hand, and then he placed his other hand over Claudia's and indicated that she was to take his arm, and immediately Jack offered his to Mrs. Locarno and off they went.

"The Admiral and Mrs. Harris are in the little drawing room," said Captain Locarno. He leaned in to Claudia's ear. "Don't worry about running aground in the drawing room. Harris and I go back a long way. I'll float you off."

Claudia laughed and tossed her hair without thinking. It was a natural thing for her to do, but she knew it was cruel and thoughtless to have done it in front of Mrs. Locarno following right behind. She knew how women get their wires crossed. Mrs. Locarno might be imagining her husband making love to his mistress and suddenly in her mind she sees Claudia Wyler tossing her beautiful hair and laughing. That would do it. Jack kept her occupied as they went along the hallway to the drawing room, but Claudia could feel the eyes.

There was an informal line moving in front of the two armchairs where Admiral and Mrs. Harris sat and, while they waited their turn and stepped forward foot by foot, Claudia glanced around the room, admiring the bookcases and tasseled lampshades. Every so often she nodded to the drift of Captain Locarno's conversation. He had noticed many fine houses on the island, and he was studying real estate. He was planning to go into business. He said Hawaii was going to have a big tourist industry, and he was going to make a fortune in hotels. Pretty soon Claudia realized it wasn't just a line. He was looking for investors. He had the idea that Jack had a lot of money.

The Admiral acknowledged Captain Locarno with "Jim," as they shook hands. Mrs. Harris, a thin, very alert, white-haired lady, smiled radiantly at Claudia.

"Oh, Martha," she said to Mrs. Locarno, "Aren't the young wives stunning. I'm so glad we don't have to compete with them."

"It might be more of a contest than any of them would think, Betty," cautioned Mrs. Locarno in a flat voice.

"You're sweet to say so, dear," said Mrs. Harris.

They moved on with the line and found themselves back in the main hall, where Captain Locarno finally released Claudia.

"I'll stand by, Jack. I think Harris wants to slip down to the game room and broadside me at billiards, and Betty likes talking with Martha. I want to keep my shore duty, you know."

"We'll mingle," said Jack. "Thanks for the introduction."

Captain Locarno again took Claudia's hand and said, "A pleasure meeting you, a real pleasure." Then he whispered, "Don't forget what we talked about. Hotels."

Claudia smiled as warmly as she could at Mrs. Locarno, and she smiled back and touched Claudia's arm tenderly. It meant everything in the world to Claudia. It meant that Mrs. Locarno was very kind, or very forgiving and gracious, or just uncommonly wise for a middle-aged woman. Or maybe she knew something.

Claudia followed Jack down the hall on his arm, lightly shouldering through the mob of gowns and dress whites, looking for the nearest bar setup, when a face in the crowd suddenly lit up, and a very bright, eager-looking young man accosted them.

"Jack—and Claudia!"

"Oh, Froggy."

"So this is the beast?"

"So it is," said Jack.

That was a surprise for Claudia. She never heard Jack be jocular before.

"Claudia, Lieutenant Ransome. Froggy, this is Claudia. Frog was in my class at the academy."

Froggy shook her hand enthusiastically. "I heard you were a real looker, but navy men are such goddamn liars. How long have you been here, Jack?"

"Just got here."

"Did you go see the big man?"

"Already taken care of."

"You know you can check your hat. There's a room down the hall on the left by the front door. You just take a ticket."

"Thanks, Frog. Wait here, Claudia. I'll be back in a jiffy."

Froggy leaned back against the wall and looked at her, so she looked at him. He was one of those very extremely white boys with curly red hair and freckles. He was kind of goofy looking, even in the dress whites.

"I only came to this thing to see you," he said. "You really are hot stuff."

"You're kind of cute yourself."

Claudia didn't bother to catch herself. It just came out, but she didn't care, and she was feeling the daiquiri. Ransome wasn't on the list, so she knew Froggy must be single and there was no wife to worry about. Claudia leaned back against the wall beside him to let the people go by.

"I was going to warn you about the girl at the office," said Froggy, "but you have nothing to worry about, sister. You got it all over her."

"You mean Annette?"

"You know about Annette?"

"Jack tells me everything."

"What did he say about me?"

"Nothing." Claudia laughed.

"Come on. What did he say? I know he said something. You just came here to get a look at me, didn't you?"

"You're like a little brother."

"He said that? I'm flattered, but I thought it was more like the other way around."

"He didn't say it, I did."

"That's like always a bridesmaid," said Froggy.

"Well you started it. You called me sister."

"That's just an expression they use in America. You know, the big island. We get America on the radio. It's the only way to keep up with what's happening uptown, downtown, crosstown."

"Don't worry about me, Mister Froggy. I keep up."

"I see you do. That's some dress."

"Jack got it for me."

"On his measly twelve hundred a year?"

"I don't know. I guess so."

"That's why I'm single. I can't find a dish like you to marry me for twelve hundred a year."

"That's probably not the only reason—" Claudia couldn't help herself. It felt so good to have fun talking, and Froggy was the kind of boy you could do that with, and it didn't have to mean anything.

"What's his secret? I mean, why Jack?"

"He's perfect," said Claudia. "Perfect in every way."

"Yes, we all know Jack's perfect. What eludes me is how can you stand it?"

"He needs me."

Froggy laughed. "What does he need you for? He's got me. He's no good at math you know. I got him through the academy, and then he turns up here. Somebody should tell the government they're getting one man for the price of two. Woops—"

His hand came up quickly to cover his mouth, and he spoke between his fingers. "That's top secret," he said

"Acknowledged, Lieutenant Ransome."

"Call me Froggy."

"I forgot."

"How can you forget Froggy?"

"I was trying." Claudia could not remember the last time she had anything to laugh about. It felt so good, and Froggy was funny, and she was keeping up pretty good herself, for being so out of practice.

"How did you get that silly name?"

"I don't know. Everyone in the family was named Ransome."

"No, you silly. The Froggy part."

"Well, that's easy. We'd go out after frogs. Frog legs got us through the Depression. I spent my callow youth in the swamps. Never went to school."

"So how did you get to Annapolis if you never went to school, mister?"

"I found a box of books in a barn when I was ten and learned Greek and mathematics by myself. Then one day we were hunting frogs by the bridge, and our congressman came by in one of the cars he stole across the border in Mississippi and asked if anyone wanted to go to Annapolis. I said sure. I thought it was a Greek restaurant—imagine my surprise. All I had to do was learn the King's English, and they let me out of Alabama. Five years later, I wind up here under the palm trees. I never knew what hit me." Then he smiled a big one and said, "I wouldn't lie to you, sugar."

He had nice blue eyes, not too watery, and his teeth were very straight and white, which was good because he smiled as he talked and you could see them all the time. It was just the curly red hair.

"So Mister Frog, do you think you're going to find a princess to kiss you at this party?"

"How did you know I was looking?"

"You've got that look on your face. Any princess would see you coming a mile away."

"What harm would a little kiss do?"

"Don't ask me. I've already got a prince."

"Yeah, well, you'll have to explain that to me sometime."

Jack came through the hallway toward them. Claudia could see his head over most of the others. It wasn't that he was tall as much as it was his posture. Officers did not have to stand up straight, or brace, like Jack called it, but Jack did it naturally all the time. He was carrying another Tom Collins and a daiquiri. Froggy was saying something but stopped when she wasn't paying attention. She hoped Froggy noticed the way she looked at Jack. There wasn't any hope for anybody else with Jack around.

"There was a crowd at the bar." He gave Claudia the daiquiri and pulled a bottle of beer out of his jacket and tossed it to Froggy.

"Hey, thanks, Jack. Say, does anyone want to go dancing?"

"Dancing. Oh Jack."

"Can't leave the party."

"No," said Froggy. "Right here, downstairs. Come on."

He took Claudia by the hand and pushed off into the flow of gowns and whites with Jack following. He led them around the corner and through some swinging doors into the kitchen, with all the busy cooks in chef hats, pots and pans hanging from the ceiling, trays and platters everywhere, and waiters standing around on break smoking. No one even looked up as they went through and down a side staircase. At the bottom of the stairs was a dark corridor and then a room with music and voices. There was a bar set up on one side and a record player, and the chairs had been moved out of the way for a dance floor. Some couples were dancing to the "One O'Clock Jump," and a bunch of young navy men and their girls were hanging around the back walls in the dark. Everybody was their age. It was like college.

"Welcome to the rumpus room," said Froggy. He leaned into Claudia. "That's where the Admiral keeps his rumpus."

Jack hung back in the doorway and looked over the room.

"Oh, Jack—can we dance?"

Jack drew her away from Froggy and whispered to her. "We're not supposed to be here, and nobody here is supposed to be at the party. I don't know how they got in."

"Can't we just dance one or two? It would be so much fun."

"You can. I'm going topside."

"I'll come too."

"No, you stay here," he said. "Frog, can I dock Claudia with you for a while?"

"Sure thing."

"No, Jack, I want to come with you."

"No," said Jack. "You stay here, dance a few and come back up when you're ready. Okay?"

"All right, but just a few, and then I'll come find you."

Froggy stepped in, and Jack disappeared down the corridor.

"This is wonderful, Froggy."

"Let's go."

"No, I want to watch a minute."

They leaned against the wall with some other couples. It was pretty dark, and some of the couples were kissing along the wall. They had to move over to make room, and soon Claudia found herself leaning against Froggy, and he had his arm around her waist. He kind of snuck that in, but it would be there anyway if they were dancing. Just the same, she only let him get away with it because she was tipsy and because he was the kind of man who didn't matter that much. It's funny how many rules and exceptions you have to learn—dumbfounding, really.

"So what's your waistline?" he asked. "If I may be bold."

"You mean fresh."

"Okay, fresh."

"Nineteen." Claudia could smile to herself in the dark without him seeing. She was very pleased with her numbers, and it was something you didn't bring up yourself.

"You picked up a few pounds on the island, huh?

"You're a jerk."

"I just heard it was less."

"You heard wrong, buddy. Let's go dance."

They kicked off with "Skyliner." She knew that one. Claudia took off the heels and slid them under a chair on the side. It was a little fast, and Claudia was rusty, but she caught up. Froggy held her tightly when they came together and let her go all the way out when they flew apart, gripping her hand with only his fingertips. She loved it so much and laughed every time he got out of time. As they tried to speed up, they tripped over each other's feet, but he never stepped on her toes. When the record ended, they stood together catching their breath while someone changed the record. Froggy knew all the songs and brought her up to date. They passed on "The Flat Foot Floogie," but "Bounce Me Brother with a Solid Four" brought everybody to the dance floor. It was the perfect dance number, and Claudia and Froggy lit into it with the others. Soon Claudia was aware of perspiration coming out on her forehead and upper lip. She was really drunk now, and when the song was over, she went back to lean against the wall. She knew she shouldn't dance anymore and go find Jack, but it was hard to stop having a good time.

"Great records, Froggy," she said breathlessly. "Admiral Harris must have a side of him Mrs. Harris doesn't know about."

"It's easy to make that mistake with Harris," said Froggy, "but, no, the platters-that-matter are my roommate's. He used to be a hepcat before Annapolis. He's got all the big swingin' hits."

While Froggy was talking, he pulled a white handkerchief out of his pocket and dabbed off the perspiration on her forehead. "Hold still," he said, and he dabbed her upper lip too. He should have just offered the handkerchief, but it happened too fast for her to stop him. As quick as that, the handkerchief was back in his pocket, and he was grabbing the arm of somebody.

"Dan, I want you to meet somebody. This is Jack's wife. Claudia. Claudia, this is my roommate, Dan. He's the one with the records."

Claudia had pictured a hepcat differently. He was like Jack. He looked more mature than the other young officers, and he was dazzling in his dress whites. He said, "How do you do" like he was doing business. It was hard to imagine them as roommates.

"I like your records," she said.

"Thank you. I try to keep a balanced collection."

"Good one coming up," said Froggy. "An oldie but still doin' it, for your listenin' pleasure, little treasure."

Claudia recognized the long beginning of "I've Got a Crush on You." Dan and his girl excused themselves to dance, and Froggy stepped into Claudia and put his arm around her. She figured him to be the type with all hands, but that's as far as it went. The hands were strictly regulation, and he was a perfect gentleman. He took her hand, and she rested her head against his shoulder like you're supposed to do. Somehow she thought he was short, but up against him she found she fit like she fit with Jack, and if anything, he might even be a little taller than Jack. He just seemed less significant. She closed her eyes. It was a dreamy song in the true sense of dreamy because she remembered how she dreamed to it when she was twelve years old. She dreamed of getting a boy of her own. Then she grew up and found out you get a man.

When she opened her eyes, she found herself looking right into Dan's eyes. The floor was full, and the couples weren't able to turn very much, and it was like floating down a river, looking at each other from two rafts. She smiled over Froggy's shoulder, and Dan smiled back over his girl's. It would be fun to make up a man from pieces of men you liked. Froggy would let her get away with anything if she was his girl, and she knew she didn't want that, but just the same, maybe she'd take a thing or two from Froggy.

The song ran out, and someone started it over, and more of the lights went out, so Claudia knew it was time to get out while the getting was good.

"Froggy," she said, "can you help me find my shoes?"

"You don't have to go, do you?"

"I think Jack needs me." She was grateful Froggy didn't twist it around and make something funny out of it. He was very good and found her shoes. She had snagged one of her nylons at the heel. Another $1.25 out the window, but it was so much fun.

"Thanks for the dance, beautiful."

"I had fun, Froggy. You're sweet."

"I'll walk you back up."

"No, you stay here. I have to go to the powder room."

Froggy said okay, but then he held her back for a moment and looked her in the eyes. Claudia couldn't make out the red hair and freckles in the darkness, but she knew they were there, and he really didn't have much of a chin, at least not like Jack. They say you can fall in love with anyone, but how can that be true?

"Do me a favor," he said. "You know what I said about Jack?"

"I don't remember."

"About the math. Just forget that, okay? I don't want to end up on middle-watch iceberg duty off the Aleutians on Christmas Eve. That happens to guys with big mouths."

"Don't worry," she said. "My lips are sealed. Thanks for the dancing, Froggy."

She gave one of his hands a light squeeze, and she went into the dark corridor toward the stairs and the brightness behind the swinging doors of the kitchen. A little squeeze was a good way to get out of a tight spot. A man will always let you go if you give his hand a little squeeze.

CHAPTER EIGHT

Claudia was surprised by the powder room. It was under a back staircase, but it was huge. There were two toilet stalls that looked somewhat navy in origin, but everything was painted in the most delicate shade of rose. There was a carpeted lounge area with two chairs set before a makeup table with a tall mirror and lighting that didn't make you feel miserable about yourself. She was glad no one was there and hurried to use the toilet and look at her burn. Dancing was probably not the greatest idea in the world. She heard someone come in, and she quickly flushed and came out.

One girl was already in the other stall, and Claudia heard her complain, "God, I hate taking everything off." Another girl was sitting at the makeup table brushing her hair. Claudia sat down next to her, smiled, and turned her face from profile to profile, wondering if she needed to get her hairbrush out of the car.

"So what do you think, Brenda?" the girl in the stall called out.

The girl in the chair beside her was putting on her lipstick and did not take her eyes off the mirror. "I don't know," she said.

"He's fair game, isn't he?"

"Well, I know, but still—"

"But still nothing. She had her chance, and if she muffed it, well that's tough."

"I feel bad for her."

"You better get over that." The girl in the stall flushed and came out. "You go on, Brenda," she said. "I have to do my hair."

"Okay, see you out there."

"Go get 'em, tiger."

When Brenda left, after blocking the mirror with last minute adjustments of her dress and trimming ship, it was as if Claudia's view had been obstructed by busy tugboats, a flotilla of small craft, and the fountains of harbor fireboats in salute; for gliding through the narrows of the stall door came the magnificent stacks and sleek lines of a regular transatlantic liner of a girl. She came up behind Claudia and exclaimed "I love it! The dress. It's perfect. Stand up and turn around. Let's see." Her hair swirled around her shoulders as she spoke.

Claudia stood up and turned around, not knowing what to say.

"Oh, I'm sorry. I'm Annette Anisinelli. I work with Jack. I helped him pick out the dress. You're Claudia, aren't you?"

Annette embraced her, and Claudia's face was plunged into the raven night of her hair, and as they separated, her eyes dropped into the deep cleavage of a noteworthy pair of bosoms, elevated by a tight bodice of daring horizontal pleats that hoisted their cargo up to the main deck. Below that, the dress was a sheath of shimmering white satin with black panels. Annette was statuesque, regal, and earthy at the same time, with hunter's bow lips, and eyebrows like sculpted wings over the arch of an aquiline nose. She was wearing Jeanne Lanvin My Sin. It figured.

"And I love your hair. That turned out very well. Mr. Anthony's great, isn't he? You look like someone in the movies."

"Ann Sheridan."

"Maybe a little."

"That was the idea. Jack's idea anyway."

"That's one thing men are good at, isn't it? They have such vivid imaginations. They can pretend they're making love to anyone they want."

Claudia had never heard that. It never crossed her mind. But it all fit. At one stroke, Annette had altered her universe. She tried to laugh along, but her heart had stopped. She didn't think there was any laughing matter that could do that.

"We have to brush your hair," said Annette. "What have you been doing?"

"Dancing, downstairs. It was a stupid thing to do. Oh, I forgot. Thank you for the list. I wanted to say thanks and say how much I appreciated it."

Annette sat Claudia down in the chair again and remained standing behind her, gently drafting her hair back with her hands. "It wasn't any trouble. I have all that information on everybody. Did you bring a brush?"

"It's out in the car."

"You don't mind my hairbrush, do you?"

"Oh no. You have beautiful hair."

"I can't figure out what to do with it in this climate, so I just leave it alone."

Annette got her hairbrush out of her bag, and Claudia watched her in the mirror as she brushed her hair. She was deeply tanned. There wasn't a trace of where white lines should be, anywhere. She had beautiful eyes too, hazel but not quite.

"Oh, I know," she said. "You look like Veronica Lake. If you didn't have the bangs and let it down over one eye—"

"I know—me and a million other girls with their hair in their eyes."

Annette laughed. "I guess you'd notice that. See, I wouldn't because there's no way in the world I could look like Veronica Lake. I'm too dark. When I came back from Radcliffe, I was pale as a ghost, but it didn't take long to get dark again. I have a lot of Italian in me on my dad's side. He works in the Agriculture Department, studying pineapples, if you can believe that. My mom's French. You must be Swedish or something?"

"I'm married to Jack, remember? It's like being in the Foreign Legion. You have no past. Toujours Jack."

Annette laughed. "It's good to have a sense of humor about it."

"Somebody has to."

"You noticed that too? The man has no sense of humor at all, does he?"

"I never really thought about it, but no, I guess he doesn't."

"You know what we're doing, don't you?"

"No, what?"

"I think it's called comparing notes."

That made Claudia a little uneasy. Where did people get off? But she tried to laugh, and Annette laughed too and packed up her bag.

"He's right outside."

"Jack?"

"Mr. U.S. Navy himself. He's waiting for me, so let me go out first, and we'll surprise him."

Claudia waited a moment after Annette went out the door. Again, where did people get off? She did not feel like seeing anything that would make her jealous. So far, she had been able to do all the housework and cooking without a second thought and put up with the loneliness of being alone most of the time while he was working with tanned Italian girls from Radcliffe all day, and he could pretend he was making love to anybody he wanted. He had given her the wrong impression. She thought Annette was just an ordinary office girl. She even thought Annette might have been Hawaiian because there were so few white girls on the island. And then he was always bumping into her.

When Claudia came out of the powder room, Jack was trying to get away, and Annette was holding him down. She had both hands on him. One hand was where his belly button was, the other was around the side. Claudia knew he thought the girls set him up, and she did not care for the implicit complicity between herself and Annette, but there was nothing she could do about it now. She went right to his side and put her arm around him, and Annette backed off. Jack smiled confidently.

"Well, I hope you two can put your heads together and come up with a shortcut to lieutenant commander for me. I'm tired of shining my own shoes."

"I didn't know you needed directions," said Annette. "You should have asked. Nearest lieutenant commander just two doors away—as the old crow flies."

Jack and Annette laughed, and Jack explained that she meant Bobby Rodgers, and Bobby Rodgers liked Old Crow whiskey.

"Let's put it this way," said Jack. "He likes it a lot."

Then he and Annette both said at the same time, "—and a lot of it!"

Then they both laughed, and Claudia tried to laugh too.

"He was the one on the radio, wasn't he, Jack?"

"That's him, and we're probably just in time to catch him sober. Come on."

As they walked around the main entrance hall again, looking into the rooms full of people holding drinks and laughing, Jack whispered to Claudia that Bobby Rodgers's wife never came to the parties. It was a reputation problem, he said. Annette put her hand on Claudia's shoulder from behind.

"It wasn't her problem. It was his," she said.

"That's what I meant," Jack said, glowering over his shoulder.

"No, Jack. You said it as if Cynthia Rodgers had the bad reputation."

"She knew what I meant."

"No, I didn't," said Claudia.

"You see, Jack. It's like that orientation directive the other day. When you're indiscriminate with your pronouns, it confuses people."

Jack and Annette stopped and turned to face each other, like drawing up battle lines.

"Everybody knew who was who."

"Then why was I on the phone all day explaining it?"

"All right. Next time you write it."

"That's what makes me so goddamn mad, Jack. I do write them. All you have to do is signoff and pass them to the pool. You mess up every one I give you."

"Go to hell, Annette."

"No, you go to hell."

Annette slapped him across the face. He grabbed her wrist, and she slapped him again with the other hand. He tried to grab that wrist too but missed, and she got both hands free. Claudia heard Jack say bitch, and then Annette slapped him again. He feigned a punch toward her face, and she abruptly turned and disappeared into the people going by.

It was almost too fast for Claudia to take in. Jack laughed as if he had been caught playing a joke on someone and looked around, but he didn't have to bother. Nobody notices much at a party. It was after midnight, and a lot of people had drunk too much. Claudia could tell Jack had a few while she was dancing.

"Shouldn't you go find Annette?" she asked timidly.

"She'll get over it. Annette's just hotheaded like that. She's Italian."

"But Jack—"

"It happens all the time, don't worry about it. She can be a bitch sometimes, that's all."

Claudia followed Jack into a room where there was something drawing everyone to a big table. He had never used that word before. She had never seen him physically fight with anyone, let alone a girl, and when he feigned the punch at Annette, it made her heart go to her throat. It was the navy. If it ever happened again, she would have to write to *Woman's Home Companion* for advice. She would have to write it with different names and a different naval base, but the postmark would say Pearl Harbor, Hawaii, and the navy wives who read the magazine and saw her letter would think it was Mrs.

Rodgers who was writing in about her husband, because, as far as she knew, Jack didn't have a bad reputation. Not yet anyway.

Jack approached the group bending over the table and touched one man on the shoulder, who pulled out of the group and turned around.

"Commander Rodgers, I'd like you to meet my wife, Claudia."

Commander Rodgers straightened up and turned fully around, and Claudia was happy to see his face brighten up.

"Good to see you, Jack. My pleasure, Mrs. Wyler. Delighted to meet you."

He looked about fifty and was good looking, like all the navy men in their dress whites with the stiff collars and the epaulets. They called them boards. What would she do if *Woman's Home Companion* told her to get Jack out of the navy? She loved the uniforms so much. Life was full of impossible choices.

"I'm glad you could make it to the party, Mrs. Wyler."

"It's been so much fun."

"What are we doing on the map, commander?" Jack asked.

"Oh, just pushing the boats around. Why don't you look in, Jack. I've had enough war games for the night. I think I might take some air."

"Claudia was just saying the same thing."

With that, Jack exchanged a nod with Commander Rodgers and made for the vacant place at the table. Claudia felt Jack left her high and dry, but Commander Rodgers was quick to throw her a line.

"Maybe a daiquiri—a small one," she said.

Rodgers headed for the other side of the room where a bar was set up on card tables, with ice buckets and fizzy dispensers and every brand of liquor you could imagine, looking like a city skyline of bottles. There was a Hawaiian bartender in a white shirt and black vest standing behind the tables, polishing glasses with a towel, inclining thoughtfully into the conversation of a group of five or six wives standing around.

Claudia looked over Jack's head and between the navy men at the big table. It was a large, circular oak table with a glass top, and under the glass was the biggest map of the Pacific Ocean she had ever seen. Jack turned his head and whispered to her to go with Commander Rodgers.

"But I want to see what you're doing."

"It's just maneuvers and war games. Go on."

Claudia could tell Jack was getting short, and when he told her to go, she could see his lower front teeth because his jaw was so tight. Then he turned his back on her and put his elbows down on the table between two other officers, shoulder to shoulder, who said, "Hey Jack," and then everyone was looking at the map and moving little boats around with long poles. Somebody threw out a pair of dice, so she knew it was only a game. But she figured Jack had something up his sleeve and wanted her to leave him alone. He was looking after his career.

When Claudia came up behind Commander Rodgers at the bar, he was just turning around with her daiquiri and a cocktail napkin in one hand and something tall for himself in the other, and he almost lost the daiquiri.

"Oh, I'm sorry," she said.

"A close call."

"You're very quick," she said.

"I've had some practice."

"Well, I've had some practice getting in the way."

"I don't see how you could ever be in the way," he said.

"Jack could tell you some stories."

Commander Rodgers laughed. "The only things I've heard out of Jack wouldn't make your ears wiggle."

"Ears wiggle?"

"Haven't you ever heard that? It must be Midwest. I'm from Kansas City, not the Missouri side, the Kansas side."

"Oh, that's right. There's two—and both of them sound like the real Kansas City, don't they?"

"Come on," he said, "Let's find a place to sit down."

He led her over to some very plushy armchairs by the windows. The breeze was coming in and drafting off the smoke that was coming from the war table.

"This is very nice," she said. "It's like a restaurant on a pier. You can see all the lights of Honolulu. I'm from Connecticut—I don't know if Jack told you, so this is all so new to me. But I love it here."

"Most people do. I've been looking into some properties around the city. I think it would be a great opportunity to put together the right group of investors."

Another one, thought Claudia.

"After the war, of course," he added. "We're bound to get in it."

"You sound just like you did on the radio the other day."

"Oh, you heard that."

"I just caught the last part. You have a very good voice for radio, commander. You could advertise your hotels on the radio."

"Oh, no hotels for me," he said. "Retirement homes is the way to go."

There was an outburst of laughter and whistles from the map table. Claudia thought the boys were done, but Commander Rodgers said not by a long shot. He said they were playing a game someone from his office invented in his spare time. He explained why it was okay, as long as it wasn't written on navy paper. That was the word from document control. Then he explained the game. Claudia felt her eyelids getting heavy.

"Say," he said. "It's such a nice night out, I was going to take a drive. Would you like to come along?"

"I'd love to, but I think we're leaving soon."

"Oh no. They'll be at it for a while, if I know anything about my crew. I'd love to show you the bay. Won't take long at all."

"Oh gosh. That sounds so good."

"Let's go then."

Commander Rodgers stood up, and Claudia followed his lead but stopped herself abruptly.

"I really can't," she said. "I have to wait for Jack."

For a moment, Commander Rodgers looked like some rug had been pulled out from under him, but he bounced up quickly.

"I can't change your mind?"

"No, really, but thanks so much for the offer."

"Well then, I'll shove off. It's been a pleasure to meet you, Mrs. Wyler."

"And a pleasure for me as well," she said.

"Don't forget what we talked about."

Claudia was getting the idea that Jack had made a certain kind of impression at the navy yard. For the first time she saw that getting ahead in the navy had its own rules and exceptions. Jack had to navigate and master them. It was the first time she had seen him in action. That's why it was bewildering. How could she learn what Jack had learned? How could she possibly be of any help to him in his career? For just a moment, because she was tired and had too many drinks, she thought—to hell with it. Jack could just keep towing her behind in the rowboat, for all she cared. She didn't have to understand everything.

She looked out the window, at the lights down in Honolulu and started to fall asleep, but then she snapped out of it and straightened up. There was work to do. The wives were still at the bar talking. If Jack could do it, she could do it, too. Claudia got up on the pretext of getting another daiquiri and moved into the periphery of the group, holding her glass in front of her in both hands, one on the stem and two fingers of the other on the base. It felt sophisticated. They had all seen her with Commander Rodgers.

One girl looked at her drink and right away said, "I thought the bartender couldn't make daiquiris."

"I don't know. I just asked for one."

"How does it taste?"

"I wouldn't know the difference. Want to try it?"

"Sure."

"I'm Claudia Wyler."

"I'm Rebecca Ogden, but call me Becky."

Claudia knew Ogden from the cards. Her husband was a lieutenant like Jack. So far so good, but the introductions to the others came faster than Claudia's flash cards.

"I don't think I'll remember all the names."

"Don't worry about it," said one girl with a southern accent. "We've known each other for a long time. I love your dress, Claudia. I had to go shopping with Katie last week—"

"You make it sound like I dragged you," said Katie.

"Well I don't want to give a new girl the wrong impression. I don't like shopping anymore."

"Oh come off it, Margie. You love it."

"I do not."

"You should see her shoe closet," Becky confided to Claudia, but everyone heard.

"Why are y'all picking on me?"

The girls mimicked the y'all in unison.

Becky asked Claudia where she lived, and suddenly everyone listened at once.

"In the little shoe box," she said. "No, that's not right."

They all laughed.

"You mean the little white houses?"

"That's it."

"Oh, we know about them, don't we," said Becky.

Then they all started talking at the same time.

"Do you still have to take the washer out of the back closet?"

"I don't mind that," said Claudia, "but the worst thing—"

"No bathtub," someone said.

"I'd have died for a bathtub," said someone else. "Three years without a bathtub."

"A year for me."

"I got you all beat. Four years."

"I was only there six months."

"You got off so easy, Ruthie."

"You call having a baby easy? They still weren't going to let us out. I had to go chew out Albert's boss, that Captain—oh, I don't remember, Captain So and So."

"I bet he really was a so and so."

"They all are."

"Except for the ones who are dopes. Remember that real dopey one, Beverly? The one Jimmy played golf with. He took the prize for dopes, believe me."

Somebody asked Claudia what her husband did, and she said he was in Intelligence and worked in the top secret office. Katie grabbed her arm and asked if he was the one with the car.

"What car?" said Beverly.

"That real nice one. You know. What's it called, Becky?"

"A Roadmaster."

All of them gasped.

"Oh God. You're married to the Roadmaster?"

Two more girls came in, and Ruthie pulled them over.

"Carol and Sandy, this is Claudia. Guess what? Claudia's married to the Roadmaster."

"No kidding," said Sandy. "He's as dreamy as the car."

"Don't mind her, Claudia. Sandy's harmless."

One of the girls whispered loudly "home-wrecker," and they all laughed.

"Looks like the boys are breaking up," Becky said.

"Let's go pick up the pieces, girls."

The girls started putting their glasses down on the bar and the windowsills.

"Now we get to drive them home and put them to bed," said Beverly.

"Don't you get sick of it? How would they like it if it were the other way around?"

"I wish I had a penis," said Ruthie.

"Me too," said Sandy. "I wouldn't mind dishing it out for a change."

"Me too."

"Shut up, Carol. You do not."

"How about you?"

"Hell no," said Becky.

"Oh, look. We finally got Rita's attention. The magic word."

"Gets the rabbit out of the hat for me, girls," said Rita. She batted her eyes around like Groucho Marx, and Claudia laughed along with everybody else.

The girls broke up as the men turned away from the map table, and each one went to her husband, and then it looked like the party was over and everyone was leaving. Claudia was so happy the wives turned out to be just regular girls. Becky introduced her to her husband and said they would have to get together. Claudia was going to introduce Jack, but he was coming up with such a frown on his face that Becky took the hint and pulled her husband away toward the door.

"What are you doing here?" said Jack.

"I was waiting for you."

"I thought you went for a ride with Rodgers."

"I wouldn't do that, Jack."

"That's what I meant."

"What do you mean?"

"When I said you go along."

"I thought you meant over to the bar."

"Oh, Jesus. Where is he now?"

"He left."

"What did he say?"

"I don't know. He said he was going for a ride."

"Oh swell. Come on."

Claudia followed Jack into the main entrance hall. He went to get his hat and then said see you later to a few of the officers still hanging around. One or two of them had their collars open. The admiral and his wife had retired long ago, they said. The only ones left were the drunk ones downstairs.

Jack was really mad. He held the door for her because he was a gentleman, but she could tell he wanted to slam it on her fingers. Whenever she saw the amazing self-control Jack possessed, it renewed her deep admiration of him. It was the essence of masculinity. Some girls wanted to be like men and thought it was as easy as having a penis. Well it isn't. They could take a lesson or two from Jack Wyler about how hard it is to have self-control when you're married. Jack had to drive all the way home without saying a single word.

As far as her own conduct was concerned, the only problem that Claudia could see was that she did not always know what Jack expected of her. She would do anything for him if she only knew what it was. The party wasn't bad at all. She got to dance, and she liked the girls she met. She and Becky might turn out to be best friends.

Then she remembered Annette, and she felt like some kind of hobo compared to her. But then Jack called her a bitch and said it right to her face. She knew she shouldn't worry so much. Tomorrow was Sunday and she had a feeling Jack would want to make love to her, even if he was still mad. She thought about him almost hitting Annette. She hoped her poor peaches would be healed by tomorrow afternoon. If men were really that good at imagining, Jack had a lot of self-control to get out of his system.

CHAPTER NINE

Claudia opened her eyes at eight thirty. It was sunny, and she could hear Bill cutting his grass next door. She knew the blades were dull and he was having a hard time pushing it. She hoped he would sharpen them up before she had to borrow it again. The best part about Sunday was she had Jack all day to herself. They needed time to mend. You can't go a long time without any excitement and then have a lot of it all at once like last night. They needed time to be alone. Jack didn't understand what could happen to a couple who let themselves grow apart. He didn't read *Woman's Home Companion*.

Claudia got up as quietly as she could and went to the kitchen to start the percolator. She poured the bit of leftover coffee into a glass, looked around for her Chesterfields and sat at the table, leafing through *Life*. The percolator started to gurgle and spurt up in the little glass top, and it reminded her that she was going to have to be resourceful about dinner tonight and she better step on it.

She took out *The Newlywed Cookbook* and started looking. They usually went to the market Saturday night. They could have gone Saturday morning, but Jack had wanted to get his tan on the north shore, and he never went shopping by himself unless he was planning to bump into Annette. Apparently.

That wasn't fair. She had to remember never to say it like that. He didn't like to get into uniform on Saturday just to go to the market, and she didn't know how it felt to be in a uniform all the time. But Jack never complained. That was self-control. It was the counterpart to self-confidence in women. She could see it in his face whenever he was losing his temper.

So much depended on his mood, and Claudia hoped he wasn't still mad about whatever it was last night. It could be a good Sunday or not so good, depending. Either way, she would have to ask him to make up the list for the market. She could go tomorrow, and Mary Ann could give her a ride home if Jack dropped her off. Tonight was the problem. She wished she were a wizard in the kitchen like Betty Crocker.

Claudia made the batter for Jack's Sunday pancakes with the last four eggs and added some cinnamon and then put in some nutmeg and tasted it. It was so good, and she brought the bowl over to the table and went back to *Life Looks Back*, where it had pictures from years ago. Then she made herself read the war news from England. She identified with Princess Elizabeth sometimes, pictured on the lawn at Balmoral Castle in the tweed jacket and the pleated kilt. She had an outfit just like it when she was her age. Keeping up with current events was important, and it was fun when there was a personal connection like that. Before she knew it, she noticed that she was running her finger around the bottom of the bowl and Jack's pancake mix was gone.

"Oh no," she said.

"What's oh no?" Jack called out from the bedroom. "Coffee done yet?"

"I was just trying something. Coffee's almost ready."

Claudia didn't know what to do. She couldn't put the bowl in the sink. Jack would see it. She went to the cupboard under the sink and hid the bowl in the trash bucket. Jack came out of the bedroom just then in his Annapolis bathrobe and sat down at the table. Claudia brought him his coffee, and he lit a Chesterfield. She sat down and lit one for herself.

"Well, what about breakfast?" he said.

"I thought I'd sit with you a minute. I didn't get to see you very much last night."

"Whose fault is that? You had to go dancing."

"I know, Jack."

"You're a bright girl, but you don't think before you say something accusatory."

"I know," she said. "I'm sorry. I wasn't blaming it on you."

"But that was the inference." Jack shrugged his shoulders. Then he smiled. "I guess I have to make the best of it," he said.

"I'm glad, Jack. I love you so much."

"I love you too, sweetheart."

"What are we going to do today?" she asked excitedly.

"Don't know."

"We can do anything you want, Jack."

"Well, thank you very much."

"I didn't mean it like that."

"I hope not. I get one day of the week for myself. I better be able to do what I want. You don't have to tag along if it irks you so much."

"It doesn't irk me, Jack. I just want to be with you. I'll do anything you want."

"Then how about my pancakes?"

"We can't have pancakes today. We didn't get to the market yesterday because of the party, and we're all out of eggs."

"There were four in there yesterday. What happened?"

"I don't know. They're gone."

"How can they be gone?" He got up and looked in the icebox. Then he started looking around, and he found the bowl with the eggshells in the trashcan.

"What's this?"

"The pancake mix," she said quietly.

"What happened to it?"

"I ate it."

"What?"

"I ate it."

Jack put the bowl in the sink. "I'm going to go shave."

He went into the bathroom, and Claudia went outside to open the window and hook up the hose for his shower. She waited at the sink, looking at the ocean and holding back the tears, and when he came out, she turned on the water for him. He would not look at her. She thought she had a good idea and got out a bowl and put it in Jack's place at the table, got out the Kellogg's Corn Flakes and filled up the bowl, and set out the little pitcher with fresh milk and the big spoon he liked to eat cereal with.

Jack came back in with the towel wrapped around his middle and went right into the bedroom. Claudia got up to turn off the water and put the hose away. Presently she heard Jack humming to himself and it lifted her spirits considerably. Maybe today would be a good Sunday after all. But when he came out, he was in his uniform.

"I'll just go down to the Brown Derby," he said. "Is there any of that money left?"

"I'll get it for you, Jack." She went to the bedroom and brought back a two-dollar bill. "Can I come too?"

He looked at her with incredulity. "What for?"

"Just to come."

"You already had breakfast," he said. "Yours and mine too. It would only waste money to have another breakfast."

He was already out the door, and he tossed off, "Back soon, love you, bye."

Then he came back and put his head in the doorway. "You know it isn't the pancakes," he said. "If you asked me if you could eat up everything in the house, I'd say sure, go ahead. That's because I love you, and I wouldn't deny you anything. It wasn't the pancakes. It was the lying. That's hard to take, Claudia."

From behind the door, Claudia listened to the car go out the driveway. Everything turned out so wrong. She poured the milk over the corn flakes and ate it all and went to lie down on the bed. Jack would never trust her again. He was doing everything he could to get ahead in his career and get them out of the little white house, and this is how she repaid him. He worked so hard every day, and now he couldn't even have a little peace on weekends in his own home. She was making his life hell and only thinking of herself. It was driving him away, and what would she do without Jack?

The tears welled up in her eyes, and she cried out loud. She had not had a good cry for a week and did not try to stop herself. She thought of home and Mom and Dad and how far away they were, and Dad still working because all his savings were lost, and spit shining Jack's shoes, for all the good it did. At the party he said he was tired of shining his own shoes, but he never shined his own shoes, and she thought of Annette, with her black hair and her red lips and those sunbaked bosoms she was shoving under Jack's nose all the time, and her own little white flapjacks that Jack never paid any attention to, and all the other usual things that made her cry.

Why in the world did she eat the pancake mix? She was intelligent and resourceful, but to Jack it must look like she only used those traits to deceive and manipulate him. He had every right to say she was failing to make the grade. She wondered for the first time if it was her own psychology tripping her up. Maybe she did things on purpose because subconsciously she wanted Jack to fail in his ambitions. But why would she want that? What did women want? That was Freud. What a stupid question. All he had to do was read *Woman's Home Companion* or *New Girl* or *Modern Housewife*. He would probably get distracted by the advertisements. The new Hoover Deluxe with patented Air Flow that gets out the hidden dirt would appeal to him. Well, for all she cared, the dirt could keep hiding.

There was nothing in psychology that was going to make her feel better, but it got the wheels turning, and it suddenly occurred to her that dinner could be bacon sandwiches and pea soup with croutons. She felt much better and prospects for a good Sunday were looking good again. Spicy croutons can really wake up the flavor in ordinary pea soup. There was one apple left and one pear and one tomato—oh, and one can of fruit cocktail. She could leave everything until half an hour before dinnertime, while Jack was having his drink, and pretend to just think it up at the last minute. He would be so impressed because he knew there wasn't any food in the house, and he could only conclude that he had married a wiz in the kitchen.

Jack could get home any time, so she quickly hooked up the hose and took her shower. She dried her hair and brushed it a hundred strokes. It was three days after the permanent, and it looked terrific. Today was white shift, deck shoes and blue hairband. She made the bed and straightened up and began waiting for Jack to come home. It was twelve thirty. You could get breakfast any time of day at the Brown Derby, and he probably bumped into someone. He would never tell anyone about the pancake mix. He would say he liked the Brown Derby Sunday specials or Claudia was busy with her household accounts, even though he handled all the money, and she didn't know anything about it.

Claudia sat at the kitchen table with her Chesterfields and her coffee and read her book, *The Heart Is a Lonely Hunter*. It was very popular. Becky Ogden had probably already read it. They could read books and have discussions about them if they became best friends. You couldn't do that with Mary Ann. She wasn't intellectual. But maybe Becky wasn't intellectual either. Just because she was the only one who didn't wish she had a penis did not make her an intellectual. Not necessarily. You could not correlate one with the other. Or maybe there might be no relationship between the two things at all.

It would have been a good one for her class in logic at Sweet Briar. Ellen Talbot was having an affair with Professor Callan but you couldn't get a word out of her about it. They both loved logic. She was killed in a car crash in the spring of freshman year. Professor Callan finished out the term but never came back. They probably didn't know that their lives were not following the logic of professor and student. When they became a love story, it followed the logic of an ill-fated romance. It was so sad. Humanity might be a social and communal species, but sometimes it sure looks like people are all wrong for each other.

Claudia went outside. She walked to the end of the driveway and looked down the road. No Jack. She went around the house and walked down to where the grass stopped and lifted her head to the wind coming off the ocean. Her hair fanned out behind her, and she felt wonderful again and so grateful for her hair and her slender arms and graceful hands. She was twenty-three. She was married. Other girls her age were still single and living at home and worried about the other thing, being a virgin. What a relief when she got that out of the way. And Jack was a real, honest-to-God catch. They lived in a pretty place, and life was all ahead of them.

The beach looked quiet and beautiful today, but she did not want to be so far from the telephone, so she stayed on the grass and walked around the yard in her bare feet. She sat down with her chin on her knees and looked out over the ocean and felt it like the pull of the moon on the tides and how smooth her legs were as her hands ran up and down her calves. Her heart began to beat faster, and she wanted Jack to kiss and hold her and feel how good her body felt, and she breathed out oh Jack, and that little grab down there happened again.

Jack still did not come home. It was two o'clock when Claudia came inside and checked the clock on the back of the stove. She had a 7Up and a Chesterfield and read more of her book. She would have gone to lie down and read in the bedroom, but she was afraid Jack would come home and find she had fallen asleep. The least she could do was try to stay awake while he was out doing things he needed to do.

Suddenly she heard the Roadmaster in the driveway, and she looked up at the clock. It was four thirty. She had been sound asleep. She shook her hair and patted her cheeks and ran to the door. Jack had a bouquet of flowers, and he was smiling.

"Oh, Jack, I'm so glad you're home."

"Here, sweetheart. I got these for you."

"Oh, they're lovely." She was so glad he was smiling.

"I figure I can't be upset with you all the time," he said. "What kind of life would that be?"

She hugged him hard and kissed him all over his face. He hugged her back and tried to keep moving into the house.

"I could use a drink," he said. "What a time I had."

Claudia let him go and ran ahead to make him a drink, and he sat down at the kitchen table and took out a Chesterfield.

"What did you do to your face?" he asked.

"I don't know, what?"

"You have a crease across the side of your face." He put out a finger and traced it in the air.

"Oh," she said. "I must have fallen asleep on my book."

"Oh, Claudia."

"I'm sorry, Jack. I just got tired waiting all day. What happened?"

"Nothing much. I got tied up. One thing and another. I bumped into Froggy and Annette at the diner, so I had breakfast with them."

"Did they say anything about last night?"

"Not much."

"I mean about me. Did they say anything?"

"They liked you. Don't worry."

"What did they say?"

"I don't remember every little detail. They said they liked you."

"I wish you could remember something specific."

"Oh God, Claudia. The world doesn't revolve around you, you know."

Claudia lowered her eyes. "I know. I'm sorry, Jack." Then she tried to brighten up and said, "I liked both of them. Froggy is real nice."

"Well, don't get too attached to Frog. I've got to get rid of him."

"What do you mean get rid of him?"

"He's in the way."

"I thought he was your friend."

"Sure. It's nothing personal. It's just how the navy works promotions. Believe me, if the shoe was on the other foot, Frog would throw me overboard in a minute."

"Oh Jack. That's really too bad."

"You can't worry about things like that. When you get somewhere, you can look back, but if you look back before you get somewhere, you never get anywhere."

Claudia laughed and asked him to say it again, but he couldn't remember how it went, and he started laughing too. Then she tossed her hair and looked away for a minute, pretending to look at the clock on the stove, stretching backward a little so her shift would ride up on her thigh. She knew his eyes would follow that. It was probably a bad idea, but she wanted to be close to him when he was being so sweet.

"It's only ten after five," he said. "Come on. Let's lie down a while."

He led her to the bedroom and they lay down and kicked off their shoes. She got him to put his arms around her, and then he was pulling her shift up, and she let it go over her head and over the side of the bed. Then the panties were off. Claudia wanted to be kissed and held more, but she knew he was already too far along.

"Get over," he said.

It was the way she didn't like. But it was the only way he ever wanted to do it, so her heart sank, but she turned over and pulled the pillows under and buried her face in them, same as always. Then she had to wait like that while he stood at the back of the bed and took off his uniform. She knew he was looking at her, and it took him so long to undress.

He always spit on his hand. He must have thought it made her ready, but it never did, and this time was worse than ever, and it hurt like all hell. He bumped and bumped and slapped her bottom, and then he started doing it fast like the jackhammer, and it hurt so much she opened her mouth wide into the pillow. She had to come up to breathe but she kept her eyes at the headboard so he wouldn't see the tears on her face. Then he slapped her bottom again. He was probably thinking of Annette and calling her a bitch, and then he went back to the jackhammering and kept going until he was done. He got off her like a man jumping off the back of a streetcar, and Claudia slumped down flat. He lay on his back, panting. Claudia could not even move to pull the sheet over herself. After a while he said, "I don't know why you're so tired. All you have to do is lie there. I'm the one who has to do all the work."

It was dark when Claudia got up. She put on her robe and limped into the bathroom. She sat down and looked at herself. It didn't look that bad. It just hurt so much. Jack was sound asleep. She turned the light on in the kitchen and got out the package of bacon for his bacon sandwich. She could not help crying. At ten o'clock it was *Swingin' New York* with Arthur Franklin that Jack liked, and she had just enough time to get everything ready. She cried all the way through frying the bacon and getting bread out and the pea soup cooking and slicing up the last apple, last pear, and last tomato. The croutons brought up the rear because croutons had to be piping hot or Jack didn't like them. She tried to wake him up at quarter of ten. He was dead to the world, except for the last time she tried, when he woke up and told her he didn't want dinner and to leave him alone.

Claudia sat at Jack's place at the table and turned on *Swingin' New York* very low while she ate the bacon sandwich and pea soup with croutons and the rest. Then she got out the ironing board and pressed a clean shirt for Jack and a clean pair of pants. Then a good shine for the shoes. She put Vaseline on her hurt parts and went to bed. She fell asleep whispering into Jack's ear how much she loved him. It was called somatic suggestion, and she had read about it in *Woman's Home Companion*.

Claudia tried out another one the next morning. She lit a Chesterfield and blew the smoke toward the bedroom and blew across the top of her coffee mug in the same direction.

"Can't you just stay for one cup of coffee?" she called.

"Not if I have to get breakfast in town."

"You have plenty of time, Jack." She sent another puff toward the bedroom. "How about just one. It's the taste that satisfies."

Jack came out of the bedroom, straightening his tie. "Just one," he said. "Come on, coffee."

Claudia jumped up as he sat down and poured him a mug of coffee. She was very optimistic about the potential in somatic suggestion. Jack was totally unaware of how he had been influenced by suggestion. There might be other things she could learn to make him do. Maybe it wasn't fair, but if men didn't bother to read *Woman's Home Companion*, well, it was at their own peril.

Claudia lit his Chesterfield and took out another for herself so she could smoke with him and drink coffee together, as she had always imagined marriage to be.

"I don't have time to do the grocery list now," he said, "so you'll have to go tomorrow. What have we got for dinner tonight?"

"Pea soup and crackers."

"Okay, you can have that, and I'll pick up something in town. I'll need some money. And don't worry if I'm a little late. I may have to smooth things over."

"What things?"

"Claudia, you're really difficult sometimes, you know."

"I don't know what you mean," she said.

"You know, with Bobby Rodgers. Sometimes I think you're trying to scuttle everything on purpose. I guess I should figure that one out before we go on much longer."

"You mean you wanted me to go with him in his car?"

"It wasn't any big deal."

"You didn't tell him I would, did you?"

"No, of course not. We were just talking the other day."

"What did you tell him?"

"I just said you like driving along the coast at night."

"With you. Not anybody else."

"Well, it could have helped my career. But I guess you didn't see it that way."

"I didn't see it any way, Jack. I wouldn't go out in a car with a man at night."

Jack snuffed out his cigarette and would not look at her. "I guess we know that now, don't we?"

"I don't know what you wanted me to do, Jack. He has a bad reputation. You said that yourself."

"All right," he said. "Let's drop it."

"No, Jack. I want to know what you told him."

"I already did."

"You didn't tell him I'd do anything, did you?"

"I already told you what I told him. Now will you leave me alone? I've got to get going." Jack got up and took his jacket off the back of the chair and picked up his briefcase. "See you tonight," he said. "Oh—that money for breakfast—and dinner."

Claudia ran to get the money from her drawer in the bedroom. He was already in the car, and she gave him a five and then another five when he frowned at the first one. He rolled down the window and started backing out. Claudia did not know what she wanted to say but she followed him down the driveway, staying at the driver-side door and getting her arms scratched by the bushes. When he turned the wheels, it pushed her all the way into the bushes and she fell, catching a sharp stick in the corner of her mouth.

"Claudia, will you get away from the car?" He got to the end of the driveway and turned and put it in forward.

"Jack, could you talk to me more?"

"I can't, sweetheart. Got to get to work."

"Please, Jack."

"Got to go. See you tonight. Love you, bye."

Claudia stepped back from the car as it started moving ahead. Then something welled up inside her, and she kicked the rear of the Roadmaster as hard as she could. Jack put the brakes on and jumped out. He came around the car and looked at the indentation in the metal.

"That was a stupid thing to do. You've got to get hold of yourself, Claudia."

"Oh, Jack." She still didn't know what she wanted to say.

He put his hands on her shoulders and looked at her. It was the only thing that kept her from crying. "Claudia," he said. "I love you so much."

"I love you too, Jack."

"I just don't know if I can live with the way you are."

Claudia had to put her head down.

"You know what I mean?"

"I'm sorry, Jack. I'll try."

"All right. You go in and calm down. Have some coffee and a smoke, and you'll feel better. I'll see you tonight. Okay?"

"Okay Jack."

"That's my girl. See you tonight. Love you, bye."

He got back in the car and drove off and Claudia went back in the house. She ate the last little handful of Kellogg's Corn Flakes. The milk was all gone. Then she had another cup of coffee and a smoke and soon she felt better, just like Jack said she would.

CHAPTER TEN

An hour later Claudia was on the road down to Honolulu. She started out fine, but after a few miles, her foot swelled up. She hadn't realized how hard she'd kicked the Roadmaster, and now every step hurt worse than the last. She started looking around and pretty soon came across a good stick about the right size for a crutch and, padding one end with her scarf, kept plugging away. Walking made the burn hurt too. It still wasn't right, and there were bloody scratches on her arms from the bushes. When she switched hands carrying her paper bag, she got blood across the middle of her white dress. If that wasn't enough, her whole lower lip was swelling up from the branch that stuck her in the corner of the mouth.

How could this have happened to her? She was a natural blonde with good posture. She was first in her class at New Haven Select Academy and had gone to Sweet Briar, and now she was married to a naval officer. But here she was, in the hot sun with her dress soaked through and clinging with perspiration. She could have gotten out of making love to Jack and had another week to heal her burn. What was wrong with her?

She should have known it would be the usual. He just liked bumping from behind—and then he was always bumping into Annette here and bumping into Annette there. He was so sweet when he wooed her in the ballroom at Sweet Briar, kissing her behind the ear when the chaperones weren't looking. It was romantic and wonderful, and after that it was a hard adjustment to getting jackhammered every Sunday afternoon. No older women ever told her about that. Maybe it was just her. She held on tightly to the paper bag, stopping every few minutes to switch hands while she wiped the perspiration from her arms off on her hair.

Claudia finally got to town. She left the stick at the side of the road where she could find it and limped into the navy yard. The guards held her up at the gate when she asked for Lieutenant Wyler. They were looking suspiciously at her paper bag, so she held it tightly in front of her with both hands where they couldn't grab for it.

"Excuse me," she said politely. "Admiral Harris told me that if I ever have trouble at the gate to ask for Bobby Rodgers."

The two guards looked at each other and raised their eyebrows.

"What's the name, miss?"

"Claudia. Just say Claudia."

"One moment, miss."

One guard went into the gatehouse and picked up the phone, and in a moment he came out. "Commander Rodgers will be here shortly, miss," he said.

Claudia thanked the guards and turned backed to look at the street. Maybe she would regret it, but she was proud of herself. She had never done anything like this before. She had never needed personality because she was beautiful, but now Jack would see she had personality, lots of it, and when she had to get to her man, she meant to do it, and nothing could stop her.

The guards saw Commander Rodgers coming and let Claudia through the gate. She tried not to limp, but he caught it, and his smile faded quickly when he saw the state she was in. She tried to smile as if nothing was unusual, but her lower lip was so out of whack, it felt like it came out crooked.

"Mrs. Wyler," he said. "What an unexpected pleasure."

"Commander Rodgers, good afternoon."

"What happened to your foot?" He bent down to look at it. "Oh, that doesn't look very good. We'd better have someone take a look at it."

"Oh no," she said quickly. "I hurt it shopping in town. Jack can take care of it. I don't know where his office is though. I was hoping you could show me."

"Certainly," he said. He took her arm and led her back to the guardhouse and ordered a car brought around. There wasn't any breeze, of all days. Claudia knew Commander Rodgers could smell her perspiration. Her dress was sopping wet, and her brassiere was showing, and there was the blood on her dress. She did not want Commander Rogers interested in her, but she didn't want him thinking this was her real self. Without thinking, she let him take the arm with the scratches. To her horror she noticed perspiration had made the blood runny, but so far he hadn't noticed the red smear on his uniform.

The car came, and Commander Rodgers put her in the back seat and told the driver which building and to wait for her. As they drove off and turned a corner, Claudia saw him looking down at the front of his uniform. Now he had something difficult to explain, too. Drat. That's exactly how word gets out about what kind of girl you are.

There ensued a short drive through the complex. Claudia was so relieved to be off her bad foot. It was swollen so badly that she could hardly touch it, and when she got out of the car, the pain of her weight on it again sent her through the roof. Holding her paper bag tightly, she went through the doors and followed the corridor down to a set of steel doors with the black-stenciled letters "G-4" on the glass.

Claudia looked through and saw a row of desks and immediately spotted Froggy's red hair. Annette was the only one standing up. She was dressed in a tailored gray suit with a short skirt, and her hair was pulled back in a bun so tight it seemed to bring her cheekbones into alignment with her gull-wing eyebrows. She walked right by the door, and Claudia ducked back.

Peeking in again, she saw about twenty men in the office, diligently looking over papers, except for one, who was Jack. His desk had white paper cartons all over the top, and Annette stopped when she got to him. He looked up, and they laughed about something. Then she took the papers she had been holding against her chest into one hand and accepted the fork Jack offered with the other. She bent over to eat something that looked like coleslaw, and Jack picked up another fork, and they were eating out of the same little paper carton with their heads close together. It looked like Annette's bosoms were heaving out of her brassiere right in Jack's face.

Claudia did not want to see any more and went back down the corridor. She was so hurt and upset that she limped all the way around the inside of the building before she came to the G-4 door again and realized she had gone the wrong way. At last she got to the outside door. The driver jumped out and held the door for her and returned her to the main gate. As she walked off the asphalt of the navy yard, she wondered how she was going to manage the walk home. She didn't think she had enough personality left to do it.

Claudia was glad to see her stick was still there. Her foot was in bad shape. How would she ever make it home? By five o'clock she had hardly gotten to the first milepost. A car pulled up behind her. It was an old heap with a taxi dome on top, and the driver popped his head out the window to ask if she wanted a lift. He was an old oriental man.

"No, thank you," she said.

"You look beat. You come ride in my taxi."

"I don't have any money," she said.

"That's okay. You come ride in my taxi anyway. You get special deal."

He kept waving her to come over. She was going to tell him no, but she didn't want Jack to drive by going home and see her like this, so she did not resist when the old man got out and assisted her to the car. She noticed that the taxi dome was made out of sturdy paper glued to the top of the car, with a light bulb under it.

"Where you wanna go, lady?"

"Straight up the road to the little white houses, if you please."

"Good," he said. "I know where you go. You never get there on bad foot. Much too far. How you hurt your foot?"

"I kicked something by accident."

"You let me fix it. I know good way."

"No, thank you," she said. "Just take me home, please."

"First we go to my house and fix foot."

"No," she said firmly. "Just home." She thought that was the end of it until they slowed down and turned off the main road.

"Please just take me home," she said.

"First we fix foot. You see."

He drove around a series of curves that made the fenders on the old car rattle, and down a dirt road of piled-up little houses that looked like the ones in Japan she saw in *Life*. She should never have gotten into the cab. It wasn't a real cab. She should have known when she saw the paper top. What if they held her for ransom?

"My name is Takeo. Who are you?"

"Claudia Wyler. My husband is Lieutenant Jack Wyler. Please take me home now."

"We fix your foot, Claudia Wyler. Then take you home. Don't worry." He pulled up in front of a little house even smaller than Claudia's. As he helped her out of the back seat, an old Japanese woman appeared at the door with white hair put up with sticks in the back, just like the pictures in *Life*. She came down the short walk and took Claudia's other arm, and they helped her into the little kitchen and set her down in a bamboo chair.

"This my wife, Siuri. This is Claudia Wyler."

Siuri bowed and Claudia said hello, and then Siuri went to fill up a basin with water at the sink. Takeo and Siuri together lifted the heavy basin out of the sink and brought it over. Siuri carefully removed Claudia's shoe and gently lowered her foot into the hot water. Takeo went to a low apothecary cabinet. As Siuri called out names, he pulled drawers and added to a black lacquer bowl he held, big or little pinches of different herbs that filled the room with pungent scents.

"We get you fixed up fine," he said.

Claudia started to cry. Takeo and Siuri looked at each other, and then Siuri got up and put her arms around Claudia, and Claudia put her head on the shoulder of the old woman and cried her eyes out. How could she go back to the little white house when it was dark inside and there was no food and Jack had to go out for dinner? Her life was ruined, and she could not say how it happened. It was just ruined. She had not let go of the paper bag, and she felt Siuri trying to take it from her.

"No, no," she said. "That's mine." But she wasn't fast enough and Siuri put the paper bag on the table.

"Bag right here where you can see it," she said.

"It's my husband's lunch." Claudia stopped crying and wiped her eyes.

Siuri returned to her knees and started massaging Claudia's foot in the water steaming with herbs.

"It was for today, but he didn't want it. It's cream cheese and jelly. And a can of fruit cocktail. That's all we had in the house."

"Maybe you eat it now," said Takeo.

"Would you like to try it?" said Claudia, brightening.

"Sure," he said. "Cream cheese, you say. Jelly." He looked in the paper bag, glanced over at Claudia for approval, and pulled out a folded nylon stocking.

"I didn't have any waxed paper," she said. "Here, I'll get it."

Claudia unfolded the nylon stocking and rolled it back to the toe where the crumpled sandwich was. Takeo flattened it on a cutting board and cut it into strips for them, and he and Siuri ate their pieces with expressions of astonishment. Claudia was very pleased with their reactions.

Takeo nodded and said, "New one on us—cream cheese, jelly." Siuri nodded too.

"We make something for you now."

Before Claudia could protest, Takeo went to the little icebox they had and took out a large bowl with a plate over it. She could not see what he was spooning out, but she was afraid it might be poi. She had to do it, so she ate a little bit and it tasted so good. What a surprise. She ate two more bowls.

While Claudia's foot soaked in the warm water, Takeo brought out colored paper and showed her how to fold it into shapes. He taught her how to make square boxes and a round ball that lay flat until you blew into a small hole and the folds popped out. They made a monkey family with a big monkey, a medium monkey, and two little monkeys in red and orange paper, and they looked like monkeys Picasso would have painted. Cubist monkeys. As Claudia stood them up in line on the table and moved them into a family, they looked more and more like real monkeys, and she felt a quirky kind of love surrounding them that warmed her heart.

After an hour or so, Siuri lifted Claudia's foot out of the water and dried it. It looked so much better, and they wrapped it tightly in cloth from a long bandage roll. Then they helped her to the car. Siuri said goodbye and placed the paper bag with the fruit cocktail and the nylon stocking on Claudia's lap. They drove off through the dark, quiet neighborhood, and soon Claudia was leaning over the front seat to point out the little white house where she belonged.

"Come back tomorrow, and I'll pay you," she whispered.

"Okay. I try to come back tomorrow," he said. "Here, I give you my taxi card."

He reached into the glove compartment and gave her his card.

The Roadmaster was in the driveway, and she squeezed by it and turned around to wave to Takeo. The orange paper dome on top of the taxi looked so pretty with the light on. It reminded her to ask Jack sometime why they didn't have any pretty things in the house.

It was still tender to walk on, but her foot was much better. The house was dark. She listened at the bedroom, and it sounded like Jack was sound asleep. By the light of the moon coming in the windows, she could see the grocery list Jack had made up and the ashtray full of Chesterfields and his coffee cup. She was so glad they were both safe at home and had come through the trials of the day. She brushed her teeth and washed her face and saw that Siuri had cleaned and treated the scratches on her arm while she had been dozing. Criminy, all that poi.

It came to her in a dream that night. She was pregnant. It explained everything. Claudia decided to tell Jack the first time he brought up something she had done that could be construed as irrational, and with this strategy in mind, she made the coffee and lay in wait for Jack the next morning. She busied herself about the kitchen. All there was in the house was coffee and the can of fruit cocktail in the paper bag. When she went to take it out of the bag, she found four flattened paper constructions. It was the monkey family. She was so delighted and set them up on the kitchen table in front of Jack's place. Jack was still in the bathroom. He had plenty of time for breakfast at the navy yard, and Claudia was all ready to go along to the market. He came out straightening his tie and sat down for his coffee and Chesterfield.

"What's this?"

"It's a monkey family, Jack. I made them."

He looked at them closely and smiled. "That's really good."

Then he looked up and noticed her dress and the beret. "What's the occasion?"

She knew he would have something to say about it. It was her light green shirtwaist with straight shoulders and a matching beret.

"I felt like wearing something nice today."

"Great for carrying dirty bags in the heat. That's your best dress, isn't it?"

"Do you want me to change?"

"No, it's just interesting."

"How so?"

"Oh, never mind." He looked like he was being playful.

"Well, if you're not going to tell me, you can't blame me for whatever it is," she said.

"Okay, then I better tell you. You may be intelligent, and I know you are, darling. It's just that you don't have good sense. That's the missing part."

"Is that all?"

"For now"—but he said it in a good-natured way.

Claudia was going to tell him she was pregnant right then, but it was getting close to time to leave. She sat in his lap and took a puff off his Chesterfield. He put his arms around her and blew his smoke in the other direction.

"I'll let you think that, mister," she said.

"Silence denotes consent," he replied with a Nick Charles cocky smile.

Then he kissed her, and they got up to go. He was being so sweet and it was like they were Nick and Nora again. For the first time in so long. They were good movies. Myrna Loy always stole the show in her opinion. She had brains. Jack thought William Powell had more brains but he didn't mind looking at Myrna in that skimpy underwear they wore back then. It was different now. No more skimpy underwear. Bosoms were back in style, backed up with sturdy brassieres, and if you were a small-breasted girl like Myrna, well, you might as well ship your oars. She bet Jack was getting a good education on lift and separate, eating coleslaw with Annette every day. She didn't want to think about it—as long as they were going to be Nick and Nora again. Nick and Nora might not last long.

Jack didn't say anything about last night. Another man would get jealous and suspicious, but not Jack. He probably just assumed she went out visiting someone late. He respected her privacy. He did not feel a wife had to be home all day and do nothing but wait on her husband hand and foot.

He noticed the way she was favoring her foot as they got in the car, and she could see he was getting cross, remembering she kicked his baby. The dent in the Roadmaster really showed up in the light. He sank into quiet as they drove along and only brought it up when they got near the navy yard.

"She goes into the shop next Tuesday," he said.

"Can't someone at the yard fix it?"

"It's a pretty bad dent."

"I'm sorry, Jack. I didn't mean to hurt your car."

"No, I understand." Then after a long pause, he added, "You meant it for somebody else."

"No, I didn't."

"Well, I guess I shouldn't expect you to understand."

"Understand what, Jack?"

"Psychological transference."

"What?"

"Let me explain."

"I can guess what it means, Jack."

They were just getting to the navy yard, and Jack pulled over. He had never brought up anything psychological before. Claudia thought he must have been talking to someone. He wouldn't have read anything like that on his own.

"Something in you is not happy with living in a situation—like marriage—that depends so much on cooperation."

"Now why would that be?"

"I don't know," he said. "That's what baffles me every time you run us off course and steer for the rocks."

"I don't think I run us off course."

"That's the point. You're unaware of it, darling. The advantage to marriage is teamwork. I need a ship with a good crew."

Claudia glanced at the clock on the dashboard and knew he still had plenty of time for breakfast. He never asked her to come along, and all she'd had was coffee. She could not mention the baby now, and Jack was close to making her cry, even though he was being tender. He smiled and placed his hand over hers on the seat. Maybe they really were coming through the first year with flying colors. She had to go back and read that article "Are You Doing Your Best to Make Your Marriage Stand the Test of Time?" in last month's *Woman's Home Companion*. She shouldn't be afraid to take the quiz.

"I'll try, Jack," she said.

"I know you will, darling." He kissed her, and she got out of the car.

"I'll start tonight," she said.

"Can't wait, darling. Love you, bye."

Jack drove through the gate. Claudia was glad there were different guards on duty. She had to walk to the grocery store, and she was worried about her foot since she had taken off the bandage. She had it in her purse and sat down on a bench to wrap her foot. It made the shoe a little tight, but she got to the market fine and gave the man her list. It wasn't busy in the morning. They had a soda fountain, and pretty tables by the front windows. Claudia got a coffee and a plain donut. Mary Ann got off work at eleven so she bought the new issue of *Modern Girl* with her own money.

Claudia went up to the counter when the clerk totaled up her groceries and asked him to put the perishables in his icebox until her ride came, and then she got six more donuts and ate them while she read her *Modern Girl*. At eleven she called the filling station and asked Mary Ann to come get her.

Claudia was so happy to see Mary Ann, and Mary Ann was happy to see her too. She asked Claudia about her foot and her lip right off the bat, and then Claudia told her about the party, except for the part about Annette and Commander Rodgers. She had not realized how glamorous it was until she told it, and then she told Mary Ann she was pregnant, and Mary Ann almost veered the car off the road.

"Have you told Jack?"

"I was going to this morning, but I wasn't sure."

"You mean you're not sure if you're pregnant?"

They had to shout because all the windows were down and the wind was whipping the tops of the paper bags in the back seat and Mary Ann had the radio turned up.

"No, just when to tell Jack. I'll probably tell him tonight."

"That'll be interesting. I remember when I told Bill about Edgar Lee. It was while he was fooling around with someone else, so he wasn't all there. He was more interested in the second one, but then I lost it."

"I'm so sorry. I didn't know."

"Oh yeah. It was a girl, and she only lived eleven hours. All kinds of things went wrong after that, and I couldn't seem to get knocked up anymore."

"Oh Mary Ann. Do you think I could lose my baby?"

"Don't start worrying now, sweetie. You've got a long stretch to go."

"I got you some donuts." Claudia turned around in the seat and pulled out the white paper bag of donuts for Mary Ann.

"And how many did you eat while you were waiting for me?" she asked.

"Only six. No, maybe eight, I think."

Mary Ann laughed. "I hope they got enough donuts around here for nine months of you, babe," she said.

It was nice to have food in the house again. Claudia made shepherd's pie. While it baked in the oven, she did her accounts, the only thing with money that Jack let her do. Beside each item on Jack's list, she wrote the price and multiplied it by the quantity and added down to a final total. Jack could get so mad if it did not work out with the change she brought home. She had no idea what he would say if he knew about the cans of poi she bought with the money out of her drawer. One moment she wanted to tell him about the baby, and the next moment she did not want to tell him at all. She had to write to Mom. Mom would want to come to Hawaii and stay the whole nine months. Jack would probably move in with Froggy and Dan if that happened. It would be so nice if Becky Ogden gave her a call and they got to be best friends. She felt like picking up the telephone and calling to tell her she was pregnant. She was so happy about it all of a sudden. It was a good basket to put all her eggs in.

Jack got home about eight o'clock. He had gone out for a few drinks. It was Annette's birthday, and he said he had to go because everyone in the office went. Claudia put the dish of shepherd's pie down on the table and served him and sat down with hers.

"I might as well tell you, Jack. I'm pregnant."

He paused for a second with his fork in midair and then went on eating. He made a sound like "hmm," looked at his watch, and reached to turn the radio on. He held on to the volume knob with his arm outstretched until it warmed up, and then he left it on low.

"I think it's wonderful," she said. "I know it might seem like a burden to you right now, but I think we're going to be very happy. You don't have to do anything. I'll take care of the baby and everything. It won't be any trouble. Just love me, Jack."

He looked up and very sincerely said, "I do, Claudia."

"That's all we need then. I know we'll do fine. What's the matter?"

"Nothing," he said. "I have to think. This is kind of sudden, you know."

He turned the radio up. Claudia brought over the string beans and the salad, and afterward they had their coffee and Chesterfields and the radio dramas, and it was just like dinner on any other night. Jack went to bed early. Claudia ironed a new shirt for him and pressed his pants. When she went to hang up his uniform jacket, she noticed one of the pockets was turned out, and when she went to straighten it, she found a scrap of paper. It was a note Jack had written. He had jotted down a few notes, "good sense" and "run us off course."

Now she was pretty sure Jack was talking to someone in psychology. She had heard of couples being advised to write down their criticisms of each other to bring problems into the open. He was probably trying to do that, all by himself, and Claudia resolved that as long as Jack showed that much commitment to their marriage, she had to make every effort to be the best wife she could be and not complain when everything did not go her way.

She slipped into bed that night beside her husband with a renewed dedication to him and a strong awareness of the new life inside her, feeling that the love between the three of them in their little white house by the ocean would abide. Her old family, her mother and father and Barb and Harry, had played out its years and was far away and scattered to the winds, as she herself had once been scattered to the winds before Jack. Now the baby was coming, and she would be the rock of the new family, and Jack would advance in his career and be the salvation. She knew it would be hard and a lot of work and days of trial, but she was finally coming to understand the wisdom that lay beneath it. It was really very simple. All she had to do was lash Jack to the mast.

CHAPTER ELEVEN

The next day at the beach, Claudia told Mary Ann about telling Jack, and she could see Mary Ann was going to be critical.

"You mean he didn't say anything at all?"

"No, he said he had to think. I can understand that. It was so sudden."

"Sounds like he's looking to get rid of you."

"You're so cynical, Mary Ann. You always think the worst."

"You would too if you were always finding out your husband was up to no good."

Claudia sat up to put on more lotion. She didn't bother asking Mary Ann if she wanted any because she just laughed at lotion, even Golden Tan Hawaiian with seven moisturizers. She looked at the label once and called it bacon fat. Now she was looking around, squinting. She didn't have the best eyes in town either. Claudia spotted Edgar Lee and Petey playing in the shallow ponds where the waves ended.

"They're fine."

Then Claudia looked down at her belly, and Mary Ann caught it.

"You're not going to see anything yet," she said. She sat up and gripped one of the Michelins going around her middle. "This is what you'll look like in five months."

"Oh dear."

"Your boobs hurt yet?"

"Not yet. I don't think they'll ever get big."

"Boy, are you going to be surprised," she said. "You have to get new clothes, and the bras look like something they make for the army."

It had not occurred to Claudia that she would get bigger up top, and she was delighted for a moment, for Jack's sake, but then she looked at Mary Ann lying propped up on her elbows with her bosoms lolling around, and the picture of herself with that much extra weight made her enthusiasm droop.

"Don't worry," said Mary Ann. "Yours will go away. You just get a chance to take some big ones out for a spin once in your life."

"I was going to use formula. I want my baby to have all the right vitamins and minerals."

"Then you better start putting cabbage leaves on them right now so you won't get milk."

"I never heard of that."

"You just put them in your bra every day for a couple of months before the baby comes."

"Then what?"

"Then you just have the damn baby, give him the bottles, and hope your husband doesn't turn out to be a crap like mine."

Mary Ann smiled and seemed in a better mood. She had a good heart and meant well, but she just couldn't get away from thinking everything was the man's fault. At least she had not said the bad word or been critical of Jack. It was different now, she and Jack and the baby were a family now, and Jack wasn't a crap like Bill.

After lunch, while she was rolling dough for chicken potpies, Claudia wanted to feel close to Jack in the most desperate way and, acting on the impulse, found his office number in her book and called him. A young man answered and put Jack on right away. The minute he knew who it was, he slipped into his navy voice.

"What's wrong?" he said.

"Nothing. I just wanted to call you."

"You can't."

"Oh, you can't talk now."

"Right."

"I won't bother you then. I just wanted to feel close to you. I'll see you tonight."

"That would be fine. Goodbye."

Claudia hung up the phone and had to laugh. Jack was all navy. But just hearing his voice made her feel warm inside. She made her potpies and brought in the sheets and made the bed and then lay down with the little cat. Curling up made her feel good. She knew she could be the perfect wife, but uncharted waters were ahead. Could she learn to be the perfect mother?

Mary Ann might be a good resource, but there were obvious limitations. She would have to look for different magazines, ones that provided essential information to new moms. As a new mom, you could go wrong with what to do with a crying baby or scheduling nap times or potty training, and you don't want to traumatize a sensitive child. She was sure she had seen magazines like that. Hawaii had everything they had in America, just like Jack said.

Jack got home after six, and he was in good spirits. He had stopped at the Italian bakery and gotten four slices of tomato pie and some bottles of beer. It was a nice change having beer and tomato pie for appetizers. Jack thought the potpies turned out great. He listened to his radio shows and read his newspaper while Claudia did the dishes, and then she sat down to have a Chesterfield with him before he went to bed. She pressed his pants and a clean shirt and shined his shoes. Her foot was much better. Tomorrow was Thursday, and *Life* magazine would come. She could end her next letter to Mom with "Life couldn't be better!!" and paste a cutout "life" from *Life* where she wrote "life."

Nothing happened on Thursday, but *Life* came, and at breakfast Jack said he had to go to San Diego next Tuesday for briefings and would be gone two weeks. That was a shock. He still had not said anything about the baby. Claudia did not bring it up either. It was a big responsibility, and sometimes she wished it might not happen. It felt like it was at a stage where she could will it to be true or will it not to be true. But whenever she willed it not to be true and contemplated going back to the way it was with Jack and her alone, she knew she wanted to go forward and have a baby, especially if he was going away for two weeks right after a bad stretch like they'd had. Nothing had changed with Jack really, but Claudia realized that she felt differently toward him since she had conjectured her pregnancy.

Jack could be remote. It did not matter that much now because she had her chores and her own life. But the baby would change that. She would have to insist that Jack spend time at home. She would serve meals at the right times, and he would be expected to be there. He would have to put his newspaper away, and they would converse with one another like a family, and then if he wanted, he could have one radio show to himself for half an hour when she and the children would not bother him. He would have to give her money and not watch the accounts like a hawk if she was going to prepare wholesome and nutritious meals. And if he could not agree to that, she would have to put her foot down and say, "I've had it with you Jack." Or she could say, "That's the limit, Jack." By then, with all their children, Jack would have to give in. She knew he would. That was how it was supposed to be, and everybody knows it.

On Friday morning she sent Jack off to work, as usual, and he still had not said anything about the baby. She sat at the kitchen table with her coffee and her Chesterfields, looking at *Life* again, and began to think that she was imagining her pregnancy and living in a fool's paradise, when she suddenly felt sick to her stomach. For the next hour she sat by the toilet throwing up. That settled the question. She went to the back of the icebox and got the head of cabbage that she bought with her own money to make coleslaw so that Jack could eat coleslaw at home with her and not out of paper cartons with Annette—if he liked coleslaw so much—and she took off some leaves and put them in her brassiere. It wasn't as easy as she thought. She kept patting them down and pulling them back from the sides while she did the laundry and went around with the sweeper and the dust mop.

Claudia talked to Mary Ann for a few minutes when she came over to borrow the *Life*. They weren't going to the beach today because Edgar Lee had a fever, so Claudia had lunch and got a head start on another letter to Mom. She wasn't going to tell her about the baby yet, and she had trouble thinking of a snappy ending, so she just wrote in pencil in the margin, "Baked Chicken Tonight!!" and then went to get the chicken out of the icebox. Maybe she could put some diced peppers in the rice for a zesty flavor and something in the string beans, and as she washed the chicken and greased the roasting pan, she got the urge to call Jack again.

A girl answered this time. She said Lieutenant Wyler was unavailable. Claudia left a message that it was Mrs. Wyler calling. The girl said, "All right" and hung up. Claudia knew it wasn't Annette. She liked Annette. There were always a few mean girls in any office, but it was annoying. She knew Jack would never get the message. He would come back to his desk and ask who called, and the girl would say, "Oh, nobody." Claudia drew the water for the rice and string beans and sat down with another Chesterfield and got ready to call again.

The same girl answered the telephone. She said Lieutenant Wyler was still in a meeting and would be tied up until the office closed at five. Claudia knew it was no use, so she said, "Thank you very much. Goodbye." She thought she said it with dignity and poise. The girl said "Goodbye," but before the receiver went down on the hook, Claudia heard the girl say, "—Your wife."

When Jack came home, he seemed happy to see her at first. Claudia fixed his gin and tonic, and he said the chicken cooking smelled good. She lit a Chesterfield for him and one for herself, and he took off his jacket and tie, and everything seemed fine until she was telling him about her day, and then he acted bored to tears and said he was getting a headache. He finished his drink and went into the bedroom to lie down until dinner.

Maybe something had happened with Annette. She was probably throwing herself at him and getting him confused. She had to admire Jack's fortitude. When Jesus was up on the mountain and Satan tempted him, all he had to say was get behind me, Satan, or something like that—and just like that, the devil gave up. How hard was that? Annette on the other hand, didn't look like the kind of temptation who would take no for an answer. Poor Jack.

Claudia got the chicken out of the oven. The roasting pan was old, and the bottom was so warped that it was hard to carve the bird without it slipping around in the grease, so she had to concentrate and not think about Annette until she was done with the chicken and the wobbling roasting pan. She put out the rice and the string beans and turned on Jack's radio show. She went in to wake him up, but try as she might, he could not be roused, so she took off his shoes and covered him with the bedspread. Nothing really mattered on Friday nights because the week was over, but it left him so tired out, and it showed how hard he worked. Once he had pulled over to the side of the road and fell asleep and did not get home until ten. At least that was what he said. He was probably doing extra work behind her back because he knew how much she wanted to get out of the little white house.

The chicken went back in the oven, and she covered the rice and string beans. He might be coaxed out by the radio, so she left it on and waited, sitting at the table with her book about hearts being lonely hunters, and had a Chesterfield and a 7Up. At eleven she tried to wake him up again. It was no use, so she lay down beside him and went to sleep too. In the middle of the night, she woke up because Jack was nudging her.

"What's that awful smell?"

"I don't know, Jack," she said. "I must have drifted off to sleep."

Jack fumbled with the alarm clock on the night table. "Jesus. Four thirty. God, what smells so bad?"

"I don't smell anything."

"It's something cooking. What the hell did you do now?"

Jack got out of bed, and Claudia followed him into the kitchen. He looked at the stove, lifting the covers of the two pots and sniffing over them. Then he looked in the oven.

"Oh swell. The chicken's been out all this time."

"It's still all right, Jack," she said.

"That's how you get food poisoning. I don't feel like spending the night in the hospital. You can't leave meat out in eighty-degree temperatures."

"It's not eighty degrees."

"It was when I got home."

"All right. I'll throw it out."

"Thank you. I wish you didn't always have to put up an argument."

"I'm sorry, Jack. I just wanted to have a nice dinner."

He was still looking around the kitchen. Then he went outside and looked around and came back in. He was regaining his composure. The bad smell was a mystery.

"What the hell is it?"

"I don't know. What does it smell like?"

"Something cooking, like cabbage." He turned towards her, and just then he seemed to determine that it was coming from where she stood.

"I think I know," she said. She unbuttoned her blouse. The cabbage leaves were soft and limp and very warm to the touch. "I think I cooked the cabbage," she said.

Jack stood with another of those incredulous looks on his face while she pulled the leaves out of her brassiere and put them on the counter. She tried to sound informed and authoritative.

"You do this when you plan to raise your baby on one of the new high-vitamin supplement formulas. It prevents troublesome lactation, but it can sometimes result in unpleasant odors."

She felt her face redden and knew Jack could see right through her. He sighed and ran his hand through his hair. One side was sticking up where he had slept on it. He sat down at the table and looked like he was at his wit's end.

"I'll get you some coffee," she said.

Claudia poured some coffee from the percolator into the small saucepan and put it on the stove. She had a feeling this was going to be bad.

"I can hardly believe this is happening," he said. "It's almost five in the morning, and I haven't had dinner yet. You leave the chicken out, and all the lights in the house are on all night like money grows on trees."

"It was only the kitchen light, Jack," she said softly. She poured the coffee into a clean cup and set it down in front of him.

"It's not just a little thing here and there. Sit down, Claudia."

Claudia sat down across from him and took out a Chesterfield. Jack was very serious, but he did not look mad. He looked gentle, and it gave her a good feeling that he was learning a better way to help her understand what he needed from her.

"It's like this," he began. "Everything you do has an impact on me and what I'm trying to do for us. It's getting to be too much." He paused to think, drew on his cigarette, flicked an ash, and bent over with his elbows on the table, the way he looked when he listened to *Mr. District Attorney*.

"What do you mean, Jack?"

"It's dragging me under."

"What is?"

Jack moved his coffee cup to one side of the table and reached to take both her hands, and then he looked directly into her eyes.

"Your instability, honey."

Claudia pulled her hands away and folded them under her arms.

"Where are you getting this stuff, Jack?"

"I've been talking to someone. It's gotten so bad, I had to."

"Who?"

"That doesn't matter."

"It's Annette, isn't it?"

"All right," he said. "—Annette."

"Well, what does Annette know?"

"She majored in psychology at Radcliffe. She's a very intelligent girl, and she can tell a lot about a person just from one meeting. She's very concerned about you."

"My foot."

Jack sighed deeply and looked away. "She thought you might respond in a negative way if I tried to talk to you. It's one of the signs."

"One of the signs of what?"

"An inadequate personality." He said it like everybody in the world knew.

"So Annette meets me for five minutes and says I have an inadequate personality."

"No, that's the difference. It's not something you have, it's something you are."

"Oh, come on, Jack."

"Annette can explain it better than I can, but it all fits. It shows up in everything you do."

"Do what? What am I doing that looks so crazy?"

"Not crazy—inadequate. You're not up to it. Living, I mean. Just ordinary living."

Claudia had to look down. She wished she had her big robe on so she could put her head in it and cry. Jack was waiting for her to say something, and she pulled herself together. She had to show him that she was up to a dressing down, and she could take it.

"So what have you and Annette decided about me?"

"It's not me and Annette."

"Of course it is," she said. "You just want to fuck somebody else for a change, don't you?"

Jack was surprised. He put out his Chesterfield and got up with his coffee cup. He put it in the sink and quietly said he was going back to bed.

"You've changed, Claudia," he said. "I guess you can see it for yourself now."

Claudia never felt worse in her life. She followed into the bedroom right behind Jack and tried to get close to him, even though he turned away from her. She could not blame him at all. She thought he might be hiding his face in the pillow so that she would not see him break down. There was so much on his shoulders, and she only complicated his life. When he tried to help, she was arrogant and threw it in his face and said a bad word he never heard her say before. She put her arms around him and coaxed him, and finally he turned over.

"Jack, I'll do anything you say. Just tell me what to do."

He lay quietly for a while, looking up at the ceiling. It was already light out, but the shades were down, and she could just make out his strong chin and forehead in the dark.

"We think it would be a good idea for you to see someone," he said.

"Oh, Jack, I don't want to."

"I know you don't, sweetheart, but this has gone on a long time. Annette knows someone very good."

"You mean a doctor."

"You just talk to him. It isn't anything to be afraid of. You don't have to go back if you don't like him."

"Promise?"

"Promise. I think it would help. I need you behind me a hundred percent."

"I want that, Jack. I really do."

"Then I'll call him Monday morning. Is that all right?"

"I guess so. You aren't going to put me in the hospital, are you?"

"Maybe we won't have to," he said. "But don't worry. We can tell people you had to go back to the States for a while."

Jack turned to her and held her in his arms and was so tender. She wondered if any of it was true. She thought there were good reasons for everything she did, and maybe sometimes there are good reasons why the cheese doesn't go in the hot dogs. But if the only time someone looks at you is when you have cheese on your fingers, you can't blame them for thinking something's not right. But then she thought—who am I trying to kid?

CHAPTER TWELVE

They slept late Saturday morning. Claudia got up first and hurried to put the coffee on. She took the chicken and rice and string beans and went out front across the road to where the jungle started and dumped them. She didn't want anything around to remind Jack. They were going to start over. The little cat went right for the chicken. He didn't know he could land in the hospital eating things like that.

Claudia made Jack a big breakfast with bacon and eggs and French toast. Then they had their coffee and Chesterfields and read the paper together. She had not seen Jack look so contented, and it made her feel better about the new plan.

"One thing," he said, looking up from his paper.

"What, Jack?"

"No more cabbage leaves."

"All right. No more cabbage leaves."

"And don't tell anyone about it, okay? Especially you-know-who."

He gestured over toward Mary Ann and Bill's house.

"Oh, I never tell her anything," said Claudia.

Later on they changed into their suits and went down to the beach together. Jack put lotion on her back and was very nice and even played a joke on her by untying the strings of her suit without her knowing it. A couple of sailors were walking down by the water and if she had gotten up when Jack asked her to get him a Coke out of the bag, they would have gotten an eyeful. Jack said the look on her face was priceless, and they ended up laughing so hard. It was so much fun to laugh, and right then she had a good idea.

"You know what I want to do tonight, Jack?"

"What? Anything you want."

"I want to go to a nightclub."

"Sure," he said.

"We can?"

"Sure. I know a good one." Jack looked at his watch and said if they were going to a nightclub, they'd better get back to the house and get ready.

Claudia made them bologna-and-cheese sandwiches and a little fruit plate, and they ate at the table without the radio. It was nice to be close to Jack when he was smiling and happy, and to be going on an expedition together. She always loved driving with him at night.

"I think we'd better take a cab," he said. "There won't be any place to park in town on a Saturday night."

"I know a good cab. I'll call him while you're taking your shower."

"Tell him to come about eight."

Claudia found the card Takeo had given her and called him while Jack was outside. She talked to the wife and said her foot was fine now, and she was very glad that by the end of the call she remembered her name was Siuri. Then she went out in her blue robe to take her shower right after Jack. He didn't go in like he usually did. He held the hose over her, and then he soaped her up. Feeling his hands go over her like that, she closed her eyes and didn't care she was standing up naked, right where Mary Ann or Mrs. Bigalow could see her if they were on their roofs. Suddenly she didn't want to go out anymore, she just wanted to stay home, but then Jack snapped out of it and left her with the hose.

They were still getting ready when the cab pulled up outside. Jack went to the front door, and Claudia heard him call out, "Claudia, get out here. What the hell is that?"

She did not remember the car looking that bad and only remembered how pretty the lighted paper dome on top was, orange with black calligraphy for the word taxi.

"I'm calling another cab," he said. "I can't show up at a club in a heap like that. You get rid of him."

Jack went back to the kitchen to make the call and Claudia went out to talk to Takeo. She said they had changed their minds about going out and she gave him a five-dollar bill for the other night and for his trouble. It would have worked out fine except that Takeo could not start the old car, and he was still trying to get it going when the other taxi arrived. Jack told her to keep walking and get in the cab. Claudia felt terrible walking by Takeo like that when he was so sweet and complimented her on her dress. It was a full-length black strapless satin from New York she had never worn. Mom didn't know anything about it.

They got in the regular cab and started down toward the lights of Honolulu, and Jack leaned over the seat to tell the driver where they were going. Claudia had heard of the Palmetto. Mary Ann said it was where all the rich people went. She knew they were going to have fun, and she needed it. Jack must have known it too. She wondered why it took her so long to realize things about herself. Jack always said that putting herself in his shoes would be a good way to begin to understand what was wrong with her.

The Palmetto was much better than the party at Admiral Harris's. There were just as many people, but they seemed more interested in kicking up their heels than bowing and scraping for promotions. They got a nice table on the edge of the dance floor and ordered drinks. There were Hawaiian dancers with torches, a girl singer, and a comic to warm up the crowd. The headliner was a bandleader from the States who Jack liked on the radio. The spotlight came down on him and he said into the microphone, "Let's get swingin', folks." That's all it took to fill up the dance floor.

Claudia felt like drinking a lot tonight, and they put away two rounds of gin and tonics and daiquiris and had another one coming when Froggy came out of the smoky crowd and joined them. Claudia burst out laughing when she saw him. He was in black tie and looked pretty good, surprisingly good, except for the curly red hair, and it was such a shame he didn't have a stronger chin.

"What's so funny?" He had to shout because the club was so loud.

"You," Claudia shouted back at him.

"You don't get out much, do you, toots?" He eased in by Claudia.

They had another round, and Jack and Froggy started talking shop, shouting across her until she got up and let them sit together, which left her feeling third wheel, but she didn't mind it one bit with all the people to look at. She just let her eyes roam. And then she was aware of someone bending down to speak to her and a hand with a big Annapolis class ring appeared on the white tablecloth. Her eyes followed the starched white cuff into the black sleeve of a tuxedo.

"Dan Almay," he said. "You might remember me from the party."

"Oh, certainly. The one with the records. Froggy's roommate."

"Would you like to dance?"

"I'd love to," she said, even though she wasn't sure if she could stand up anymore. She had lost count of the daiquiris, and she had nothing but half a bologna sandwich for dinner, and Jack had eaten all the rest. She only shaped up because Dan was so serious.

Jack was busy talking to Froggy and hardly noticed when Claudia tapped his shoulder and said she was going to dance with Dan. They got on the floor, and Dan led her by the hand to the middle, packed with couples on all sides. There he turned and took her in his arms and held her close in the dark. It wasn't even dancing because the place was so packed, but she felt their bodies moving together, like a river deep down.

"I wanted to see you again," he said.

He did not pull away to say it. He whispered it into her ear, as if he were in a confessional, whispering to a priest through the blind of her hair. She felt herself wanting to give way to sin, and it wasn't the sin that was bugs under a rock. It was birds in a cage, and she wanted to fly. Her lips were at his neck and then on his lips, and suddenly they were kissing. She wanted to lie naked with him and writhe in ecstasy. It was her last night to let loose before Jack called the doctor, her last chance before she was cured. She could tell the doctor about dancing with Dan, and he could explain to her why she wanted to do bad things with Dan so much.

When the swing stuff came back, Dan led her back to the table. There were two girls there with Jack and Froggy, and Froggy introduced them as Elaine and Fitzy. The table was only big enough for four, so they were practically sitting on top of each other, and some of the dancers on the floor kept knocking into their legs. Fitzy was with Dan but he hardly paid any attention to her, and Elaine was with Froggy, who was still talking to Jack. The two just lit each other's cigarettes and looked bored. The boys kept the drinks coming while the band was on break, and Claudia tried to be nice and found out that Elaine and Fitzy were girl doctors at the navy dependents clinic and had an early shift, so they were just drinking ginger ale. At first Claudia had thought they were prostitutes, but everything made sense now, and she couldn't stop laughing. That brought the boys around.

"Do you think this girl has had enough to drink?" said Froggy.

The daiquiri Claudia was drinking went up her nose and everyone started laughing and pushing each other. Dan was the only one who wasn't in the swim, so Claudia thought she would nudge him under the table with her foot. She slipped out of her shoe and brought her foot up between his legs, right where it counts. She didn't have time to feel anything because he grabbed her foot and held it away. He wasn't going to let her touch it. He wasn't going to let her tease him, so now he was teasing her. No one knew what was going on because Dan was so serious.

"You get more wet blankets in here like Dan, Mr. Anthony, and the place will drop dead," said Froggy.

Claudia turned around, and there was Mr. Anthony with his hand on the back of her chair.

"Everyone is welcome here," he said. "I trust you are enjoying yourselves."

Froggy and Mr. Anthony exchanged a few words, and then he smiled around the group and went on to another table. Fitzy leaned into the middle and said, "Who's he?"

"He owns the place," said Froggy.

"He looks like a gangster," said Elaine.

"Yeah," said Froggy. "I think he's got his fingers in everything in town."

At that, the daiquiri went up her nose again and Claudia couldn't stop laughing.

"Will you cut that out?"

"Oh, Jack, don't be such a stuffed shirt," she said. "I want to have fun tonight."

"Your stupid daiquiris are costing a fortune and most of it is going down your dress."

"Am I showing?"

"Not much," said Froggy, and then the beer went up his nose too.

"Jack, he's picking on me."

"Frog, stop picking on Claudia."

"She's not going to remember anything," said Elaine. She turned Jack's wrist over to look at his watch and said it was after two o'clock.

"Let's go, Fitzy. Early shift tomorrow."

They both had big handbags hanging over the back of Froggy's chair, and they moved him forward to get them as they stood up. Claudia caught the look that Elaine sent to Fitzy and the look that Fitzy sent to Elaine. It said what are you doing with Dan? and do you want to be alone with Froggy?—the stuff that flashes between girls in two seconds getting up to leave. Claudia didn't have to bother with that anymore.

They all went out together, winding their way single file through the tables. Claudia was so drunk she could hardly walk, and it was nice to get out on the street with the fresh air and the wind off the ocean. Jack held her up and waved for a cab, and the others walked off down the street with their arms around each other.

On the way home in the back of the cab, Claudia put her hand in Jack's pants and got him going. She didn't care if he thought it was an unbecoming thing to do to an officer in the United States Navy. She wouldn't mind if he slapped her face, and she wouldn't mind slapping him back. He liked getting slapped by Annette. She was going to find out all his likes and dislikes so he wouldn't have to go somewhere else to get slapped. He could get his face slapped any time he wanted to at home.

She was glad Takeo and his cab were gone when they got home. They didn't even turn any lights on. They just went in the bedroom and took their clothes off and left them on the floor. Jack began bumping her right away, and she almost got something out of it this time. She thought she would have with Dan on the dance floor if there had been one more slow song, even with all her clothes on. But nothing ever happened getting bumped in the bedroom. Maybe the doctor would explain what was wrong with her. It was out of her hands now. There would be no more excuses, after she was cured.

PART TWO

"Keep Your Beauty on Duty"

—EMILY CHRISTIAN SANDYS, *WOMAN'S HOME COMPANION*, JUNE, 1943

CHAPTER THIRTEEN

It was only eight o'clock in the morning and sunny, but there were big sounds like thunder outside. Claudia got out of bed and made it to the bathroom, where she threw up everything from last night. She heard Jack going out through the kitchen, and she heard him say, "Oh God." She got to her feet as soon as she could and went outside. Jack was standing in the grass, barefoot in his shorts, looking toward the navy yard, and there were a lot of airplanes in the sky.

"What's going on, Jack?"

"Oh God, I think we're under attack." He rushed into the house, and she followed after him.

"Hook up the hose. Quick," he shouted.

He came out of the bedroom naked with his towel in his hand, and when he saw her fumbling with the hose, he took it away from her and screwed it on the faucet himself and ran outside. He was done showering in a moment, and a few minutes later he was coming out of the bedroom with his hair wet and tying his tie. There were some thunderous booms, and Claudia knew if they could hear them in the house, all the way from the navy yard, it must be bad.

"You aren't going down there, are you? Can't you call?"

"Calling won't do any good. I've got to report to base."

"I don't want you to go, Jack," she said. "It's Sunday."

"Oh Jesus, Claudia."

She followed him out to the car.

"You stay here," he said. "Stay in the house. Put the radio on, and do what they tell you to do, okay?"

"Okay. Oh, Jack, be careful."

"All right. Love you, bye."

He pulled the Roadmaster out of the driveway and roared down the road. Claudia ran back to the other side of the house. There was a big fire going in the navy yard now, and a tall, black column of smoke was rising into the sky. All she could see of the yard was in rolling red and black clouds and fire, and little planes were buzzing over it and diving into it, and there were more explosions. Mary Ann was out in her yard too, in her bathrobe.

"Do you know what's going on?" she called.

"Jack thinks there's an attack." She didn't think that was Top Secret. Not anymore. She ducked through the bushes to Mary Ann's yard.

"I just had the news on at six, and there wasn't anything about it," said Mary Ann.

"Jack just left."

"Bill's on rotation. He was supposed to get off at seven, but he always hangs around with his buddies. He better be on his way home, that's all I can say."

Mary Ann was looking straight out over the rise to the ocean. She winced whenever there was another explosion. Claudia came over to her and clutched at her bathrobe. Mary Ann put her arm around her. It was far enough away that they saw the flash of an explosion, and the boom came a split second later. The whole navy yard was sending up smoke, and Claudia could hardly see the ships.

"What a goddamn mess," said Mary Ann.

That did it, and Claudia dissolved into tears in Mary Ann's arms. Mary Ann held her and said comforting things like maybe it looks worse than it is, but Claudia knew it was probably the other way around.

They watched until the planes were gone, and then they went back in their houses. Claudia turned the radio on, but there was nothing but static. She got the percolator going and noticed her hands were shaking. Jack was down there. She had to go throw up again. She shouldn't have gotten so drunk last night. She wanted Jack. It was his day off, and he shouldn't have to go to work. They could have attacked on Monday. Everybody knows Sunday is a day off, and even if you don't go to church, you're not supposed to make a lot of noise.

Claudia went outside to look again. The explosions were over, and she couldn't hear anything from the navy yard, but she could see the fires and smoke and knew there must be sirens and fire trucks and men running all over and people shouting. It was like an old silent movie. The Bigalows were out in their yard, and so was the Johnson girl next door to Mary Ann. Claudia thought she saw her at Admiral Harris's party. Her husband was a lieutenant. His old Ford had been right behind the Roadmaster going down to the navy yard.

Claudia ran the mop around and then did the sweeper on the rugs. The airplanes came back, and more of the navy yard blew up. Her stomach was gnawing at her, but she did not want to eat anything if Jack wasn't eating. She only had coffee and smokes, because she knew that whatever happened, the navy always had coffee and smokes and Jack would be all right on that score. She had to concentrate on her jobs. She washed the sheets, but it was hard to hang them on the line without looking over at the burning navy yard, and she wasn't used to doing laundry on a Sunday. The air was beginning to smell so much like gasoline and smoke that she would probably have to wash the sheets all over again. Mary Ann and the Johnson girl were out on the road, and Mary Ann called out to her.

"We're going to find out what happened. Wanna come?"

Claudia hung up the last pillowcase and hurried to join them. The Johnson girl didn't even say hi. She was telling a story to Mary Ann.

"So he told me to get off the phone," she said.

"I don't think you would have found out anything," said Mary Ann.

"He could have been more polite, that's all. I mean Joe is an officer. He came out of Annapolis, and this fellow is just a clerk or something. I should have gotten his name."

Claudia did not like her very much. She didn't know how Mary Ann could be friends with her. Claudia didn't think they were close, but Mary Ann was always out back talking to her over the fence. Maybe she just tolerated the Johnson girl. Then again, maybe Mary Ann just tolerated her too. Jack said enlisted men hated officers, so why wouldn't it go for the wives too?

Claudia had never seen the Johnson girl up close. She was a petite brunette with zero bosoms and small, delicate features that looked like they never got out of a snit. She was wearing short pants and sandals. Claudia walked behind her, listening to her gripe about one thing and another. Her sandals flipped against her heels, and her buttocks pulled her shorts into the crack between them like the rollers of the electric wringer. She had a cute little behind though and, Claudia had to admit, great legs. Her hair was one of her assets too. Girls always knew what they had, and this one knew she had the hair, a cute behind, and great legs, but all the same, Claudia knew Jack would be glad he wasn't married to the Johnson girl if he ever had to listen to her complain.

There were many other people on the road as they got farther down. Mostly it was navy wives, but there were some Hawaiians who worked in town and were off on Sunday. People were beginning to come back up the road the other way too, and they said the road was blocked off ahead by MPs. Nobody going down was turning back though. They wanted to see for themselves if there was anything to find out.

A crowd was milling around two brown army cars that were parked across the road a little ways down. Two MPs were standing on the running boards shouting. Mary Ann and Claudia and the Johnson girl tried to get up close. All they could hear was everyone should go home and stay inside, and that information would be broadcast over the radio. All military personnel who had not done so were to report to their duty stations, and those already there were restricted to base. No one was supposed to use residential telephones until notified, and a general blackout was in effect from sundown to sunrise.

There was nothing to do but go home, so they joined the others marching back up the road. It felt like the beginning of a long bad time. The Johnson girl wanted them to stay together, but when it came to deciding at whose house, they each thought it was best if they stayed home and waited in case there was a call. Claudia knew Jack would call home if he had a chance, and the other girls felt the same way about their men too.

Army trucks were patrolling the beach. About every half hour one would go by with armed men in the back, under the canvas top. Claudia sat on the back steps drinking coffee and smoking her Chesterfields, listening to static on the radio inside, and watching the black smoke rise from the navy yard. A few ships had gone out of the harbor and they sat on the horizon like black silhouette pop-up targets in a shooting gallery. The war had finally gotten around to them, all the way out in the middle of the ocean. How could we be losing already? She was glad there was food in the house. She pulled the sheets in and took the line down. Then she spent the rest of the afternoon sitting on the porch with her head against the doorway.

There was hamburger cooking at Mary Ann's, and over on the other side, Mrs. Bigalow was cooking a ham. Mrs. Bigalow was lucky to have an old retired husband who didn't have to report anywhere. Claudia was starving to death, but she did not have the will to make anything. It was going to get dark soon, and she would not be allowed to turn on any lights. She gave up on the radio and went to lie down. She lay curled up in a ball on the bedspread with the little cat and prayed to hear the Roadmaster come in the driveway. She couldn't live without Jack. She couldn't do anything without Jack.

Morning came, and Claudia opened her eyes to find herself still alone, with all appearances suggesting that what happened yesterday was really true, and she had not dreamed it. She only got up because she was going to be sick again. She lay on the floor by the toilet for a long time. Jack was dead, she knew it. She was so weak that she thought it would take nothing more than breathing out her last breath and not drawing in the next one to take her away to heaven. Jack and she could get a place together since they were married. It wouldn't matter that their little family would never be real. You probably could be happy in heaven without a lot of the stuff you need down here.

Mary Ann found her on the bathroom floor and brought her into the kitchen and put her up in a chair. She said she was going back to her house to get some mashed potatoes, and when she returned, she made Claudia sit up straight and swallow each spoonful she fed her. She kept saying that Jack was fine, and presently Claudia regained enough strength to feed herself and cry.

"You saved my life, Mary Ann," she said through her tears.

"Will you please cut it out?"

"I don't know what I'd do if anything happened to Jack. Oh, Mary Ann, what are we going to do?"

"We're going to sit on our buttinskis in the house like they told us, that's what."

"Is the radio back on yet?"

"No, just static. But I've got to get back. I don't want to miss a phone call. I haven't seen Bill since Saturday afternoon. Now you fix yourself something else to eat. You're eating for two, remember?"

"All right," said Claudia. "Thanks, Mary Ann." She felt much better.

Claudia got out one of the cans of poi. It was a tall, four-pound can, and believe it or not, she ate all of it with a spoon, listening to the static on the radio. That helped a lot, and she went outside to the backyard and looked over to the navy yard, where smoke was still rising up to the sky. At the base of the black smoke it looked like it was rolling fast, and she knew that meant there were still fires. Jack was down there somewhere. Claudia sat on the back steps and watched it, and late in the afternoon, Jack came home.

She heard a car coming up the road and ran into the house. Through the front windows, she could see the Roadmaster pulling into the driveway, and she flew out the screen door and into Jack's arms as he was getting out of the car.

"Oh, Jack. You're safe. Thank god you're safe."

He hugged her briefly, and they went up the path to the house with arms around each other. She had never seen him wearing a gun belt, the kind with the leather strap over the shoulder.

"I have to shower and shave and get back to base in an hour," he said.

"Oh no, Jack. Please. I can't be alone."

Jack looked at her with an expression that made her ashamed of herself. He looked haggard, and his eyes were tired. His uniform was creased and rumpled, but he seemed not to care. She could see he was a different man, a man of action, pared down to essentials, and it rallied her spirit. As he stripped off his shirt and ran the water in the bathroom sink, it seemed to her as if the United States Navy itself, embodied in her very own husband, Lieutenant Jack Wyler, had thrown off its showy accoutrements and readied for battle, and it was evident in the way he shaved, with sure broad sweeps through the lather and focused quick strokes like the jabs of a boxer coming back from the ropes. Claudia ran to hook up the hose for his shower, and he was right behind her.

She set out clean socks and underwear on the bed while he showered, and got out a clean pressed shirt and trousers. They passed each other in the narrow hallway like crewmen on a ship called to action stations, moving quickly, each to his duty. An overwhelming and joyous feeling rose up in her. They were a team. Without hesitation or doubt, she knew what was expected of her. She made a bologna-and-cheese sandwich. She poured a tall glass of milk. Coffee. Spearmint Gum. Two packs of Chesterfields. Fill the lighter. "Toilet kit," she said, reminding herself.

Jack was halfway through his sandwich and nodded. Claudia went right to the little bathroom closet and fished around until she found his black leather toilet kit and packed it with his tube of shaving cream, shaving brush, razor, toothbrush, Ipana, Wildroot Cream-oil. Comb, Aqua Velva.

"Here, Jack," she said, putting it down beside him on the kitchen table. "You don't have to check. All accounted for, sir."

The milk and sandwich were gone, and he was at coffee and Chesterfields. Claudia quickly grabbed one and took some fast drags to catch up to where he was. She hoped he would have time for another one, but she would not try to hold him back.

He bent over the table, holding his cigarette over the coffee with both hands around the mug, the way he listened to *Mr. District Attorney*. He told her they were trying to determine where the Japanese were. He told her what they did to the women in China and what they did to pregnant women in particular. The navy base was as good as wiped out, and the Japs had hit the airfields too. Most of the planes were gone, and the island was defenseless, like a sitting duck. The Japs needed Hawaii. Now they could just march in and take it.

He could not stay to have another Chesterfield, and Claudia followed him out to the car. Smoke was rising in a line on the seaward side of the house. Jack threw his jacket on the front seat and reached over to get something on the floor.

"We're laying down a smoke screen," he said. "We don't know where they are. We don't want them to know where we are either. They could be on the other side of the island. Listen to me, Claudia. If they land on the other side of the island in raiding parties, you won't know it till they come out of the jungle in front of the house."

Jack had a big revolver in his hand. "I might not be able to get back here," he said. "It's loaded, and the safety is right here, see? You just flick this, and then you can pull the trigger."

"I don't think I can, Jack."

"Don't worry," he said, "You'll be able to do it if you have to."

He put the gun in her hands and made her flick the safety on and off.

"That's good," he said. "Hold it with both hands, like this. Then you aim and pull the trigger. Always aim low. Remember that. Aim low, got it?"

"Yes, sir."

"Good girl." Jack smiled and kissed her and held her, and when he drew back, he looked in her eyes in a way that took her back to the beginning of Jack and Claudia.

"You've got what it takes, Claudia," he said. He got behind the wheel of the Roadmaster. It was already warmed up, so he did not wait long before he backed out of the driveway.

Claudia held the heavy gun with both hands and walked around the side of the house, where she could see the full horizon of ocean. The few American ships out there were now hidden in the smoke screen, and the wind was sweeping the smoke across the whole line of the sky, where the sun was beginning to go down. She went back around front and sat on the porch steps with the gun in both hands, pointed across the road at the jungle, which was getting dark and foreboding.

She liked direct orders from Jack. She was a true-blue navy wife after all. She could follow orders and measure up. Jack said it himself. He said she had what it takes. If Scarlet O'Hara could shoot a Yankee, she could shoot a Jap. She did not want to be tied to a wagon wheel and bayoneted through her belly. Suddenly she let go of a whole afternoon's worth of pee all down the steps, and the courage Jack had inspired in her took to the hills. What was she going to do when she needed courage? Maybe you don't need courage to go down fighting, she thought. Maybe you just had to have what it takes. She would fight. She would fight to the end. It was no use hiding in the jungle. They would find her. Even if they didn't find her, she would have to come out sometime. She could not make herself eat a grub.

She heard Mary Ann's creaky screen door and got up quickly and went into the house, bending over to hide her wet sundress and the gun. She put the gun under the bed and stripped off her dress and panties and washed herself in the bathroom with the washcloth. Mary Ann was calling her. She got into her blue robe and went to the back door and leaned out to see Mary Ann's head over the bushes.

"Can you come to the hedge? I want to be where I can hear the phone."

"Sure," said Claudia. "I'm in my robe though." Claudia went over, and they talked over the bushes.

Mary Ann had that cocky little smirk on her face. "I guess you got a chance to ride the old meat pole," she said.

"What?"

"You know—Jack was home."

"Oh," said Claudia. "Oh, no. Jack didn't have time for meat poles. He shaved and took a shower and had to go right back."

"So what did he say?"

"They don't know anything."

"Is that all?"

"That's all."

"Well, I guess I better go back in and get Edgar Lee something for dinner. I'd chew all my fingernails off if I didn't keep busy. The radio is back on, and they said stay calm, but the men are still restricted to base, and I haven't heard anything from Bill. Did Jack know anything about the ordinance yard?—that's where Bill works."

Claudia knew Mary Ann would chew off her whole fingers if she knew the truth. "No really, he was only here for a half hour, and he didn't say much."

"Well, I got to get back. If I hear anything, I'll let you know."

Mary Ann went back to her house, and Claudia went back inside and made some Campbell's Tomato Soup. She was calming down, but she realized it can be a self-delusion when you make yourself be calm when there's no reason to be calm. She wondered how you could talk Japs out of bayoneting you when they don't speak English. Should she tell Mary Ann the truth or not? Some people might not want to know ahead of time if they're going to get bayoneted.

Late that night, Claudia sat on the tile floor of the bathroom in her blue robe, looking closely at the crochet hook her mother sent with all those balls of yarn. She wished she had tried it. After tonight, she probably wouldn't. Her heart was beating fast, and her hands were shaking so badly she had trouble getting the top off the jar of Vaseline. Then she suddenly thought she should sterilize the crochet hook, so she took it to the kitchen and put it in the saucepan with water and a handful of salt and set it on the burner. There were night birds outside and little noises coming from the edge of the jungle that she had never listened to before, and she was so alert it made her legs feel weak and wobbly. After the water boiled for a while, she took the hook out and let it air dry on the way back to the bathroom. There she sat down on the floor again where the light from the bulb over the medicine cabinet was coming from the right direction.

Scooping out a glob of Vaseline, Claudia covered the crochet hook with enough to make it slide easily and put it into herself carefully. She didn't feel anything through the wood and her fingers holding it, and did not feel anything inside, so she pushed a little further up and tried to move the end of the hook in a circle. It was impossible to tell if she was getting anything, so she started pulling it out and looking, and then putting it back in. So far nothing, but she felt better and more confident because nothing hurt and because after all the thinking, she was finally getting on with it. She moved herself into a better position on the floor. She thought she got the hook around the corner of something and was deeper in. Nothing seemed to be doing anything, so she poked around with a little more gusto.

Suddenly there was a terrific cramp that took the hook out of her fingers and made her eyes pop out, and in an instant she was dripping with sweat that came out of nowhere. Another cramp followed and another that doubled her over and expelled a length of the crochet hook. She felt so dizzy that she lay down with her head on the tiles. She thought that must have done it and wondered if it really could have been that easy. When the dizziness passed, she pulled out the rest of the crochet hook and looked at the end, but there was nothing there. She wiped the sweat off her face and then she noticed blood coming out of her. It was just a little bit, but it made her afraid, and then she couldn't stop shivering. Lying back down helped, and she calmed herself by tucking the robe around her face and not looking anymore.

Jack said, "You've got what it takes, Claudia." The way he said it made it sound like the only sincere thing he had ever said in his life, and he had said it to her.

CHAPTER FOURTEEN

Claudia thought it was Mary Ann standing in the doorway of the bathroom.

"What the hell, Claudia!"

She found herself lying in a pool of blood that had spread out to cover almost the entire floor of the tiny bathroom, and she started crying.

"Oh, Mary Ann. What am I going to do?"

"You just leave this to me. We'll talk about it later."

Mary Ann got rags out of the closet and got busy right away cleaning the blood off her legs and the arm that had been under her head, using the blue robe to sop up the blood on the floor. They looked, and as far as they could tell, the bleeding had stopped, so Mary Ann got her out of the bathroom and put her to bed.

"You stay right there," she said. "I'm going to make you something to eat."

Before long Claudia smelled Campbell's Cream of Mushroom Soup. After Claudia had the soup and some crackers and drank some coffee, she started feeling better. Mary Ann did not say anything, but Claudia noticed she was wearing a crucifix around her neck. She had never seen Mary Ann with one of those before.

Mary Ann made her stay in bed all day and kept coming back to bring her food and take her to the bathroom and do the laundry. She saved the blue robe with her Tide Miracle Wash and made a big point out of that because Claudia swore by her Rinso so much. They were up half the night going to the bathroom because Mary Ann made her drink so much water.

The next day Claudia felt better. There was no indication if she got the you-know-what, but she wasn't going to try again. She wasn't going to think about it. Mary Ann went back to work in town. There was still no word about Bill, and she was going to go by the navy yard to see if she could find out anything.

The telephone rang around nine o'clock, and she carefully got up to answer it. It was someone from Jack's office. He said that Jack had been hurt in a car accident, and he was in the Presbyterian Hospital in town, which was taking overflow from the base hospital. There was nothing more he could tell her except Jack was out of the OR and on the floors, and that it was okay to use the telephone again.

Claudia felt bad about Saturday night, but she wanted someone familiar to go with, so she called Takeo. He said okay and told her he would be around soon. Claudia dressed quickly and put her hair up and was on the front porch when he pulled up. Takeo jumped out to open the back door for her, and she told him to please hurry to the Presbyterian Hospital. She didn't want to say it was about Jack.

They only got a few miles along when they came to a tow truck parked on the side of the road. The driver had one foot on the running board and was leaning against the cab of his truck, smoking a cigar. They slowed down, and Claudia could see the wreckage of the Roadmaster, turned over halfway down the hillside.

She had Takeo pull over. A crowd of people were around the Roadmaster, banging on it with hammers and trying to pry off parts of it with crowbars, and a hundred or more people were fanned out through the scruffy brush in the vicinity. They were bent over looking for something. Claudia wanted to know what was going on, and Takeo pulled up to the tow truck and asked the driver.

"There was money flying around everywhere," he said. "They won't let me take the car."

When he saw Claudia, he came over and put his head through the window of the other side, but he kept the hand holding the cigar up on the top of the taxi.

"Do you know anything about the driver of the car?" she asked.

"I just got here, lady. That happened sometime the other night. I couldn't get out here until now, what with all that going on in town."

He looked down the slope where the people were combing the ground.

"Sure don't take long for news to spread. People around here started finding money all over the place. Somebody figured out it came out of the wreck, so they're taking the damn thing apart piece by piece. There was hundred-dollar bills flying around. See out to where them trees is? People were finding bills all the way out there, and there were a few up here on the road too."

He fished a few out of his pocket and showed Claudia and Takeo.

"I ain't greedy," he said. "I just got to wait till they're done. Long as they keep finding money, I ain't gonna fight them for the wreck."

Claudia told Takeo to go on. She did not cry. It was over for the baby, and the Roadmaster, but she was not going to go to pieces. The night Jack came home to give her the gun, dire circumstances had forged them into a team. It was a small thing to make Jack's sandwich and get his personal care products ready, but she felt she was part of a fighting team, and she promised God that if He made Jack okay she would shape up and do her duty. As Takeo sped up and they rattled into town to find Jack, Claudia felt sorry for the Japs. With men like Jack Wyler and wives like her, they didn't stand a chance against America.

Honolulu looked the same as it did just a few days before, before the war, but there was a bad smell of fuel and smoke everywhere. There were not as many sailors walking around free, but there were enough to make it look almost normal, except they were all wearing helmets. At a stop sign a bunch of them crossed in front of the taxi, and they all looked over because they saw her blonde hair blowing out the window, but then they noticed Takeo and slowed down, and the expressions on their faces began to change. Claudia put her head out and called out that her husband was Lieutenant Jack Wyler, who was gravely wounded, and the taxi man had pulled him to safety when his boat was bombed. Takeo did not make the slightest move, like a man standing before a pack of dogs, and they shrugged their shoulders and kept on crossing the street.

Takeo let her off at the front door of the hospital and told her he would park where he could watch the entrance. There were two MPs at the door, but they let her through to the front desk. The man looked for Lieutenant Jack Wyler on a list of names he had on a clipboard but could not find him. An orderly came up and stood over his shoulder.

"They must have brought him in Monday night," she said. "It was a car wreck."

"Oh, that." He pulled out a different folder and flipped through it.

"We're a little backed up. We haven't gotten to Monday's work yet, ma'am. Wyler, let's see. They set up an officers' ward. That's where he'd be."

The orderly bent over the man looking over the papers and said, "I don't think he made it that far, Bob."

"Says here he did."

The one at the desk told her to go to the second floor and ask to talk to one of the doctors. He advised her not to talk to anyone but a doctor. The two of them looked so uncomfortable that it made Claudia worry, and she asked where the stairs were and set out to find Jack.

Claudia went up the stairs and got directions down the long hall to the officers' ward. She would have gone right in, but she looked through the glass and saw Annette hanging over a gurney in the entranceway. There was a sheet over the man, but Claudia knew it was Jack. She waited outside the door because she wasn't going in with Annette there, especially when every time she looked through the glass, Annette had her hands all over him.

A while went by, and Claudia was beginning to worry that she would start to bleed again or faint if she had to stand up any longer. A doctor came down the hall with two orderlies behind, and she stood aside to let them enter the ward. As Claudia watched through the glass, the orderlies bent down to release the wheels of the gurney and turned it toward the door. Claudia stepped back again and stood behind the door to allow the gurney out, and right behind came Annette weeping, with the arm of the doctor around her.

They went the other way down the hall, and Claudia followed the gurney to a service elevator, where the wheels bumped over the door channel and

Jack's shoe fell off. Claudia picked it up immediately and stepped into the elevator just as the door closed behind her. The two orderlies stood still, looking ahead into the wall, and Claudia found that she was holding Jack's shoe, along with the foot inside it and about two inches of his leg. She did not want to look surprised in front of the two men, so she held the shoe tightly and looked at the wall too. That way they would know she was his wife and not somebody else.

They went down to the basement of the hospital. Claudia tried not to look to either side as she followed the orderlies pushing Jack's gurney past rows of others, some with naked men who had their skin burned off and some gurneys with just body parts piled on them. There were corpsmen with clipboards walking through the rows. Jack was left at the end of one of the rows and both orderlies gave Claudia a little nod as they left.

Claudia pulled the sheet off Jack's face. His eyes were half open but lifeless, and his mouth was open too, as if he were saying, "What is it this time, Claudia?"

"I brought you your foot, Jack."

He would have said, "Oh, thanks honey."

Claudia could see his head was almost cut off by a deep laceration in his neck, and all his blood was gone, probably out on the ground where the people were looking for money. It was such a shame. All the money Jack had saved to pay her parents back was gone. There was blood on his collar, and she said, "Jack, I just ironed that shirt. I thought you said you had a job where you didn't get dirty."

Jack would say, "That's the navy for you." And he would have the same expression on his face that he had now, with his eyes rolled up. But his mouth would be shut, so she closed his mouth with her fingers.

"That's more like it," she said.

Claudia untied the laces of the shoe on Jack's good foot and took it off, and then she did the same for the loose foot and put the foot under the sheet. Thinking it might get lost, she changed her mind and pulled the sheet down to his middle, where she loosened his belt and tucked the foot under it into his trousers.

"I know it doesn't look so nice," she said, "but it's more important to have both your feet, and you shouldn't be so self-conscious about how it looks."

Jack would not always agree with a statement like that. He thought looks were very important. Of course they were, but they weren't always the most important thing. Women are more practical.

"You're lucky to have me," she said. "If you had married Annette, your foot would be up on the second floor now without a dog tag, and no one would know whose dog it was."

She tried to look into Jack's eyes like she did when he told her she had what it takes, but his head would not stay straight and kept flopping to the side. The rest of him was pretty stiff. Claudia wondered what kind of relationship Jack and Annette had. She thought that maybe they had fallen in love without being aware of it, and then they had the dilemma of Claudia. Annette was the perfect girl for him. He could have fun playing with her big bosoms and get lost in her wild Italian hair, and they could admire their tanned bodies when they went to the beach with practically no clothes on.

Claudia realized she could no longer be selfish with Jack, now that he was dead. She would have to let him have Annette. She would have to get used to him going to see her and not coming home so much. He could bump into Annette at the Brown Derby or the Grand Hawaiian or eat coleslaw out of paper cartons at the office, and it wouldn't create a scandal because he would be invisible. He could bump into her all he wanted, and he wouldn't have to put up with Coney Island hot dogs without buns. She was glad she came to the hospital. She just wanted to see that he was really dead before she let him go off like that.

"I'll shine your shoes, Jack," she said.

"Love you, bye," he would say.

Holding Jack's shoes tightly in her hands, Claudia went out a side door and walked around the hospital to the front. Takeo came up right away in the cab and opened the door for her. She said she had a nice visit with her husband, and she tried to be seen smiling in the rearview mirror all the way home.

CHAPTER FIFTEEN

When Claudia got home, she gave Takeo two dollars and made him keep it. He drove away, and Claudia got up on the porch where she could see over the top of the bushes because she noticed a big brown army car in Mary Ann's driveway. She didn't want to be snoopy, she just wanted to see. Then she went in the house and put Jack's shoes away, and suddenly there was a long, despairing wail coming from Mary Ann's house. That was why the army car was there. Bill was dead, too. Poor Mary Ann. Poor Edgar Lee. Poor Petey the dog. It sure wasn't a good day for the little white houses. The Army car left Mary Ann's and went up the road, not down the road, so there were some more dead navy men. The mail was late too.

Claudia sat in front of the mirror in the bedroom and brushed her hair. It was time to take stock of her life. The situation was different now, with Annette in the picture and Jack being dead. She could say, "Well, Jack, if you're going to be off with Annette all the time, of course I have to find another man to fulfill my needs." But Jack wouldn't know anything about her needs, so why bother? She would only say it to make him jealous, but he would see right through her. He would say "All right, well, suit yourself. Love you, bye."

She didn't want that. In a way it worked out to her advantage because Jack being dead meant that she had a second chance. Sure, there were going to be bad days like this in even the best marriage, but if Jack was going to be away for a while—and she couldn't blame him one bit—she could examine everything she had done wrong and correct her mistakes before he got back.

Claudia brushed her hair and lost count of her strokes, so she just kept going. She sat back from time to time and studied herself in the mirror at different angles, as if she were going to be placed in a museum and had to choose one pose. It was time for American Girl to become a standard of beauty and proportion, like the classical Greek girl did. And who could be more American Girl than she? Even when she was down in the dumps, looking at her perky, upturned nose in the mirror, her bright eyes and golden, flowing hair and perfect proportions brought her spirits back up. What more could you ask from physiognomy? She could do so much good for the world if it all were well-rendered in marble.

Claudia felt much better for having taken the time and given some thought to examining her life. Just like Socrates said. It was really worth living when you examined how beautiful you were, or something like that.

Taking stock also brings up so many other questions, she thought. How could she compete with Annette? Her features were so different. They were luscious and passionate, not perky. Her black hair. Her dark eyes and sensuous lips. The Hollywood tan really put the icing on the cupcakes. She wondered where Annette got her brassieres. She should try to find out. Maybe a place with a large selection would carry a decent A-cup for grown women that did not lose your bosoms and go all over the place under your dress trying to find them.

How was she going to get in touch with Jack now that he was dead? She could not remember what she was just thinking about. Jack would have kept her on track. Even if he was listening to his radio shows and not paying any attention to what she was saying, he would stop her and say, "Wait. You lost me." Well now she really had.

Claudia realized she had been brushing her hair for a long time, and it was getting dark, and Jack was dead. She didn't know where she had been, but she was back now, and she felt her life had crashed into a mountain and she was sitting stunned in the wreckage.

Tomorrow she would have to get up and make coffee, eat something and brush her teeth, do the laundry, clean the house, shine Jack's shoes, take her shower, and she suddenly had no will to do any of it. Damn, damn, damn. It was all meaningless crap, and she saw it for what it was. It was for people who could forget that they loved someone enough not to be able to live without them. That's what the meaningless crap was for. Every tedious act of living keeps your mind on crap all day. Then you go to sleep at night and get your strength back for the next day of meaningless crap.

Claudia went to the bedroom and got Jack's gun and took it into the bathroom and sat on the floor. This had to be fast. She put the end of the barrel to her temple, but it was too heavy to hold there, so she held it in both hands with the barrel in the middle of her forehead between her eyes and used her thumb on the trigger. She forgot the safety. Then she didn't want to do it in the bathroom because it took her so long to clean the tiles with a toothbrush and vinegar when they moved in. She wanted to be outside in the dark, in nature, with the wind off the ocean.

When she came around the side of the house toward the ocean, the wind had died away, and Claudia could hear Mary Ann crying in her house. It was so pitiful. She couldn't leave Mary Ann like that. Claudia put the gun down in the grass and pushed through the bushes and went in Mary Ann's door without knocking and right to the bedroom, where the crying was coming from.

Poor Mary Ann. She was a mess. She was sitting cross legged in the middle of the bed, holding a Bible under the night table lamp, and Claudia could see, as she sat down beside her and put her arms around her, that Mary Ann did not know anything about the Bible because she was in the beginning part where everybody was begetting everybody else. She had crumpled and torn the thin pages and wet them with tears, looking for comfort in the wrong places.

"Where's Edgar Lee?"

"I don't know," she said, "In his room. Playing with his toy soldiers."

"Come on, Mary Ann. We have to make dinner."

"No, Claudia. I just can't."

Claudia took her hands and looked at her firmly.

"We have to. It's dinnertime. American women have to get up and make dinner."

Claudia stood her up and wiped her face with her handkerchief and tried to smooth her hair, but that was hopeless. She led her by the hand into the kitchen and turned on both of the lights there and the one in the living room. Mary Ann blinked her eyes. That reminded Claudia to run around and pull the curtains.

"We have to brighten up the place, Mary Ann, and don't you be sad in front of Edgar Lee. He'll be fine if he sees you are, so you have to be brave."

"I'll try, I'll try," she said, rubbing her nose with a hanky.

"Why don't you go find him, and I'll get something going for dinner."

Mary Ann went into Edgar Lee's room, and Claudia could hear her talking softly to him. She looked around the kitchen cupboards and in the icebox. Petey had seen the lights on and came scratching at the door, and Claudia let him in. He was a young, bright-eyed, little fox terrier puppy and seemed happy to see people, so she put a whole can of Pard in the back porch dog dish. Maybe a whole can was too much. She didn't know. She remembered the gun was still out there with the safety off, so she ran over in the dark and put the gun back under the bed with the safety back on. Close call.

Claudia started rice and unwrapped a package of sausage links and put four of them in the iron skillet. She wanted everything going when Mary Ann came in. There was a whole crate of apples that Bill's uncle had sent from the States on the back porch and she went and got some. Making applesauce was good for passing the time. She thought Mary Ann might be getting worried about her kitchen from all the clattering of pans that was going on, but that was good for her, too. By the time Mary Ann came into the kitchen with Edgar Lee, Claudia had the rice cooking, the sausages sizzling in a pan, apple chunks bubbling away in a big pot, and she was cutting up lettuce for a salad.

"You can stir the apples," said Claudia. "Can Edgar Lee have some bread and butter?"

"Oh, sure," said Mary Ann. She was just sniffling a little but looking better.

Mary Ann put Edgar Lee into his chair and fixed him a piece of bread and butter, and when she came over to stir the apples, she almost looked like her old self.

"I was going to get to making applesauce," she said wistfully.

It sounded like not making applesauce was a regret that Mary Ann would carry with her to the grave as an enduring reproach, so Claudia nudged her and gave her a look that almost made her smile. Claudia surmised that she had not yet told Edgar Lee about his father. She did not know much about children, but maybe he would not notice for a while if Mary Ann could keep herself pulled together.

Claudia turned on the radio to one of Jack's shows, and they had a nice dinner with the music in the background. Edgar Lee played with his blocks in the living room, and Petey went to sleep under the table while they cleaned up. Mary Ann's house was much nicer than her house inside. It was cozy, like people really lived there. That was because Bill and Mary Ann were not ambitious, and they knew they weren't getting out of there. Suddenly her own little white house did not seem so small anymore, and Claudia decided she would have to make it cozy like Mary Ann's. Cutting Edgar Lee's sausages and wiping applesauce off his chin got Mary Ann back, and Claudia felt she could relax now. She was glad she had not shot herself in the head. There was always a reason good enough to sign up for another hitch. That's what Jack said once.

Mary Ann asked if Claudia could call her boss at the filling station for her and tell him she couldn't come in for a few days, but Claudia convinced her it was better to go to work and persuaded her to keep her life regular for Edgar Lee's sake. It seemed to make sense to Mary Ann and kept her from crying again. Mary Ann put Edgar Lee to bed at eight o'clock. She looked pretty beat, so Claudia made her brush her teeth and get ready for bed.

Claudia was going to stay overnight. She sat on the bed and tried to brush Mary Ann's hair and read the Psalms to her until she fell asleep. The sundress was so wrinkled up that it didn't make any difference, and Claudia slipped into bed and turned out the light. Mary Ann held on to her through the night, and Claudia knew how Jack must have felt with Annette. It was very comforting to lay your head on big soft bosoms. Maybe she and Mary Ann could be best friends now that Jack and Bill were away. She was going to cry, but she had not told Mary Ann about Jack yet, and she didn't want to get her upset again. Claudia drifted off to sleep, and her last thoughts were how everybody says live one day at a time. It's an easy thing to say, but living that way is living without a carrot at the end of the string or a gold ring to grab on the merry-go-round. Living without hope. But you have all the meaningless crap you need.

Claudia got Mary Ann up early to go to work. She made breakfast for them and left the house at the same time so that Edgar Lee and Petey could be locked in without thinking anything was up. It was only for half an hour. Mrs. Bigalow would be over at seven. Claudia waved confidently to Mary Ann as she drove off. Then she went home and lay down on the bed. She knew she could not stay for long. Jack's shoes had to be shined and there was the housework. Then she felt a funny sensation and a cramp, and she got up and went into the bathroom.

It was the baby coming out. It was a sorrowful little brown thing. Coming out, it had shaped itself like one of the sausages she had cooked in the skillet last night, and shed with it was a bloody membrane that she had to pull out with her fingers while the baby dangled over the water in the toilet. She could not look at it and flushed all of it down the toilet right away. Only after it was gone did it occur to her that she should have buried it in the backyard, but that would have been hard to do, and she knew she had already done enough for any woman to feel bad about. She could not let herself tend a grave or think she could have had a little Jack if she hadn't worried so much about getting bayoneted. It was water under the bridge. That meant she wasn't going to let herself think about it anymore.

There was the dust mop and the sweeper. After that, Claudia hooked up the hose and had her shower on the cement patch and put on a clean sundress. The radio had all the regular shows, and it did not sound so much like the Japs were coming. People were just nervous, and the patrols still went by on the beach every hour. Mary Ann came home around eleven thirty, as usual. She seemed all right and had her housework to do and Edgar Lee to look after, so Claudia let her alone and went back to her laundry.

A big brown army car came up the road about two o'clock and pulled into the driveway. An Army officer and a WAVE got out. Claudia had seen pictures of the WAVES in *Life* magazine, rows of them standing at attention, just like soldiers. She liked the adorable hats. They had several different outfits, and every one of them looked as if it had been designed by somebody who knew his way around the female figure. She wanted to ask how you got into the WAVES, but the one getting out of the car looked serious, and she knew they were here to tell her about Jack.

When it was clear that Claudia did not want to talk about it and did not need to be comforted, the WAVES girl deferred to the army man, who took out a folder and informed her that Jack's benefits would entitle her to $2 a month for the rest of her life. Claudia signed his papers, and they left. Two dollars wasn't very much. But she would still be getting it if she lived to be eighty. How strange it would be if she lived to be eighty and her husband was twenty-four, since Jack would always be twenty-four. Being dead was like the Fountain of Youth.

Mary Ann ran over with horror on her face after they left. Hearing about Jack got her started again, and she cried with her head down on Claudia's kitchen table. Edgar Lee followed her over, and then he was crying too. Mary Ann had told him when she got home, but he didn't understand. He just did what she did. Claudia lit a Chesterfield for Mary Ann and told her not to waste it, and then she picked up Edgar Lee and took him down to the beach. She knew Mary Ann would not be far behind, and once they were all there, it would be easy to get them to go back for their suits and towels like a regular afternoon.

Mary Ann proved easy to distract. When they were lying in the sun and Claudia sensed that Mary Ann was thinking that their husbands were alive the last time they were at the beach like this, only last week, she sat up quickly and asked her how much she was getting.

"Oh dear. Five dollars a month. Something like that."

"How come I'm only getting two?"

"Seniority."

"But Jack was an officer."

"Doesn't matter. He only had a year in, not even that, right?"

"Well, why don't they count the four years at Annapolis?"

"Because they're having fun. That's why."

"Annapolis wasn't fun, Mary Ann. Did you ever hear anyone call Annapolis a party school?"

"Oh, get off it, Claudia. It's college, isn't it? Besides, anyone who went to Annapolis wouldn't need the money anyway."

"That's not really true," said Claudia.

Claudia told Mary Ann about Jack's father going to prison for fraud and how her father had invested money and lost his entire savings. Jack had dedicated his life to paying her father back for what his father had done. He was hiding the money in the Roadmaster, and when it crashed, people took the car apart and got all the money. Now that she said it out loud, it did sound like a tight spot she was in. Jack was gone and both families were broke.

"What are you going to do, Claudia?"

"I don't know."

"You can't live on two dollars a month."

"I have some money."

"How much? —if you don't mind my asking."

"Some. Fifty maybe."

"You know what? I can get you a job at the filling station."

Claudia made a face.

"All the men are leaving. I know Mr. Sterrin would hire you, and he's so nice."

"But I can't do anything in a garage."

"You can pump gas. It's easy. I always do it when Mr. Sterrin goes to the post office and the fellas are busy. The only one too old to go in the army is the mechanic in back, so I'm sure we'll need help."

Claudia was thrilled to hear it, but she did not want to get her hopes up. Jack didn't want her to work. He was adamant about that, and if he came back, he would be so cross. But it would be fun to work with Mary Ann, pumping gas in a bustling town like Honolulu, and she decided she could do it behind his back, and if he didn't like it, all she had to do was bring up Annette. So she said yes.

That night they were both so excited by the idea. They had dinner in their own houses to get used to it, but Mary Ann asked her to sleep over again because she missed Bill so much at night. Claudia came over in her nightgown after Edgar Lee was asleep and brushed Mary Ann's hair while they talked on the bed. She thought Mary Ann might have begun to see the difference in her hair.

"Even dull browns can become lustrous," Claudia said. "You don't have to do anything but brush it."

"I don't want to bother."

But Claudia could tell that Mary Ann liked being pampered for once in her life, so she went back to get her manicure set and did her nails too. It was good practice because naturally they looked terrible. Mary Ann was going to be a real project. When they were getting into bed, Claudia ventured to mention some of the benefits in wearing a good brassiere at night. She may have gone a little too far because Mary Ann only looked at her funny and said, "You're too much, Claudia."

CHAPTER SIXTEEN

Claudia loved her blue jump-suit coveralls. They were a dollar twenty-five at Bermanders. She purposely got them two sizes too small so they would be snug around the legs. They were boys' coveralls actually, so the hips fit fine. She bought two bandannas, blue naturally, one for her head and one for her back pocket, which was more like an accessory to the outfit. The last things were a man's shirt for under the coveralls and a little red bowtie. All dressed up in front of the mirror, she stepped back and said to herself, "Stow that gear. Clear the decks. The USS Claudia Wyler stands off for the open sea."

Every morning she came into town with Mary Ann and they walked into the garage behind big burly Leo Sterrin, with the keys, at five of seven. Mary Ann went to make coffee and get out the till for the cash register, and Claudia swept the concrete out front by the pumps. The mechanic, Mr. Knight, Mr. Sterrin's son, Billings, and the two helper boys were always late. Next up, Claudia pulled the chains that got the doors up on the four bays, which was fun, like hoisting the sails, and then she started sweeping the inside, dropping her broom to run out whenever a car pulled up for gas. She always said a cheery good morning to the customer, flipped the lever on the pump, and cranked it up like Mr. Sterrin showed her. She gave just the right amount of gas, looked at the ration card like she was Mr. District Attorney, got the money, cleaned the windshield, and checked the oil.

It only took a few weeks before Claudia was very proud of herself because she learned to do everything right. She liked that in the working world people showed you what to do and did not assume you already knew how to do it—not like being married. It was just fun to be in town too, with all the people walking around and seeing the Christmas decorations going up. You wouldn't know there was a war on. She adored her little red bow tie and the green Texaco cap she always put on to go out to the pumps.

After the morning rush was over, Claudia sat on a stool by the office door in the sunshine where Mr. Sterrin had his tomato plants growing. Through the window she could just see the top of Mary Ann's head inside where she was doing the accounts. It was comforting to know she was there, and for the first few days, when eleven o'clock came around and Mary Ann packed up to go, Claudia remembered how she felt when her mom dropped her off at school for the first time. They had a quick smoke together, but then Mary Ann had to get home to relieve Mrs. Bigalow and let Edgar Lee and Petey out. Mrs. Bigalow didn't like to let them loose in the yard and sometimes Petey peed on the rug if Mary Ann was late.

It was like being homesick at first, without Mary Ann there in the afternoon, but it did not last long because she and Mr. Sterrin got familiar so fast. The only annoying things about that were when she had her back turned, Mr. Sterrin would flip her ponytail with his finger, and every night she had a grease smudge in her hair. He also snuck up behind her a couple of times every day and picked her up around the waist in a bear hug that lifted her feet off the ground and squeezed the air out of her. He thought it was the funniest thing in the world.

Mr. Sterrin looked like he was in his mid fifties. He told her that before he came to Hawaii with a dredging crew, he'd had a farm in Pennsylvania and worked in the coal mines. Claudia thought that was where he must have gotten the barrel chest and great big arms. He looked German and had a bulldog face and a few missing teeth, but it looked like he was glad that the flukes of life had left him in a nice place, and he walked around the garage smiling all the time.

The first day he pointed proudly to a framed picture on the wall of the little office. It was out of *Life* magazine from 1936. *Life* had matched up a team of Pennsylvania coal miners against a team of lumberjacks from the Pacific Northwest in a tug-of-war. The caption of the picture said the coal miners won, and she could see Mr. Sterrin in the picture pulling hard on the rope. From the looks of those arms, she guessed Mr. Sterrin could have pulled those lumberjacks to kingdom come all by himself. He married his wife, Dot, when she was only fifteen. She didn't like the islands very much and wanted to go back to her people, who were mostly in West Virginia. She never came down to the station. Claudia heard him on the phone in the office, making promises sometimes.

Mr. Knight was big boss in the back of the shop, and Claudia felt at ease with him right from the start. He was an old, thin, and very tall Negro man. There seemed to be nothing he did not know about cars, and Mr. Sterrin treated him very well. He always addressed him as Mr. Knight and kept anyone out of the garage who might make trouble for him. He and Billings worked hard back there, but Mr. Knight made sure they had fun while they did. At least it sounded like that.

Billings had grown up working in the garage and was close with Mr. Knight. He was built exactly like his father, but had it not been for that, and being as pale and white as Mr. Knight was black, Claudia would have taken the two of them for father and son, the way they talked and jived each other in the back. Billings didn't seem to have much to say to his father and lowered his eyes whenever Mr. Sterrin poked his head into the shop. He went home at noon every day for some reason. Mary Ann said he had a drinking problem and didn't get along with his father very well over it.

When the two helper boys went into the army in January, Mr. Knight began to teach Claudia garage mechanics, since he needed help in the afternoon. It did not take her long to learn how to change the oil in cars and how to put in spark plugs, replace points and condensers, cap, rotor, wires, and use a dwell meter. Soon she was changing belts and hoses and doing brake jobs by herself. Mr. Knight said she caught on fast, and after a while he only looked over her work if she asked him. He let her use his tools and showed her how to wrestle with the tire changer and calibrate the huge metal lathe that lined most of the back wall of the shop. He said she cut brake drums real good, and he showed her how to plane heads and grind valves so she would be able to do it by herself when they called him up.

"You pay close attention now, girl," he kept saying, "'cause they gonna call me one day. You can bet on that fo sure, yessuh."

Then he would laugh because he was eighty or more, and he knew the army wasn't going to take him. Sometimes a few of his friends would stop by the garage, and if Mr. Knight hung around talking to them too long with work to do, Mr. Sterrin would put his head out the door of the office and say, "You get that call from the army yet, Mr. Knight?"

"Not just yet, Mr. Sterrin, no, sir. Looks like them Jap's lucky streak still goin' strong, ain't it." Then he'd doff his old Sinclair hat with the dinosaur on it to his friends and go back to work.

Claudia soon learned that as happy and sociable as he was, Mr. Knight needed time to himself. At lunchtime he always ate alone in peace. While Claudia sat in the sunshine outside the door of the office with the tomato plants and ate her sandwich, Mr. Knight went into the cool dark recesses of the parts room, where he had a comfortable chair that used to be the rumble seat of an old Ford. It was so dark back there that whenever Claudia looked into the garage, all she could see through the door of the parts room was a white sandwich going up and down to a set of white teeth and eyeballs. When Claudia told him what she was laughing at, they put Mr. Sterrin in Mr. Knight's seat back there after he had gotten soot all over his face from a muffler job and had him take some bites out of a sandwich, just to see what it looked like. It was fun working there. Billings was the only one who didn't laugh too much around the place, at least when his father was around.

Claudia took the taxi home every night the first week at the garage. She called Takeo, and he came down to get her in his cab. The first night she was surprised to see that he had changed out of being Japanese. The cab still had the orange paper dome on top, but the calligraphy writing was gone. Now it was just a light. Across both doors was professional signage that read: SKIP SANTIAGO'S ALL AMERICAN CAB INC. There were four brand new whitewalls on it, good ones too, Goodrich Silvertons, and the car looked ten years younger with a terrific yellow paint job.

Takeo got out of the cab to hold the door for her. He was wearing a colorful Hawaiian shirt and straw hat. On the drive home he told her he was Filipino now, and no one bothered him. He was getting many fares with the new sailors coming in and took them to hot spots in town.

"You call me Skip now," he said. "I had name change. Now I am Skip Santiago. Siuri is Louise Santiago. All official. My friend Mr. Anthony take care of it for me. He make some calls and papers with new names come in mail."

Takeo only charged her fifty cents, but when the money in her drawer ran out, Claudia realized she was going to have to do something different. She was only making $.25 an hour, which was $2.50 a day, which was $15.00 a week. That made $60.00 a month, plus the $2.00 for Jack being dead. Rent for the little white house was $40.00 a month. With two trips on Saturday because Mary Ann was off, the taxi was going to be $14.00 a month.

Claudia figured with the pencil and paper every day, and it always came out the same. It looked like there was only eight dollars available every month for food, clothes, and Chesterfields. That was when she decided to hitchhike home. She knew she could get rides, and if worse came to worst, she could walk it in two hours.

As luck would have it, on Monday night of the first week hitching home, after she said good night to Mr. Sterrin and stepped off the curb with her thumb out, a car pulled over like it had a mind of its own. It was Joe Johnson, the one married to the Johnson girl, who lived next door to Mary Ann. Claudia would not have known him, but she recognized the car because it had a little carved airplane hanging off the rearview mirror. He got gas at the Esso station a block down, and once or twice she had seem him get out of the car. She ran up and put her head in the window.

"You must be Joe," she said. Joe looked surprised, so she quickly added, "I'm Claudia Wyler, Jack's wife. We're on the other side of Mary Ann. Are you on your way home?"

"You bet," he said. "You need a ride? Hop in."

"Oh, thanks, Joe," she said as she got in. "It's nice to meet you. It's so funny, we've lived two doors down for a year and never met. I guess everyone is so busy, and now the war, of course."

"I didn't know you've already been there a year. Whaddya know."

"A little bit more than a year, actually."

"I think I might have talked to Jack once, out back, but I never saw you."

"Well, I only saw your car go by a few times," she said "—with a flash of khaki and blond hair. I thought you were going to look more like Leslie Howard."

"Oh geez, I wish I did."

"Oh, I think you're much better-looking."

She just tossed it off. Claudia knew she was flirting, but she didn't care. She needed the ride. The Johnson girl never said a word to her when they were walking down the road to find out about the attack. She acted so impatient when Claudia said anything, as if—all because of Claudia—she wasn't going to have enough time to complain about every little thing in the world that needed complaining about. Joe was safe anyway. He could stop to let her out and go on to his house, and because of all the bushes, even Mary Ann wouldn't see her get out of the car. Maybe he could bring her home every night.

He did not know that Jack had been killed, so she told him, without mentioning that it was a car crash. Jack was going into the big new cemetery with all the men who died in the navy yard and at the airfield. He was on navy business at the time, so what was the difference? She could always say he got strafed by a Zero if the Roadmaster ever came up. She went right on talking so Joe would not feel uncomfortable about Jack getting killed and told him about her job and then asked about his job, to loosen him up. He was an ordinance supply officer. Claudia could tell he liked having a pretty girl in the car flirting with him, and when she got out at her house, she leaned back in to say an intimate kind of "Thanks, Joe," before closing the door. She knew she would see him tomorrow. Joe was the type. She made a mental note never to complain about anything, unlike some people she could mention.

Claudia was so bushed that she took off her overalls and lay down on the bed for a few minutes. When she got up and turned on the light in the kitchen, Mary Ann came right over. All Claudia had for dinner was some cheese and crackers and Campbell's Green Pea Soup, but it was so nice to be with Mary Ann over Chesterfields and coffee at the kitchen table together.

"You didn't have to worry, I got a ride right away."

"Yeah, I knew you would. Lots of men around here," said Mary Ann, with one of her little smirks. "So what was all the brouhaha back there this morning?"

"Oh, Billings just lost the clip for a wire harness down the drain grate."

"Yeah, I figured it was a major catastrophe like that. He's a nice kid, but when he's been sneaking liquor, forget it."

"How did he hurt his leg, anyway?"

"He was pulling an engine and lost his grip on the chain. They couldn't get his leg back together right, so now he's got that bad limp—Oh, but that wasn't what started him drinking. That was his brother, Leo junior. Now there was one wild kid. He got killed in a motorcycle crash on the north shore."

"Oh," said Claudia. "I was wondering about him. His toolbox is in the back. Mr. Knight won't let anyone touch it."

"Well, Billings was only sixteen then, but that's when he started drinking. Everybody's got a story, huh?"

Claudia had to think about that. She didn't want Mary Ann to go, but she was so tired she couldn't think of anything to say. She was just dog-tired. She never really thought about other people having stories.

"Well, better get to bed, missy. They said six o'clock is going to be at the same time tomorrow morning. Just heard it on the radio." Mary Ann gathered up her smokes and matches and coffee cup. "Maybe we can get together when you get home every night, but just for one smoke because both of us need our sleep. We can try to figure something out so you don't have to hitch rides."

"Oh, I'll be fine, Mary Ann."

"You know I'd come get you if they weren't rationing the damn gas. And get this, I got a notice on my door today about the spare tires Bill had on the side of the house. I'm supposed to turn them in at the town hall garage. I wonder who snitched."

Claudia lay awake that night thinking. She would miss long talks with Mary Ann, and she would miss seeing Takeo, but that wasn't keeping her up. The ride home problem was solved, which should have made her feel better because it was a load off her mind. It would leave her with fourteen more dollars in the kitty every month. But prices were going up because everything in the stores had to come through submarine infested waters, so she could probably knock the fourteen back to seven worth of purchasing power. All the calculations swimming around in her mind gave her an ominous feeling.

She had never thought much about money before. She had never needed to think about it. There was always some money in a drawer or in the pocket of another jacket. She never had to do anything to get money, so it was never put to the test what she would do to get it, or what she wouldn't do to get it. She was suddenly feeling a little afraid. She was aware that you can make people jump for money, and she didn't want it to happen to her. By unkind twists of fate, it had come about that staying in the little white house meant more to her than anything else, and it had become a new vulnerability, laying out the snares of beg borrow steal.

At last Claudia gave up thinking around and around. Maybe sometimes you just feel strong, and maybe sometimes you just feel weak. That was no reason to abandon what you were trying to do. But she reminded herself not to leave confusion out of the equation. She didn't want to learn anything the hard way.

Her instincts kept her from telling Mary Ann about Joe, and she knew she ought to stick to that. That bothered her too. She didn't want to keep secrets from Mary Ann. It wouldn't be hard to believe she always got a ride. She was pretty, even in dirty overalls. She could get to sleep pondering over that one.

Now Claudia knew what it was like being Jack. He had weekends off, but she only had Sunday, so she was worse in the soup for free time than he ever was. Forget the radio shows and sleeping late. The housework fell behind, and the laundry piled up, and the grass in the yard got high. A month went by, and she was still sleeping in the same sheets with the blood from the baby.

Every morning she told herself that she would work when she got home, and every night she told herself that she would get up an hour early and get some work done, but neither one worked. All she could manage was shower, breakfast, and dishes in the morning, then shower, dinner, and dishes at night and a smoke with Mary Ann if it wasn't too late when she got home. Sometimes Joe wanted to talk and pulled over a little before they got to their street, and she couldn't cut him off. It kept her from thinking about Jack though.

What to do about Jack's things was a problem until she decided it was no problem leaving them where they were. *Life* magazine got through, but not a single letter had come from the States since the attack. Jack's parents must have been notified. She had already written Mom and Dad and told them about Jack and not to worry about her. It took her two days to think of something happy to say at the end. She settled on "Looking for that Silver Lining!!" She still had not heard back from them.

One day when she got home, there was a note from Froggy on the door. It said he had been up to the house to see her a few times, but she was never home. He was sorry about Jack, and he ended by writing down his number and letting her know to call him any time she needed a friend. Claudia made herself one of Jack's gin and tonics and had a Chesterfield while she read it. She liked Froggy and she would love to see him, but she knew that he wanted to be more than friends, and she wasn't interested. She had not thought of having another man. She was fine the way she was. How could any man measure up to Jack? No one was even close. He was the perfect man and long-suffering husband. Their year as husband and wife was filled with trial and error—whose wasn't? —but his last words came to her again whenever she doubted herself. "You've got what it takes, Claudia," he said. That was enough to live on for now.

It seemed to her that if she ever had another husband, it would give her life an importance it did not deserve. She felt her real life ended with Jack and she now existed in a phantom world. Everything real had gone off with Jack. Jack was like a train moving down the tracks. A switch had been thrown to change the track, and Claudia fell off the train. As she sat by the side, all the cars went clattering by after the locomotive, all the lights and noise of everything real went by her, and when it passed, the darkness of this phantom world closed around her. What was alive in a phantom world? To seek love and marry and hope for happiness were things of the living world, where Jack was. She was the dead one, and sometimes at night alone, she could hardly bear it.

Spring came. But spring didn't make her feel better. There weren't daffodils standing up in little patches of snow. She wasn't expecting to see the first robin in the yard. It was the same as it always was in Hawaii, and it wasn't going to look right until the calendar caught up with the weather and said it was July. On April 18, Jimmy Doolittle landed a punch and gave the Japs a blackeye. Everybody was pretty excited about that, so it kind of felt like spring after all.

It came down to practicalities. It was war, and all bets were off. After two months at the filling station, she had needed money to meet the rent on the little white house. Joe had been picking her up every night at the corner. Claudia had asked him for five dollars and he had it for her the next night. She had let another two weeks go by and asked him for another five, and she got it.

Two months went by like that, getting ten dollars a month out of Joe. She decided she could not go on talking about the loan, so she decided to force the issue. One night she said, "I don't know how I'll ever be able to pay you back, Joe."

He said not to worry about it, and she wasn't sure if he was catching on.

"I mean I can't keep asking," she said, "because I know I can't pay you back. It just isn't right."

She took off her bandana and shook out her hair. "I don't think you should take me home anymore," she said.

"Claudia—"

"No, really, Joe. I feel I'm taking advantage."

"There's no reason to feel that way," he said.

"I can't help it. You've been so sweet and unselfish."

"Well, I like you."

Claudia lowered her eyes and spoke softly. "I like you too, Joe," she said.

"So it's no big deal then. I like driving you home, and we talk."

"But I'm taking advantage of you."

"No, you're not."

"Yes, I am. I'm taking money from you."

"I don't mind," he said.

Claudia laughed. "Sure, nobody minds giving money away for nothing."

"It isn't for nothing," he said. "I like your company."

"So, you're paying me for my company now. Boy, that sounds nice."

"You know what I mean."

Claudia looked down again. "I know what you mean. I'd be flattered the other way too."

She could tell he was finally getting the idea, but he was scared. He was scared of getting caught and scared of his wife. It could go either way.

"I don't know if you would want something like that," she said quietly. "It would have to be so discrete."

Joe pulled over to the side of the road where there was an overlook for the tourists. Claudia knew he had only pulled over to talk, but she moved over on the seat and put her hands on him, and he gave in. They got back on the road and took every side road that went off, looking for a secluded place in the jungle brush, but every one seemed to lead into pockets of houses, and one of them was where Takeo lived. They went right by the taxi with the paper light on top. Joe was only getting more and more nervous and sweating through his uniform, and his heart must have been going a mile a minute. It didn't mean anything to her. If it worked out, she could count on an extra ten dollars a month. No loan.

When they finally found a place where there weren't any houses, Joe pulled in where the hood went under the bushes and he stopped the car. It was getting into twilight. Claudia opened his shirt. They were out of the sea breeze, where it was hot and steamy, and they both sweated getting out of their clothes even though the overalls were easy. Then it was just her panties, the sight of which, and her smooth legs coming out of rough blue jean, was almost too much for him. She didn't give it a second thought. In for a penny, in for a pound. She opened up his fly and just climbed on. Mary Ann had given her the idea when she said ride the meat pole. It was one of those expressions that sticks in your mind, and then you suddenly figure out what it means. Joe was done in a second, and she pretended she had never had anything like Joe before. Then she got off him and they put their clothes back on and got out of there fast.

Joe dropped her off where the road branched off to the little white houses. He had to go back to the base to take a shower, and Claudia walked up the road to her house. When she took off her shirt to go shower under the hose in the dark, she found it wet with a little milk because her bosoms still expected they'd be going to work, and Joe really went to town on them. She was so sorry about the baby. It seemed like a long time ago, but it really wasn't.

CHAPTER SEVENTEEN

That was the only time they did it in the car. They drove around to a little hotel called The Nomad and stayed about an hour. Claudia loved having a hot bath and brought along a folded-up sundress in her bag so she did not have to put her dirty overalls back on. Joe tried to get away without paying once, but she held him to it. It was going to be ten dollars a time, she told him, not ten dollars for a month with a lot of times, even though she got the hot baths.

She knew Joe thought she had feelings for him because she pretended so well. Pretending was part of the deal. She told him that straight and pointed out that he would not want someone to really fall in love with him because it would wreck his marriage. After that he was satisfied to have her pretend, and some months he had the money to pay for two times. Claudia didn't know where all that money was coming from, but she was glad she was on the right end of the stick this time.

Occasionally Claudia felt bad about Joe because she had led him astray, but she didn't let it bother her for long. Joe had a choice. He could have stuck to the straight and narrow, and he could back out any time. She didn't have any other way. She had to be like Jack now. Jack knew what he had to do to get ahead. You didn't have to be ambitious. The same thing applied if you were desperate and didn't want to go under. She didn't want to feel sorry for herself, but working for twenty-five cents an hour to keep a roof over her head put the water right up to her chin.

From time to time, Claudia caught a glimpse of the Johnson girl out in the backyard. She always had that mean, screwed-up face, like everything was wrong with the world. You give up giving someone like that the benefit of the doubt after a while. Claudia guessed the main thing Joe liked was having a pleasant, blue-eyed blonde who smiled at everybody when they walked into the Nomad. And wasn't he the cock in the barnyard walking by the old men reading their newspapers in the lobby. She knew it also appealed to him to have an older woman. He was twenty-one, and she was twenty-four. That made her a mystery woman, and she had enough brains to know you had to have some mystery to you if you expected to be a man's mistress for long.

Claudia liked everything about working in the garage, even fixing flats and hot patching tubes and knocking out ball joints with the fork and sledgehammer. Mr. Knight didn't like welding because he was so tall that the apron let sparks get under, so he showed Claudia, and then she did most of the pipes and mufflers that came in. She still had to drop everything to go out to pump gas, so Mr. Sterrin hired a high school kid named

Ricky to cover the pumps and gave her a raise. She had been there only eight months, but he put her up to thirty cents an hour, and he always had sandwiches brought over from the diner across the street, so lunch was free. He still flipped her ponytail when he went by and picked her up in bear hugs and squeezed the air out of her, but Claudia didn't mind because he was sweet.

Best of all, she liked when the four of them, she and Mr. Knight, Mr. Sterrin, and Billings worked together, shoulder to shoulder, on a deadline job like rebuilding an engine on a farm truck. It made her feel like part of the war effort.

She grew to admire Billings. He knew as much as Mr. Knight and he was smart besides. It was fun to watch him reason out a problem. He might blow his top when little things went wrong, but when big things went wrong, like dropping the rear of a car into the pit, he was steady, even if he had been drinking a little. He never looked directly at her, and when he explained something to her, he always talked to the ground. At noon he left to go home for lunch and did not come back. Mr. Sterrin said his mother could not do anything with him.

One night after hours when they were waiting for the tanker truck and talking seriously, Mr. Sterrin confided to her that Mrs. Sterrin had her woman's parts taken out several years ago and was gun-shy about relations. Claudia already knew he had a Hawaiian girl in town. She stopped at the station sometimes and brought homemade pies. She was sweet, and Claudia liked her. She already knew something was going on. Claudia said she was always on the side of the wife, but she understood.

Claudia could talk about anything with Mr. Sterrin because he accepted her both as a mechanic and as a woman. It was all the same to him, so sometimes he talked to her rough and bawdy like a man would talk to another man, and sometimes he talked to her respectfully, the way men talk to women. Claudia knew he hoped she would marry Billings and get him straightened out, and one day he came out and said it.

"You two could run the place," he said. "We'd give it to you for a dollar. Me and Dot could go back to Pennsylvania and get a little farm, or West Virginia where her people come from. She'd be so happy. Think about it, Claud, just think about it. Dot would be so happy. You could straighten out Billings real good."

He closed his eyes and smiled, as if he were imagining it, and then went back to sweeping out the bay. Claudia and Mr. Knight were finishing up a brake job on a beautiful Packard Super Eight convertible that belonged to the president of the Honolulu Merchants Association. It was on the last boat that came over with new cars before the war, and it was a beauty. Up on the lift in the driver's seat, Mr. Knight was pumping the brakes for Claudia underneath and he was pretending to be driving the car through his old hometown in Mississippi.

"Yessah! Yessah!" he shouted out the window. "Look at dat wind blowin' my hair!" He took off his cap and ran his hand over his bald head and laughed. "Yessah, Yessah, look at me now."

Mr. Sterrin put up his broom again and came under the car. "She'd be so happy, Claud. She never liked it here. If you and Billings got together and took the place over, I could take her home. She's sick, you know, and she don't want to die here. You look good together, you and Billings. I seen you two workin'. I knowed he'd stop drinkin' if he was your man. You could change him, Claud."

"I think he likes drinking more than me," said Claudia.

"No, he likes you, Claud. He just shy. He likes you a lot."

To be honest, Claudia had to admit that Billings was a very good-looking boy, and she might have been interested if he didn't have so many problems. She was a working person now. She didn't think about self-confidence anymore. The old life was over. She was a mechanic, and she knew what she was doing. She could almost say she didn't need anybody, but that would be arrogant. Just the same, she thought about Billings. He was quiet and shy, and she liked looking at him. Sometimes she thought about him when the morning work was over and she sat on the bench by the tomato plants eating lunch and looking up into the nice sunshine, watching him limp around the corner on his way home. He didn't try to stand up straight either. She could make him do that. There was nothing wrong with owning a garage. Sometimes she could see it.

Mr. Sterrin thought Billings never got over the death of his brother, but from what Claudia heard, she thought it was Dot Sterrin who never got over it, and she had no time for Billings. Mothers had a lot to do with how men turned out, like the Achilles' heel story. Achilles' weakness wasn't his heel, the weakness was the mother. That was what Claudia got out of the story. Since she'd known Billings anyway.

There was always a lot of stuff to fix if you didn't have a good mother, Claudia thought. And then she thought about her own child, the little bird she flushed down the toilet last year. She had not thought about it for a long time, and remembering was like getting hit over the head. Since she had been working in the garage, there had been nothing to cry about, except when she stopped getting that time of the month. She gave up waiting for it. It was her own doing, and she realized what it probably meant. The only baby she would ever have was dead in the septic tank.

"Been almost a year now, girl," said Mr. Sterrin, one night when they were closing up.

"Since what?" she said.

"You know. Since you had a man."

Mr. Knight caught just enough to find it a good time to get out the door. "Uh-oh," he said. "Soun like you two gonna sass each otha. Time for me to git along. Goodnight, everybody!"

He ducked as if they were throwing things at him and went for his lunch pail and the door.

"Don't worry about me," said Claudia. "I'm getting plenty."

"Plenty, my eye," said Mr. Sterrin. "I don't see no admirals comin' round here to fetch you."

"That's because you wouldn't catch me with no old admirals. It's young sailor boys for me."

Mr. Sterrin roared with laughter. "I know you ain't gettin' any young sailor boys, Claud, you too stuck up."

"Sez you." She turned around to put the tools away in Mr. Knight's box and Mr. Sterrin put his big arms around her middle and picked her up off the ground. She hit her fists against his sides but it was useless.

"Cut it out, you big palooka."

"Young sailor boys, huh?"

"Plenty of 'em," she said. "Anytime I want."

He squeezed her carefully, just enough to squeeze all the air out of her. He was such a big lout, and his arms around her middle were like hams made of rock, and the only way to get out was to not say anything or resist, and then he put her back down.

"You in a bad mood again, ain't you, Claud," he said.

"Leave me alone."

"Now I done it." He pretended to be so remorseful. It was the way the routine went, and after Claudia threw him a grudging okay, he got back to being serious about how happy Dot would be to go home. They stuck the storage tank for the end of the day with the long pole, wrote down the numbers, and finished closing up. Outside the door Mr. Sterrin hung the keys back on the belt that disappeared under his big tummy and said, "She'd be so happy Claud, she'd be so happy. You just think about it. We'd give you the station. I knowed you can straighten out Billings. He likes you. He'd do what you tell him. You could be happy too. He's a good boy. You know that. Just think about it."

Claudia told him she would think about it, and he said goodnight and went to his truck and got in. She paused on the step to light up a Chesterfield. The minute she stepped off the corner, Joe would pull over in his car. She saw him waiting on the other side, parked at the curb.

Everything was different now. Jack wasn't coming back and she was on her own. With Jack, she was something. Without Jack, she was nothing. Being selfish and delusional had kept her going and gotten her around the need to be strong. But it still left her with herself, which was nothing. If she had to be someone alone in the world, she would rather be Jack. She saw things from his point of view now. Jack knew how the world worked, and now she did too. She had been a sap. That was one thing you couldn't say about Jack, and now she was no sap either. Everything was going great, and she was getting plenty. All she had to do was be like Jack, or be Jack if she could.

Joe pulled over and she got in. He had the look on his face that meant he had gotten his hands on another ten, and tonight she was going to get a hot bath.

CHAPTER EIGHTEEN

Sometime that night, Billings and Mr. Sterrin had a fight. Billings was drunk and picked up a hammer and hit his father over the head and killed him. Mary Ann and Claudia had no idea what had happened when they got to the station the next morning. They waited for an hour in the car, but no one came to open up. Mr. Knight and Ricky sat on the curb and got up every time a car pulled in for gas and waved them on, saying the place wasn't open yet. A police car came about nine thirty, and the officer told them what had happened. They stood around not knowing what to do. Mr. Sterrin had been taken to the hospital and pronounced dead, and Billings was tied up and taken to the same place and put in a ward where they held crazy people. Mr. Knight got tears in his eyes and pulled the bandana out of the back pocket of his overalls and put his face in it. Mary Ann and Claudia got close around him and tried to comfort him.

"Oh, I ain't worried about the boss. He's a good man. He's gone to Glory, I'm thinkin' bout dat por boy an da trouble he in now. Mercy me, mercy me. Dat por boy."

Mary Ann and Claudia drove home and had lunch together at Mary Ann's house. It was strange to be home in the middle of the day, and Edgar Lee and Petey were glad to get out of the house early and were playing in the yard. Mary Ann was deep in thought since the drive home. After some coaxing, she finally said, "I don't know about you, but I'm going to need another job pretty fast."

"Me too. But you know what? I think we can do better than just a job."

"How do you figure that?"

"I've been thinking. All we have to do is go see Dot. We can run the place for her until she wants to go back to West Virginia, and then we can send her a little money every month and buy the place off her. What do you think of that?"

"We can't run a garage."

"Sure we can. Why not?"

"We don't know anything about running a garage."

"You do the bookkeeping, and Mr. Knight and I can do the rest. What else is there to do?"

"There's other things—"

"We'll figure them out. And we'll be together. Well?"

"Well what?"

"What do you think?"

Mary Ann stopped and thought, leaving the door of the ice box wide open, which was very unlike her. Coming back with Edgar Lee's glass of milk, she smiled and started getting excited about the idea and said, "Okay, Miss Claudia, let's give it a go."

They decided to look in the paper the next day or two to see when the funeral was going to be and get hold of Dot right after it was over. The more they talked about it, the better it looked. They called Mr. Knight and lined him up, and for the next two days they were on cloud nine thinking about having their own business. Claudia pointed out an article in an old *Life* magazine called Women at Work. She explained it was called a human-interest story and if they were successful they might get a write-up in a national magazine as the first full-service garage owned and operated by girls. Mary Ann said she'd be happy if they just made money, and then Claudia had to explain the value of promotion.

"So you think anybody in Ohio is going to come here to buy their gas?"

Mary Ann was just being contrary, so Claudia smiled back and said, "Sure, why not?"

Very late that night, Claudia heard a tapping at the bedroom window. It woke her up, and for a second she thought the Japs were coming out of the jungle. But then she thought the Japs would not bother tapping on anyone's window, and it was probably Joe. He must have snuck out, and he had to be crazy to take a chance like this, one house down from his wife. He wouldn't come without the ten dollars, but she wasn't in the mood for Joe and certainly did not feel like pretending anything at three o'clock in the morning, other than pretending she was asleep. She didn't know how long he tapped because she was completely dead to the world in two minutes.

On the day of the funeral, they went to pay their final respects and to meet Dot Sterrin. When people were going back to their cars and Dot was unattended, they made their move. As it turned out, they had all the time they needed to make the pitch because no one was in a hurry to pick up the ball with Dot. Those who attended the funeral were probably relieved that Claudia and Mary Ann were willing to take her on and backed away to their cars to get over to the buffet at one of the hotels.

After it was all over and Claudia and Mary Ann were driving home, they agreed there was no hope for these particular girls to have the first full-service garage owned and operated by girls. Dot was a thin, bitter little woman who thought everything that had happened was just what she had expected and both the men she had lost were damn fools. She was the only one with good sense, and she was selling the station to a man named Mr.

Anthony, who was going to make it into a sidewalk café like they have in Paris. So that was the end of that. Another success story for somebody else.

CHAPTER NINETEEN

The next day was Saturday, so they looked through the classified section of the *Honolulu Times* and the *Honolulu Advertiser* at Claudia's over coffee and Chesterfields while Edgar Lee and Petey played in the yard. The plan was to go into action Monday morning, so Sunday was going to be beauty day.

They were shooting for the working girl look, not glamour, and if Claudia had not spent a year in a garage, it would have been easy for her to come down to working girl level. Now it was going to be a job getting up that far. Her nails were the worst, and her hair was so bad with split ends from trying to get grease out every night for a year that she had Mary Ann cut a whole inch off the bottom. They did the cuts and other drastic measures like Mary Ann's hair on Saturday night so that all of beauty day would not go to just one or two big projects.

They went to the beach a little on both Saturday and Sunday and got a little color in their faces while they worked on eyebrows and mapped out the placement of curlers to set the wave for Mary Ann's hair. It was easy for Claudia to feel like a girl again, and she was glad that Mary Ann finally came around to see how worthwhile it is to look for your strengths and get back to basics. They set up in Mary Ann's kitchen on the big table.

"You want to put your best foot forward," Claudia said. "Hold still."

Claudia was putting one lipstick color on half of Mary Ann's lips and a different shade on the other half. Mary Ann was getting impatient and wanted the mirror.

"It doesn't have to be your best foot," she said. "All you need is enough foot to put in the door."

Claudia tried not to get frustrated and let her have the mirror.

"You want to be pleasing to look at, don't you?"

"I'm not pleasing to look at?"

"No, not all the time, to be honest with you."

"Well, what's so wrong?"

"It's not any one thing, Mary Ann. It's an amalgamation of little things. It's how you project. It's what goes into 'the look.'"

"Okay Miss Amalgamation. What bugs you most about my look?"

"Well, I know you're not going to like this, but it's your bust."

"I knew it."

"No. Listen Mary Ann. You're never going to look right in a dress until you find the right brassiere."

"You and your bras, Claudia. Jesus."

"I'm just trying to help."

"You're talking about men, right?"

"Well sure. All the bosses are men."

"Let me tell you, Claudia, they aren't that picky. They'll fuck anything."

Claudia was exasperated and sullen, but only for a moment. She wasn't going to let Mary Ann get her down with either her bad attitude or her language.

"We're supposed to be helping each other," she said. "It would be nice if you could be more cooperative."

Claudia was firm about it, so Mary Ann said she was sorry, and then Claudia said she was sorry too, even though it was not her fault that Mary Ann had a mental block when it came to brassieres.

"We'll concentrate on your hair," said Claudia.

On Monday morning they left Edgar Lee and Petey in the house with Mrs. Bigalow and drove into town and parked behind the Grand Hawaiian. It was right in the middle of everything and a good place to meet. Then they went off in different directions with plans to get back together at noon in front of the hotel. Mary Ann was going for a few bookkeeping and general ledger jobs, and Claudia was going to go around to the other big garage before she tried anything else.

For the first time in her life, Claudia knew she had a useful skill. They might not recognize her at Alonzo's because she was all dolled up, but she knew who to talk to because she had picked up a couple of cars at Alonzo's with electrical problems they didn't know what to do with. Mr. Knight was good with electrical and had taught her how to read schematics in shop manuals. They were bums at Alonzo's, but they had tools and equipment, even though they didn't know what to do with them. The boss was Mike somebody. Nobody knew who Alonzo was.

Walking by the old shop, Claudia spotted Mr. Anthony standing at the front door peering inside. She crossed the street and went the other way before he turned around, and she glanced back to see that one of the bay doors was going up and Mr. Knight was getting his tools out. His daughter was backing their old truck up to the door.

When Claudia got to Alonzo's, Mike laughed at her. She told him that she was the girl who worked over at Sterrin's and that he himself had tried to give her twenty cents an hour more to come work for him. Then he stopped laughing and listened to her. Mike was nice but said he was full up in the garage with men the army didn't want, and meanwhile he had just hired Mr. Knight, who he could not pass up, so he was all set for now. While they were talking, Mr. Knight's truck came up. Mr. Knight looked hard through the picture windows when Claudia waved at him. He had to look twice before he recognized her, and then he took off his Sinclair hat, not to wave it but out of respect for considering himself in the presence of a lady, even though he was out in his truck. Emily Post had nothing on Mr. Knight.

It was too bad about Alonzo's, but Claudia was happy for Mr. Knight. Mike wasn't a bum at all. She could have worked with him. She went around to another shop but it was the same story, and they were afraid of getting their gas cut back. It was only ten o'clock. Next she went to the public library. They did not need any help either, and Claudia felt as overdressed there as she had at Alonzo's. The ladies looked down their noses at her as if she couldn't be smart enough to work there, looking so good in a snappy outfit and having silky blond hair with lots of body. It almost killed them to be polite.

The newspaper office was next, the *Honolulu Star*. They had been so good in their editorials about protecting the resident Japanese on the island after the big attack, and Claudia could easily see herself leading a committed life, working for a sane and moral organization. Her instincts told her that the boss would hire her. All she had to do was get through the girls they had at the front desk.

Claudia went successfully through two check points, claiming to be the bearer of an important communiqué, which took her into the interior of the floor, which was like a beehive, with everyone running every which way between the desks and all the typewriters clacking away. The other secretaries must have called ahead because the one Claudia now faced showed her immediately into the office of the top banana. The banana sat on the edge of his desk, looked up from some papers and put out his hand. Claudia said there was no communiqué. Just her. She wanted to be a reporter. She told him she was a girl who could work well under pressure in a fast-paced environment and do what it takes to get the scoop, as he should be able to see from her clever ruse. The banana said they were fully staffed but he'd make a couple of calls while she waited outside. An hour later he called her back in and said the *Times* wanted her, but she'd better get over there fast.

"So much for morals," said Claudia.

They were looking forward to having lunch at the Grand Hawaiian to celebrate getting jobs, but even from a block away Claudia could see that Mary Ann had nothing to be happy about either, so they walked around until they found a café on a side street that didn't look too expensive and sat outside under the umbrellas.

"He was playing a joke on me. The people at the *Times* just laughed. I had to take a cab across town. That bastard."

Claudia pulled the folded classified page out of her purse and showed all the other places she had crossed off.

"Nobody liked your looks, huh?

"Don't be silly, Mary Ann. It's so discouraging. You always have to get past the girls to get to the men."

Claudia put the paper back in her purse. They both had the turkey club with cottage cheese and pineapple slices, coffee, and a few Chesterfields. Lots of sailors were walking around town, and it was fun to catch some cute ones looking them over.

"Been a long time," said Mary Ann with a smirk.

Then it was back to pounding the pavement. They split up again and agreed to meet back at the hotel at five. Claudia went down the long boulevard with palm trees and began looking in at every office and store along the way. There were girls at front desks everywhere, and it was no use. The Outdoor Circle sounded nice. They worked to abolish billboards on the island, and Claudia liked the thought of driving around looking for billboards. The girl at the front desk was so nice it almost made her cry, but it turned out to be all volunteer.

Farther down and off on side streets, Claudia found the water works and tried it, and a place where they made bags for the sugar refinery. Then she swung back towards town and tried a bakery and wholesale fish place that smelled terrible. That was enough for one day.

Mary Ann struck out too, so they went into the Grand Hawaiian and had a drink at the bar. Mary Ann had the skills but had never worked on machines before. Everybody had machines now, she said. They wanted to hire her at one place and tried to teach her a big machine with cards that you fed in while you pushed numbers. It had a big carriage that flew back and forth with so much noise you couldn't talk over it. It was that old-dogs-new-tricks thing. She just couldn't do it.

Even though they were down on their luck, Claudia began to feel more in her element at the Grand Hawaiian. There were some naval officers at the bar. Mary Ann reminded her about Edgar Lee and Petey back at the house, so Claudia drank up and they called it a day. It was not an auspicious first day, but they tried. When the gun goes off, you're supposed to run. Jack said that once.

At least the bread box was full. Claudia looked in her cupboards. The six Campbell's soups in two lines of three looked good but not much else was sitting on the shelves. Too bad she couldn't eat the poi. She still had three big cans. Well, the day might come, you never know. The groceries she got with Mary Ann on the way home filled up four bags, but when she got them unpacked, her cupboards still looked like a movie theater with a lot of empty seats. Claudia put the rest of the money back in the money can on top of the icebox. Not exactly a sellout crowd in there either.

That night she left a light on in the bedroom and lay down on the bed. Around midnight, Joe came tapping at the window again and she let him in. He had the ten dollars, and he really gave it to her because it had been so long. Afterward he went to sleep on top of her, which was annoying when it's dead weight like that, so she gave him a couple of nudges, and then he wanted to do it again and got going without asking. It was a bad precedent, but she was too tired to argue. She made sure he knew she was mad about it. Then she had to hook up the hose and wait for him to have a shower outside. No hot bath for her this time. Later, when she sat on the toilet and looked down between her legs, it looked like Joe wasn't saving anything for his wife, and he better watch out.

It was just gossip, but Claudia wished she had not heard it. They were at the little café again. Mary Ann said Jan thought her husband was having an affair. Claudia didn't know who she was talking about.

"You know, the Johnson girl."

"Oh, her. I didn't know her name was Jan."

"Yeah, that's her name. She was out back the other day and we were talking. She said Joe, that's her husband, is always picking fights and then drives off in the car."

"Do you want any dessert, Mary Ann?"

"Better not."

Claudia asked the waiter for the check, and they had a little more coffee. It was day two, lunch break. They weren't setting the world on fire again.

"I don't want to go back out there," said Mary Ann. "My feet hurt. So what do you think?"

"I don't know. Maybe he just drives around in the car."

"Come on, Claudia. He's got to be seeing someone."

"Well, maybe it's someone he doesn't really love and it'll blow over."

"How do you know that?"

"Oh, don't ask me, Mary Ann. Remember what you said about Bill? You said he just wanted to do it with somebody different."

Mary Ann leaned over to her and whispered, "He hasn't wanted to do it for months. With her, I mean."

"She told you that?"

"Yeah. She thinks of me like her mom or something."

Claudia figured Joe must be hiding the car somewhere and walking back up to the little white houses. It sounded like the stakes were getting higher if Joe was working that close to the wire. She felt bad about Jan, but she couldn't let that stop her. She needed the money. But there were still principles she could stand on. It was going to be ten dollars for each time, not all you can eat.

"I wouldn't be telling my mother anything like that," she said.

"Me neither," said Mary Ann. "Jan's just going through a rough time."

Claudia got up and pulled her purse off the back of the chair. "We better get going, or it's going to be a rough time for us too," she said.

The afternoon went like the morning. It was the same with day three, four, and five. They were staying together now and going into places like laundries and tattoo shops that they had walked past before. Mary Ann had given up on bookkeeping and was just tagging along as they looked into every place that might need a couple of girls. At five o'clock on Friday, they sat on a bench in a little park opposite the Grand Hawaiian and took off their shoes. It was so pretty there under the palm trees with all the flower beds around them. Neither one of them felt like going home without any prospects and worrying about it all weekend.

"I'm just beat," said Mary Ann.

Claudia thought Mary Ann needed a boost. She could tell that Mary Ann's self-confidence had suffered in the week they had been looking for jobs and that she would revert to her natural tendency not to care about her personal appearance. Claudia realized that she had been too critical and had left out the key ingredient in any beauty program.

"You don't look half as beat as some of the girls we've seen out looking for jobs. Even the much younger ones," said Claudia.

"Get out," said Mary Ann.

"I mean it. No one would know you've been walking all over the city for five days straight. Some of those girls look terrible. You look very fresh."

Mary Ann started laughing, but Claudia knew there was a part of her that wanted to believe she could be beautiful. It was all in the article "Believe You Can Be Beautiful" in this month's *Woman's Home Companion.* Self-confidence and believing in yourself inspired morale, and today it wasn't only for individual people or girls. You could see it in the patriotic posters going up every day on walls and telephone poles. We were all in this together. *Woman's Home Companion* and the United States government were on to something. It didn't matter what you were. It was more important to believe you were something better.

But then Claudia thought more about it, and she saw that she and Mary Ann were in different situations. Mary Ann had Edgar Lee to look after, and that would make her better and stronger than she thought she was. She did not need compliments or praise.

Being alone, what did she have, when it came down to it? Beauty day had gotten her on the wrong track of expecting to rely on herself. Her strength was still Jack—as she had known him, as she understood him now, as her acknowledged failings stood out so starkly against his shining example, vindicating and absolving him of all blame in her memories of their year together. Jack would show the way.

And there, on the park bench with Mary Ann under the palm trees, looking over to the great hotel, with the flags of the allied nations waving over marble steps, a transfixing vision came to her of Jack, standing at the entrance to the Grand Hawaiian, and an idea flashed into her head with all the brilliance of his dress whites and bright Ipana smile.

CHAPTER TWENTY

There was another note from Froggy on the door when she got home but she didn't have the strength or patience to read it. She knew what it probably said anyway.

Claudia fell into bed exhausted. Every bone in her body ached, and her hands throbbed, but she felt good because she had a job. Both of them did, and she was so happy she would be working with Mary Ann. They got home at midnight. She was starving, but all she could do was make a bowl of Campbell's Cream of Mushroom Soup and open a pack of saltines. She would do better tomorrow.

She would work out a schedule and find a way to get some sleep and get everything done around the house. It wouldn't be easy to get used to the work and figure out the money. If she didn't move up the ladder fast enough, she would still need Joe. She didn't know how she would fit him in, but in the meantime, it was cast off all lines, hoist the mainsail and set her into the wind.

The next day was Sunday, December 6. The day of the big attack would fall on Monday this year, but she decided to count today as the one-year anniversary because it was a Sunday, quiet and reverent like Sunday, and nice sitting outside in the sunshine with her coffee and Chesterfields. There were black clouds in the mountains, but they tore away and kept going eastward over the wide ocean to America. She never thought of leaving the little white house now. She thought of Jack in the wreckage of the Roadmaster and her baby in the septic tank. If she were Dot Sterrin, she would say this is where her people were buried. So much had happened in a year. If this is what a year feels like, she felt like she and her people had lived a hundred of them here.

It looked like Mary Ann slept all day. Edgar Lee and Petey stayed inside, and Claudia gave up looking for them when it started getting dark and the lights went on in Mary Ann's house. Claudia came in and sat down at the kitchen table with her coffee and her Chesterfields to write to her mother before she made dinner. She said she was now an official working girl but didn't tell her what the job was. She would have to make up something. For the last line, she said she was going to try Chase & Sanborn, but it didn't look right with exclamation marks.

Before she went to bed, Claudia took off her engagement ring and put it in the black-and-red Chinese vase on the dresser. The wedding band was plain, and that was okay but the engagement ring would attract too much attention at work. She decided never to take off the wedding band unless it was for another man, and that didn't look like it was going to happen in the new job.

The next morning, Claudia ambled over to Mary Ann's and waited for her by the car. It was sure better than going to the garage so early. All they had to do was get there by eleven. On the other hand, it wasn't so nice getting home at midnight. Claudia leaned against the car and did some figuring in her head. Thirty cents an hour wasn't going to set the world on fire, and then she started singing in her head "I don't want to set the world on fire, I just want to start—(pause, pause) a flame in your heart." It was the only line she knew, but it was kind of cute.

"You be good, Edgar Lee," Mary Ann called back inside the door. "Mrs. Bigalow will be over soon and Auntie Jan will come make you dinner, so you be good. Petey, you watch Edgar Lee. Good boy. Bye-bye."

Mary Ann locked them in and got behind the wheel. She had a bag lunch too, but hers was more like two bags compared to Claudia's. Claudia figured this job would either thin Mary Ann down, or her bag lunches would get bigger. It was going to be interesting to see which.

"I don't know about this job, Claudia," she said.

"I like punching in on the time clock, don't you? It makes me feel like part of the war effort, like the girls they show going to the factories in *Life*. Some of them have cute outfits, and it's interesting to see what they do with their hair. I guess it depends on what kind of factory where you're punching in."

"I never gave punching in any thought."

"Oh gosh, Mary Ann. You've punched in before?"

"Sure. No great shakes. So, I was thinking about it last night. The job, I mean—"

"We have to start somewhere, Mary Ann. You don't have the Johnson girl coming in for Edgar Lee, do you?"

"Yeah, she wanted to. Midnight's too late for Mrs. Bigalow. But about the job, I thought we were going to be cooks. I wouldn't mind that so much."

"They can't just start us as cooks. I know we'll move up, but they like to see everybody start at the bottom. You just wait. Someone will be out sick or something and we'll be right there, in the right place at the right time."

It was such a pretty day that Claudia wished the drive was longer. On one side of the road there were the mountains and clouds and all the palm trees and grasses and vines shot through with flowers of every color on earth. Then she could turn and look out over the ocean on the other side and see little parts of the beach flash by.

"I'm going to miss going to the beach."

"We'll go to the beach," said Claudia.

"Sure. Like when? It's not the same at two o'clock in the morning."

"Oh God, Mary Ann, you're such a gloomy gus. We can bring flashlights."

They both laughed.

"I'm glad I have you," said Mary Ann.

"Ditto."

"Ditto, kiddo."

The dishwasher was a long sheet-metal tunnel with a conveyor inside that clanked and sprayed water and shot steam so much you couldn't hear anything up close to it, but while you waited for the dishes to come out, you could back off and hear the radio. Larry kept it going all the time because he liked to jive to the music as he did the pots and pans in the sinks. Mostly he only jived his fanny because he could lean over and rest his arms on the sink and take the weight off his bad foot.

Claudia liked him a lot. He was just a kid. He got his foot crushed in the navy, during the attack and they discharged him. He did not want to go home the way he was, so he stayed in Hawaii. He was a good-looking boy, but Claudia could see he didn't care about that because his blond hair was grown out long like Prince Valiant in the comics, and since he was too light to need to shave every day, sometimes he looked a little unkempt. And then there was the Southern accent.

Larry was a strange mix. The blue eyes and blond hair and fine features made her think of the boys at Washington and Lee in their smart tennis sweaters and pressed white shorts, but the Prince Valiant hair and the fuzz on his face threw her off. So did the ain'ts and y'alls. He could have had a proud and manly demeanor even with his light frame, but he looked down at the ground when he talked to anyone, and his posture was terrible. He was like Billings in that way. But Larry did not drink and did not have another side to himself. Claudia tried to find a word for it and came up with self-possession—if that meant that he seemed to completely understand what he was. Every strength he needed came from inside. Ergo, every gift was freely given. He was a different kind of man, all right.

When the kitchen got too hot, Larry took off his T-shirt, and the sight of his smooth shoulders and chest and his flat stomach knocked her out. The first time Claudia saw his belly button, she gasped and looked around to see if anyone else noticed it was showing. Men were supposed to keep their pants up. It was like girls can show cleavage all they want, but other girls will let you know right away, with disapproving looks, if your nipples are showing. You can count on your mother-in-law for that too. Claudia could not help looking at Larry's belly button. On busy nights with lots of dishes and steam coming out of the dishwasher like crazy, she couldn't wait for the shirt to come off. She didn't mean to obsess, but it was nice to have something to look forward to in a job like this.

Claudia didn't think it ever entered Larry's mind that girls would look at him. He had a girl back home. Claudia saw her picture once when he was outside smoking and she had wandered into a back room off the kitchen. It was Larry's room. He slept on a cot back there so he could put hams in the ovens at four o'clock in the morning every day. His better clothes were on hangers against the wall. He didn't seem to have much else. The picture of his girl was in a silver locket on the floor beside the cot. She was cute and very young-looking like he was. He said she liked to go dancing, so he was going to stay in Hawaii until his foot got better. As far as his girl knew, he was still in the navy.

When Larry jived at the sink to the music, it was almost too much for Mary Ann. If Claudia caught her looking at Larry's fanny, Mary Ann would throw her drying rag over her shoulder and cock her hips like a hooker in the movies and push her bosoms up with her hands and make kissy lips. The cooks always turned around to see what was so funny when Claudia and Mary Ann got going like that.

Larry didn't catch on that they looked at him. They admitted to each other on the way home the first night that Larry was downright sexy. Mary Ann had her glasses on for driving at night and was hunched over the wheel and squinting into the lights of an on-coming car. "Forget it, Claudia," she said. "We're old ladies to him. Don't kid yourself."

Claudia knew she would have to keep reminding herself. Larry always came over to lift the racks off the conveyor when they were loaded with the big dinner plates, but it was because he was nice, and he knew they were heavy. Fully loaded, each rack was probably fifty pounds, but Larry picked them up like they were nothing. If he had his T-shirt off, Claudia could see the muscles of his abdomen clench in rows as he hefted, and the waistband of his navy pants dropped a full three or four inches below his belly button and held across the arc of his pelvis like a suspension bridge over a canyon in shadows. It was enough to make her heart stop. As he turned to go back to the pots and pans at the sink, he always hiked his pants back up and told her not to forget to shake the silverware basket while it was hot so there wouldn't be water spots. She always forgot to do that when he helped her because she got lost imagining in her mind for a while.

It was easy to let her mind drift, waiting while the racks went clunking through the long tunnel. She remembered reading the *Aeneid* in Latin. She used to know what a Geissler tube was. She used to know how to use a slide rule and conjugate French verbs. She used to be able to play two of Mozart's piano concertos by heart, and she used to know the names and dates of the Lake Poets. If Larry ever said that something in the kitchen of the Grand Hawaiian transcended post-modernism, she would have known exactly what he meant. But Larry wasn't going to come up with any surprises like that, was he?

Claudia realized that she had been bred for one kind of man. That was what all the preparation was for, the dancing classes, riding lessons, clubs, tea parties and horse shows, prom, and cotillion. New Haven Select Academy and Sweet Briar served the purpose well, affixing a mischievous little corollary to the rules of biological imperative. Claudia put a lot of two and twos together like that, standing in the hot steam with her yellow rubber gloves and rubber apron in that dead hour after closing, when it was just her and Mary Ann and Larry cleaning up.

In the first hour of the day before the dishes started coming down, she could lean back against the dishwasher and study what the line cooks were doing on the other side in case she and Mary Ann got their big break. It wouldn't do much good to get called up to work with the salad boys, but it would get her to the middle island and close enough to the line cooks to glance over and take mental notes.

They were a pretty motley crew, touchy and real good with knives, and they hid things from each other. One liked the little towels they threw over their shoulders and kept bags of them hidden in the meat locker. Another one could only use a certain shrimp cleaner and kept it in an inside pocket of his white jacket. Another one had his favorite garlic press and snatched it out of Larry's hands right after he washed it, and if he wasn't using it, it was nowhere to be found.

At the end of the line of five big stoves was Big Jim, the head chef, an Irishman with a red beard. The line cooks wore the white jackets and chef hats, but Big Jim wore a big Hawaiian shirt and drank beer while he cooked. The sous chef was a quiet Chinese man who was very skilled with pork, insistent on protocol, and immaculate in dress, but Claudia could tell he was much entertained by Big Jim, who laughed and swore and kept going through bottle after bottle of beer through the night. One of the hostesses had a crush on Big Jim and frequently came down the stairs to ask someone how many beers he had had or to say that some dignitary was about to come through. In that case Jim would duck to the pantry and wrestle into his white jacket with all those buttons and put on his chef hat, which was taller than the ones the line cooks wore.

One time, the under secretary of the navy came through the kitchen with a photographer from *Life*, but Claudia got pushed out of the picture by the line cooks. It was just as well. If she had made the picture, she would have had to make up a story for Mom to explain the boots and rubber gloves. Maybe she could have said that the word in her circle was that the under secretary had a disease.

Claudia and Mary Ann sat on the back steps of the kitchen for their breaks. They could see the parking lot and everyone going around to the front and coming back to their cars. They commented on the clothes and imagined what the relationships were because more than a few did not look much like married couples. Sometimes they played a game where they said the tenth man to walk the parking lot in either direction would be Claudia's man and the fifteenth man would be Mary Ann's man. They always laughed at the lucky numbers. If they weren't in uniform, something was wrong with them. Whether you could see it or not, you knew it was bad enough to keep them out of the service.

There was a Pacific Fleet again. It had beaten up the Japanese at Midway and took the Marines to Guadalcanal and the Solomons. Everyone had gone to war. Vitalis and Nesbitt's Orange drink had gone to war. Elgin watches had gone, and Westinghouse had devices on bombers. Canada Dry was there. As far as Claudia could tell from the ads in *Life*, 7UP stayed on the homefront, but her Pep-O-Mint LifeSavers went, and she was very proud of her Chesterfields. They were fighting for America all over the world. She bought a carton for two dollars and got a free brass pin with the Chesterfield emblem that said, "Keep 'Em Smokin." Five cents from the sale of each carton went to the war effort. Claudia wore her pin every day and felt good when she lit up with Mary Ann on the steps at break time.

Everybody was working too. Even steel mills had girls now, and some of the ads in *Life* showed girls in overalls doing man jobs. Claudia brought in her *Life* for Mary Ann to look at when they ate their bag lunches at dinner-time. They got half an hour at five o'clock, after the luncheon dishes were done and before the dinner rush started.

Claudia found it inspiring to look at the ads. In the ads with photographs, the girls were always brunettes or redheads, but in the drawn or painted ads, where the artist had to imagine a girl, he always imagined a blonde, and her hair was always beautifully rendered. It was a comfort to Claudia to see that they could not find enough blondes for the photo ads. Natural blondes were like a national treasure of America. Mary Ann always took what she said about that the wrong way and had to be negative.

"Now look at this one," she said.

Claudia looked over at the page and then took a sip of 7Up and gave her a blank expression.

"Not a smudge on her and every hair in place," said Mary Ann.

"Maybe she's very careful walking around all those piles of coal."

"Oh, my eye, Claudia. Maybe she's really a model."

"No, they can't do that. It would be against the law. In advertising it has to be a real girl, and a true-to-life situation."

Mary Ann gave up on that one and kept turning pages while Claudia confidently smoked her Chesterfield and drank the last of her 7Up.

"How about this one. How long does it take to put in a transmission?"

"A couple of hours maybe."

Mary Ann held the magazine away from Claudia.

"Okay. Suppose you did five in one day. Do you think you'd look like this?"

She folded back the *Life*, which made Claudia cringe, and she turned the side with the ad around for her to see.

"She probably had her hair in a bandanna," said Claudia.

"No, look, she's doing one right here in the other picture."

"Well those are brand new tanks, Mary Ann. There isn't any transmission fluid in them yet, and they're clean. Twelve bolts and there you go."

"With that?"

The wrench in the girl's hand looked like something she got out of her purse, and Claudia had to look at it twice.

"Maybe it's a special wrench. There's lots of special wrenches, but you wouldn't know that."

"Oh, God, Claudia, you're the limit. Anybody with nice hair."

"It's not that."

"It is too. It's like Bill telling me all the girls on his dirty calendar were virgins. What bullshit. You believe anything they tell you."

"I do not."

Larry came to the door with his apron on. He snapped the fingers on his rubber gloves, and looking down at the floor drain in the concrete at the bottom of the steps, he softly said, out of the shy smiling corner of his mouth, "Time to boogie woogie ladies."

Mary Ann had some meat on her bones, but Claudia was not holding up so well. Her hands hurt from grabbing the big plates, and standing twelve hours a day or more on the concrete floor made her ache all over. The worst part was working six days a week. At least they had the car and weren't stuck in the middle of nowhere in the little white houses with no gas.

Mary Ann had a thing going with one of Bill's old friends. Every Tuesday night they met Richard in the alley behind the hardware store, and he put a sloppy five-gallon can of gas in the trunk. He was a heavy, bald petty officer from the Midwest, and he was obviously in love with Mary Ann, because Claudia could tell that nothing else but love could ever make a guy like him commit a crime. The can always looked like it had been filled up in the dark in a big hurry by somebody with shaky hands. She thought he might be married, but she wasn't going to ask. Before she took on Joe she would have, because it was between girls, but if you didn't know it before, there were plenty of posters up to remind you. Loose lips sink ships.

It might ease Mary Ann's conscience about what she was doing with Richard if she told her what she was doing with Joe, depending on what she was doing with Richard. It was hard to say. Mary Ann was wearing a cross around her neck all the time now, and her language had cleaned up a little. For all her bawdiness, Mary Ann was really a straight arrow.

Some of the drives home were pretty quiet. Claudia liked to rest her head on her arm out the window and look over the dark ocean. There wasn't any invasion coming. The Japs weren't going to come out of the jungle in front of the house. The navy had sunk almost all the Jap boats, and now the Marines were giving it to them on one island after another. She wanted to tell Mary Ann about the bad business with Joe and cry on her shoulder like she used to. She wanted her conscience back. It was too hard, living every man for himself.

"Do you need any food or anything, Claudia?"

"No, I'm fine."

"You look like you're losing weight."

"No, I'm the same. One ten."

"You didn't have to tell me the exact number, damn it."

"Why? What are you?"

"Oh, shut up. You know."

"No, I really don't. One fifty?"

"I wish."

"One fifty-five?"

"No, one sixty."

"Well," said Claudia, "that's because you're big-boned."

They both had to laugh, and Claudia felt very close to Mary Ann. She never would have been able to laugh if she were the fat one, but she still wanted to tell her about Joe and cry in her arms.

Christmas came and they both had to work even though it was supposed to be a day off for everybody in the world. They worked Christmas Eve and all that week without a day off because of the special parties and banquets. On break they sat out on the back steps and watched people go around the side of the hotel to the big marble steps of the entrance. Claudia was so miserable. She saw Dan one night with the girl doctor and Froggy with the other one. He never came back or called or left notes anymore. By now the four of them were probably items with each other, and she had missed the boat.

Annette went by once. She was with another naval officer, and it did not seem to bother her that she was being unfaithful to Jack, after all they went through together. Claudia could not help thinking that if she had lost a man like Jack she would have died of a broken heart and would not be going out with other men, and of course, then she realized the absurdity of the thought, and the cruelty of the absurdity almost made her cry. Anyway, she could not blame Annette for going on with her life, and from then on, all Christmas week it seemed she kept seeing Annette every time she set foot out the back door in her apron and boots and yellow rubber gloves. It put her down in the dumps, catching a glimpse of Annette in her beautiful tropical gowns, but she couldn't keep herself from looking for her.

New Year's Eve went on forever. All the cooking was done by eleven, so the cooks knocked off and started drinking. The hostess came down the stairs pretty liquored up herself and hung all over Big Jim. Tons of dishes showed up all at once from the private parties going on upstairs. Then the regular dining room's late dinner dishes came down, and a wagon train of bus pans showed up, which had to go ahead of everything else because they needed the glasses back at the parties. Jim and the cooks and the salad boys helped break down the bus pans and load the racks.

It was a long night. Claudia and Mary Ann never had their dinner break, and then they drank a few bottles of beer and got done cleaning up around four in the morning. One by one everyone went home. Claudia wanted to flop down on Larry's cot and close her eyes. She was dead tired and drunk, and she wanted Larry to make love to her, and it didn't have to mean anything. She knew he wasn't interested, or so it seemed, but he was a man, after all, so you never know. Don't let that boyish stuff fool you.

Larry was outside having a smoke, and he wasn't drinking anyway. Mary Ann was crazy with worry about Edgar Lee, so they got out of there and said happy new year to Larry as they walked to the car holding on to each other. They had not realized how drunk and tired they were until Mary

Ann started driving, and then it was all four hands on the wheel and looking so hard at the road that their eyes almost popped out of their heads. But they got home okay and Edgar Lee and Petey were fine. Jan Johnson didn't look too happy, but nobody would have noticed a difference.

Claudia lay down on the bed with all her clothes on. She did not know what might have happened with Larry. Throwing herself at any other man would have been predictable. Maybe it was fear of rejection. Maybe it was her better judgment. He was too young for her. He was not a naval officer from a good family. Just the same, you never know who will turn out to be important in your life. All these characters get pitched at you. Most of them turn out to be false leads or brief appearances, and you never know who might show up later. It was like reading a frustrating novel.

It was strange the other way too, how everyone was so interchangeable. She could be mated to any man who walked the earth. She could find out all his likes and dislikes and everything about him. The only drawback was doing it one by one. Claudia fell asleep missing Jack and wondering how many men she could know as well as she knew Jack if she kept marrying them, one after another.

CHAPTER TWENTY-ONE

Claudia slept all day. She got up briefly to go over to see if Mary Ann was all right or needed help with Edgar Lee, but Mary Ann was dead to the world, so she made breakfast for Edgar Lee and fed Petey. She left a note on the kitchen table, tiptoed into the bedroom to get Edgar Lee's Johnny Jeep hat, and took boy and pooch to the beach. Keeping her eyes open was hard to do, but Claudia watched Edgar Lee and Petey all the time in the little waves along the shoreline. No one was around. The whole island seemed to be sound asleep. A little swim perked her up, and she had fun with Edgar Lee. She showed him how to make sandcastles by dripping sandy water through his hands, and he made her do it with him a million times.

It was the first day of 1943. Her baby would have been six months old, or around that. She wondered if she should set a birthday day for him, but then she thought the day she chose could only be both the day he came into the world and the day he left it. She imagined him looking like Jack, and she imagined standing for pictures with him at his graduation from Annapolis. A shudder went over her that she had almost killed him and flushed him down the toilet when he was a little brown sausage with broken wings, and then she stopped dreaming. She had actually done that, and there would never be a young Jack graduating from Annapolis. He wasn't alive like Edgar Lee, who would grow up and live in different places. He would always stay here in the backyard, dead in the septic tank.

Claudia played around with Edgar Lee. How funny little kids are. Too young to figure out yet—just funny. He took after Mary Ann more than Bill. She was so tired, and tears were coming into her eyes, but she did what Edgar Lee wanted her to do, turn his little bucket over and make a sand fez, as many times as he asked her. She wanted to give Mary Ann a chance to catch up on her sleep, so she brought Edgar Lee back to her house and made him a peanut butter and jelly sandwich, and then they went back to the beach.

The sun was going in and out of the clouds, but on the whole, it was a gray day. Edgar Lee went to sleep on the blanket, and Petey stretched out under the grassy dunes. Claudia did not know what she felt like doing. She didn't feel like reading. She lay down beside Edgar Lee with her arm over him and her face into the mushed top of his Johnny Jeep hat and drifted away with the nice sound of the waves. She needed sleep so badly. She needed to fall apart and collapse. It was the first day of January. A new year. It was about eighty degrees with a light breeze moving the palms, like it was every day, but something seemed wrong. Maybe it was just her, but she was getting a feeling that everything was wrong.

When they came back from the beach, Mary Ann was up, and the house smelled of hamburger and onions cooking, and Claudia could only thank God because it was a big responsibility watching a five-year-old. She had done her good deed for the day and just wanted to get home, but Mary Ann wouldn't let her.

"No, you sit down in that chair, girlie," she said. "I'm going to take care of you now."

"I'm fine."

"You look like hell."

"I do not. You're so jealous, Mary Ann."

"Jealous? Oh sure. Go look in the mirror—no don't. How do you want your hamburger?"

"Well done, I guess."

"That's the only kind I do. Imagine us as cooks, will ya?" Mary Ann shoveled the burgers around in the pan and took them out just as the pan began smoking. Then she put in some bread to fry up as buns.

"After this we're going to take a bath, aren't we, Edgar Lee? And then Aunt Claudia is going to have a nice hot bath too, and then we're all going to bed."

"I don't want to take a bath," said Edgar Lee.

"Aunt Claudia doesn't want to take a bath either," said Mary Ann, "but you have to when you've been at the beach all day. Aunt Claudia isn't fussing about it, is she? You aren't fussing, are you?"

"No fuss from me," said Claudia.

Bill had been good with tools and had known a lot of practical things, so when they got to the little white houses, instead of the business with the hose out the window, he had built a little shed off the kitchen and put in a real bathtub with ornate feet and faucets that looked like something from the palace of the Grand Poobah. Claudia wanted to ask Mary Ann where Bill got it, but she remembered what Jack had said about enlisted men. Claudia never told Jack about the bathtub. He wasn't a handy man. They were better off if he put his brains to work getting them out of the little white house. So she was stuck with the hose out the window.

Mary Ann would not hear of her cleaning up. She cleared the dishes and put down a hot cup of coffee for Claudia and dropped the newspaper in front of her on the table. She turned the radio to one of Jack's shows and went to give Edgar Lee his bath. Claudia could hear the water running. It was such a nice sound. Ocean waves are great for outside, but inside, nothing beats hot water filling up a tub.

Darkness was coming over, and Mary Ann was going around closing the blackout curtains. It was just out of habit. Nobody ever came over bombing. What to do with the gas masks? One lady down the road had hers in the window with flowers in it. Mary Ann had her sleeves rolled up, and Edgar Lee must have gotten a good scrubbing. Claudia hoped she could stay awake for her turn.

It was like heaven. Claudia was so weak getting out of the tub that Mary Ann had to help her. She put a big beach towel around her and dried her off while she hung limp.

"You're going right to bed, young lady."

"Where are my things?"

"Your bathing suit is hanging up to dry. You shouldn't have been sitting in it all that time—listen to me, I'm getting like you. Now get going to the bedroom."

"I can't stay over, Mary Ann. I don't have my things."

"I went and got them when you were in the tub."

Mary Ann wrapped the towel around her and shooed her into the bedroom. Her nightie was folded in a neat little square on the bed, and Claudia was so touched to see one of her brassieres and a pair of panties and her toothbrush. She put them on and went to brush her teeth.

Mary Ann was running the water in the tub. "I'm going to be a while," she said, "so you just go to sleep."

"Thanks, Mary Ann. I love you."

"I love you too, blondie."

Claudia was so comfortable that she fell asleep right away while the bath water was still running. She woke up when Mary Ann came to bed. She turned over, and Mary Ann was so tender to hold her that she could not stop herself and started to cry. She didn't even know what she was crying about. She cried and cried with her head in the pillow so Edgar Lee would not hear, and then she fell asleep with her head on Mary Ann where the crucifix disappeared between her bosoms like a mountaineer down a crevasse.

In the morning Mary Ann made breakfast, and Claudia felt so much better. She was just run-down and they were both overjoyed when Larry called and told them not to bother coming in until Friday because it was going to be slow and he could handle it. It was like a snow day back home. Mary Ann got off the phone with Larry and yelled "No school!!" Things were looking up.

It was wonderful getting a day off. First, they went back to bed in their own houses for a couple of hours, and then they took a picnic lunch to the beach. That evening, they left Petey in the house and drove into town to see a Roy Rodgers cowboy picture. Mary Ann covered Edgar Lee's ears, and Claudia covered his eyes during the newsreels about the war. The Wild West and the cowboys swept them away, and then it felt so strange to come out of the theater into the bright lights of town and the high palms waving in the night breeze. Claudia would be willing to bet that people in New Haven right now would not mind walking out of a theater and finding themselves in Honolulu. It was probably around zero degrees in Connecticut.

The blackouts were unofficially over, and everyone was back to having a good time. They walked along the sidewalk and got ice cream cones. When they got home, Claudia had another hot bath while Mary Ann got Edgar Lee to bed. They stayed up late, sitting at Mary Ann's kitchen table in their bathrobes, drinking coffee, and smoking Chesterfields. Mary Ann told Claudia about the boys at all the places she worked, and Claudia told about the girls in school and the boys she met. She did not want to sound snooty, so she told all the stories as if they had happened in high school. Thinking back, she kissed more boys in high school than college anyway. She didn't know anything back then, compared to Mary Ann.

Mary Ann grew up in Philadelphia in the part she called South Philly, like it was a different country, and went to Bishop somebody High School. She met Bill at the beach in Atlantic City. It was a good story, but Mary Ann skipped over parts, so it sounded like things happened faster than they probably did.

"I was in ninth grade at the time, and I had tits out to here. He fucked me under the boardwalk the first day I met him. Right through my bathing suit."

"Oh God, Mary Ann."

"No kidding," she said. "The first day. I was that stupid." Mary Ann took a sip of coffee and a very long draw on her Chesterfield. "You know my sister, Louise? Well, she isn't really my sister."

Claudia was flabbergasted. She still did not want to tell her about Joe, even though it was just girls talking between girls. When you had something worse, it didn't mean you had to tell it. You have to let the other girl win once in a while.

"I lived with my aunt and uncle in Florida for a year," said Mary Ann. "Then I came home with my new baby sister. I got to hand it to my mom. She could come up with some doozies explaining it to people. South Philly is like a small town."

"Did you tell Bill?"

"Why bother? It was a girl problem. He was out fucking other girls anyway. My little sister probably had a lot of cousins I didn't know about."

"Well, God, Mary Ann. If he was out fucking other girls, why did you marry him?"

Mary Ann smiled, thinking about it a moment, and then she got tears in her eyes, but she wiped them away with the edge of the tablecloth and came up smiling another smile, but a little sadder one. Maybe she was thinking about things that were only between her and Bill or just thinking about Bill being dead, or maybe she was thinking her life should have been better.

"I don't know," she said. "I just liked him." She said it the way girls always say things, as if there was a question mark at the end.

Claudia slept over again that night, and this time she didn't cry. Compared to Mary Ann, she'd had a pretty good life, and there was no comparison at all between Bill and Jack. Jack did not go for just anything in skirts like Bill. Annette was a cut above the rest, and who could blame him for falling in love with her? She was glad that she could smile about it now because it was one of the private things she shared with Jack. She knew Jack appreciated her. She came through for him in a pinch. When you're dead and your foot falls off, you really want your wife around and nobody else.

The next day it was back to work. Heigh-ho, Heigh-ho, it's off to work we go. At least the hours were good on one side of the day. Eleven o'clock gave them plenty of time to wake up and not feel rushed. The late morning air felt so good as they drove down the road to town, and they liked everyone in the kitchen. It was such hard work though, and they always had to stay until the last dog was hung. Around ten o'clock they started looking out the narrow horizontal windows at ground level to see if any headlights were turning into the parking lot. If there were, it meant another two hours before they got out.

Claudia vowed then and there never to be the last one in a restaurant. Even if her date were Errol Flynn. Even if they were talking intimately and at any moment Errol might move the candle away and kiss her across the table, the memory of waiting for the last plates to come out of the dishwasher would be foremost in her mind.

"Errol," she would say. "We must go. No, I beg you, do not ask me why—"

"But Claudia," he would reply, "They are open weekdays from 11:00 a.m. to 11:00 p.m., Saturday 11:00 a.m. to 2:00 a.m., and Sunday Brunch 11:00 to 3:00, with extended hours for holidays and special occasions."

She would never tell Errol Flynn about her old job. She would remain a woman of mystery. She learned her lesson with Jack. He knew her too well. Why did she ever let him see all of her naked, especially in that way? It would have been better had he beheld and cherished only her lovely hair and beautiful face, but the picture that probably stuck in his mind was the USS Claudia Wyler going down hard by the bow, stern up in the air. She made that mistake with Jack, but she wouldn't make it with Errol.

Everyone was a little down and glum after the holidays. Larry turned up the volume for *Swing Favorites*, but he did not jive around so much as he had leading up to Christmas and New Year's Eve. Claudia scraped dishes and scooped the cigarette butts with lipstick out of the bottoms of coffee cups. Some girls are such tramps. Big Jim had given up drinking on the urging of his hostess girlfriend, and he was getting crabby about her coming down to check on him every five minutes. She said she was so proud of him, but Claudia knew Big Jim was thinking all he had to do was ditch the hostess and he could go back to beer, but more power to him—he was sticking to it. Claudia just did her job. She had a lot to think about.

She was going to have to stop sleeping over at Mary Ann's. It wasn't healthy. They had gotten into a habit. She knew she was getting a crush on Mary Ann because she thought about her all the time and she liked sleeping over, and they got along so well. It wasn't like the crush she had on Debbie Snow in high school. That was so innocent. Mary Ann was already fucking Bill and giving birth to her little sister when she was that age. It was just confusing her sometimes.

Claudia did not want to ever fight with Mary Ann. She did not want to be accused of trying to run her life or trying to take over Edgar Lee, but she wanted to do both those things. But how could she help it? Mary Ann could do more with herself, but she just didn't care or know how. And Edgar Lee needed more pep in his diet, but Mary Ann did not pay any attention to the symptoms. They were right there in the advertisements in *Life* every week. Claudia knew she could do wonders with Edgar Lee, and Mary Ann too, if she were in charge.

The rent was coming up in exactly one week, and Claudia had not heard anything from Joe. Now that she was over at Mary Ann's so much and right next door to Joe and Jan, she tried to listen, but not a peep came out of the place. Claudia left the night table light on, but Joe didn't come the first night she was back in her own house. There was no sign of him for the next four nights either and she began to worry. With all the army and navy officers coming to Hawaii, the man who owned the twelve little white houses would jump at the chance to get her out and raise the rent on the newcomers, so Claudia knew she was on thin ice.

Joe finally came the night before the rent was due, and he had the money. Claudia was so tired because the hotel had hosted a late dinner and meeting of the Rotarians that did not get them out until after twelve. When she got home, she turned on the light in the bedroom. She went to the kitchen and made a sandwich and then stalled around with her coffee and Chesterfields until two thirty. No Joe. She finally went to bed, not knowing what she was going to do. Forty dollars had to be in the office downtown by ten the next morning or she was out. Mary Ann wanted to go in early to take the rent and have coffee in town before they went to work.

There was a tapping at the window, and Claudia woke up. It was three o'clock on her travel alarm clock, and she could hardly drag herself out of bed, but it was Joe at the back door. She was saved. She opened the door a crack, and he said hi.

"Oh, hi Joe," she said.

"Can we do it?" he whispered.

"Sure, Joe. Come on in."

"You aren't too tired, are you?"

"No," she said. "I just need some coffee. Want some?"

"No, thanks. I'll just sit."

Claudia poured a little cold coffee out of the percolator into a saucepan and warmed it up on the stove. She didn't really want any, and the first puffs of her Chesterfield made her feel sick, but she knew he would take the money out, and she wanted to count it without looking like she was counting. It was all in ones so it wasn't easy. She let her robe fall open so he could see some of her, and while he was distracted, she spread the bills a little, reaching for her coffee. It looked like it was all there. She was glad she could count on Joe.

He was getting fidgety, and she wanted to get it over with and go back to sleep, so she put out her Chesterfield and said, "Okay, let's go." She turned off the light in the kitchen and then the one in the bedroom, and Joe followed along. She took off her robe and lay down, but he wanted to hold her standing up first, so she got up again and then had to wait for him to get out of his clothes.

"You sure it's okay?" he said.

"I'm sorry, Joe. I'm just a little beat."

There was almost a full moon, and it was coming in the window like daylight. Joe sat cross-legged on the bed watching her bend over for the right place with a dab of Vaseline, and his thing was standing up like a flagpole.

It was good for her in other ways besides the money, she thought. She knew she liked men when it came down to it, but she had drifted away, being with Mary Ann so much. She had been with two men, and she liked seeing them get excited just by looking at her. While they were on her, she could let her mind go anywhere it wanted because they were busy and not paying any attention to her.

It was the only time she had ever fallen asleep. She only woke up because Joe was trying to flip her over and get in another round.

"No, that's it, Joe," she said.

He didn't say anything or stop. He was always trying to get away with something, and she was fed up. Not this time. She squirmed and pushed away, but he wasn't being gentle anymore. He had his hand between her legs trying to get them apart.

"Goddamn it, Joe," she said.

"Shh."

"Get off me."

She raised her voice, and Joe put his hand over her mouth. Then she really fought him, and he couldn't keep his hand over her mouth, so he got both hands around her neck and choked her breath off. She went limp because Joe didn't seem to care if he strangled her. So she let him have his other round. When he got off, he said he was sorry.

Claudia just lay there after he left. It felt like Joe had crushed something in her throat. She could breathe again, but she did not know if she could talk. The lights were still off, but she heard him in the kitchen, so she got up and put her robe on. His uniform was on the floor in a heap, and he was standing naked over the sink, trying to screw the garden hose onto the faucet in the dark. When he heard her, he looked over his shoulder and then back to the sink. He wasn't taking her seriously. The big chef knife was in the drain board, and Claudia grabbed it.

"Get the fuck out of here," she said. It came out raspy, and it hurt.

"I'm just going to take a shower."

"Not here you're not."

He wasn't paying any attention, so she jabbed him in the back with the knife, and he jumped.

"Ow. You bitch. That hurt."

"Get the fuck out of here."

"I just want to take a shower."

"Go someplace else."

"I need to take a shower. I can't go home like this."

Joe turned around and picked up the end of the hose. He didn't think she'd do it, but she nicked him in the back again, and he whipped around.

"Cut it out."

"Get the fuck out."

"No."

"I'm telling you—get the fuck out of here."

"Not till I take a shower. It'll only take a minute."

He said it like he was going to wait for her to come to her senses. Claudia thrust the knife in the air in front of him, but he stood his ground.

"I just want to take a quick shower, and then I'll be out of your hair. Just calm down."

It made her so mad. She had to do something. She dove forward and aimed low like Jack told her and got him between the legs where it counts. The point of the knife must have caught the bag thing because it put some drag on the blade.

"Ow, fuck." Joe almost forgot where he was and shouted. It stopped him, but then he suddenly lunged toward her with his hands out to grab the knife. She only had a split second to dodge, and then to show she meant business, she stabbed him in the stomach and stood back. It was just a little poke, but she knew it broke the skin. Joe looked at his stomach and gave up on the shower.

"You fucking bitch," he said.

He put on his uniform without buttoning anything and picked up his shoes and socks and went out the door. Claudia threw the end of the hose outside and closed the window over the sink. It was four thirty, and Mary Ann would be tapping on her horn in four hours to go down to pay the rent, and then it wouldn't be worth coming home. They would just drive over to the Grand Hawaiian and go to work. She was dead tired and shaking with exhaustion. She couldn't swallow very well, and her throat hurt. It wasn't even worth crying over. It was just the wasted time. She needed her sleep, and she was so mad at Joe. It didn't occur to him that some people had to go to work in the morning.

CHAPTER TWENTY-TWO

Work got worse as the day went on. Claudia was so tired but she knew she'd better start thinking fast because she wasn't going to get the money out of Joe anymore, and the next rent was only a month away. Instead of taking her dinner break, she went upstairs to the offices to see Mr. Bing. It took her a while asking around to find out who to go see because no one in the kitchen had ever asked for a raise before.

Mr. Bing saw her right away and was very polite. Claudia sat in a chair in front of his desk, and Mr. Bing smoked a cigar as he talked to her. He said it was impossible to pay her more than thirty cents an hour as a dishwasher, but there were opportunities for her to move up as a salad boy or one of the runners who brought the trays upstairs. He wrote her name down and said he would let her know when an opening came up.

Claudia was disappointed. She had to line up her forty dollars. She would have gone for a Joe-deal with Mr. Bing, but he didn't ask, and she was not sure how to pitch the idea to an older man. On the way back to the kitchen, the smell of the wood in the old part of the hotel made her think of the cabin at Jerryman's Cove, where she and Caroline Mulney barged in on Jenny Hughes and her boyfriend to save her from a fate worse than death. Now that Claudia knew what the fate worse than death was, it was easy to see there were fates worse than the fate worse than death. There was getting kicked out of your house. Mr. Bing was kind of cute, but he looked like a tough businessman. Claudia knew if she negotiated a Joe-deal with Mr. Bing, he would open at thirty cents an hour. It wouldn't be right. She needed forty dollars.

The rest of the night was hard to get through, but finally they were back in the car, and the city lights were dropping behind them. Claudia wanted to go to bed, but when she turned on the kitchen light, there were drops of blood on the floor, and she had to get out the bucket and sponge. There were a few on the back steps, and Joe had dropped one of his socks. Claudia got the flashlight and went over the grass, but it had rained during the day. Jan Johnson looked like the type who would snoop around. The knife was still in the sink but there was nothing on it. Claudia didn't know what to do about the sock. It was regulation navy, and it could have been just as easily one of Jack's, but she decided to put it in the trash basket under the sink.

Just as Claudia was falling asleep, her instinct woke her up. The sock was bothering her. She got up and pulled it out of the trash. What now? She walked around the house looking, but there really wasn't a good place to hide it. Then she had a good idea and went to get her sewing basket. She cut a piece out of the big toe and sat up another hour darning the hole. It was worthy of *Mr. District Attorney*. There was a handful of coins in the little dish on top of the icebox, and she dropped it all in the sock. Now it was Jack's spare change sock. Into the sock drawer it went with the other navy socks. *Finis!* The second sock she had ever darned in her life. She had wasted so much time being innocent and stupid. Now she was going to have to use her brains, and she was glad to see she had some. She popped the cutout piece of sock into her mouth and ate it. Jan Johnson could snoop around till she was blue in the face. No Joe here.

Army cars woke her up the next morning. They went by and up the road. It was after eight, so she got up and made the coffee. Then a police car went by. If she had not known in her heart that it had something to do with Joe, she would have gone out to the end of the drive and looked. But she knew it did, and she knew the army cars and the police would be parked outside the Johnson house. Time to lay low.

Claudia took her shower while the coffee perked. She hugged the wall of the house in case any men were up on roofs, hosed off fast, and got back inside. Ordinarily she hung around in her robe, but this close to trouble meant prepare to repel boarders. So she got dressed for work, and around nine, two MPs and a man in a striped suit came around to the door. She let them in and tried to look innocently inquisitive.

The one in the suit introduced himself as Detective DeNante. He already knew who she was. Time to dummy up.

"May I offer you gentlemen some coffee?" she asked.

Detective DeNante said sure and sat down at the kitchen table. He was middle-aged but good-looking, with a nice haircut and a little mustache that made him look like he spoke French. It was clear to her that the two MPs were there to poke around.

"You don't mind if we look around, do you?"

Claudia said no and brought over his cup of coffee.

"This is the new Chase & Sanborn," she said. "It's supposed to have smooth, full-bodied flavor that won't let you down—but I'm not so sure."

Claudia knew from *Mr. District Attorney* that she should just be her natural self and act normal.

"I'd like to ask you a few questions," he said.

Then she remembered what she was supposed to say. "What's this all about?"

"A disappearance. Joe Johnson. Two doors down."

"He disappeared?"

"—A little more than that. I'm afraid he's dead."

It wasn't a game anymore. Claudia put her hand up to cover her mouth. "Oh, no."

"You knew him?"

"Just by sight, I mean—oh, God. I don't believe it. How did it happen?"

"Then you did know him."

"I just saw him go by in the car. The last time was when the Japs attacked. He was right behind my husband, Jack. They were going down to fight. Jack was killed."

"I'm sorry, Mrs. Wyler."

The two MPs were in the bedroom. Claudia saw them out of the corner of her eye. They would find the jar of Vaseline under the bed. If her husband had been gone for almost two years, what was it doing there? She would just act incredulous and say, "Petroleum jelly soothes chapped skin and lips, softens dry skin overnight, heals minor burns and scrapes, and removes eye make up. Where have you been?" That's exactly what she would say.

"We'd like to know if you heard anything unusual the night before last."

"No, I don't think so. What kind of things?"

"Anything unusual. Gunshots? Loud noises?" Detective DeNante took a small black notebook out of his jacket. There was a Lord & Taylor label on the inside pocket, just as she suspected. She couldn't always tell a Lord & Taylor. Some of the better Hart Schaffners gave her trouble, too. High-end menswear can be tricky, and you have to trust your instincts. When she closed her eyes and Detective DeNante was waiting to hear if she remembered hearing any unusual noises, she was listening to her inner voice. It was saying Lord & Taylor.

"Oh, no. I didn't hear anything. I didn't know anything was going on."

"You work at the Grand Hawaiian, I understand."

"Yes, that's right," she said.

"What time did you get home the other night?"

"I guess around eleven thirty."

"Your neighbor," Detective DeNante thumbed over a page in his little book, "a Mrs. Plithe, a few doors down, said twelve thirty."

"Oh, that's probably right. The Rotarian dinner was that night, and I got home late." She didn't know Mrs. Plithe was up that late.

"So, you want to change your story?"

"Yes," she said. "Put me down for twelve thirty."

"And you didn't hear anything?"

"No," said Claudia.

The MPs came back to the kitchen, and Detective DeNante exchanged looks with them. One of them was holding Jack's gun by the barrel. She had forgotten all about that.

"Oh, that's Jack's gun," she said.

Detective DeNante had a questioning look on his face, but Claudia could tell the MP standing behind her was probably indicating to him that it had not been fired and was not a strong piece of evidence for anything.

"It's just routine, Mrs. Wyler," said Detective DeNante, "but we're going to have to impound the weapon and run some tests. I'm sure you understand. You'll have it back in a day or two. You can give me a call if a week goes by."

He took out a card and put it on the table, between the salt-and-pepper shakers and got up. "Well, thank you, Mrs. Wyler," he said. "I'll be in touch, and be sure to contact me if you remember anything, even if you don't think it seems important."

"I'm afraid I wasn't much help."

"You've been fine," he said.

Claudia was very glad to see them out of the house and gone. She looked out the front window and saw them going around the corner to Mrs. Bigalow's, but the one with Jack's gun was going to the cars.

They were good searchers, she thought. Nothing in the bedroom looked amiss. She never would have known they had been there, but her instincts might have divined that everything in the bedroom had been moved, or altered in relation to other objects by just a little. She would have felt uncomfortable in the bedroom. The feeling would have persisted until her hands had gone over everything and changed the room back by a sixteenth of an inch, or whatever it was. Then the record would go around without the skips.

It was not that she did not care about Joe Johnson. When Joe tried to strangle her, she did what any woman would do. She crossed him off her list. The same with Mr. Anthony. When he put his finger in her, she crossed him off her list. That meant those two birds were invisible nobodies to Claudia Wyler. If Joe weren't dead, she could have a perfectly good conversation with him, and he would never know he was off her list. And she could go down to the Palmetto club tonight and let Mr. Anthony buy her drinks, but if either of them asked her for a favor, she would have some excuse. So if Detective DeNante asked her if she had ever been naked in her kitchen with Joe Johnson or if Mr. Anthony had ever put his finger in her, she would look up with no expression on her face whatsoever and say no, I'm sorry. Those two gentlemen are not on my list.

On the way down to work, Mary Ann said they found Joe's uniform on the beach. Parts of him had washed up on shore, and it looked like he had gone into the water and something had eaten most of him. The police and MPs were looking around because there was a lot of blood on his uniform. They were looking for a missing sock. The speculation was that he had been shot, but they did not know why he would take off his uniform and go into the water at night with a bleeding wound and sharks around. Jan was taken to the police station for questioning because the neighbors on the other side heard them fighting that night. That was what Mary Ann got out of the mailman. He knew everything.

"I heard them going at it too sometimes," said Mary Ann. "But not that night. Did you hear anything?"

"No," said Claudia.

"You aren't getting sick, are you? Your voice is as bad as yesterday."

"Just a little sore throat. It sounds worse than it is."

Claudia felt bad for Jan Johnson. She would have to come forward if Jan were accused of shooting Joe. She would run in and confess at the last minute. But it sounded like a shark got him. That made it just one of those things, like the war. Lots of people were getting killed. Getting killed was different from dying, and Joe and Jan Johnson had been at war. Not like she and Jack. They had their troubles, sure, but they came through. Not everybody can do that.

"Well," said Mary Ann, "it's one for the books all right."

Claudia looked out the window at the white patches of beach that flashed by and thought it was safe to assume Mary Ann did not know anything. When you're innocent, everything is a mystery to you, isn't it?

Day after day the dishes came down in full bus pans. There were some new bus boys who piled plates and glasses and silver all together. Then Mary Ann and Claudia had to take apart the piles without letting anything slide off and crash on the floor. January was busy all month. Claudia's hands got red and sore. Her back, her arms, her legs, and feet hurt. She thought she would get used to it, but midway through January it seemed everything got red and swollen and just stayed that way. In February, she had to borrow some money from Mary Ann.

One night Mary Ann was looking out the ground level window at the parking lot to get an idea of how busy they were going to get, and she gave a start, put her hand up to her mouth, and started laughing.

"Come over here quick, Claudia."

Claudia rushed over, and Mary Ann stood aside to give her a good view through the narrow window. "Get a load of that, will ya?"

It was Jan Johnson, all dolled up, disappearing around the corner of the hotel in the company of a smartly dressed officer. He had an arm around her.

"He's a dreamboat, isn't he?" said Mary Ann.

"I didn't get a good look."

"Well, he's older. You can see that. Not too much. Maybe my age. But he sure ain't no low-life sailor boy."

"Where the dickens did Jan Johnson dig him up?"

"Just look at the car, Claudia. Like they say, read it and weep."

Claudia squinted through the parking lot. There was no doubt about it.

"Oh my gosh, Mary Ann. He's a navy chaplain."

"Yeah, well I saw the car up there by her house a lot lately, but I didn't think anything of it. I thought she was crying on the shoulder of some old padre. That guy is no old padre. Hubba-Hubba."

Mary Ann couldn't stop laughing.

"Cut it out, Mary Ann."

"I'm sorry, Claudia. I couldn't help it."

"Don't you think that's a little fast?"

"Well, that's Jan Johnson in a nutshell." Mary Ann touched her rubber glove tenderly to Claudia's rubber glove. "I'm sorry because it should have been you."

It could have been. From the little she caught of the chaplain, she knew she could have fallen in love with him. He looked like Jack, and mid-thirties wasn't that old. If she hadn't kissed off the army man and the WAVES lady and looked so independent, they would have sent a navy chaplain, and she could have sorted through the old padres till she got the right one. It wasn't fair.

"Well, don't be blue, Claudia," said Mary Ann. "You still got us." And she spread her arms out wide to take in Big Jim and the line cooks, the salad boys and runners, and Larry jiving away at the sinks, the hostess peeking down the steps, the steam coming out of the dishwasher, the whole sorry lot, downstairs at the Grand Hawaiian.

Claudia said she was looking for jobs when they split up the newspaper at dinnertime every night out on the back steps of the kitchen. She did not want Mary Ann to know what she was doing until it was all settled, so she pretended to scan through the want ads when she was really looking sideways down the columns of rooms to let. Mary Ann would want her to move in with her and Edgar Lee. Claudia wanted to do that more than anything because she loved Mary Ann and she wanted Edgar Lee to be her dead baby. Mary Ann would say they would get along great, but she was so naïve. Claudia knew she would run Mary Ann's life and take over Edgar Lee. Mary Ann wouldn't want Jack moving in with her, but that's what she would get. As much as Claudia wanted to live with Mary Ann and raise Edgar Lee, it would not be fair, and she could not allow herself to do it. She had to go her own way.

When the rent for March came up, Claudia did not have the forty dollars but the contingency plan was ready, and when dinner break came, she told Mary Ann she had to go someplace. The Barrymore was four blocks away. Within half an hour Claudia walked over, looked at a room on the second floor, signed the lease, plunked down her fourteen dollars, and got back to the Grand Hawaiian in time to catch a quick smoke on the back steps with Mary Ann and Larry.

Claudia told her on the drive home. At first, she was mad. She said everything that Claudia expected her to say, so it wasn't hard to argue back.

"I couldn't borrow any more money from you, Mary Ann," she said. "What would happen next month and the month after that? You can hardly afford your own rent."

"Well, you could have told me."

"It isn't your problem."

"But I care about you, so it is."

"Well, I care about you, too. That's why I didn't tell you. You worry so much."

Mary Ann just looked straight ahead at the road. Her face was very set. The dashboard lights illuminated her like the Lincoln Memorial. Since they weren't going to talk, Claudia took out a Chesterfield and put the pack back in her purse.

"Thanks for offering," said Mary Ann.

Claudia took the pack out again and went to pull one out for Mary Ann at the same time Mary Ann reached for it and the pack fell on the floor between them.

"I'll get it," said Claudia.

"No, leave me alone. I'll get it."

They both fished around on the floor in the dark, and their hands came to it at the same time, and they fought over it.

"Jesus Christ! Look out, Mary Ann!" Claudia's heart jumped, and Mary Ann swerved just in time to avoid going off the edge of the road into the jungle.

"Shut up, Claudia. Don't say that."

Claudia thought that was strange. "What?"

"The Lord's name in vain."

"You almost got us killed."

"But I didn't. Everything's okay."

Mary Ann said Jesus Christ all the time. At least she used to. She used to say it as often as she said fuck. But, come to think of it, Mary Ann kept saying fuck but had not said a Jesus Christ in a long time. Something was definitely up.

"I'm sorry, Mary Ann."

"That's okay. You were just scared."

"I'll say fuck next time."

"That's okay with me, babe."

"Do you want this smoke?"

"I guess not."

"You just wanted to crash the car then, huh?"

They both started laughing. Claudia asked her if they could take a carload of her things down on their way to work the next two days. She thought two trips ought to do it. Mary Ann was sad, but she said it was all right since that was what Claudia wanted to do. At least they would see each other every day at work, and Mary Ann could come around to the Barrymore anytime.

When they got back home, Mary Ann asked her over for a drink, so she got out of her work clothes and put her robe on over her nightie and went over. There was a note from Jan on the kitchen table about Edgar Lee eating all his dinner and Petey going out to pee, and Claudia noticed it was signed Love, Jan.

"I'm glad nothing happened to her," said Claudia.

"I know you don't like her, but she's nice. I mean, she isn't like you think she is. How about some of this?" Mary Ann was at the cupboards holding up a bottle of brandy.

"That looks good."

"We can finish it off. I mean, between tonight and tomorrow night."

Claudia pulled out her Chesterfields while Mary Ann went for the little wine glasses on the top shelf.

"I don't know," said Claudia. "She just seems stuck up."

"She isn't really. Her face just looks like that. She can't help it."

"Well, she could smile once in a while. That constant sneer. You should tell her, Mary Ann. Since you're friends."

"We're not really friends. I mean I wouldn't call it that. I don't think I could ever be close with her. Not like it is with you. You know what I mean?"

As far as Claudia was concerned, Mary Ann never had to ask that question. They talked half the night and killed half the bottle of brandy. It didn't do much for Claudia. It was just four little glasses, but she liked sitting with Mary Ann and talking. It was very warm out and still. There were little beads of perspiration on Mary Ann's upper lip, and being plump made her cheeks flush in the heat. They both kept brushing their damp hair back from their foreheads and looking into each other's faces.

It was so warm, and there wasn't any air moving, even with all the windows open. Mary Ann was going to sleep with nothing on and just the sheet. Claudia took off her nightie, and on second thought she wanted to be cool and naked, so she took off her brassiere and panties too.

"Whoa," said Mary Ann.

"It's so hot tonight."

Mary Ann paused with her hand on the bedside lamp.

"Well, turn the light out, Mary Ann."

"I just wanted to look. So shoot me—no don't. Poor Joe."

Suddenly it was dark, and Claudia momentarily lost her bearings and had to feel out ahead of her for the bedpost on her side.

"I don't want to think about Joe," she said and slipped under the sheet.

It didn't matter how hot it was, it felt good up against Mary Ann. Her eyes got used to the dark. Their faces were close together, and she could feel Mary Ann smiling.

"What?"

"You're so skinny, Claudia. You're like bones. You're like I used to be."

"Before you got unboney?"

"Don't you mean over-unboney?"

They both burst out laughing and rolled around a little. It was nice being naked with somebody in the dark without expecting to get bumped and jackhammered the next minute. That wasn't any fun. She was glad she could finally say something to herself about that.

"We've got to get to sleep," she said.

"I know."

"Can you stop laughing, Mary Ann?"

"I'll try. I promise."

Claudia went to her side of the bed. Mary Ann calmed down and settled on her back with her hands folded on her tummy and her eyes shut tight with a look of determined trying. It was one of those nights when the room was dark but full of moonlight and everything was silvery. Claudia wanted to lean over and kiss Mary Ann, but she couldn't do it, and anyway she didn't want to find out what she had been missing all those years kissing boys with thin lips. She lay on her back too and fell asleep with her side against Mary Ann's side, and they slept soundly there until morning, when Edgar Lee came in to bounce on the bed.

Claudia had to hurry to get the first load packed into Mary Ann's car. There wasn't that much after all. In terms of material goods, it did not look like the life of Jack and Claudia had amounted to much, but you can't go by material goods alone. What was that thing about storing up riches in heaven? If that were true, she and Jack would run out of closet space up there.

Most of her clothes went into the steamer trunk from Connecticut. She didn't have any boxes, so Jack's uniforms went over the back seat of the car, and everything from his drawers went into bags from the market. Mary Ann had some bags too, and when time got short, they just started dumping everything in the bags.

Mary Ann parked right in front of the Barrymore, and they each took a couple of bags up first. They went up the stairs to the second floor and walked down a dark corridor with little nightlights. There was no one around, and it was so quiet in the hallway that it made them both whisper.

"I don't think you're going to meet anyone here," Mary Ann whispered.

"Just ghosts."

"Oh, stop it, Claudia."

Claudia could tell Mary Ann thought the place felt creepy but wasn't going to say anything. She would probably like the room though. The sun just poured through the windows. There were two big ones, and she knew she was going to have to do something about curtains. Claudia turned the key to the door of number 210 and stood back as she opened it so Mary Ann would see all the sunshine.

"Oh, it's nice."

"Let's just drop everything in the middle. There's at least two more trips and then the trunk."

"I'm surprised it's so nice," Mary Ann said as they were walking down the stairs. "It's not bad at all."

"I can walk to work too."

Mary Ann held her hand all the way down the stairs. "I'm going to miss you so much," she said. "So will Mrs. Bigalow's little cat."

Claudia did not want to get sentimental or cry on her last night. They got home by eleven because it was slow at the end of the night, and Larry said he could handle the rest of the dishes. Mary Ann hung around while Claudia went through the cupboards, asking if she wanted this or that. The soups could go to the room because she was going to get a hot plate. When it came to the five big cans of poi, she was just going to leave them in the house, but then she thought of Takeo, so she gave him a call, and he came over in his cab. He said it wasn't late for him because he was always taking sailors around the clubs.

He was very pleased to see the monkey family still on her kitchen table. Claudia told him how she cherished the monkey family and would take them everywhere she went, and she wasn't just saying that, it was true. She said that to her the monkey family stood for kind people who were good to each other, and Takeo was very touched. She ended up giving him a lot more stuff, anything that Mary Ann couldn't use. By the time he left, the taxi was full and Claudia felt good about it because it might make up for the night she and Jack went to the Palmetto club and would not ride in his cab.

The last thing was the icebox, but there wasn't much left in there, and Mary Ann said she could get it tomorrow. She said she had the bathtub all filled up for Claudia to go first, so they closed the windows and turned the lights out and walked over to Mary Ann's. The tough part was done. Leaving in the light of day wouldn't be so hard. It would not feel so much like she was leaving home.

The bath was heavenly, even though she was so tired. Claudia sat at the kitchen table in her bathrobe and had a few Chesterfields while Mary Ann had the next bath. She got the brandy out and glasses, and soon Mary Ann came out in her robe, smiling from ear to ear.

"What's so funny?"

"Not funny, just—I don't know. It's nice to come out and see you here."

Mary Ann sat down with her legs under her, and they touched their hands.

"Have some of this," Claudia said.

"I don't know if we can finish it off. Can we?"

"Sure, it's only one o'clock."

She poured Mary Ann's glass and watched her sip at it. Then Mary Ann took a Chesterfield and leaned over for Claudia with Jack's lighter.

"Your hair looks nice," said Claudia.

"I'll try to pay attention to it."

"You better," said Claudia. "I'll still see you every day at work."

"Oh, Claudia, you can't go."

"You'll have Jan."

"She's no good."

"You're so two-faced, Mary Ann."

"I am not."

"So, what's suddenly no good about Jan?"

"She's stuck up. I thought that was what we decided."

They laughed, and Mary Ann said she was going to miss her so much. They stayed up talking about Edgar Lee, and Mary Ann tried to tell Claudia how to make curtains. When she got to measuring yardage, she finally gave up and told Claudia she would make them for her.

They finished off the brandy and went in the bedroom without turning on the light and threw their robes toward the chair. They held a little just to feel cozy, and the moonlight coming through the windows glistened on Mary Ann's lips, and there was a faint wisp of brandy between them. Mary Ann closed her eyes first, and Claudia lay back with her thoughts and waited for sleep. It was her last night with Mary Ann. It wasn't healthy what they were doing. She was glad she had made the decision and got the room. It was for the best. Mary Ann would get to be best friends with Jan but not be close, and Edgar Lee would have to get along without pep.

CHAPTER TWENTY-THREE

Claudia sat on the bed in her room, number 210. Sunshine was pouring in like the wall wasn't even there. It was nice but a little too much. She would have to hang something over the windows at night for the time being. There was a set of sheets, a blanket, and bedspread left in a neatly folded stack on the bed when she came in last night. The card with the house rules said you got a fresh set every week, and you could leave your laundry outside the door any time, which cost $.25 a bag. That was what the bag with the stenciled 210 was for. The bag and the sheets and the stenciled number looked like navy surplus. Claudia felt right at home. "That's the navy for you," she said to herself.

Claudia looked around the room, which still looked barren because everything she owned was still in a pile on the floor. She sang to herself "Here we sit like birds in the wilderness." The senior class of 1940 made it their theme song. They were rebels that year. The girls sat all the way around Main Porch with their legs hanging over the edge, singing that song to protest the new curfew hours on weekends, directing it boldly toward the administration building like it was the big revolution. College was great. She wouldn't mind a life like that. It went by too fast. Why did life have to go fast through the good parts and stop dead on the bad parts?

It sure had stopped on a bad part here. Even if she were here for only a year, it would seem like four, while the four at Sweet Briar had gone by like one. Four years here would seem like the twenty-five she already had under her belt. The bed was so soft in the middle that she ended up there no matter where she started, and sitting up, she could not get out of the middle enough to hang her legs over the side and sing about being a bird in the wilderness.

Down the hall was the bathroom. The men's was to the left, and the girls' was farther down, but Claudia could still see it from her door. She was afraid she might have to wait, but there was no one using it when she went with her bathrobe and towel. The shower was nice, and there was plenty of hot water. No one knocked at the door, so she took her time drying her hair and then scampered back to her room in her robe.

There was a little sink in the room, fitted into the corner. It was strange having a bed from a bedroom, a table from a kitchen, an armchair from a living room, and a sink from a bathroom all together in one room. It was like each one had run away from home and ended up here. Of course, she was here too, but she wasn't running away. She was laying low. She was going to figure out what to do and get out.

Claudia plugged in the percolator. She would need some extension cords. It was getting to be a long list of things she needed, but they were all little things. A shade for the overhead light was another one. Mom's letter was on the table, the last mail to the dear little white house. Harry was dead. He was on maneuvers in Colorado for being in the mountain troops. He fell and broke his neck. It happened way back before Christmas. If she had known about it then, she would be over it by now. She would be done crying and not thinking about Harry so much, and memories would not keep coming into her head every time she turned around. Maybe she could pretend that was the way it happened, that she heard about Harry getting killed the day he got killed. You could do that with anyone who died, she thought. Now she knew four who died. Jack, Bill, Joe, and Harry. Jack was twenty-four, Bill was thirty-five, Joe was twenty-two, and Harry was nineteen. It was just as she suspected. In war the old guard did fine. It was the young guard that got killed off. She remembered Harry from when he was no bigger than Edgar Lee. She remembered playing with him on the beach at Nantucket and playing marbles with him at home, and then she had to remind herself that she was pretending she had known he was dead for three months and the crying was over.

Claudia woke up the next morning thinking, whew, don't we get slapped around. What a dream. She lay on the bed almost breathless. She and Jack were at the Brown Derby. Beautiful Broadway showgirls who looked like Annette were dropping their bosoms in Jack's coleslaw. People were laughing, and when Claudia turned around, there was a studio audience behind her. And then she was in Mr. Bing's office at the hotel. He was making her pay for a dish she had broken. It wasn't actually broken, but it was ruined because it was an origami Japanese paper dish and she had put it through the dishwasher. Just before she woke up, she was crying and writing out a check to Mr. Bing for $1,900.

How are you supposed to get up and be normal after a dream like that? It was so crazy and so real, the way all dreams are. And they can stay with you for a while. She didn't know how she was going to shake the feeling that people took advantage of her. Nineteen hundred dollars was too much for a paper plate. She should have said something.

Claudia decided to go down to the diner around the corner to make herself feel better with a fried egg on toast and a muffin. People from the Barrymore got a ten percent discount because it was owned by the same man who owned the hotel. All she had to do was show her room key, and the waitress put the charge on her tab. It was a nice place. It was called the New Yorker, and it was open all night. She could go there at three o'clock in the morning, and there would be people around.

The egg on toast and the muffin hit the spot, and it was pleasant to sit at the counter with her coffee and Chesterfields and look out the window at the busy street with cars going by, with plenty of time to get over to the Grand Hawaiian. She was on her own now. That wasn't bad, but she was not around the people she was meant to be with, and she sure wasn't in the place she was supposed to be. What was worse, she had started to think about things she had no business thinking about. She was supposed to be with a man and married. That was just nature, and when you go against nature, maybe that's where bad dreams come from.

Claudia looked around the room to make sure she unplugged the percolator and the radio before she went off to work. On the way down the hall, she listened at the door of the girl's bathroom and then went in. There was no sign that anyone had been in after her. She wondered if there was any girl on the floor but her. She looked for hair in the shower drain or on the sink. The tile floor gave no clues, and neither did the mirror or the toilet. If there were another girl on the floor, it would have to be the neatest girl on earth. Some girl's bathrooms are atrocious. Claudia made a mental note to turn the faucets with the heel of her hand to avoid disturbing any fingerprints she might be able to detect. It wasn't a mystery yet. She needed a piece of evidence first.

Larry was out on the steps having a smoke. It was only quarter to eleven and Mary Ann wasn't there yet. It was nice getting Larry alone, and he looked really lanky today.

"I heard you got a new place," he said.

Claudia moved over on the concrete step so he didn't have to get up on his bad foot to light her Chesterfield. "It's at the Barrymore," she said.

"You like it?"

"So far. You'll have to come see me."

"That's four blocks," he said. "Take me all day to get there."

Claudia leaned back against the upper step, cupping her elbow in her hand and holding her Chesterfield away like Katharine Hepburn. She smiled, and Larry glanced up from under his blond Prince Valiant hair long enough to see it.

"I'll wait," she said.

Larry turned his face away and gave a thoughtful little laugh and took another drag on his smoke. Claudia liked the kind of boy Larry was, and not just because he wasn't taking the bait. There was something about Larry that made her think he was wise and deep. Being around him was good for her. Mary Ann's car pulled into the back parking lot. They waited for her, had a last smoke together, and then went to put on their rubber aprons, boots, and gloves and get to work.

Claudia was saving money now, being at the Barrymore, and everything was looking up. The war had spread all over the world, and the men were fighting in white snowsuits here and fighting in undershirts and short pants there. Americans were in North Africa and Burma and Russia, and *Life* magazine had maps with big black arrows showing how Italy had been invaded. There were maps and black arrows for the Pacific too, but it was more like dots in the ocean. The Marines were the ones connecting the dots. Every little dot filled up the hospitals in Honolulu. The town was swarming with sailors, so many that people just said sailors when they would have said navy men just a year or two ago.

Living in town at the Barrymore, Claudia was beginning to think of them as sailors too. All night long they went by the hotel on the street right under her window, singing and laughing and shouting at each other and breaking beer bottles. A little after one group passed, another group would come along with swear words and fooling around, and sometimes you could hear a girl with them.

It was two months before Claudia found out there was a girl on the second floor after all. She went in to check one morning before going to work, and there was a piece of the brown toilet paper in the trashcan under the sink. Claudia grabbed it and took it back to her room. She opened it up in the sunlight through the windows and found a piece of chewed gum. It had the small impressions of girl teeth in it, and there was a hint of a lipstick smear on the paper. There wasn't time for a thorough investigation before work, so she fished around in the bags from the house until she found the empty Sucrets tin she was saving and put the little square of paper in. She knew it was a gold mine of information.

When Claudia got home that night, she went straight to the Sucrets box and lifted out the piece of toilet paper with a pair of tweezers. First, she made impressions of her own teeth on different kinds of chewing gum, a top left incisor and lower left second molar, if she wasn't mistaken. Then she put her samples up to the gum in the toilet paper and got a pretty close match. That established age of mystery girl as about her own, which made sense. The gum was Wrigley's Wintergreen. That was easy. But Wintergreen was hard to find in Honolulu. Only the navy commissary had it.

The magnifying glass had to come out for the smear of lipstick. It was definitely not the beetroot juice they were using now. It was either a prewar Helena Rubinstein or an Elizabeth Arden Victory Red. Claudia went with her instinct on that one and fingered Helena and old money. At first the lipstick smear looked like bright red, but that didn't fool Claudia. The discoloration in the corner was Vaseline, which meant the base color was actually a deep red with a little highlight—the telltale Vaseline. That meant a girl with skill. Claudia sat back from the light over the kitchen table. A picture was beginning to take shape in her mind. Mystery girl was about her age, moneyed background in reduced circumstances, access to navy commissary, motor skills, and good eye-hand coordination. It added up to office girl. Detective DeNante had nothing on girl detective Claudia Wyler.

It was another month before the next clue. Claudia discovered a long black hair in the shower drain and an eyelash or eyebrow in the space between tiles on the floor. Under the magnifying glass, the long hair revealed a slanted cut on one end, indicating professional expertise. The short piece was assuredly an eyebrow. No one was doing eyelashes these days. One thing was obvious to Claudia. Mystery office girl wasn't trying to cover her tracks anymore. She put the long hair and eyebrow sample in her Sucrets tin with the gum in the toilet paper. Exhibit A, B and C.

It could be Annette. Claudia daydreamed as she waited for the racks to come out of the dishwasher. She imagined Annette taking a shower and washing her hair and rinsing until one hair came lose and shot the rapids between her bosoms and cascaded over the swell of her belly and sluiced down the narrows of her inner thigh to the water parting over the bone of her ankle and down to the drain.

The dishwasher shut down abruptly, and Claudia glanced up at the clock. Mary Ann was looking at her funny.

"Hey," she said. "Break time. Let's go."

They went out the back door and sat down on the concrete steps with their Chesterfields and coffee. Claudia knew what was coming. Maybe Mary Ann knew about the other girl in the Barrymore. There wasn't anything going on, and even if there were, Mary Ann should understand that it was only natural that she would have more in common with Annette because they were sharing Jack. And anyway, Mary Ann had Jan to be friends with now.

"I just have things on my mind," she said.

"What things? You're up in the clouds somewhere tonight, girlie."

"Just things."

They were both holding their Chesterfields like Katharine Hepburn. Mary Ann was looking her up and down critically as if she hadn't seen her in ages.

"You're too skinny. It's only been a few months. What are you eating? Did you get a hot plate?"

"No, I go down to the diner most of the time."

"That's no good. You have those cans of soup, you know. I carried them up all those stairs."

"You can have them."

"I don't want them."

After a long silence, Mary Ann asked if she was seeing anyone, and if that was the reason she went to the diner all the time. When Claudia said no, she wasn't seeing anyone, Mary Ann relaxed a little. There wasn't any reason to break up with Mary Ann. She still loved her.

"So how did Edgar Lee do on the reading test?"

Mary Ann smiled and was warm again and moved over close. "Oh, that wasn't any trouble for him. He's really smart. He misses you so much. He says you're more fun than I am. Oh, Claudia, come back. I know you want to be independent, but it was so nice having you there. You can still save money because we'll just have one house, and it would make Edgar Lee so happy."

"I can't, Mary Ann."

"You could if you wanted."

"It's not that."

"Then what is it?"

"I have to figure out what I'm going to do. I might go home to Connecticut. I don't know. I have another idea, too."

"What?"

"I don't want to say anything yet. I haven't figured out any details."

Larry appeared at the screen door and said it was time to boogie-woogie, so they put out their smokes and helped each other up.

"Well, you better not tell anyone else before me."

"I promise," said Claudia. She gave Mary Ann's hand a squeeze, and they went back to work. She really did love Mary Ann. She was sweet to care so much, and she had kept up with her hair like she said she would.

Claudia let a little more time go by so she could help Mary Ann with the fourth of July crowd. It was exactly four months since she had moved into the Barrymore. At eleven thirty that night, Mary Ann knocked at the door, and Claudia braced herself. The minute she opened the door, Mary Ann looked her right in the eyes.

"What happened?" she said.

"Come on in, Mary Ann."

Claudia already had the armchair pulled up close to the table, and she sat in the kitchen chair and left the armchair for Mary Ann.

"What happened, Claudia? Why did you quit?"

"It's a long story."

"You said you would tell me before you did anything. You promised."

"I promised I would tell you what my idea was."

"You know what I mean, damn it."

"I'm going to tell you everything. Don't worry. It's about you, too."

"What is?"

"My idea."

"Okay, let's hear your idea."

Mary Ann finally sat down in the armchair, and Claudia poured her a glass of brandy. She had everything out on the table because she knew Mary Ann would come over right after she got off work.

"I was thinking about it for a long time," said Claudia. "There we were, working six days a week for thirty cents an hour, and you with Edgar Lee, trying to support him on that. We should have been out finding husbands."

"Who has time for that?"

Claudia leaned forward in her chair. "That's just what I mean, Mary Ann! We didn't have time to do what we should have started doing right away after Jack and Bill."

"Okay, and just how were we supposed to do that?"

"Well, that's the point, Mary Ann. We didn't have any time. So I saved up enough for two months' rent and expenses, bought a couple of new dresses, and I'm going to go out and find a husband."

"I thought you wanted to be so independent."

"That was part of what was all wrong."

Claudia looked away toward the windows a little because she did not want Mary Ann to be hurt, thinking it included sleeping over at her house and saying it had been wrong. If it made her mixed up for a while, it was her own fault. Not Mary Ann's.

"I mean, I shouldn't have to be independent, Mary Ann. I should have a husband. I'm supposed to be somebody's wife."

Mary Ann just laughed. "Who did you have in mind?"

"I thought of somebody."

"Oh, you're so smug, Claudia. Who?"

"I'll tell you later."

"No, tell me now. Who's the lucky guy?"

"Dan."

"Dan who?"

"I don't remember his last name."

"Oh, that's great."

"Don't laugh at me, Mary Ann. Dan. The one I told you about from the club."

"Oh, the one with the doctor girlfriend, and you kicked his dick or something."

"I didn't kick his dick. I just flirted with him under the table, and he flirted back."

"I think he just wanted you to kick his dick."

"Shut up, Mary Ann. I'm not going to tell you anything more if you're just going to laugh at everything I say."

"Well, what are you going to do about the doctor girlfriend?"

"She wasn't so much. I can take care of her."

"That's pretty crappy, isn't it?"

"She's a doctor, Mary Ann. She's one of those independent girls. She doesn't need Dan. And he doesn't really care about her anyway, or he would have married her by now."

"You can't say that. You don't know anything about it."

"I know what I saw."

"That was, what—two years ago, sweetie. I wouldn't count on it."

Claudia finished her brandy and poured them both another one. She should have expected Mary Ann to argue about it. People always argue back when they know you're right. "It wasn't two years," she said quietly.

"Well, almost," said Mary Ann.

"I have to start somewhere, don't I?" she said.

Mary Ann got out another Chesterfield, but she looked up at the clock too because it was getting late and she must have been thinking about Edgar Lee and Petey.

"I don't know why you think you have to start anything. You were doing fine." She got out the lighter Claudia had given her even though Claudia's was on the table.

"I still use it all the time."

She was going to try to talk her into coming back home to live with her and Edgar Lee. Claudia just knew it. She didn't know if there was any way around tears at the end.

"I just want to get things back the way they're supposed to be. You know what I mean. The wife stays home and takes care of the babies, and the man goes out to get the buffaloes."

"Get the what?"

"You know. Like the caveman days. The men go out to get the buffaloes, and part of the wife's job is to make sure they do that. It's the natural order."

"Listen, Claudia, I know you're not lazy. Remember how you liked working at the garage? I know the kitchen is hard, but there are good things about it. Everybody likes you. You have friends there. If you just need a little time off to catch a breather and rest up, I know they'll take you back."

"No, Mary Ann. It's nothing like that. I'm supposed to be the wife of a naval officer. And that's work too. You don't just stay home doing nothing."

Mary Ann did not come back with anything smart. She just sat there looking like a beaten-up boxer sitting in his corner who expects to get knocked out in the next round.

"I'm not getting any naval officer, Claudia. Let's face it."

"No, that's why I'm telling you this. You can. They're all over the place now."

"I'm thirty-seven years old, and I got a kid. Now really."

"You can get one of the older ones. Not a real old one. I mean one like the chaplain, the one Jan got. Someone like that. There are plenty of them around, but if we don't hurry up, the war will be over, and they'll start going home."

"Oh, God, Claudia."

"We have to do it now. That's why I quit the job."

"Well, I can't just quit the job. I got Edgar Lee. Don't you remember how hard it was to find a job?"

"Mary Ann—I wish you'd listen to me."

"I better go. I got work tomorrow." Mary Ann stood up and went to the door.

"Mary Ann, come back. Please."

"I've got to get home."

Claudia got up too and went to the door. Mary Ann stood in the hallway for a moment. She didn't get the idea at all.

"I guess I'll see you around. Everybody in the kitchen misses you. We're like a family, you know."

"I miss them too."

"I think you're really fucked up, Claudia." She smiled a kind of weak smile. "But I still love you."

"I still love you too, Mary Ann."

Claudia had to let her go, and she watched Mary Ann go down the quiet, dark hallway. They should have hugged.

CHAPTER TWENTY-FOUR

Claudia did not see Mary Ann again for two months. By then she was living with Dan. Not exactly all the way, because he kept his things on base where he roomed with Froggy, but he moved her into a nicer hotel called the Captain Cook and paid the rent. She still wore her wedding ring from Jack, so no one gave her any trouble, and it was safe to wear her nice engagement ring with the delicate gold filigree.

It was a three-room apartment with its own bath and a telephone. Dan gave her the money to buy anything she needed. She stocked up the little kitchen, but mostly they went out. Sometimes they went to the Grand Hawaiian, and walking in from the parking lot, Claudia always looked for the steam rising out of the back. Once she saw Mary Ann and Larry out on the steps but she looked away quickly. She still loved Mary Ann. She still loved Larry and Jim and all the rest of them, even the silly hostess. It really was like a family. It made her sad, thinking back.

Dan liked to have a lot of people around. He wasn't comfortable with just the two of them home alone. He didn't seem too comfortable out with people either, but it didn't bother Claudia. It only meant that he was a different kind of man, and it was her job to get to know him. It was like reading a book, a little every day. She took notes on his likes and dislikes, and there was another list she made of what she found out were his expectations of the perfect mate, who, come hell or high water, was going to be her.

Snagging Dan turned out to be easier than she thought. The night after she quit at the Grand Hawaiian, Claudia turned out at the Palmetto club in a Toni Hill sheik rayon that stretched taut across her tummy and hips, with spaghetti straps and lots to invite the eye. The maître d' did not quite know what to do with a single girl, but since she was so decked out, he waved her in, and it didn't take her long to spot Dan. It was really Froggy she noticed because of the red hair. They picked up right where they left off. Froggy was with Elaine, and Dan was still with Fitzy. She laughed so much that night, and the daiquiris were so good. Besides the mission, it was so much fun to get out.

Claudia made up that she was waiting to hear if she had been accepted for Red Cross nurses training. Unexpectedly, Elaine offered to put in a good word for her at the hospital if it was anyone she knew, and Claudia had to think fast. She said she could not remember the name of the person she mailed the application to. Then she left early. Timing was everything. She paused, standing behind Dan with one hand lightly on his shoulder, to say it was good to see the old gang again.

They didn't show the next night. Claudia made small talk with Mr. Anthony at the bar, and he bought her a few drinks. He wasn't such a bad guy, but he still gave her the heebie-jeebies, and he was always looking sideways to make sure everyone was in the right place. There were a few men in the club you knew were goons, one by the side of the stage where there was a door, and one or two by the main entrance.

Another week went by. Claudia checked in every night around nine. The next time they showed up she pretended she was just leaving and let Froggy talk her into joining them. They had another good time, laughing and drinking up a storm. Froggy must have seen right through her, but she knew that pretty soon Dan wouldn't listen to anything Froggy might say about her. It's just what happens when you become a couple.

Claudia was waiting for ginger ale night, and when it came a few nights later, it could not have gone better. It was only Dan and Fitzy. They still had fun, but around ten o'clock, Fitzy had to go because of her early shift at the hospital.

"What a shame," said Claudia. "We were having so much fun." Then she looked furtively around and said, "I don't think I know anyone here tonight. You'll come back, won't you, Dan? Oh, please."

Dan said maybe he might, just for a nightcap. Fitzy shrugged her shoulders and said, "Come on, Dan. Gotta go. You're my ride."

Claudia knew he'd be back, and sure enough, not a half hour went by and there was Dan, making his way through the crowded club toward her table. He walked like a man coming in to buy a new car, and Claudia smiled like it was so nice to see him, determined as any slick salesman that this one was going home with a slightly used blonde, right off the showroom floor.

Mary Ann was at the market on Kaiulani, looking over the produce. Claudia saw her from the used bookstall across the street where she had been looking for mysteries she had not read. She decided to just go over.

"I saw you too," said Mary Ann, "but I didn't know if you wanted to see me."

"Of course I do."

"I went over to your room once. A fella came to the door and said he never heard of you."

"I moved to the Captain Cook."

"Oh, I wasn't sure. There was someone in the bed. I thought it might be you and you changed your name—you know, back to your maiden name."

"No, Wyler's still my name, and Claudia's my game. You know how it is."

"You look good, Claudia."

"Thanks, so do you."

"Looks like you put on—but that's good for you. You must be eating right."

"You know, Mary Ann, I always thought I'd die if I gained an ounce, but now I don't care anymore. I'm more secure."

"You got your buffalo then, I take it."

They both smiled and held each other's hands.

"I just stay home and keep house," said Claudia. "Dan goes out for the buffaloes. He's doing great. He got to meet Admiral Nimitz. He shook his hand and everything."

"That's a pretty big buffalo."

Mary Ann leaned against the bean flats and took out a Chesterfield, and Claudia had one too. Dan did not smoke. Mary Ann agreed that was too bad. She said Dan would probably want her to quit, but Claudia explained that Dan never criticized anything about her. Mary Ann thought that was rare in a man.

"So what is it? Are you going to get married?"

"I'm working on it."

"He doesn't know he's doomed, does he?"

"I'm not such a bad catch."

"I'm sorry, Claudia. I'm happy for you. I really am. Do you want to have lunch?"

"I'd love to. Where's Edgar Lee?"

"Jan's got him."

They had lunch together at a nice little place outside. Mary Ann was still at the Grand Hawaiian and told Claudia about everyone and their little intrigues. Claudia told Mary Ann all about Dan. This time she could tell her everything because they didn't have husbands with different ranks, and when Claudia left her at the car, she gave Mary Ann a hundred dollars. She folded up five twenties under the table at the café when Mary Ann wasn't looking and pressed it into her hand. She made her take it for Edgar Lee.

Walking home to the Captain Cook with a light shopping bag of produce, Claudia felt so happy being back together with Mary Ann. It had been a lonely two months, but it had made all the difference. She had come so far from the sparse living of the Barrymore and the hard work of the Grand Hawaiian. She was with Dan, and Dan was on his way up. And to prove it, she only had to look down and contemplate that a hand that had shaken the hand of Admiral Nimitz, that same morning, only a few hours earlier, had been between her downy blonde peaches. It was like she was part of history.

But it wasn't easy. It was entirely different from how it was with Jack. Her efforts there had been to make herself worthy of Jack and fulfill his expectations, and she still held Jack and herself up as an example of perfection in a marital relationship. How could she see it as anything else? But Dan did not make his expectations of her known. He never asked her to do anything. He sent all his laundry out and kept everything on base except his financial papers. He was going to work in the stock market after the war, and he was already doing it with brokers he knew on the exchanges. He had a time-zone chart on his desk and made long-distance calls early in the morning. She heard him ordering buys and sells, but there was never any emotion in his voice. The desk was in the living room of the apartment, covered with stacks of papers and manila folders. Every morning when he came in to say goodbye to her, he always said, "Don't touch anything on the desk."

Claudia never touched anything. Dan's desk was like the corral where he had his buffaloes rounded up. They were going to go far together. She knew she could learn the ins and ouches of the market and help him. Dan was only in the navy because he came from a long line of navy men and his father was an admiral in the War Department, but whenever he mentioned his family, it was only to say that none of them knew how to make money.

Dan did not say much otherwise and was always so serious, and Claudia had to guess at most of what she knew about him. It was not like reading a good book after all. She inferred that Dan did know how to make money and that he was itching to get out of the navy and head straight for New York. Instead of personal stories, he told her stock market stories about bulls and bears. She liked best the Jesse Livermore stories and the risky moves he pulled off. It was interesting to know you could make money when the market was going "down the toilet," as Dan put it. Claudia did not care for vulgarity, but it was a good image. The navy only depressed him. It was going to be her job to keep him in the navy and get him through the war so he could go after the big buffaloes on Wall Street.

Dan went to bed early and got up early to make his phone calls, so Claudia put him to bed by eight thirty or nine. She tucked him in and kissed him and closed the door to the bedroom. Then she stayed up late, listening to Jack's radio shows and eating cakes and pies. Once she ate a whole chocolate cake in one night, but her real weakness was cookies because they were easier to eat while she read mysteries.

It all started when she did not know what to do one night after the radio went off the air, so she picked up a mystery that was on the bookshelf when she moved in. Ever since then she had devoured one mystery after another. Twice a week she went to the outdoor used bookstalls with the books she had read and slipped them back on the tables. Then she bought at least two or three new ones. She liked the little Hawaiian man who worked the stalls, and now she had plenty of money to do any little good deed that came to her.

She didn't know why she liked mysteries so much. She even liked the gruesome murder mysteries, as long as they were good stories and the murderer did not turn out to be the one she thought it was. The best one so far was one about a man who killed girls for the little fatty pillows on the sides of their bosoms. He put them in mason jars of formaldehyde. That was how they caught him. He bought too much formaldehyde.

"He'd sure love me," Claudia said to herself. She pressed her arms to her sides and the little pillows there almost rivaled her bosoms, but the bosoms had gotten a little more heft to them too. She bought a postage meter scale and weighed them every night when Dan was asleep. They were nothing like Mary Ann's, but they were definitely going places, and Claudia knew better than most what the right brassiere could do for you. By the time she bumped into Mary Ann at the market, she could tell they knocked Mary Ann's eyes out.

The nineteen-inch waist was long gone, but she felt good, packed into her all-in-ones, and she loved it. Looking sideways in the long mirror in the bathroom without her clothes on, the shapely curves and differentiation were still there. She thought she looked good in her clothes too, and since Dan kept all his at the base, he let her have both bedroom closets and money to fill them up.

Claudia went to bed around four o'clock in the morning and snuggled up to Dan to wake him up for his phone calls. When he was planning a big foray in the market, it was easy to get him going. She liked being the instigator though. It made her feel like an equal partner, not just one person bumping the other person out of the way.

There were so many other good things about Dan, and one way or another they all derived from his love of regularity and his commitment to responsibility and consideration. He had breakfast sent up to her every morning promptly at eleven from the restaurant across the street. Every day it was something different. One day it might be two eggs with French toast and sausage, fried potatoes, a pineapple muffin, a few Danish pastries, and a basket of biscuits. Whatever it was, she always ate everything and then went back to bed to sleep a few more hours before she had to get up and get pretty by six.

Dan was always home at six on the dot, even if there was some big operation going on out at sea with task forces. Dan could get out of anything. Claudia thought it was due to his father, Admiral Almay, back at the War Department, who was a terrific letter writer. He always had an axe to grind with somebody, Gandhi, George Bernard Shaw, Henry Ford, Elsa Maxwell, the pope, you name it. When he was mad at everyone at the same time, a letter from Admiral Almay under an assumed name appeared in the *New York Times*, but you could tell who it was.

They had a drink at six while Dan looked over the financial section of the evening papers, and then he lay down in the bedroom to think by himself for thirty minutes. Then it was out on the town for dinner. When they went to the Grand Hawaiian, Claudia would always break a roll in half and discretely wipe her plate clean, thinking of Mary Ann down in the dungeon. No one they bumped into, including Dan, knew that she had worked there. She kept saying she had not heard back from the Red Cross about nurses training.

When they were out to dinner, it was a good time to tell him about her day, and Claudia always asked about his. Just like Jack, his days were always fine, but she managed to get enough out of him to tell that he didn't like Annette. She saw no reason to worry anyway. Dan did not go for passion or personal relationships. When he pulled out his little notebook and made some notes during dinner, she went right on talking, even though he wasn't paying any attention. She knew he wasn't writing down her likes and dislikes. One girl was enough for him. One girl was all he could take.

They usually got home by eight thirty, and Dan went right to bed. Claudia went to the kitchen to look for something good to eat and settled on the couch to listen to her radio shows with the volume down. She read her mysteries and weighed her bosoms and wrote down what they were, and she wrote home once a week to say everything was fine and she was still waiting to hear from the Red Cross. She had not had a good cry since she cried on Mary Ann the first night she slept over. This week she could end her letter to Mom with "Nothing to Cry About!!"

On Saturday nights they went to the Palmetto, which was where Claudia really earned her keep because Froggy liked to pick on Dan for being so serious and quiet. It did not help to get him drunk like you would expect because he only got more serious. The Palmetto was always packed, but Froggy was usually there with Elaine on Saturday nights, and they saved seats for each other. One night Annette was there with a new date named Walter. None of the boys wanted to dance that night, so Annette and Claudia got up and danced together. Lots of girls danced together when their men were out on the boats somewhere.

They got going pretty well with "Fascinating Rhythm," and that was lots of fun. "The Breeze and I" came up next. The boys over at the table looked like they were getting tips on the market from Dan, so Annette and Claudia looked at each other and decided at the same time, what the heck, and put their arms around each other.

"Okay, who do you want to be?" Annette asked.

"I'll be the man," said Claudia.

They just went through the steps on that one, getting the feel of it. Claudia thought they were doing really well, and she could tell Annette was pleased when they got the little moves right to the rhythm of the song. You never got that with a man. With a man it was just one, two, three.

The band went right into the next number, and everyone kept on dancing. It was one Claudia hadn't heard before. Annette said it was "Where Was I?" by Charlie Barnet. They kept dancing too. It was nice to hold the real Annette and not be just imagining it. As they moved together with the others crowding the dance floor, Claudia felt herself relieved of the workings of her imagination and everything about Annette that had ever gone through her mind. They could be just regular girls together. She had her man, Dan, and her best friend, Mary Ann, and she could be regular girls with Annette. Regular girls didn't have to be a big deal.

It seemed to her that sex was the big monkey wrench in the picture. It turned you into predator or prey. It was one of those little design flaws in human beings. If you let sex become what was wrong with your life, you were a cooked goose. She had Dan. She was back to normal. So was the world, except for the war, but even that was kind of normal. Another design flaw.

She had to help Dan get through the navy and take care of their home when he was after the buffaloes. The sex part was even up with Dan. Sometimes she thought it wouldn't hurt to teach him some emotion even though he was doing so well without it. It was like putting up curtains. You need a woman for that. A man doesn't always see the need.

"Where Was I?" drifted to an end, and Claudia blinked herself awake and came out of the transforming revelations she'd had while dancing with Annette. She smiled back at Annette and was pleased with the great stride she had made. It was like skipping over squares on a game board, and she had landed on normal. What a surprise when revelations get you somewhere nice, considering that when she had walked out on the dance floor, all she wanted was the satisfaction of going eyeball to eyeball with Annette with her new bosoms—now that she had such a respectable pair.

The band went on break, and they made their way back to the table. Froggy was smirking when they pulled out their chairs and sat down and sorted out whose drink was whose.

"We'll dance the next one, huh, Dan? No, on second thought, I'll dance with Valentino."

"His name is Walter," said Annette. "You better be nice to him, Froggy. Where did he go?"

"He went to the head. You shouldn't lose track of your men, Annette."

"I'm not worried."

"I'm sorry," said Froggy. "I misspoke. There's nothing to worry about. For a woman your age, Annette, you still got the goods."

Elaine gave him a little slap. "I thought you didn't notice other girls."

"Oh, sorry. You're right," said Froggy. "Gosh, Annette, I never noticed how you still got the goods."

Elaine smacked him again and knocked her glass over. Everybody got their elbows up fast, and Froggy put his hand up for a waiter. Some towels appeared instantly and then another round of drinks came.

"Please, Elaine, no more hysterics," said Froggy. "Save it for later."

"Listen to this guy," said Elaine. "I have to put him in the back seat on the way home. It's the only place in the car he won't fall out of when I open the door back at base."

"Lies. Don't listen to her."

"You're not awake five minutes after we get out of here."

"Well, at least I'm awake while I'm here. Look at Dan."

Dan's eyes went up right away. "I'm awake."

"Yeah, well, I know you can do that with your eyes open too."

"Stop picking on Dan," said Claudia.

"I'm fine," said Dan.

"Dan's fine," said Froggy. "But that wasn't always the case, you know."

Dan wasn't looking at his watch yet, so Claudia knew she still had a little time to have fun. Walter came back from the head and squeezed in beside Annette. Claudia was glad for Annette, but she could see what she was doing. She was looking for another man like Jack. He didn't look much like Jack, but anyone could see he was the next best thing. Froggy bent toward her in a confiding way, but not so the others couldn't hear.

"Dan had that awkward year, you know. Before he made his first million."

"You're so full of baloney, Frog," said Elaine. "Listen, if you want to dance, you better get going."

The band was coming back. Elaine didn't know how to dance to anything but a waltz, but she was a good egg and wanted to see Froggy have a good time. "One of you can have him," she said.

"Not me," said Annette, "I'd need more to drink."

"Let's go, babe. Looks like it's you and me," Froggy said, extending a hand to Claudia. She got up, suddenly feeling a little unsteady because of her last daiquiri, and nodded to Dan, who looked at her and tapped on his watch.

Out on the floor, Froggy took her in his arms and gave a deep sigh at her ear.

"What now?" she said.

"I like you this way."

"What do you mean, Froggy?"

"Oh, you know. You're a little more substantial these days. I didn't like you the other way. I never said anything at the time, of course."

"Is that so."

"You may have noticed me averting my eyes."

"I thought it was something else."

"For heaven's sake, what?"

"You know, hopeless despair."

"I think I would have remembered that."

"No, I distinctly remember hopeless despair. Are you sure it wasn't you?"

"What did he look like?"

"Something like you, only more handsome and manly."

"Well, I guess you can write him off as the one that got away. But if you will permit me to offer a modest consolation, I could go for you now in a big way."

"What about you-know-who?"

"Elaine?"

"Remember her?"

"Yeah, well, there's no future there. I'm trying to establish dominance, and it's not working."

"That's because she's independent. Why can't a girl be independent?"

"It never works out."

"Well, I'm sorry about that, but don't look at me. I'm taken."

"That won't last. I'll get you in the end."

"Fat chance, buster."

"We'll see," he said. "The worm turns, you know."

"You can turn your worms all you want, Froggy. It won't do you any good."

"Then I presume you intend to remain taken."

"That is correct, lieutenant."

The song was over, and everyone at the table looked ready to leave. Another revelation came to her as she walked off the dance floor. She liked Froggy a lot. He could be a good friend, and she didn't have to do anything. He probably was in love with her, but it wasn't going to get in the way. It wasn't fair to Elaine, but loving different girls didn't seem to bother men. It was like Dan rebalancing his asset portfolio.

Late that Sunday afternoon, Dan told her he had been ordered back to Washington and had to leave Monday morning. Claudia's heart dropped like a stone, but then he said he would be back in two weeks, depending on how long the meetings ran. After the initial shock, she realized she would have a chance to do some things she had been putting off, and two weeks was not such a long time. It might make Dan miss her and see how vital she was to his life. Two weeks away might be just the thing to bring him around to proposing.

They went to the Grand Hawaiian for dinner, and then she got him to bed by eight. She tucked him in and left him alone for a good night's sleep before the long flight to America. It made her jittery and anxious just thinking about it. The Japs didn't have any Zeros left, but his plane could still go down, either on the way there or on the way back, and California to Washington was no sure thing either.

Claudia turned on her radio shows to keep her from thinking about all the ways to get killed. There was the peach pie to finish off and then the bowl of Chinese noodles she had made yesterday. That got her through *Mr. District Attorney* and *New York Variety*. She was trying to save the cookies and chocolate-covered macadamia nuts and the coconut date rolls for reading time.

The mystery was a particularly good one. The girl was found hanging on a big clock tower. She was tied to the hands of time. It was deeper and more sophisticated than the ordinary mystery, and you would never guess who did it. Mary Ann would like it too. It would be hard not to give away the end, but all the fun of a mystery depended on it. In fourth grade back in Connecticut, she had discovered how important it was not to give away the ending of a book and capitalized heavily on the principal. She ended every book report with "And if you want to find out the ending, you'll have to read the book." It was kind of like her trademark. She had mentioned it to Edgar Lee, and Mary Ann said he used it all the time.

Claudia ate a vanilla pound cake and went to bed at four to get Dan up. Since he would be gone for two weeks, he wanted to do it, and she made sure he had a good time so he would be thinking about it while he was gone and would decide to marry her. She didn't ask for happily-ever-after like it was with Jack. You take your chances. They had been together for almost three months and had never argued over anything so it was a good bet. Everything was easy with Dan, right from the start. She just put her line in the water, and he jumped into the boat all by himself.

Now he was putting on the jacket of his uniform and closing his briefcase and going to the door. He was so casual about leaving, as if he were just going down to the corner store. In mysteries, you knew the character was about to disappear. Anytime a character went down to the corner store, you knew. It was always to get a pack of smokes or the newspaper. That was the only thing about Dan's leaving that made her feel better. The character who disappeared was never going down to the corner store for a meeting at the War Department.

"Don't touch anything on the desk," he said.

He was already out the door in the hallway, and Claudia had to grab his sleeve to make him turn around.

"Kiss me," she said.

"Oh, okay."

Claudia tried to look into his eyes with deep meaning, but he was in a hurry. He kissed her without holding her because he was changing hands with his briefcase to get the car keys out of his pants pocket.

"See you in two weeks," he said.

"I love you."

"Love you too. Don't touch anything on the desk."

Then he was off down the hall like any other morning. Only today, he looked like one of those men in the movies getting out of prison, where you get a new suit and ten bucks, and the friendly guard closes the gate behind you and says "Don't let me see you back here, Johnny." And you walk off down the street looking up into the sunshine.

CHAPTER TWENTY-FIVE

Claudia was glad she had her idea the night before Dan left. First, it was important to keep to her schedule, so she went back to bed until eleven, when breakfast came. The boy told her that Lieutenant Almay paid two weeks in advance for her breakfasts, so she needn't worry. A dinner menu came with her tray, and he said that if she liked, she could select a meal for the evening, which would go on Lieutenant Almay's tab and could be brought up whenever she requested. The boy said she could leave her dinner order outside the door on her breakfast tray. It thrilled her when he left saying "Thank you, Mrs. Almay. Good day."

After breakfast, Claudia went back to bed again and slept till four. She found Takeo's card and called him for a ride to the store where he bought the paper for his origami and she got a box the size of a suitcase in all different colors. Takeo carried the box up to the apartment, and Claudia gave him a dollar tip for showing her how to make paper monkeys. Her plan was to surprise Dan by filling up the whole apartment with paper monkeys.

The original monkey family was on a shelf over the bed, and she wanted to keep them separate, so she decided to do just the kitchen and living room. Takeo thought it was a clever idea too and helped her make monkeys for more than an hour before he had to go.

"Monkeys good luck," he said. "Your new man get the idea all right, you see."

Claudia realized that she needed to bring an organizational concept to her monkeys before going any further. She had six colors of paper and needed husband monkeys, wife monkeys, and children monkeys. Her final plan called for one husband monkey and one wife monkey, each the size of a full sheet of paper. All the rest would be children monkeys. Another consideration was that, while filling the rooms with monkeys was important for an effective presentation, recognition was critical. She decided to solve the recognition problem by watching at the door for Dan, and when he came in, she would jump out and exclaim, "They're monkeys, Dan!!"

Dinner arrived at seven, and it was the only time she stopped making monkeys. She had roast beef with mashed potatoes, two barbecued chicken breasts with wild rice, asparagus, a vegetable lasagna, a basket of rolls, and a basket of baked breads with cheese in half of them and a sweet apple-and-pear mix in the other half. She used up the whole quarter pound of butter on the rolls, and they were so delicious. Choosing more than one entrée was a completely original idea of hers, but why not? They knew her from breakfast.

Dessert that night was chocolate cake. On the menu she had checked off chocolate cake and put an asterisk beside it. At the bottom of the menu where there was room, she carefully printed "Whole Cake Please." Their cherry tarts were irresistible, but she decided to put off ordering those until tomorrow. She didn't want to be a pig.

Claudia dozed on the couch and listened to music on the radio. She wondered if there was something besides the leftover chocolate cake for later. It was only nine thirty. Everything close by was closed by midnight on weekdays, and she would not be going to bed until four. Breakfast came at eleven. She decided to leave a note to include a few cherry tarts with breakfast every day, planning to conduct experiments on the extras. She already knew one thing she could try—cream cheese and pineapples on cherry tarts. She could keep a journal of her experiments for each time she had a baby so that she would know what foods to keep on hand.

Claudia looked at herself with satisfaction every morning, naked in the full-length mirror. It was so pleasing to see how formidable she was getting, with rump, thighs, and belly so pleasantly portentous, and bosoms standing out, so fulfilling of prophesy. Standing back, taking it in all together, she thought Claudia Wyler presented a perfect picture of fecundity. There were so many ingenious ways evolution had come up with to protect the young. There were eggs in nests, burrows, and pouches, and there were little pods hanging from trees, egg sacks tied to weeds underwater, seeds in puffballs that floated in the air. All kinds of crazy Rube Goldberg ways. Mammals were the only ones to think of keeping the baby all the way in the mother. That was the best idea of all because it seemed like you only got killed or eaten after you came out. She didn't know anyone who died inside, except for one.

Dan would marry her right away. He might be dull but he was true blue. She knew she could count on him. It was a roundabout way of getting to the right place, but it was wartime and they were in a far-flung outpost. Nothing counted out here. When they got back to America they could make up dates and co-ordinate their stories and get on the up and up.

They would live in Manhattan. When they had more children they would move to a farmhouse in Connecticut, and Dan would take the train to the city, where the buffaloes roam. She had plenty of time to think it through that week.

All week, Claudia made monkey children and did not leave the apartment. One night she talked to Mary Ann for two hours on the telephone. It wasn't just chatterbox talk. Mary Ann told her more about Richard, the petty officer who was giving her the gasoline. It sounded like Mary Ann was losing her nerve or something. From her mystery stories, Claudia knew that when you lost your nerve, the jig was up. She cut and folded little monkeys all during the long telephone call, and then she didn't go to bed at all so she wouldn't oversleep and miss breakfast.

Saturday was the day Claudia weighed herself. Her bosoms weighed one pound two ounces each. Big jump from last week, and they didn't hang down. They stood out proudly like the ones on figureheads in the days of sail. Total girl, at five foot four inches, was 182 pounds, four ounces. In the full-length mirror in the bathroom, where she could view the whole kit n' caboodle, everything looked ready for action. She couldn't see her peaches anymore. They had retreated to the safety of the hollow space between her legs, but she had a feeling it wasn't hollow there anymore. Mother Nature was at the helm now.

On Sunday morning Froggy came around. It was an unexpected surprise, but she didn't mind. She had her monkeys done. He sat on the window settee while Claudia ate breakfast. She only had her silk robe on, and she knew he was looking, so she had to get up and go to the bedroom to put on a brassier and panties and a slip and a sundress and slippers. It was also annoying that she could not lick her fingers and lick the plates, but it was nice to have company after thirteen days. It was Froggy's day off, and he was dressed civilian in a short-sleeved Hawaiian shirt that was blue-and-white in an ocean wave pattern, white shorts, no socks, and deck shoes.

"You look like a tourist, Froggy."

"That's me. Carefree. Maybe I can stow away on a boat home."

"Well, I know you're dying to ask. They're monkeys."

"What are monkeys?"

"Don't tell me you didn't notice."

"I don't look around girls' apartments."

"Oh, come on."

"I'm sorry. Go on. What are monkeys?"

"All the origami paper monkeys."

"Am I free to look?"

"It's a surprise for Dan. All right. You can look."

Froggy turned and looked around the room and seemed impressed as Claudia watched his eyes go over the hundreds of paper monkeys in six different colors that covered every surface, the ones perched on the window ledges and on top of the bookshelves, the ones pinned to the drapes and arranged in groups in the corners. For once he did not have any smart aleck thing to say. He just breathed out, "Oh God, Claudia."

It was a real triumph after all that work, like the Pyramids and the Lord's Prayer engraved on the head of a pin, grand scale and meticulous detail right there in one magnificent explosion of art. He looked around at the monkeys, stepping carefully and looking up at the high-up monkeys like a man in the Louvre, with his glasses on and arms behind his back.

Claudia offered him one of the cherry tarts that she was holding out for an experiment with cream cheese, but he politely declined. He said he heard from Dan. All the papers on his desk had to get shipped to Washington.

"I have a box out in the hall," he said.

"Go right ahead," she said. "I don't know why he didn't ask me, but I guess he doesn't want his buffaloes touched by a girl. He always tells me not to touch anything."

"It'll only take a minute," said Froggy.

"I have to brush my hair," said Claudia. "Just put the monkeys on the floor for now. I can rearrange them later."

Claudia went into the bedroom and brushed her hair one hundred strokes, which was taking more time these days because she got tired keeping her arms up. She was surprised Froggy didn't ask about the buffaloes. Not many people would skip over a reference like that and wait for a context to explain it. As far as she knew, buffaloes did not come in a large variety of contexts. When she came out, she was surprised again, this time to find Froggy hurriedly dumping the desk drawers into the box. All the papers and folders from on top were gone, and she could see one box was already out in the hall.

"What's going on, Froggy?"

"I'll just get this one out of here."

Froggy closed the flaps of the cardboard box and took it out to the hall. Then he sat down at the table and took an envelope out of his shorts, from under his big Hawaiian shirt. Claudia sat down and waited.

"Dan got transferred back to the States. He wanted me to tell you."

"That didn't go through the mail, did it, Froggy."

Claudia reached for the envelope, but he jerked it away.

"I'll show you later."

"Where's Dan?"

"I have to explain something."

"Where's Dan, Froggy?"

"He's in Washington. He really was called back."

"What's going on? Why didn't he tell me? He knew he wasn't coming back here before he left, didn't he?"

"I'm trying to explain. Will you please let me explain?"

"Okay. What happened?"

"Well, first of all," said Froggy, "he wants you to have this." He pulled a stack of bills in sleeved packets out of the manila envelope. "It's $200 in twenties."

"What's that for?"

"It's for the restaurant and the rent. To cover you for a while."

"He told you this before he left, didn't he?"

"No, honestly," said Froggy.

"Well, where did you get this?"

"He left it on his bed at base."

Froggy gave the letter to Claudia. It had "Please Open" with yesterday's date on it. It started with "Dear Frog." It just said everything Froggy had already told her, except it ended with something that made her mad.

"I'm only letting you see it so you'll believe me," said Froggy.

"What are you supposed to tell me, and why does he say make sure you get the papers out of the apartment first?"

"I guess he didn't know how you would take it."

"Take what?"

"Him getting transferred."

"What's the other thing?"

"Well—"

"Froggy!"

"Dan's married."

"Oh fuck, Froggy."

"No, he is. Really."

Claudia stood up and threw her coffee cup across the room. Then she turned over the breakfast cart, and Froggy jumped out of the way.

"Why didn't you tell me? You knew, didn't you?"

"Not till just recently. He let it slip one night. And I didn't know if you knew."

"That's bullshit, Froggy. I'd never be with him if he were married. You should have known that."

"I thought we were all just drinking and kidding around."

Claudia kicked the breakfast cart and started to cry.

"Why would I be just kidding around? Look at me. I'm going to have a baby. What the hell am I supposed to do now?"

Froggy sat with his eyes lowered and his hands together between his knees, looking at the floor like someone at a funeral.

"I don't know," he said. "I guess you could get in touch with Dan, but I don't know if it's a good idea."

"What did he think he was doing?"

Claudia sat down across from Froggy and made him look her in the eyes.

"What was he doing with me, Froggy?"

"I don't know."

"No, Froggy. Explain this to me. What was he doing?"

"Well, I know he liked you."

"No. Come on."

"I guess he thought of you as his mistress. You know, the apartment and the clothes and everything. He liked giving you things, I know that. He looked all over town for that pearl necklace."

Claudia sat up straight and couldn't believe what she was hearing.

"He never gave me a pearl necklace."

"Well, no, he never found one. The right one, I mean. He wanted a certain size pearl."

"You're lying to me." Claudia grabbed his shirt at the shoulder and everything loose about the shirt pulled to one side. "I'm going to tear your shirt to pieces if you don't tell me the truth. Do you have another place to go?"

Froggy winced away from her, but she pulled tighter on the shirt until his shoulder was coming out of the neck.

"Are you supposed to go to another apartment after me?"

"Yeah," he said sullenly.

"Oh, that bastard. Oh, god damn him."

Claudia got up and kicked the breakfast cart again and again. Then she fell down on the settee and cried. Froggy stayed where he was, sitting the way he was before she grabbed his shirt. Claudia turned away and cried full tilt for a few minutes. Then she looked back at Froggy, not bothering to wipe her face. She was too mad to cry anymore.

"How many apartments are you going to?"

"Just one. Nobody you know."

"Who?"

"I don't know. Jean somebody. She never came to the club."

"Did you know about her?"

"No, honestly I didn't. He didn't tell me anything about her."

"How could he be such a bastard? How could he have another girl? He slept here every night."

"Don't ask me. I never knew where he was—except out of the office a lot."

Claudia came back and sat down beside Froggy on the window settee. She got out a Chesterfield, and Froggy lit hers and took out one of his Luckys.

"You want some coffee?"

"Sure," he said.

"God, Froggy, what am I going to do?"

"Are you sure you're expecting?"

"What else could it be?"

"Search me." He said it sincerely, as far as Claudia could tell.

"That would make a big difference," he added.

"What a bad thing to do. How could he be so awful to two girls? How could he be so awful to his wife?"

"I don't know, but you can't blame anyone for not telling you. Nobody knew. I only found out a little while ago. I thought maybe you knew."

"Well, go to hell, Froggy. I wouldn't even look at him if I knew he was married. What's the matter with you? I thought he was up for grabs."

"So did I. So did everybody else. You can ask Elaine—or Fitzy."

Claudia brought up what a good husband Jack had been and how they had come through their first year with flying colors. Froggy did not have much to say about it, but he could only agree that a good husband would never treat his mistress so badly. Then he had to go because it was getting late and he had another stop to make.

"I'll be back in a few days," he said. "I want to help you figure things out. Your finances, I mean. Maybe I can help."

"Thanks, Froggy. You're a good friend. I'm sorry I got so upset."

"I understand," he said and leaned in to touch his cheek to hers with a little kiss sound. "Maybe I can get away Thursday night, okay?"

"Sure," she said.

"And get all your papers together, okay. Things like bills and bank stuff. I'm good with that, and we'll figure something out."

"Thanks, Froggy."

Claudia squeezed his hand once and let go.

PART THREE

"When Just Us Girls is Just the Thing"

—PATRICIA "PATTY" PRESCOTT, *WOMAN'S HOME COMPANION*, APRIL 1944

CHAPTER TWENTY-SIX

Everything changed by Thursday. After Froggy left, Claudia put the breakfast cart outside her door for the boy to pick up. She could not straighten out the bent parts, so she leaned it up against the wall and placed all the broken dishes on it along with the pieces of the coffee cup and orange juice glass. She went back to bed like she was supposed to, to keep the schedule, but she didn't feel like lounging, so she got up to pace, and that did not do any good either. She walked around the apartment saying to herself that bastard, that bastard, if I ever get my hands on you.

She composed a letter to Dan's wife in which she asserted that she was Dan's true soul mate and revealed that she was having his baby. His wife might send him packing back to Hawaii if she had any sway with the War Department. Then she could tell him he was a bastard to his face and slam the door. Claudia wrote letters all day to Mrs. Almay, a different one every time her mood changed. Finally, she threw them all away. It would be worse to be Mrs. Almay.

Dinner came at seven on a new trolley, and Claudia ate everything. There was nothing to do but get over Dan, and she already had two weeks to get used to him not being around. What came to mind were phrases like "good riddance" and "so, who needs you?" and "drop dead." By the time Froggy came on Thursday night, Claudia was changed into a girl of action, a girl who could roll with the punches and come out swinging.

Froggy came after dinner. Claudia didn't feel like getting out of her shift, but Froggy was a man, after all, and he was coming to her apartment where they would be alone, and she did not want to give him any ideas. So she went with brassiere and girdle and a nice loose sundress and put in the time with the hairbrush. She was going to have to look herself over and take stock since the USS Claudia Wyler was weighing anchor and taking to the high seas again. Hell's bells and oh, phooey.

When she came out of the bedroom, Froggy was looking over the dinner dishes piled up on the cart, and he had that expression on his face like he was looking at the aftermath of the Battle of Waterloo. She thought a smart remark was coming, but he didn't say a thing about it. Maybe he would back off for a while. Dan was his buddy, and he should have known, so he probably felt guilty.

"I don't know if you can afford to keep this up," was all he said.

"I'm not," she said. "There's still some coffee in the carafe. Want some?"

They sat down on the couch and had coffee and got out the Chesterfields and Luckys.

"You look good, Claudia."

"Thanks, Froggy. You're sweet. At least my face is still the same, don't you think?"

"Oh yeah, and you look good—healthy."

"Okay Froggy. Well, on to the lean years."

"You got some papers to show me?"

Claudia cleared the coffee table and went to the bedroom to get two shoeboxes that she put all her bills and papers in. She was more organized than she had let on, but she knew Froggy wanted to help, and she was glad to have him. No matter how bad life could get, you weren't lost if you had a man somewhere in the picture. It did not have to be a romantic man, just some kind of man.

Froggy looked over the bills. Claudia had been going to the hairdresser's. Every week she got a beauty analysis consultation with her beauty team. It was worth the money if she was going to look for a husband, but Froggy said it had to go. The room service from the restaurant had to go, and so did clothes shopping. He said the best part about Hawaii, if you were expecting to be on a limited income, was that you only had to have a one-season wardrobe. That wasn't quite true, but Claudia did not want him thinking she was a clotheshorse.

"Now we'll look at income and available cash," he said. "This is where we see what kind of strategy we need. Let's see what we have here."

He turned to the other shoebox with the bankbooks and money. He looked at the bankbooks first. "You keep it in the mattress, huh?"

"Dan put all his money in the stock market."

"Okay, let's see how much cash you have on hand."

Claudia went ahead of him and lay out the bills from several envelopes and straightened out all the folded corners. He counted out the bills and wrote the number down on his scratch pad.

"What happened to Dan's two hundred?"

"I loaned it out. A hundred of it."

"When?—Well, that doesn't matter. Who'd you loan it to?"

"My girlfriend Mary Ann needed a hundred dollars."

"When are you getting it back?"

"She's really in a bind, Froggy. The landlord raised the rent, and she has a little boy, Edgar Lee."

"Then you aren't getting it back, are you?"

"I guess not."

Froggy considered this as he put his hand to his chin and then ran it through his red cowlick and sighed.

"So you're the one in the tight spot now."

"Nope," she said resolutely. "We have a plan."

"Who is we?"

"Mary Ann and me. She's a nice girl, Froggy. She wouldn't have asked me for the money if she had known about Dan leaving."

Claudia had the percolator going in the kitchen and got up to get them more coffee when the blurp blurps stopped. She heard Froggy call out, "I hope you have a good plan."

Claudia brought out the coffee and the little pitcher of cream and settled into the couch beside Froggy. It was embarrassing how far down into the couch she sank and how high up he was, so she shifted around a little, and Froggy shifted around a little, and they were almost even.

"Here's the plan," she said. "Mary Ann and Edgar Lee and I are moving into the Barrymore down the street. That's the plan. We're going to pool our resources. The rent is only fourteen dollars a month. I mean fourteen for each of us. We have two rooms beside each other."

Froggy was surprised. He didn't know she was a girl of action.

"That's not all set, is it?"

"Yeppers. Mary Ann and Edgar Lee moved in yesterday, and I'm moving in next week when the guy next to her leaves. I still have another two weeks to go here, but I want to grab the room next to Mary Ann. It's all signed, sealed, and digested."

"I think you mean delivered."

"I thought it was digested."

"Well, okay, so what are you going to do then?"

Froggy lit another Chesterfield for Claudia, and she sipped her coffee.

"I don't know," she said. "But I had to get out of here, right?"

"Well, I thought we were going to consider that."

"I'm not stupid, Froggy." She quickly reached over and took his hand. "I wanted you to help me get organized, and I'll need your advice, I really will. But I know I can't stay here. It's much too expensive, and I knew you would bring that up right off the bat, so I put my mind to just that one thing. I thought you'd be impressed."

"Oh, I am."

"I'm not hopeless, am I?"

"No, you're very bright, Claudia. I just thought we could work out something where you didn't have to leave this place after you've gotten used to it. You've had a bad shock, and you need the stability of familiar surroundings. You know."

"What are you talking about, Froggy? I don't have any money."

"I just thought I could help you out for a little while until you were ready to make a change like that."

For the first time, Claudia detected a nervous little quiver in Froggy's voice. She knew the bush he was beating around. She'd had an inkling last Sunday. It didn't matter to him that she had lost her figure, and it didn't matter that he had a something going with Elaine—or maybe he didn't. Maybe he figured he had nothing to lose. But when you have nothing to lose, you're not supposed to care if your shot in the dark doesn't hit a target.

She wasn't going to start anything with Froggy. It wasn't just being put off by the red hair, the white skin and freckles. She might be able to live with that. It was a worse problem. She liked him, but she couldn't imagine loving him. He would be the one taking notes on her likes and dislikes, not her. She wouldn't have to bother. But that went back to his looks. The zing wasn't there. She couldn't help that. The zing is the reason you mate with someone. She wasn't a girl who zinged for red hair, white skin, and orange freckles. He'd have better luck in Ireland. Anyway, it was wrong what people did to each other, when they knew they could have helped it by not getting involved in the first place.

"I'm kind of off men right now, Froggy. You know?" Claudia stretched up to the coffee table to put out her Chesterfield and looked into Froggy's eyes. It was good to know that she could be serious with Froggy.

"It was just an idea. That's all. I didn't know if you could pull yourself together."

"I'm all right," she said. "I guess Dan wasn't the one. How did girlfriend number two take it?"

"Not bad. She was only in it for the money, so the two bills cheered her up."

Claudia could laugh at that, so Froggy did too, and it got them back on track.

"Dan should have left you $200 for doing the dirty work, Froggy."

"You would think so, right?" he said. "I should have gotten combat pay. That's why I've always avoided beautiful women. They're much too volatile."

"That's been a big problem for you, hasn't it?"

"Yes, indeed. Starlets, models, bombshells—I do my best to stay out of serious relationships with them. They get too passionate."

"They can't help themselves."

"Is that it? They can't help themselves around me?"

"Oh yes, Froggy. They're powerless against the surging tides of attraction."

"You're speaking now as a bombshell, right?"

"Strictly professionally, yes. Ask me anything."

"What's not to like about me?"

Claudia dropped the game and put her hand over his on the couch.

"You're sweet, Froggy."

Claudia took her hand away, and he took another puff of his Lucky and a thoughtful sip of his coffee.

"Nobody seems to get too passionate over sweet," he said.

"Somebody will, someday."

"I hope I live that long," he said.

Froggy said he had been up to see her at the little white house a few times, but she was never home. Claudia had a bottle of brandy, and they drank half of it while Claudia told him about her job at the filling station and learning about cars and the Grand Hawaiian and dishes. He was so surprised. He said he never would have figured her for a mechanic. He didn't have much to say about Elaine. He made it sound like she just liked going somewhere on Saturday nights. When it got late and he had to go, Claudia remembered what she wanted to say when he was talking about Elaine. She thought it would boost his self-confidence.

"You looked cute in the big shirt the other day, and those white shorts," she said.

"You looked cute, too," he said.

"I don't remember what I had on."

"Your robe."

"No, I put something on after that."

"I only remember the robe."

Claudia gave him a little hug at the door, and he went weaving a little down the hall. It wouldn't be hard to be close friends with Froggy and keep everything else at arm's length. The only two things she would have to remember were not to lead him on and not to take advantage. When he turned the corner at the end of the hallway, she closed the door and leaned back against it for a moment, thinking.

"Can you do that Claudia, old chum?" she said to herself.

CHAPTER TWENTY-SEVEN

A couple of trips over to the Barrymore with Mary Ann's car took care of the moving. She could have stayed longer at the Captain Cook, but Mary Ann and Edgar Lee brought some life to the Barrymore that made the apartment at the Captain Cook feel so lonely, so Claudia decided to just make the move.

They were rooms 216 and 218. Claudia could knock on the wall any time and go in to see Mary Ann. Her hot plate was always going, and the whole second floor smelled good, with tomato sauce and garlic and basil and onions. It wasn't a house by the beach, that's for sure, but they kept up their spirits having each other. Edgar Lee missed Petey. Mary Ann had to give him to the Prestons, who lived two doors down. Distraction was the key. You walked out the door of the Barrymore, and the whole busy, bustling city was right there, and Edgar Lee took to it right away. Mary Ann let him walk around the block by himself, and he picked up a couple of little kid friends. He was almost seven and didn't need so much watching, especially in a city with all the people around.

Edgar Lee had big stacks of comic books. In the little white house, he would sit on the toilet and read them for an hour at a time, but he would not be able to do that at the Barrymore. He didn't like the men's bathroom, but they figured it was just because he wasn't used to men. Claudia or Mary Ann would watch him go down the hall in his little bathrobe, holding his soap and his towel. He would look from side to side down the hallway when he got there and knock on the door before he went in. He would take care of business, have a quick shower, and come running back, mostly wet. If a man came along when Edgar Lee was in the bathroom, either Claudia or Mary Ann would run down to head him off and say "Edgar Lee is in there!" That's because Edgar Lee would be too scared to say anything if somebody knocked on the door, and the man might think there was someone dead in there.

They sold the car for fifty dollars. Mary Ann could walk to work, and they needed the money more than they needed the car since they were right in town. The only thing Mary Ann did wrong was to give the money to the church. Edgar Lee started at the Catholic school a few blocks away, and every morning Mary Ann walked him over and went to mass to light candles and put money in the box. Then she came home and slept until ten o'clock, when Claudia came in and made breakfast while she got ready to go to work. She wanted Claudia to come back to work at the Grand Hawaiian, but Claudia was determined not to go backward.

"We'd do better with two of us working," said Mary Ann. "We could save money then. I thought that was the idea of pooling our resources, like you said."

"You can see it from a different angle too, Mary Ann. The advantage is that one working frees the other one up to think of good ideas."

"So you're the brains of the outfit."

"That's right. Eggs on toast again?"

"Sure." Mary Ann got out the plates and silverware. "So, when are you going to start thinking, Mister Brains?"

"Oh, I already am. I'm going over to the Palmetto club tonight."

"Not that again."

"It worked once, didn't it?"

"There was one little fly in the ointment, as I recall," said Mary Ann.

"This time I'm going to check their references. You never know, Mary Ann, I might meet someone who would be perfect for you. Wouldn't that be great?"

"Just so you hold the reception at the Grand Hawaiian so I can get into my rubber boots and punch in if it doesn't pan out."

"Stop being so negative, Mary Ann. I'll get someone nice. You have to trust my judgment."

"No marines, please. I want someone who's starting with a life expectancy of more than zero."

"If you really cared about true love, it wouldn't matter. I mean, just look at Jack and me. If your love is true, it will go on until the end of time. That's what you should be looking for in a man."

It was so nice having breakfast with Mary Ann every day. They always found something to talk about. They had been through some things together, but they had come through, better than ever. Claudia cleared the dishes and got out a couple of nice-looking Chesterfields for their coffee.

"Yeah, well, what good does it do if he kicks the bucket in six months?"

"I'm just saying that you shouldn't limit yourself."

"Okay, then marines are back on the table, but make sure he's the right type, like what you said."

"Oh, Mary Ann. There's no way to tell about that by just looking at a man. You might get one whose love might only last until the mountains fall into the sea and the sun no longer shines, but that's not eternity."

"How can you tell the difference?"

"You can't."

"Well, then, just get me one with a big you-know-what."

"You can't tell about that either."

"Oh, sure you can," said Mary Ann. "You can tell."

"Oh bull, Mary Ann. How?"

"You can just tell. That's all."

"Well how?"

"You know, by their build. Big guys have little weenies, little guys have big weenies. Then there's variations. You think they can't tell about us?"

"That's crazy. What are they going to tell? How big our holes are?"

"No, stupid. The young guys look for girls who are going to be easy, and the old guys can tell who's going to be nothing but trouble. That's what the deal is with men."

Mary Ann looked at her watch. "It's so great being able to stay home till ten of eleven," she said. "You should come back to work, Claudia. We'd have such a great time."

"I want us to go places, Mary Ann." She reached over and held her hand. "We can't go backward. I know it's hard work. You're keeping us going, and now it's my job to think of something so you don't have to keep working so hard. I don't want to let you and Edgar Lee down."

"I know you won't, babe. Okay, we'll give it a chance. But if it doesn't work, you're coming back with me. So, what time are you going?"

"I can put Edgar Lee to bed first, and then I'll go about nine. I'll just tap on the wall if I'm late."

"I don't care how late it is, I want to know what happened, so come over."

"Okay, but nothing might happen. You don't get a buffalo every time you drop your line in the water, you know."

The Palmetto club was eight blocks away. Claudia did not want to get all sweaty, so she walked as far as the Grand Hawaiian and took a cab from there. It was a little disappointing when she got to the Palmetto because the club was only about half full and the crowd looked disappointed that they weren't more of a crowd. People were at the tables and the bar, some dancing and milling around, but there was an unusual amount of space around each person. There was more excitement and energy to the place when you were packed in like sardines.

A single girl didn't just roam around, so Claudia went right to the bar and ordered a daiquiri, and sure enough, it was not long before Mr. Anthony slid out of the darkness. She was glad to get it over with on the first night.

"Hi, Mr. Anthony," she said. "I come in a lot with my friends. I'm Claudia Wyler. I don't know if you remember me."

Mr. Anthony put his fingers to the knot of his tie and then pointed at her in a recollective gesture.

"You come in with your husband, the dark, quiet gentleman."

"Oh, no. My husband was killed."

Mr. Anthony looked shocked. "Just recently?"

"No, that was two years ago. In the attack. The one you're thinking of was just a friend. He's been transferred back to the States."

"Condolences all the same."

"Have you seen any of my crowd tonight?"

"I'm afraid—"

"Oh, I'm sorry. You wouldn't know. You have so many people to remember. I could never run a big club like this."

"I've no doubt someone will come along. It should pick up any time now. In any case, I hope you'll stay for the late show. We've got something new that I think you'll like. The Palmetto Review."

Mr. Anthony touched her shoulder and drifted along down the bar, and Claudia settled in to wait. That's the only thing you can do when you're bait. You just sit there and try to keep the hook under cover. She smoothed her dress down. It was a light-purple A-line with a black sash. She had taken out the shoulder pads to allow for her new bust measurement, but it was hard not to look one hundred and eighty pounds, sitting on a bar stool.

Mr. Anthony still gave her the creeps, but she was catching on that he was all business, and he was right about it picking up. People were starting to come in from dinner and drinking at other places, and the Palmetto was filling up like a big vat of perfume, flowers, cigarette smoke, aftershave, and Tennessee bourbon, barrels and all. The place was as noisy as a thousand people talking in her ear at the same time.

There was a captain who bought her two drinks who said she reminded him of his wife back in the States. The next one reminded her of Mary Ann's Bill, one of those guys who was in the navy for twenty years and looked a little beat. She waited for the limpy conversation to drop dead and said, "Well thanks for the drink."

Then a good prospect came along—right age, nice face, good build. She never thought about the size of a man's thing until Mary Ann said you could always tell. How the hell did she know? He sat down and lit her Chesterfield. Wedding ring. Claudia sensed that he wanted to cheat on his wife in the worst way, but he was going to have to be dragged into it against his will. "Thanks for the drink."

Claudia made a deadline for herself at twelve o'clock. If no one good came along by then, she was going to leave. She was working on her sixth gin and tonic. Six free and the daiquiri she started with. At almost twelve, she lit her last Chesterfield and looked down into the ashtray in front of her and started singing over and over to herself the line "gonna dance with the one that brung me."

All of a sudden the lights went dim, and Mr. Anthony was on stage in a spotlight, quelling the noise and introducing his Palmetto Review. The curtain behind him went up with a flourish from the band, and Claudia was astonished to see a magnificent chorus line of girls poised for a number. There were twelve of them, in grass brassieres and grass skirts. They were tall and bosomy, and Claudia wondered where Mr. Anthony had found so many pretty girls. The bandleader kept looking at Mr. Anthony while a thunderous applause rose, and at a signal from Mr. Anthony as he stepped aside, the band ripped into it, and the girls took off. It was spectacular, just spectacular.

Mary Ann must have been waiting up, looking out the window, because she helped Claudia out of the cab when she got back to the Barrymore and almost had to carry her up the stairs. That's all Claudia could remember in the morning, but she woke up after eleven, and Mary Ann was already gone. She remembered peeing in her pants in the cab, but the ones she had on were dry, so Mary Ann must have done that, and the brassiere she was in was the one she always slept in. Dear Mary Ann.

The first battle of the campaign had not gone well. Mary Ann probably figured that out. Claudia got up and started the coffee. There was one of those little bottles of Jack Daniel's that she picked up on the train to San Francisco when she and Jack were heading for his new assignment at Pearl, and she dug it up to have with her first Chesterfield while the percolator went through its blurp blurps.

Claudia knew she was going to have to think this out better. She couldn't go to the club on Friday or Saturday nights because she didn't want to run into anyone she knew. Only Froggy would know what she was doing there alone, but she didn't want to waste all the time and trouble of an appearance on a night she couldn't hunt. That left her with five nights, but she felt better. Lots of people have five-day work weeks. The whiskey tasted pretty good with her Chesterfield.

A month went by. At least it turned out she wasn't pregnant. Claudia was cheerful with Mary Ann and Edgar Lee, but privately she was getting discouraged. She got her drinking under control with a little whiskey every morning before breakfast. Regulating it like medicine and taking it at the right time were essential. Then she picked up a few bottles of Jack Daniel's and a bottle of Listerine so that Mary Ann wouldn't notice she'd been drinking a little when she was over there. Every night she tapped on the wall, two little soft taps that bespoke a girl in control. No more peeing in taxicabs. After a while, Mary Ann did not wait up anymore.

Another month went by, and Claudia had to borrow her fourteen dollars from Mary Ann for the rent. Mr. Anthony must have talked to the bartender because her first drink was free now, and she had breakfast at Mary Ann's and always ate something when she made dinner for Edgar Lee, so there was no excuse. Her only expenses were the Jack Daniel's and Listerine and cab fare. There was no way around what was looking more and more like failure. As little as she was eating, she could not cross the 180 line. No baby either. Maybe it was time to raise the white flag and march out of the fort, but what would she do then? Mary Ann would get her back at the Grand Hawaiian. Then they were lost.

It was a low point. Monday night. Claudia was down in the dumps. She'd had four gin and tonics, not a single man had come along, and the gin wasn't getting along with the whiskey she'd had in the back of the cab on the way over. A sailor sat down on the stool beside her, but Claudia was looking the other way and the periphery of her vision gave her the impression of a kid climbing into a barber chair.

"Hi," he said.

Claudia looked sideways at him. "Hi, kid."

"Can I buy you a drink?"

"No, thanks. I'm over my limit."

"I guess it's hard meeting nice people here," he said. "You should go to the library or a museum."

"They don't serve drinks."

For a moment he didn't know what to say, and since Claudia was getting ready to give up and leave, she wasn't particularly interested in getting him going.

"I'm John Wales," he said.

"I'm Claudia."

Now she knew what was going on. There was a table of young sailor boys a few rows in from the dance floor, and when she glanced over in their direction, they put their heads down. The empty chair at the table was where John Wales came from. He looked like a kid with a fresh haircut off to summer camp, but he must have been a least eighteen because he was in the navy.

"Are you waiting for anybody?" he asked.

"Mr. Right," she said.

"I've been looking at you all night. You're really beautiful."

"Thanks, buddy." Claudia turned to look him over a little more and felt the inclination to be rude and snippy going away. She was just discouraged and disappointed. She was letting Mary Ann and Edgar Lee down, but that wasn't anybody's fault but her own, and she shouldn't take it out on a kid.

"I wanted to ask you out," he said.

"You mean ask me on a date?"

"Well, yeah. I guess."

"Where to? What do you feel like doing?"

John Wales looked like he might be losing his nerve. The bartender came over, and he ordered a rum and coke for himself and another of what Claudia had.

"Did you want to have a date next week or something?"

"No," he said. "I was wondering, you know, maybe tonight."

"The library and the museums are closed now, John Wales."

"I thought maybe we could—you know, go to your place."

That made Claudia smile. "Oh," she said. "Then you do know what you want to do, don't you? You were just being a gentleman. Well, I hate to tell you, John Wales, but it costs twenty dollars."

"I got a twenty," he said quickly.

Claudia really didn't want to drink anymore, but it was in front of her, and the conversation was getting interesting.

"You have twenty dollars? On you?"

"Yeah." He fished into his pants and took out a folded bill with the number showing in the corner.

"Cab fare too?"

"Yep," he said and pulled out another little fold of ones.

"Do you want a date with me then?"

"Yeah."

"You sure?"

"Yeah."

"You're on, John Wales."

Claudia took the twenty and unfolded it. She was going to put it in her brassiere because she always wanted to try that, but she changed her mind. She called the bartender over and asked him for two tens. He had to go to Mr. Anthony, who was standing by the side steps to the stage. Claudia watched them put their heads together, and Mr. Anthony went into the pocket of his striped jacket, and they exchanged bills. The two tens were crisp new ones without a fold or a crease on them. She wouldn't have been surprised if Mr. Anthony had just run them off in the back office.

"I want to wait a minute," she said. "Drink up and have a smoke."

Claudia gave him one of her Chesterfields, and he lit up like he knew what he was doing. She looked around and sipped at her gin and tonic, waiting for a good time to make a break for it. John Wales looked like his Adam's apple was giving him trouble, and the end of his Chesterfield was jittering over the ashtray. She wanted to get out without his table of buddies seeing them. It was a good crowd now. The lights went down, and all eyes went to the stage, where the curtain was going up for the Hula Girls.

"Let's go," she said.

It took him by surprise, and he fumbled getting off the stool, and then he tried to go back to put out his cigarette. Claudia had to grab him by the arm.

"Leave it there," she said.

Claudia got them through the crowd and out the door. A cab swooped in and picked them up, and ten minutes later they were walking down the dark quiet hall of the second floor of the Barrymore and slipping in the door of 216. She turned on the light on the table and put a kitchen towel over the shade, and the room turned a subdued brown. She led John Wales over to the bed and started undressing him. She could hear him swallowing.

"This is the kind of date you had in mind, isn't it?"

"Yeah," he said. "I guess so."

John Wales was standing like a statue, but then he came around and helped her get that tight navy shirt over his head. Then there were all those buttons on the pants. His briefs were civilian, and nice ones. It was amazing how the right weave of cotton could stretch, she thought. It really was a miracle fiber, just like they said, providing matchless style, perfect fit, and money-saving economy. Claudia was looking for the label on the band as she pulled them down, and his thing almost hit her in the face. She didn't want to touch anything yet.

He got his shoes off by himself, and she pulled the cover, blanket, and top sheet all the way off the bed. She sat him down and turned to have him unzip her dress. The last thing would be the brassiere, she decided, so she slipped out of her panties and got on the bed in front of him, and when the straps came off and the white brassiere fell, John Wales started squirting. He had a look on his face like he had run two blocks to catch a bus and just missed it.

Claudia knew she shouldn't laugh, but she had all those gin and tonics under her belt. She waited for him to stop and asked if he thought he could do it again in the right place. It was only fair. He said yes, so she lay down, and after a little bit he got on top of her, and she felt she really earned the money that night because she had to show him how to do everything.

CHAPTER TWENTY-EIGHT

One thing Claudia learned about the young first-timers, they could usually muster up if they goofed the first time. It was just messy, and she had to ask for an additional twenty-five cents to cover the extra laundry. She seemed to attract the young sailors. Maybe she reminded them of a girl in high school. There were lots of girls in high school who hadn't lost their baby fat. Their imaginations wouldn't know the difference.

Claudia always got her twenty dollars up front. That was the best part, but it was also kind of sad. The bills were always folded as tight and flat as they could be, sometimes with tape marks on them. Claudia imagined those sailors' moms, working at Woolworth's or cleaning houses or washing dishes in a restaurant, saving every penny for the day when they could go to the bank and turn in all that hard-earned loose stuff for a twenty-dollar bill. Then it got folded up tight and flat and put in a letter. It must have made the mothers feel they had done everything they could for their boys far away. That twenty-dollar bill could get them home when the war was over. Wherever they might be when the music stopped, they could get home, like Ashley Wilkes coming home from the war on the dusty road, dirty and ragged, but home. The moms thought the twenty-dollar bills would bring their boys home alive. Claudia knew because she would have thought that too.

They were the moms who had not flushed their babies down the toilet, and the boys in the sailor suits were their babies grown up. With the young ones, Claudia could feel she was helping them with their education about women and relieving them of the terrible stress of innocence and inexperience. She could be kind and gentle and show them what women liked. The older males were more dangerous, and she had to watch her step. It was like the animal kingdom. Either way, she worked hard to please, and she always changed the twenty-dollar bills from the young ones for two tens at the bar to keep from thinking about the moms and how many of their boys might not be walking down the dusty road home.

Claudia cut out most of the drinking after John Wales. She did not want to do it that way, and she didn't want to go on without thinking about what she was doing. It looked like the only way she had, and she didn't have to give up the idea of finding a husband while she was at it. It was just a job.

She had a family now, Mary Ann and Edgar Lee, and she had to make a decent living to support them.

Men worked. All men worked. Some of them had bad jobs, but they remembered the Depression, and they didn't gripe. They worked in sewers or garbage dumps or slaughterhouses. There were men who had the job of bashing cows on the head with sledgehammers and cutting off the heads of chickens and bleeding hung-up pigs to death. How could you not hurt in your soul if you had a job like that? But they had to feed their families, and they had to do what it takes. That was the only way to think about it. It was the only way to get her and Mary Ann and Edgar Lee to a better life.

It was a rare night that at least one man did not come home with her from the Palmetto club. Most nights it was two, sometimes three, and one night she did four. That was eight trips in the taxi. She wished she could have given the business to Takeo, but she did not want him to lose respect for her. Funny thing though, when she thought about who might lose respect for her, she knew, ironically enough, Takeo would be the last one.

Claudia went to work her five nights a week after she made dinner for Edgar Lee and put him to bed. Either she got the men in and out early, before Mary Ann got home at eleven or eleven thirty, or she stalled off until after twelve, when she knew Mary Ann would be asleep. Then she was in the clear. The Palmetto closed at 2 a.m. Once in a while Mary Ann would say "I heard you last night," and Claudia would have to confess that her fictional new boyfriend, Lieutenant Reed, had come up to the room, and he was pushing his luck a little. Mary Ann warned her about giving too much away if she really wanted this guy to marry her.

The twist to that was what she was giving away and who she was giving it to. She was making big money now, sometimes $200 a week, and she started putting some in the jar Mary Ann kept in her cupboard for food and rent. When Mary Ann figured it out, Claudia just said Keith—that was his name—was aware of her circumstances and was very generous. It kind of irked her to think that every day Mary Ann walked Edgar Lee to school, the church was making big money too.

"I guess if he can afford to go to the club five nights a week, he must be loaded," said Mary Ann.

"His dad owns a factory in Cleveland and has a big war contract."

"I thought you said he was from Richmond."

"Oh, he is. They just keep the factory in Cleveland," said Claudia.

It was tough keeping the story straight because Mary Ann had a good memory and asked questions about him. Claudia would forget from one day to the next what she had said. The persistent question was "So when am I going to meet Mister Moneybags?"

One night a banquet at the hotel was postponed, and Larry said he could handle the rest of the night. So Mary Ann came home full of beans at nine thirty, thinking she could go along to the club. There was no way around it. Claudia had to come up with a strategy for the night while Mary Ann flew through the shower. There was nothing jazzy enough in her closet, so they went over to Claudia's. When something she tried on was too big for her, Mary Ann said she didn't think the color was right for her or something else was wrong, but Claudia knew what she was doing. She was bigger than Mary Ann now.

It was a big change of plans for Claudia. What was she going to do if one of her regulars came in looking for her? Mary Ann was running over with excitement. She had never been to the Palmetto and was acting like she had never been in a taxi either. She said Bill never took her out.

"Oh, gosh," she said. "It must be ten years."

She flopped back in the seat of the cab and closed her eyes with pleasure.

"I think I'm hearing the thunder of buffaloes," she said.

Claudia did not know what she was going to do when they got to the club, but at least Mary Ann was finally getting the right idea about buffaloes.

It was pretty crowded for a Wednesday night. Claudia took Mary Ann through to the tables.

"They don't reserve tables here," she said. "It's hit-and-miss, unless you know Mr. Anthony. Keith and I always sit over there."

Claudia threaded her way between tables to a small corner almost hidden by a column and a potted palm.

"You can hardly tell there's a table back here," said Mary Ann.

"Keith will find us if he's here tonight. This is where we always sit."

"But you can't see anything from here."

"Do you want to meet Keith or not?"

Mary Ann sat down in a bit of a huff. "Well, I wanted to have fun too, you know."

She bumped her chair around the column a little so she could see the stage. The nearest waiter looked a mile away over the tables and dance floor, but Claudia caught his attention with a wave, and soon they had some drinks sitting on little cocktail napkins in front of them.

"You think he's going to find us here?"

"If he comes in tonight," said Claudia. "He might not be able to get off. Some nights I wait hours, and he doesn't show. It's unpredictable. He's very important in communications."

"I thought he was in intelligence."

"Oh—that's what they call it now. Intelligent communications. Sometimes he gets phone calls here and has to leave."

"So what do you do then?"

"I just come home."

"So you think he's the one?"

"He's perfect."

Mary Ann fixed her gaze on something, but Claudia couldn't see what it was around the column.

"That isn't him, is it?"

"No," said Claudia.

"You didn't even look—but don't look now. He's coming over here."

A good-looking man in a tuxedo was making his way across the floor between the tables, and he did seem intent upon getting to the corner where they were. When he got to the column, he put his hands on it as if he had been hiding behind it and peeked around.

"Good evening, ladies," he said. "Getting away from it all?"

"Oh, no," Claudia said. "We're waiting for someone."

"At a table for two?"

"It's just my date."

"How fortunate," he said, focusing his attention on Mary Ann. "Then might I ask you to dance?"

"I'd love to," said Mary Ann, lighting up like a Christmas tree.

She stood up, and with her back to the gentleman she raised her eyebrows at Claudia and asked her to watch her purse.

Claudia sat back behind the column with her gin and tonic and thought to herself, well whaddya know. It showed you the reason for advertising. Mary Ann only had her head sticking out from behind the column and the palm tree, and a handsome man had spotted her from all the way across the tables and dance floor. It was like All-Bran. She probably never would have tried All-Bran if they hadn't run the ad in *Life* with the cute cartoon of *The*

Captain and The Kids. "Himmell! Dis suff oxplodes!" Claudia moved over to Mary Ann's chair and hung her head out, just for the hell of it, to see if lightning would strike twice, and she saw Mr. Anthony headed her way. But when he got to the column, he wasn't fooling around.

"May I join you?" he asked, but he sat down without giving her a chance to answer.

"Mrs. Wyler—"

"Mr. Anthony."

"We seem to be seeing a lot of you lately."

"I like it here. And you've been so nice about the drinks."

"We're glad to have attractive ladies frequent the establishment."

Claudia took out a Chesterfield, and he immediately went to his pocket and produced a gold lighter with a nice jet flame.

"I'd like to ask you, though, if you don't think you might be spending too much time with us."

"I'm looking for a husband, Mr. Anthony," she said. "To be perfectly honest about it. The war isn't going to last forever, you know, and all these men will be going home. I want to go home with one of them. And your club is—well, it's the center of everything around here. Everyone comes here. It's the perfect place to meet someone."

"I thank you for the compliment," he said. "I was concerned for you because it did not escape my notice that you have been conducting interviews for the position you hope to fill."

"I guess you could say that, yes."

"A great number of interviews in fact."

"You can't let a good prospect slip through your fingers."

"No, of course not, but some of the men you've interviewed really do not look suitable. You are not alone here in your wish to find a husband, Mrs. Wyler. There are many women who come here with that intention, and on their behalf, I must let you know that I have received a number of complaints."

"Complaints?"

"They feel you are conducting too many interviews. Perhaps they feel you may be leading on some gentlemen who would otherwise avail themselves of other opportunities."

"I'm awfully sorry," said Claudia. "I didn't think it would cause anyone distress."

"But what would anyone expect? You are a very beautiful woman and certainly sure to draw the attention of men. That cannot be helped, but it was not really a significant problem until tonight."

Mr. Anthony then seemed to become deeply thoughtful, and his dark eyebrows met over lowered eyes. He touched the tip of his finger to the thin line of his pencil mustache and ran it down to the corner of his mouth.

"Your friend is very attractive as well," he said, "and we are concerned that if she is also looking for a husband as diligently as you—well, there won't be enough available men to go around. You must surely understand."

"Oh, Mr. Anthony," Claudia said. "There's a misunderstanding I must clear up. Mary Ann isn't here to find a husband. She has someone she's nuts about. She just wanted to get out for a night and have some fun, and I've told her so much about the club. She'd die if she thought anybody thought she was interviewing for a husband. She's dancing with a gentleman right now, but she'll discourage him. Don't worry."

"Well, that is certainly nice to know. I'm glad we had a chance to talk frankly with each other, Mrs. Wyler. And I'm sure you understand my position."

"Oh, I do," said Claudia. "Completely."

"And I was wondering," he went on, "since we are speaking so honestly, if I might ask how long you think it might take you to secure a good prospect."

"I really couldn't say, Mr. Anthony. It could happen tomorrow, or then again, I might have to keep looking for a long time."

"I suppose what I really mean to ask is, how many nights a week do you anticipate for this campaign?"

"Oh, I'm not sure. Maybe three or four?"

"Could you make it two?"

"All right. I guess two would be manageable."

Mr. Anthony smiled warmly.

"Thank you so much, Mrs. Wyler. You know I am only the messenger in this kind of thing, and I'm so glad I can return with a favorable report. Thank you."

That part was a lie. You could tell Mr. Anthony was the boss. It just made it easier for him to say he wasn't. He was good at getting to the point, though, and she wasn't stupid. She didn't have to get hit over the head, and she didn't want Mary Ann getting hit over the head either. It dawned on her then that Mister Tuxedo was a decoy.

Mary Ann came off the dance floor head over heels, but her new boyfriend left pretty much the same way Mr. Anthony did. Claudia told her not to get her hopes up too high. It was almost eleven thirty, and Claudia convinced her that Lieutenant Keith Reed wasn't going to make it. Mary Ann had already had two drinks and enough to dream on her pillow about, so she didn't fuss. They walked home for the fresh air and the lights and the cars going by and the wind blowing the palm trees around, and Mary Ann was seeing stars all the way.

CHAPTER TWENTY-NINE

June came, and then everyone was celebrating the big D-Day in France, on the other side of the world. It looked like more people were getting killed than usual on this side of the world too. After a worrisome delay, *Life* finally found her at the Barrymore, and there were a few past issues to catch up with, which provided a helpful distraction for Mary Ann, who wanted to go back to the Palmetto and kept asking questions about Lieutenant Reed. It was getting complicated.

Early one morning Claudia heard someone pounding on Mary Ann's door. She went out to the hallway and found Richard the petty officer making all the noise.

"You stop that," she said. "What's the big idea, waking everybody up?"

"I want to talk to Mary Ann. I know she's in there."

"No, she's not. You're scaring Edgar Lee. You just stop that right now."

Claudia pushed Richard away from the door. He was a big man and her hands sank into the stomach part of his uniform. He said "Ooff—" and his hat fell off. Claudia shouted into the door, "Don't be scared, Edgar Lee. I'm out here. I'll send the man away."

"I know she's in there."

"No, she's not. Now you get going."

"Not 'til I've talked to Mary Ann."

"She doesn't want to see you. She told me that."

"I don't believe you."

Claudia pushed him again. She wanted to keep him moving and not let him think they were going to have a talk about it. She didn't know what was going on, and she didn't want to come on too strong if Mary Ann really wanted him.

"Just get out of here," she said. "Get going."

"I only want to talk to her."

"I can take a message."

"No, I want Mary Ann."

"She'll be mad if you scare Edgar Lee. If you go away now, I promise I'll give her the message."

Richard stopped pushing back against her and looked at his watch.

"Okay, I'll go, but tell her to wait for me tonight when she gets off work, okay? I just want to talk to her, and I'll leave her alone if she wants, but I have to talk to her, okay? I'll come to the back steps where she goes to smoke, okay?"

"Okay okay," said Claudia. "I got it."

Before he picked up his hat and walked down the hall, he made her say the message back to him twice. That's the navy for you.

Claudia knocked softy on the door when she was sure Richard was gone, and Mary Ann let her in. Edgar Lee was sitting like a stone at the table on the kitchen side of the room.

"You're very brave, Edgar Lee," she said. She knew that Edgar Lee looked up to her and that she inspired confidence. He was at the age when he would have been looking up to Bill if he were around. She was the next best thing. Probably better.

"What was that all about, Mary Ann?"

"A misunderstanding," she said.

Mary Ann made eyes at her that they couldn't talk until Edgar Lee was off to school. He was all ready to go in his little gray blazer with the emblem of Our Lady of Good Counsel on the breast pocket. He had a light green shirt and a darker green, little-boy tie that was only about a foot long when you stretched it out to tie around his collar. Mary Ann put a white scarf over her head for Mass and looked at herself in the mirror on the wall beside the door. Then she went to the cupboard to get money out of the jar. Claudia turned away because she didn't want to get aggravated seeing any big bills coming out.

"I won't be long," she said. "Will you be around?"

"Just bang on the wall."

"Okay. Thanks, Claudia."

Claudia went back to her room and got the percolator going. It was only a quarter to eight. Most mornings she got up around nine or ten, depending on how late she was up and if it were a club night or not. She remembered the Captain Cook when she stayed up all night and slept all day. Last month's *Reader's Digest* said you can't change your sleep schedule after the age of twenty-four, and here she was twenty-six. Thinking about it made her want to have coffee and a Chesterfield and count her money to make herself feel better. She got the Campbell's soup can out of the cupboard and sat down with her coffee and Chesterfields. She didn't want to begrudge Mary Ann anything, but there would have been so much more if she hadn't given it away to the church. Private school for Edgar Lee was bad enough. She didn't even want to think about it. What the hell was wrong with Mary Ann?

Claudia counted $1,200 dollars. It was more money than she had ever saved up on her own. They needed to get ahead, and now Mr. Anthony was telling her she could only come two nights a week. That was a serious blow. It meant that she'd have to push hard on her two nights. For all Mr. Anthony knew, she was just doing it for fun, like a hobby. That's what people think when they see you going beneath your dignity. They wouldn't believe you would stoop so low for real.

Claudia put the Campbell's soup can back and pulled out her pile of back issues of *Life* to see if she had missed anything. No letup in the war. The new B-29s had enough range to get to Japan now. There were pictures of them being built in the factories, and most of the jobs were done by girls. There were no jobs like that around here. Before she knew it, there was a tap on the wall. Mary Ann was back. They had a nice little breakfast and got down to coffee and Chesterfields.

"I'm sorry about this morning," said Mary Ann.

"You heard the message, didn't you?"

"Yeah, three times."

"Are you going to talk to him?"

"I guess I have to."

"Just tell him he's a creep and say get lost."

"But that's the problem," she said. "He's not a creep. He's a wonderful man."

"You mean like this morning."

Mary Ann leaned over the table in earnest.

"He's not like that, Claudia. He was only that way because—"

"Because what? You haven't said a word about this guy for months."

"Because I broke it off. That's why."

"Well, thanks for telling me. I didn't even know you were an item, and now you're not."

"I thought you knew something was going on."

"I just knew about the gasoline."

"There was more to it."

Claudia could see Mary Ann was having a rough time getting to the point. Something was up. Mary Ann had a lot of savvy about the bottom strata of life. Somebody like Mr. Tuxedo at the club might throw her off, but Richard the petty officer shouldn't. Something was definitely up with Mary Ann. She just wasn't her old self.

"So why did you break up with him?"

"It's best for him."

"Well, what about you?"

Mary Ann had started to sniffle, and the tears were coming to her eyes.

"He's married, Claudia. I knew it from the start. I shouldn't have let anything—now he wants to divorce his wife. He's Catholic too. It's a sin, Claudia. He can't divorce his wife. And guess what?"

Mary Ann stood up and came around to Claudia's side of the table. She smoothed her dress over her belly. There was nothing to see, but suddenly everything with Mary Ann made sense.

"Oh God, Mary Ann."

"I went too far with him once. I didn't mean to. It just happened. He doesn't know about it. I don't want to take the chance of him finding out—that's why I don't want to see him."

Mary Ann burst into tears, and Claudia put her arms around her with her face sideways against her belly. She could feel Mary Ann's tears falling on the top of her head.

"It'll be all right. It'll be all right. We'll do fine, Mary Ann, don't worry."

When Mary Ann recovered herself, she went back to her chair and drank some more coffee and lit up another Chesterfield without remembering the one in the ashtray.

"I was thinking," she said. "I was thinking Benito and I might get together."

"Who the hell is Benito?"

"You know. The guy at the club."

"You're crazy, Mary Ann."

"No, I have a good feeling about it."

"From dancing with him one time?"

"No, it was two dances."

"Oh, excuse me then."

"Don't be that way, Claudia. We talked about everything under the sun, and I just have a good feeling about him. That's why I want to get back to the club so much."

"Well, you can't. At least not for him."

"I don't know why you're so dead set against it."

"He's married. That's why."

Mary Ann stared at her in disbelief.

"I asked Froggy about him. You know. The guy with the red hair? I didn't want to tell you. Honest, I didn't. I thought it would blow over. He's been with lots of girls. He's no good."

They were all lies, but there wasn't any other way. Mary Ann just stared into space. At least she wasn't crying anymore. Claudia reached over and stroked her hair, and after a few minutes her mind was back on its feet. Mary Ann sat back in the chair, took a big drag off her Chesterfield and blew the smoke out her nose.

"Well, so much for that half-assed idea." It was the last words of the old Mary Ann, and then the whole thing collapsed. "What am I going to do, Claudia?" she said. "In a couple of months, I won't be able to hide it, and I'll lose my job. What am I going to do then?"

"We'll get along. Don't worry."

"How can you say that? You don't have a job either."

"I've got Keith in the background."

"You can't keep taking money from him, Claudia. If he's not going to marry you, it's not right. It's a sin, I think."

It was hard for Claudia to hold her tongue when it came to Mary Ann and her new preoccupation with sin. It was just the money. They could be frugal all they wanted, but most of the money Claudia slipped Mary Ann from the fictitious Lieutenant Keith Reed was going out the door on Mary Ann's layaway plan for sins and misdemeanors. She did not want to see what was left in the jar in Mary Ann's cupboard. She just knew from a quick glance whenever she put more in, that there was hole in the bucket.

Claudia brought up going back to the States once, because it crossed her mind. Mary Ann said everyone she knew in South Philly wasn't there anymore or was dead. Her little sister, who was really her daughter, lived in Oklahoma with her husband and a new baby, so she was actually a grandmother. She said maybe someday but not now. Hawaii was home.

Claudia felt the same way. She didn't want to go home with her tail between her legs. Larry was that way too, so he washed pots and pans and waited. It wasn't a bad place to sit tight. They said it was going to be a state of the union someday. Then all the misfits would have to find someplace else.

She'd heard some talk around the Palmetto that there would be a land-office business in hotels after the war. That got her thinking about real estate, and she remembered Captain Locarno. They could save up and go in with him. All she had to do was round up enough investment capital and stay one step ahead of Mary Ann and baby-on-the-way. That would be hard to do with only two nights at the club. If they were going to get out of the rut, she was going to have to take a risk. She decided to try for a third night at the Palmetto.

Mr. Anthony did not go for it. Claudia spotted Froggy and Elaine coming in and left her seat at the bar just as Mr. Anthony was leaving his office on a collision course—two points off the starboard bow and closing fast. Annette and a new man were right behind Froggy and Elaine, Fitzy with someone new, and a few new people from the office were tagging along. The night was shot anyway, so Claudia slid into the safety of the convoy and had a few drinks and a few laughs and got to know more people she would have to avoid. So much for a third night at the Palmetto.

Claudia sat out the rest of the week. She got up every morning to make breakfast for Mary Ann and Edgar Lee and got them off in the morning. Then she waited to have coffee with Mary Ann when she got back from walking Edgar Lee and saw her off at eleven. She washed the dishes in the little sink in the corner and cleaned the hot plate and coffee pot, made the bed, and straightened up the corner where Edgar Lee slept cramped up on a baby mattress, and then went back to her room to rest a few hours before it was time to walk Edgar Lee home from school. *Life* magazine came on Wednesday in town. She wrote to Mom and made up good stories about Lieutenant Keith Reed. She didn't know how she was going to get out of that one, but they were fun to write. She counted her money. She had more than $1,500 now. She figured she needed at least $2,000 before she went looking for Captain Locarno, but she knew he must have so much money tied up here that he would finagle a way to stay in Honolulu even if the war ended.

In his escapades out on the streets, Edgar Lee had acquired a best friend named Nick. Three or four times a week, Nick's mom was going to be late getting home from her government job, so he had permission to go to the beach with Edgar Lee. The three of them walked a few blocks to Waikiki and swam and played on the beach for an hour or so. On the way back, they stopped at the market and picked up a bottle of milk and something for dinner. Then Claudia was on the phone at the end of the hall with Nick's mom about who was staying over, who was having dinner, and who was picking up who when. Nick and Edgar Lee played card games and listened to the radio and made a lot of noise. It didn't bother Claudia at all. She liked having them around, and she liked talking to Nick's mom on the phone.

Mary Ann had Wednesdays off and did not know what was going on at home half the time. Claudia had to explain that Nick had to be walked home or Edgar Lee had to be walked home, but sometimes Nick's mom could meet you halfway if it was a Monday or a Thursday. If it was a Tuesday and Nick was going to be over, you could call Nick's mom at work, but only before two o'clock. If you called the office number after two, you only let it ring once and hang up. Then Nick's mom would know.

"Know what?" Mary Ann would say.

And then Claudia would have to start all over again. She knew she couldn't blame Mary Ann. Work was so hard, and every night when she came home, she couldn't find her towel or the spatula or something because Claudia had found a better place to put it. Sometimes she would say, "Where's my damn towel?" and scare Edgar Lee, and sometimes she would just dissolve into tears. The baby was making her more emotional. She couldn't make up her mind about anything, even the smallest things. She was really going to pieces. Claudia tried to be patient with her, but Jesus Christ.

Claudia walked over to the navy base one day and brought home some heavy cardboard they shipped boat parts in and made a fort for Edgar Lee. It was heavy-duty stuff, but she scored it with a knife and folded flaps here and there and cut out gun-slit windows, and when it was tied and taped together, it was such a solid box she could put heavy things on top and make better use of the space. Claudia was on the phone at the end of the hall with Nick's mom that night when Mary Ann came home. Sometimes she and Nick's mom just talked, and she was so involved that she didn't see Mary Ann go in the room, and naturally she banged into Edgar Lee's fort in the dark. She scratched her cornea and had to go to the hospital early the next morning, and for the next four days she had to go to work with a big bandage over one eye. She had the worst luck.

The best times were at night when Mary Ann came home. Claudia fixed her a sandwich, and they talked quietly at the table with a candle between them and their coffee and Chesterfields. Edgar Lee was usually asleep in his fort, but if Nick was over, they would be reading comic books with flashlights. When the little noises out of the fort stopped, Claudia crawled in on all fours to turn off their flashlights. She could take off all their clothes and get them into their pajamas and tucked in without waking either of them up. Mary Ann would be asleep with her head on the table by the time Claudia was done with the boys, so Claudia would get her undressed and to bed too, and in the morning, Claudia was the only one out of the four who could remember how they came to be waking up in their pajamas.

Mary Ann said everyone at work knew that she was expecting, but no one had said anything yet. The baby was only about three months along, and she said she could work fine. But one day she came home early. Mr. Bing had called her up to his office that afternoon and had told her that the Grand Hawaiian had to let her go because of the baby. What they could do, he said, was to give her $7 a week to help cover her expenses, in view of the fact that her husband had been killed in the big attack and she had no other way to support herself. The Grand Hawaiian, he said, would be pleased to have her come back to her job at such time as she was able. In the meanwhile, they would make do with temporary help.

Claudia was so surprised. It meant half of Mary Ann's wages would still be coming in, plus her $5 a month from the navy for Bill. She smiled at Mary Ann in the candlelight when she told her because it meant everyone at the Grand Hawaiian liked her. They didn't have to do anything, but they wanted her to come back, and they wanted to take care of her because they liked her so much.

"Now we'll have more time to do something about your hair, Mary Ann. You'll be so pretty."

"Sez you."

Claudia leaned over the table and stroked her hair. Mary Ann looked so dog-tired from the baby that Claudia knew she could go to sleep in two minutes, so she rousted her up.

"Time for bed," she said, and lifted Mary Ann up from behind.

"Okay, okay."

"Big day tomorrow."

"What's up?"

"I'm going to try fingernail polish. Club night."

"Can I come?"

"They don't let pregnant ladies into the Palmetto. Half the men would run out the back door."

That made Mary Ann laugh, and she let Claudia help her out of her dress and into her nightie. Claudia tucked her in and sat on the bed looking down at her in the dark.

"I'm glad about what happened at the hotel. I'm so proud of you. You got everyone to love you."

She could see Mary Ann smile in the dark. She smoothed her hair and told her she loved her too, and then she tiptoed out so she wouldn't wake up Edgar Lee in his fort.

CHAPTER THIRTY

Claudia had never used fingernail polish before because she grew up thinking it made you look cheap. Well, it does, but the more she thought about it, the more she began to see the value of it in her current working life. The trick was to make astute choices of color and shade—for an effect that would unify other elements of her beauty as she casually ran a hand along her hip or touched her shoulder and allowed her hand to alight at the wavy edge of her hair. She tried to explain it, but Mary Ann did not know what she was talking about. Mary Ann did, however, have years of experience and a great little box of prewar stuff that couldn't be beat.

"Try this one," she said, holding up a bright red.

"No, Mary Ann. You're not listening to me. Why would a man want a girl with what looks like blood on her hands?"

"Well, what about lips? Who wants a girl who's been sucking blood?"

"No, that's different. Lips are lips, right? Red lips suggest something else to a man. With nails, the only referent is claws, and you want to get away from that. You want your nails to put an entirely different image in the man's mind."

"Like what?"

"Like maybe peaches. Got any nice peach in there? Not too bright. Something subtle. You don't want to make it too obvious."

"Oh God, Claudia. Here. You look."

Mary Ann pushed the box across the table and threw up her hands. But she was more than willing to patiently show her how much to put on and how to use the brush so it didn't make streak marks. Claudia proudly held up her hands for Mary Ann as she blew lightly on them. It was just what she wanted. Advertising was everything, and Claudia felt she was developing an eye for it.

She went out looking for earrings to try instead of her regular button pearls and came back with some real finds, a set of little dangling bananas and a pair of little peaches. The bananas would immediately suggest something to men, and since she was a natural blonde, the peaches would hint that she was as pretty as a peach down there too.

All day as Claudia went about doing ordinary things, jingles and slogans came to mind. She tried to concentrate on tourism and hotels, thinking ahead to working with Captain Locarno. If she could get a portfolio together of advertising pitches, maybe he would ask her to be in charge of marketing, and then she'd have a real career. Good advertising campaigns could play a critical role in the success of their ventures. The key to it was catching the attention of the subconscious mind. A slogan like "The stay of a lifetime!" on a billboard or brochure, for example, might read to the subconscious mind as "The lay of a lifetime!" Who wasn't interested in that? You could make people believe that if they stayed at a Locarno Wyler Hotel, they would get stupendous sex. There was so much potential there that just thinking about it made Claudia feel like chewing her peach nails right off with anticipation, waiting for the day when she had $2,000 to go into business with Captain Locarno. She thought that was a good round number.

She only had about $500 to go, but that was still a lot of men, and now she was supporting Mary Ann. Claudia knew she could not let herself become impatient. She would have to ride it out, settle into a nice routine with Mary Ann and Edgar Lee, work her two nights a week at the Palmetto and stick to it.

When Mary Ann had a bad morning, Claudia was glad to walk Edgar Lee to school and save the money Mary Ann would have dropped in the church box. It was encouraging to look in the Campbell's soup can in her cupboard and see a bigger roll of bills every week. The money jar in Mary Ann's cupboard was holding steady. She found out the secret was not putting too much money in, so it always looked low, and then Mary Ann didn't give so much away. Things were looking up.

At the club, Claudia held out for twenty dollars. She got to be friendly with the bartender, a big native Hawaiian man named Billy, and he helped her out by lining up prospects. He did it on the sly, just because he liked her. He knew he could get in trouble. Some Wednesday and Thursday nights he had a full schedule booked before she even walked in the door. It was gratifying because she noticed a significant jump in sales when she taught Billy to use such phrases as, "if it's quality you want," and "at no extra cost," and "the choice of millions," and "limited time offer." He seemed to remember most of what she told him, and she trusted his bartender's judgment on men. In fact, Billy signed most of her nice-guy regulars. Everything was going smoothly until the price war.

The problem was Mr. Anthony's twelve hula girls. Claudia had to hand it to him for recognizing the shortage of white girls in Honolulu, and he had good instincts about the girls he imported from the mainland. On stage, they were stunning, and when they walked through the club, you realized why. All of them were at least five eight, and a few were probably six feet, with sleek bodies and lots up top.

They could do no wrong on stage, but that was largely because the audience was mostly men. For Claudia it was easy to see that Mr. Anthony's talents were limited to the acquisition phase of the business. She had to really think to figure out what was missing. It wasn't marketing. That took care of itself. Claudia tried to put her finger on it and decided that what was lacking was product development. Costuming and choreography did not get enough attention. Just the same, the Hula Girls packed in a crowd even on Wednesday and Thursday nights.

The Hula Girls did two floor shows a night. Between shows they circulated through the crowd and hung around the bar. Claudia put two and two together when one of her regulars went by her with a sheepish expression on his face. He was trailing behind one of the Hula Girls, and Claudia watched them disappear behind the side steps to the stage. Looking around and keeping track, she began to see that a lot of the Hula Girls were leading men over to the same place. Of the twelve Hula Girls, only four or five were ever on the floor at any one time between shows.

Ordinarily, Claudia lost a few customers who did not like the price or could not afford her. Someone else always came along, but one night she didn't get anyone who could come up with the money, and a few of her prospects went off with Hula Girls. She cut the price to ten dollars by the end of the night and finally got an older man who made her work hard for it because he said he could have gotten a Hula Girl and a few drinks for that kind of money.

The next night, Claudia opened at fifteen and was glad to see prices had stabilized and the Hula Girls weren't going to drive her to the wall. Some of the other independents Claudia had come to recognize had gone back out to the streets to head off the clientele, but she wouldn't dream of doing that. You look more respectable if you are associated with an established business, and some of the girls who worked on the street looked pretty fly-by-night, frankly. Claudia did three the first night and three the second night and made $90 for the week, which was nothing to complain about, but it should have been $120. So she decided to go back to twenty.

As if that were not enough aggravation, Richard was skulking around the Barrymore. Claudia spotted him sometimes at the corner of the building, holding up a newspaper in front of his face. Mary Ann didn't want to talk to him, and when he caught her, she always came back to the room in tears. She was getting to be a bundle of nerves. She just wanted him to leave her alone and go back to his wife and kids when the war was over. Claudia shooed him away whenever she saw him around the building. She told him he was scaring Edgar Lee.

On Claudia's two nights at the club, Mary Ann kept the radio and the lights on all night. She and Edgar Lee went for their last trip to the bathroom just before Claudia left and then locked themselves in. Claudia was glad for that because it made it easier to slip men in and out of her room on club nights. Mary Ann would just attribute anything she heard outside the door to Richard prowling the hallway.

They both walked Edgar Lee to school in the mornings when Mary Ann was up to it, and on the way back Claudia waited outside the church while Mary Ann went in and paid her sin lay-away. Back home, they had a nice big breakfast with their coffee and Chesterfields, and then Mary Ann went to lie down for a rest. Claudia cleared the dishes, went out shopping, and came back to straighten up the room and the mess Edgar Lee made in his fort with his comic books, candy wrappers, and other stuff he hid in there. Sometimes she lay down with Mary Ann for a while.

For once in her life, Claudia was glad she wasn't having a baby. Mary Ann could hardly do anything without getting tired. Claudia went to the library one day and started looking for books on having babies. There wasn't much there. They must think women know what they're doing. There was one by a Doctor Brody that said babies got into everything, so you could not leave your cleaning supplies or sharp objects lying around. He made it sound like babies didn't have the brains they were born with, but no use saying that to a baby, is there? Dr. Brody was big on enemas, and as Claudia read through the chapter, it began to make good sense. On the way home that day, she stopped at the drugstore and bought a big rubber syringe with a big red ball on the end.

At quarter of three they went to walk Edgar Lee home from school. Then they changed and went to the beach. It felt good to swim every day, and Mary Ann perked up in the cool water. From then on, with the cooler temperatures of evening, Mary Ann regained her energy and was her usual self. Later on when it got dark, she was more jumpy about Richard. Edgar Lee was happy to have Claudia sleep over on her non-club nights because then it was more like a family, and he knew Claudia could take care of anybody who pounded on the door.

Edgar Lee did not fuss about his enemas. Whenever he was cranky, Claudia put him in his little bathrobe and marched him down to the women's bathroom with her red rubber syringe and Vaseline in a paper bag. She scrubbed part of the floor first and then put Edgar Lee down on his side on a towel. She talked to him while she was doing the water, and then Edgar Lee dozed while they waited. Dr. Brody never said anything about trust, but with Edgar Lee, Claudia saw that trust was very important. On the other hand, all Claudia did was mention it once to Mary Ann, and she said,

"You're not getting near me with that thing. Forget it." But maybe she was just cranky that day.

Edgar Lee went to sleep over at Nick's one night, so Claudia and Mary Ann decided to go see a picture. They walked a few blocks to the Carnet and saw *Woman of the Year,* with Spencer Tracy and Katharine Hepburn. It's funny how you can get a wrong idea in your head. She had been smoking all wrong when she had tried to smoke like Katharine Hepburn. Movies were good for pointers on how to do almost anything. Walking out of the theater, she remembered how John Dillinger got it, and she caught herself looking around for Richard.

"This is silly," she said.

"What?" said Mary Ann.

"Richard isn't going to drive up in a car and shoot you, is he?"

"Oh, God, no," said Mary Ann. "It's not like that. He just wants to talk to me, but I just can't. I can't talk to him. I start giving in. It wouldn't do any good."

They stopped at the soda fountain place across from the Carnet and got ice cream cones and sat on the low wall in front with some other people and watched the wind go through the palm trees overhead.

"Well, I think it sounds like you want to take the deal," said Claudia.

"Oh, I do," said Mary Ann. It seemed like a load off her mind to say so. "Bill was—well, you know what Bill was like. I mean, I loved him, but Richard is the first man I ever felt was right for me. I know I made a mistake that one time. I shouldn't have done that to his wife. No matter how much you want something, you can't let it make you do something wrong." Then she looked up at Claudia and said, "You know?" Then she looked back at her ice cream cone. "We can't tell Edgar Lee we did this," she said.

"He's probably eating ice cream now anyway," said Claudia.

"Do you think Nick's mom will make him brush his teeth?"

"Mary Ann, for Pete's sake. One night. Who cares?"

"I don't think Nick's mom pays any attention to what they do."

"Well, you're right about that one, but I wouldn't worry about it. He doesn't need his mom hanging over him all the time."

"Did he tell you that?"

"No, don't be silly."

"Oh," she said. "I guess you just wanted me to feel bad."

"For crying out loud, Mary Ann. It was just conversation. He's a real boy now. You have to accept that."

Mary Ann looked sadly down at her ice cream cone.

"Why did you tell him he could have a bike?" she said.

"Well, he can, can't he? I mean someday."

"I don't think he understands that. I think he thinks you're going to get him a bike."

"All right. I'll get him a bike."

"We don't have enough money to get him a bike."

"We've got plenty of money. Don't worry about it."

"How can you say we have plenty of money? We don't have jobs."

"Look out for your ice cream cone, Mary Ann. No, the other side."

Claudia grabbed the cone out of Mary Ann's hand and licked the big drip about to fall off the bottom. Then she licked all around the base of the ice cream to stop the drips just starting to go over, and handed it back. Ordinary life was getting too fast for Mary Ann.

"You have to pay attention, Mary Ann."

"I'm sorry."

It was all too much for Mary Ann, and Claudia could tell she was on the verge of getting weepy.

"Let me get your hands."

Claudia moistened the middle of her napkin with her tongue and rubbed Mary Ann's fingers one at a time. Then she changed hands with the cone and did the other hand.

"There it goes again," said Claudia. "Look out."

Mary Ann licked quick and caught the new drips. Claudia gave her a big approving smile and encouraging words of "good job, girl" and Mary Ann smiled, too. Another catastrophe avoided. When they were a little more in the clear with the ice cream cone, Claudia asked her why everything these days seemed to end in tears.

"That's just the baby," she said, lowering her head again.

"Stop it, Mary Ann. You've got to pull yourself together."

"I'm sorry."

"I wish you didn't have to say that so much."

"I'm sorry."

Claudia kicked her legs. "Hey somebody—get the dither-brain out of here."

They both laughed, and Claudia put her arm around her. Mary Ann, with her head on Claudia's shoulder said, "Which dither-brain?"

"I love you," said Claudia. "Don't be a dither-brain and forget that, no matter what I say."

"I love you too, blondie."

They got up and walked down the street under the palm trees holding hands. No one would think anything about that.

Claudia knew that Mary Ann could not take much, so she kept her worries to herself. Top priority was figuring out how to get more out of her two club nights and watch over Mary Ann and take care of Edgar Lee. She could see how vulnerable they would be without her, and in that respect she could lump Mary Ann right in with Edgar Lee. It was up to her now. She felt strong, strong enough to keep quiet in the back of her mind a thousand worries that did not trouble Mary Ann. She still could be close and be regular girls with Mary Ann without letting her get the feeling she was taking over.

One night when Edgar Lee was sleeping over at Nick's, they were really talking like old times, sitting around Mary Ann's kitchen table in their nighties with just the one light on with their coffee and Chesterfields between them. Claudia went back to her place and brought over one of her bottles of Jack Daniel's, and then it really started feeling warm and cozy. She didn't know how they got on the topic, since they were going from one thing to the other, but it got around to intimate things, and Claudia suddenly felt like asking Mary Ann if she ever felt that little grab.

"I don't think I know what you're talking about," she said.

"It's a little grab kind of feeling. You know, down there."

"Down where?"

"You know. In your girl parts."

"Oh," said Mary Ann. "Let's have more of that whiskey. This is getting interesting."

"It's the greatest thing, Mary Ann. I have to tell you about it."

Claudia told her about her discovery of the hot water and how it felt so good with the little grabs down there, and she told how she got carried away and burned herself, and that she was going to try it again, only not burn herself on the next try, but then the war started. At first Mary Ann looked confused, but the lines in her face smoothed out as she heard more, and then she was smiling.

"I don't know where we can get a hose around here," said Claudia, "or how we could set it up because of all the hot water you need, but then I started thinking about the thing I've been using for Edgar Lee's enemas."

"You and your rubber hoses, Claudia." Mary Ann put her chin up and exhaled a full cloud of smoke, but Claudia could tell she was laughing.

"Don't laugh, Mary Ann. It's the best feeling in the world. I know you'll love it. Sometimes you get two or three grabs out of it."

Mary Ann came down to earth and leaned forward with her elbows on the table like Mr. District Attorney.

"I want to ask you a few questions," she said. "How long were you married?"

"A year."

"And Jack was your only man."

"Of course." It was such a lie, but Claudia knew Mary Ann wasn't expecting any other answer, and she was glad to see she could pull off a lie like that if she ever had to. It was fun with Mary Ann being her old self.

"Okay. Did you ever feel the grab with Jack?"

"Not really."

"Did you ever feel the grab at any other time, other than the night in question with your hot water hose? Think carefully, Mrs. Wyler."

"Once when I was thinking about Jack."

"Hmm," said Mary Ann. "Let me ask you this. Did you ever poke around down there by yourself?"

"You're not supposed to."

"Is that a yes answer or a no answer?"

"Definitely a no." Turning to one side, Claudia added, "The court will record the witness answered no and wishes to include in her testimony that you aren't supposed to."

"I have no further questions," said Mary Ann.

"Well, what's the verdict?"

"Here," said Mary Ann. "Have a little more of this stuff, and then I want to show you something."

She filled up Claudia's glass with the Jack Daniel's and lit them up a couple of Chesterfields. While they smoked and drank up, Mary Ann looked at her with such a bemused smile. Claudia knew she knew about the grabs. When they put out their smokes, Mary Ann led her over to the bed and sat down beside her. She reached over and got her sleep mask off the night table.

"Now I want you to put this on and lie back. You can keep your nightie on, but you have to ditch the bra and get out of your panties."

"I don't know, Mary Ann."

"This is strictly business. I want to show you something."

Claudia did what she asked and put on the sleep mask and lay back on the bed. Her head was swimming a little because of the dark and the whiskey, and she was trying not to giggle.

"Now listen to me, Claudia. You don't have to be so tough now. You can be a marshmallow. I want you to just drift in the dark. Don't think about anything. All right? Just be a marshmallow."

"I'll try."

"Okay, now I'm going to give you a massage."

Claudia felt her hands running lightly over her nightie, around and over and up around her neck and down to her knees and up her thighs, and then they were under her nightie and pressing down and letting up as they kept moving over her bosoms and her tummy. Sometimes a hand went away while the other kept going, and then it came back down in another place, and then the other hand left and came down somewhere else, always moving. It was starting to make her breathe in short little gasps, and she was getting that feeling. Mary Ann took Claudia's hand and placed her fingers in one spot.

"Feel that little button? That's where your grabs come from."

Mary Ann let Claudia's hand go and went on with her own, slipping her fingers over the place, and every time they went over it, Claudia felt a jolt that made her heart go faster and her breath come quicker, and she tensed all over, and her pelvis started rocking all by itself and suddenly everything was letting go.

"Oh, something's coming, Mary Ann. Something's coming—" And right after she said that, it did.

When Claudia took off the sleep mask and opened her eyes, she could hardly believe the world was still in one piece. She felt as if she had been tumbled in an avalanche, dropped off a cliff, flung high into the sky, roasted alive, burned to a cinder, electrocuted across high tension lines in brilliant flashes of ecstasy that were too much to bear, and it would not stop until she pushed Mary Ann's hand away. She didn't know how she had lived through it. But the room was as quiet as before, with the little fan on the bureau going tick, tick, tick, as it whirred. In the half-light through the windows, the silhouettes showed everything in the same places. It had all happened inside her, without a sound. You wouldn't have known anything had happened except for the sweat and how wet she was.

Mary Ann lay beside her and stroked her hair. Claudia wanted to do it for Mary Ann, but she said no. She said maybe they could do it together after the baby came. They got up and turned the light on and sat at the kitchen table and had a last smoke together. Claudia felt a little stupid with her idea about the hose and the enema thing.

"Just wanted you to know," said Mary Ann.

It was like one of those life-changing experiences she read about in *Reader's Digest*. It made her wonder why she had not figured it out herself. She wondered how many women knew about it. Maybe she could make it happen with one of her men. She could pick a nice one and have her grab at the same time he had his grab. It really should cost more if you weren't faking, but men probably couldn't tell the difference. Their grab was more like smashing a champagne bottle over the prow of one of their stupid boats. Claudia couldn't help being a little down on men. Some of her customers were pretty insensitive and rough. She didn't feel like going to work the next night, knowing she was going to have to try for four, but with a two-day workweek, she had to make an extra effort.

There were a few young sailor boys who looked interested, but they got snagged by the roving Hula Girls after the shows. On stage the Hulas really made you want a Hula Girl. Claudia wrote down the phrase "and nothing else will do" on a cocktail napkin and put it in her purse for future use in her real estate career. She only got two that night. The Hulas were tough competition, and she couldn't lose weight and become a goddess overnight, just like that.

Froggy and Annette showed up unexpectedly on Thursday night, and Claudia had to go over because she knew they'd see her. Apparently, Elaine had told Froggy she thought they were in a rut, so Annette was going to explain it to him at the club over some drinks. Annette said psychology would interpret it as an ultimatum for Froggy to overcome his fear of intimacy. He was a smart aleck about it as usual. He could be so nice by himself, but when he got around other people, he turned into a jerk. She was on Annette's side. Everything she said was so true. She didn't blame Jack one bit for wanting a girl like Annette.

It was already after twelve when they were ready to leave. Claudia pretended to go call for a cab and went back to the bar after they left. She still had time to get one client, and fifteen or twenty dollars was nothing to sneeze at, but all she wanted now was to go home and have coffee and smokes with Mary Ann. She promised herself that's what she would do after she got one. She just couldn't go back empty-handed. A nice-looking civilian came along, and they started talking. He was one of those with a glint in his eye, and her better judgment was against it, but it was almost closing time. She didn't get the money up front either.

When he was done, he got dressed and started looking around the room. Claudia asked him for the twenty dollars, but he said he wasn't going to give it to her because he wasn't satisfied. He kept looking around and turning over the boxes of things on the floor that she hadn't found places for. She was getting scared, so she told him he could have her again no charge if he wasn't satisfied. He wasn't interested, and he didn't reply to anything she said. He just kept rooting around and knocking things over.

When he found the Campbell's soup can, Claudia jumped off the bed naked and charged into him. He pushed her off and kicked her in the stomach when she was on the floor. It wasn't a hard kick, but when she got up and tried to stop him at the door, he really swung at her with his fist, catching her on the shoulder and spinning her around. She fell on the floor, stunned, and he put his shoe on her head and pressed down like he was going to crush her head, and she stopped moving and lay very still. She thought he was going to do it, and then suddenly the door swung back, and something plowed into him from behind.

Claudia didn't know what was happening. There were fists flying, grappling in the clinch, growling and snarling, and from where she was on the floor, Claudia thought she saw Mary Ann's nightie, and what was a wild animal doing in Mary Ann's nightie?

"Mary Ann!"

The man was on the floor getting pounded, and Claudia jumped up and got in a couple of licks herself. His face was bloody, but he was holding tight to the Campbell's soup can and managed to get to his feet and out the door. Claudia was too beat to chase him down the hall. Mary Ann was crying and shaking like a leaf. Claudia was crying too, but it was for the lost money and all her hopes down the drain. He got away with almost $2,000. Mary Ann was crying, the room was turned upside down, there was blood on the floor, and she was standing in the hallway without any clothes on.

Claudia peeped down the hall, ducked back inside, and closed the door. Good thing she lived in a building with heavy sleepers, or people who minded their own business. From her investigations last year, she knew there was at least one. Office girl. Claudia tried to comfort Mary Ann. She pulled the blanket off the bed and put it around Mary Ann's shoulders and the sheet around her own.

"You're a pretty good fighter," she said. "We should put you in the ring."

"But I'm having a baby," said Mary Ann through her sobs.

"That's okay, champ, Joe Louis can wait." Claudia patted Mary Ann's head soothingly as she held her courageous and wonderful friend.

Mary Ann wasn't stupid, and Claudia knew they were going to talk about it when they got back from walking Edgar Lee to school the next day. He had slept through the whole thing in his fort. Mary Ann held one of his hands, and Claudia held the other hand as they walked along, as if they were holding tight to the only steady part of their lives, the part they still understood about each other.

The man was obviously not Lieutenant Keith Reed. There was all the money she had, and the clothes she bought for her club nights, and how her room sometimes smelled like hell, and the mornings when Mary Ann asked, "What was all that noise last night?" It all added up.

Mary Ann hardly said a word to her on the way home, and that was probably what she was adding up in her head. The silence was okay because Claudia had some figuring to do too. Some women had no idea what their husbands did for a living. The men went off on the train every morning and came home at night and said their days were fine. She knew Mary Ann wasn't going to let it go at that.

Claudia sat down at Mary Ann's kitchen table and got out her Chesterfields while Mary Ann started the coffee. Then they sat together. Mary Ann had her eyes down like she didn't want to be the first one to say anything. Now Claudia knew how Jack felt. Women can make you feel so guilty. It's always their first move.

"Well, what is it?" said Claudia.

"Claudia—" Then there was a long pause. It didn't used to take Mary Ann so long to get to the point. "What are you doing?"

"I just made a mistake," she said. "Keith wasn't the right man."

"Oh bullshit, Claudia. I wasn't born yesterday. There is no Lieutenant Reed, is there? You're having men come up to your room and they're giving you money, aren't they? Is that what you're doing?"

"What do you think?"

"I think you're being a whore."

"I'm trying to make a living, Mary Ann," said Claudia. "For us. You and Edgar Lee and me. Where do you think we'd be if I didn't make money for us?"

"You could have come back to the hotel and washed dishes with me."

"You can't make money there."

"I did."

"And it wasn't a whole hell of a lot, was it?"

"I tried," said Mary Ann softly.

"But it wasn't, was it? You couldn't raise Edgar Lee on that."

Mary Ann admitted that it wasn't much and that it would be hard to raise Edgar Lee on it. Then she sat quietly with her head down again. She got out a Chesterfield, and her hands were shaking as she lit it.

"At least it was better than what you're doing," she said.

"You can't think like that, Mary Ann. We can't afford to. We've got Edgar Lee and now the baby coming. We've got to make some money."

"Well, what am I supposed to do about that?"

"I don't know. You sure can't do much."

"That's just hurtful, Claudia."

"Well, I'm sorry, but if you're going to be so high and mighty, there isn't a lot you can do in this world, is there?"

"I couldn't do that—"

"If I can, anybody can."

"Oh God, Claudia, I could never do that."

"Nobody's asking you to. If you're too proud to do a little dirty work to take care of your kids, don't worry. I will."

"It isn't pride, Claudia. It's my soul. I've been praying for you, too, Claudia."

It was so exasperating. Claudia poured more coffee and started another Chesterfield. Mary Ann could sit there and pass judgment, and there was nothing she could say about it because it was her religion.

"There's nothing I can say about it because it's your religion," she said.

Mary Ann quietly looked around the room and back to her coffee cup.

"I'd sooner you said something about my religion than hurt my feelings," she said.

"I'm sorry, Mary Ann. I never mean to do that."

"Maybe you could come with me to church sometime."

"I don't think we can afford it."

"No, church is free. Didn't you know that?"

"It's not free. Look at all the money you give them."

"But that's a gift. It goes to charity, to people less fortunate than us."

"Well, I got news for you, Mary Ann. We just joined the people less fortunate."

"All right," she said. "I won't give away any more of your money."

"It's our money," said Claudia. "That's the point. I'm trying to take care of us, so it's not my money I'm worried about. It's our money."

Claudia sensed they had finished getting everything out in the air and were softening up and could smooth it over. Mary Ann had taken it better than she expected. She reached over and put her hand over Mary Ann's arm and tried to bring her eyes up.

"It's just what I have to do now, Mary Ann. It isn't forever. I just want us to get somewhere and not be living hand to mouth like this. I know you'll see that when we're out from under, but I need you to understand that now and get out of the way and let me do my job. I can't do it with you slowing me down. I can't afford to let you push us off course."

"I'll try," she said, but there was still no smile. It wasn't right yet.

"Okay. Now I've got to go back and get some sleep because I've got to go out tonight."

"I thought you wanted to get Edgar Lee with me and go to the beach."

"I can't do everything, Mary Ann."

"He was counting on it. I know he'll be disappointed. He has so much fun with you."

"Mary Ann. You're not helping me. If you can take him to the beach yourself, I'd appreciate it."

"I thought you loved Edgar Lee."

"I do," said Claudia. "And I love you too."

"I love you, too," Mary Ann said quickly. She smiled and looked more encouraged. "I love you, Claudia. I'll try to help, I promise. And I won't give away any more money."

"Okay, okay," said Claudia. She got up and hugged Mary Ann and kissed her on both cheeks. She looked back as Mary Ann closed the door and said, "I'll probably be late tonight, so I'll see you tomorrow morning. Love you, bye."

Claudia slept the rest of the day and got up around eight. She took a shower and made a bowl of Campbell's Cream of Mushroom Soup and ate a pack of crackers with it. She was determined to start losing weight. She had to start looking like a Hula Girl. The room was a mess, but she left it. There was the whole rest of the week to houseclean, but tonight she had to get busy making enough money to get into real estate deals. Even if it took another year or two at this rate. It was important to keep the goal out in front. She fixed herself up pretty nice, blended a little rouge over the abrasion on the cheek that got ground into the floorboards, and took a cab to the club.

The Palmetto was up and running full steam, and Claudia felt herself breathing easier the minute she walked in the door. She liked the atmosphere. Everybody was drinking and dancing and having fun. Nobody was talking about bills to pay or the kids or the baby on the way. It never ends. Home can be depressing. It was nice to be able to go off to work.

Claudia sat at the bar and got a gin and tonic and lit up a Chesterfield. Billy didn't have anything lined up, but it looked like tonight wasn't going to be a problem. Claudia looked over the floor and saw plenty of men who didn't seem to be part of a group. She looked around, caught a few eyes here and there, and turned back to the bar to wait. Someone would be tapping her on the shoulder any minute. She was surprised when it turned out to be Mary Ann.

"What are you doing here?"

"Come on. We'll get a table," she said. "Then they'll know we're a team."

Mary Ann was already going for a table, so Claudia picked up her drink and followed. Mary Ann took out her Chesterfields and ordered bourbon on the rocks, and looked determined. Claudia was amazed. Mary Ann had set the wave just right and her hair came out Hedy Lamarr fabulous. The lipstick caught every twinkling light in the club, and one of the dresses out of Claudia's closets pushed her bosoms out so much it took all the attention away from her belly. You could hardly tell for sure if she was pregnant or just big, and she looked like a pretty good whore except that she was obviously scared to death.

"So what do you think you're doing, Madam X?"

"I want to help you." Her voice was quavering all over the place.

"For Pete's sake, Mary Ann. Drink something."

Mary Ann sipped at her bourbon and then drank the whole thing right down.

"I think I should have another one," she said.

"Where's Edgar Lee?"

"I sent him over to Nick's for the night."

Claudia held up her hand as a waiter went by. When the next round came, Mary Ann drank about half of that one right away, too.

"How do I look?"

"Like a million dollars. God, Mary Ann. You really do."

"I didn't think that would be so surprising."

"I always knew it was there. I'm not surprised at all. And it's good to see you here. The Palmetto is like my office, and it's like you dropped in."

"So how much money do I have to charge these guys?"

"A million dollars."

"It doesn't look like there are a lot of millionaires here tonight."

"You only need one. Listen, Mary Ann, if you get one for a million, you bring the money right back to me."

Mary Ann drank the rest of her bourbon, and her hands weren't shaking so much.

"Let's be serious, Mary Ann. You don't have to do this, you know."

"I know."

"I really don't want you to. That wasn't what I was talking about."

"I know, but I want to help. I really want to do it. I thought about it a lot today, and I made up my mind I can do it. I did my hair and everything, so I can't back out now."

"What if I don't want you to?"

"Well, I am, so shut up. If we're fighting it'll scare the boys away."

"You're not doing it, Mary Ann."

"Yes, I am. We're in this together."

Mary Ann put a fierce look on her face and dug her nails into Claudia's arm.

"Okay," said Claudia. "We'll see."

"No. I'm here."

"Okay then. You just tell me when you're ready. I'll get someone nice."

"Let me have another drink first."

Claudia got two more drinks coming, and they both lit up their Chesterfields and looked around. She explained how it worked and tried to tell her the signs to look for in men. It surprised her that she knew so much without ever having written anything down on the topic, but Mary Ann already knew a lot about the seamy side of men, so it was more like a refresher course for her.

"How about them?" said Mary Ann.

There were two young sailor boys just inside the entrance, taking in the scene. They looked like they had never been to the Palmetto before. They were pretty far away but they looked like good kids who wouldn't be any trouble.

"Okay," said Claudia. "Are you ready to go into action, Madam X?"

Mary Ann swallowed hard and said okay.

Claudia didn't ordinarily go up to anyone, but these two looked perfect for breaking in Mary Ann. They would be easy pickings for the Hula Girls though, and there wasn't much chance that two fresh-faced blond boys, who slipped out of convoy and strayed into the Palmetto, could make it through the water to the bar without getting torpedoed.

"You wait here," she said.

Mary Ann looked up like her head was on the chopping block, and it was so pathetic that they both had to laugh. Claudia moved quickly through the crowd. The boys were heading in the direction of the tables, but a two-girl wolf pack of Hulas had sighted them and was moving in for the kill. Claudia zeroed in on the boys so fast that she bumped one of the Hula Girls off course when she got there.

"Oh, I'm sorry. Excuse me," she said. She caught one sleeve of each boy, and brought heads together for a few discrete words.

"Do you fellas need dates?"

They looked at each other and said sure.

"We have two dates for you over here," she said.

Out of the corner of her eye, Claudia saw the two Hula Girls veering off to submerge and look for other prey. She grabbed a hand of each boy and led them back to the table. Mary Ann turned up with a pretty convincing smile.

"I'm Claudia, and this is Mary Ann."

"Hi," said Mary Ann.

"I'm John, and this is—"

"John."

"Why don't we all sit down," said Claudia.

The boys had rum and cokes. They all talked about how great the club was. Claudia prodded Mary Ann under the table to remember to keep smiling and not let the boys' eyes wander. When she thought the time was right, she said, "We'd sure like to get to know you boys better, but you know, we work for the club and we're supposed to be circulating around."

Neither of them knew what to do next, so Claudia had to go on.

"So if you paid us, you know, for that amount of time, we could stay and get to know you better. You see what I mean?"

They looked back and forth at each other like they were trying to figure it out. At least they seemed to know something was expected of them that had to do with money.

"We don't have to stay here either, not if you're paying for the time. So we could even go back to our place and get to know you better."

It sank in finally, and one of them asked how much.

"Twenty dollars. For each of us, I mean."

The two made eyes at each other, and Claudia could tell they were getting ready to abandon ship. She would have let them go, but they were perfect for Mary Ann, and she wanted her to have a good experience the first time.

"Well, maybe we can do better if you'll take care of the cab fare and tip."

Claudia hated to do it, but she went down to ten. She should have known better, and it didn't turn out very well. In the cab to the Barrymore, the boys had their hands all over them. It turned out they both wanted the older one, Mary Ann—who knows why—and Claudia ended up standing outside her door with one of them while the other one was playing with Mary Ann.

What was worse, they tricked her, and the one who was coming out let the other one come in first, and then they quickly closed the door and locked it. Claudia didn't know what she ought to do about it because she could hear the boys giggling, and they were just being boys. She waited to hear Mary Ann call out if she needed help, and she was ready to break the door down and fight them like a tiger if she had to save Mary Ann, but there was no SOS.

Claudia waited with her ear to the door for almost an hour. Just normal sounds, and she could hear Mary Ann was okay. The boys came out giggling stupidly and goofing around and buttoning all those buttons on their pants. She could see Mary Ann getting dressed, and she seemed okay. They fessed up they had each done Mary Ann twice. Claudia tried to argue with them over the money, but they said they only used one girl, so the twenty dollars was enough, and it was all they had on them anyway. They weren't mean and let Claudia look through all their hidden pockets to prove they didn't have any more money, so there was nothing to be done about it. They were going to walk back to base.

Mary Ann came to the door and didn't look very happy. Twenty dollars. That meant she had gone for five dollars, and that wasn't anywhere close to a million. Claudia went back in the room with her and helped her clean up. She wasn't crying, and she didn't seem upset. It was her baptism of fire, like in the war, and she took it. Mary Ann went down the hall in her robe and slippers and took a long shower. They had coffee and Chesterfields at the table at Mary Ann's and tried to put it behind them.

"It'll just take a while to get used to it," said Mary Ann. "It wasn't so bad. I thought it was going to be worse, but it wasn't so bad."

"Thank you, Mary Ann. But you don't have to do it anymore."

"No, I want to help. It wasn't so bad. I can do it."

Claudia reached for her hand across the table.

"You've got what it takes, Mary Ann," she said.

PART FOUR

"Follow Your Instincts, or Listen to Your Better Judgment?"

—BETTY DUNSFORD ROY, *WOMAN'S HOME COMPANION*, DECEMBER 1946

CHAPTER THIRTY-ONE

Mary Ann was dead to the world the next morning, so Claudia let her sleep. She went over to Nick's to pick up Edgar Lee and walked the boys to school. Then she came back and had breakfast by herself. It was some saint's birthday, so Edgar Lee was getting out at noon. That would be perfect. She could pick up some donuts, go get Edgar Lee, roust out Mary Ann, and they could have a nice afternoon at the beach.

But first she wanted to go look for a present for Mary Ann. Easier said than done. She walked all over town and couldn't find anything right. It was turning into a problem and taking too long, so she had some coffee at the French Café to think. The present had to represent what she wanted to say. She had already decided not to let Mary Ann help her anymore. It was good for her to have a taste of what she had to go through, but it wasn't right to make her do it. Even if they had a big fight over it, she wasn't going to give in. A lot of boys weren't nice, and she couldn't stand the thought of anyone mistreating Mary Ann. What could say all that?

As if the universe approved, she got lucky on the way back and found a little ivory carving of two polar bears hugging. It was the perfect thing. One of them kind of looked like Mary Ann, but she wasn't going to tell her that. She thanked her lucky stars for finding something so perfect. Last stop was donuts, and it left her just enough time to get back to the Barrymore, get Mary Ann up, and go for Edgar Lee. She hurried along and got a little sweaty, but she felt so happy about the polar bears and couldn't wait to argue with Mary Ann and show her how adamant she felt. The polar bears hugging would just melt her heart and show how much she loved her.

Claudia went to knock on Mary Ann's door and was surprised to find it open. The curtains were drawn, and it was stuffy inside, so she went right over to the windows and drew back the curtains, and when she turned around, she saw Mary Ann lying on the bed with her arms stretched out over the sides. Her dress was up, and her panties were stuffed in her mouth. Her throat had been cut.

Claudia stood and stared. Struck dumb. She dropped the bag of donuts. Mary Ann was dead. She went over and knelt beside her. The sheets were bloody. Oh, Mary Ann, oh no. Mary Ann was dead. There was nothing to do about that. There was nothing to say but "Oh, Mary Ann, oh no" over and over, and she kept saying it as she took the panties out of Mary Ann's mouth and closed her eyes. She pulled her dress down and put her legs together and her arms at her sides. Then she went to the bureau and got out some clean underwear. It was hard getting the brassiere on straight.

"I'm sorry, Mary Ann. I know you hate this, but it's important to look your best now. You're so pretty, Mary Ann."

And then she suddenly remembered Edgar Lee. He would have started walking home by himself. She had to head him off. At the door she stopped and turned around and looked at Mary Ann again.

"I got you a present, Mary Ann." She looked around the floor, thinking she had dropped the ivory carving, but she found it clutched in her hand and held it up. "It's two polar bears hugging. Polar bears in Hawaii—what are the odds? They look just like us. I'll keep them for us. I love you, Mary Ann. Goodbye, Mary Ann. I love you, I love you."

There was blood on her hands, and some on the front of her dress, and on the polar bears but she didn't have time to do anything about it. She had to catch Edgar Lee and every second counted now. Why didn't she think of that five minutes sooner?

Edgar Lee was coming the other way on the sidewalk, and Claudia crossed over.

"Where's Mom?"

"You mom's not feeling well, Edgar Lee."

"What's wrong with her?"

"She has a sore throat." It's all she could think of.

"I'll go see," he said.

"No, you can't. She's lying down."

Edgar Lee took off running with his book bag flopping at his side, and he wouldn't stop when she called him. Claudia ran after him, but she couldn't run fast enough, and Edgar Lee disappeared around the corner. She had to catch him, she had to. She tried to make her legs go faster. She pumped her arms, and her heart was pounding. It was so hot, and she couldn't get enough air in her lungs, but she had to catch Edgar Lee. She couldn't let him see his mom dead. She kept trying, but she couldn't catch up. She got to one corner, and he had already gone around the next. Her legs gave out, and she couldn't run anymore. She lumbered on as fast as she could, stumbling, and she started to cry and beg God not to let Edgar Lee see. Nothing was worse than this. Oh God, why didn't she lock the door.

Before Claudia even got near the Barrymore, she heard Edgar Lee screaming through the window, and people were running from all over. By the time she struggled up to the second floor, pulling herself by the handrail, she had to push through a crowd in the hall, and there were lots of people in the room. Claudia couldn't see over their heads, but she could hear Edgar Lee, and her strength came roaring back.

"I'm his mother. I'm his mother," she cried. She shouldered into the mob at the door and pushed into the room and barreled through blindly with her head down, shoving and pushing her way toward the wails of Edgar Lee. She fought her way through and wrenched Edgar Lee out of the hands and arms that held him. "I'm his mother. Get away, I'm his mother," she cried. She had to get him out now, and she twisted and turned out of the grasping hands and made it back to the hall. Edgar Lee kept screaming with his eyes shut, and she held onto him for dear life as she pulled out her key and got them into her room and pushed the door closed against all comers. She put Edgar Lee down on the bed and lay with her arms around him, and soon the hysteria and crying stopped, and he was just limp, staring into space with his eyes wide open. She held his little body against her and said it would be all right, it would be all right.

The police came and asked her questions. It was Detective DeNante again. Edgar Lee was asleep on the bed. Claudia had made him some Campbell's Cream of Mushroom Soup and made him eat a pack of crackers so he would fall asleep. She didn't think she should be giving him any Jack Daniel's, but the thought had occurred to her. Detective DeNante did not ask too many questions. She knew he could tell it was a professional job. That put it in a whole different ballpark. Nobody living at the Barrymore was going to get the third degree. He said all that stuff about not leaving town and patted her on the back when he left, like they were old friends.

CHAPTER THIRTY-TWO

Claudia and Edgar Lee moved down the street into a room at the Strickland. It was about the same as the Barrymore but a little cheaper, just one room with everything. She wanted to make Edgar Lee another fort but decided to stay away from anything that would remind him of what happened or the life they had there. That life was over for both of them, and it was up to her to start a new one, at least for him.

There was $100 in the pot in Mary Ann's cupboard that she hadn't given away to the church. In the quiet after the police left and after Mary Ann was taken away, Claudia got in with her key and grabbed it without anyone noticing. Claudia was surprised there was that much. So they moved into the Strickland with a hundred dollars, a pile of clothes, the *Life* magazines, the steamer trunk, a percolator, and a hot plate. She went out and bought a bigger mattress for Edgar Lee.

The first few nights, Edgar Lee slept with her in the big bed and had screaming night frights and wet the bed. During the day he was sluggish and in his own world. Looking at the *Life* magazines was all he would do. Claudia tried holding him and talking to him, but when he looked up from the magazines, he just stared into space. When he talked, he just kept repeating "All Ashore for Bosco! All ashore for Bosco!" It was the only thing he said, so she went out and got a jar of Bosco and kept a couple of milk bottles in the icebox because it was the only nourishment he would take. Claudia didn't know what to do. She only knew him as a normal little boy, and now he was something different.

After a few bad nights, Claudia called Annette at the base and told her what happened, and she came over. They had tea, and Annette tried talking to Edgar Lee. Nothing seemed to work. Edgar Lee stared out the window and said, "All Ashore for Bosco!" So Claudia got up to get him a glass of Bosco. Annette put her hand on her arm to stop her and blinked her eye a tiny bit. Claudia took the hint and took her leave.

The police station was a few blocks away. She found out where Mary Ann was and took a cab to the municipal cemetery. All she had to do was look for a patch of fresh earth in that big field, and there it was, with just a little wood marker that had her name on it. Claudia sat down on the dirt and took some up in her hands, as she had seen Mary Ann do with her rosary beads, and said, "I'm sorry, Mary Ann, I'm sorry, Mary Ann," as she cried and let it fall through her fingers.

She didn't know how long she was there, but she made herself get up and leave when she felt herself staring at nothing and thinking about Bosco. Walking back to the cab, she remembered when they had been talking like regular girls, and Mary Ann had said she liked the idea of a big funeral in Philadelphia someday. Claudia didn't guess there was much of a ceremony here. The paper only said a prostitute was found murdered, and that isn't the kind of funeral you go looking to attend, is it? They didn't say it was Mary Ann, and why would the paper say she was a prostitute? It looked like Mr. Anthony was stacking the deck. What else could she think?

When Claudia got back to the Strickland, Edgar Lee was eating a pork chop and green beans. Annette was at the hot plate making toast in the frying pan, looking pretty pleased with Edgar Lee. They had some coffee and Chesterfields after getting Edgar Lee into his new bed and putting a shade over the light on the kitchen table. He still had that faraway look about him, but he called Claudia Mom when she kissed him goodnight.

The night frights ended, and he never wet the bed again. Claudia didn't know what Annette did to bring Edgar Lee back. Maybe there were things he could only talk about with Annette. It wouldn't be the first time. But Claudia could not begrudge Annette anything. She got her out of a jam with Edgar Lee, and she seemed to know her way around psychology. Annette was really not the kind of girl Jack thought she was at all.

Annette came every day after work for the next few weeks and stayed with Edgar Lee a few hours. He seemed back to pretty normal and talked like he did before, but there was something like a blank spot he had to get around. Sometimes in the middle of saying something, he stopped dead—then started up again on another track. That happened less as his mind built roads around, and bridges over the blank spot. That's what Annette thought it was. He went back to school and called Claudia Mom, and she got a chance to go out looking for a job and do her shopping and try to figure out what she was going to do when the money ran out.

When it did, Claudia went to see Mr. Anthony about a job. Her better judgment was against it and every fear inside her rose up, but she knew it was her only chance to get working. From the first day she started pounding the pavement, it was in the back of her mind that she would end up at the

Palmetto. During the next two weeks, as she stuck her nose in every shop door and garage in town, the idea came forward in her mind, not only as an expedient, but as the recognition of an old reality of life that she had read about but had never experienced herself. The privilege of her upbringing and her marriage to Jack had sheltered her from the evil of the world. Her careless ways had stirred it, and it struck down the one following in her path. For Mary Ann's sake, she resolved not to forget, turn away, flee, or grant herself pardon. But how were the weak to confront evil? It came to Claudia as she walked the streets that the only way to defy evil, to turn it back against itself into good was to seek it out and go to the heart of it with false supplication and feigned submission. Strengthened to that purpose, with a tight grip on the rope, she would lower herself into the dark, bide her time there, look around, and see what evil wanted to do with her.

Claudia sent her name in with the secretary, with word that it was business of a personal nature. She expected to be ushered into Mr. Anthony's office right away, but he took his time. Then he forgot her name. He did not remember they were arch foes either. Well, never mind, but she was through starting at the bottom.

"I'm so sorry, Mrs. Wyler," he said. "As you know, the Hula Girls are a special group of young ladies. Exclusive would be a better word, perhaps. We've gone to great expense to find the best the United States has to offer."

When Claudia pointed out the lesser expense of training a local girl who was a natural blonde, Mr. Anthony looked like a good idea just crossed his mind, and he made her an offer to be the thirteenth Hula Girl. Claudia did not want to jump at it too fast.

"What would the compensation be for the position?" she inquired coolly.

"Fifty dollars a week salary, plus ten percent of your personal initiatives."

Mr. Anthony went on to explain that the Personal Initiative Program, or PIP, at the Palmetto was one of his own ideas, submitted to the board of directors, of course, and so approved. As a Palmetto Hula Girl, you were offered the opportunity to circulate among the clientele when you were not participating in a floor show. During that time, each Hula Girl was free to pursue her own personal initiative and arrange dates with the clientele. The dates were a set fee of twenty dollars, and at the end of each week the amount was tabulated, and you received ten percent of the total. Tips were expected to supplement the income, he added, but he understood anecdotally that they usually exceeded the commission.

It sounded to Claudia like laying down for two dollars, but she didn't want to be independent in this business anymore. There was nothing in the want ads, and there wasn't any more time to waste. Fifty a week was a fantastic amount of money. It would give Edgar Lee stability, and she could go into real estate sooner rather than later, so she took it.

Mr. Anthony scheduled her for a training and orientation session the next morning at nine. He had two other new Hula Girls starting, replacements for two who were getting married, and all twelve were coming to the rehearsal, so the new ones could learn to work as a team. He said he would expect her to catch on quickly and be ready to go on the same night in the floor show. There were two shows a night, and the hours were 9 p.m. to 2 a.m., six nights a week, with Sunday off. Claudia and Mr. Anthony shook hands on it like proper adversaries, and that was that.

Having a regular job was important to making a family life for her and Edgar Lee, and it was going to pay more than the garage and the Grand Hawaiian put together, not to mention how exciting it was to be getting into show business. Claudia figured she could forget the PIP and make out fine on just the fifty a week. She had not crossed men off her list, but she was getting close.

The girls were nice too, as she found out the next day. If you had to work with girls and they weren't nice, you were a cooked goose. The trainer was an older man named Max, who was sweet. He took them through the dance routines, and Claudia caught on fast. It was fun being on stage. The dances were designed to make your bosoms bounce and get your fanny wiggling. Even with the girls in their regular clothes at rehearsal, "The Grand Finale" of the second show got all the bosoms flying, and Claudia knew it was going to be fabulous. It was easy to imagine being picked out by a Hollywood producer, and Claudia had to remind herself it was just a hootchy-kootchy show and she should not get her hopes up. Nothing brought her down to earth like the back rooms.

Max took Claudia and the two new girls through a corridor that ran by Mr. Anthony's office, just down from the stage. There was a row of small rooms.

"You get the money first, ladies, and then you put it in your box," said Max. "Can everybody hear me?"

The two new girls behind Claudia piped up, and he went on to say that nobody goes into the rooms until the money is in the box. They said they understood. Then he took out some tape for temporary name tags and cut three pieces off the roll, one for each box on the last three doors at the end of the corridor. Poised with his pen, he said:

"Gimme your stage names, ladies."

Claudia picked Jasmine. The two other girls said they were going to be Starfire and Moonglow.

"Like the song," said Moonglow.

"Now when we go in the rooms," said Max, "you'll see you got your bottle of disinfectant in the corner. This is important because you want to wipe down your pad after each customer."

The room was not much bigger than a closet. There was a narrow, metal-framed bed along the wall with a long rubber cushion on it that was about four inches high. Each girl lay down to get the feel of it, and it turned out to be really cushy and comfortable. Max pointed out the hooks and hangers on the walls and a button you could push in case you had any trouble. He said someone would be right there if you buzzed. He showed how you could turn the light switch to make the overhead light dim, and they all tried it, giggling as the lights went up and down. Max then pointed to a metal box bolted to the wall beside the bed.

"In here's your club rubbers. Every customer's got to have a club rubber."

Claudia began to see how the club made money. You were only allowed to be with a Hula Girl if you were wearing a regulation club rubber. Max warned them that some men might say they had an extra from their last visit, and it may even look exactly like a club rubber, but it didn't count. A club rubber cost a dollar, and the money went in a slot on the side of the box. Max told them not to worry about the additional cost because if the customer got this far, his pants were in the driver's seat. Claudia knew that anyway, from as far back as Joe, but it sure hit the tail of the donkey on the head how he said it.

Max was a nice guy. He was a little heavy, and Claudia was surprised how light on his feet he was. They ran through the dance numbers a few more times and got out by 2 p.m. Claudia hung around with Max afterward because she really wanted to know the ropes of a real professional troupe. Max said he was from New York and had done some Broadway in the hard days of the Depression. He came to Hawaii with a touring group and got to talking to Mr. Anthony at the bar one night.

"That's where the idea of the Hula Girls came from," he said. "I know we're doing good right now, but we could do more. You've seen the show, haven't you? Mr. Anthony doesn't go for new ideas much, but he called me this morning to tell me he had a good one. I shouldn't tell you this, Jasmine, but it has to do with you, and I want you to be ready. I can see you got potential. Just keep an open mind tonight and remember, whatever happens, the show must go on. You got that? I know you'll do great. Tonight, just remember to keep going. You got all the steps down, so you'll do fine. Remember, just keep going. No matter what happens."

Claudia took a cab over to the school, and she and Edgar Lee walked home. It was a completely different way to the Strickland than to the Barrymore, and Claudia thanked Annette in her mind every day for Edgar Lee being normal. She had no way of telling how fragile the peace was in Edgar Lee's mind, but she didn't want to take any chances with stray bullets stirring up memories.

Everything was working like clockwork. Working nine to two at night was perfect for having a child. She could get him up in the morning, take him to school, bring him home, make dinner and get him to bed. All she needed was someone to sit in the room for five hours at night.

Annette saved the day again. She called back almost right away, and by eight o'clock that night, when Claudia was getting ready to leave, there was a very pleasant Hawaiian lady named Mrs. Butter at her door. At least it sounded like that, so Claudia called her Mrs. Butter. Thirty cents an hour was going to be fine with her, plus cab fare. Edgar Lee was in his pajamas and came over from his comic books on the bed to meet her. He seemed to like her and seemed to like Froggy, too.

Froggy came right in behind Mrs. Butter since he had brought her over, and he put his navy hat on Edgar Lee as he walked in. Froggy always knew how to get on the inside track. Mrs. Butter and Claudia sat at the table, and Froggy sat with Edgar Lee on his bed looking at comic books while Claudia briefed Mrs. Butter on the bathroom and the telephone down the hall and Edgar Lee's likes and dislikes. Then she had to get going and kissed Edgar Lee and left with Froggy, who said he'd drop her off.

"Where to, babe? Back to the salt mines?"

Claudia wasn't expecting to see Froggy, so she didn't know what to say. She couldn't hide where she worked for very long.

"Not exactly," she said. "I'm working at the Palmetto club now."

He pulled out into the street and said. "That's terrific," without seeming to have anywhere to go with it until he had more information.

"I'm one of the new Hula Girls."

"Good for you."

"You don't believe me, do you?"

"Sure, I do."

"Okay, don't believe me. Next time you're there, you'll see."

"Then I have to say, congratulations. I understand it's a very exclusive group."

But it didn't look like he really believed her.

"Oh, yes," she said. "We're known all over. And it isn't just because the girls are pretty. Since I started working with them, I've discovered that they're talented and gifted show business professionals."

"I thought it was your first night."

"I mean in rehearsal. There's a lot to learn with the routines and the dance steps and getting everyone coordinated. You get to know everybody in a troupe pretty fast."

"I know. Don't forget, I work in a troop, too."

It was a difficult conversation. She was nervous enough about performing without having to contend with Froggy, but he lay off about being a Hula Girl and got pretty quiet on the way over. When he pulled over in front of the club, he jumped out to get the door and wished her good luck.

"I don't want to give you the jitters on your first night," he said, "so I'll catch the show later."

"Thanks, Froggy."

"We should talk some time. Maybe we could get away somewhere."

"I'm kind of busy now. And I have Edgar Lee."

"I know. Sometime, I mean."

Claudia walked around to the side entrance and up the steps. There was plenty of backstage action going on. It was the first time she had ever been around the people who did lights and microphones. The guys in the orchestra were walking around in white tuxedos with shirt collars open, smoking, and there were so many wires running everywhere on the floor that she had to watch where she was stepping. Some corridors led only to brick walls, and she had to ask how to get to the dressing room. Then she got lost a few times and walked in late.

It was a long, narrow room with a big mirror across one wall, with bare light bulbs along the top. The other girls were getting into their grass skirts and show bras, so no one was really sitting down to do their hair and face yet. The old hands asked Claudia, Starfire, and Moonglow if they were nervous. They said funny things to each other and talked to their reflections in the mirrors. It was fun being part of the group, even when Claudia got out of her dress and saw herself naked beside the others in the mirror. She had to be four inches shorter and sixty pounds heavier than any of the other Hula Girls. She already knew she was at least six years older than everybody, but that didn't show as much.

Claudia knew she had a pretty face and beautiful hair, her big assets. They were the basics. But of course, you had to have the basics, and she told herself that Mr. Anthony must have seen the diamond in the rough, the princess in the pea, and he was willing to take a chance. He believed in her. It was so encouraging when she thought of it like that, and Max believed in her too. Edgar Lee depended on her, and she knew she could lose weight and become the best of the Hulas. She could practice the dance routines at home and lose weight.

Claudia resolved not to be self-conscious about displaying her body in the line of duty. She opened up her costume package, the one with "Jasmine" on it. The show panties and show bra were on top. Both were black, with little sequins that flashed all colors under the light, and the panties had a cut so high it made her gasp when she pulled them up. One tug on the waist and the little strip of sequined cloth in back went right up between her buttocks and was gone. Oh dear. And something was wrong with the bra. It was much too small, and on close inspection it looked like it had been turned in and sewn down with a double seam. The side sections of the cups weren't all there, either. The other Hulas looked fine. There wasn't time to do anything.

Max came to the door and said, "Let's go, Hula Girls," and everyone started filing out. Max called to her from the door, "Suit up, Jasmine. Let's go. Come on. Come on."

He came down the narrow passage through the chairs and helped her out. He hooked her bra in back so she could use both hands in front to stuff. They weren't going to stay in for long. She knew that.

"I think it's the wrong bra."

"No, it's right," said Max. "Just this one time. Just this one time. Let's go."

Claudia was so nervous that she started for the door without her grass skirt, and Max had to call her back. There were only about six inches of grass around it. All the other ones had grass down to the knees.

"What am I supposed to do with this?"

"Just put it on and get up there."

"But it's too short. I can't wear this."

"No, that's how it's supposed to be," he said. "Just for tonight. Mr. Anthony wants to try a new thing. Just put it on."

She needed the fifty dollars. She put the grass skirt around her middle. It was too small there too, and the strings came together but the grass didn't. It left most of her show panties showing, either in front or in back, whichever way she turned the skirt, and she couldn't make up her mind, which was worse.

"Remember what I told you, Jasmine," said Max, "Just keep going, no matter what."

They lined up behind the curtain, and Claudia took her place at the end of the line with Starfire and Moonglow. The old hands were in the lead on the other end. She couldn't worry about her costume now. There were the dance steps and routines and remembering to smile. This was show business. She had to look like she enjoyed what she was doing. She could hear the noise of people on the other side of the curtain quiet down as the spotlight swooped down on the master of ceremonies, Mr. Desmond Gandolfo. He introduced the fabulous Hula Girls. The orchestra hit it, the curtain went up, and off they went.

It was more exhilarating than anything Claudia could have imagined. The lights, the applause and whistles, and she, linked arm in arm with the twelve other Hulas, kicked her legs as high as they would go, spun around to the count, swung her hips, and thrust out her bosom in perfect unison with the line. She fought to keep smiling through the exertion of such energy and counted one, two, three, in her head, and glanced at the lead Hulas for cues. Lo and behold, she was doing it! Starfire and Moonglow were looking to her, and they were keeping up too.

The place was packed, and what a crowd. It sounded like the Army-Navy game. And then it sounded like it wasn't just the roar of the crowd in the stadium. There was a wave of laughter going over, and then another. Something was catching the attention of the people in the dark beyond the tables, even way over at the bar. More and more men began to come through the tables to the dance floor and then to the edge of the stage, carrying their drinks in their hands, whistling and hooting and cheering them on and laughing. Claudia was afraid it was her costume. It felt like all eyes were on her. A turn was coming up, and for a good fifteen seconds, she knew that the line would be dancing with backs to the audience. The others were covered by their grass skirts, but almost all her whole behind would be showing. It wouldn't even look like she had panties on because she felt the little strip was already out of sight.

When they made the turn, the noise from the sailors and marines and army men drowned out the orchestra. The only thing Claudia could do was try to cover herself with a hand, which she alternated as the Hulas danced, backs to the crowd, six beats with one arm up in the air and six beats with the other arm up. It didn't work because when she started changing the hand that covered her behind, it only drew more attention, and the Palmetto thundered with applause and whistles and cheers.

Finally, the line swung around, mostly on the timing of the lead Hulas, because no one could hear the orchestra anymore, and they set up for "Hulas Reach for the Sky." Now Claudia could see that all eyes were on her, and she missed some steps and got out of time and took a spill. Since Starfire and Moonglow were rookies, they broke ranks to help her up, and the crowd loved that, too. Claudia was so glad her bosoms stayed in the basket for "Hulas Reach for the Sky," which brought the house down, and then it was exit stage left, none too soon. The crowd was roaring, and the curtain came down like Niagara Falls right on their heels.

Claudia felt like crying, but the Hulas gathered around her and said she was great and the star of the show and a good sport. Max came and scattered them away to go circulate and told her she was great too, just like he said she'd be. She didn't feel like circulating though. She went to her room in back and sat on the blue rubber mattress and cried. It was so humiliating, and now she knew what Mr. Anthony's big idea was. Any one of the girls would have been funny in a real short grass skirt too, but it was funnier because she was the only heavy one. Just the same, you couldn't even get hired to be a Hula Girl if you looked like a moose. You had to be pretty, or you didn't get in. She knew that, so a little humiliation wasn't worth crying over.

If there was anything to cry about, it was Mary Ann. But it was like Jack always said. Whenever he found her crying over something he would say, "Well, it's too late for that now, isn't it?" You could say that about everything.

Mary Ann, Jack, the war, people fighting all over the world, people when they weren't nice. You'd never stop crying if you let yourself think about all the things to cry about.

And as far as humiliations go, Claudia decided she wasn't going to let this one get her down. Save it for the next one. That's what you say to yourself. That's how you take your stand. And this wasn't *The Blue Angel*. She wasn't going to pieces over anybody. This was her job. She was a show business professional. Claudia decided then and there, no more tears. She had to raise Edgar Lee. Like the song says, we're all between perdition and the deep blue sea, but she was on a mighty mission. Already she heard the sounds of the sliding bolts and locking doors of the Hula Girl rooms along the corridor. She had to go make money. Battle stations. Man the guns. Praise the Lord and pass the ammunition.

Claudia came out of her room and bravely went on the floor to circulate. Max said to stay away from tables with women. You were supposed to walk around with a gracious smile, asking if the gentlemen were enjoying the show, and give them time to approach when you swished back to the bar. Claudia circulated and circulated for the next two hours but didn't have any luck. She knew what it was. She was too conspicuous, and any man asking her for a date would be conspicuous, too. That was all right with her for now. She still got the fifty a week, and she didn't have to look at men with their pants down.

At eleven o'clock, they came backstage to get ready for the last show. Max told Starfire and Moonglow to move up the line for the last number of the routine behind the lead Hulas, Fury and Tender Trap, and for Sassy and Venus to drop back. Claudia knew that put her on the end of "Hulas Crack the Whip." She signaled for an aside with Max, and he brought her over to the edge of the curtain where they could talk privately.

"Yeah," he said, "I wanted to talk to you, too."

"It's the bra, Max. If I'm on the end of "Crack the Whip," they're going to come out."

"I know."

"Well?"

Max looked for a moment like he was thinking, with his arms folded in front and a hand on his chin, but time was getting short, so he dropped the pose.

"It's like this, Jasmine," he said. "It's a test."

"No, I'll do it, but I know they're going to jump out—"

"No, it's not a test for you. You're a trooper. It's another kind of test. You'll see. We don't have much time now. We'll talk. But what I wanted to talk to you about now was—it really raised the roof when you missed steps and fell. We want you to do it in the last show too, okay?"

Claudia took a last draw of her Chesterfield like Dietrich and said, "You got a stunt double for me, Max?"

"Good girl," he said.

The last show went like the first one. The late crowd had trouble getting in because the early crowd didn't leave like they normally did, and it looked like everyone was there for the show. Claudia did a few missteps and a couple of slips, and a fantastic pratfall on "Hulas Crack the Whip" because she pretended to be trying—but really was—to hold her bosoms in. It worked that time, but in "The Grand Finale," when the Hulas leaped and kicked their legs up, they jumped right out. There were still eight bars of the music to go when the Hulas linked arms, so everyone at the edge of the stage got an eyeful. There were people falling out of their chairs at the Palmetto that night.

The next night, there was a line outside the club waiting to get in. Claudia went to the side entrance, but she had to pass the marquee in front. The Hula Girls were featured on the poster, and it looked mostly the same until she got closer and saw that the Hula at the end of the lineup had been painted over. Now the last Hula Girl was a cartoon hippopotamus, painted purple and dressed in a tiny show bra and a grass skirt that looked like a ballerina tutu. That was really the icing on the cake, but it came down to needing the fifty dollars and wanting to keep Edgar Lee in the Catholic school for Mary Ann. What worried her a little was that the hippopotamus was wearing high heels.

CHAPTER THIRTY-THREE

Every night the Hula Girls danced to a packed crowd and standing ovations. The test Max talked about turned out to be whether or not the act would get shut down because of Claudia's bosoms getting loose at the end of the second show. It was made to look like an accident, but it happened every night. Anyway, nobody went blabbing to the newspaper or the churches, so they got away with it. At least Claudia got Max to give her a regulation show bra and grass skirt for circulating between shows, but she still didn't get any dates when she walked around the club. Max said it was because she was the star of the show. A few weeks into the job, one night he told her confidentially, "See that marine over there at the bar? Yeah, the big guy. I was talking to him. He's seen a lot of action. Got wounded a couple of times. That's why he's back here. Nothing that guy's afraid of—except one thing. You know what that is?"

"No, what?"

"You. That big guy is scared of you. You're what they call intimidating. That can happen to the one who stands out in a chorus line. I've seen it many times back in New York. It just takes a little time for customers to get used to you. You're through the worst of it now."

Claudia thought it was too bad the worst of it is not a standard amount of time for every experience in life. This one was already going on too long. Part of it was her own fault because in the next weeks, she perfected slips, missteps, falls, and other accidents to a high level of professional expertise. Max even altered some of the routines in order to showcase her talents. The trouble came when something went amiss on its own and Mr. Anthony wanted to add it to the show. One night, on "Hulas Crack the Whip," Atlantis missed the catch, and Claudia went sliding off the edge of the stage, and guess what?

The next day Max told her Mr. Anthony wanted her to do it that way every night. For the next two weeks, marines, sailors, and army boys crowded the edge of the stage waiting for it, and when she went over the side they tossed her up in the air and got as many hands on a girl as was possible to get on a moving target. When she didn't land back on stage, the Hulas rushed to the edge to rescue her and jumped down and fought the boys off. After the surprise of the first night, when it happened by accident, the orchestra just kept on playing through the melee. It was a big hit.

Claudia was worried about her girls and the integrity of the act and went to see Mr. Anthony with a reasonable concern. She pointed out how important it was to retain their women clientele. A man could suggest cocktails and a show at the Palmetto, but the woman would kill the deal if the place had a bad reputation. Mr. Anthony saw the logic in that and agreed to let her stop going over the edge of the stage.

"It will still work for us," Claudia noted, "because the boys know it can happen, so they'll be at the footlights waiting for it."

Flushed with the encouragement of finding it possible to reason with Mr. Anthony, Claudia brought up the matter of the high heels that only she had to wear, and a few other issues of low buffoonery that the girls didn't like. Mr. Anthony pulled the old excuse that none of them were his ideas. He said he was only following orders and could not have thought up any of those things himself. Then he sat back in his chair, looking more like a gangster than ever, and said, "Do I look like a comedian to you?"

The girls were the best part of the job. They were so sweet. Claudia knew they were putting money in the box outside her door because she started getting a check every week like the others from the Personal Initiative Program, the PIP. She did not have a single date in the first two months, and they must have felt bad about it because they were getting so many clients out of the act. When her PIP checks kept coming and kept getting bigger, she told the girls she knew they were putting money in her box and they had to cut it out because it was important for young women to be independent and have their own money. She said the jig was up, but then the girls started a new jig that had to do with their boyfriends.

Hula Girl boyfriends were banned from the club because the management felt their presence would inhibit the girls' performance. A short time after she made the girls stop putting money in her box, Claudia began to get some dates, and some of the faces looked kind of familiar from the parking lot. The girls were not good at keeping secrets, and one night Thunder, with a coy, sideways face, asked, "Remember that guy you had last night?"

"Sure," she said.

"Wasn't he cute?"

"Now that you mention it, yeah, he was."

Thunder came over close and held her arm and whispered in her ear. "I bet he was great, wasn't he? Wasn't he great?"

Of course, it was going to come out that he was Thunder's boyfriend, so Claudia had to say, yes, he was great. Thunder said her boyfriend had heard about Claudia from his buddies in the clerk typist pool at the base and had come to the club on his own initiative against the rules, and when he saw her, he wanted to have her so much. Thunder said he confessed. It was his own money too, she said. In time, Claudia had all twelve boyfriends, and she always found out the same way:

"You know that guy last night?"

"Yeah?"

"Wasn't he great?"

Claudia waited in the parking lot after closing every night before she called Takeo to come get her. She sat by the bushes along the side with her Chesterfields and coffee and stayed until each one of her girls got picked by her boyfriend, just to be sure they were safe. After she went to see Mr. Anthony again, she got a table with an umbrella and two chairs put out there, and she whiled away the time with one of Mr. Anthony's goons, Rivoli, who, she found out later, had volunteered his time.

Claudia couldn't figure out Rivoli from any angle. He didn't have a wedding ring and never said a word about his personal life. In a roundabout way, she asked Max about him one day when they were looking over some drawings Claudia was playing with for new Hula Girl costumes. She was going to take them to Mr. Anthony after Max looked them over.

"Oh, it's nothing to do with you, Jasmine," he said. "Just protocol."

"Didn't know that," said Claudia.

"In that line of work, you don't want people to know anything about you. You know. Something could happen."

Max looked over to the door of his office to check if anyone was out there and bent in over Claudia's drawings. "The other guys Mr. Anthony has working for him talk too much. They get lax out here because it ain't New York or Chicago or Kansas City, but Rivoli's solid. I never saw one like Rivoli. There's only one thing I know about him."

"What's that?"

Max knew all along what she was getting at.

"I know he likes you."

Claudia shrugged it off. "So you're not going to spill any beans, are you?" she said. "Now, what do you think of this one with the tight bodice and cross straps?"

It was nice having something to smile to herself about. But she was left with observation and deduction as her only tools to figuring out Rivoli. He had that lustrous Italian hair, close at the sides but wavy on top. His eyes were always in the shadow of his brow, but Claudia knew they were always moving and watching, and he had a scar along one cheek that would have been the envy of any German duelist. There was a rugged look to him that went strangely well with the impeccably tailored Canali suits he wore. Even the pinstripes were so good you couldn't tell he had a shoulder holster under there. He still looked gangland, but classy. All she knew for certain was the aftershave. Miagonelli Tadera. No doubt about it. They had good talks over their coffee and smokes. Takeo liked him too, and sometimes the three of them stayed late talking after the girls got their rides.

Claudia couldn't complain. The little boyfriend activity broke the ice with some of the regulars at the club, and she started getting some business of her own. Dan would have called it a trend in the market. Now she was making some money, and she couldn't pass it up because she had started making promises to Edgar Lee about things he wanted, like a bike.

Some of the Hula boyfriends were nice, but Claudia could tell some of them were loafers, living off their girlfriends. She didn't want to say anything about that because it would only interfere and hurt people's feelings, but how could you send your boyfriend to another girl like that? And why would the boy do it if he really loved his girl? The Hulas also began to ask her privately how the other girl's men were, and Claudia had to draw the line.

It was up to her. She was the oldest and the most experienced. She knew the girls looked up to her, even the old hands, because she had a keen eye for the assets and vulnerabilities of each one of them, and gave good advice when they came to her. Maybe they came to her because she was the only one who looked different from the others. Who knows? But as the months passed and Claudia saw them remain just a ragtag batch of beautiful girls, she began to understand what leadership and unit cohesion could do for them, and she came to the inescapable conclusion that she was the one to forge this scrappy bunch into something they would all be proud to be a part of.

The Hulas had started gathering around her in the dressing room before they went on every night. It was just to give them a little pep talk like the boys do in locker rooms, but it was always about the act. She had never addressed the chatter about the back rooms, and one night she decided it was time to establish professional standards for the ensemble. She explained to them that the Hulas were like doctors, lawyers, and priests.

"Sometimes men act in ways they would want to keep private," she said. "So you must consider yourselves professionally bound to client confidentiality. That means you don't say anything about what happens in the back rooms to anyone but your supervisor."

"Who's that?" said Sassy. "Max?"

Everybody thought that was so funny.

"No, not Max. You can use me for that, but I don't want to hear anything unless it concerns your personal safety. Not the usual stupid stuff, no matter how strange it might be."

"Strange like what?" asked Moonglow.

Then they all started laughing and talking at once and swatting Moonglow with their grass skirts.

"No, no, no," said Claudia, holding up her hand to quiet them down. "You can't say anything about what goes on back there."

"That isn't any fun," said Pinkie and Hot Lava, almost at the same time.

"Or in here either. What we say in here between ourselves is for Hula Girls only. You have to see it as part of our job."

"We're just dancing whores."

"That's beside the point, Kitten," said Claudia. "Get back in here, Sassy, this is for you too. Listen to me, girls, it's an important job. It may not be fun, and it isn't work that anyone back home would understand, but it's what we can do for the morale of these boys and make the war safe for democracy."

"I thought we only had to get their dicks up," said Hot Lava.

Claudia laughed along with the others but then she bore down. "Sure that's what we do, but every one of you is in a bigger picture, a picture bigger than all of us. Oh, I know. Nobody in a show bra and a grass skirt is going to save the world. We aren't punching in at factories, turning out airplanes and tanks, or plowing the fields. But on stage and in the back rooms, we inspire the manhood of America. To them, we are the wives and girls they left behind. Some of these boys may never come back. Some of those boys who lay down with you may even now lie under the grass of foreign fields where crosses grow between the poppies row on row. Let the ones who have passed this way, those boys who have whispered in our ears and spent their passions in these rooms, let them go forth with cherished memories of American womanhood in their loins, memories that stir their hearts to fight on with their last full measure of emotion. God bless America. Now let's get out there and show them what we're made of."

The girls shut up because they always listened to her, and then they cheered her and went up the stairs ready to take on the world. It was just a shame that after a good speech like that, Claudia had to stuff her bosoms into a rigged show bra and put on a cut-off grass skirt that made her look like a hippopotamus in high heels. Rivoli told her that he heard the cheers up on the floor, even with the orchestra going full tilt. It got a little smile out of him. He must have known the cheers were because of her.

CHAPTER THIRTY-FOUR

Claudia didn't think Froggy came into the club very much. Anyway, she didn't see him, and she avoided circulating on weekend nights because she didn't want to run into anyone she knew, even though she went on the floor in regulation show bra and grass skirt. Annette knew about the job because she was over for Edgar Lee, and they talked all the time. Claudia never mentioned the PIP, but it might have been common knowledge that something besides dancing was going on. Whenever she saw Annette at the club, she always went over to chat and brushed off any men who asked her for a date on the way back to the bar.

The first few months, Claudia had worried that Froggy might come in some night solo with twenty bucks for a session in the back room. But it didn't look like he was going to do that, thank God. He must have seen the show, and maybe he knew about the back rooms, but maybe he didn't notice since he was always with people and putting on an act of his own, except that one time at the Captain Cook when he tried to help her after Dan left.

She didn't know why it even bothered her. She just missed having a man friend like she thought he was going to be.

When Claudia saw him at the club one night with Annette, Elaine, Fitzy, and some new men, it was like old times. Claudia was just the one in the grass skirt and show bra. When she moved on to check on the clientele at other tables, Froggy gave her a special look that made her feel good. She wondered why it made her feel so good. She decided it was because people who knew her before her present situation accepted her for what she was now. But what she was now was changing too. Annette was the first one to see it printed on the program, and she showed it to everyone else:

"Floor Show Produced and Directed by Max Levine and Jasmine Lambeau."

"That's you, isn't it, Claudia?" she said.

It started with "Fighting Hulas of America," a new routine Claudia thought up, modeled after the endless parades she sat through at Annapolis. Max helped her work out the choreography as she explained what she envisioned—Hulas marching in place, splitting off, wheeling, coming back together, and fanning out across the stage in a big finish. They needed a traveling step for so much moving around, and they came up with a slide and skip that had lots of versatility for covering ground. It was a real effort to get the girls to come in early, but after a few weeks it got easier when they saw how fantastic it could be. They worked with the orchestra to coordinate the music, and when they opened the show with it, "Fighting Hulas of America" was a big hit and put the Palmetto Hula Girls on the map with the *Honolulu Star Gazette*.

Max and Claudia followed up with a dance step they named The Tendardee that they added to "Hulas Reach for the Sky." In production, The Tendardee was top secret. They had to get a gym teacher in to train the girls. Even with all the stunts they performed in the back rooms, the girls had to train hard for The Tendardee. Claudia was surprised she could do it, since it incorporated a split and a twist, chest up with a bounce, some hip rotation, a great leap, and lots of legs. She invented it sitting on the floor. The trick was doing it in midair. She brought it to Max, and they pondered over it long and hard and finally came up with a way to sequence it. The Hulas were sworn to secrecy.

The night they set to debut The Tendardee was a tense one for Max and Claudia. They sat in his office, drinking coffee and smoking, tossing their doubts back and forth. Two months of training. Were the Hulas ready? The girls were waiting in the dressing room for a final decision. Everybody was tense. There was a cloud of smoke coming through the dressing room door.

"Maybe we need more time," said Max. "We still haven't had one rehearsal without somebody falling."

"I don't know," said Claudia. "They've had a lot of training and a lot of practice. It would be bad to see more time give us diminishing returns."

"They won't have rails or mats up there, ya know. Somebody could get hurt."

"I know," said Claudia.

There were so many factors to consider. She thought Max would have a firm opinion, but he went back and forth like she did. There was a long silence while they looked down at their smokes over the ashtray.

"Rhapsody's weak," said Max in an abject, distracted way.

"We can put her between Starfire and Kitten."

"How's that gonna help when they get to the split? I don't know if we're ready to go tonight, Jasmine. Too many things can go wrong."

"But we picked tonight," said Claudia. "If we postpone, it will look like we don't think they can do it."

"Do you think they can?"

"I don't know, Max, but right now they think they can. If we put it off a night or a week, it'll destroy their confidence. They've got the confidence now. I don't want them to lose it. I'll be in the lead. They'll follow the cue at the number three take-off. That's half way there."

"You know your girls."

"I say we go."

The decision was passed next door to the Hula Girls dressing room. D-Day. The word was greeted at first with boisterous spirits, hugs, and pats on the back. Then a quiet fell over them as they suited up. Fury, Thunder, Sassy, Tender Trap, Pinkie, Venus, Rhapsody, Atlantis, Hot Lava, Kitten, Starfire, Moonglow. Tonight was the night. After the weeks and months of secrecy and training, tonight they were going up there to do The Tendardee. Claudia stood at the dressing room door and bid each of them good luck. She stayed for a moment alone, feeling the heavy burden of command. Was she sending them to injury, ridicule, and humiliation? They were trained. They were ready and their spirits were high, but could they do it? Watching the grass skirts go up the circular metal stairs one by one in close file, Claudia thought it was nice that sometimes life left a window open and let you try to fly. Then she turned out the light and followed her girls up.

All it took for The Tendardee to sweep the world of nightclub entertainment was a flawless performance and a chance photograph taken from the floor at just the right moment. There was also the audible gasp of five hundred soldiers and sailors that would live in the memory of anyone who could say he was there that night. A week later, a reporter and photographer from *Life* magazine were in Mr. Anthony's office, and two weeks after that, the Palmetto appeared in their spread, "*Life* Goes to a Nightclub." It turned out to be Claudia's second near miss with getting into *Life* magazine. She was out back having a smoke with Rivoli when *Life* came.

Claudia had some leverage with Mr. Anthony now. From what she had heard from Doris in bookkeeping, the Palmetto was breaking records because of the Hula Girls. A week after the spread in *Life*, Claudia got her girls more money up front at $100 a week, twenty percent on the PIP, and the price up to $50 for the back rooms. She gave the girls a lecture about money, and during the next week she took them one at a time over to the Honolulu City Savings and Loan and showed them how to open a savings account. She had to learn how to do it herself first, so it was like everything else in her life.

Negotiating with Mr. Anthony was another thing Claudia learned to do. He understood business and making money, so she had to tie that in with what she wanted for her girls. She avoided confrontation and particularly ultimatums after the first time she tried one, when Mr. Anthony sat back in his chair and said, "Or else what?"

She got the regulation show bra and grass skirt for circulating and got him to let her get rid of the high heels, but the one point he would never concede was the trick bra and her bosoms popping out in "The Grand Finale." He would not even consider it. Claudia tried to convince him that it was more than just a nightclub act now. The Palmetto had drawn national attention. The Hula Girls were held in high esteem, and she showed him where *Life* reported in a follow-up that even the choreographers of the Bolshoi Ballet could not figure out how they did The Tendardee. Why would you want to detract from that with a two-bit vaudeville stunt?

Max explained it to her later. "Because it's what they call in show business an old chestnut," he said. "Mr. Anthony might be—you know—sentimental about it."

On April 12, the President died. Everyone was shocked. He wasn't looking good in the newsreels, but no one thought there wouldn't be a President Roosevelt anymore. The club was closed for three days and nights, but they made up for it not long after that when the Germans threw in the towel. The VE Day party at the Palmetto went on all night for two nights. Claudia tried to keep control of her girls, but all the Hulas got drunk, and she and Max abandoned the floor show for the next three nights. Mr. Anthony didn't care as long as the people kept crowding up to the bar. The sailors and marines and army boys overran the Hula Girl private rooms like the Alamo, and Claudia had to press the goon button more than a few times to get the boys off the Hulas. Mr. Anthony's men were always stone cold sober. Service boys knew you didn't fool with goons, and Mr. Anthony's goons looked real.

Everyone was glad the war was over in Europe. Hitler was dead, and they were rounding up all the big Nazis. Now Japan was really going to get slaughtered. Claudia had a few clients in back, regular nice married guys. They missed their wives, and sometimes they just liked to talk and didn't want all that jazzy sex. It felt about right to her because she was older, twenty-seven, and still had not lost weight, and she had stopped kidding herself about it. How could she? The other girls were so gorgeous. One dropped out every so often to get married, and the new girls from the States she interviewed for Mr. Anthony were like a new generation of gorgeous. The corridor now had part of the wall as a Hula Hall of Fame, with pictures of the greats of yesteryear. Someday her picture would hang there too, but she wasn't finished being great yet.

Mrs. Butter turned out to be a gem. One night when she came home, Claudia asked her if she knew any seamstress ladies, and it turned out she knew a whole church full. It was a case of the right people at the right time, and that's just what she told Mr. Anthony. He wouldn't go for a costume shop in the club, but he agreed to hire them on as outside temporaries for a limited production run. Mrs. Butter and her ladies went to work on their sewing machines at home and knocked out some of Claudia's designs. Before long, there was a new, original, eye-catching look to the Hulas every week.

Mr. Anthony didn't like the money Claudia spent on feathers, but he quit grousing about it when he saw the reviews in the papers the day after "Hula Girls Aztec Splendor" hit the boards. Believe it or not, it was in the fashion pages. Claudia never figured him for a publicity hound, but it got easier to get money out of him for a costume shop when the Palmetto Costume Shop took home most of the awards at the 1944 Honolulu Theater Guild convention. That was a week before the costume shop existed.

The Hula Girls did a special show for the ceremony in the ballroom of the Grand Hawaiian that night. It was themed "Hulas in Paris" and featured a gay 90s cancan with the Hulas in petticoats, and a Tendardee finale that knocked everybody on their keisters. Accepting the awards were Mr. Anthony and Mrs. Butter. Jasmine Lambeau was unable to attend because Claudia stayed home with Edgar Lee making grilled cheese. What's the point of an alias if your picture is going to be in the papers? Renovations for the Palmetto Costume Shop started the next day in two large storage rooms of the club, and it turned out fabulous.

Edgar Lee wanted to see the show at the club. She told him that he was too young to go in the Palmetto because they served liquor. That was an easy out. It was getting hard to keep him in the dark about her job, and she wasn't sure how to explain it yet, and she didn't want to ask Annette. When she first started working with Mrs. Butter, there were some repairs going on at the Palmetto, and the Hulas had to come around to the Strickland for their costume fittings. Edgar Lee came home early because it was some saint's birthday and walked in on twelve girls in their underwear, and some of them were sitting on his bed reading his comic books. Claudia told him she and Mrs. Butter were helping with a high school play. Of course, the girls were all over Edgar Lee because he was so cute. After that, he couldn't wait to get to high school.

Every night when she came home from the club, she looked at Edgar Lee sleeping. He was too big for his boy bed now. That wouldn't be a problem. There was plenty of money. There was enough to move into an apartment with more than one room, but she didn't want just a little for Edgar Lee. She wanted everything for him. And that meant saving every penny she could and getting into real estate before the rush left her behind. In the meantime, she was learning, and that was as important as the money. She was learning about men and the world and business. It had never been part of her experience, and as she learned those things, she tried to raise Edgar Lee and keep a wary eye on the world that was coming.

CHAPTER THIRTY-FIVE

It wasn't much of a life for Edgar Lee, but he did not seem to remember any other life but the one that started and ended every day in one room at the Strickland. It was harder on her than on him. He didn't have a past as far as Claudia could tell. A year had gone by since "All Ashore for Bosco." She was the one with a past, and now there were her big plans for the future. Too bad you have to live through the present to get there.

Annette dropped in to see Edgar Lee a few times a month as a maintenance check, and every Thursday Claudia had coffee with her at the French Café. Claudia could not resist telling her about the $8,000 she had saved up in the Hulas and her plan to go into real estate with Captain Locarno. Annette was all ears when it came to big money and wanted in. They put their heads together and got very excited thinking ahead to the day when they would have a respectable amount of money to make a pitch.

Annette didn't have much saved because she was such a clotheshorse, but she thought she could go in for $1,000. Claudia knew she was going to have to rein in Annette's expectations, but it was nice thinking she had a trustworthy business partner who was good with psychology. Captain Locarno had seemed more interested in making money than beautiful women at the Admiral Harris party. But he was still a man, and since men have psychology too, you know women are in there somewhere, even with Captain Locarno.

Claudia never asked Annette how she brought Edgar Lee back. She regarded it as a matter of client confidentiality, like the men she had at the club. She could have told Annette some doozies about men, and she suspected Annette could tell her some things about eight-year-old boys that would make her head spin, but they only alluded to such things in a general way. Claudia tried to advise her on the men who came and went in her life, and Annette gave her things to consider about Edgar Lee. They discussed the possibility that someday he might be able to remember his real mother without trauma and whether that would impose a moral obligation upon Claudia to tell him the truth. For the moment, they were both pleased with his progress. The night frights were gone. He slept in his own bed, and he had given up crayoning in red on the walls.

Claudia went to every PTA meeting at the Catholic school, where Edgar Lee was in second grade. She just sat and listened because she did not want to attract attention to herself, but when they held parents' night at the school, she always talked to his teacher, Miss Alcott, and sat at Edgar Lee's little desk. She always left him a note inside that said, "I love you Edgar Lee." She knew she wouldn't be able to do that for long, but he was still at the age when he liked it.

Just when everything was going so great, the Department of Social Welfare Services for Children lowered the boom. They abducted Edgar Lee. Annette came right over to the Strickland. Claudia thought working at the club had made her tough, but this was a flank attack and a drive for the soft underbelly. She was so upset that she was lighting one Chesterfield after another. Annette put her hands over Claudia's to stop them from shaking.

"I'm sure I can help, Claudia," she said. "Just tell me what happened."

"I'm sorry, Annette. I'm so glad you could come over. Do you want some coffee?"

At first Annette said no, but then she said yes, probably because it would give her something to do besides shaking like a leaf and chain smoking. Claudia was glad to see that psychology worked even if you knew you were getting tricked, because after she cleaned the morning coffee grounds out of the percolator and got it started up, she felt better. She came back to the table and lit up another Chesterfield and picked up all the cigarettes she had dropped on the floor.

"I went over to get him at school, but he didn't come out with the other kids, so I went into the office and asked where's Edgar Lee, and they said he had been removed by the Department of Social Welfare Services for Children. They said a man and a lady had come in that morning with a court order, and they took Edgar Lee out of his class and drove off with him."

"Okay, so he wasn't kidnapped."

"Well, they just took him, Annette."

"But we know who has him, I mean."

"Well, anyway, then I ran home as fast as I could so I could call them, but there was a man and a lady here, coming out of the room with Edgar Lee's suitcase, and they had another court order. They wouldn't listen to anything I said. They gave me a card. Here."

Annette looked at the card and turned it over. "What's this?" she said.

"That's my writing. I'm supposed to call the number of the juvenile court in two weeks to get a case number and a hearing date. Two weeks, Annette. Edgar Lee can't take it two weeks. He'll go back to being crazy."

"No, he won't," Annette said quickly. "You leave it to me. I'll go back to the office and make some calls, and I'll call you in an hour. Now you just relax, Claudia. You've got the full weight of the United States Navy behind you."

She got up and grabbed her purse and was out the door in a minute.

After she left, Claudia felt much better. She was so worried about Edgar Lee, but she knew Annette would come through. She had some more coffee and smoked one Chesterfield after another and kept saying to herself, "That's the navy for you."

An hour later, right on time, Annette called her back on the telephone out in the hall. She said it didn't look good. Edgar Lee was being held in the juvenile detention center, pending placement in a foster home. The case would be reviewed in three weeks, and if she wanted to hire a lawyer and file an affidavit for custody of Edgar Lee, it would only be considered if she quit her job, got married to someone with a verifiable salary, and moved into a single-family dwelling. Then she said, "There's someone here who wants to talk to you." It was Froggy.

"Hi, Claudia," he said.

"Hi, Froggy."

"Can I come over?"

Claudia knew what was coming. She didn't have any choice. When Froggy came over, it was obvious that he had detoured from the office to shave and shower up and put on aftershave. She made him coffee. He proposed taking her out to dinner at the Grand Hawaiian, but she wanted to stay home, so they sat at the table quietly and put away some cheese and crackers and got out their smokes for the parley.

"You can marry me, Claudia," he said.

"What about Elaine?"

"It's not going anywhere."

"Does she know that?"

"We talked already. She knows how I feel about you. She knows I'm here now."

Claudia let that settle for a minute while she tried to think of a way to say something honest.

"How would you feel about marrying someone who didn't love you?"

"I wouldn't mind."

"It's not supposed to be like that when you get married, Froggy."

"I know. But I think you might love me after a while."

"What makes you think that?"

He smiled with a lot of confidence and said, "You'll get to know me."

"I think I know enough right now."

"Not really."

Claudia didn't want to go through this anymore.

"I like you a lot, Froggy, I really do, but when you get married, you get together in an intimate way, and you should want to do that, you know? If you still want to marry me knowing I don't feel like that about you—I'm sorry, this is awful."

"No, I want you to be honest about it. I know that's how you feel now."

"Well, do you still want to marry me?"

"I sure do."

They sat looking at their coffee cups on the table and smoking. Then Claudia put her hand over his and said she would let him know tomorrow. He said he could come back around four in the afternoon. He gave her a little hug at the door and told her not to worry about Edgar Lee. It would be all right.

Claudia put a scarf over her head like Mary Ann did and went to the church. She knew she had to marry Froggy. It wasn't that. She prayed for Edgar Lee. He was so fragile and helpless, and she couldn't do anything to help him. All the weeks for this and weeks for that and lawyers and courts. She could get through it. Froggy would be her husband, and they could buy a nice house, and it would turn out to be the best thing for Edgar Lee if he could wait that long and not go crazy. She prayed for Edgar Lee with a contrite heart, and presently, there in the cool dark of the church, an idea came to her.

Claudia walked home with a gathering confidence that made her want to run the last block. When she got there, she went right to the telephone and called Mr. Anthony. He listened to the whole story and said he would look into it.

Edgar Lee was home by seven o'clock that night, accompanied by Rivoli and another of Mr. Anthony's men. Claudia had no idea who was at the door and hit Edgar Lee like a tidal wave of hugs and kisses and oh God, oh God, oh God. Edgar Lee was fine. She rushed him in and locked the door and sat him at the table and could hardly make him cheese and crackers for running back and forth kissing him.

"I knew you'd spring me from the slammer, Mom," he said.

"Spring you what?"

"It was a real jail, Mom, with bars and everything."

"Where did you learn to talk like that?"

"The guys. There were big kids too, not just babies. Some of the guys were on the lam and got picked up by the fuzz. I told them you were going to spring me, and they said, yeah, sure, but then the two heavies came. Boy, were they surprised."

Claudia stood him up under the light right away and checked him for lice. She pulled off his clothes and thrust them into the laundry bag, and then she marched Edgar Lee down the hall in his bathrobe to the men's bathroom. She scrubbed him head to toe in Pine Sol, marched him back, and cooked up a pork chop with applesauce and peas and carrots. She let him eat his dinner sitting in the big armchair with the tray across, like a special day when she let him stay home from school pretending to be sick.

She was getting ready to go to work when there was a knock at the door. She thought it was Mrs. Butter a little early, but it turned out to be Rivoli. He took off his hat and extended his compliments and those of Mr. Anthony and handed her a handsome leather binder with a law firm name embossed in gold. He apologized for the delay in the paperwork.

Edgar Lee did not just come home, he came with papers. There was a birth certificate, a baptismal certificate, a passport, a notice of confirmation in the church, a complete medical history, and even two years of report cards with good grades. He had gotten all E's since first grade and only two G's in music. It was all so authentic looking that it made Claudia want to go talk to the teacher about the G's in music. He was now officially Edgar Lee Wyler and, according to the paperwork, he had always been the natural child of Jack and Claudia Wyler.

Included in the packet was a photograph out of the newspaper of the first-prize winner of the 1937 Waikiki Beach Baby Parade. The baby in the stroller, captioned as Edgar Lee Wyler, was pictured in a headdress that looked like one out of the Palmetto club costume shop. Nice touch.

Edgar Lee was now hers. Officially hers. At first Claudia was overwhelmed with her feelings for him because some part of her had always held them back, but now he was hers for keeps. She loved him with a true mother's love. She may not have actually brought him into the world, but that did not matter anymore. She was earning her motherhood badge every night when she strapped on her show bra and grass skirt and with every man she lay down for in the back room and with all the hours she put into making the show. She was catching on to the world and getting smart, and by golly, she was going to earn Edgar Lee with all her heart and soul. From that day on, Claudia thought of Edgar Lee as her own boy, and if anybody ever asked, she would make no bones about it. She was glad her prayers had been answered and Edgar Lee had not gone to pieces in the slammer. But the way he fussed in the shower, she had a feeling it was the last time he was ever going to let her see his penis. No enemas either. He was a little man now.

When Claudia got home from work that night, she asked Mrs. Butter if she could stay a little while longer. She pulled Mary Ann's box out from under the bed and made sure Edgar Lee was fast asleep before she got the key and unlocked it. She separated out all of Edgar Lee's real papers and put them on top. She could not make up her mind about the rest, so she put it all back in and took the whole box down to the beach.

It was a beautiful, calm night with a nice white moon almost full. She sat down and opened Mary Ann's box and took out Edgar Lee's real papers. She dug a hole in the sand and put the papers in and started a little fire. One minute she wanted to put everything in, and the next minute she changed her mind. Finally, she decided to only burn up Edgar Lee's papers. She saved Mary Ann's papers and the couple of baby pictures of Mary Ann with Edgar Lee that Bill had taken with his camera, and little notes Mary Ann had written her. By the moonlight she looked into Mary Ann's face in the pictures, and it hurt deep in her heart.

Claudia held the ivory polar bears in her hand and into the ashes of the fire she said, "I'll take care of our polar bears, Mary Ann. You never saw them, but they're just like us, and they're hugging. We'll always be together, Mary Ann. We'll always be together."

Then she took the ashes in her hands and walked down to the little waves coming in, walked out to her knees, and gently spread the ashes on the dark water.

"Goodbye, Mary Ann," she said. "Goodbye, Mary Ann. I love you. I'll take care of Edgar Lee. I love you, Mary Ann. Goodbye."

CHAPTER THIRTY-SIX

The only missing ingredient was a husband. Edgar Lee was going to need a father. She could tell it would not be long before all those male misconceptions and dangerous fallacies started seeping into his blood. A dad would show him how to control that stuff. All she knew was how to charge the right amount of money for it. But she knew about girls, and that might be useful information for Edgar Lee later on, so that might keep her in the picture. She didn't even have to take notes. The young Hulas with their emotional turmoils with boyfriends kept her jumping.

Froggy had already heard the news from Annette, but he still came over at four o'clock the next day. They had coffee and smoked some Chesterfields and Luckys and talked. Claudia thanked him for his kind offer, but he stopped her from going on about it. She realized he saw the difference between how desperate she was yesterday and how calm and happy she was today, knowing she did not have to marry him, and he probably didn't want it rubbed in his face that she was so relieved. He just said, "Well maybe next time."

Claudia felt bad about it, but she never said she would marry him. That was a great relief, too. She would not have gone back on her word if she had agreed to marry him last night. Edgar Lee could have come back safe with all his papers, and she would have been stuck. Then, she supposed, it would have been up to Froggy. He would have known she did not love him, and she had accepted under duress, and now saving Edgar Lee had been removed as the reason for it. Claudia wondered if Froggy would have had enough confidence in his lovability to go through with the deal or if he would have let her off the hook. But she didn't spend much time thinking about it. It was just the road not taken.

Annette tried to help her out, and Claudia tried on a couple of her hand-me-down men, but nothing caught fire. That was a good way to put it. It was hard to explain any other way, but when they had coffee at the French Café, Claudia felt they really got into the deep issues.

"So what was wrong with Froggy?"

That was what Annette jumped into, before they even sat down and got out their cigarettes. Claudia said, "Well—" and let it hang while they hung their purses over the chairs and pulled them in under the big umbrella so they could both be out of the sun, and then she said another "Well—" to hold them until the coffee and Annette's chocolate cake appeared.

"Well?" said Annette.

"Well, you know. First of all, there's the name."

"It's John C. Ransome. The C is for Calder."

"Oh," said Claudia. "I could never call him that."

"For Pete's sake, why not?"

"Because he's just Froggy."

"That's funny, but I kind of understand. Okay, so what else?"

"Well, Annette, I don't want to sound shallow, but it would be hard for me to fall in love with a face like that. I mean, it would take an effort, you know? White skin with orange freckles and red hair never appealed to me. He's great, and I'm flattered he would have married me to save Edgar Lee. I could love him for that, but—" Then she had to pause to think of the right words. "But you fall in love with a face. That's the difference. You're going to be—you know, intimate with the one you marry, so you want to be able to get excited for those times and have a nice face to look at while you're doing it. That's what I mean." And then she quickly added, "They like it more if they think you're excited."

"I guess you'd know more about that than I would," said Annette, "since you've been married, I mean."

Claudia was pretty sure Annette knew she was a prostitute or had figured it out, but Annette seemed to accept people for what they were. She was never critical of anyone and would never ask questions that might make someone feel bad. Claudia thought it was a good example to follow and never asked her what she had done with Jack. It was like the Code of the Hulas.

"So let's get practical," said Annette. "What kind of man do you want? You have to give me some guidelines."

"Someone like Jack."

Annette put a piece of chocolate cake into her mouth and brought her teeth down like a stunning white portcullis on the tines of the fork as she drew it out.

"Mmmmmmmh," she said. "He was nice."

Annette could eat anything she wanted. She had not gained an ounce in four years or lost any of her looks. Once or twice, when the light came from the right direction, Claudia caught sight of a strand of gray, but it disappeared into the dark lovely night of rich black all around her face like it had jumped its cue and ducked back behind the curtain real quick.

"That's a tall order," she added.

"I know, but that's what I want."

"What was wrong with Glenn Franklin? He kind of looked like Jack."

"Well," said Claudia, "nothing really. He took me to a restaurant on the north shore. I didn't have the heart to tell him that Jack and I sat at the same table once, so I just thought about Jack the whole time. Then he took me sailing. Now, Annette, tell me. Would I look good in a boat?"

"Oh, Claudia, you'd look good anywhere. You have such nice hair."

"A fat lot of good that does when you have to cut the date short to get back by three o'clock to get your son from school."

"So what was wrong with that guy Alec?"

"Nothing. He was perfectly fine. The zing just wasn't there."

"Who needs zing? Look at James."

Annette was seeing a middle-aged man from the U.S. Geological Survey. Claudia had met him at the club.

"I think I really love him," said Annette. "But no zing. You have to get over the thing about zing, Claudia."

Claudia took out another Chesterfield, and Annette got out another Lucky. The wind off the ocean was picking up, so they lit up with their faces together and their hair swirling around.

"The zing is important," said Claudia, sitting back in her chair. "I mean, as long as you're under thirty, there's going to be, you know, intimacy, right? So I'm looking for the zing. A man's looks have to slay me." Then she leaned forward and whispered, "You know that little grab you get sometimes?"

The question looked dead on arrival. Annette had a blank expression on her face. For as close as she felt to Annette, there were private, intimate topics outside the Code that they had not talked about. Maybe nobody did. Mary Ann knew about it. She wondered if Annette knew. What if she didn't? What the hell—Claudia leaned in again and whispered.

"There's a little grab you can get sometimes when you're around a man," she said. She lowered her eyes. "Down there."

"Okay—" Annette looked like she might have had a grab once and was interested in hearing more.

"Well." Claudia leaned back for a long draw on her Chesterfield and then looked around to be sure no one was near enough to hear and leaned in again. "Well, if you've ever felt it, you know. But what you may not know is, it's nothing compared to the follow-through. It's like an earthquake hit you."

That seemed to hit home, and Claudia was glad she didn't have to try to explain it a better way. Tidal wave or getting electrocuted were up next. Now it was Annette leaning in. Her hair spread over the table as she brought her face in close and whispered.

"Are you talking about an orgasm?"

"I didn't know there was a word."

"Oh, sure. I have them sometimes."

"With men?" Claudia was shocked, but she tried not to show it.

"Oh, no. What do you think I am?—Oh, I didn't mean it like that. It's just that I've never been with a man. In that way, I mean. I do it myself. Not a lot. Just sometimes. I take it you have them, too. Some women can't, you know. How often do you do it?—No, I shouldn't ask. You don't have to tell me."

Suddenly the foot was on the other shoe, but Claudia didn't care. She liked Annette so much and now they had become such good friends. They could turn out to be best friends. It would make her feel so good to have someone.

"I've only had two," Claudia said. "Well actually only one that I'm sure of. The other one was kind of by accident."

"You can do it yourself, you know. It's easy," Annette whispered.

"Oh, I know. But you're not supposed to. I try not to think about it. I'm saving it for when I'm married." Then she brightened up with the whole idea. "Besides Edgar Lee, that's another reason why I want to get married."

"Well, I'll keep trying to get you somebody with zing," said Annette. "Do you want any of this?" She held up the last piece of chocolate cake.

"Oh, no thanks."

"You never eat anything, Claudia. You aren't on a diet, are you?"

"Not now," said Claudia. "Probably next week. I want to get back to one ten before I go on any more dates in boats."

Annette looked into her coffee, and Claudia knew she was holding something back.

"What is it, Annette?"

"Well, it's just that I don't think you're ever going to do it."

"Yes, I am."

"No, you aren't. I think you're going to stay heavy."

Claudia crossed her legs and narrowed her look on Annette.

"Is this something psychological?"

"Yes, I think it is, Claudia."

"Then don't you think you should tell me?"

"All right. It might help. I think you don't really want to lose weight. You want a man to accept you for what you are."

"Why would I want anyone like that?"

Annette had to laugh, but Claudia knew immediately that she was right. She had faith in Annette, and after seeing the good she had done for Edgar Lee, she was beginning to trust psychology more. It seemed to get to the bottom of why people behave the way they do. Psychology mostly explained the bad things. Everybody took the good things for granted and only expected psychology to explain the bad ones. Maybe psychology should try looking under the pretty rocks sometimes and not just the bad rocks. But for now, Claudia could accept Annette's insight as to why she had a weight problem, and it sure sounded like a pretty good excuse for getting one of those donuts she had been admiring at another table.

"I'm that way, too," said Annette. "There are things I want James to accept about me that I can't change—until he accepts them."

"Oh sure, like what?"

"Just things," said Annette.

Then she did it again. Annette could arch her eyebrows, one higher than the other, narrow those sultry eyes, flare her nostrils, and slightly part her perfect hunter's bow lips, all in one expression. Talk about a face to fall in love with. It always knocked Claudia flat. She could be in love with Annette in a second, as easy as rolling off a log. Anything can happen in life, she thought. But she also knew that a lot of things don't happen. Life is full of things that don't happen.

In the next few weeks, Claudia went out with a few more men that Annette found, but nothing had any get-up-and-go. She kept coming back to thinking about Rivoli. Maybe it was because they sat out at their table every night, drinking coffee and smoking Chesterfields, waiting for the last Hula Girl to get picked up, and the nights were so beautiful under the palm trees with the wind off the ocean. He was so good-looking and such a sharp dresser, and he treated her like the princess of the Hulas, not the grande dame, and she definitely felt the zing for him.

But they were both employees of the club, and it was against the rules. It was a rule she made up herself for the Hula Girls, and she got Mr. Anthony to put it before the board of directors, and it soon appeared in a new version of the Palmetto Employee Handbook. It was on that occasion that she asked Mr. Anthony if she could attend a meeting of the board as a representative of the Hula Girls, who were now so famous. All he said was, "No. They don't live around here."

It was too bad about Rivoli because Claudia knew she could go for him in a big way. She just didn't want to be married to him for twenty years and find out he was the one who cut Mary Ann's throat. It didn't help thinking that if any man could keep a secret like that from his wife, it would be Rivoli.

Froggy came over to the room at the Strickland one night. He walked in with a big Hawaiian shirt, short pants, and leather sandals. He said he was in the neighborhood. Edgar Lee was over at Nick's for the night, and it was her night off at the club. Annette was the only person who knew she was going to be alone, so he must have gotten it from her. It was too much of a coincidence that he had gin and tonic and limes in the car, along with a bottle of bourbon, a big can of pretzels, his record player, and some albums.

Claudia felt like letting her hair down a little with Edgar Lee away, so she let Froggy bring all of it in, and they got a little drunk. It was nice to play whatever songs she wanted, and they danced a few boogie-woogie ones until the neighbors downstairs knocked on the ceiling. Then they turned the music down and put on some mellow stuff and had a few more drinks. They ended up lying on the bed, with Claudia lying the right direction and Froggy lying the other way with his head propped up on the extra pillow at Claudia's feet. They were really drunk, and when Froggy stopped talking and closed his eyes, Claudia wiggled her toes under his chin.

"I heard it's over with Elaine," said Claudia.

"Yeah, she wanted to get married to somebody else." He was looking up at the ceiling and started throwing one of Claudia's shoes up in the air and catching it.

"That's too bad," she said. "Are you broken up about it?"

"Nah, it didn't take me by surprise."

"You'll find somebody else. There's plenty of fish in the sea, Froggy. Will you stop throwing that shoe?"

"Okay, okay. Be nice to me. My life has been shattered."

"You don't look too shattered to me."

"It's just a brave front."

"You don't have to do that for me, Froggy. We're friends."

"Yes, well, about that—"

"No, we can just be friends, Froggy. You've been a good friend to me, and I want to be a good friend to you. Sometimes being friends means just being friends."

"I thought that was what it always meant."

Froggy sat up like someone who had sobered up from one minute to the next and made a decision.

"On that note," he said, "I must bid you adieu. Good night, my dear."

Claudia helped him carry his bottles and record player and records down to the car. He leaned over and kissed her on the cheek, got in his little car, and swerved off around the corner. Claudia walked up the steps to the long hallway and went back to her room, hoping she would not be reading in the papers that he had been eaten by a shark or was in jail. With Froggy it was hard to tell. If she really wanted to be his friend, she should have kept him there and talked until they got to his hurt feelings and consoled him. But they were probably too drunk for that.

It was three o'clock in the morning, but Claudia was wide awake. She poured out the bottom of the percolator and sat down at the table with a Chesterfield and a cup of cold old coffee. She was a prostitute. Annette knew. Something tonight made her think Froggy knew, too. She wondered if prostitutes could really have friends. *Woman's Home Companion* said it was important to accept yourself for what you were, but it probably never got letters to the editor from prostitutes. She felt like a vacant building, the kind with broken windows and tattered curtains.

Claudia didn't bother to wash her face and brush her teeth. She turned off the light and took off all her clothes and left her brassiere and panties on the floor and lay down on top of the covers with an enormous sigh. There was a nice breeze coming through the window that felt so good going across her naked like that, and she put her hand down there and started feeling herself. Pretty soon something was coming, and she let it come closer and closer. She closed her eyes tight and moved her hand up and down faster, and it got closer, and suddenly she was afraid it would be too much for her to take, but it was too late, and it hit her like a freight train. She convulsed onto her side with her legs clamped together and her arms clutched around her middle. She thought she screamed, but all she heard out of her mouth was a tiny oh, oh, oh, oh, oh. Then it threw her off the tracks like a pile of leaves and sticks, and Claudia lay back, panting and breathless, with her arms and legs spread out wide across the bed.

"Wow," she said to herself. "No wonder you're not supposed to do that."

CHAPTER THIRTY-SEVEN

The next few weeks were big at the Palmetto. The Japanese didn't have any boats or planes left, but they wouldn't give up, and every little island on the way to Tokyo was Custer's Last Stand. The papers said we were going to invade Japan like we did with France. The war was supposed to go on another year, but nobody was worried about us winning it anymore.

Claudia took Takeo to lunch at the French Café one afternoon when she saw him waiting for a fare outside the Grand Hawaiian. They just talked about ordinary things because Claudia did not want to make him feel bad that his people were losing, but it came around to the war anyway because of all the new men in town and the construction going on. The navy base looked like Grand Central Station. Takeo did not look sad, but he looked deeply concerned. He shook his head slowly back and forth and thought for a moment before he held out his hands as if he was holding a football at arm's length.

"Japan is like big wasp nest," he said quietly, "very dangerous to go near." And then he shook his head again slowly back and forth and reached down to put his cigarette out on the pavement.

And then, suddenly the war was over. They dropped a new kind of bomb on Japan. Then they dropped another one, and even though the Japs started it, you had to feel sorry for them because they sure got it in the end. And then Claudia thought of all the children and old people with their chickens and donkeys and little birds in cages and hamsters running on their wheels just before bombs fell.

Of course, it had been going on all through the war, everywhere except the States, but she was only really thinking about it for the first time. Maybe because she was older now and had Edgar Lee and they had a room of their own that was home. She just glanced at the pictures in *Life* and turned the pages, but the pictures she saw were not in a magazine or in the newspapers. They were in her imagination, and the pages there were harder to turn.

All those poor people and birds and donkeys and hamsters. They thought they were safe at home. They thought it would be an ordinary day. Home was where you had ordinary days. Home was where you kept your old people and babies. That's what made her cry and hold Edgar Lee when the news came on the radio. The war was over. They said the world was safe again, but people knew better. You couldn't trust ordinary days anymore.

In Honolulu it was like one of those baseball games when someone hits a home run with three men on base in a late inning when they were way ahead anyhow. The men started going home, and new ones weren't coming in. For four years at the Palmetto, there had always been new men coming in. The only new men still coming in were the wounded.

The Hula Girls were like Miss America. That's what Claudia told her girls one night in her pep talk before the show. The incidental fact that they were prostitutes didn't matter, so she didn't say anything about that, but she knew the girls would like the Miss America business.

"People look up to us," she said. "We have a moral obligation to stand for American ideals. We have to start doing what Miss America does."

The girls went for the idea in a big way because they all wanted to be Miss America, and Claudia went to see Mr. Anthony about arranging for the Hulas to make public appearances. The hospital was a natural place to start, and the first visit was a big event, with all thirteen Hulas in full dress, the latest from Claudia's drawing board and Mrs. Butter's costume shop. Following them as they proceeded six blocks to the hospital in parade ground formation was a herd of photographers and reporters from the papers and a crowd that grew quickly and began to block traffic.

For an hour they strutted through the wards in a group and retired to the lobby for a catered luncheon, where they ate little sandwiches and mingled with the reporters, who looked small and shabby alongside those giant girls with their bosoms on and feathered headdresses three feet high. Mr. Anthony thought it went off very well, but Claudia had doubts from the minute he first picked up the phone in his office to arrange it. After the appearance at the hospital, she knew she had to take it out of his hands.

That was the first and last official public appearance of the Hula Girls at the hospital. Once a week they went for a press event in costume at the Firemen's Relief, The Benevolent Society, or somewhere else for fundraisers, but Claudia claimed the hospital and got her girls an extra ten dollars a week if they wanted to do it.

Her instincts told her that wounded soldiers would rather get visits from ordinary girls in regular clothes, and just one, not thirteen of them, at one time. It was better for everyone. Each Hula could go when she felt like going, but if you missed a week, you didn't get the extra ten, and you could only go by yourself. Claudia kept a notebook for Doris in bookkeeping, and she put each girl on her honor if she went that week or didn't. Claudia went several times a week and sometimes took Edgar Lee along when she visited the boys who weren't banged up too badly, but she never put in for the extra money. It made her feel like Mary Ann, paying for her sins at the church.

Most of the time, Claudia went into the wards that she knew the Hulas would probably avoid, where the men were in bad shape or dying. She sat beside them and held their hands, and if the nurses weren't around, she held their heads and kissed their faces all over like their moms would have. One man died in her arms. He was unconscious, but when she held him, a little smile came over his face and he said, "Snow day, no school." In his mind he must have been a boy like Edgar Lee, looking out the kitchen window at the snow coming down. Mom was cooking breakfast on the stove, and Dad was out in the garage looking for the snow shovel. He smiled that little smile, and then he died. He made it home after all. It was the only time she got teary. A nurse came and put her arm around her and led her away.

"I'm sorry I'm so much trouble," she said at the door, taking another tissue from the nurse. "I just don't want the boys to feel they're alone."

"Oh, you don't have to worry about that, honey," said the nurse. "Your girls are in here all the time. I just have to keep a lot of tissues on me."

The war ended so suddenly that it caught Claudia off-balance, and now she had to scramble. She called Annette, and they talked about it and agreed to invite Captain Locarno to lunch at the French Café on Thursday to talk business.

"What are you going to wear?" Annette asked.

"I was going to ask you the same question."

Annette favored business apparel—white blouse, pleated skirt, fitted jacket, and flats. Claudia didn't have anything like that that still fit, and she knew none of Annette's office-girl victory suits would fit her either, so there was no point to going through Annette's closet, but it was nice of her to offer. They were on the phone for half an hour telling each other what each other looked good in, like Annette's bolero jacket and Annette's red wool-weight, rayon A-line and Annette's long-sleeved, belted jacket with the shoulder pads. At last, they settled on plain black dresses with wide brimmed hats, but five minutes later Claudia had to call her back.

"We don't want to look like two spiders waiting for a fly to come along," she said.

Their breezy prints felt just right on Thursday as they sat under the umbrellas of the French Café in the glorious sunshine. Across the street, the wind moved in the stand of high palms, and the flags of the allied nations snapped over the façade of the Grand Hawaiian down the block. At noon the waiters went around the tables tilting the angle of each umbrella to suit the patrons. Annette and Claudia took off their sunglasses, and Annette removed her scarf and let her hair play around her face. They just sat looking at each other, sipping their coffee and smoking their cigarettes and listening to other people's conversations. Claudia's contentment displaced any of her concerns about meeting Captain Locarno. She was so pleased having Annette as her business partner. She could sit and look at Annette all day. There was never anything wrong with her black wavy hair, hunter's bow lips, and gull-wing eyebrows. You could look all you wanted.

Maybe that's what she wanted in a man. Someone who would look at her the way she looked at Annette. Mary Ann would have just laughed at that, like she laughed at the ads in *Life*. Annette would understand. Life was different when you were beautiful. You had reason to expect romance. She could not imagine how ordinary-looking people could have extraordinary passions and great loves like *Wuthering Heights* when they had to get those feelings by looking at each other. How could you ever feel or inspire such soaring flights of the heart if you weren't beautiful?

Claudia knew she had to stop thinking that way. Maybe she was missing something. It was a matter of what you thought was beautiful. There was a little, wrinkled old man sitting at the next table with an equally old and equally wrinkled old lady across from him, and he was looking at her like she had come down from Mount Olympus. Everything you needed to know about love was in the face of the old man, the look she wanted to see in a man looking at her. One person who loves you best. That's all you need. She had been such a fool.

"Are you crying?" said Annette.

Claudia touched her napkin to her eyes and said, "No, it's just all the damn flowers around here. You got your checkbook, Miss Rockefeller?"

"Right here," said Annette, patting her purse. "How about you?"

"Right here," said Claudia, patting her purse too.

"I can't make up my mind how much I want to put in though."

"They say you aren't supposed to gamble with more than you can afford to lose."

Annette suddenly looked concerned.

"I didn't think it was a gamble," she said.

"Well, I don't think we can go wrong, but you can always lose money on things, even if they seem a sure thing."

"What are you going to put in?"

"I was thinking that we should listen to the deal, and if it sounds good, I'm ready to go all the way."

"How much have you got?"

"Ten thousand dollars."

"Wow, Claudia."

"How much do you have?"

"I've got two."

"That's not bad. So together we can go in for twelve."

"If you think it sounds good. I mean I trust your judgment but I'd hate to lose my two. It's all I've got after five years in the department. That's the navy for you."

Claudia knew it was not really a case of that's the navy for you. Annette lived pretty high. She had a nice, two-bedroom apartment with a kitchen, living room, and full bath, a closet full of clothes, a jewelry cabinet, hats, gloves, shoes, and handbags. Her shelf of fragrances looked like an aircraft carrier with more planes than had room to take off. The first time she saw Annette's place was like walking into Neiman Marcus. It was strictly girls only. At the club, Claudia never met a date of Annette's who ever gave any indication that he had been inside the Forbidden City. Getting to know Annette's prudish nature better was restoring her faith in Jack—funny enough.

Captain Locarno came right on time at twelve thirty. He bustled over like a little dynamo and put his navy hat on the edge of the table as he sat down. He ordered a whiskey sour and sat up straight, with his hands clasped way out ahead of him. He must have been close to fifty, but he looked as trim and fit and plucky as he did four years ago. His blond hair was cut shorter, and he was still wearing the wedding band, so Claudia figured his poor wife was still in the picture. She was such a sweet dear.

"I understand that you ladies have some capital to invest," he said briskly.

"Yes," said Claudia. "We talked once at Admiral Harris's, and I remember being impressed with your ventures into real estate on the island."

"Well, happily, I am able to report that those ventures have done well in the interim."

"Annette and I were hoping you might provide—an avenue, shall we say, for us into this kind of area."

His whiskey sour came, and he took a sip and smacked his lips.

"I would be happy to do that. What do you want to do?"

"We aren't sure," said Annette.

"We would like to hear of some opportunities," Claudia added.

"Hotels," he said. "That's the place to be. How about hotels?"

Annette and Claudia looked at each other and said sure, hotels were perfect.

"I think so, too," he said. "No one comes to live here. Let's face it. It's an island. There's nowhere to go. But everyone will want to come on vacation, and a lot more will have the money to do it. So they'll need hotels. It's very simple. Hotels are going to go up all over this area, and now is the time to jump in."

Captain Locarno leaned forward confidingly and raised each eyebrow in turn to beckon their heads low over the table.

"I have a golden opportunity right now. The old Maycomber. It's been sitting for years. I don't know if you've ever heard of it. The sign came down before the war. But it was big when I came in '38. Then it had a few bad years, changed hands a few times, and eventually became a migrant hotel for the Chinese who came here looking for work. Two years ago, it finally closed down, and it's been sitting ever since."

"Is it for sale now?" Claudia asked.

"Not exactly."

"Who owns it?"

"Well, that's the thing," he said. "I checked into it, and it turns out the Maycomber is owned by the *San Francisco Clarion*. You know, the newspaper. They acquired it through a merger of some sort. I got hold of the financial officer for the newspaper, and they're willing to give it up for a song to get it off their books. Now the trouble is, I need some money to close the deal fast."

"How much?"

"How much have you got?" He said it with a straight face, then broke into a smile that seemed to be a new direction for the prevailing lines of expression on his face.

They all laughed. Then he said, "No, but I mean that in all seriousness. I doubt that you have enough floating capital to invest, but if you can take the edge off what I need, I can borrow the rest. So it does hinge on how much you've got."

Annette was going to pipe up, but Claudia put her hand on her knee under the table.

"Could you tell us what you would like to do with the Maycomber, Captain Locarno?" said Claudia.

"Certainly," he said. He relaxed and tilted back in his chair. "Luxury hotel. The Grand Hawaiian, but more contemporary and more style. The Grand Hawaiian is nice, but it's plain as white toast. The Maycomber could have character and charm along with all the modern conveniences. Just look at the building."

"I think I know the one you mean. It's across from Exclusive Ladies Footwear," said Annette.

"That's right."

"Oh, Claudia, it really is a beautiful building."

Captain Locarno let his chair come down, and he leaned forward over the table again.

"I need twenty thousand. I need it right away, or I miss the deal because it's going so cheap and their fiscal year closes at the end of September. The paperwork is going to take weeks, but the money has to be in the bank. What do you think?"

Claudia and Annette looked at each other and then Claudia spoke up because she knew you had to buy well, and Captain Locarno sounded like he knew what he was doing.

"We might be able to come up with twelve."

Captain Locarno's face turned down a little, but he didn't say anything. He took a notebook and pen out of the inside pocket of his tunic and began working numbers. Claudia and Annette sipped at their drinks and shared a Chesterfield.

"All right," he said. "I think we might be able to do it. We need a down payment and enough to get a head start with contractors on the exterior to shorten up our wait time on the revenue side. I think I can get the rest of the money we'll need if I can have a commitment on your twelve. What do you say?"

"I think you want to do it, don't you, Claudia?" said Annette.

"If you do."

"I'm not sure."

"I'd like to know by noon tomorrow," said Captain Locarno.

"That would be fine," said Claudia.

Captain Locarno was getting up to leave, but before he could put his hand out to shake, Annette indicated that she wanted a private word with Claudia, so he retired to the door of the café and waited.

"I know you want to do it," Annette whispered.

"Only if you do. We can talk about it."

"No, let's settle it now. I want to go in with you. I can say yes right now."

"You're sure?" said Claudia.

"Yes, I think we should."

They agreed to go through with the deal, even with the caveat. Captain Locarno impressed upon them the need for patience with a real estate investment. He said it might take two years, possibly three to get the hotel up and running. In the meantime, there would be expenses. Claudia grit her teeth and wrote out her check to Captain Locarno for $10,000 and Annette wrote out one for $2,000. Captain Locarno said he would get in touch when he had a contract written up and a figure on the amount they would have to pay every month on the mortgage. He said he was on his way to the bank, and he would get the ball rolling.

Claudia and Annette sat down again and had a few more drinks. They were pleased and elated, and any reservations Claudia had about investing her entire life savings were pushed aside by her new self-confidence. She and Annette were business partners, and they had rounded up their first buffalo.

CHAPTER THIRTY-EIGHT

The enterprising spirit was in full swing at the Palmetto as well. With the fighting men going home, a quieter crowd began to come out of hiding. They were the office workers in departments and agencies Claudia had never heard of, and they were coming in with their wives. Soon it was hard to remember the last time someone climbed up on the stage and tried to feel the girls. Mr. Anthony was adept at catching the general drift, and he let Claudia and Max tone down some of the routines.

The new crowd was more sedate, but they still wanted to feel they were in a nightclub, so Claudia became more bold and creative with her costume designs, and she and Max put together some dazzling new steps to jazz up the dance numbers. The only constraint to a new dance step was whether or not Claudia would be able to do it, but that was understood between the two of them and left unsaid. So far, she was still able to match her girls, even though she was eight or nine years older than some of them. To make the big feature of the show a little easier, Max moved The Tendardee to the end of the first show while the girls were still fresh. Claudia took a double Tendardee to the drawing board, but Max said it couldn't be done. Privately, Claudia thought she was the Hula who could do it, and she worked on it at home when Edgar Lee was in school.

Mr. Anthony had the purple hippopotamus on the marquee painted over. He said the board of directors made him do it after the great write up the Hulas got in *Paris Match*. The only difference to her costume was a little string to the hook of her show bra in back. In the second show finale, they changed the music to "June is Bustin' Out All Over" from the new Broadway show *Carousel*. When they got to the end with "Hulas Reach for the Skies," Claudia spread her arms out wide, singing "Just because it's June, June, June!" And right then she could pull the string, and her show bra would fly off. She could pretend she didn't notice or cover herself, depending on the sense she got from the audience. Then she would run for the curtain with the Hulas hurrying after. The audience loved it. Even the women. To be charitable, Claudia attributed it to being glad it happened to somebody else and not them.

Claudia got more for her girls out of Mr. Anthony since the club was doing better than ever, and the back rooms got nicer because each Hula got a decorating allowance. Their taste in colors and décor was sometimes surprising to Claudia, but she was never critical as she would have been before the war. Being surprised only meant that she did not know enough about her girls and she should try harder to put aside her leadership role and get to know them better as individuals. There were only twelve of them, for Pete's sake. It wasn't like she was General Eisenhower.

The Hulas also got meals brought in when they came in early for rehearsals and late suppers for staying after hours for meetings. The new girls often asked her about the early days of the Hulas when they walked down the corridor of the Hula Hall of Fame and saw the framed pictures, and Claudia always brought the stories around to a good ending with a phrase she made up herself. She would say, "That's the Hulas for you."

With the circulating part of the job confined to the bar area and the clientele older, Claudia was picking up more dates. All she had to do was swish by. She usually had three or four a night. They were perfect gentlemen and left her big tips of five or ten dollars. Together with her PIP check every month and her base salary, she was doing well, but she needed all of it to stay above water in the real estate game.

After Captain Locarno signed the paperwork for the Maycomber, her share of the mortgage hit her like a ton of bricks every month. She called it call money. She tried to explain what she learned from Dan about call money and margin and the stock market to Annette once, but her eyes wandered too much. Annette was no dumb bunny. She came out of Radcliffe, after all. She just wasn't interested. Claudia could not hold it against her, because the situation was so often reversed when Annette went on about handbags. Being business partners was like being married. You don't have to see eye-to-eye on everything.

Within six months of closing the deal on the Maycomber, Captain Locarno had contractors working on the old hotel. Claudia's share of the mortgage and monthly expenses came to $500 month. It was going to be tough to keep up that kind of money, but Captain Locarno said if they could do it and have the hotel up and running in less than eighteen months, they could pay everything off and be showing a fourteen percent profit on their investment by the year after.

Claudia and Edgar Lee walked by the site almost every day on their way to the beach. She told him that she and Annette were part owners of the hotel, and he brought up something that had never occurred to her.

"Can I have my own room?"

"What do you mean?"

"We're going to live there, aren't we?"

"You know, Edgar Lee, I never thought of that. I'll have to ask Captain Locarno."

"Who's he, anyway?"

"Captain Locarno. He was a friend of Daddy's. Daddy and I used to go to parties at Admiral Harris's house, and one time we got talking about hotels. He told me how much it cost to buy one, and that's why we've been saving our money. Now we just have to keep saving our money to pay for fixing it up. Oh, look at that, Edgar Lee."

The workmen were hoisting a pallet of buckets up the side of the scaffold with a block and tackle on either side. The Maycomber was ten stories high, and all the window frames were knocked out, like the bombed-out buildings in Germany. *Life* was full of pictures like that. There were bombed-out buildings all over the place.

"They're fixing all the cracks in the façade with concrete. Do you know what façade means, Edgar Lee? It's a French word that means the front of a building."

Edgar Lee leaned up against the chain-link fence that ran for a block around the whole property. He watched the men on the scaffold looking down and the men at the foundation looking up as the pallet was hiking up from one floor to the next.

"Where did you get the money?" he asked.

"We saved it up. Slow and steady. That's how you save money, Edgar Lee. Every week I put some in the bank from the money we have left over and little by little it adds up. Next year we'll go to the bank to open a savings account for you, and you'll see how it grows."

"Well, where am I going to get any money to put in it?"

"I'll give you some of what we earn from people staying at the hotel to get you started, and then I can give you an allowance every week for chores around the house."

"You mean around the room."

"Well, all right. Chores around the room."

Claudia tried hard to be patient with Edgar Lee when he got snippy. Ever since he turned ten, he was sometimes very critical of her, and some of the things he said were hurtful.

Annette said it was just the age, but Claudia knew it was as much attributable to the circumstances. It was hard to say how another year had gone by, but it had, without any of the changes that would have made life interesting for Edgar Lee. For her, work at the club was exciting, as she brought to life her creations in costume design and innovations in dance with Mrs. Butter and Max. Her endless negotiations with Mr. Anthony for Hula rights kept her on her toes, and lunch every week with Annette kept her straight. Just the same, there was no accounting for the time that whizzed by.

Edgar Lee only had school and his friends. Some of his friends weren't the best influence either, especially that Nick. She was going to have to figure out what to do about that. There wasn't much room to manoeuver, living in one room. Literally.

She knew Edgar Lee wanted privacy. He didn't like living in one room with her anymore, and he hated going down the hall to the bathroom. She could leave him alone at night now when she went to the club, but some of the neighbors complained to her that after she left, Edgar Lee would go down to the phone in the hall and stay on it for an hour, and then he had the radio on too loud in the room.

"Come on, Edgar Lee," she said. "I've got to get dinner started."

Edgar Lee picked up a stone and threw it toward the hotel. It almost hit one of the workmen, who turned around and shouted, "Hey!" Edgar Lee was already down the block, and the man thought Claudia threw it because no one else was around. That was the kind of thing he would do. He already knew, probably from what he did with his friend Nick, that when you threw a stone, you didn't wait to see who you hit. You ran like hell.

Annette still came to talk to him every week, but now they would go out and walk along the beach for an hour or two. He probably had an aggravated case of puppy love, but she trusted Annette. Claudia respected the confidentiality of the relationship and did not ask what they talked about, and she did not mind the thought that he was telling Annette all his true feelings and not telling her anything. She didn't care about that or get resentful. She wanted him to have what he needed. When they had lunch at the French Café and the topic of Edgar Lee came up, Annette stressed that you have to be firm and consistent with children, especially at the stage when they get rebellious and discipline is required.

Claudia listened attentively, but inside she was kind of shrugging her shoulders. Maybe Annette was just learning you can't control all the crazy things about men, even at an early age. It was different with her. All she could do was love Edgar Lee, and all she hoped was that he would love her back. The rest could take care of itself. Everybody grows up eventually.

There was no one else in her life to love that way. It was probably her own fault. She had let herself go. How was she going to find a man now? When Edgar Lee was in school in the mornings, Claudia weighed herself and looked at herself without any clothes on in the full-length mirror on the inside of the closet door. She was five foot four inches and still at one hundred and eighty. The rolls around her middle still rolled there gracefully in place, and they were trying hard, but there were signs that defying gravity much longer would be too much to ask. Her face was still young-looking, and her hair, of course, was her crowning glory, but the rest of her, oh Jesus.

The men at the club still looked at her with that distinctly male slant of lust, but Claudia was aware that her priorities had changed. She needed to find a husband all right, but she wanted a good one, a man who would be a good father to Edgar Lee and set a good example for him, and she didn't think she was going to find a man like that at the Palmetto, paying two dollars for a club rubber.

In the meantime, the only hope of getting out of the present situation was the hotel. It heartened her greatly to see it coming along. All she had to do was keep going for another year or so, keep saving every penny, and not live beyond her means. She had to deny Edgar Lee so many things he asked for, and it made her feel so bad that she finally sat him down and explained the value of money to him. That night he had nightmares because of what she had said about slipping backward into destitution, and she had to go sit on his bed and hold him until the nightmare let go. She told him how much she loved him and that everything would be okay, and if he could be patient a little longer, all his dreams would come true—the happy ones, not the nightmares. That was the funny thing about being his age. He could be a little boy who needed her, and then the next minute he could push her away and say, "Why don't you get lost."

There was a lot of Mary Ann in Edgar Lee. He had her brown hair and dark eyes and a cute face, just like her. But he was skinny and was probably going to be tall and lanky like Bill. He had a temper, but he could be so sweet and tender, the way she was, the way she had been, the way Claudia remembered her best.

Before she woke him up each morning, Claudia looked at him sleeping, feeling she could look at him so long that the hair over his eyes and his lips slightly apart and the peace in which he dwelt could so easily draw her in like the slowly spinning spiral on a hypnosis wheel. That's how it happened, she thought. That was how a mother always thinks of her child as her child. You get mesmerized.

Edgar Lee woke up sweetly too, and he ate his breakfast quietly, reading the back of the cereal box about things he could send away for. It was usually only a quarter, and he always enjoyed filling out his name and address on the order blanks and putting the box tops into the envelope and then waiting for the mail to bring him a game or a police badge or a special kind of whistle or something like that. He did not like going to school because it made his stomach hurt. He was a different kid when he came home after school, but in the morning he just wanted to stay home with her. He liked to suggest things they could do and places they could go, and he liked when she poured a little of her coffee into his glass of milk.

"We can get a car," he said one morning.

"Why, Edgar Lee. What a dreamer you are."

"Everybody has cars now, Mom."

"Where did you get that idea, little man?"

"*Time* magazine said so."

"That's in America, Edgar Lee. It's different here. You don't need a car on an island."

"What about Dad's Roadmaster?"

"He had to get to the navy base every day. He was very important."

"Did you ever drive it?"

"Oh, no. Why would I ever drive it?"

"Just to drive around, Mom."

"We never did that very much. Your dad was too busy."

Claudia took out a Chesterfield, and Edgar Lee sprang up to get the lighter, and he lit her cigarette for her like a gentleman.

"Thank you, Edgar Lee."

She didn't know where he learned to do the fancy flip with the cap of the lighter, but it must have been from Nick or one of the other little hooligans in the schoolyard. She didn't want him smoking at ten. Everybody knew it would stunt your growth. She smelled his hair every day when he came home, and she had a lecture ready. So far he was clean.

"We could get a car and drive around, Mom. Don't you ever want to go anywhere?"

"Sure I do, Edgar Lee. It's just the money now."

"It's always the money."

"Well, now it's different. Before, we were saving up, but now the money is going to work for us. That's what you call it when you invest your savings in something that makes money like a hotel. Now we have to buckle down. It's only for a year or maybe just a little more. Then the money will start coming back to us."

"So, we can get a car in a year?"

"We'll see."

"Why can't you ever say something for sure?"

Claudia ended up promising that they could buy a car next year. Edgar Lee went to mark it down on the calendar he had tacked up by his bed.

"So, in exactly one year we'll get a car," he said. "May 15, 1948. Get Car. Mom promised." He said it as he wrote it down.

That put an end to the discussion, for the time being.

"Can I pick out the car?"

"Yes, Edgar Lee. You can pick out the car. You better get ready for school now and put some pants on before you go out."

"It's just to the bathroom."

"I don't care. Go put your pants on. I won't have you walking in the hall in your underwear. It shows a lack of respect for others, and you know better."

"I'm just going to take them off in the bathroom anyway."

"I don't care what you do in the bathroom. In the hallway you wear your pants. What would people think if I walked down the hall in my underwear, young man?"

"Everybody would run."

He was getting into his school trousers and grumbling, and he went on grumbling out the door and left it wide open. He could be such a little bear sometimes. The things he said. It made her heart hurt. She hoped he would get older and not remember the things he had said when he was young. Not remembering was the only way to have a clear conscience and be happy in life. There were people who could do that. It was a mystery to her, but she knew there must be people like that, and she wanted Edgar Lee to have a happy life. There were so many things she wanted for him. Promising him a car was small potatoes.

Claudia still walked him to school. Edgar Lee had a little gang of friends and didn't want them to see her, so he only let her get within a block of the school and made her go home without a kiss.

Claudia always walked by the hotel on the way back to watch what was going on there. All the new windows were in, and they had brought in a giant crane to get at the roof. Usually she stayed at the fence and watched the workmen for half an hour or so.

There was one man on the crew she knew from the club, and when she didn't have Edgar Lee along, she stayed until he came out of the building or out from around a pile of boards or jumped off the back of a truck. His name was Andrew. He was nineteen. He always waved when he saw her, and if he was going on break he came over to the fence and talked, and they had a smoke together. It was good for business. She kept it just club talk and was careful about that because she thought he might have some big ideas. Claudia always upbraided her girls when they got in trouble with a man, and she had to maintain professional standards in her own life if she wanted to be a good leader.

Andrew came to the club every Friday night and sat at the bar and always picked her. She might be overweight and ten years older than he was, but he never looked twice at any of the other Hulas. But they sure tested him because he was such a beautiful man. One after another they swished around him, pushing up their bosoms and brushing against him with their sleek hips, but he didn't pay any attention. Jasmine was the only one for him. Claudia could hardly believe it sometimes, but then she remembered the two times in her life when she was on the other end of that stick. Thinking you were in love was the worst kind of mental block against facing reality.

He was just young. He looked like a blond, blue-eyed, young Jack, and watching him get out of his clothes in the back room took her breath away.

She felt the grab feeling, and a few times when he went slow, she felt it coming and getting closer, and all she needed was a little more time, and she would have gone off like an A-bomb. There were a lot of close calls, but she never let it happen because it wasn't professional, and Andrew was satisfied with her pretend ones. Sometimes she daydreamed about letting go of the helm, but that was what daydreaming was for. It never gets you anywhere.

"Mrs. Wyler."

Claudia almost jumped out of her skin and turned to see Captain Locarno coming down the sidewalk with his brisk walk. His navy car was parked on the other side of the street.

"Oh, Captain Locarno," she said. "I didn't expect to see you."

"I just dropped by to check on some details. Nothing pressing. But since you're here, would you like to take a little tour of the operation? I would be pleased to officiate."

"Certainly," she said.

They went around to a side gate off the street, and Captain Locarno asked a workman to find them some safety helmets. He brought out two army helmets painted orange, and Claudia fitted one carefully over her hair.

"I never tried on one of these," she said. "They don't have them where I shop."

"I can assure you, Mrs. Wyler, you would look perfectly lovely in any hat."

"I could wear the phone book, huh?"

Captain Locarno looked at her strangely. Either he didn't get the joke or didn't think women could be funny, or maybe he just wanted a serious business partner. Who knows. He led her to the hotel through a muddy no man's land of puddles and rubble, tiptoeing across boards that had been laid out, and once safely standing on the remnants of the paving in front of the grand entrance, he turned to describe the view he envisioned.

"All this will be landscaped with palms and flower beds, and in the middle of the circular drive in front will be a fountain, right about there." He leaned in and whispered, "I'll tell you about my plan for the north side later."

There were workmen gathering in the main entrance on break. They took off their helmets for her and offered her cigarettes. Andrew was among them, and she took one of his Chesterfields. When she first met him at the bar at the Palmetto, he was an Old Gold man, but he changed over to Chesterfields for her. Captain Locarno asked to see Pete, the foreman, and when he came out, they talked for a few minutes, and then Captain

Locarno led her inside the building. Andrew threw her a questioning look, and she gave him a wiggle of her little finger that none of the other men would catch.

Inside the Maycomber, it was busy like an anthill. Men were going back and forth in front and behind them as they stepped cautiously over wires and boards and buckets. The older men touched the brims of their helmets and lowered their eyes, and the younger men turned around and craned their necks. Captain Locarno said it was lucky he kept his feelers out because the crew was on loan from another construction team that was held up on a job. The men were available at the right time.

"It was a good thing I already had the plans ready for the interior. We have a very good architect on the project, a very imaginative young man, and he makes his deadlines."

He turned and pointed up to the second and third floors, which she could see from the bottom of the big staircase.

"We decided to go with a concept of units and suites. The architect worked out a ratio of units to suites, based on optimal use of space, and the accountant figured the same ratio by revenue. There were a few options, but we went with the one that best aligned with projections of postwar holiday travel."

There was probably very little that Captain Locarno had not planned for. It gave her confidence as an investor, but when he mentioned that starting early on the interior would speed up the project by an estimated four months, Claudia was delighted but skeptical. There had already been delays. The foundation had to be worked on. Then a steel shortage.

"I wonder if this is a good time to ask you something," she said.

"Go ahead."

Captain Locarno was bright, alert, and attentive. He flipped over the loose pages on his clipboard and hugged it to his chest in his folded arms. Claudia had never seen a man stop what he was doing like that. He was all business, no nonsense, hustle and bustle, but he came to a full stop and stood with his legs apart and his arms holding his clipboard to his chest and gave her his full attention. In the worst way, she wanted to work with him on this and the next project and the next one and learn everything she could about making money in real estate. He was a straight-up guy, and not many of those come down the pike.

"My son was asking if we could live here."

"Mrs. Wyler, you can do anything you want. It's your hotel."

"We could live here?"

"You're a partner in the project, Mrs. Wyler. You can take one of the suites and pay nothing but a nominal lease. In fact, if you become available, we could set you up as hospitality coordinator for the hotel. You could run the travel agency that we have planned for the lobby. I thought you or Miss Anisinelli might be interested."

Claudia did not know what to say. It was beyond her wildest dreams. She said Edgar Lee would be so excited about living in the hotel. The prospect of being on site as a travel agent for the guests was a very attractive offer, she said, and she would seriously consider it. It was probably no secret that she danced with the Hula Girls, but she had no idea exactly what he knew. She had never seen him in the club. He certainly did not look like a man who wasted his time in clubs, and she suddenly felt bad that she was in an occupation that made people waste their time. You got them to waste their time and pay you for it. It was a depressing way to think about it.

"You can let me know in the next few months. As for your personal living accommodations, we have six ocean-view suites going in on the top floor, with one more we planned to squeeze in—a little smaller, but two bedrooms, bath, kitchen, and living area. It should be ready for you to look at in a few months if all goes on schedule. It will be yours if you want it."

"It's difficult to imagine anything you arrange not being on schedule," said Claudia, "except for unforeseen events."

Captain Locarno tapped his finger on his clipboard. "Well, we try to plan for them too," he said. "But unfortunately they have an effect on the money. Oh, it's nothing to worry about, but accelerating the work on the interior meant another capital demand. To be very honest with you, Mrs. Wyler, when I calculated the amount needed to start the crew on the inside, I realized it was going to be beyond the resources of you and Miss Anisinelli. I thought it best to approach the other investors."

"I didn't know there were others."

"Originally it was just the three of us and my wife—on paper. When the present opportunity arose, I felt it advantageous to bring in Mr. Sellman—Art Sellman from the Honolulu Business Association—and another gentleman from their membership, Mr. Anthony, whom you must know from the Palmetto board of directors."

Claudia was a little surprised Captain Locarno bought the board of directors story, but not at all surprised to hear about Mr. Anthony's fingers getting into another pie.

Captain Locarno brought her around the hotel to the side that faced Bermander's Department Store.

"I didn't want to say anything in front of the men," he said, "but I think we might want to discuss buying that building. Mr. Anthony owns the property on the other side, the gift store, and he said he would be willing to cash out for expansion of the Maycomber. With the two additional properties, we could add another wing in a configuration that would allow for a courtyard here and a swimming pool over there. Do you see? We could add twenty-five percent to our total units overnight."

Overnight sounded like Jack saying, before you know it. She realized she had become more practical about things taking more time, but she did not want to give Captain Locarno any doubts about her commitment to the project.

"I suppose it would be a good move," she said.

"It will delay completion of the hotel by a few months, but it will be worth it and save us a redesign of the basic layout."

"I guess I could live with that.

"Then I can count on your vote?"

"I'd like to look over the cost projections," Claudia said. She thought that came out sounding good. She had never heard anything about voting. It might be a good idea if she and Annette looked at the envelope with the partnership contract Captain Locarno gave them. It was in a box under her bed.

They walked back to the gate where they had come in, and Captain Locarno had to run, so she let him go and bent down to hook the wire at the bottom. When she stood up, Andrew was right in front of her on the other side of the fence.

"Oh, you scared me," she said.

"I'm sorry. Hi, Jasmine."

"Hi, Andrew."

God, he really was cute. He didn't have a shirt on, just those work jeans without a belt and big brown muddy boots and a blue bandanna around his head.

"What are you doing here?" he asked.

"I'm one of the owners of the hotel."

"Come on."

"No, really."

"So is Locarno your boyfriend?"

"None of your beeswax, kid." Claudia tossed her hair and laughed. It was the way to be with a client. Well, I've got to be on my way. See you around."

"Will you be at the club tomorrow night?"

"What's tomorrow night?"

"Friday," he said. "My usual."

"I don't know. Maybe."

"I'll see you then, Jasmine."

"I'll put a candle in the window."

Claudia walked down the sidewalk with a little English on the hips that brought her dress into the breeze. She heard Andrew get some ribbing from his work buddies. He was cute, and he seemed polite and considerate. Too bad he was nineteen. That could override a host of positive qualities. Nineteen was why he was going to the club in the first place.

On the way home, Claudia stopped into the paper store. She was so encouraged after talking to Captain Locarno that she wanted to get Edgar Lee a car magazine. She ended up walking out with *Automotive Digest, Car Buyer's Showcase* and *Hot Wheels and Street Dreams*. She noticed that this month's *Boys' Life* had a picture of a boy and his dad on the cover, working on the family car, so she bought that, too. She thought they could pick up some tools when the hotel money started coming in and they got the car. She could teach Edgar Lee how to work on it. The dad in the picture was going at a bolt with the wrench turned the wrong way. She wondered how many letters to the editor they would get for that faux pas. She and Edgar Lee could live in a farmhouse in New England, out in the country, with a garage in back or an old barn, and spend Saturday afternoons in the fall working on their cars. That's what she'd like to do. She could marry Annette, and let Annette take over as Edgar Lee's mom. What a nice life that would be.

She thought about some pretty stupid things sometimes.

THIRTY-NINE

When Claudia got home from walking Edgar Lee to school every day, she finished off the coffee with a few Chesterfields and devoted some time to thinking about her life. She didn't have to walk Edgar Lee anywhere anymore, but she liked the regularity of it, and Edgar Lee didn't fuss as long as she let him go the last block alone. Thinking about her life was well suited to sitting at the table with coffee and Chesterfields, but it was never long before she ended up lying on the bed with her eyes closed. Then she had to hurry through thinking because working six nights a week made her fall asleep whenever she stretched out.

Claudia tried many ways to look at her life, but she always ended up feeling lucky, even when she had her eyes open, looking at the cracks in the ceiling plaster and all the other little inconveniences of where she lived with Edgar Lee. She was lucky to have a job where she could work creatively with a nice man like Max. The only drawback was the Personal Initiative Program, but she needed the money, and she had to show her girls that she could get out of the trenches and go through the wire like they did every night.

She was grateful to have a regular life, and chalking up another year with the Hulas made her feel regular. It would have been better if working at the Palmetto had been a normal job. Better yet would be to be married and not working a job at all, and not living in one room with a kid who was growing up fast. But being regular made her feel one step closer to normal, so she felt just lucky enough. Normal was shaping up to look like a time in the distant future when she would not always be waiting for something to pull the rug out.

She was lucky to have Annette. They had lunch together every Thursday at the French Café, and it was nice being regular girls. They actually had a lot in common besides Jack. The circumstances were different, but they were both looking for husbands, and they both had a plentitude of men in their lives. Claudia thought her can of worms was nothing like Annette's kettle of fish, but they felt free to speak in an advisory capacity about what they had in their buckets.

Nevertheless, it was hard for Claudia to determine if Annette knew anything about the low side of her job at the Palmetto, and Friday mornings while thinking about her life, she always sorted through the previous day's luncheon conversation for hints. Today it was mostly a blank except for recollections of trying not to be too opinionated.

"You're too picky, Annette," she said. That wasn't so bad.

"I just have high standards," said Annette. "I mean, for myself. Everybody has high standards of their own. It's just a matter of how important one thing is over another to different people."

"Well, if you ask me—" Claudia had to pause, not sure how much she wanted to say. Being obliged to lie down for every man with fifty bucks does not exactly elevate the value of your opinions on romance, but she couldn't help it. Every week Annette came to the French Café in a new outfit. It looked like a small fortune was going into presentation of the merchandise, but Annette wasn't letting anybody play with it. Her advice to Annette would be to stop giving herself all those orgasms and get serious while she still had the goods. You don't have to become a whore.

Annette turned her head back from blowing her smoke away and said, "I'm sorry, Claudia. Were you saying something?"

That was about it for yesterday, except for a new pastry they had, which was out of this world.

Claudia felt lucky to have Froggy in the background too. She knew he hung around the Brown Derby on Sunday mornings, so she walked by one time and let him catch her. It seemed like he had given up being in love with her, and now they could just talk like friends. In a few months he was going to decide if he wanted to stay in the navy or not. He had put on some weight. He was going to be thirty soon too, and they decided they both still looked pretty good for all the wear and tear. They put pennies in the weight scales outside the diner and laughed at what came out. Froggy said they shouldn't trust it because he said it looked a lot like the random number generator at base engineering, where he was working. Sunday morning at the Brown Derby with Froggy became a regular thing. But good little talks were as far as it went, and that was just what she wanted.

Andrew was another lucky break. Claudia kept up her professional persona with him but was starting to admit she thought about him more and looked forward to the back room on Friday night. He had just gotten out of the navy after a two-year hitch when he first came into the club. It looked like the navy was about as conscientious about checking ages during the war as the goons at the door of the Palmetto. He went for her in a big way, and even though he had her in the back room every Friday night, nothing seemed to satisfy his curiosity about her. She dodged the questions with Hula Girl club talk, but not to string him along. He did that to himself, choosing her every week. Every other man she'd had liked variety. Even some of her regulars had Pinkie once in a while, and she and Pinkie were as different as apple pie.

Andrew was working construction jobs and living in the basement of the Barrymore for almost nothing to save up money for college. He had already sent out some applications. The way Jack was about the navy was the way Andrew was about the career he foresaw for himself in law. Above all, he was just himself, and he was nuts about her.

Most of all, Claudia was grateful to have Edgar Lee. That was usually where she fell asleep while thinking about her life, before she got to the details. It was just as well. With the way he was getting difficult, sometimes it was easy for her to stray out of gratitude and into the minefield. Every month that went by, Edgar Lee looked more and more like he was pushing a boulder up a hill, just coming in the door. She dreaded the day when he would bring up the car. She needed every penny for the hotel. At least she was smart enough to know she couldn't get away with hiding his calendar and hoping he would forget, but she didn't feel much smarter than that when it came to Edgar Lee.

Edgar Lee was usually still asleep when Claudia got home from breakfast with Froggy on Sunday mornings. She knew he was sneaking out Saturday nights with his friend Nick and roaming all over town, but she pretended she didn't know. Rivoli told her one night when they were sitting at their table in the parking lot, waiting for the girls to get their rides.

"They just fool around and throw stones at the street lights," Rivoli said.

"Well, I'm his mother. Don't you think I should say something?"

"Nah. I'll let you know if you need to. I'll watch out for him. Don't worry."

"I don't know when you ever sleep, Rivoli."

"Night work," he said with that little smile at the corners. "You know how it is."

Claudia knew she didn't have much self-confidence when it came to Edgar Lee, and he wasn't even a teenager yet. But she had Annette to ask questions about boy psychology and Rivoli watching over, so she wasn't alone. She was lucky to have them. And as she lay on the bed thinking about her life, Claudia didn't count Edgar Lee as lucky to have because he was more than a part of her life. He was everything that her life was. He was where all her love went, and he didn't even know it.

Claudia got up to have a sandwich and a 7Up for lunch, and then she wrote to Mom and Dad. Dad was still with Towers, Anderson & Jacobi, and Mom was still at Woolworth's in New Haven. It was six years since Harry was killed. Barbara met a 4F man at Woolworth's and got married. She lived close by and had a baby boy, so Mom did the babysitting. Claudia sent them pictures of her and Edgar Lee that Annette took on the beach, and she told them a version of everything that had happened to her. She said she was Creative Director at the club. In a way it was true, in the same way the other stories were true. True in a way. She wrote about the hotel deal she was in and how sharp Captain Locarno was, and today she wrote about Andrew. She left out that he was nineteen years old. She said he was a strong possibility, and in a way it was true. She ended her letter with "Looking for that pot of gold!!!"

At three o'clock every day, Claudia went over to the school to get Edgar Lee. She waited a block away, out of range where his friends couldn't see her. Back home, inside the doors of the Strickland, she hugged him hard like a bear and said, "I love you, Edgar Lee, you little dickens." Most of the time he hugged her back. She fixed him a snack, and then they went to the beach for a couple of hours.

Edgar Lee was starting to look at girls. Claudia gave him Jack's navy sunglasses for his twelfth birthday. She gasped when he wore them at the beach and turned toward the girls with that contemptuous scowl of his. My God, she thought. It's happening. He was getting long legs with downy blond hair on them and hair under his arms. She didn't know when boys started getting wildcat boners, but she thought Edgar Lee was starting because after lying on his stomach, he sat up and waited a while before he would stand up to go in the water. She wondered if boys knew what was going on. She would have to tell him about sex soon. For a second, she thought she could take him to the club and let one of the Hulas teach him. Pinkie would be good. Then she felt like slapping herself across the face. It's just that he looked like he was seventeen with Jack's sunglasses on.

They usually stopped to get some things at the market for dinner on the way home. Edgar Lee washed the vegetables in the little sink and cut them up for their salads while Claudia cooked whatever they were having on the hot plate. Sometimes they sang songs together as they made dinner, or they turned on the radio. Claudia sat at the table to eat, and Edgar Lee sat on the settee in front of the window, and they listened to one of his radio shows. It was no use trying to have conversations during dinner because Edgar Lee did not like to hear her chewing. She was such a pushover.

After dinner, Claudia helped him with his homework. Sixth grade math wasn't very difficult, but she found it hard to explain why you did certain things, and Edgar Lee got frustrated easily. At eight o'clock she went down the hall in her robe to take her shower, and by nine she was at the club. She straggled home around three in the morning and fell into bed, staying awake only long enough to hear Edgar Lee's breathing, count the night's earnings in her head, and yearn for the hotel to come through and deliver her and Edgar Lee from the daily life she felt so lucky to have. Sometimes she stayed awake long enough to ask herself how mixed up that sounded.

Claudia could hear herself saying it, just like one of her girls, when she tried to explain it to herself. "It just happened." But there were no other words for it. One Friday night in the back room, she had an orgasm with Andrew. She felt that little grab when he was getting aboard, and before she knew it, every moving part in her brain shut down like five o'clock at a factory, and her girl parts went off like the Fourth of July and Macy's Parade.

When Claudia returned to her right mind, she decided to rule it inadmissible evidence in the case of Claudia Wyler vs Andrew Taylor, currently litigating in that right mind. But her defenses were falling anyway, and she knew she was breaking all the rules of the profession. Andrew was a winning kind of guy. That's what did it. They had long conversations at the bar that took up most of her circulating time every Friday night, and when the show was over, she frequently found him at a table with perfect strangers, espousing her talents in dance and costume design. He might have been too young to see it in himself, but he was swaying a jury with everyone he met at the club. He was a natural, and he was swaying her, too. Tipping the scales in the matter was a surprise witness.

"I don't know," said Annette. "But from what you told me, I think you want to let it happen."

"Well, sure I do. That's not it."

"What I mean is, you're ready to let it happen."

When Annette blew the smoke out of her nose and raised one eyebrow, it always knocked her out. Claudia drew herself up closer over her coffee and said, "But it's against my better judgment."

"Well, you know what that is, don't you? Better judgment is only internalized social convention. It can be misleading you into thinking you are doing the right thing."

"I thought that was what social conventions are for," said Claudia.

"But you have to do what's right for *you*, Claudia. You have to discard old ideas of what's right and wrong. If it were turned around and you were twenty, and he was twenty-nine, would that seem all right to you?

"Sure."

"That's social convention. There's nothing wrong with looking at it differently. If you can do that, it might look like it's right for you. This is just my opinion, but if you want to let it happen, and you're ready to let it happen, why don't you let it happen?"

"And see what happens?"

"Exactly."

So, on good authority, Claudia let herself go and let it happen. That Friday night, Andrew came in the Palmetto and took her to the back room, and she let go of her better judgment. Friday nights with Andrew after that were so terrific that they probably killed off half her brain cells, but she didn't care. She didn't need her brains anymore because she wasn't going to stop counting her orgasms until she got to three hundred million billion. What a way to go!

When better judgment went by the board, so did the lesser judgments. Andrew asked to see her outside the club, and she said yes, against all the rules. She didn't want to end up like poor Bunnylove, the Hula from Iowa they found in a cane field with her brassiere tied around her neck, but he had been coming around to the club for more than a year and she trusted that he was thoroughly no more than exactly what he seemed to be. Just the same, she made it for late Monday morning breakfast at the Whaler's Rest.

Claudia wore a light green print with a neckline low enough to make it interesting. She wanted to ask Edgar Lee what he thought, but he was at school. It was Hawaiian and meant to be loose, but she decided to wear a sash for the little definition it gave to what was once her figure. The thought of being outside of the club with Andrew in the light of day made Claudia long for the girdle days. Bermander's didn't have anything her size. Nobody did. Maybe some of those German scientists they were bringing to America could work on women's plus sizes in their spare time. It's supposed to be the land of opportunity, isn't it?

Andrew came in a nicely tailored blue suit. Outside the Whaler's Rest, they stood like strangers for only a moment before he put his hand lightly around and touched between her shoulder blades in that way men have of guiding the girls they possess into restaurants, and Claudia liked the feeling that she had been claimed by such a handsome specimen. They were shown to a table with a window overlooking the ocean, and Andrew held out her chair like he knew what he was doing in civilization.

"It's so stormy out there," she said.

"When it means a day off for me, it improves the view," he replied. "I didn't feel that way about it before I met you, Jasmine."

The waiter came over and dropped menus, silverware, and water glasses in front of them in what seemed one motion, and swept off to the next table. While the Whaler's Rest was not as common as a diner, it wasn't a full step up. But it had some atmosphere, some hanging fishnets, big corks and buoys, hooks with heavy rope, and stuffed fish mounted on varnished plaques on the walls.

"This is very nice," she said. "My husband and I came here a few times."

Andrew was looking down at the menu, but he caught that pretty fast.

"I thought I was going to have to trick you into revealing your past."

"I know. I trick myself."

"You know all about me, but I know very little about you. Does that seem fair and equitable to you?

"Club rules."

"That's why I wanted to see you outside the club."

"I guess I can even it up a little."

The waiter came with the coffee. Claudia ordered scrambled eggs with bacon, toast, and fried potatoes. Andrew ordered the same thing, and they both had a Chesterfield with their coffee. Andrew looked at his Chesterfield as if it had just appeared between his fingers out of nowhere and said, "I liked my Old Golds, but these are much better. Thanks for the tip—so what can you tell me?—without incriminating yourself, of course."

"Jack, my husband, was killed on December 7."

"I'm sorry to hear that, Jasmine. Did you meet him at the club?"

"No, that was way before I started at the club. He was a naval officer."

"Was he a friend of Locarno?"

"They knew each other. A little more, maybe. Captain Locarno used to borrow Jack's car. Jack had a real nice car."

"Are you seeing Locarno?"

"God no, Andrew."

"Are you interested in seeing Locarno?"

"God no, again. Relax, buster."

Andrew held his hands up, palms out, and said, "No further questions." And just then the waiter slipped their plates and platters under Andrew's hands and onto the table.

"I just wanted to establish the parameters of your current situation," he said. "In your opinion, would you say I came along at the right time?"

Claudia did not feel like putting on any club talk or telling stories. Andrew was infatuated with her before he knew she was part owner of a hotel, so it wasn't money he was after. She was ready, just like Annette said.

"I have a twelve-year-old son."

"You do?"

Andrew looked around the room as if he expected to see a twelve-year-old walk in. It was like telling him there was a person at the party he hadn't met.

"Junior?"

"No, just Edgar Lee. Edgar Lee Wyler."

"Then you must be Jasmine Wyler."

"No, my real name is Claudia. Jasmine is my club name."

"Claudia. I like that. Claudia Wyler. Can I call you Claudia?"

"I guess so, but only outside the club."

"Then I hope I'll be calling you Claudia a lot."

They both lifted their coffee cups at the same time, with mingling smiles.

"I guess that depends on the weather," she said. She tried to make it sound coy, but she was losing her grip on coy. She hoped she would not be sorry about all this later.

Andrew wanted to come with her to pick up Edgar Lee at school. They went to the Strickland first, and he waited outside the door while she changed, and then she waited outside his door at the Barrymore while he changed.

"Feel better?" he asked.

"Frankly, yes. Let's get going."

As they walked up the basement steps of the Barrymore and out the door, Andrew said, "I see we're doing the same thing, living on the cheap and saving up. You have all your money in the hotel, don't you?"

"It's not just for me," she said. "It's for Edgar Lee. His future."

"I know how you feel. You had no direction in your life, and then Edgar Lee came along and provided the inspiration. Am I right?"

"That's it," she said. "That's exactly it. You're very psychological, Andrew."

"I just know how it feels. I've had an inspiration come along, too."

Claudia lowered her eyes. "—Better finish building the hotel first."

Andrew laughed and told her what a good crew they had and how the hotel was really going to be beautiful. He said she could easily walk away with a million dollars.

"Why would I want to walk away?"

"That's what an entrepreneur does, Jasmine."

"Claudia."

"Claudia, sorry. You have to keep your liquidity so you can take advantage of opportunities that arise in other places."

"What other places?"

"I don't know. Anywhere. You don't want to stay here all your life, do you?"

"I never thought about it like that. I mean, as an entrepreneur. All this time I just didn't want to go home a failure. It would be great if I could come home rich and help my parents out."

"That's what I'm thinking with law school, but I probably won't be making much in the areas I'm interested in."

Andrew told her about labor relations and civil rights law and his ideals, but Claudia had to cut him off because they were getting to the corner where Edgar Lee made her wait for him.

"I'll remind you where you left off," she said. "But I have a quick comment. You have to have some fun too, you know."

"That's not so important," he said.

"I guess I shouldn't worry about that. You came to the club, didn't you?"

Andrew looked away, smiling. She caught him on that one, and it was a good clean catch.

"You were out looking for trouble, weren't you?"

"Well, not exactly."

"You can admit it. You were looking for some action."

"No," he said. "I was looking for you."

Andrew looked into her eyes with one of those clear, honest faces you only have when you're young, and she knew he was telling her the truth, in a way. She wanted to give him a snippy, club-girl reply, but she wasn't Jasmine now. She was Claudia head over heels. Recovering quickly, Claudia explained about waiting at the corner. She didn't want Edgar Lee to get mad at her.

"It sounds like you need a good lawyer," he said.

"Too late for that."

"Not necessarily, Mrs. Wyler. I'll take the case. Come with me," he said.

With that, he took her arm, and they stepped off the curb.

They came out on the street with the stone church and its twin spires that towered over the modern brick school building. There were boys playing baseball in the schoolyard, and Andrew brought her right up to the fence.

"Is Edgar Lee in that crowd?"

"That's him with the dark hair. He just pushed his sleeves up."

"I see him. Okay."

"I wonder what he did with his jacket."

"How long do we wait?"

"Well, he saw me, so I don't think he'll come out till I go back to the corner."

"Would you like me to represent you?"

"Don't make Edgar Lee mad," she said.

"You worry too much. Watch this."

Andrew walked right into the schoolyard and interrupted a play. He bent over Edgar Lee for a moment and started walking back. Edgar Lee stood looking at him, and then he got his books and his jacket off the steps and lumped after him.

"What did you say?" said Claudia.

"I told him we were going to come play baseball. You, me, and him against everybody else."

"Oh, dear."

Edgar Lee came up behind Andrew. "Who's he?"

"This is Mr. Taylor, Edgar Lee. He's a friend of mine from the club. He's also working on the hotel."

"Hi, Edgar Lee."

"Hi."

Andrew asked him if he wanted to tell the other guys about the challenge, and he said no, so they started walking back home, and after a little while, Edgar Lee said, "You can't have a three-man team anyway."

"Sure, you can," said Andrew.

"Like how?"

"Three batters come up. Base hit, base hit, home run. Then you do it over again."

"That wouldn't work."

"Why not?"

"Mom's fat. She can't run."

"That's easy," said Andrew. "Mom bats last. First you, then me, then Mom gets the homer."

Trailing behind them, Edgar Lee thought it over.

"How about the other way. You have to have men in the field."

"No, you don't. That's a myth, Edgar Lee. All you need is a real good pitcher and a catcher. Your mom and me. You can sit on the bench and rest up so you can run fast when you get your base hit. Your mom and me would be mad if you got tagged at first. Then it wouldn't work."

Andrew pretended to whisper to Claudia. "Maybe we better get somebody else."

"I'm better than Mom," said Edgar Lee.

"You never saw her pitch for the Honolulu Wave Riders."

"That's not a real team."

"Well, sure. Not anymore. Now they're the Brooklyn Dodgers. I thought you knew this stuff. Your mom is always telling me you could teach me a thing or two about baseball. Well, I guess no one can know everything. You know about Big Dynamite McGan, don't you?"

"No," said Edgar Lee. "Who's he?"

"Why he's the only major league hitter who ever got a home run off your mom. And that includes all those Yankee sluggers."

Andrew turned to Claudia and put his arm around her. "I know you don't like to bring up the bad times, Claud, but it's part of history. Anybody can have an off day. Tell you what," he said, looking at his watch. "Let's go look at the hotel, and by then it'll be dinner time, and we can pick something up. You're getting a suite in the hotel and your own room, aren't you, Edgar Lee?"

"That's what Mom says. I hope she not telling a story—like you."

"I'm not telling stories, Edgar Lee. Your mom is one of the greats. It's time you knew."

Claudia's heart was in her throat the whole time. Andrew put Edgar Lee in the bucket of the big crane and shot him up to the tenth floor of the hotel. He worked the controls and jostled Edgar Lee around a little to give him a thrill, and that's when Claudia made him bring Edgar Lee down.

"How about the Dog House for dinner?" said Andrew.

"I like the Dog House," said Edgar Lee.

"When were you at the Dog House, young man?"

"Nick's Mom took us."

"Oh. All right," she said. "Tuck in your shirt, Edgar Lee."

The Dog House was something like a diner, but it had a big hot dog on the roof. Claudia had never been there, so she was interested to see if they had Coney Island hot dogs on the menu. They did, and she got four of them for herself, and a basket of french fries. The dogs came lying in their buns as pretty as sleeping babies, split in two with bright orange blankets of melted cheese tucking them in.

"Now that's a great looking Coney Island hot dog," said Andrew.

He had worked on Coney Island the summer he was sixteen. He lived with his grandparents in Queens and took the subway all over the city and had interesting experiences. He told Claudia the secret to Coney Island hot dogs, and he showed Edgar Lee how to win at arm wrestling. Both were simple as pie once you knew the secret. Before he rolled his sleeve down, Andrew propped his elbow up on the table and told Edgar Lee to look closely.

"I don't have a tattoo on my arm, as you can see, but this would be a perfect place to put a hula girl tattoo, wouldn't it? Right here, see?"

Edgar Lee agreed.

"All right now, Edgar Lee, imagine the hula girl right there, and where would her fanny be?"

When he said the word fanny, he bent close and whispered it to Edgar Lee, and Edgar Lee pointed to where he thought the hula girl's fanny would be.

"That's just about right. Now concentrate on that spot and watch what happens. One, two, three!"

Andrew flexed his muscles and Edgar Lee's eyes almost popped out. They were like a couple of kids.

Later that night, when Claudia was getting Edgar Lee to bed, he said Andrew was really keen. There was always some new expression.

"Did you see his muscles? The muscles on his arms are like this big."

"They aren't that big, Edgar Lee."

"They are, too. You didn't see. He's a real hombre, Mom."

"What's an hombre?"

"That's a guy with big muscles. You don't know anything."

Claudia tucked him in bed. He would be up the minute she walked out the door, but she liked to see him safe in his bed before she left for the club.

"That's what you keep telling me, young man, but as a matter of fact, I do know some things. I know what isn't going to happen tonight."

Claudia pointed a finger at him and mustered every bit of advice Annette had given her about being consistent and firm with children.

"Let me tell you what isn't going to happen. You and your friend Nick are not going to go out roaming around town and go over to the hotel. You aren't going to sneak under the fence and get the key from where Andrew hid it, start up that crane and break your necks falling out of the bucket. That isn't going to happen, do you hear me?"

He listened to her perfectly still, and then he promised not to do what she said. Claudia was surprised how easy it was. She figured her stock just went up a couple of points. She was seeing a real hombre, and obviously she was somebody a real muscleman hombre would want to be seen with.

On Friday nights, Andrew sat with her and Rivoli, waiting for the girls to get picked up in the parking lot. Strange to say, Rivoli liked him. They talked about Italian food, and Andrew brought him dishes he whipped up on his hotplate at the Barrymore, which Rivoli swore were as good as his mother used to make. Takeo liked him, too. They talked about Chinese food with him.

When Andrew got her back to the door of the Strickland, he held her in his arms and kissed her. Claudia knew how to make men fall in love with her, but she didn't have a hand in this one. She never laid a glove on him, but look what happened. He came to the Palmetto club every Friday night to bang the hell out of Jasmine, but he had it in mind to marry Claudia, his lovely blonde virgin Claudia. And Claudia had to admit, she was in love with the whole idea, too.

Claudia took Andrew to the Brown Derby one Sunday morning to meet Annette and Froggy. Annette had been dying to meet him, and Froggy was just along for the ride. She never brought up Andrew when she and Froggy had breakfast together on Sundays, but she was sure he must have heard something from Annette. Anyway, he didn't look surprised when they walked in together.

Andrew had been working all night on the hotel because the big push was on, so he was in his gray sweatshirt, work jeans, and boots, but he looked as bright as a new penny and was ready to dig into a big breakfast. Annette and Froggy were still working up to the morning with their coffee and Luckys. Froggy stood up, and they shook hands all around. Then Andrew said he had to excuse himself to wash up and knock some of the dried mud off his boots and jeans.

"Can't we order first?" said Claudia.

"You order for me, Claud," he said. "I don't even want to sit down in these pants without a brush off. Go ahead and order, you know what I like—anything you do."

The minute Andrew disappeared around the corner, Annette lurched forward and said in an astonished whisper, "Oh my God, Claudia."

"How old is this kid?" said Froggy.

"Old enough," said Claudia.

"Maybe you should ask him."

"Don't you say anything, damn it."

"Don't pay any attention to Froggy," said Annette. "He's gorgeous, Claudia. Oh my God, I had no idea. You look good together too. You really do. I'm so jealous."

"Wait a minute," said Froggy. "You aren't going out with this guy, are you?"

Claudia wanted to slow it down a little, so she paused and took the napkin out of the bamboo ring and fiddled with it, and then she looked at Froggy in a serious way without saying anything.

"Well, I hope you aren't planning anything long-term," he said.

"I don't know—what if I were?"

"You don't have that much long-term left."

"That was cruel, Froggy," said Annette.

"It's all right," said Claudia. "I know. He's younger than I am. It doesn't bother me."

"No, it's not all right," said Annette. "You could be nice and be happy for Claudia, but you're being a fucking asshole, Froggy."

You could have knocked Claudia over with a feather. She had never heard Annette say a bad word, and now two at once, and she said them with such careful precision, as if she were afraid of getting the expression wrong and would have liked to check it first in a reference book.

"Annette!"

"No, Claudia, don't stop me. I don't know what's gotten into you, Froggy. You're always taking little snipes at people. I heard what you said to that new girl—"

"You didn't hear the whole story."

"Well, I heard there was a personal remark. It hurt her feelings. I think you need a girlfriend, Froggy. You were much nicer when you were with Elaine."

"I'll go along with you there," said Froggy.

"Are you going to apologize to the new girl?"

"Sure."

"Okay. Good," said Annette. "Then I'll start looking for a girl for you."

"Get me an old one, please."

Claudia was relieved they were back on track. She remembered when Annette slapped Jack at the party and was afraid her dander was getting up. What a mess it was being single at an age when everybody is supposed to be married. Freud was right. Everything had to do with sex one way or another, at least until you were thirty. That's where Freud missed the boat. After thirty it was too much trouble. You got married for companionship. Thirty had already swooped up Annette and Froggy, and her too, and despite all those terrific orgasms, sometimes Claudia felt thirty hadn't come soon enough.

Andrew came back in a nice pinstripe jacket and some tan trousers the Brown Derby kept in the back. The pants were a little too tight, but he sure looked good. Over breakfast they talked about the navy and then got into rebuilding Germany and Japan and the trouble in China. Shoes and handbags did not make an appearance in the conversation, as it went on mostly between Froggy and Andrew, but Annette sat in rapt attention, waiting, it seemed to Claudia, for the moments when Andrew turned to her. Then her eyes jumped right into his like circus dogs through hoops.

When Andrew talked about the American worker and labor laws, he became very passionate. Annette brought up women workers losing their jobs to men now that the war was over, and Claudia and Froggy moved their chairs back to let them go at it. Claudia could almost smell Annette's arousal. Andrew was just being Andrew, but the intensity in Annette's eyes and the almost imperceptible movement in her lips as she listened to him, the arch of an eyebrow, the flare of a nostril—well, that was just Annette being Annette.

"You know, Annette, I think we're going to see some court decisions there. I'm itching to get into the thick of it. I might have missed the shooting war, but I'm not going to miss that—what do you always say, Claud? Pile on the canvas?"

Andrew pivoted Claudia's chair back to the table. He took a few sips of his coffee and lit up a Chesterfield for Claudia and one for himself.

"But, in the meantime," said Andrew, "I think you're thinking the same thing I am, Frog. They shouldn't call it a Big Island Omelet if they're going to use so much Swiss cheese, and I don't know if you noticed or not, but I think they're using the shank portion of the ham."

"I didn't notice that," said Froggy. "But what do I know?"

Annette scowled at him while Andrew was turned away.

"Can you cook, Andrew?" Annette asked.

"It's more like what can't he cook," said Claudia.

"I just put together some little things on my hot plate," he said. "You know, when I got out of the navy, I knew I was going to miss the food. What terrific chow, huh Frog?"

"You bet," said Froggy, raising his eyebrows.

"I went to the library and dove right into the cookbooks and learned a few things. It helps to have a good audience." Andrew looked at Claudia and took her hand on the table.

"You have Rivoli, too," Claudia said. "Andrew makes Italian food for a guy who works at the club. He loved that thing you made the other night."

"That was pasta carbonara."

"I don't know how you do it."

"Well, I'll tell you, Claud, I have two hot plates. You never saw the other one. I keep it hidden. That's the secret. I plug it in on the other side of the room where it's on a different circuit. Then I run back and forth."

"Sounds like a lot of work to me," said Froggy.

"Oh, sure, but you can't just sit back and eat out of a can. It's bad for morale. You feel better if you take care of yourself."

"That's so important," said Annette with genuine sincerity, "caring enough about yourself."

"I think so, Annette. And I think, Frog, you'll find that others respond well to that kind of—I don't know—what's the word I want, Claudia?"

"Outlook."

"That's it. Thanks, Claud."

"An uplifting outlook."

"We could sure use more of that around here," said Annette.

She nudged Froggy like a wife waking up her husband during a long lecture. She put one of his Luckys in his mouth and lit it for him. Claudia knew Froggy wanted to say he needed a more uplifting outlook like a hole in the head.

"Does anybody feel like playing golf today?" said Andrew.

The others were lukewarm about it, and Claudia knew Andrew had been working all night and had not gone to bed. He needed his sleep, so she put her foot down even though he made a very persuasive argument about how much fun it would be.

Claudia thought the breakfast at the Brown Derby went off quite well. She knew even Froggy would come around to liking Andrew, but it would be an adjustment, and it would take time. It was like getting a puppy after you got used to the old dog that died.

CHAPTER FORTY

A few weeks before Christmas, Andrew got the letters he was waiting for. He showed up at the Strickland all excited on a rainy Wednesday morning after she had walked Edgar Lee to school with his big project.

He had been working on a relief map of the African continent, shaping plaster of paris on a board the size of a bakery sheet cake. Very meticulously, he had carved topographical details from a color map in a geography book into the plaster and painted it with hobby paint. Then the board sat high up on Claudia's pile of unpacked boxes to dry. When the day came for his class report, it was raining to beat the band, so Edgar Lee wrapped the African continent in his raincoat with Claudia's raincoat over his, and they walked to school—Edgar Lee with his big board and Claudia holding the umbrella over both of them, heading into the wind.

When Claudia got home, she went back to bed, feeling it was a nice, dark, rainy morning to lie in bed with the windows open, listening to the rain, and dreaming. And that was exactly when dreamboat came to the door. Claudia slipped back into her dress and opened up.

"Guess what?" Andrew said.

"You got accepted, Mister College Boy?"

"You betcha."

"Where?"

"Everywhere."

"Well, come on in and show me."

Andrew kissed her quick on the side of the face and went right to the table, where he sat down, took out his letters, and spread them out.

"Syracuse, University of Chicago, University of Pennsylvania, UVA, UCLA, and Ohio State—that was my safety. Get over here, Claud."

"I thought you'd want some coffee."

"Sure, but hurry."

"You're worse than Edgar Lee."

"It's just that I have to decide pretty fast."

Claudia set up the percolator and went over to read Andrew's letters.

"Oh, this one sounds nice. Ohio State. I know you don't want to go there, but they sound nice."

"How about UCLA?"

Claudia shuffled through them and read UCLA again. It was so-so.

"I still like Ohio State best. Look, they are 'very pleased' and 'looking forward to meeting you.' They aren't beating around the bush like some of these other ones."

"Like which ones?"

"Well, here, The University of Chicago sounds like they're doing you a big favor."

"They're giving me money along with the GI Bill."

"But they all are, aren't they?"

"Yes—"

"Then why can't they be nice about it? I wouldn't go to Chicago if I was going to be with snooty people like that."

"Okay," said Andrew. "One down."

He took the Chicago letter out of her hand and turned it face down on the table. Then he spread out the other letters like a dealer spreads a deck of cards. Claudia watched him and thought how like a hand of cards it really was. You picked a school, and everything that happened to you after that was determined by that choice. Who you met, who you married, what you became, where you lived. Your whole life came out of that hand. She was watching it happen right now to an innocent. Andrew was picking out what the rest of his life would be, and he had no idea he was doing it.

"Any other ones you can rule out?"

"Andrew," she said, "I don't know anything about these schools."

"Then how about location? What appeals to you as a place to live? That's really a better way to do it. Pick one."

"I can't pick one."

"You must have a preference on a place to live."

"Sure, I do, but this is your decision."

"Just look them over and tell me where you'd like to live. Purely hypothetical."

"All right, but I'll be thinking of you too. It won't be all me. Like, for instance, California would be nice, but I know you wouldn't get any work done in California. Nice weather is bad for school. You need snow. So I would rule out UCLA off the top."

"Okay, that's good," said Andrew, and he turned UCLA over with Chicago.

"Syracuse is more snow than you need, and if you have New York tags on your car, everyone thinks you're from the city and the police pull you over out of state just for spite. Does that take care of Syracuse?"

"Okay."

"Let's see. What's next. Ohio State. Well, I know you don't want to go there, so here—"

Andrew turned that one over on the pile, too.

"University of Virginia. Everybody drinks too much. That's out."

"I don't drink that much, Claud."

"That's the trouble."

"Okay. Then I guess it's Penn."

"In my considered opinion, yes," said Claudia. "You can see how much thought I put into it." Then she reflected on her choice of Sweet Briar ten years ago. That was a shot in the dark, too. "Actually, Penn is kind of nice. I went up there for a dance sophomore year."

"This was a big help, Claudia."

"Can I have my coffee now?"

Claudia got up and brought the percolator over and poured them out two cups. She sat down across from him and took out a Chesterfield. Andrew had one too, which surprised her because it was only nine thirty, and he never started smoking that early.

"I wanted to talk to you because I have to let them know right away," he said. "I can get in the spring term but I probably have to be there by end of January."

"Oh no, Andrew," she said. "I didn't think it would happen so fast."

Suddenly, around the corner was the end of the fantasy life she had been living. She felt like one of those little flies that only lives a day—if it ever looked at its tiny body and fragile wings and could tell that it was not meant to last any longer than a day. Running out of time is a sorrowful thing.

"Yeah, it is pretty soon, so I wanted to talk to you. I want you to come with me."

"Oh, Andrew."

"I want you to marry me."

"Sure."

"Come on."

"No, really. Sure thing. I don't know why I didn't think of it myself."

Claudia looked at him right between the eyes and blew her smoke over his head like an airplane taking off, just missing the power lines.

"That's Jasmine talking," he said.

"Now you're catching on, kid."

"I'm asking Claudia."

"You don't know anything about Claudia. You only took her out a couple of times."

"I think I know her well enough."

"You think so? Try this one on for size," said Claudia. If her life was going to be over, why drag it out? "I like playing with girls."

Andrew's eyes opened up a little wider, but that was it.

"There's a lot you don't know about Claudia, or Jasmine for that matter."

"Then tell me," he said.

Fair and square. Over their coffee and smokes, Claudia began to tell him everything. She started with Mary Ann. Andrew listened intently and looked like his mind was going to work putting pieces of a puzzle together. Then she backed up to tell him about Jack and where she got her high standards for marriage. That explained the magnitude of the debacle with Dan. Andrew didn't believe the mechanic part, so she rattled off some engine specs on early model Oldsmobiles and went on to dishwashing at the Grand Hawaiian. Then getting into the bad girl business with Joe Johnson. She stopped at the Palmetto because of professional ethics.

She did not say anything about her dead baby in the septic tank. He would be seven years old by now. Everything would have been different. There wouldn't be any Andrew. Then she remembered she was going to name her baby Andrew. There wasn't any more irony to the rest of the story. Just a straight drop to the bottom.

They filled up the ashtray and drank all the coffee. It was nothing like a weeping confession in the movies. It was more like a deposition. She just wanted to get it out. He said nothing in her past mattered. It was over and done with, and they were two people living in the present. But that's what anyone would say.

Claudia got up to empty the ashtray. He got up too and made her put it down. He took her in his arms, which he must have known was the best thing he had going for him, but she was going to be tough. She wasn't going to let him appeal to the lower court of Claudia Wyler and end up having to change her damn underwear. Not this time.

"You haven't answered my question," he said.

"I can't now," she said. "I'm not in my right mind."

"No, you're in your right mind right now. Will you marry me, Claudia?"

She laid her head on his shoulder and closed her eyes and gave up. She was Claudia in her right mind all right, throwing her better judgment out the window. If she said yes, it meant a fresh start. If she said yes. All she needed to say was yes. Penn was nice, it was a pretty campus, she had walked across it one night in springtime, the spring of '38, and here it was, on a silver platter, a chance to start over, and she had to say yes because she was in love and it was the best thing for Edgar Lee. The war was over. America was busting out all over, and it was going to be such an exciting time for young people.

"Yes, I'll marry you, Andrew Taylor," she said.

Edgar Lee was thrilled to pieces. If it had been anyone but Andrew, it would have been a battle because Edgar Lee was getting independent and imposing the rule of a father over him would have been King George and the Revolution. He was already in low orbit around Andrew and did everything with him, from going to the beach to kicking around the hotel every chance he had. It was even better than having a father. Andrew was more like a big brother, a tough, flat-stomached, lean, lanky, muscled-up arms and shoulders hombre. Andrew could say things like "Hey Edgar Lee. Quit being a jerk." And Edgar Lee would quit being a jerk right away.

When they wore their sunglasses, they looked like two young navy men. Put Claudia between them, and they could pass for father and son, she thought, looking like the three of them belonged together. It was going to be a whole new life. And now there wasn't much time to get rid of the old one.

The University of Pennsylvania confirmed Andrew for the spring semester, starting January 28th, 1950. They sent a big packet of forms to fill out. They were going to live in a new building for married veterans, and Andrew would get a stipend of twenty dollars a month if he wanted to do four hours of work in the library every week. Enclosed was a brochure of The Towers. It was a new high-rise building with modern apartments. Edgar Lee was going to get his own room, and Claudia would have a kitchen. It listed all the schools in the area and bus routes that stopped in front of the place. Claudia helped Andrew with the paperwork, and they got it out the same day it came in. When a telegram came back saying they were registered, Annette manned the phones and got them lined up for a military transport plane to Wake Island, then one to Guam, and one to San Francisco. After that they were on their own.

Andrew wanted to buy a car and drive across the country. They wouldn't have much time to stop anywhere, but Edgar Lee was off his nut about the idea, and Claudia was beginning to get with it. So that's what they were going to do, and it looked like everything would be ready by the second week of January.

Christmas day was quiet because it was just the three of them in the room, and the details of the trip were not completely worked out. Edgar Lee gave Andrew a pair of sunglasses for Christmas, and Claudia had a feeling he stole them. That was another good reason for leaving, getting Edgar Lee away from his little buddy Nick once and for all and his life of crime.

January 4, 1950 was Claudia's last night at the Palmetto. She wanted to keep it low-key, but Mr. Anthony must have had something up his sleeve because the place was packed. The Hulas got a standing ovation when they came out on stage, and flash bulbs went off all over the club during the first show. It brought tears to her eyes, but that was only the beginning. She told the other Hula Girls as they gathered around her backstage that she was fine, but she wondered how she was going to do the last show without crying through "June is Bustin' Out all Over."

Between shows, Claudia sat at the bar with some friends of Andrew who distracted her while a big valentine heart was brought out on the stage. There was a fanfare of trumpets, and Claudia turned around to see Mr. Anthony under the spotlight. He called her up on stage and put his arm around her and summoned Andrew out of the wings. Andrew asked Claudia to marry him over the microphone, and she leaned forward to say yes into it, but she got too close and the microphone made a big tweek sound. The audience roared.

Claudia tried again, and she said, "Yes yes yes yes yes yes!"

Andrew put the engagement ring on her finger. She didn't know anything about it, and she gasped with amazement. It was so beautiful. It had a little diamond set in gold filigree like her first one from Jack. She flung herself into Andrew's arms, and the crowd went crazy with cheers and whistles. As she looked over Andrew's shoulder, across the bright footlights of the stage into the darkness of the crowd with flash bulbs popping all over the place, she felt it was so easy to believe in finding love, and here it was for everyone to see and believe, and believe it could happen to them too, because it was based on a true story.

In the last show, Claudia gave it everything she had. "June Is Bustin' Out All Over" went off without a hitch, but she did not pull the strings on her show bra because now that she was engaged, she didn't think anyone should be looking at her bosoms but her husband to be. But it gave her the time she needed. She had been practicing for three weeks, and she was ready. She didn't know if she could pull it off, but she didn't care. She wanted to go out with her best effort. Live in fame or go down in flames.

When the Hulas readied to rush her offstage, instead of doubling over to cover herself, Claudia sprung up, executed a perfect Tendardee, then touched down on one foot so fast no one would be able to tell she landed, and spun in a death-defying flying Double Tendardee, never before attempted on stage or screen, and she landed right side up. She did it. The Double Tendardee was in the record books.

There was a stunned silence. The Hulas stood with their jaws dropped and mouths open. The orchestra struggled back to life as a tremendous ovation erupted from the crowd. The Hulas took it as their cue to rush Claudia, and this time they put her up on their shoulders like she was no heavier than her old 110 and swept off stage in a swirl of grass skirts.

There were curtain calls and a presentation of roses to Claudia and Andrew when he came up to bow with the Hulas. Tears filled her eyes, and she made no effort to hold them back. She had done the Double Tendardee. She was getting married and going to a nice place that had civilized seasons. Her head was swimming. She couldn't tell if she was never so happy in her life, or just relieved.

After the show, the lights in the dressing room suddenly went out and someone yelled, "Surprise." Hot Lava and Atlantis, totally naked, carried in a big sheet cake with so many candles it looked like a thousand candles in the mirrors, and all the girls stood around it arm-in-arm, naked as jaybirds, and sang "For She's a Jolly Good Hula," with bawdy verses they made up themselves. Claudia pulled the strings on her show bra. It flew off while everyone clapped wildly, and she wiggled out of her grass skirt and stood naked with them in the flattering light of the candles. They crowded her to the cake and made her look at all the details before she went for the candles. It was in the shape of a big island, painted green with food coloring, with Diamond Head and Hula Girls and sailors, kind of like Edgar Lee's mock-up of the African continent. The writing said,

"Good Luck to Jasmine from Us," and below that were many X's for kisses. Claudia huffed and puffed, and everybody laughed and helped her out, and there were so many bosoms hanging over the candles that Claudia worried someone was going to get burned.

They ate the whole cake before they got dressed, then turned the lights out in the dressing room and left. For Claudia, the last one to leave, it was for the last time. Each of her girls kissed her and hugged her goodbye in the parking lot when their rides came, and finally it was just her and Rivoli and the wind going through the palms up high. She knew Rivoli was in love with her, but there was never a crack in his man's-man demeanor. She felt like walking home, so Rivoli walked her down to the Strickland. He offered his congratulations and best wishes and said goodnight the way he always said goodnight, as if he would see her again tomorrow. Then he walked off down the dark street and back to business. If she ever wanted a man without ups and downs or bad moods, it would be Rivoli. No questions asked—just the way he would want it.

Edgar Lee was sound asleep when she got in. Sometimes she wanted to tell him about her life, but she knew it wouldn't be right. Maybe someday. It was so late that she got into bed without washing her face or brushing her teeth. It was sad to think her career was over, and she tried to think it was keeping her awake, but another little thought was trying to say something, and it would not go away.

She couldn't get the Hula Girls out of her mind. They had never been naked together in a group like that, in the candlelight of the dressing room. All those shapely bottoms in the mirrors and perky bosoms swaying over the cake. Even then, every one of them had a few years on Andrew. She was easy to pick out of the crowd with her rolls, lines and sags. What business did she have going off with a twenty-year-old? If it didn't look ridiculous now, it wouldn't be long before it did. Andrew would have to make excuses and hide her away from the important people he met as he pursued his ambitions. Even worse, as a man, he would open his eyes and see what he was missing. The girls his age were so gorgeous. She could not bear losing him that way. She would be forty before he got to thirty. He had ten more years of being young. The only way she got herself to sleep that night was deciding to sleep on it.

The next day, Claudia made herself keep packing and making lists of what she had to do. She sat at the table and smoked her Chesterfields and found herself twisting her hair around her fingers while she looked at the latest *Life* magazine. She had a 7Up and another Chesterfield. There wasn't much left to do. No more club to get ready for, and Edgar Lee was probably out busting up the town with Nick. She started thinking about what to make for dinner at eleven o'clock in the morning. *The Newlywed Cookbook* was already packed in a box. There were ten boxes and all the shipping labels to write and glue on, but she did not feel like doing it.

The next night, Froggy showed up at the Strickland. She should have known. She'd had lunch with Annette at the French Café earlier and had mentioned Edgar Lee was over at Nick's for the night. He came in the big Hawaiian shirt, short pants, and those awful rubber tire sandals, and a straw hat that he tossed over to the bed when she told him to make himself comfortable.

"What's up, Doc?" he said, pulling a chair up and looking in his big pockets for his Luckys.

Claudia came over with the labels and a pen and sat down with him. She had not seen him for a month. He had his hair cut very short, so there was less red about the general impression of his face, but the freckles were still there. He said he was going to the beach more and watching the surfboard riders. He said he had some ideas about that but did not want to say anything yet.

"That was a big send-off they gave you at the club the other night. I don't know how the new girl is going to fill your—"

"Shoes, Froggy. Please don't make any smart remarks. I'm not in the mood."

She wiped away some beads of perspiration on her upper lip and tried to address a label. "I bet you want to see my ring," she said absently.

"Sure."

Claudia offered her hand, and he took it and brought the ring up close to his glasses. "Nice."

"Andrew has good taste," she said.

"Nothing much wrong with him, is there?"

"Not much." Claudia felt herself giving way, and she could not look at Froggy. A tear came out of nowhere and fell on a label she had just written and blurred the ink.

"Oh, goddamnit," she said.

"What's wrong? Sorry—I left my handkerchief in my formal wear."

Claudia wiped her eyes on her sleeve and let it blurt out.

"Am I only thinking about myself, Froggy?"

"You'll have to fill me in," he said.

"Andrew could have any girl his own age, but I came along and manipulated him into thinking he was in love with me. Now I'm going to weasel him out of the fun he should be having in his college years. But what do I care? I'll get the best part of his life. That's what I mean."

Froggy did not have anything to say. He just looked at her like he was waiting for an erroneous conclusion.

"I don't think I should marry Andrew," she said.

Froggy leaned back in his chair and said, "Whew. That's a big one. How are you going to back out of it now?"

"I don't know, Froggy, but I think I should. I can't do that to him."

"I don't get you. What can't you do to him? Backing out?"

"No, going through with it. Tying him down with a wife and a grown-up boy. He's only twenty. He doesn't know what he's doing."

"That's not the impression I got. The kid knows what he wants to do, and he has his whole life planned out. I don't think you have him pegged right."

"So I'm going to look like the heartless bitch again, aren't I? I know that's what all your friends think of me already, isn't it?"

Froggy looked down over his coffee cup, and Claudia caught one shoulder of his Hawaiian shirt going up in a non-committal shrug that quickly decided to retire. She didn't know why she was going back to something trivial that didn't matter anymore. It just irked her.

"Well, I don't appreciate that. I know the story from Annette."

"That's not what anybody thinks," he said softly. "I never said we were anything but friends."

Claudia said she was sorry and put her hand out to touch his arm, then picked up his pack of Luckys off the table and turned it over in her hand a few times, just for the feel of its squareness. They were much more satisfying packs to hold in the hand than the larger, rectangular Chesterfield packs. Maybe she should be getting more out of her smoking experience—but she felt too old to change, and that seemed to be the direction of the prevailing winds all of a sudden.

"Well, some kind of story got around. It doesn't matter. But this is crazy, Froggy, Andrew marrying an older woman with a teenage son and going off to college."

Claudia got up to get the last of the coffee.

"I don't think you're giving him enough credit," said Froggy.

"No, he should be going off to college alone, like everybody does. He's not even a year behind the others. He hasn't been away at the war like us. Remember when the war started, Froggy? It's like yesterday, isn't it? Andrew was back home in the States. He was twelve. He was Edgar Lee's age when the war started. It's ancient history to him. It's true, isn't it?"

"Well, maybe, I don't know. I can't argue with you because, well, you know, I have a conflict of interest."

At the door, Froggy said he would see what he could do about those ugly, coldhearted bitch rumors, which left her with a bit of a smile. Claudia dreaded the next day. She knew what she had to do. She looked at the boxes stacked up in the middle of the room and the half-done labels on the table, and she wished she did not have to undo her new life before it had even started, and tie the old one back down.

CHAPTER FORTY-ONE

Claudia told Edgar Lee the next morning when he came home from Nick's. She said she had to change her mind, and they weren't going after all. Edgar Lee said he wasn't going to talk to her ever again, but first he called her every name in the book, and then he stomped out, slamming the door. He was gone all day.

Rivoli brought him home around dinnertime, when she was getting worried, along with three flat boxes of Italian tomato pie with cheese that were so hot that Edgar Lee, who was carrying all three, hurried to the table to put them down. Rivoli had a bottle of red wine in the crook of his arm.

Claudia invited Rivoli to stay for dinner, and he graciously accepted. She turned on the little fan because it was so warm in the room and she made Rivoli take off his beautifully tailored Ramanson jacket. She motioned him to sit down at the table with Edgar Lee while she got plates and silverware and cut the first tomato pie into pleasing triangles. He had on a pressed white shirt with smart creases, a tie that matched the jacket, and a shoulder holster with a gun that instantly riveted Edgar Lee's attention.

There was very little difference Claudia noticed about the off-duty Rivoli, who sat across from her. Whenever he looked up from cutting his tomato pie, his eyes went from side to side, not in a conspicuous way, but she knew he was watching for a sudden attack from any quarter. His manners were beyond reproach.

"Elbows off the table, Edgar Lee," she said.

A glance from Rivoli ensured the execution of this directive, and Claudia was relieved she wasn't going to have it out with Edgar Lee, at least not while Rivoli was there.

"Listening to your mother is important in the Sicilian culture," said Rivoli. "Their wisdom is highly esteemed. You discover that later, Edgar Lee, when you turn out to be a good man, as no doubt you will." He opened the bottle of wine and set a glass in front of Edgar Lee, too. As he raised his glass in a toast, he said, "*Piaciri di canuscvi*—that means a pleasure to know you in Sicilian." Then he added, "Like this, Edgar Lee." He decorously sipped, and Edgar Lee followed suit with only a minor jolt after the swallow.

Rivoli told stories of where he grew up in Sicily, of Roman ruins and olive groves and roaming the hills hunting rabbits, enthralling Edgar Lee and carrying Claudia away. Edgar Lee asked him if the scar under his eye was from the war.

"Edgar Lee!" said Claudia

"Ah," he said, smiling as he turned to Edgar Lee. "When we are old men, we'll talk about that. I'll tell you about my wars, and you will tell me about yours. We'll smoke cigars, drink brandy from big round glasses, tell stories of our wars, women we have loved, and our mothers. You'll see."

Rivoli only drank as much wine as he had poured out for Edgar Lee. When they had finished the third tomato pie, Rivoli looked at his watch and said he must be going, as he had obligations elsewhere. Claudia thanked him for dinner and led him to the door. Edgar Lee watched him walk all the way down the hall and then turned and gave Claudia a huff and went to sit on his bed and read his comic books. She was glad he was safe at home and glad for Rivoli popping up at a good time. Gangsters probably had better luck with their kids.

Edgar Lee was gone in the morning. All his school uniforms were still in the closet, so he was out playing hooky, roaming around Honolulu and probably getting into trouble. There was going to be hell to pay for this particular lapse of her better judgment. She didn't know how she would ever get Edgar Lee back.

With her heart in her throat, Claudia walked over to the Barrymore and went down the steps to the basement. Andrew's door was wide open. She could hear Edgar Lee in there, so she went in without knocking, and there was Edgar Lee, sitting at Andrew's table, shuffling a deck of cards, with a cigarette in the ashtray in front of him. He had a marine fatigue hat on and his navy sunglasses. There was boogie-woogie music on the radio, and Andrew was over at the bed, turned around with his back to the door, putting his knee on a stuffed suitcase. It didn't look like Edgar Lee had told him the news.

"Edgar Lee," she said, "You put out that cigarette this minute."

Andrew turned around when he heard her and said, "Hey, Claud."

"You're just in time to sit on his suitcase, Mom," said Edgar Lee.

"Don't be impertinent, Edgar Lee. Will you please go home immediately. I have to talk to Andrew alone. And leave the hat here. And don't you budge out of that room until I come back, do you hear me?"

The tone of her voice meant business, so Edgar Lee slid off the chair and threw the hat across the room and went right out, right past her, without saying anything.

"Edgar Lee? Did you hear what I said?"

Claudia heard him mumble from the stairs, and then the door to the outside slammed.

"He'll catch up on his sleep on the plane," said Andrew. "He looks a little beat today."

"Why are you letting him smoke, Andrew?"

"Oh, well—I didn't think it was a big deal."

"I don't want to get him started."

Andrew shrugged his shoulders.

"I thought you were going to help me with Edgar Lee," she said.

"I am."

"You're letting him smoke."

"Everybody smokes."

"Oh, for heavens sake, Andrew. Everyone knows it's bad for children."

"He's not a kid anymore—"

"He's thirteen years old, Andrew. He's acting like he's sixteen, and you're encouraging him. And now you're acting like a thirteen-year-old too. I can't raise both of you."

Andrew sat down on the bed and started laughing.

"Come over here and sit down," he said.

"No, Andrew."

Claudia sat down at the table. She took off her engagement ring and put it in front of her. Andrew froze solid. There was no going back now. It was a hell of a thing to do to him. It was crushing her too, and she wanted them to die quickly and not suffer. But suffering was all there was to this, and it would stay alive a long time, coming back whenever she remembered the time of day, the tattered curtains in the windows, and the flowers painted on the table—and here she was, choosing a fate like that.

"I can't go with you, Andrew," she said. "I'm not going to pretend it has anything to do with Edgar Lee because I know you would make the best father in the world. I didn't tell you that I can't have children. I told you everything but that because I wanted you so much, and even if you say it doesn't matter, well, it does matter, because you'll want children someday, and you should be with someone who can do that."

Whenever she spoke seriously, Andrew listened carefully, like a lawyer, and made sure she completed her thoughts and he had a clear understanding of them. She could take out a Chesterfield and take her time, but there was no point to that. It was better to get it over with and leave.

"Look at what you're packing," she said. "One suitcase. That's because you're twenty. I can't pick up and go like that. I have a son and a lifetime of junk from a husband and other men and shares in a hotel I have to figure out what to do with. That's because I'm ten years older than you. It's too much of a difference."

At this, Andrew lifted his head to protest, as she knew he would, but she kept going.

"I can tell you all about college," she said. "I've already done it. Pillow fights in the dorms and getting drunk for the first time. I loved every minute of it, and you should too. You don't belong with the married students. I can't do that to you, Andrew. When you're young and you go to college, you have to be free. It's the time of life for that."

That was all she had to say. She stood up to leave and held up a hand to stop everything he tried to say.

"I'll come to say goodbye to you at the plane at four o'clock, but I don't want to see you until then. I've made up my mind."

Then she left and walked back to the Strickland. It was so hard to do, but she knew she was right. He thought he was going to study hard and blaze through college in three years by working extra hard and go on to law school, but she knew what school was like. He would go to a party or a mixer and meet someone wonderful, and love would mess up his plans because he couldn't just walk into her dorm room every Friday night with fifty bucks and fuck the dickens out of her. He would have to romance her, and all the work that takes would pay off in the end because he would marry her and have children of his own, not a juvenile delinquent from his has-been old wife. He was so young he didn't know boys never have pillow fights in the dorms, and he was so young he didn't know he could change her mind.

Edgar Lee wasn't in the room when she got back. He probably doubled back to Andrew's, or he was out roaming around Honolulu going into stores and shoplifting. What was she going to do with him now?

Claudia set up the percolator for coffee and lay down on the bed. Jack wouldn't have stood for it. He would have said, "Go apologize to your mother." If she could still be married to Jack, everything would be all right. He wouldn't stand for her going off with a younger man. She and Jack were so good together, but what's the use of thinking stuff like that?

It was only noon. Four hours to go. She felt so bad and sick at heart, but it was too soon to give up and cry. Andrew could come to the door and beg her to go, and she would go. She could leave everything behind and take just one suitcase. She prayed that Edgar Lee was with Andrew. What would she do if he weren't? How could she find him in time to catch the plane? She could call Rivoli at the club. He'd find him.

Claudia made herself doze on the bed while the percolator went blurp, blurp, blurp. Then she got up and had some hot coffee and a few Chesterfields and watched the clock, waiting for a knock at the door. When she went down the hall to the bathroom, she left the door to the room open and a note in the doorway. It took her a while to think what to write because either Andrew or Edgar Lee might show up. She finally wrote "Edgar Lee. Stay here. We might be going after all." And then she had to run as fast as she could down the hall to make it to the bathroom in time, after all that coffee.

It was all for nothing anyway. Claudia came back and had a few more Chesterfields and more coffee. She went down the hall to check if the phone was properly on the hook. This would be the one time, wouldn't it?

Her mind was going one way and then the other way, and it made her stomach hurt. She had some crackers, lay down, got up, had more coffee and a smoke, and lay down again. Watching the clock, waiting, hoping that Andrew would quit being an extraordinary man for once in his life and be a normal, regular one who didn't listen to a thing she said. She thought she could pack a suitcase and one for Edgar Lee and bring them in the cab to the airfield, but when three o'clock came, she decided against it. What she knew was for the best was still for the best. She did the right thing, and she had to stick with it.

At three thirty Claudia called Takeo, but he wasn't home, so she went out to catch a cab on the street. She didn't know where Edgar Lee was. There wasn't any point to leaving him a note. It looked like they weren't going. When they got to Hickam Field, she stuck her head out the window and shouted, "Wake Island?" at a guard, and he signaled them to drive out on the asphalt where an old, brown army plane was loading. Claudia got out and looked around for Andrew among the jeeps and trucks buzzing around, and it turned out he was already on the plane and spotted her from a window. He came down the stepladder that was propped against the open cargo doors.

They hugged and then drew back, looking each other up and down, holding each other's arms. Claudia smiled.

"You have to smile, Andrew," she said. "I want to think of you smiling, and I want you to think of me smiling when you think of me, and when you get back on the plane, you can't turn around and look back at me, okay?"

Andrew smiled, and she knew he was trying as hard as he could.

"I love you, Claudia. I have the ring. When you come out to school, we'll have another engagement party."

"I love you too, Andrew, but I want you to go off and have a good time. If you say anything else, it's only going to make it harder for me to see you go. Just smile and hold me and kiss me goodbye."

He kissed her and they held each other, and Claudia's mind stopped racing so she could just feel him against her for the last time and remember it.

"Write to me, Andrew," she said. "Maybe I'll be able to come when the hotel's done and you're settled. Smile now. Goodbye, Andrew. I love you. I love you so much."

Andrew smiled, and she gave him another quick kiss and turned him around toward the plane. She watched him climb the steps to the door, and before he could have a chance to turn around at the top, she ran back to the cab and told the driver to get going.

The last two times with Andrew were so hard. They were the worst one-sided conversations she'd ever had, two in one day, and they really hurt. This was the one that broke her heart. Why did her better judgment have to pick this, of all times, to come back from vacation?

PART FIVE

"What Makes that Man in Your Life so Difficult?"

—CASSANDRA A. HENDERSON, *WOMAN'S HOME COMPANION*, MAY 1950

CHAPTER FORTY-TWO

Now the man in Claudia's life, to whom she pledged her love and vowed to cherish for better or worse, in sickness and in health, till death do ye part, was Edgar Lee. She knew the vow hung around her neck only, not his, and driving back from the airfield in the cab, it felt like a millstone or a hangman's noose. The island was shrouded with clouds, and it started raining like crazy when they pulled up in front of the Strickland.

Claudia rushed upstairs to close the windows, but her bed was already wet, and the wind had driven the rain to the stack of boxes in the middle of the room. It looked as miserable a place to come home to as it could possibly be, but there it was, home, and she was Edgar Lee's mom, even though he would hate her for this day, maybe till death did she part.

But in the face of that forgone conclusion, Claudia rallied and made her stand. There was work to do. She tore through the boxes, unpacked all their worldly possessions, and put each one back in its place in the closet or on the shelves or hanging off a hook. She carried the soggy pile of cardboard to the end of the hall and let it fall down the stairwell to the basement. She'd worry about that later. No time to lose.

It was just a chance, but worth taking. Claudia left the door open in case Edgar Lee came home, grabbed the umbrella and walked to the Barrymore through the rain as fast as she could. She slipped and fell down most of the steps to the basement but didn't hurt herself too badly. Andrew's door was unlocked. She looked around like a burglar and stole inside. It smelled of Andrew, Ivory soap, Old Spice, and his boots. She felt around for the light switch but could not find it, groped her way to the bed, where she wanted to lie down in his sheets and die, but kept going for Edgar Lee, over to the wall and across to the table, crouched over, waving her arms in front of her in the pitch black windowless pit of the basement. The last thing she needed was poking an eye out on something. There it was. She found it with her hands. The hot plate.

Claudia got that home under her dress and went out to the store. Hot dogs and baked beans were Edgar Lee's favorite, so she got four dogs and a can of beans and four hot dog rolls. When she got back it was after six o'clock, and there was just enough time to make the room smell good and cozy, if Edgar Lee's delinquency kept regular hours. She did what Andrew did and set up his hot plate on the other side of the room so it wouldn't blow a fuse, and then she got the hot dogs cooking on one skillet and the baked beans going at the same time on the other. She stirred the baked beans over low heat and looked into the pot as she stirred, calming herself down. She had to keep her mind on little things now.

Edgar Lee came home around seven o'clock. He was still wearing his navy sunglasses, and now he had the marine fatigue hat on again, so he must have gone back to Andrew's room. She told him to take the hat off in the house, like she would have anyway, even though he had come home, and she wouldn't have cared about the damn hat because she was so happy he was home.

"You mean the room," he said.

"All right. Would you do that for me, please?"

Edgar Lee took off his hat and threw it over to his bed.

"Maybe the sunglasses too."

"Leave me alone," he said.

"Edgar Lee, I don't know how you can see anything in here."

"That's the idea."

"Don't be impertinent, Edgar Lee. And get the hair out of your eyes."

"Why don't you leave me alone," he said. "I wish you would just leave me alone for once."

"I thought we could talk tonight."

"Talk about what? You're so stupid."

"Don't talk to me that way."

Edgar Lee started over toward his bed. Claudia knew he was going to get the hat, and if she didn't put her foot down now, he would be going out the door, and God knows when he would come back.

"Edgar Lee," she insisted, "you're not leaving this house. I have dinner ready, and I want you to wash up and sit down at the table."

"It's a room. It's not a house."

"I don't want to hear any more back talk from you, young man," she said. "Now you go wash up right now."

He clumped over to the corner and washed his hands in the sink and came back to the table. Claudia pulled out two grilled hot dogs and fried two rolls up with butter in the pan and served them with generous dollops of baked beans. He ate it all while she cooked up the other two hot dogs and fried the rolls, and then he ate those and the rest of the baked beans. She turned on his radio show for him and stayed over by the hot plates and sink so she wouldn't bother him. When he was finished with his hot dogs and baked beans, she brought him two squares of chocolate from a Hershey bar and sat down across from him at the table with the last of the afternoon coffee and her Chesterfields.

"I'm sorry about the way things turned out," she said. "I wish I could change it, but I can't, and we're going to have to do the best we can for a while."

"How long is a while?"

"Until the hotel is done and we can move in. It will probably be a few months, but they'll go by before you know it."

"No, they won't. Besides, that's what you said about the car. You broke your promise."

"I thought you understood about that, Edgar Lee." There was nothing else she could say. She had gotten herself into a big mess. And it was her own fault, allowing herself to think everything was going so well. It was, for her. Not for Edgar Lee. She hadn't been paying attention.

"Do you want to go to the beach tomorrow afternoon?" she said.

"I'm going with my friends."

Claudia wanted to put the whole day behind her, turn the lights out, and go to sleep, but she knew Edgar Lee was miserable too, and she had to show him how you take bad news and go on, how you see it through, how you get through a day, how you suffer what you have to suffer and come up smiling, and how you can be strong without being mean. There was no one else to do that for Edgar Lee, and she could not let him stop her.

Edgar Lee was lying on his bed with his comic books. Claudia was at the sink in the corner, washing his plate and the skillet and pot. She might as well get it over with.

"You have to go back to school tomorrow," she said.

"I know."

"I thought I was going to have to fight you on that one."

"What's the use? You'd just make me go. You only care about yourself."

"Honey, please. I'm trying to do the right things."

"Well, why couldn't we go with Andrew? We were going to get a car and drive across the whole country and have fun. It was all planned out, and then you changed it. I already said goodbye to everybody at school. They're going to laugh at me."

"No one is going to laugh at you, Edgar Lee. If they're really your friends, they'll know there must be a good reason."

"No, they won't. What am I supposed to say?"

"You tell them—" Claudia had to stop and think a minute. "You tell them you changed your mind. You say 'I changed my mind. Thought I'd stick around a while.' That's what you say. You only get in trouble when you talk too much. It's always best not to say a lot and let people wonder."

"What was that again?"

Claudia went to the box under her bed and took out the pen and her airmail writing paper. "I'll write it down for you so you can practice your delivery. That's how you say something when it's like a speech." Then she wrote it out at the table while she repeated it. "I changed my mind. Thought I'd stick around a while."

She gave him the piece of paper, and he looked at it critically, sitting on his bed in the middle of a batch of comic books.

"Don't say anything else. Just what I wrote down. You'll be the mystery man. By the way, it works on girls too."

It was the only idea she had, but in the flash in which it came to her, it seemed like the best idea she'd ever had.

"What works on girls?" said Edgar Lee.

"Being a mystery man."

He took the bait. He was going to be a man someday, and she had to remind herself that he was already halfway there. She did not like to plot against Edgar Lee, her own son, but it was the only way, and he was asking for it every time he made her cry. She didn't have to be such a hurt mom all the time. She could try to think of him like one of the young sailor boys at the club and give him a little Jasmine club talk. It was going to be tricky. She didn't want to tip him off to what she did for a living.

"I know a lot about girls, kiddo," she said.

"Oh yeah? Like what?"

"You're asking me what I know about girls?"

"Yeah."

"Everything. And you know what else?"

She lit up a Chesterfield and crossed her legs and held her cigarette like Katharine Hepburn. "I never promised not to tell."

"Tell what?"

"Wouldn't you like to know."

"Come on, Mom."

"All right. Are you ready to get serious? Okay, I'll tell you how to be a mystery man."

"That's stupid."

"Look, do you want to get girls or not?"

"Okay."

"You want to be a mystery man?"

"I guess so."

"If you want to be a mystery man, Edgar Lee, you have to want it more than that. You have to commit yourself—that's when you try real hard. And you have to be able to accept criticism. There's no point in me telling you what you're doing wrong if you're going to be stubborn. It takes practice. And hard work. And you'll have to listen to me and pay attention."

"It sounds too hard," he said.

"Don't get discouraged, Edgar Lee. It's worth it in the end when you get girls. You won't get girls right off the bat, but you'll see."

Claudia stood him up and pretended she was looking him over. She brushed off his shoulders and smoothed the unruly hair out of his eyes.

"Hmm," she said. "I think we have some good raw material to work with."

Then she could not resist anymore and hugged him tight. He was getting tall, and the top of his head fit just under her chin without any room to spare. She said, "I love you, Edgar Lee," and she would not let him go until he stopped fussing and hugged her back. He didn't have to say anything, but she thought she heard the begrudging grumble she wanted to hear.

After Edgar Lee was asleep, Claudia got up very quietly and opened a pack of crackers and ate four of them. It was the only food she'd had since yesterday. She sat at the window with her last smoke and the little bit of old coffee left at the bottom of the percolator and looked at the stars coming out after all that rain. She wondered where Andrew was now and longed for him, watching the smoke disappear into the dark sky. Maybe she could sneak off the next time her better judgment decided to get away from it all. But for now, she thanked God for helping her with Edgar Lee. One down, one to go. Next stop was Mr. Anthony.

CHAPTER FORTY-THREE

Claudia wanted her old job back, but it wasn't going to be easy. The first thing Mr. Anthony was going to bring up was her interest in the hotel. Annette let Captain Locarno buy her out when she needed money for Christmas a few weeks ago, and he said that Mr. Anthony had picked up all the outstanding shares of the investors at the business association. It was just the three of them now, and that meant Claudia's monthly call money was going to the moon. As far as Mr. Anthony was concerned, she did not know if that made her shares in the hotel her ace in the hole or the sword over her head.

Claudia got in to see him without any wait, and he welcomed her with his usual inscrutable and impassive courtesy, motioning her to the plushy swivel chair in front of his desk. He took out a cigar and lit her Chesterfield, sat down, and leaned forward over his desk in an attitude that said, let's be honest with each other.

"I believe you were supposed to be going somewhere in an aeroplane," he said.

"The trip has been postponed, Mr. Anthony. That is why I wanted to see you."

"Perhaps you've come to a decision about your shares in the hotel?"

"No, another matter."

"Before we get to that," he said quickly, "have you considered the advantage to your present circumstances it would be to have ready cash and be relieved of the monthly commitment to the hotel?"

"I have," said Claudia, "and to be perfectly honest with you, I would like to reserve the favor of your interest in my shares, but for the moment, my son and I are planning to move into a suite in the hotel as soon as it is available. After that, I would definitely consider liquidating my holdings at a fair price and a suitable lease arrangement for maintaining a residence in the hotel."

Mr. Anthony smiled. "I see you believe business need not involve risk."

"Oh, no," said Claudia. "I've lived with risk ever since I became a part of the hotel. That's why I accepted the construction delays. What I am looking for now is the reward. I'm sure you understand."

"Certainly I do, Mrs. Wyler. This is what I have to say. Wait no longer. I assume you would like to get out of the hotel what you have in it, and with a reasonable profit."

"You're in it, too, Mr. Anthony, so you must know. Captain Locarno has led me to believe there's going to be a good return."

"But it can go the other way, too. Sometimes one can get out just in the nick of time."

Claudia sat back and crossed her legs and tried to appear unconcerned. She looked over toward the window to make him think she was giving it some thought.

"There seems to be no trouble since the delay over the variance," she said, "but it's nice to know I can come to you if I get worried."

"By then I would be worried, too, Mrs. Wyler. I may not be able to give you what you want for your shares. I can afford a loss. Forgive the presumption, but I daresay a loss would be more than an inconvenience for you. Right now I can get you out of it with a fair profit. I am prepared to give you two thousand above what you have invested. Would you mind telling me where you stand now?"

"Not at all. Could you pass me paper and a pen?"

Claudia leaned over to figure on the corner of Mr. Anthony's desk, the same way she had done so many times negotiating for the Hulas. This time was different. He was the one making the proposal. He was the one with leverage.

"There was my original $10,000 plus $24,000 for the last four years. So I come in at $34,000 total investment, not counting next month coming due."

"Then why don't we say three thousand over that? I can give you a check right now for $37,000. You'll never have to worry with cash in hand. We can get together with Captain Locarno and negotiate a modest lease for you and your son. You may even choose to change your plans. I'm sure you may have certain decisions to reconsider."

"No," said Claudia, "I won't be changing my mind about that. In fact, Mr. Anthony, that's why I'm here. I will keep your offer in mind, but meanwhile, I would like to discuss the other matter."

Claudia was glad he gave her the opening. A week ago, Mr. Anthony had been lukewarm about buying her out. She was in a rush to convert her assets into cash for a new life in the States. He said he would think it over. Now it was clear that he wanted her shares, but he didn't have to put the squeeze on. All he had to do was wait for her to need money badly enough, and he could buy her out for next to nothing. Mr. Anthony was never going to give her the job back.

"I was hoping I might get my old job back."

"Oh, Mrs. Wyler," he said. "I'm afraid we can't do that. The new girl is working out so well. It wouldn't be fair to let her go. She's worked so hard, and the audience has taken her into their hearts. As for behind the scenes, you were so indispensable to the act that we were forced to go through an agency in New York to secure the services of a full-time costume designer and a choreographer to work with Max. They should be here any day now, so you see—"

Mr. Anthony thought a moment, turned toward the window, and then swung back around abruptly.

"One question. Could you do the Double Tendardee again?"

Claudia looked him straight in the eyes and said with all the confidence in the world, "No."

"I didn't think so," he said, leaning back in his chair.

"It was one in a million. I got lucky."

They both looked toward the window as if dreaming of a better time.

"Isn't there something I could do at the club?" she asked.

Mr. Anthony puffed on his cigar, narrowed his eyes down, and then brightened with the same look on his face that Claudia remembered from the day he first hired her. An idea had come down from the sky.

"The Palmetto Community Outreach Program," he said. "It's something new, an experiment. I don't know if you would want to try it."

"I know I would," she said.

"We were looking for someone with the right skills to get it started. Maybe you're the one. The idea is to bring the show to people in the countryside who are unable to get into the city. A traveling Palmetto show. What do you think?"

"I love it," said Claudia.

"Of course, we can't anticipate the response, so we could only pay you a per diem for each show. Say, $50 a performance."

"That sounds good to me," she said.

"We can't guarantee the number of shows until we confirm locations and schedules. We're just trying it out, you understand."

"I understand completely. Then it's up to us to make it a success?"

"Precisely."

"I think we can do it. You're on, Mr. Anthony."

"All right," he said. "Why don't you come in Thursday at eleven and suit up. I'll make a few calls and see what I can put together."

They stood up and shook hands across the desk like real business partners, and not a peep out of her better judgment.

Claudia walked home from the club because it was such a beautiful day and she felt so good having a job. She needed it badly. If Mr. Anthony had not hired her, she didn't know what she would have done. Just to stay in the game with the Maycomber meant $500 a month, according to Captain Locarno's latest assessments. The hotel felt like an albatross around her neck when she and Andrew had gotten engaged, but now it was back to being her only chance. It was the baby in the bathwater, and she'd drink all that dirty bathwater if she had to, before she let the baby get away.

She could not think about Andrew. She was with him only twenty-four hours ago. She had to think of Edgar Lee and his future. $37,000 was a lot of money, but it would kill the golden goose, and Edgar Lee had a long future to go. On the way home she picked up some hamburger for dinner, vegetables for a nice salad, and a few cans of fruit cocktail. If she could make $50 a show and did five or six shows a week, there wouldn't be any worries about money and she could keep up with Locarno. Thinking that over and running numbers in her head, Claudia walked two blocks back to the store because she knew Edgar Lee would love the chocolate cake in the glass counter. Before she left, she had two more bags of things Edgar Lee liked and struggled home desperately clutching four paper bags with nary a Boy Scout in sight.

Claudia put the chocolate cake in the middle of the table so Edgar Lee would see it when he came home from school. She dragged her finger carefully through the icing, making a groove that formed the words "I love you, Edgar Lee." She had a cup of ice cream sprinkles that she brought home from Annette's birthday party and lay them down like colored seeds in the grooves of "I love you, Edgar Lee."

When Edgar Lee came in the door, he looked at the cake as he went by and did not say anything. He put his school blazer on the bed and flopped down on top of it.

"Hi there, Edgar Lee."

"Hi."

"Did you see the chocolate cake?"

"Yeah."

"I thought we'd have a nice dessert tonight."

"You can."

Claudia went to the bureau where she kept kitchen things and got out the wax paper to cover the cake. Edgar Lee just lay there looking up at the ceiling. She was going to have to say something about getting creases in his school clothes if he didn't take them off soon.

"I thought you were going to the beach with your friends."

"I don't have any friends."

"What about Nick? And the boys you play baseball with?

"He's a jerk. They're jerks, too."

"What's wrong, Edgar Lee?"

"Nothing."

"Something's wrong. I can tell. Did you gain weight today? Is that it? You look like you put on fifty or sixty pounds since this morning."

"Stop it, Mom."

"I can't keep letting your pants out, buster. I'm going to call the school and tell them to stop giving you all those fried potatoes."

"Mom—"

"Well, what are you so morose about?"

"This kid in my class."

Claudia waited. Then she went over and sat on the corner of Edgar Lee's bed. She took off his tie and unbuttoned his collar. She thought she might be able to get all his school clothes off him and the blazer out from under without him noticing. She hated using the iron. She always burned herself on the tummy. It was one of those things people should not do without their clothes on.

"What about the kid in your class?" she asked.

"What's a whore?"

Claudia was taken by surprise, but she didn't think she showed it. She knew she was going to have to keep her wits about her on this one.

"I don't know why something like that would come up at school, Edgar Lee."

"This kid had a picture that he showed everybody. Nobody knew it was you, but I did. His dad took it."

"What kind of picture?"

"You have a hula dancer dress on, but just the bottom part. You don't have any top part on. It's pretty bad, Mom. It was you, wasn't it?"

"Well, I don't know, but I suppose it might have been."

"He said it was a picture of a whore at that club."

"Well, you know I work at the Palmetto, Edgar Lee—"

"So, what's a whore?"

"Well, a whore is a lady at a club. There are lots of different jobs at clubs like ours. The whores arrange get-togethers between people. Now, I work with the Hula Girls and make up dances for them. We also bring people their drinks and see that they have a good time, and then we do shows on the stage. That's why I come home so tired, because I help them out sometimes. We do lots of dancing, you know, like the show we did for the hospital last year. You remember that, don't you? Remember the costumes? I help make them up. And sometimes we do authentic Hawaiian dances where we only wear grass skirts. You know, that's how Hawaiian girls used to dance all the time, and nobody ever said a thing about it. But the boy's father never should have taken the picture because it's an ancient Hawaiian ritual and pictures are forbidden by the Hawaiian people's gods. It's also against club rules. He could be banned from the club."

Claudia stopped there. That was going to be it for now. When he knew better, there might be a chance he would understand better too.

"Okay?"

"Okay," said Edgar Lee.

Claudia got his good shirt unbuttoned and off him and pulled off his good school trousers while he was still looking up at the ceiling. She got the blazer too and hung everything up in the closet.

"Why don't you go down to the beach?"

"I don't want to."

"Edgar Lee, you can't let people see you down and blue. Then they make up stories behind your back. You have to look calm, cool, and collected."

"Nick knows it was you in the picture."

"Well if he says anything, you just say, 'Aw, what do you know, Nick.' Then he'll just drop it. But if you don't go to the beach today, they'll start picking on you, and the girls will find out about it. You don't want that to happen, do you?"

"I guess not."

"Then you better get going, mystery man, but be back by six thirty, and tonight we'll eat the cake."

After Edgar Lee left, Claudia sat down with a Chesterfield and a cup of the cold coffee from morning. She figured she was off the hook for now, but she knew it would not be long before somebody was going to wise up Edgar Lee to what whores are, and she was going to have to tell him a little more than the standard government issue facts of life. How do you put whores in a good light? Facts of life are easier to take when they don't involve your mother.

Claudia hoped there were not circulating on the school ground any old pictures of the early Hula Girl shows with her bare bottom hanging over the edge of the stage, getting pawed by marines and sailors. It would be tough to sell as an authentic Hawaiian ceremony, and Edgar Lee would never buy it. She had seen one or two snaps that went around the club, and it really was true, the camera always adds ten pounds. She knew she was fat, but she wasn't that fat.

After dinner, when Claudia and Edgar Lee were about to go for the cake, there was a very soft knock at the door, and Claudia was surprised to see a little crowd in the doorway. Annette, Froggy, and Pinkie from the club. Annette and Pinkie hugged her as they came in, and Froggy bustled through them with a game box and a couple of shopping bags.

"I know I'm being selfish, but I'm so glad you didn't go," said Annette.

"All the girls miss you at the club. Hot Lava's in charge now, and she stinks."

"Oh, that's not nice to say, Christine."

"This is Christine, Edgar Lee," said Froggy. "Christine, this is Edgar Lee. Let's sit on the floor. Not enough chairs in here. We brought along some stuff and—drum roll please—Parcheesi!"

Froggy held up the box of Parcheesi for all to see and then moved the table and chairs to the side and sat down on the floor with the bags and started setting up the Parcheesi board. First on the ground was Pinkie beside him, and then Froggy gestured for Edgar Lee to sit beside Pinkie, and then Claudia plopped down on the other side of Froggy, and then she had to give Annette a hand getting to the ground like a giraffe at the zoo because of her tight skirt.

"I'm surprised you two know each other," said Claudia.

"We met at Palace Steps just yesterday," said Pinky, "The new shoe store."

"Christine has excellent taste, Claudia. Just look at that dress. She won't tell me where she got it. You find out and tell me."

Pinkie was decked out, all right. Sitting down with her knees together and her legs to one side and practically leaning on Edgar Lee, with the hem of the little Hawaiian pattern she was wearing almost up to her panties, Pinkie could have stepped out of *Li'l Abner*. The plunging neckline made Claudia remind herself to cover her bosoms better around Edgar Lee. He was probably getting started on that scrapbook men keep of the sex pictures their eyes are always taking.

Edgar Lee was at full alert sitting next to Pinkie, obviously imagining this blondie with blue eyes and ponytails was a girl he had acquired in one of his mental adventures. As they got down to Parcheesi and gobbled bags of popcorn and bottles of Hires Root Beer, Claudia felt so grateful to Annette. She knew it was all her doing, and she knew she did it for Edgar Lee. She and Annette went down the hall to the bathroom together.

"She's a real nice girl," said Annette. "I knew she would perk up Edgar Lee."

"He sure looks perked up to me. Gee-zu, Annette. That was just the thing. I didn't know what I was going to do with him. Thank you, thank you, thank you."

Coming back to the door, Annette stopped her and hugged her before they went in. Then she drew back and held her around the middle with her face up and smiling.

"I'm so glad you're still here, Claudia," she said. "Everything is going to be fine. Just don't worry. I know you'll miss Andrew, but someone else will come along and you'll be happy again. I know you will."

Froggy was learning Chinese for the navy now, and when Claudia and Annette came back in, he was saying Chinese words and making Edgar Lee laugh because of the accent he was overdoing and the way he raised his eyebrows way up when he said them. Pinkie was in stitches too, turning into Edgar Lee with her bosoms and ponytails bouncing around so much Claudia was afraid Edgar Lee was going to blow a fuse.

Froggy said he re-upped with the navy, so they made him a lieutenant commander for his trouble.

"I don't know what I'm going to do with all the money," he said. "I just toss the paychecks in the closet."

"Don't get any ideas about this guy, Christine," said Annette. "He's loaded, but he's tight."

"I've been known to loosen up."

"Like fun," said Annette. "Christine, look at what Arnold gave me." She thrust her chest out over the Parcheesi board to show an exquisite gold chain around her neck, and Christine and Claudia bent over to get a good look, Claudia with a hand over the opening at the top of her dress.

"I bet that relationship is going nowhere, isn't it?" said Froggy.

"You're damn right," said Annette.

Froggy put his arm around Edgar Lee. "Learn the ways, Edgar Lee. Learn the ways."

It made Claudia so happy. Edgar Lee did not catch half of what went back and forth, but she could tell a new world was revealing itself to Edgar Lee, and the realization might be dawning on him that it was bigger than he thought it was.

"It's puberty," said Annette, the next day at the French Café. "But not the awful, anxiety-ridden things girls deal with. Boys get muscles and erections. Nothing bad about that, right? In Edgar Lee's mind, the muscles and erections are associated with Honolulu by positive reinforcement—that's where Christine comes in. You see what I mean? The trip you didn't take is going to look more and more like kid stuff to Edgar Lee. He'll be glad he didn't go."

"That may be too much to hope for," said Claudia, "but at least he's not moping around anymore."

"He's probably getting erections then," said Annette thoughtfully.

"Jesus, Annette, will you lay off the erections?"

"Okay, okay. Let's have some pie and you can tell me about the community outreach program. I'm so proud of you, getting into philanthropy."

CHAPTER FORTY-FOUR

The next morning after Edgar Lee went off to school, Claudia went down the hall to take a shower and get ready to go to work. It looked like everything was working out okay. No upsets at school, but for all she knew, Edgar Lee would find out about whores somewhere along the line. Who knows with boys? He might be a big hero on the playground, making up stories about her cavorting with ten men at once or doing it with the president when he came to Pearl Harbor. But so far so good.

Claudia caught a cab to the club and got there just at eleven. Max was in his office and glad to see her back. He gave her a box with her costume, so she went in the dressing room and changed. There was her picture, along the wall in the Hula Hall of Fame. It was a great shot, taken at the moment she completed a Tendardee in a midair split with both arms raised to the sky. She didn't remember when it was taken, but it was a good one to leave behind. If there was anything she would bequeath to her girls and those that followed, it was an inspirational expression of a can-do spirit, caught in a moment of triumph. Sometimes it can be downhill after that. She went in the office and gave Max a kiss on the cheek.

"You can leave your purse and everything in your old locker, Jasmine," Max said. "Mr. Anthony said something about you going out to a site."

"We're doing a show in the countryside. It's called community outreach."

"Something new?"

"Yeah, we're going to see how it goes over."

"What are you doing for dance numbers?"

"Old stuff, I guess."

When Claudia came out of the dressing room in her hula costume, there were two of Mr. Anthony's men waiting outside Max's office. One was Rivoli. The other one was much older. He was probably too old for the job, but the word was that he was Mr. Anthony's uncle, the Palmetto's goon emeritus.

"We're supposed to drive you, Miss Jasmine," said Rivoli.

They escorted her out the back door to one of Mr. Anthony's big black gangster cars. That's when Claudia began to get nervous. She was the only Hula Girl there. Rivoli held the back door for her and then got in the front beside Emeritus at the wheel. They took off down the alley.

"Where are we going?" she asked.

"Don't worry about it," said Emeritus.

Rivoli did not say anything. He looked different with his hat on. He didn't look like the man she knew. But what did she ever really know about him? Claudia suddenly understood what was going on now. She was going to get a bullet in the head today.

Emeritus seemed to take every back street to get out of town, picking up speed as they cleared the outskirts. Then it was country, pineapple and sugar plantations and all that lush, green, tangly jungle stuff and red dirt on the side of the road. What was going to happen to Edgar Lee?

Mr. Anthony couldn't kill a boy. The hotel shares would pass to Edgar Lee, and he couldn't do anything about that. Maybe he had lawyers. She didn't know. Maybe he was just getting rid of her because she was trouble, because she had fought for hula rights, and better pay. If she was a thorn in his side, Mr. Anthony wouldn't care if Edgar Lee lost another mother. And that made Claudia think of Annette. Thank God for Annette. Annette could marry Froggy, and they could adopt Edgar Lee. They would do it for him. They would settle down, and Froggy would be a good father when he stopped being a cutup and knuckled down. He could talk rings around Edgar Lee if he didn't mind his p's and q's. He looked like a grown boy's father since he put on weight. He looked like a dad who would come out on the porch and say you weren't going anywhere until you cut the grass. Then a sense of peace and transcendence came over Claudia there in the back seat, thinking how good it would be for Edgar Lee to end up with Froggy and Annette. She just had to get out of the way.

The car slowed down and pulled off on a dirt road. This was it. The road led back into the jungle a few hundred yards until it opened up to a clearing and the road disappeared into scruffy grass. It must have been part of a plantation. Emeritus drove twice around the clearing, honking the horn again and again, and pulled up by a little aluminum trailer, shaded by a clump of low palms. Rivoli and Emeritus got out and pulled a thick board with hooks on the sides and a blanket out of the trunk. Rivoli opened the door for Claudia. Men were coming out of the jungle and down the road.

"Mr. Anthony wants you to dance on top of the car," said Rivoli.

Claudia couldn't believe it. Emeritus threw the blanket over the roof of the car, and Rivoli helped him lift the board on top and tie it down. She was glad she wasn't going to get the bullet in the head, but she wasn't sure how glad she should be. There were an awful lot of men coming toward the car. Emeritus, with his back against the car, pulled his gun and held it pointing up while Rivoli helped Claudia climb onto the board on the roof. She managed to stay on her feet once she stood up and got the feel of it. Emeritus turned on the car radio with the volume all the way up and got some dance music.

Claudia started dancing. She did some hula and some of the easy ones from the club. It probably didn't matter to any of the men coming up to the car and forming a circle around it, but she tried to adapt slower movements to the faster rhythms coming from the radio. The board wobbled when she tried to go faster, and this was one stage she didn't want to fall off. The men looked pretty rough. There were about twenty of them and more were coming out of the bushes. The radio had commercials and the time and weather forecast, but she danced to that too, and the men started to get rowdy.

When the time seemed right, they turned off the radio, and Rivoli helped Claudia get down. Emeritus waved his gun to clear a path through the men to the trailer, and once there, he unlocked the door, pulled out a card table and metal cash box and set up beside the door. Rivoli motioned to Claudia and held her arm as she mounted the stepladder. The heat was stifling inside the trailer, so they cranked the windows out first thing, and then she looked around.

There was a plain metal-frame bed with a dirty, bare mattress on it that filled up most of the space inside. There was also a chair that Rivoli moved to the head of the bed, where he sat down and kept his eyes on the door. There was a box of club rubbers on the bed.

"Oh, God. This is really awful, Rivoli," she said.

"Mr. Anthony said you get a percentage. He said to tell you that. You just tell me when you want to stop."

"Where do I put my costume?"

"I'll hold it," he said.

Claudia gave him her grass skirt, and he folded it carefully over his knee, and then he did the same with her show bra and panties. Rivoli was respectful. She lay down on the mattress and waited. There were a lot of loud voices outside.

"This is really bad, isn't it."

"There are some things you might need under the bed," said Rivoli.

She reached under the bed and pulled out a jar of Vaseline and some towels.

"Thanks, Rivoli."

He looked away while she got ready, and then they waited. The voices got louder outside. It was probably about the money. Rivoli had his gun trained at the door. Then it quieted down. Claudia had to hand it to Mr. Anthony. He knew how to make money when the market was going down. She was a fading Hula Girl, a depreciating security, and Mr. Anthony was selling short.

The first man in the trailer didn't know he needed another dollar for the club rubber. He didn't have it, so Rivoli kicked him out and shouted to Emeritus outside that you can't spring that on a farm guy without a wallet. From then on, they came in with the extra dollar. Rivoli made sure they got the club rubbers on right, and then he sat in the chair right by the head of the bed. Now the gun came out. While the men were on her, Claudia could hear Ravoli slapping it from one hand to the other, and if anyone got too rough with her, he pointed the gun right at the man's head. She could see the barrel in the upper corner of her peripheral vision. Rivoli didn't take it away when the man eased up, either. He kept it aimed right between the eyes. It was a wonder they did any business at all. If it wasn't sex, you probably couldn't get anyone to do something that way.

Claudia tried to keep count because she knew she was going to have to check Mr. Anthony's figures. He acted so polite and nice, but he really was about as low as you can get. She tried but lost count. She had to turn off her counting mind and think about nice things like driving the shore road in the Roadmaster and Edgar Lee laughing at Froggy's Chinese and how kind Takeo was and the monkey family and the ivory polar bears hugging, and Mary Ann, oh Mary Ann, oh Mary Ann. She was so sorry, and she wished she was going to get the bullet in the head after all so Edgar Lee could be raised by decent people like Froggy and Annette.

Finally, it hurt so much that she could not take another man and she told Rivoli she had to stop. He and Emeritus scared all the other men off, dropped the curtain, and closed the show. On the way back to the club, Claudia stared out the window, thinking about nothing. She was beginning to wonder if she was ever going to cry again.

CHAPTER FORTY-FIVE

Claudia knew she had to go to the club Friday morning. Mr. Anthony had to see she was tough. He gave her an envelope with the $50 per diem and another envelope with her percentage. She opened them, standing in front of his desk, and he asked if she was interested in continuing the program. When she said yes, he said they should clarify the details, and they both sat down.

"I gather you don't feel it necessary to invest much in production," Claudia said.

"Within reason."

"A bed pad, one out of the back rooms. And an ice bucket. A fan."

Mr. Anthony wrote these down on a pad and looked up.

"That's it for now," she said.

"Well then," he said. "How often can you do the show? Looking over the expenses, I find that two shows a week are a minimum requirement for the club to make a worthwhile profit."

Claudia looked at the checks again. $50 for the show, $50 for the percentage. She did not know what Mr. Anthony was charging or what her percentage was, but she did not want to ask. The checks were decent. It was more than she expected. It just seemed like an awful lot of men.

"I can do it Mondays and Thursdays," she said. "At ten. We quit when I want to stop. I'll pick up my checks Friday mornings."

"Agreed," he said. "Welcome to private contracting, Mrs. Wyler. I think the outreach program is off to a good start."

They stood up and shook hands across the desk, and Claudia left the office standing as tall and proud as she could but walking funny because she still hurt. Two times a week was going to be rough. Monday would tell if three days was enough to recover, and then Thursday would be the test if two days were enough. Maybe she could load up on Thursdays and go light on Mondays. There was a lot to work out. She could be back before Edgar Lee came home from school. He wouldn't know the difference.

Monday went like the first time. Rivoli was good at keeping it down to a low roar in the trailer, and Thursday she kept to a full schedule and saw it through. The little fan that worked on batteries did a good job. Rivoli kept it pointed at her on the bed, and after each man left the trailer, Claudia got up and redirected it at him in the chair against his protests. Looking out for Rivoli was the only thing that made her feel good about her workday. She knew it wasn't easy on him either.

She wasn't holding her breath for things to get better anymore. The hotel would take a few months, and she had to slog it out. It was a war of attrition. You won if you lasted longer than the other guy. But the other guy wasn't Mr. Anthony. The other guy was life. You never win against life. You just stay on your feet and last as long as you can. She had to do it for Edgar Lee. If it came down to it, she had to last at least until he was strong enough or old enough to go on by himself, whichever came first.

After the first time in the trailer, Claudia felt as lonely for someone to talk to as she ever had in her life. But now the need to talk was set aside by the finality of her decisions, by facing facts she could not get around, and there was no point squawking about it. It was easy to be Jack when she was on top. Now she had to be Jack when she was at the bottom, the bottom of the barrel, and she was glad to find that thinking of Jack still made her strong. She could do what she had to do. Jack said, "Claudia, you got what it takes." She had to remind herself. Some days she forgot how it went.

Claudia endured her two days a week, and the weeks went by, and a month went by and another month, and trying to be Jack landed her in the dependent's clinic at the navy base hospital. She sat on an examining room table in a blue string-tie gown, waiting for the doctor, and she heard a familiar voice outside the door saying, "I'll take this one." Elaine walked in with a stethoscope around her neck, white coat, and a clipboard in hand.

"Claudia," she said, "it's so good to see you."

"Oh, Elaine, I'm so glad it's you," said Claudia. "I heard your voice out there and I didn't know if I'd get you. I'm so glad. Oh, let me see your ring. I was so happy for you. How's married life?"

"Just like I thought it would be," said Elaine, sitting down on a little stool beside the table. "Well, actually, I could tell you stories, but that's not what you're here for, is it? Why don't you tell me what's wrong?" She looked at her clipboard. "It says here 'girl problems.' Okay. Well, let's take a look."

Claudia lay back, and Elaine put on her glasses and pulled a penlight out of her breast pocket.

"Oh," she said. "That must hurt." Then she shifted over to talking to herself in a low voice as she wrote on her clipboard between looks. "Labial hypertrophy, possible bacterial vaginosis, possible trichomoniasis. Oh, wait a minute. What have we here?"

"What?" said Claudia, looking up at the ceiling fan.

"You can get up now, Claudia."

Elaine wrote more on the clipboard and took out a prescription pad.

"Pthirus pubis," she said. Then she looked up over her glasses and said, "You have crabs, dear. That's what those little critters crawling around down there are. It's nothing to be alarmed about. We'll take care of that first. Then you get some needles. I'm going to have Dante shave you first."

Elaine bent in close and said, "Don't worry. He's not interested in girls. He's very gentle. The girl on shift is a little rough, but Dante's good. I'll send him in. I'm going down to the pharmacy. Back in a few minutes. Just lie back and relax."

Claudia didn't need to hear that twice. She was asleep in two minutes, even as the paper covering the table crinkled at her ear every time she breathed. The next thing she knew, there was a quick knock, the door swung open, and it had to be Dante. All Claudia could make out, just opening her eyes in the bright light, was a blue surgical gown and lots of colors.

"A pleasant afternoon to you. I am Dante. And you must be this person, Claudia Wyler," he said, looking at the chart on the inside of the door.

He was young, tall, and slender. Some kind of Asian. Over his arm was a pair of purple rubber gloves that matched a streak of purple in his hair, which was pulled back to a knot in the back with bamboo slivers through it. From there it stood up like a parade-ground shako. She wanted to ask him where he got the gold and turquoise earrings and who did his nails as he swept gracefully around her, pulling a basin from this cabinet and a razor from that drawer, and then adding on a lathering brush, soap, and towel. Then he sat down on the stool beside her and looked her right in the eyes.

"Do you understand why I am here, Miss Claudia?"

"Yes," she said.

"Good." He slapped his hands on his knees and got right to work.

Claudia lay back and let him move her around a bit this way and that. All she felt was a little wetness, a little soapy, little flickers and whisks that she would have taken for the touch of feathers, and dab, dab, dab with a soft towel. Then, in the middle of the discussion they were having on Jean Peters in "*Captain from Castile*," he said, "All done!" Dante covered her legs and sat her up. "—but I completely agree with you Miss Claudia, Hollywood overdoes it with the makeup. You don't know what they have to cover up though. Now when it comes to you and me, Miss Claudia, we just go natural, don't we?" Then he laughed and left the room in a flourish of blue, purple, and gold.

Elaine came back with the needles and a handful of creams, salves, and ointments. The needles were big horse needles and went in the rear, and while Elaine was doing that, she explained what each of the tubes was for.

Then she turned her back over, put on surgical gloves, and showed her how to apply the gooey stuff. Claudia was expecting a lecture because Elaine knew she wasn't married, but all she said, as she finished writing on her clipboard and putting her glasses back in her jacket pocket, was, "You're going to have to tell your fella to take cold showers for a while. Two weeks. And go easy after that."

Claudia felt better already as she waved for Takeo's cab at the gates of the navy base. She wished she did have a fella. She would tell him it was doctor's orders, and she would get two weeks off. Twenty guys in the jungle was a different story. She had two days R&R, and then it was back to the front lines in the trailer.

Claudia got to the French Café a little early and ordered coffee and a plate of cinnamon buns and got out her Chesterfields. She divided the buns in half, ate all of hers, and was considering nibbling into the six she saved for Annette on the other side of the plate when Annette showed up.

"I didn't know if you would remember changing our day," said Claudia.

"Memory like an elephant."

It was true. Annette could remember every party she had ever gone to and what everyone was wearing. She said last time Claudia came in the blue shift with a sash, straw pumps, and that cute little black cloche that looked so good with her blonde hair.

"You always look good, Claudia, but honestly, you've got to let me take you shopping."

Annette took out her Luckys and ordered a cup of coffee. She peeled off the outer ring of one of her six cinnamon buns and told Claudia to eat the rest, which Claudia immediately set about to do, between generous swigs of coffee and puffs of her Chesterfield balancing in the ashtray.

"I like your nails, Annette. What color is that?"

"It's new. It's called Coquette. I just did them at the office. It's always slow on Wednesdays."

"Oh, I bumped into Elaine today. I hadn't seen her since she and Froggy broke up. Have you seen her ring?"

"No, but I heard it's a big rock."

"Well, it reminded me I want to ask you something, but I want Froggy in on it too, so I don't want to ask you now."

"How about with Parcheesi on Friday night?"

"I don't want to say anything in front of Edgar Lee and Christine. Maybe Sunday at the Brown Derby. You two going to be there?"

"Yeah, it's kind of a regular thing with him now," said Annette with a note of exasperation. "I don't know what's worse. Before he quit the navy, we just talked about office stuff. Now the only thing he wants to talk about is that silly surfboard riding. Maybe having you there will get him off the subject. Wear something provocative—oh, let's go shopping. I saw something the other day that would knock him right off his surfboards. I don't have the figure for it, but it would be perfect for you."

"No, thanks. Not interested in a quest for perfect today."

Claudia went shopping with Annette anyway, but she didn't buy anything. She just waited while Annette auditioned new dresses for her closet. She counted the money in her purse. There was just enough to stop at the market on the way home and pick up something nice for Edgar Lee's dinner.

The last thing in the world Claudia wanted to do was encourage Froggy. It was fun seeing him on Friday nights for Parcheesi, but she didn't want to give him the idea he was her fella. The jury was still out on Andrew. Every few days a letter came from Philadelphia. His handwriting was as beautiful as his thoughts, and one letter was fifteen pages long. If he kept it up through this semester, the summer courses, and into the fall, she knew she would be at odds again with her better judgment. She and Edgar Lee would be living in the hotel suite by then. Claudia didn't understand why you always have to give up one thing to get something else, considering most of us have two hands.

It was so important to have cooking smells to come home to, so Claudia got some onions started in the skillet on one burner and a pot of water going on the other burner across the room and cut up her vegetables for a savory stew that she could serve with a salad and oyster crackers. It would prep Edgar Lee for New England, which was taking shape as Claudia's next plan for flying the coop.

Maybe it was selfish of her to want to hold onto Edgar Lee when Annette and Froggy could raise him so much better—not that she would have liked the bullet in the head, but she wouldn't have minded so much if it made life better for Edgar Lee. She would have to talk to Annette about her obsession with erections. She wouldn't want Edgar Lee having a new mom who would be checking on him about that. Maybe it was just Annette's scientific curiosity. Earlier today at the French Café, Annette fessed up that she had never actually seen one in the wild.

"Hi, Mom."

"Hi, Edgar Lee. What's doin'?"

Edgar Lee walked in like he had just trudged halfway across the Yukon, and dumped his books on the table and flopped on his bed.

"I'll be glad when we get a car."

"The Maycomber is closer to your school, so we won't need a car."

"Aw, Mom."

"I'm just teasing, Edgar Lee. I want a car too, you know. It'll be the first thing we buy, and you can pick it out for us. You better take off your school clothes."

"Aw Mom."

"Is that all you know how to say?"

Edgar Lee took off his blazer and was going to throw it at the chair, but Claudia took it from him and waited for his shirt and trousers.

"What happened to Petey?" he said. "I just remembered him."

"Oh, your dog Petey. We had to give him to the nice lady who moved in next door to our old house when we came here. You were about five years old. Do you remember the little white house and going to the beach every day?"

"Kind of."

Claudia kept her head down over the big pot and waited for the memory clouds to blow over. Edgar Lee had never remembered anything before. She wished Annette were here. She didn't know what to do but act normal.

"I want to go see Petey," he said.

"We can do that someday."

"I mean now."

"You have school, Edgar Lee."

"Then how about we go on Saturday?"

Claudia said all right, and then he made her promise, so that was that, come what may. She could call Annette and ask what to do.

"Oh, quick, Edgar Lee. Get the window."

Wind blew the curtains almost straight out, and the room was thrown into a twilight darkness by ragged black clouds, and rain started pouring down outside. Edgar Lee got one window, and she got the other one just in time.

"I guess you aren't going to the beach today, buddy."

"I have to read this book for school anyway," he said.

"I was going to read, too, and the stew has to simmer for a couple of hours."

Then Claudia remembered there wasn't any stew. Jesus, she was getting like she was with Jack. Edgar Lee wasn't going to feel cozy at all finding out his mom had been cooking a pot of water for two hours and that was dinner. He had started joking about sending her back to the Mom Factory, and he could sound just like Jack when he wanted to.

"You get reading, Edgar Lee. I have a few things to add to the stew."

In a minute she had a pile of little meat cubes on the cutting board, which she seared in the skillet with onions from the other hot plate. Then it went in the pot with half the vegetables she had ready. Now it was really getting dark and windy out.

"Turn on your light, Edgar Lee," she said.

Claudia wiped her hands and went to lie down on her bed and read her book, *Arctic Tales*, from the library, about polar explorers. It was nice and cozy when she turned on the little clip light over her bed. Edgar Lee still had not turned on his, and she was going to say something about it when he came over, still in his underwear, and asked if he could read with her.

"Sure, honey," she said, moving over.

Edgar Lee got on the bed and lay down on his side with his back to her. Claudia propped herself up on one elbow and draped her other arm over him. He read his book, and she could see hers well enough after she got it balanced right on the pillow above his head. Pretty soon she noticed Edgar Lee's pages weren't turning, and then his hand tipped over the edge of the book and lay still. Claudia gave up on her book and lay her head down into his mussed hair. The wind blew the curtains around through the little bit of the windows they left open for air, and she began to smell the cooking of the stew. She gently held Edgar Lee close, under her wing. There was nothing she could do about him becoming an awful teenager in the coming years, but that was the future, and sometimes you get a moment in the present that's perfect, when your love going out and the love coming back meet each other in the middle. She closed her eyes but would not let herself go to sleep. She wanted to feel perfect for as long as her turn lasted.

CHAPTER FORTY-SIX

On Saturday morning Claudia got Edgar Lee up at eight o'clock. Start to finish it was going to be a special day. On the phone, Annette said that as long as everything Claudia pointed out for Edgar Lee's memory was pleasant, there should be no sudden traumatic throwback to the day his mother died. If he remembered Mary Ann, Annette said to tell him she was a lady who babysat for him.

First, they walked down to the Brown Derby for a big breakfast, and when they were ready to leave, Claudia called Takeo from the telephone booth and asked if he could come down to the Strickland around ten thirty and take them up to white house row. On the walk home they picked up some ice at the store and some cold cuts and 7Ups and root beer and Dixie Cups. It was in the low eighties, so Edgar Lee ran ahead to put everything in the cooler before it melted, and Claudia trailed behind, lumbering along the sidewalk like an old bear. It wasn't the best thing for her girl parts after the other day in the trailer. She hoped Petey was still around. She hadn't thought of that.

Back home, they took one of the Strickland laundry bags for their towels and bathing suits and another one for the bread and crackers and dry non-perishables. Claudia got her sunglasses and extra money, an old *Woman's Home Companion*, and Edgar Lee's Swiss Army knife for a bottle opener.

"No telling what we might need," said Claudia.

"We're taking everything but the kitchen sink, Mom. It isn't going to be any fun if we have to lug all this stuff along."

"Oh, the sink. I knew I forgot something."

"You're so corny, Mom."

"I bet if you were in the Sahara Desert, you'd be glad you had a kitchen sink."

"If there was water. But what if it was a mirage like in *Beau Geste?*"

"Well, Edgar Lee, everybody knows mirages hook up to regular plumbing just like ordinary water."

"You're pretty good, Mom."

"Thanks, Edgar Lee. But you know I'm waiting for the day."

"What day?"

"The day you outsmart me."

"I don't want to tell you, Mom, but the day already came."

"No, I would have remembered."

"Not if you were outsmarted, you wouldn't. So there."

"You're a little dickens, Edgar Lee."

Takeo came in his cab, and they drove up the shore road. He and Edgar Lee threw Japanese words at each other in the front seat whenever they rode together because Edgar Lee had some Japanese kids in his class at school. He sounded pretty good, and sometimes Takeo looked back at Claudia with his eyebrows way up when he said a particularly good word.

"Look how far you can see from up here, Edgar Lee," Claudia said, as they cleared the jungly stuff and got higher, where the little white houses first came into view. As they went in and out of curves in the road, Edgar Lee hung out the window with both arms, and his hair blew around, and it was such fun for Claudia to see him so happy and free.

Takeo slowed down when they got to the row of little white houses. Claudia pointed out the little white house where she said she and Daddy and Edgar Lee used to live, and she had Takeo pull over at the next one. She glanced over at the one that Joe and Jan Johnson lived in before Joe got eaten and Jan moved back to the States with her chaplain, and she looked for a quiet moment at Mary Ann and Bill's house, thinking a world of sad things.

There was a little sign with the name Preston in the flowerbed around the mailbox out front. As Claudia and Edgar Lee approached the door, they heard barking, and when the lady of the house opened up, Petey jumped right out the door and into Edgar Lee's arms.

"Oh, my word. You must be Edgar Lee," said Mrs. Preston. "And I remember you too. Weren't you with Mary Ann when she came around with Petey?"

Edgar Lee was so busy getting his face licked that he could not have seen the little eye signals Claudia sent Mrs. Preston.

"Yes, I'm Claudia Wyler, Edgar Lee's mom. I almost didn't remember which house was ours. It's been so long. Edgar Lee was wondering about Petey."

"I guess you can see for yourself he's doing fine."

"He remembers me," said Edgar Lee.

"Well, sure he does," said Mrs. Preston. "Remember I told you he'll always be your dog. Why don't you two come in."

"We planned to go down to the beach for the day, so I wonder if we could just walk through your yard."

"Oh sure. I was going down myself. I always take Petey."

Claudia ran back to the cab, and Takeo helped carry all their things through the yard and down to the beach. They arranged to meet out front at six o'clock to go home. Edgar Lee and Petey ran ahead, and Claudia had a chance to tell Bobbie Preston about Mary Ann dying in a car accident and how it upset Edgar Lee so much that he didn't remember her. She said she wasn't sure what Edgar Lee remembered, now that she had adopted him and he thought she was his mother.

"Oh, dear," said Bobbie Preston, taking off her glasses to wipe her eyes.

Bobbie was a stout little woman, somewhere in her forties, and a brisk walker who only slowed down to hear the story that Claudia needed time to tell. She put her arm around Claudia when they both started to get weepy over Mary Ann. At the beach, they made a little encampment, and Bobbie stayed for lunch. Then she took Petey back for a nap because it was getting too hot for him on the beach, and she said they would be back in a little while. Petey jumped into her arms, and they went up over the dune.

"He seems happy here, doesn't he?" said Claudia.

"I guess so."

"Mrs. Preston said her husband plays with him every night when he comes home from the navy yard, and he sleeps with them in their bed."

"Well, he was my dog first, Mom."

"Oh, honey, I know. But it's best for him to be up here. He has a yard, and he isn't going to be hit by cars, and he has people who love him. You can tell he loves them too."

Edgar Lee looked like he was thinking about something that was going to upset him, and Claudia wondered what she would do if he stopped talking and went catatonic again. But then he pulled himself out of it. He said he didn't like the idea of giving dogs away to different people.

"It gets them all confused," he said.

"I thought Petey was fine. He wasn't confused at all. He remembered you because he knows he'll always be your dog. But he's smart, too. He knows you have to go with other people sometimes, so he got used to the new people and loves them, too. You don't have to forget the old people you loved to love new people, Edgar Lee."

Claudia knew she was on thin ice and wished Annette was around. She would know what was going on in his mind. Maybe nothing else was going to bubble up.

"Dogs are like people, Edgar Lee. Someday you're going to marry one of the girls you get, but it won't stop you from loving me, will it? Of course not. Well I certainly hope not. Everybody loves their moms, no matter who else they love later on. And you know I'll always love you."

"What if I give you to the neighbors?"

"Oh, you're a little dickens, Edgar Lee."

They walked the beach all the way down to where a wrecked boat used to be, and when they came back to their encampment, Claudia went a little farther and up the dune to look over the edge of her old yard. There were sheets on the laundry line and girl underwear and lots of black navy socks. The line was just where she always hung it, and the back of the house looked the same with the little cement patch, and a hose was leaning up against the house. It was all the same except the different lives inside.

With Andrew, it was going to be apartments and rooms for the next ten years. She wanted a house of her own now, for Edgar Lee, with a yard. She wanted to worry about what color to paint the living room, what furniture went together, and how to best utilize her kitchen cabinets. There were so many new appliances coming out now. It was in *Life* and *Woman's Home Companion*, and every magazine on the newsstand.

There was a postwar boom in America. Housewives and babies covered the land like bison on the Great Plains, from one horizon to the other, as far as the eye could see. What were she and Edgar Lee doing here?—limping along, falling behind the herd, prey for wolves.

Claudia let the thought disperse. She wasn't going to let herself think about it. What they were doing here was having a nice day together, and that's all there was to it. Bobbie Preston and Petey came back and they all played in the water, splashing each other, and throwing a stick for Petey. It was fun watching the little terrier run around with his eyes on the floating stick, trying to make up his mind when to make a dash into the waves. Edgar Lee took such delight in watching Petey jump in, and Claudia took delight in watching Edgar Lee. He had a whole world to take delight in, and she wished it for him. For herself, it was enough to take delight simply in one other, the one who was hers. That's what she was doing here, drying off in the sun in their little camp, sharing their Dixie cups, and marveling at the sculptural simplicity of the little wooden spoons.

On the way home in Takeo's cab, Edgar Lee said he remembered the neighbor, but the way he told it, Claudia figured out he had it the wrong way around. He thought the person he was describing—Mary Ann, for sure—was the neighbor, and he insisted he remembered hearing from her, his mom, that the neighbor lady was stuck up and thought she was better than everybody else. Claudia asked him if he remembered her saying anything else about the neighbor, because once she realized that Edgar Lee had it backwards, she was curious what else Mary Ann really thought of her back then. She was a bit surprised what Mary Ann said around little pitchers with big ears.

Claudia also asked him what he remembered of his father, and from what he said, she knew he was describing Jack from the pictures she had on her bureau and in the box under her bed. What a work of alchemy it was. Then he began asking questions, and Claudia had to make up things. She told him he was born in the hospital in New Haven. He was a colicky baby and cried a lot, she said. The dates would add up in such a way that she had Edgar Lee in the middle of her sophomore year at Sweet Briar, but she could worry about that later. What she was doing in the trailer two times a week was where she didn't want to get tripped up with her stories.

Claudia told Annette and Froggy about the expedition to the little white houses the next morning at breakfast. She went over to the Brown Derby while Edgar Lee was still asleep. It was going to be a day with two breakfasts. Annette asked about Edgar Lee right away, and Claudia found out that most of what they talked about was baseball.

"Well, Holy Moses, Annette, I thought you were working your psychology and solving his problems."

"I am," she said. "Talking about baseball with a noncritical person is what he needs."

"I'm not critical."

"Well, I'm sorry, Claudia, but yes you are."

"I have to go along with Annette," said Froggy.

"Stay out of this, Froggy. You're not being serious."

"Sure I am. Think of some of the things you've said to me."

"That's because you get fresh. I actually have a high opinion of you. No, really, I do, and that's why I wanted to ask you something. You and Annette."

"This ought to be good."

"I'm serious, Froggy. Edgar Lee likes you a lot, and you know how he feels about you, Annette."

"Who wouldn't mind curling up on a couch with Annette talking baseball?"

"Froggy, will you please?"

"Okay, I'm sorry. Go ahead."

Two Luckys and a Chesterfield came out and they passed Froggy's lighter around.

"I was wondering if you would take Edgar Lee if something happened to me."

"Who?"

"Well, both of you."

Annette and Froggy looked at each other. The breakfast plates arrived, and a moment after the waiter left with his big brown oval tray, Annette said, "Sure, Claudia. Don't worry."

"That goes for me, too," said Froggy. "He's a good kid."

Simple as that. Then they talked about surfboard riding. Froggy was taking lessons. It was all he had done since he got out of the navy. Claudia had to admit he looked good, with his tan and his hair growing out and the beard, which was a little reddish but not as bad as she had expected. Annette said she missed him at the office. The peacetime people weren't as much fun as the wartime people had been.

"I don't like *that* very much though," she said, directing a disapproving look at Froggy's beard.

"It's part of the lifestyle. Since the war's over, and I jumped ship on the navy, I don't worry so much about getting detained by a foreign power. It's had a liberating effect on me. Now I just ride the waves and be myself."

"You'll get tired of being a beach bum."

"Just goes to show, Annette. You think you know me, but you don't. Claudia, you should bring Edgar Lee out to see me surf. Any nice day. I'm learning at Pops on Waikiki right now. We're usually there from about ten in the morning on."

"You're going to break your neck doing that," said Annette. "Don't let Edgar Lee get started, Claudia. No son of mine is going to be a surfboard rider."

"Well, as a matter of fact, Claudia," said Froggy, "I was going to ask you to take care of Annette here if anything happens to me."

"Oh quit it Froggy. I was serious."

"I know, I know, I'm sorry. Seriously, don't worry about Edgar Lee. We'll take care of him."

"Are there any civilian jobs in your office, Annette?"

"No jobs anywhere, I don't think. I thought you liked philanthropy."

"It's great, I mean ideologically, but there's no money in it."

"Don't look at me," said Froggy. "I'm just a beach bum."

"A beach bum with a pension," said Annette.

"Only way to be a beach bum."

"I'm beginning to wonder if I should sell my shares in the hotel and get out of it while I have the cards in my hands," said Claudia.

"You could start a business," said Annette. "A fashion business."

"Better yet, I can let you in on the surf board business, Claudia. Surf riding is going to catch on big."

"It hasn't so far," said Annette.

"That's because the boards are too big. I designed a better board."

"You can't let a day go by, can you."

"Don't look at me like I'm crazy, Annette. I'm an engineer, remember? I trained in naval aviation. It's just aeronautics in water. That's all it is. Here's what my board looks like, Claudia."

Froggy started drawing his surfboard design on a napkin, explaining as he went along. Annette looked bored. Claudia was a little bored too. She didn't know why she even brought up selling her shares. She had to stick it out. Captain Locarno was already taking reservations for rooms in group lots with travel agents in California. He projected that her share of expenses would level out at three hundred a month, but she could count on a return of twelve hundred every month if it was booked at full capacity year-round. She and Edgar Lee could live in a suite until he finished high school, and then she could say good riddance to the Palmetto Community Outreach Program and hello New England any time they wanted. Edgar Lee would love Dartmouth.

Froggy zeroed in on her after Annette left and they were standing out in the parking lot. He was going to give her a lift home in an Austin-Healey he had just acquired. It was kind of a rattletrap, but it had style. There were a couple of broken surfboard pieces jutting up out of the little crescent of a back seat.

"I'm really serious about the idea," he said. "I put in an application at the patent office. As soon as I have the patent, I can get a guy I know to build a prototype. Then we just work out the bugs. I could always use some help with paperwork."

"Oh, Froggy, I don't want to get your hopes up. I have to think of Edgar Lee. I think I have to stick with the hotel, but I'll give it some thought."

Claudia had a last smoke with Froggy, leaning on the Austin-Healey, and decided to walk home so she could do some thinking. She realized she wasn't so hot on the idea of moving into one of the hotel suites now. Not since she saw the little white house again. She wanted a house and a yard and a dog and a husband. The hotel could always flop—you never know—and right now would be the best time to get the most money out of Mr. Anthony for her shares. Froggy might have a good business idea, and she could go in on that and have money left over for a down payment on a house. But that was a bigger gamble than the hotel. She decided to stick with the hotel and give it two or three months of operation. At least she could quit the trailer business on grand opening day.

Just after Claudia got Edgar Lee off to school on Monday morning, another letter from Andrew came. He said he missed her like crazy. He was going to start looking around for a little house in the country. It was like he had read her mind. There was another way now. Meanwhile, it was back to the trenches. At least she had something to think about in the hot trailer today, and it would take her mind off making a living the old-fashioned way.

Claudia took a cab over to the club and got into her costume. Two goons came down the stairs at ten. Rivoli wasn't there, and it made her nervous. One of them was a guy she didn't like, and the other one was new. It didn't look like he had much upstairs. As they drove out of town, Claudia tried to make conversation, but they didn't say anything back, and she just looked out the window and at the back of their heads most of the way. She wondered if Mr. Anthony was getting a tax break hiring war-surplus goons from the national goon stockpile. Either one looked like he could put a bullet in the back of her head—by mistake.

They kept her dancing longer because only ten or fifteen men came out of the fields, and when the men started milling around like they weren't interested, the goon she didn't like made her take off her show bra and started banging time on the roof to speed her up. That helped. The men who were there stayed, and a few more straggled in from the jungle.

When it looked like there was a quorum, the goons led her through the men, waving their guns around, and put her in the trailer. Claudia was afraid the mean one was going to be the guard inside, and sure enough, he was. It was so hot in the trailer that he took off his jacket and put the fan on himself and didn't help her crank the windows open. It was going to be a rough day.

He sat right by her head like Rivoli, but he didn't protect her at all. He liked seeing her get it, and the rougher the better. She did about eight or nine before she said anything. She got up on her elbows between clients and told him.

"You better make them take it easy," she said.

"Whatsa matter?"

"They're getting too rough. I don't like it. And you better be sure they get the club rubbers on right. That's all I have to say."

He didn't say anything, but he heard her fine. The next two were real rough and she'd had it.

"I quit," she said.

"You can't quit till we're done."

The next man was coming in, and Claudia told him to get out. He wouldn't go, so she got up and shouted him out the door. There was some laughing outside, and when Claudia was at the door closing it, she could see there were still plenty of men out there, more than when she got down off the roof of the car.

"If you aren't going to protect me, I quit," she said.

"You can't quit."

"Get somebody else because I am."

Claudia expected him to pull his gun and threaten her, but he stood up and put on his jacket instead.

"We'll let you think about it a while."

He ducked out the door, and Claudia heard the key turning in the lock.

"Hey," she shouted. "You can't leave me in here."

She jumped on the bed and looked out the louvers of the window. The two goons had the metal cash box, and they were waving their guns around, going back to the car. They got in and drove out of the clearing. Oh God, she thought. What now?

There were voices outside, and men starting to jump up to look in the windows. They got their hands in the frames and started to bend them out, so she quickly cranked them closed as far as she could. Through the slats she could see twenty or more men. There were a few nice voices, but those went away, leaving only the bad-sounding ones, getting louder and talking faster. Knives must have been coming out, because she heard blades snapping off in the doorframe. They started pounding on the door and on the sides of the trailer. Big dents in the shape of boots began to appear in the crippled aluminum.

Claudia was getting scared. The voices were louder, and the men were trying to pick up the trailer. She put her costume back on while the trailer was rocking on its wheels, and suddenly it went over. She was thrown against the wall, and the metal bed frame slammed into her arm, and she heard something snap, and it hurt like hell. There wasn't time to look at it because the trailer went over again, and then over another time, and all she could see as the bed crashed against her again and again was more light coming through the doorframe. Then it crashed to the ground right side up and the door popped open. There was a hoarse cheer from the men, and they started climbing in.

Claudia fought them off for only a minute before she got hit in the face. They didn't mean it. It was just somebody's elbow, but it knocked out her two front teeth, maybe more, and then she stopped fighting. Her grass skirt and panties and show bra got pulled off in a second, and the first ones in the trailer kicked out enough of the others to get the bed and mattress up again. They didn't have to hold her down after the first few because she knew she was lost. Her mouth was full of blood and pieces of her teeth, her arm was broken, and there must have been more banged up parts of her she couldn't feel.

The men kept coming and there was one with a machete who was the new goon, sitting by the bed, but she had a feeling he was there to give her a final whack when they were done with her. She was glad she had talked to Annette and Froggy yesterday. They would take care of Edgar Lee. She wasn't worried about that, and she was glad for Edgar Lee. It would be a line in the paper, macheteed prostitute found in cane field. Maybe someone would take a picture that would end up in the schoolyard, and Edgar Lee would know it was her. That would be as bad as finding Mary Ann. She was so sorry about Mary Ann, so sorry, and now her teeth were knocked out, and she was broken in pieces and there was no hope of living beyond this day of battle.

Then it was all darkness and quiet around her. She made her last thoughts be thoughts of Edgar Lee with Annette and Froggy. And then she came to the river, to the waters of Babylon, and lay down, for there her captors required of her song. Under the willows she wept, remembering Zion, and by the river's edge in a foreign land, Claudia Wyler closed her eyes on all that they had seen in their days, and passed from this world.

When Claudia opened her eyes, it was still night. She didn't hurt anymore, but it sure felt like one bumpy ride up to heaven. Now a shape bent over her with a kind face shrouded in fragrant black hair. Soft, gentle eyes gazed down into hers. There was a sweet smile, and Claudia could just make out white cleavage disappearing into darkness below. What a relief to find out God was a woman, all smiles, bosoms and kind eyes. Who wants an old man with a white beard telling you what to do?

PART SIX

"What You Need to Know about Taking Things for Granted"

—CYNTHIA D. APPLETON, *WOMAN'S HOME COMPANION*, OCTOBER 1952

CHAPTER FORTY-SEVEN

When Claudia came around, it was early morning and she was still on earth, in a hospital, Honolulu, June. The war was over. No one had to tell her that. A large woman with wonderfully thick black hair framing her plump round face and falling down over her shoulders was sitting beside her, and she said, "Oh, you're back!"

"Who are you?"

"Oh, don't try to sit up, dear. That's right. You just take it easy. You had a bad accident. They're taking very good care of you here. I'm Angela, Giovanni's wife. He wanted me to watch you during the night. He comes in when he gets off work and should be here soon. He'll be so happy to see you're up. He's the one who brought you in, but I know you probably don't remember that. You've been out for a while, you know—oh, I shouldn't say anything. The doctor will tell you all about it. She's very nice, so don't be afraid. You can close your eyes and rest, and I'll go get her."

Angela so very quietly closed the door behind her, and Claudia drifted along the lapping shores of sleep, knowing Edgar Lee was probably safe at Annette's or with Froggy, and here she was, still alive. And, from what she could tell, still missing front teeth. Her arm was in a cast, and her chest and her middle were wrapped up tight. From the bad way she felt when she tried to move around, Lord knows what else. She was completely in the dark about who Angela and Giovanni were.

Elaine came in with Angela behind, and they both pulled up chairs to the bedside. Angela smoothed her hair and caressed her cheek while Elaine inventoried the disaster area. Claudia got the feeling her hair and cheeks were the only parts of her that Angela dared touch, and this was largely confirmed by the list Elaine rattled off.

"We took care of the ruptured spleen, contusions, wounds, broken arm, cracked ribs, broken ankle—let's see—" Then, with her eyes catching up to the notes on her clipboard, she added "Dislocated hip, broken wrist, multiple hairline fractures of—well, here and there—and we're monitoring the internal bleeding. We aren't sure where that's coming from."

Then Elaine took off her glasses and folded her arms around the clipboard. "That was some party you went to, missy."

Claudia looked at the little round watch that was pinned just above Elaine's breast pocket. The pin was a tri-color band that looked like a military campaign ribbon, and it was so pretty. The world of pretty things was so small.

"The police have been here every day. They want to talk to you."

Claudia held up her hand. It was hard to talk with front teeth missing.

"I want to talk to Mr. Rivoli first. He works for Mr. Anthony at the Palmetto club. Could you get in touch with him?"

"That's my husband," said Angela, putting both hands up to her ample bosom. "Giovanni. He'll be here any minute."

"Well, then, I will defer to the Rivolis," said Elaine. "I'll be back to check on you later, dear. The police usually come in around one o'clock. You don't have to talk to them today if you don't want to. Don't worry about anything, Claudia. We'll get you back in shape in no time."

Claudia rested with her eyes closed, and Angela sat by and read to her from the newspaper, waiting for Rivoli. Well, that was news to her. She would have to get used to the idea that not every man she knew was in love with her—not that she counted on it, it wasn't the end of the world, but it kind of brings you down a peg.

Rivoli was glad to see she was conscious. He kissed Angela on the cheek, sat down and reached out to take Claudia's good hand.

"I'm so sorry this happened," said Rivoli. "I was detained at another appointment, and when I got to the club and found out you left with the other two, I thought there might be trouble. I know you don't like Donio."

Just then there was a soft knock on the door, and Annette stuck her head in.

"Oh, Claudia. You're awake. I'll come back. Hi, Angela. Hi, Giovanni."

Rivoli, with his good manners stood up immediately and asked Annette to stay, but he requested a moment with Claudia for certain business communications. With Annette waiting outside, he quickly ran through the story.

"I've already talked to the police. I said you were abducted by two men and taken out to the countryside, where they attacked you. That's all you have to tell the police. Say that's all you remember. I told them I was driving by and heard screams. The men ran off when I pulled over. I took the police out to a place along the road where they wouldn't find anything. You can say you were blindfolded and didn't know where it was. Dino and the other one don't work for us anymore."

He went for the inside pocket of his jacket and pulled out an envelope and handed it to her. "Mr. Anthony wants you to have this to see you through. It's your last week's pay and severance, which, he said to tell you, he presumed. For now, I would recommend you let Miss Anisinelli hold it for you."

Rivoli stood up again and opened the door for Annette, who came in with an encouraging smile and bent over to kiss her very carefully on the forehead. Rivoli offered her his chair and stood back against the wall with his arms folded.

"They've been here every day," said Annette. "And all night, too. Thanks so much, Angela. Thank you too, Giovanni. I would be here more, but Edgar Lee is with me at my place. I didn't think you would want him here. Do you know when you can go home?"

"I don't know," said Claudia. "Could you hold on to this for me?"

She passed the envelope to Annette, and she put it in her purse without looking at it.

"How long have I been out?"

"Three days," said Angela. "They thought you were in a coma."

"Has anyone told Captain Locarno I'm here?"

Angela and Ravoli looked at each other expressionless, and Annette said, "The hotel." Then all three of them looked back and forth, as if they were wondering whose turn it was to talk. Finally, Annette seemed to come to a decision.

"Claudia, I'm afraid the hotel burned down. The night before last."

"Oh, no. No, no. All the way?"

"I'm sorry, yes. The police are probably going to ask if you know anything about it since you're a shareholder."

Claudia felt like the library at Alexandria had just gone up in flames. Goodbye ancient world. "Do I know anything about it?" she asked feebly through her missing teeth.

"Oh, no. Of course not," said Angela.

"Bermander's had a fire," said Annette, "and what they think happened was, sparks from there got in the basement of the hotel because they don't have windows in there yet, and it started up in the trash around some propane tanks. Then the whole building blew. It was at night, so nobody got hurt."

"Is it all gone?"

"I think so, Claudia. They said the firemen couldn't even get close to it. It's cordoned off, but you can see it all fell down."

"I guess that's it for me," said Claudia. She turned her head away, and they left her alone for a little while. Four years. All that money. Then dinner came on a tray. It was pretty good and left her wondering why everyone in the world could make Coney Island hot dogs but her.

Claudia was in the hospital for two weeks. Everyone came to see her, including Mr. Anthony and Edgar Lee. She couldn't for the life of her imagine why people would want other people to come visit them in the hospital. She was bruised and sore, and the arm in the cast and everywhere else they had her bandaged itched like crazy. But it wasn't forever, and the day came when she walked out of the hospital between Annette and Froggy, helping her down the steps and into the cab. The bill was over seven hundred dollars. It was ridiculous. She said the next time she invested in a building, it was going to be a hospital because that's where the big money is.

The two thousand dollars Mr. Anthony gave her went fast. Captain Locarno came to tell her they were going to have to pay for a demolition crew to knock down the rest of the hotel and clear it away. After that, they had property taxes to meet, whether there was a hotel there or not. When she asked him about insurance, she had to give him credit. He looked her in the eyes. He was straightforward.

"That was a mistake," he said.

Claudia didn't have to tell him it was a big one. But after all, it was his first hotel.

Claudia gave him most of the money and signed over her shares to him in exchange for a deed of indemnity. All the money she had left in the world went to pay the last month's tuition to Edgar Lee's school and the last month of rent at the Strickland. The next day she and Edgar Lee sat on the curb with a few suitcases and a couple of boxes.

Claudia didn't want to go on relief. For her, the embarrassment of living on the dole would not be an unjust end to her fanciful dreams, as she saw them now to be, ill-conceived aspirations that they were, built upon folly. But that was not for Edgar Lee, and that was the only reason she went for the deal.

"You're going to like it a lot, Mom," said Edgar Lee. "I liked it at Annette's, but this is much better."

"Just remember. It's only temporary, Edgar Lee. You should never get used to borrowing from other people."

"It's not borrowing if someone wants to give you something."

Just then Froggy pulled up in his rattletrap Austin-Healey.

"Sharp car, huh Mom?"

Froggy and Edgar Lee left Claudia sitting on the curb with her bad leg straight out while they loaded the suitcases and boxes into the narrow, little back seat.

"Mom can sit on my lap in front," said Edgar Lee. And then he made a sound like he was a bug being squashed, and Claudia frowned at him and said he should never say unkind things, and then she had to add—"or make unkind *innuendos.*" She added that because Edgar Lee was learning vocabulary, and it's always good to hear the word used in a sentence.

"No, you ride in back, old man," said Froggy, "and hold all the stuff down. I'll see if I can bounce you out, okay?"

He revved up the engine a couple of times, and Edgar Lee said, "Sure thing, Frog," as he climbed on top of the boxes in back, and off they went.

It was a modern building that looked like a house, but it was really four apartments. Froggy lived on the first floor on one side. He said he grabbed the one on the other side for Claudia and Edgar Lee when it came up for rent. The second-floor apartments were taken by secretaries from Froggy's old office at the navy yard.

It cost a hundred dollars a month because it was so nice and near the beach. Edgar Lee had his own room, and Claudia had a tidy little kitchen with linoleum floors and cabinets and a real stove and a new Frigidaire. It had a shower, and a beautiful tub she could soak in. Froggy was paying for it. He tricked her into it, saying it was only as much as the Strickland, but she knew the minute she walked in that it was a lot more, and she made him tell her how much it really was. He fessed up that he owned the building. She started a tab right then and there. She wasn't going to let him get away with it.

Claudia did not know what she was going to do. As pretty as it all was, it felt like rock bottom to her. Somewhere along the line since Jack, she must have started thinking she could support herself, or that it was the responsible thing to do, or that it was right thinking to want to do that. But that was wartime. Now, all the girls in the States were back at home where they belonged, and the husbands were out getting buffaloes like they were supposed to. Maybe she felt it was wrong because Froggy wasn't her husband. She didn't know. She would figure it out. First, she had to heal the war wounds.

But Claudia did not get to do that on her own either. Froggy had a list of exercises that Elaine made up, and two times a day he put her through the paces, once in the morning before he left and once before dinner when he came home. There was nothing Claudia could say about it because they were doctor's orders. She didn't like Froggy massaging her bad leg all the way up the thigh, but he kept his eyes looking into hers while he did it and told her what kind of day he was expecting to have, and in the evening, he told her what kind of day he'd had. She could tell she was getting better.

For the time being, though, Claudia's world was her kitchen, where she could have peace and quiet after Edgar Lee went off with Froggy every morning. At first she just had her coffee and Chesterfields and sat at the table with her *Life* and *Woman's Home Companion*, glad to be alive in a safe place. She started looking more closely at the ads in the magazines as she recovered, and she began poking around the kitchen. It was thoroughly modern, with all the latest gadgets and utensils. Talk about an arsenal of democracy. America had done its part. It had won the war. All those brave boys had done their part. American women could take it from here.

Takeo drove Claudia around Honolulu to used bookstalls for cookbooks, and when he had time for it, they sat in his cab and talked cooking for an hour or more. She wrote down his culinary tips and advice in a spiral notebook. Every night she tried something new for dinner, and everything was a big success—her tuna casserole, her macaroni and cheese, her grilled mahimahi, and especially her braided raisin bread loaf that was two feet long and disappeared along with half a pound of butter in one dinner. Claudia ended her letter to her mom with "And it wasn't just me!!!"

"Let's see," she always asked herself, "what else did I do?" Those were the words that always appeared somewhere in the letters to her mother. She had a reference list of stories she made up at her side as she wrote so she could untangle it sometime in the future when things were better. When she wrote to Andrew, she got out the coffee and Chesterfields and settled in. She did not tell him about anything that happened. She only wrote about her feelings, and for that she needed to think, especially since his letters were getting less and less that way.

He joined a fraternity at Penn and moved into a frat house. Classes were okay. He said Philadelphia was a great little city. There were coffee houses right off campus where just ordinary people could stand up and read their poetry. He missed her and loved her a lot. His letters began to leave her with an empty feeling.

That aside, it was a good summer. Edgar Lee was taking surfboard riding lessons with Froggy, and from all the talk at dinnertime, it sounded like they were getting good at it. Froggy still had no word from the patent office, but they were going ahead with their top-secret new board in a tucked-away garage off Pops surfing break on Waikiki. The cast on her arm came off, and everything else healed up enough that she could walk to the beach by the end of July to watch Froggy and Edgar Lee.

To Claudia, it looked like the wave Froggy caught was the one just inside the age barrier to surfboard riding. Ever since he turned thirty, it looked like his body had started swimming the other way, but he caught it just in time to try putting it on a surfboard. Edgar Lee, on the other hand, looked like a natural-born wave rider. The things he did with his legs, working the board in and out of the surf line, were dazzling. Then, when the wave was spent, he ran it out, standing erect with the contemptuous scowl of a mystery man on his face as he shot across the flat water.

Claudia, at such times, sitting on the sand under her big straw hat and fanning herself with a Japanese fan Takeo had given her, looked to her sides and perceived not a small amount of interest in the eyes of the little teenage girls present while Edgar Lee plied the waves. Whenever she mentioned it at dinner, Edgar Lee pretended not to give a hoot, but she knew the information was going into the bank that regulated the currency of being his mother. It wasn't much of a hold she still had on him that summer, but she knew it was the natural way of things to loosen the grip, and she was so glad to see him happy, even with Froggy taking him over like Sherman through Georgia.

The next letter from Andrew was routine except for the first mention of a girl in his summer-session sociology class named Caroline Merewether. July went by without any letters, and at the end of August, Claudia got a postcard from Cape Cod where Andrew was helping Caroline Merewether's dad build a sun deck on the back of the family beach house. She cried long and hard over that one. She knew she wasn't going to hear any more from Andrew Taylor.

It was the last terrible day. So passed with it the terrible year and another and another going backward until Claudia cried them all out, all the way back to the first year in this place, the only year that she had with Jack—that carefree, wonderful year.

How do you ever put the past behind you? Forgetting little things is not forgetting the past. In her head were the voices of her brother, Harry, and Jack, and Joe Johnson, Mr. Sterrin, and Mary Ann, voices that would never be heard again, and the voices of Larry and Billings and Andrew Taylor, voices that were talking and laughing somewhere with other people. The fly in the amber, the sand in the hourglass, the ship in the bottle.

"Oh Jesus, Froggy. Get out of here."

"I'm sorry. I thought you were dead."

"Well I'm not, damn it."

Claudia scrambled for her robe. She remembered falling asleep kind of drunk and naked, face down with her arms over the side of the bed, but she was facing up when she came to, so Froggy must have turned her over and seen everything there was to see.

"Keep Edgar Lee out," she said, sitting up so fast it made her head swim. "No, get away, Froggy, I'm fine."

"Don't worry. Edgar Lee went up to Waimea with some buddies. He said he'd be back by dinner."

"I don't want him to see me like this. Could you take that bottle to your place? I don't know why I kept it."

"Special occasions," said Froggy. "I saw the postcard."

"Damn it, Froggy."

"Post cards aren't confidential, Claud. I'm sorry. I know you were counting on that guy."

"Can you take Edgar Lee out for dinner tonight? I don't think I can make anything."

"Nah," said Froggy, "let's sober you up and make dinner together. It'll be good for you."

"I don't want to, Froggy."

"Come on. You'll pull through, and you'll feel better for it. You get in the shower, and I'll take a run to the store. What do you need?"

"Oh, I don't know. Take a look in the Frigidaire and think of something."

They made a great big salad together, and Claudia showed Froggy how to cut, holding the vegetables with the knuckles. But of course, then he cut his knuckles. They made pineapple grilled chicken with soy sauce over long grain wild rice with steamed green beans. They had a lot of fun. It was worth the old college try.

CHAPTER FORTY-EIGHT

Annette was always bringing it up at the French Café.

"It sounds like you're married," she said.

"Don't you want the cheese Danish? I got it for you."

"No, thanks—oh Claudia," Annette exclaimed. "I just noticed."

"Took you long enough."

"They're beautiful. Show me."

Claudia looked up at Annette and tried to draw her upper lip back in a smile that did not look too showy.

"How much did they cost?"

"Four hundred."

"Wow."

"They look pretty good, don't they?"

"Oh, they're great looking. You look like your old self again."

"They're porcelain—like the toilets."

"Oh, Claudia."

"But back to business, Annette. No, it's not like that at all. He goes back to his place every night."

"Aha—companionship. That's what you said marriage would be like after thirty. I remember you saying that. You had the yellow Hawaiian skirt with the pink top. I always liked you in that."

"Oh, that old thing. I don't have it anymore," said Claudia. "Okay, but there can be sex, too, I mean not with Froggy, but you know, when somebody good comes along. That sounded bad, but you know what I mean. I can change my mind about the after-thirty stuff, can't I?"

Annette lit up another of her Luckys and what she said next came out in a swirl of smoke.

"I don't think anybody better is coming along, Claudia. And anyway, Froggy's got you roped in. You know he always had a thing about you."

"But that's not true anymore, Annette. All he cares about is the surfboard business. He got his patent last week, and he and Edgar Lee are working in the garage with a guy who's teaching them how to make them. He's got big plans. He's going to open a shop in a few months."

"I don't know where he's getting all this money," said Annette.

"He owns the apartment building."

"Oh, I didn't know that."

"Maybe I shouldn't have said anything."

"But that doesn't really answer the question anyway," said Annette. "How did he buy the apartment building?"

"Dan taught him about the stock market when they roomed together. Froggy told me everything because he didn't want me feeling so bad about the money he's lending me. He's not loaded, but he's got plenty of money. He's putting a lot of it into getting the business set up, so he has to start being careful. We go over everything together, Annette. I help him pick out stocks to buy, and it's really fun. The library has lots of books about the stock market, and they get the *Financial Times* and the *Wall Street Journal*, so I go there almost every day. Froggy doesn't have time for that, so I'm like his eyes and ears on the market."

"Like I said," said Annette.

"What?"

"It's like you're married."

Edgar Lee started school in September and worked in the shop with Froggy every afternoon. They both came home covered with sawdust when they didn't have time to hit the beach. Edgar Lee had a beach girl and was getting pretty cocky. All he would say about it when Claudia had him away from Froggy was "Sure I kissed her." He beat out sweet-sixteen-and-never-been-kissed by a mile, but Claudia always knew he would. Her name was Di. She hung around the garage after school sometimes. She looked pretty well-developed for eighth grade. Whew.

Around Thanksgiving, Edgar Lee gave the new board design the big test. Claudia only heard about it later, thank God, because she would have either forbid it or gone along to watch. Froggy and Edgar Lee took the board up to Ehukai on the north shore in the rattletrap Austin-Healey, and Edgar Lee ran the Banzai Pipeline. Apparently the board was a big success, and so was the test pilot. Somebody they called the Big Kahuna saw him do it and held a ceremony with torches after the event, bestowing upon Edgar Lee his new title, The Wave Weasel.

"It's a gigantic big deal," said Edgar Lee.

"Now I know somebody famous," said Claudia. "I knew I felt different somehow when you two came home tonight, but I couldn't put my finger on it."

"I think I want to be a naval officer," said Edgar Lee.

Claudia turned around from the kitchen sink and wiped her hands on her apron.

"Why Edgar Lee—"

"Good choice," said Froggy. "Sounds good, too. Cadet Wave Weasel Wyler. Try saying that three times fast. That's what they'll make you do at the academy, you know."

"Your dad liked Annapolis," said Claudia.

"I liked it, too," said Froggy. Then he reflected a moment and said, "I don't think I'd like it much now, but you might, Edgar Lee."

"Where's Annapolis?"

"Back in the States, honey. In Maryland."

"Don't they have one around here?" asked Edgar Lee.

"Nah," said Froggy. "They didn't know where this place was when they built it, and now it's too much trouble to move all those bricks and parade grounds."

"I guess I have to go there, then."

Henceforth, Annapolis went on the back burner, but the idea was there in Edgar Lee's mind. He thought of it all on his own, and it became what he wanted to do from that time forward. Annapolis and naval officer were his two answers whenever anyone asked. Claudia thought her naval officer days were over, but here was a brand new one coming up, right in her own backyard. How funny is life.

Claudia kept a little framed picture of Jack on the windowsill above the sink in the kitchen. It was his yearbook picture from Annapolis. One night she was up late reading a pamphlet that she had sent away for called Felton-Simpson Market Trends for 1951, and she decided to make sourdough waffles for Edgar Lee. Annette brought the sourdough starter back from a meeting she went to in San Francisco and gave it to her. It turned out sourdough starter is something you have to keep alive, which was news to Claudia. Every month she had to remember to feed it flour and water and make something with some of it and put some of it back in the Frigidaire. The arithmetic was hard to work out. It was almost two o'clock in the morning before she had the starter in the big white bowl, making little bubbles under a towel on the counter, quietly ruminating on its future as waffles when, for no reason, Jack's picture fell off the windowsill into the water.

She went for it right away and pulled it out, and her eyes met Jack's, and she heard him saying, "You've got what it takes, Claudia." Her hands were suddenly trembling, and she didn't know why, and then she heard a twig snap behind her, and without turning around she knew the Japanese were coming out of the jungle and getting into the house. Her legs gave out, and she fell to the floor. They knew she was there. She clawed at the space under the cabinets. Bugs went under there all the time. If she could only get in there. Her nails broke off scratching at the cabinets, but she could not make herself small enough to hide. She closed her eyes, and she saw a flickering newsreel of herself taken by the Japanese, tied to the wheel of a farmer's cart and bayoneted again and again through her belly until a bloody little thing dropped from between her legs, and she saw Jack's dead, white face, and all his blood on the side of the mountain road, the cut across Mary Ann's throat, the bloody mattress, and her dead baby going down the toilet. If she screamed, they would know where she was, but she screamed, and they found her in the trailer and rocked it until the door fell off and they came crowding in with bayonets. Let them come. They had her and there was no way out. She turned over to face death and spread out her arms. She felt the bayonets go in and out of her until she could not feel them killing her anymore.

When Claudia woke up, it was time to start breakfast for Edgar Lee. She got off the floor and went to wash her face and brush her hair in the bathroom. She was afraid to look at her reflection in the mirror because she might see something behind her. Back in the kitchen, she found the waffle iron and made up a whole pile of waffles, and the nice smell brought Edgar Lee out of his room. They were so good that Edgar Lee didn't want to put anything on them, and he wrapped up a bundle to take to the shop.

"You should come down to the beach today, Mom," said Edgar Lee. "We got a new board to test."

"I didn't know surfboards were that complicated."

"Yeah, they are."

"I'd like to, Edgar Lee, but I'm going to try to have lunch with Annette."

"It's not your day."

"I know. I just want to see her about something."

"What?"

"Oh, just girl talk. Nothing you'd be interested in, little man."

"Don't call me that around my friends, Mom, okay?" said Edgar Lee.

Maybe that was a good place to start, Claudia thought. The new rules she had to live by with Edgar Lee. Annette was waiting, half turned away, looking at the people going by on the sidewalk but standing by with her coffee and Luckys, ready to counsel at a moment's notice.

"He wants me to come to the beach to watch him ride the surfboards," Claudia said, "but he doesn't want me to sit near the girls. But if I do, and they're talking about The Wave Weasel, I can say that I have heard of The Wave Weasel, but under no circumstances am I allowed to say I am The Wave Weasel's mom. Apparently, it would be too mortifying for Edgar Lee to bear. How's that for ya?"

Annette turned full around and reached for her Luckys. "That's just the age. You can't take it personally. But you already know that, so what's really bothering you? And what happened to your nails?"

Claudia began by telling Annette she'd had a bad dream, and then she told her it happened when she was wide awake and how real it was. She had never told Annette about her dead baby in the septic tank, or about the trailer, and that came out, too, but she told the trailer story as a one-time event that put her in the hospital, not that it had been her regular job. She knew Annette was shocked in so many ways. She just said, "You should have told me."

"I couldn't, Annette. What would you think of me? I'm telling you now because I'm scared. It didn't matter that I was safe at home, and there was nothing I could do to stop it. I was really there. I couldn't look away. I'm so afraid it could happen again."

"I think I know what it is," Annette said, after thinking a long time with her brows together and lips pursed. "I think you have battle fatigue."

"I didn't know it was catching—"

"No, listen to me, Claudia. A lot of men had bad experiences in the war and came home thinking they had left them behind. But sometimes they can come back, just the way your bad experiences did. From what I've read about it, they don't know what triggers an episode, but it's a good sign that you came out of it by yourself. So that's good."

"Well, what am I supposed to do if it happens again?"

"I think the only way to stop it from coming back—this is what I read—is accepting that you can't change anything that happened to you. You have to find a way to accept it."

"I thought I already did that. I mean—since I try not to think about any of the bad things."

"No, I think you have to talk about the bad things."

"Maybe I'll do that sometime. But right now I'm just trying to live. You know?"

"Well, you go on with that, and you know you can call me anytime," said Annette.

"I know. Thanks Annette. It helps thinking of it like war, and the war is over. Maybe all I have to do is think about it like that. Let's get back to normal now. How's Bernard?"

"You said that just like saying, 'What's for dinner?'"

"It's almost like that, isn't it?"

"I'm just doing what they do," said Annette. "They take you off the shelf and look at you, play with you a little, and if they don't like something, you go right back on the shelf. It's no different."

"So, how's Bernard."

"Back on the shelf."

"Batter up, huh?"

It was good to have a friend like Annette and so nice having coffee at the French Café with her like regular girls. It seemed she always learned something new when they talked about important things. Something new can always get you out of the trouble you got into with the last new thing.

CHAPTER FORTY-NINE

It turned out that the stock market was a safer place to play than real estate. It was not laying up treasures on earth where you had acts of God to contend with. You laid up your treasures in a completely man-made cloud that floated in the air between Honolulu and New York. Beechworth & Halswig had a seat on the exchange in New York, with a dedicated line, and Claudia went down there with Froggy to open a joint account. It was just one of those little practical matters they got together on since they had been settled into the two apartments for more than a year, and since the arrangement was working out so well.

Every morning, for an hour or two, Claudia sat in a plushy, red-leather armchair in the lobby of Beechworth & Halswig, reading annual reports and prospectuses on new issues, listening to the ticker tape, just audible in the alcove where they had a water fountain. She always got up at least once to get a drink and watch the tape, staying by the machine until she recognized a stock symbol coming out on the ribbon. It would take time, but she was determined to remember all the symbols and learn the ways of the market. Like Davy Crockett said, "Be sure you're right, then go ahead." Claudia resolved not to be one of those traders who just heard the go ahead part, and she needed to see the big picture to be sure she was right.

That's what she told Froggy. He set up a nice desk for her in the living room of her apartment. Then he brought over his papers, checkbooks, and bank statements, as well as the finances from his apartment house and his new business—all mixed together. She was going to take over everything.

"Ah," said Froggy, "I remember the good old days, before you got so smart."

"I was always smart, Froggy."

"Then, helpless."

"No," she said, "I don't think I was helpless either."

"Well, maybe you just thought you were. Remember when I came over to the Captain Cook?" he said.

"I think you were surprised I was so well organized," said Claudia. "I had everything in my two shoeboxes."

"You've come so far—from shoeboxes to pineapple crates."

"Well, as long as I have my file folders, crates are fine."

"What's so funny?"

"Oh, I was just thinking about when you came over to help me figure things out. You didn't know anything about money back then, did you?"

"I knew more than you did."

"Oh, I didn't mean it like that. You're a good friend, Froggy. I know you were trying to help, and I'm not going to let you down now. Just remember to bring me your mail and any receipts. And please—I know you and Edgar Lee and Johnnie are getting lunch at the shop. Get receipts for any money you spend, whatever it is. It counts for taxes."

Claudia knew she was going to have to keep Froggy in line. It helped that he was over for dinner every night and saw her working at her desk while he and Edgar Lee played cards on the floor. She took special pride in her monthly reports. Every so often, she introduced a new feature, like a year-to-date analysis, or a bar graph. She loved watching from the kitchen as Froggy reviewed her work. There wasn't really much there at the beginning, but that changed, and before long, she was able to introduce a pie chart to her monthly reports that didn't look ridiculous at all.

In January 1952, Claudia incorporated The Frog Shop with Froggy—John Calder Ransome—as President, Edgar Lee Wyler as Vice President, and Claudia Wyler as Treasurer. Since Edgar Lee was only fourteen and not of legal majority, she had to cosign whatever he had to sign, but what the heck, she was doing all the paperwork anyway.

Claudia opened a brokerage account for The Frog Shop, Inc. as it started making money, and she also started a custodial account for Edgar Lee. When she heard through the grapevine at Beechworth & Halswig that Chesterfield had plans to be the first to offer a long cigarette, she jumped in with both feet. It was her first big move in the market, buying a hundred shares of Liggett & Myers in her joint account with Froggy. It worked out that time, but she knew she was going to have to watch her sentimental tendencies. You can let that happen with people, like loving them when they are overvalued, and the only thing it does is make your heart sweet and kind. Not like the stock market.

The bad dream almost happened again, when Claudia was alone, washing dishes at night. She broke out in a cold sweat for no reason, and her hands started trembling. She felt it coming. She held onto the sink and shook her head and sang "June is Bustin' Out All Over" so she wouldn't hear snapping of twigs and footsteps behind her. The war is over. The war is over. She imagined herself writing it a hundred times on a blackboard, keeping her eyes wide open. Annette had said not to close her eyes.

It went away in a few minutes, and it left Claudia with an interesting insight. She had never been afraid of men before. She thought she might be afraid of them now—not any particular man she knew, just the gender. The men with battle fatigue were probably afraid of men too.

She had a good life now, with no place in it for the past. The past was the used-up, dead part of her. The living part could do without it, and Claudia thought if she could think of it like that, like the war being over, say it to herself, and imagine she was writing it over and over on a blackboard, it might keep the bad dreams away. And as she devised the plan and pondered getting on with her good life, Claudia felt a desire to make life happy—which was an entirely different thing from having a happy life, although she could not say precisely in what way. She just knew one was bigger than the other.

"I'm getting my self-confidence back," Claudia told Annette the following week at the French Café. "So guess what I did?"

"You started your own surfboard shop for ladies."

"No. I signed up for a training program. Guess what in?"

Annette narrowed her eyes down and gave Claudia that look with one eyebrow raised that always slayed her. "Uh-oh," she said. "What?"

"I'm going to be a Red Cross nurse. Isn't that great?"

Annette put her hand up to her mouth to hide a smile, but it peeked out.

"Well," said Claudia, "what do you think?"

"I think it's wonderful."

"You don't think I can do it."

"No, it's not that. I know you can do anything, Claudia. It's just all that icky stuff, you know. I don't want to bring it up at lunch."

"Oh, icky stuff never bothered me," she said. "There's an eighteen-month program at the hospital where you study half the time, and the other half you're on the wards. Then you come out as a registered nurse. I start Monday morning."

"Oh, you mean you're really going to do it."

"Well, sure."

"I thought you were going to think about it."

"I can't waste any more time, Annette. I'm old. I'll probably be the oldest one in the class."

"Thirty isn't old."

"Is that what you're telling people you are now?"

"I'm not telling anybody."

Then they both had to laugh since they were both thirty-four.

Annette suddenly looked like she had a good idea of her own. "You know what we should do? We should get an apartment together. I can quit my job and get in your class, and we can both be nurses."

"What about all the icky stuff?"

"We'll cheat. You can do the icky stuff for me."

"What about Edgar Lee?"

"He can stay with Froggy. He shouldn't be living with his mother anyway. He has to learn man stuff."

"He's already got man stuff down pat, Annette. He needs me to teach him the fine points, like how to get girls. Froggy was never too outstanding on that score, as you may recall."

"Well, he sure did something right. He got you."

"Froggy doesn't have me."

"Then we'll just have to make up a new designation for it, won't we—single, married, and married-to-next-door." Annette looked at her with a very self-satisfied smile.

"You don't understand how it is," said Claudia.

"No, I think you're the one who doesn't understand how it is—in fact, you may be the *only* one who doesn't understand how it is."

"Are you going to eat that last croissant?"

Seven years ago, Claudia would have jumped at the chance to live with Annette. She remembered how obsessed she was. It wasn't so crazy. After all, Jack was infatuated with Annette—obviously—and she and Jack were like-minded. It was just as easy for her to be in love with Annette. When they met each other at the French Café every week, they always hugged and kissed, and when they got up to leave, slinging their purses over their shoulders, sometimes they started walking down the street holding hands. You could be that way with a woman, and nothing would happen to you. You weren't going to have your front teeth knocked out and get raped a hundred times. You could be that way with a woman.

CHAPTER FIFTY

Claudia peeked in the window of the examining room. "Oh no," she said. "It's Mr. Berg."

"Look at your chart," said Dante.

"I don't have to—I know him," said Claudia. "He's my stockbroker. You do it, Dante. I just saw him yesterday downtown. He'll never believe I'm a nurse."

"Do I look more believable? Ha! Come on. Take the bull by the horns." With that, Dante gripped imaginary horns in the air in a way that better suggested riding a bicycle out of control down a steep hill. Then he laughed and gave Claudia a little nudge. Through the doors she went, upright and bold in her white dress, white stockings, white shoes and cap, with the little watch over her breast pocket, a stethoscope around her neck, and all the self-confidence she could muster up from a whole month as an American Red Cross cadet nurse.

"Good afternoon, Mr.—" Claudia consulted the clipboard with her eyes lowered in intense scrutiny—"Mr. Berg."

"Mrs. Wyler," said Mr. Berg without a hitch.

"Nurse Wyler," corrected Dante, standing by the Formica counter with the tube racks, trays and glass canisters of gloves and gauze.

"I see you are in for—" back to the clipboard—"insurance blood work."

"Yes," said Mr. Berg.

He judiciously offered the papers in his hand to a space halfway between Claudia and Dante without favoring either side. Dante folded his arms and looked away, leaving Claudia to receive them. With a word to Mr. Berg that he might take off his jacket and roll up his sleeves, Claudia shouldered up to Dante at the counter.

"Get your tubes," he whispered. "I'll check you. Two reds, one purple, two whites and a yellow. The labels are with his paperwork. What do you do first?"

"Put the labels on."

"Good," said Dante.

Now Claudia was nervous. Holy cow. Six tubes. That was a lot. The insurance company sure wasn't taking any chances on Mr. Berg.

He wasn't that old. He was a lean, bespectacled man with graying hair, but still bright-eyed and alert. He was looking at his bare arms when Claudia looked up from the labeling. This was it. She was through pretending. She had watched Dante do it a hundred times, and she felt fortified by the extra hours she'd put in on the arm dummy. She did not have to pretend anymore. She was almost a professional, and it was time for professional to push pretend out of the way.

Claudia squared off with Mr. Berg, taking one wrist in her hand and extending his arm, looking carefully, then the other arm. Dante stood a little behind Mr. Berg and tapped his finger at the middle of his own left arm.

"Median cephalic, left arm," Claudia said, writing it down on her paperwork and circling L for left.

When she looked up with her tubes, needle, and vacutainer in hand, Claudia expected to catch Mr. Berg sending imploring messages to Dante by means of eyebrow signals, but he was waiting with serenity. She recalled the chilling stories Mr. Berg had told her of the days when he was a broker for Hutton in the crash of '29. That was probably where the sangfroid came from.

Claudia pulled the rubber tourniquet out of her pocket with the flourish Dante always gave it, wrapped and tucked it, remembered the alcohol pad at the last minute when Dante feverishly made the gesture on his own arm, took aim, and went for the spot on Mr. Berg's arm that was pretending to be the median cephalic. Mr. Berg didn't flinch. It was a little dicey, holding the vacutainer steady for six tubes when her hands were shaking, but she got them, and then Dante tapped his own arm again to remind her to yank the tourniquet before she pulled the needle. Good thing he did.

Outside in the hallway, Dante said, "You see? Nothing to it."

In the ladies' room of the nurses' lounge, Claudia wondered where all the sweat came from. She'd have to watch that. She could not remember ever seeing a sweaty nurse. Looking into the mirror and pinning the little cap over her hair, which she was keeping in a French twist for training, Claudia thought she really did look like the real thing. She was so glad that the girls in the program got their caps the first day, so on the wards the patients would not be able to tell who was a real nurse and who was in training. She had lost some weight and was down to 160. Decked out in the tight bodice of the nursing uniform, with the double row of buttons down the front, it looked like she had a waistline again.

Cadet Nurse Claudia Wyler took up her new calling in the windowless, white cinderblock building across from the hospital, the training center for the American Red Cross. Every weekday from eight in the morning until five in the afternoon, she and eleven other cadet nurses labored over textbooks under the withering eye of stern old battle-axe nurse instructors. The first month was all about regulations, standard procedures, and hazardous materials, and there was a test every day that everyone had to pass with a perfect score of one hundred. Claudia was surprised that nobody dropped out.

Obstetrics and Gynecology were her best subjects, but she also did well in Nursing Arts, Instrument Care, Sterile Procedures, and Surgical Nursing. The class they called "catch me if you can" covered every disease there was, and the pictures in the textbook were so awful that they made her gag. Pharmacology gave everybody trouble. There were so many drugs that Claudia took Jack's old secret code cards, wrote up all the pharmaceutical names to memorize, and used them as flash cards with the other girls. The secret codes were still on the corners, but Claudia was pretty sure nobody was a spy, and she assured Jack in her mind that it was too late for her to lose the war now, even if she tried. She knew Jack would think it was her fault.

The other trainees were nice, but it wasn't Hula Girls all over again. It looked like these girls were serious and professional even before they hit the beaches of cadet nursing. They were friendly but didn't latch on to each other. And while some of them were cute, Claudia didn't think it ever crossed the mind of any one of them to hitch a wagon to her good looks or feminine wiles. Any one of them could have been in charge. Claudia could only wonder, thinking back to how scatter-brained she was at that age. Maybe the other navy wives were too, come to think of it. Cadet nurses were a different breed, all right. They were tough and serious, like men could be, and they weren't afraid of icky stuff. It was a little unnerving to be part of a group like that, to tell the truth.

Claudia was the oldest one in the program except for Grace, a colored girl who was a close second. Grace was also heavy, but again, a close second. They met at the mirror in the nurses' lounge the first day and helped each other pin on their caps. Claudia had trouble with her French twist, and Grace wasn't sure how to work with the elaborate victory rolls she had piled up on her head, and they ended up laughing so much. She and Grace were just regular girls together, and that was nice.

Grace was good at math and helped her with weights-and-measures class. When they got out for lunch every day, Claudia and Grace took their lunch bags across the street to a little park with palm trees, sat on the bench, and talked the hour away. It turned out that being heavy wasn't such a crime with colored girls. They were more interested in their hair, so Grace was right up her alley.

Grace was married to Joseph, the head chef for the officers' mess at the navy base. He cooked for all the big admirals and had received the compliments of President Roosevelt when he was on base during the war. The president loved his signature chicken dish, Country Captain. Joseph had a few more years to go, and then he wanted to retire to Scranton, Pennsylvania, and raise show cats. His Abyssinian, King KhuFu of the Nile, had taken first prize at the Honolulu Cat Show two years in a row. Becoming a nurse was something Grace had always wanted to do, and now that she was older, she was determined to acquire a good-paying practical skill because she thought Joseph was too much of a dreamer when it came to cats, and retirement wasn't that far away.

On Saturdays there was a lab practical from nine to twelve. Then they walked across the street to the hospital. There the cadets split up to go on the wards with their individual preceptors until five. Mostly it was bedpans, vital signs, sponge baths, and pushing carts back and forth to the autoclave. But when something different came along, some of the preceptors made you just watch, so Claudia's favorites were Dante, Dorothy, and Frieda. They would drop back and let you do it while they stood by with their clipboards and told you what to do. Dorothy was a very large nurse with a cute face, like the Campbell's Soup kids. When there was something interesting, she would pause before drawing back the patient curtains and ask Claudia in a whisper, "Are ya feelin' lucky today?"

Frieda was a stout little German nurse who was completely fluent in English, but her accent was so strong that when she gave instructions, Claudia always thought for a second that she had gotten conked on the head and was suddenly able to understand German. The first day training with Frieda, she drew back a curtain in the ER and said, "You bandage these people. Let's see how you do."

There were four bodies, two men and two women who had been killed in a bad car accident. The families were coming in, so the bad parts had to be bandaged over. It was so frustrating because the only way to cover up the bad parts was to make them into mummies. When it looked like Claudia was going to use up all the gauze wrap in the ER, Frieda stepped in to show

how it was done. Explaining as she went along, Frieda rolled the bodies over like logs, sometimes lifting a whole body off the table with one arm and wrapping it with the other hand. She had pretty hefty muscles on those arms and always scoffed when she did something that would have taken a couple of orderlies. Frieda looked like she had thrown a lot of bodies into piles at the end of the war, so Claudia did not want to ask her too many personal questions.

Infectious Diseases was scary, Pediatrics was sad, and Surgery was unholy gruesome. In Emergency, Claudia either spent the day smoking and reading magazines in the nurses' lounge or she didn't get a break at all. She liked her days in Obstetrics. It was a happy place because, Jiminy Christmas, everybody and his brother were having babies now.

One day, the nursing supervisor of the hospital walked over to give an inspirational talk at their morning assembly. Among other things, she told the group that no one across the street in her hospital was to die alone. Even if a nurse was busy or going off duty, if someone was dying, the nurse was supposed to sit with him and hold his hand. That really sunk in with Claudia, and one day, with Dorothy in Geriatrics, exactly that situation came up. An old man was dying, and Claudia sat down to hold his hand, remembering well her times during the war as a Hula Girl, sitting with the wounded at the hospital. In his delirium the old man kept trying to pull his hand away, and she had to keep grabbing it back.

"No, no, gimme my damn hand back," he squeaked out.

"I'm supposed to hold it," Claudia said quietly.

"I don't want you to. Leave me alone."

"I'll get in trouble," she said.

"I don't care. Leave me alone. Get out of here."

"No. It's your hour of need, and I won't leave you."

It turned into a big fight. The old man and Claudia started slapping each other's hands. Dorothy didn't know what to do. Her Campbell Kids dimples elongated into an expression of horror as she stood with her clipboard beside Claudia, watching the old man trying to tuck his hands under the bed sheet and Claudia going after them like a badger.

The old man told her later, at the market one day when they bumped into each other, that he had regained his will to live that day. He was working at an ice cream store on the beach now, had a girlfriend, and he said he never felt better in his life. Claudia was so proud of herself for that one.

Claudia came home every night and told Froggy and Edgar Lee what she had done that day and interesting things she had learned. Froggy and Edgar Lee had dinner ready for her, and Froggy made sure she had a clean, pressed, uniform for the next day. She had to admit, he was pretty good with an iron. After dinner, Claudia worked on her stocks for an hour and spent another hour on the books for The Frog Shop. Then she and Froggy went for a late-night ride in the rattletrap.

The first time Froggy suggested they go for a ride, Claudia was concerned that he was going to pull over at a make-out place and ask her to marry him, because then she would have to tell him again that she liked being friends and did not love him that way. But it didn't happen. He never tried to put her on a surfboard either.

The reason for that was probably obvious. It was the other thing that sometimes made her think. Claudia couldn't remember the last time he brought up his tender feelings for her. Maybe that changed after the trailer episode. She didn't know how much he knew about that. But that was fine with her. They were friends. They had a routine. Everything was fine the way it was. There were only a few months to go until graduation from nursing school, and she didn't want any upsets. Edgar Lee was doing well in high school, and every move she made in the market came up roses.

So dinnertime talk was a little nursing, a little surfboards, and a little trying to pry something out of Edgar Lee about tenth grade. The night drives with Froggy were mostly quiet. Claudia didn't care. She could lay her head back on the old leather seat, close her eyes, and let her hair blow in the wind. It was a nice break from nursing, surfboards, and how was school today? It was nice to live for an hour without a thought in her head. It was nice to not have to worry about something crazy upsetting the applecart—now that she had an applecart.

The Frog Shop was an instant hit, and the new boards were selling as fast as Froggy, Edgar Lee, Johnny, and two new hires could make them. They were short, only six feet long, and so light that they were easy to handle. Froggy used a combination of different woods and turned them out so aerodynamic and stylish that they made a traditional board look like it came off the side of a barn. Then he painted them high-gloss yellow-and-green, added a rubber strip for foot grips and The Frog Shop logo.

Froggy got it patented as a trademark, just like Coca-Cola. It was a crazy-looking frog in baggy short pants riding a surfboard, and around the circular border was the name "FrogDaddy" in wavy letters. Froggy did the prototype himself.

Claudia came down to the beach on Sundays to watch the surfers, and it looked like Froggy and Edgar Lee weren't kidding around. There were a lot of FrogDaddy boards out there. After a few months at the top of the hit parade, they came out with their first competition models, the Jazz FrogDaddy and the SuperJazz FrogDaddy. The SuperJazz, with three knife blade keels, set you back two hundred dollars, but they were fast and could turn on a dime, and it didn't look like the beach was going to run out of rich kids.

At the hospital, Claudia was thinking more about geriatrics. It was sad, but she felt more needed and useful in geriatrics than anywhere else. Some of the old people were always trying to get their clothes and run away. Some of them wet their beds and cried, and nobody wanted to touch them very much because, frankly, they didn't look so good. Sometimes they went around in circles with their conversations, and sometimes they didn't know who they were or where they were.

Claudia had never thought much about old people because she didn't remember seeing many of them until she entered nursing and discovered where they were. Up on the fourth floor. It was hard to believe we end up like that. It was like discovering those underground people in *The Time Machine* story. At least they didn't keep the old people in the basement. That would have been too much.

Claudia started dropping in on the fourth floor to keep the old people company and help the regular nurses on the floor after her day was over. She could never stay very long, but she came in looking happy to see them, sat with them, and asked them about their lives when they were people. She held their hands, kissed them, flirted with the old men, and brushed the old ladies' hair to make them feel pretty. Sometimes it tired her out, trying to make life happy.

Claudia graduated with her full class of twelve in June. Grace was very nervous before the ceremony, and Claudia pulled her aside while they were all milling around on the hospital front lawn watching maintenance men set up folding chairs. Grace told her she was worried about the graduation booklet with the pictures of the new nurses. She said she was the only colored person in the Indiana high school where she graduated, and when she saw the yearbook, she couldn't find her picture. All the others were in alphabetical order, but hers was by itself on the flyleaf of the book. She didn't understand until her mother told her one day, when her mother was in a temper and forgot herself, that they put her picture where it could be torn out if you didn't want anyone to see that you went to a school that had a colored girl in it.

Grace said she had never been so hurt because the people at school and the people on the yearbook committee were her friends. She was afraid it would happen again. Claudia told her not to worry because since the war America had become the greatest country of all, and down to the lowliest downtrodden of the huddled masses who had found their way to our teeming shores, all Americans knew it was up to us, and to America, to set a good example for the world and for each other, from sea to shining sea. It was kind of like one of her old Hula Girl locker room pep talks.

When the booklets were handed out, Grace's picture was in alphabetical order, right where it should be. Claudia smiled at her down the row of new nurses standing on the lawn with their diplomas, proudly wearing their new registered nurse pins.

"Whew, for once I'm right," she said to herself.

Claudia passed her nursing boards on the first try, and after she was signed off, she got hired as a floor nurse and went to work on the eleven-to-seven night shift at the hospital with Grace. The other girls hightailed it for the States, where the money was better. It was quiet most of the time, except when they rotated through the ER. Gunshot and knife wounds, accidents, shark attacks, blood and guts, and dead people. Claudia did not want to become a battle-axe, but the ER started making her feel more like Frieda. Froggy told her not to worry about it. He reminded her that it was still the same job, about which, she had once told him, she could be as warm and kind as she wanted and no one would criticize her for it.

Night shift went on for six months before she got on day shift. Grace stayed on at night because Joseph was essentially on night shift in the officers' mess at the navy yard, so that worked out for both of them. But Claudia missed her. And back on day shift, she missed having lunch with

Annette because she'd kept it up while she worked nights. Besides those two drawbacks, there was a lot to be said for normal hours. That was the main thing she thought about now. All she had to do was figure out how to make the other parts of her new life into normal.

CHAPTER FIFTY-ONE

Froggy was a good place to start. First, Claudia thought she should take an honest look at him. He always wore those big Hawaiian shirts he never tucked in, but she could tell he was getting a tummy, and he had a little extra chin that showed when they read the newspapers together at her place on Sunday mornings. At least he didn't come over in a bathrobe. He had gone back to keeping his hair at two-inch regulation navy. It was more white than red now, from so much time in the sun, and he shaved every day. Nobody in his line of work seemed to do that, shave regularly, and Claudia took it as an sign that he had one more place to go before he gave up going places.

She liked his blue eyes. He wasn't as much of a cutup smart aleck anymore. He calmed down about the same time she settled into nursing school, when he started fixing dinner and encouraging her whenever a bad day washed out her self-confidence. Peeking around the edge of her section of the Sunday paper, Claudia considered the whole picture of Froggy at thirty-five, sitting in the armchair with his reading glasses tilted at the end of his nose. Most of him probably still works, she concluded. She wore reading glasses now too.

It was on a Sunday morning when they were reading the papers that Claudia decided it was time to see if normal could go to stage two. She had been on day shift for six months, getting her sleep and living in the daytime world again. The windows were wide open, with a nice breeze coming through, and it sounded like there were a million birds out there in the palms. Froggy was reading his sections of the paper in his armchair, and Claudia was reading her sections in her armchair.

"John," she said.

Froggy did not look up, but his eyebrows rose in surprise over his eyeglasses.

"Yes, Mrs. Wyler?"

Claudia let that go and kept going. "I'm starting our taxes now," she said. "I've got mine to do, and yours, the corporate taxes for the shop, and now Edgar Lee's."

"How we doin'?"

"Oh, we're doing great. So is Edgar Lee. He has to file this year. I'm putting his wages from the shop into some good stocks, so he's got unearned income too."

"You should let him keep something, Claudia."

"No, John. I'm building for his future. When you reinvest the dividends—"

"I know. You told me before. So if the dividends are buying the stocks, then you should let him keep his wages."

"Well, he doesn't have enough stocks yet, and I need his wages to buy in round lots."

"He needs spending money." At this, Froggy put the newspaper down in his lap and looked at Claudia over his glasses. "Then I'll give him a raise. I'll give him seventy-five cents an hour. How about that? Then you can let him have some spending money."

"Okay," said Claudia, "you can afford that."

"Problem solved," said Froggy, returning to his newspaper.

"There's another thing, John." Claudia waited a moment and then went on. "The way it's set up, you can save a lot of money on taxes if you file a joint return."

Froggy's eyebrows went up again, but he kept his eyes on the newspaper.

"I guess we could find people to marry," he said. "It might be hard to get a taker for Edgar Lee, but I'll keep my eyes open."

Claudia wondered if he was going to leave it at that—if he was going to dismiss the idea with a smart remark. Being friends had worked out so well. Maybe he wasn't interested. It was her own doing. She had put him off. She remembered things she had said and couldn't blame him. Maybe he really had given up on that a long time ago. She had made her bed, and maybe she was going to have to lie in it alone.

Nothing had come along, not for a long time, that she had allowed half a chance of making her cry. Maybe he didn't want her in that way. Tears were getting ready, but holding, behind her eyes. She didn't know what was up with her psychology or her better judgment, but she knew that as much as things were fine the way they were, she wanted to be married again, and the one she wanted was right over there, reading the newspaper. Right in her own backyard. She tried to steady her voice.

"John, do you want to marry me?" she asked.

Froggy put down the newspaper, took off his glasses, and turned to her with a serious face and a short pause before he said, "I sure do."

Edgar Lee said, "So what's new?" in that condescending tenth-grade voice of his. The only ones who got excited were Grace and Annette. Claudia told Grace in the nurses' lounge, where they met every morning at shift change and had coffee and a couple of smokes together. Grace squealed and came in like a tidal wave. It's so damn satisfying hugging a big lady. Claudia said it just like that, and Grace said she noticed it too, just then, and then they hugged and laughed a lot more.

By the time Claudia saw Annette at the French Café, she had the ring back from the jewelers, and Annette almost died because it was so pretty. It was like her first one from Jack and her second one from Andrew, a tiny diamond set in gold filigree. Annette seemed to forget all about her baseless allegations that she and John were already a *fait accompli*. She asked how John proposed, when they were getting married, where they were going on the honeymoon, and circled all around the main question until Claudia came out and asked her to be her maid of honor.

A week later, Claudia Wyler, in a simple white dress with short sleeves, with a pillbox hat and little veil, and John Calder Ransome, in blue tie, white shirt, and brown corduroy sports coat with leather patches on the elbows, signed papers and took their vows before a judge in the main hallway of Honolulu City Hall. After all the somber warnings about sickness and health, the judge looked up smiling and said, "You may now kiss the bride."

It was evident to Claudia by the surprise on John's face that he had not thought of that either. They had never kissed. Suddenly Claudia's heart was racing. She had not kissed a man since Andrew. She didn't know what was going on in John's mind, but he turned to her, and she turned to him. They put their arms around each other like mountain climbers checking their rope and snaps, and then they chose which way they were going to tilt their heads and kissed. She tossed the bouquet to Annette like a football.

Then there was the other thing. As they drove out of town, Claudia was as much worried about the FrogDaddy surfboard sticking up out of the back seat of the rattletrap as the wedding night business. They pulled over to get the dangling tin cans off the bumper that Annette and Edgar Lee had contrived, and pretty soon they were on the shore road, going up to the Windjammer Hotel at Makaha, quietly talking about nothing. Claudia didn't feel different, just happy.

They had dinner at a nice place where everybody applauded the sunset because the big yellow ball lay on the line of the horizon one minute and then suddenly went plop, out of sight. It looked like quite a trick, but the waiter said it happened every evening. Claudia was so distracted by wedding night speculations that she asked the waiter, "When's the next show?" Then they walked on the beach in their bare feet, stopped in a little place for a couple of drinks, and went back to the hotel.

They brushed their teeth, let each other have a turn in the bathroom, turned out the light, and got into bed fully decked out in pajamas and nightie. They kissed and held each other, de-clothed and did it. Mission accomplished. As far as she knew, it was John's first time, but he seemed to pick up the cues, and Claudia was glad she could stand to do it after the bad time in the trailer. It was in the past now, along with everything else—but you know.

The next day turned out to be the highlight of the honeymoon. They went down to breakfast in the hotel dining room, had lunch and dinner there, spent time at the beach, and came back to the room after each outing to climb back into bed with the Do Not Disturb sign on the door. Three times that day. Claudia gave John some pointers, and she got in some rip-roaring orgasms. She didn't think sex was anything like John imagined it. It wasn't what she would have imagined either. It just felt like something good to do together, like going out for ice cream. It should have come first, but they only thought to say I love you to each other after the last time that night, before they went to sleep.

The next morning was surfboard school for Claudia. John got her lying flat on the FrogDaddy board, paddling in the shallows, and he stood by, holding the board when the waves came in. That part was lots of fun. She was fine getting to her knees and could hold on, but when she tried standing up, she kept falling off. There was no need to catch her with all that water around, but John did and felt her up a little, and then they both wanted to forget surfboard class and go back to the room. But other people were around, so Claudia kept his hands off the girl parts, and it was back to paddling the board.

The afternoon surfboard session was canceled and the honeymoon cut short because they had to go back to Honolulu to get Edgar Lee out of the pokey. The police called the hotel. Edgar Lee had apparently hosted an underage drinking party that ran between the two apartments and the place was a wreck. There were a number of people arrested for drunk and disorderly conduct, and Edgar Lee was one of them.

Claudia was just sick about it. John packed their suitcases while she fretted and paced the room. He went to the desk and settled up, loaded the bags and the FrogDaddy board, and got Claudia to stop worrying. He said everything would be all right. "I'll talk to him," he said.

That's all John had to say about it, and then he went back to making her have a good time on the drive home. It was different from the ride up because she found out how restrained and inhibited he had been before they became man and wife. He put his free hand on her knee and up her dress and in her panties. He must have been making up for lost time because he said he had wanted her since the night at Admiral Harris's party. The caressing and tickling made her feel good and got her laughing, and she forgot all about the trouble with Edgar Lee.

When she wanted peace and quiet, he left her alone to close her eyes and lie back in the seat with her hair streaming out in the wind. Everything would be all right. John would talk to Edgar Lee. There was nothing to argue over. Claudia wondered if that was going to be her new life. Maybe she could leave the problems to her husband, the way it was supposed to be. So far, nothing seemed too difficult for him.

Claudia wanted to go home first and let John get Edgar Lee, but John did not want to leave her alone there if the place really was a mess, so they both went to the police station. Edgar Lee rode home in the back with the board and suitcases. He looked like he wasn't done throwing up, and it was after dark before they got home, what with pulling over on the side of the road a few times.

John went in first and told them to wait in the car. Then he called Edgar Lee to come in. Claudia closed her eyes and lay her head back on the old leather seat, and before long John was back at the car, taking the surfboard out and putting Edgar Lee and his suitcase in the back seat.

They got two nice little rooms in the Grand Hawaiian. They met Edgar Lee downstairs in the after-hours dining room, after he had showered and changed, and they had a nice dinner as if nothing had happened. Edgar Lee and John talked waves and surfboards and speculated about a new design for heavy people, based upon Claudia's first day, which she could hardly believe was only that morning. They asked her personal questions about keeping her balance and took notes, and Claudia didn't understand why she was the one on the hot seat and not Edgar Lee.

In the morning, John fetched Edgar Lee and went down to the breakfast room early. It was a glorious morning. John left the drapes parted a little over the open balcony sliding doors, so Claudia woke up to the sound of the surf. Light morning sunshine poured in every time the wind blew the drapes apart. She felt so happy being married. She felt herself without the anxieties and burdens of the first time, when Jack needed her so much for his career. There were no tests to fail this time. The only thing asked of her was an RSVP to an invitation from a nice man, not half-bad looking, to have a good time with him for the next fifty years. She looked at the gold ring on her fourth finger and felt so happy—hungry too, because after all the talk at dinner, she had declined dessert. She had been dying for a piece of that chocolate cake going around on the cart.

When Claudia got down to the breakfast room, the hostess showed her to a table John had reserved for them just inside the restaurant. John and Edgar Lee were standing outside on the terrace with the ocean behind them. It was too far away for Claudia to hear anything but the surf or tell who was talking. She had not realized it before, but John and Edgar Lee were about the same height. Claudia sipped at her coffee and had a Chesterfield and did not take her eyes off them. John's head was inclined to Edgar Lee. Edgar Lee was looking at the ground. It was as if she were witnessing a gathering of great cloudbanks, coming together from opposing horizons, meeting over the two heads.

It looked like it was going to go on for a while, so Claudia asked the waiter to try to dig up some of last night's chocolate cake. He came back with a big piece, and she asked him to return in a minute to take the plate before the gentlemen on the terrace came in. Then Claudia had a quick order of French toast and got a new place setting before the skies were clear over John and Edgar Lee. John put his arm around Edgar Lee and gripped his shoulder in that male version of an embrace, and they broke with a nod of their heads and grimacing smiles as they turned and spotted her at the table inside.

Nothing more needed to be said, apparently. After breakfast, John and Edgar Lee went to put the house back together, and she stayed at the hotel. John brought back her stock reports, the mail, and the ledgers for The Frog Shop for her to work with on the balcony of their room. Some of the papers were still wet with beer, and Claudia had to hang them over the railing to dry. She did a little work every day, went to the beach, and kind of enjoyed being alone for the first time in God knows when, and not a moment's thought went to wondering what was going on at the house. It was still her honeymoon, and John was taking care of it.

Every night at dinner in the hotel, Claudia looked for signs in Edgar Lee. The surliness was gone and the looks of agitated impatience that crossed his face whenever she said anything longer than two sentences were gone. They talked about the shop and surfboard riding and Annapolis. It was like Edgar Lee was a different boy. He had grown up or something.

They stayed at the Grand Hawaiian for four days while John and Edgar Lee made it safe to go home. When she walked into the apartment the first time and went through the rooms, there was the smell of fresh paint, but everything was exactly as it had been. Claudia had to look closely at the ivory polar bears on the shelf over her bed to see that there was a broken arm on Mary Ann's bear that had been very carefully glued back on, and there was some scotch tape on the monkey family, but otherwise the place looked like a perfect museum restoration of Claudia and Edgar Lee Wyler's Honolulu apartment, circa 1953. It would not have felt out of place if a walkway through it had been cordoned off with velvet ropes.

Sunday was Claudia's last day before going back to work at the hospital. Edgar Lee was at the beach surfing. Claudia and John sat in their armchairs at Claudia's, reading the papers. There was no need to jinx it by asking, but now Claudia was just curious.

"John?"

"Uh-oh. What?" he said.

"What do you mean, uh-oh?"

"Well, you don't usually talk when we read the Sunday papers."

"I'm just curious. You don't have to tell me, but I was wondering what you said to Edgar Lee."

John took off his glasses and put his newspaper down.

"Well, I'm sorry we took so long out there. You should have started breakfast. You must have been starving."

"I didn't mind," said Claudia. "I was watching you out there the whole time. I wish I had the camera. You two just looked so intense."

"Didn't we though?"

"I'm being serious, John. Nothing I say seems to work on Edgar Lee, so tell me what you said to him."

"I don't remember exactly."

"Well, just give me the gist of it."

"Okay, well, I guess the gist of it was, I heard his side of the story, and then I told him what was expected of him as a man."

"Hmm," said Claudia. Then she put her glasses on and went back to the newspaper. "I didn't think you knew about stuff like that."

After a moment's pause, John said, "Come here, Mrs. Ransome."

Claudia got up with her newspaper and shuffled over in her robe and pink fluffy slippers.

"Sit here," he said, gesturing for her to sit in his lap.

No sooner had she sat down, but John began to tickle her and rough her up, and in a moment they were down on the floor.

"My glasses, my glasses," she said.

So they stopped, and Claudia took off her glasses and carefully put them on the table between the two armchairs. Then John got back on her.

"Ow—my hair." She sat up and gathered her hair behind at the neck and then went to the kitchen to get a rubber band and came back, tying her robe tightly around her, but leaving a loose knot. John wrestled her down to the floor again, got the robe off, and started tugging at her panties.

"Wait, wait. They're my good panties." Claudia leaned back and slipped out of her panties and carefully laid them beside her glasses on the table. Then he was on her again, roughhousing, sometimes releasing her for a second to let her try to escape then pulling her back, tickling her till she lost her head and left her legs apart, and then she felt his scratchy unshaven face plunge between them, sniffing and snorting like a mad bull. She could have locked her legs around his head and choked him off, but she started laughing over the animal sounds. Then she got going and had an orgasm she thought would never stop. Even with keeping an ear out for Edgar Lee, it was a pretty good time, and soon they were showered and dressed and back in their armchairs with their newspaper, coffee, and smokes.

"I didn't think you had it in you, wild man."

"Don't you forget it," he said. Then after reading a little more with his glasses down at the end of his nose, he added, "But don't expect it every time."

The hospital let her take a two-hour lunch break on Thursdays if she came in early, so Claudia got back with Annette at the French Café. Since she had gone on day shift, they'd been meeting across the street from the hospital. It just wasn't enough time, and they had to bring their own food. She wanted to hear about Annette's big surprise, so she went through the honeymoon stories and what happened with Edgar Lee as fast as she could and then settled in for the good stuff with her coffee and a Chesterfield.

"You knew something was up, didn't you?" said Annette.

"Yeah, well, you were acting kind of funny the last time."

"I wanted to say goodbye."

"Oh God, Annette. Where are you going?"

"It's not really going to a place."

"Well, what? Is something wrong?"

"No, but I didn't want to say anything until it was all over."

"What's all over? Oh, Annette!"

"Will you shut up a minute?" Annette lowered her voice and leaned in. "I was planning to lose my virginity," she said. "I figured out how to do it."

"Oh, whew."

"No, Claudia. It's a big deal."

"I know it's a big deal, but what did you have to figure out?"

Still leaning in close to Claudia, Annette said, "Well, I went to see Elaine at the clinic, and she fitted me for a diaphragm. She's so nice. She didn't ask me any questions at all. You have to be married to get one, you know. Then I had to line up a man, you know, so I chose this guy from another office down the hall who I have coffee with in the cafeteria sometimes."

"Wait. Is this guy interested in you?"

"Maybe."

"Are you interested in him?"

"Not really. I told him it would be a one-time thing."

"Oh Jesus, Annette."

Claudia and Annette let that sit while the waiter came around to the table beside theirs, loaded up the bus pan, and set a new place with silverware.

"Well, how did it go?"

"It hasn't happened yet."

"Good for you, Annette."

"What do you mean? I thought you'd be all for it. Do you think I'm making a mistake?"

Claudia sat back and considered a moment, and then she leaned back over the table.

"I think you should stick to your guns and get married first. You've waited this long. The mistake is going to be if you pick a bad husband. I'm afraid for you about that because you're just the type to do it. All these men you've been out with—perfectly good guys, and I'm so afraid you're going to pick a bad one."

"Well, how about you? Froggy was a fluke. You didn't think he was husband material, did you? And there was that guy Dan. And Jack. I don't want to say anything about Jack because of the way you have him up on a pedestal."

"What about Jack?"

Annette thought a minute and then seemed to think twice. She looked away and crossed her legs and held her short Lucky in front of her like Katharine Hepburn. Claudia did exactly the same thing, and then they went for the ashtray in the middle of the table at the same time and ended up like Errol Flynn and Basil Rathbone dueling with their cigarettes. Then they started laughing and ordered more coffee and some cherry pie.

"I just want to get it out of the way and have some fun, like you."

"You know, you can have fun by yourself, Annette."

"I know, but you're not supposed to," she said. "Remember when you told me that?"

CHAPTER FIFTY-TWO

Edgar Lee was at the wheel, and he was putting the Austin-Healey through its paces. Claudia was up front with part of the newspaper in her lap, and John was in the back, trying to sit with his arms around two FrogDaddy boards jutting up like Stonehenge while trying to keep his part of the newspaper from blowing away. Edgar Lee picked up speed, and Claudia got a little nervous. He looked so much like Jack with the sunglasses on, with that square jaw and all the confidence in the world.

"Go out Kalaki and left on Lahanihea," John shouted.

"Aye, aye, skipper," said Edgar Lee.

Claudia had to hold her scarf and turn to hear what John was trying to say. He tried again and pointed at Edgar Lee.

"Naval Aviation. I can see him in an A-4 Skyhawk."

Claudia could not see that at all.

"No thanks, Frog," said Edgar Lee over his shoulder, "Big boats for me. Carriers, or maybe a battle cruiser—or a destroyer, if I can command. Who wants to be an airplane driver if you can get a ship?"

Claudia did not know anything about the surprise Sunday morning outing. She was just doing the dishes when John sprung it on her. He had been circling ads in the real estate section of the Sunday papers after breakfast and suddenly got up and said, "Hey, let's take a ride." And that was that. Edgar Lee was always up for anything if he could drive. They put their bathing suits on under their clothes, grabbed a few towels, put a FrogDaddy and a SuperJazz FrogDaddy in the back seat, and roared out.

"Whoa," John shouted, "one coming up off the starboard bow. The one with the sign out front. Full stop, Edgar Lee."

"I don't like the flat roof," said Claudia. "Nope."

"All ahead full, Edgar Lee. Go left on Waikaloa. Down to 8th and go left again. Should be one coming up portside."

In town they went by eight or ten houses more or less that fast. There was always something Claudia did not like, so they went on to the addresses farther out, the ones on Claudia's part of the newspaper, but she deferred to John as navigator and passed the newspaper back to him because she didn't know her way around. By afternoon they were out in the countryside where the houses were tucked away in the jungley stuff, with long dirt or gravel driveways that were bumpy and full of mud holes.

One of the surfboards got bounced out of the back before Edgar Lee slowed down, and then he had to slow to a crawl, but not before they lost the muffler on the next hole. Claudia got under the car and tied it back up with scraps of wire she found doing nothing under the hood, using a pair of pliers, which happened to be the only tool left in the neglected leather pouch under the back seat. She was going to have to get some tools and teach Edgar Lee something about cars. They kept going down the dirt road to the house, just because it was the last one on the list, and they didn't want to give up after all the trouble it had taken getting this far.

It was a nice place, a trim, little split-level with lots of windows and flowers and slate walkways, and Claudia liked it right away. But another idea had entered her mind since they set out, and as a little cloud on the horizon sometimes becomes bigger and bigger until there is nothing left to be seen of the sky, the other idea in her head became the only idea up there.

"Nope," she said.

"I thought you liked the countryside."

"I do."

"So what's wrong with the house?"

"Nothing. It's a beautiful house, but it's too hot. No breeze. I couldn't live out here."

"Then you want to be in town?"

"I don't know, John."

"Just tell me where to go," said Edgar Lee.

"Let's go surfing," said Claudia.

John leaned over the seat and Edgar Lee craned his neck around so they could demonstrate to each other with wide eyes and raised brows the surprise on their faces.

"Well, I liked it so far," said Claudia, "—at the Windjammer. I liked that."

So they returned to the civilized world, where the first stop was a roadside stand that had barbecued ribs cooking in a fifty-five gallon oil drum cut in half. They ate plates of ribs at the picnic table, a lunch they agreed was worth the trip, and found a beach nearby for surfing. Edgar Lee did his wave weaseling out there on the SuperJazz FrogDaddy while John paddled Claudia around on the other board and got her up on her feet a couple of times. She actually rode a little wave for what John said must have been ten or fifteen seconds. Claudia was so proud of herself. It was just like the Wright Brothers at Kitty Hawk—fifteen seconds in the air.

Annette went with Claudia for her appointment with Elaine at the Dependents Clinic, and they sat together in the waiting room reading magazines. She thought the problem might be from getting bounced around in the rattletrap the other day.

"I don't know why I'm so nervous," said Annette.

"You're afraid it's something bad."

"Well, aren't you?"

"Not really. Now look at this, Annette." Claudia held up a magazine article with a list of warning signs. "We're girls. We get this kind of stuff all the time. If we went to the doctor every time we had nausea, tingling, rapid heartbeat, uncontrollable—what the hell—we'd be in the doctor's office every day."

"So what are we doing here now?"

"Just checking."

The nurse called Claudia in. The girl kept moving more and more weights over to the right on the scale until Claudia topped out at one seventy-two. It was probably the shoes, but she hadn't weighed herself in a while. Then she waited on the examining room bench with the stirrups. Nothing was creepy anymore since she had become a nurse, and this was the first time she realized it, so she was smiling to herself when Elaine came in. They talked a little, went through the routine questions, and then Elaine examined her.

Claudia got dressed, and Elaine wrote a lot on her clipboard. Then she sat back, took off her glasses, and crossed her legs. It was the first time Claudia ever noticed Elaine's legs or thought of her as a woman. She was going with John when he was Froggy and being silly all the time. John said it never went anywhere, just the goodnight kiss stage. He missed out on some great legs. Too late now. And wouldn't Elaine be surprised how good a husband John turned out to be. Nobody would have expected it.

"Well, Claudia, old gal, you have your period back," said Elaine.

Claudia did not know what she was expecting, but it wasn't that.

"How do you know?"

"Because—" Elaine let that sink in a moment and then continued, "I would say, as near as I can tell, you're about six weeks pregnant."

"Well, I'll be a monkey's uncle. Oh God, Elaine. I don't believe it."

"The human body is a wonder, isn't it?"

When Claudia told Annette, it was like VJ Day. She was restrained because it was in the lounge right outside the examining room, but she was so excited.

"But don't tell anybody, Annette. I have to figure out some things."

"We're still going to lunch, aren't we?"

"Sure," said Claudia. "I'm eating for two, you know."

"I thought that was what you always did."

Then they laughed and walked arm in arm down to the French Café. Annette was brimming over with baby clothes ideas, the christening, and who would be a good godmother, and things she had read, like you're not supposed to keep houseplants if you have a new baby.

"Why?"

"I don't know," said Annette. "I wasn't interested enough to read that far. I'll let you know."

On Sunday morning when they were reading the papers in their armchairs, Claudia thought it would be a good time to tell John because he had the real estate section and was beginning to circle ads that were not in last week's paper.

"This sounds like a good one," he said.

"Before you get into that, John, I have some news."

"Fire away."

"You got me pregnant."

Putting it that way was a good start—straight out of debate class at Sweet Briar. You push the blame to the other side right off the starting block. John took off his glasses and turned his head. Thinking, thinking. She knew the look.

"I want to have the baby in America," she said.

"This is America," he said.

"You know what I mean. The real America."

"Well," he said, turning back and folding up his newspaper and thinking it over, "Being as I am a man of the male gender, I don't know the good places in the real America to have a baby, so maybe you'd better tell me where we're going."

"New England."

"All right. New England."

"Okay?"

"Okay."

"And we can live there. For keeps."

Froggy pondered. "Okay," he said.

They went back to reading the papers and after a little while, John said, "By the way, congratulations, Mrs. Ransome."

Then he got up and smothered her with kisses and tickled her and roughed her up a little until she made him stop because of the baby. They went back to their newspapers and had a couple of Chesterfields and Luckys. Claudia's better judgment wanted to stop there while she was ahead, but she was batting a thousand.

"There's something else, John."

"Just say the word, Claud."

"I want you to get a real job in America. It will be good for the family and good for Edgar Lee if he wants to get into Annapolis and good for you too. I'd like to see you using your head. Annette told me what you did in the war, that thing with the radar you fixed. She said you were the only one who could figure out how to do it. You're an engineer, John. You should be doing work like that. I'm sure lots of companies would want you. I know you wanted to get out of the navy, and this FrogDaddy thing was a brilliant idea, but I think you can do more than that. I think you're ready to do more, don't you?"

'It's a good business—"

"You're not a businessman, John. You don't know that because you've done so well. You've never had any setbacks. You had a good idea, and the conditions were right, so it worked. You could take the next step and get a bigger place or even build a factory, but then you'd have to deal with employees. And if you don't want to do that, the only problem with staying small is—you know, staying small, when you're so smart and you could be doing big things."

He tried to get a word in, but Claudia thought of the other thing she wanted to say while she had the chance.

"You don't know about advertising and marketing or what to do when a competitor comes along, and I can't help you there because I don't know either."

"That's when you—"

"I know, that's when you hire people who know that stuff, but they'll change the company into something you won't like anymore. I think a lot of what you've done, John, I really do. And I'd think a lot of you too if you saw that it might be the right time to make a move. You're so good with engineering. Annette told me."

"She doesn't really know."

"I found those citations, John."

"You went through my closet?"

"I'm your wife."

"I don't go into your stuff."

"That's how it works when you're married, John."

Claudia forgot where she was going, but they were beyond the part where he tried to interrupt, so they fell back in their armchairs like fighters at the bell and went for their coffee and smokes. Then Claudia remembered where she was and jumped back into the ring.

"The Russians are after us now, aren't they? And they have the A-bomb."

"I'm not going back in the navy."

"You don't have to. They have civilian engineers. Annette told me. You can get a job like that in the States, in New England."

Then, as her closing argument, Claudia made a last, quiet but passionate appeal. Passionate because she truly believed it, aside from her own selfish motives, and quiet because she suspected he must have come to the same conclusion, and she didn't have to beat him over the head.

"You're a smart man, John. I think a smart man would see that it's time to get out of surfboards and get into A-bombs."

John took off his glasses and looked down at the newspaper in his lap. He looked a little old and tired all of a sudden. She said what she had to say. She knew he would not put it off. He would answer her here and now, once he thought it through.

She was asking him to give up his independence. She did not know what he was mentally placing piece by piece on the other side of the scale, if there were anything, even in the aggregate, that could add up to outweigh independence. A thought crept into her mind that had never been there before, that she might be too much for John and this demand was too much. It might make him realize that he could have a good life without her. She felt something inside her getting ready to die and she was afraid.

"How long before the baby comes?" he asked quietly.

"Elaine said about eight months."

"I guess I'd better start writing letters."

"John, thank you."

"Now you better get to work on the Wave Weasel."

"I thought you could talk to him," she said.

CHAPTER FIFTY-THREE

It was after dinner that night when Claudia brought up the matter. She was at the sink washing dishes. John was reading the paper. Edgar Lee was at the kitchen table writing a paper for school.

"You've already decided, haven't you," he said.

"You've never seen snow, Edgar Lee. The change of seasons is good for people. You've got spring, summer, fall—"

"I know what the seasons are, Mom."

"But you have to experience them. They're what you call an emotional touchstone for all your memories."

"I've got plenty of memories."

Claudia appealed to John. "You know what I mean, John. How fall is burning leaves and going back to school, and winter is, well, you know—all your memories get connected to nature."

"Oh, shit," said Edgar Lee. "I can't do this fucking paper."

He threw his spiral notebook and pen across the room and walked out, slamming the door behind him. Claudia heard the Austin-Healey start up, then a couple of big revs. She threw a look of terror at John, who motioned her over and made her sit down in her armchair. He gave her his coffee cup and made her take a few big gulps. She heard Edgar Lee get a surfboard out from under the house, another big rev, and the Austin-Healey roared away.

"I'll talk to him when he comes back," said John.

He lit up a Chesterfield for her and told her to stay in the armchair while he finished the dishes.

"I've never heard him say words like that, John."

"Didn't come from me."

"Is it the men at the shop? That's another reason I want to get him away from here."

"Well, it gets a little inconvenient if you have to leave a country whenever you hear a bad word."

He was only trying to be funny, but Claudia couldn't laugh. She was too worried about Edgar Lee. It was dark outside, and she could hear the wind picking up.

At eleven o'clock, John made her go to bed. He said he was going to wait out on the driveway for Edgar Lee, and he told her to go to sleep. But she watched hour after hour go by on the luminous dial of her folding travel alarm clock on the nightstand and got up at three o'clock to peek out the window. John was sitting in an old rattan chair in the driveway and had his coffee and Luckys and ashtray on the other chair beside it. It looked like he had fallen asleep. Claudia wrung her hands and felt like Lady Macbeth.

The rattletrap came home an hour later. Claudia heard it and went to look out the window. Edgar Lee was okay. He started walking toward the door, and she heard John's voice. She crouched down under the window. She wanted to hear what John said this time. It was still dark and quiet outside.

"Sit with me a minute," said John.

Claudia didn't hear Edgar Lee at the door, so she assumed she missed how John got him to stop walking away. Drat. That was always half the battle. She peeked over the windowsill and saw John and Edgar Lee sitting in the rattan chairs side by side, looking up at the sky. She went to the other window where she could hear better.

"Your mom was worried, so I told her you could outswim a tiger shark in the dark."

"She wouldn't believe that."

"I guess you don't believe that either."

"I just drove around. What's she trying to do, Frog?"

"Your mom just told me she's going to have a baby."

"Oh—"

"Surprised me too."

There was a long silence.

"Did you see that shooting star?"

"Yeah."

"So your mom wants to be somewhere settled. Women want to be in certain places when they have babies. So we got to pack our bags, Wave Weasel."

There was another long silence.

"See that one?"

"Yeah."

"Can I stay here?"

"Negative."

"Why not?"

There was another long silence.

"Do you want to go to Annapolis?"

"Yeah."

"Real bad?"

"Yeah."

"Well, you can't get there from here, Wave Weasel. It's by congressional appointment. Hawaii doesn't have any congressmen."

There was another long silence.

"Are we bringing the Austin-Healey?"

"You better believe it, kid."

There was another long silence, and then Claudia heard John say they better go inside, so she almost fell over trying to get up off the floor and back to bed before they came in. She pretended to be asleep when John tiptoed in. She heard him get out of his clothes, and then he quietly slipped into bed beside her. He got up against her a little and then went to sleep, and she lay awake looking at the clock for a while, thinking how little men talked to each other. It was a wonder there were so many languages in the world. What the hell for? They sure didn't get used much with men around.

Claudia got up the minute John begin to stir. He went back to his place to shave and shower. She had everything going by the time John came back, and the smell of coffee in the percolator rousted Edgar Lee out of his den, since he had started drinking coffee. She got bacon frying and started pancake batter and stood ready for action on the bridge.

Edgar Lee wolfed everything down like he hadn't eaten in three days.

"I don't want you going in the water at night, Edgar Lee," Claudia said. She just had to make the point. "It's dangerous. I had a friend who was killed by a shark when he went in the water at night."

"Who?"

"A friend from years ago. He worked with your father. So I don't want to hear of you ever doing that again. Do you understand me?"

Edgar Lee glanced at John as if he were his lawyer. John nodded.

"Okay," he said.

"Pancakes?" Claudia gave the batter another stir and started a couple more in the hot pan for Edgar Lee. "You know, Edgar Lee, there are plenty of beaches in New England."

"Not like here."

"No, but you're missing something important. You'll be the best surfboard rider there, with the best board anybody's ever seen. You know what that means?"

"No, what?"

"Well, I'm just thinking if I were a New England girl, I'd want to go to the beach to see for myself—this guy Wave Weasel."

It was as easy as that. She didn't know why she had not thought of it before. Shooting fish in a barrel is a good expression.

Claudia knew the next month or two would tell the tale. She didn't want to be one of those women who had to spend six months in bed because she could lose the baby. She wanted to be the pioneer type who could work in the fields, have the baby, and be back bossing her men the day after, so she went to see Elaine to find out. Elaine felt her abdomen and measured her pelvis and felt along each leg, looking at the veins, and she even looked at the bottoms of her feet. Then she looked at her insides and took some measurements with a tape measure. When she was done, they had a good talk.

"The baby's fine. Everything is shipshape," she said. "And in answer to your question—well, I'll put it like this. I've seen a lot of women in ten years, being a physician, but I've never seen anyone built for childbearing like you are. You're a regular broodmare, Claudia. I'm going to give you a calcium supplement, but other than that, you could have a baby every year that your period wants to stick around. I wouldn't have them out in the pineapple fields though."

"Pumpkin fields is more like it. We're going back to New England soon, I hope. We're not sure where yet, but probably Connecticut."

Elaine was so surprised. "Well you won't have to worry about getting great care in Connecticut," she said. "I know we don't see much of each other these days, but I'll miss you."

"I'll miss you too, Elaine. You've been such a dear. And you're such a good doctor."

"Well, I heard you're a pretty good nurse too."

"Oh, that's nothing compared to what you do. I'll always be grateful for what you did for me."

"Don't thank me. All we did was patch you up. You've got a tough constitution, and your body is one for the books. As a matter of fact, I don't think

I told you this, but I was at the Palmetto on your last night and saw you do that double thing—"

"The Tendardee—"

"Yes, the one that made the papers. Right then I wanted to measure the tilt of your pelvis. Of course, I wouldn't have asked, so I was glad to get the chance. It explains a lot."

"Oh," said Claudia, a little crestfallen. "I thought it was determination and training."

"Oh, sure, Claudia, nothing would take the place of that. But there are physical limitations. No male would be able to do it. I can say that positively. Most women wouldn't be able to do it either. I don't know how you managed to find twelve women who could manage to do one, but two in a row is almost out of the question. That's where your build and weight distribution came in."

"So I guess I can keep working."

"As long as you feel up to it," said Elaine. "I know they're going to miss you at the hospital."

"That's what I keep telling them," said Claudia.

Claudia was glad to hear she could keep working because knowing she was leaving all this behind suddenly made all this very dear to her. She loved the hospital and the patients and meeting the new Red Cross nursing cadets coming over from the training center with Dorothy, Frieda and Dante. She got to precept a cadet nurse in Obstetrics once in a while, and she got her own clipboard. It was lots of fun remembering how nervous she was when she was just starting out.

Being full time in obstetrics was great for picking up tips from the old hands that might come in handy someday, and because she had a bun in the oven and looked like an old hand herself, the girls coming in automatically trusted her. In truth, Claudia only realized when she trained her first cadet nurse that she wasn't the new girl anymore and was indeed an old hand. She knew her way around, and it was mostly a happy place, like a game at a county fair where everybody walks out with a prize.

But it had its days too. On one of those, Claudia got called down to the ER to help with a teenage girl brought in after a self-inflicted abortion attempt. It was a bloody mess. She was taking a lot of blood, and losing it, which mostly ended up on Claudia, the other obstetrics nurse Arlene, Dr.

Wolgamont, and the floor. Everybody had their hands in there, but it wasn't doing any good.

After an of hour of that, Dr. Wolgamont looked up and said, "Go get Frieda."

The aide on standby swung out the door. Claudia didn't know what possible good Frieda could do, but she had worked with Wolgamont enough, so she went on trying to plug the hole in the dike with Arlene while Dr. Wolgamont worked at the other end with the transfusion line, the oxygen and hypodermics.

Frieda came in, glanced at Dr. Wolgamont, and paused to size up the situation. Then she stood over Claudia's shoulder to watch what she was doing between the poor girl's legs. "That's good," she said. "Not too much pressure in one place. When you two get tired, change places. What's her name?"

Claudia didn't know. Neither did Arlene.

"Francesca," said Dr. Wolgamont. "She's had twenty-four units, Frieda. I'm just running plasma now."

Frieda took a place at Francesca's head across from the doctor. She bent down with her elbows on the bed and put her face at Francesca's ear, smoothing away the wet hair with her big hands. Claudia had to concentrate on stemming the blood at her end, but she could hear Frieda talking softly. She couldn't hear what Frieda was saying because her voice was so low. It went on for another fifteen or twenty minutes. When she glanced up, she saw Frieda had taken Francesca's hand and was holding it between hers as she talked. She never stopped talking, softly, right at the girl's ear until a smile came over Francesca's face. Frieda must have said something funny because Francesca gave a little laugh. Her eyes were closed against the bright overhead lights, and her head tilted into Frieda.

"That's it," said Dr. Wolgamont.

Frieda patted Francesca's hand, laid it across her chest and stood up with no expression on her face. Arlene had to wipe her eyes with her bloody hands, and Claudia got a clean towel to wipe the blood off Arlene's face. Frieda touched a hand to their backs on her way out of the room.

"Get her cleaned up nice," she said.

When they had Francesca cleaned up and the floor was dry, Dr. Wolgamont went out to tell her parents. Claudia heard the wail of the mother and then the crying. When they came in to see their girl, they didn't even notice Arlene and Claudia in fresh green gowns, standing respectfully to the side.

Claudia kept her head down, but she knew Rivoli's voice and the voice of Angela, his wife, even though she was crying. She didn't know if she should go over to them. Sometimes there's nothing you can do. She just learned that.

Claudia kept her head through the rest of the shift back in obstetrics. Two new babies hit the deck in the last hour, and everybody concerned was joyous and pleased. The old people in Geriatrics would have to do without her visit that night because she just wanted to go home. She held herself together walking home. She only cried over it when she told John what happened. Edgar Lee made himself scarce, so she cried all she wanted, with John's arms around her head. What made her cry most of all was that she didn't know Francesca's name when Frieda asked her. She didn't tell John that part. She was too ashamed.

CHAPTER FIFTY-FOUR

John was first across the Rubicon. He sold both the apartment house and the Frog Shop to Captain Locarno, who was out of the navy and building hotels again. They bumped into each other at the post exchange buying cigarettes, and they started talking business. It turned out they could do each other a favor.

John gave up the logo and patents on his three surfboard designs. Before the contract was finalized, Captain Locarno had a man fly out from California to look over the books. John brought home a set of filing cabinets so they would look more respectable, and Claudia finished moving her records out of shoeboxes and pineapple crates just before the man got to the apartment.

The accounts looked so good that the business went for half a million dollars, with another half million in two years if The Frog Shop had gross sales exceeding ten million. John thought he was taking Captain Locarno to the cleaners, which Claudia pointed out was exactly why she had advised him to steer clear of the business world. Shortly after the contract was signed, the Honolulu papers were buzzing about the new factory proposed on Oahu under the guiding hand of "Buzz" Locarno, the commercial properties mogul. Claudia was pretty sure he'd get insurance this time.

John and Edgar Lee were free to work in their shop for as long as they wanted because Captain Locarno's new wholly owned subsidiary, Frog Shop World, planned to preserve the original shop as a future tourist attraction, complete with a historical marker to be provided by the city of Honolulu. As a special addendum to the contract, John and Edgar Lee retained the right to be compensated for posing as John Ransome and Edgar Lee "Wave Weasel" Wyler in historical reenactments at the site.

Claudia put the money in the stock market. After a brief and shocking discussion with Mr. Berg at Beechworth & Halswig, she realized she was going to have to talk to someone about taxes. It turns out you don't have to go swimming at night to get eaten by something with big teeth. Ninety-one percent, Jesus Christ.

John and Edgar Lee got in a lot more surfing in August. Edgar Lee was waiting to start eleventh grade, and John also considered himself on vacation as well, before entering the servitude of the next twenty years of his life. He never complained or made her feel bad about it, and, if not for that alone, Claudia felt her esteem for him rise every day.

Every night she sat at her kitchen table with him as he typed out his letters. John was good at math, but a bad speller and impatient about looking up words, so Claudia had the dictionary by her and looked up words for him if she wasn't sure. Every morning he and Edgar Lee waited for the mailman before they went off to the shop. There were letters he wrote to get names and addresses, letters he wrote to inquire about jobs, and letters he wrote for applications. So he was waiting for different kinds of replies by day and writing different kinds of requests by night. Claudia made a chart for him to keep it straight.

The one they were waiting for was New London. It was close to Claudia's mom and dad, and John boned up on submarines before he wrote his letter. It took so long to hear back that John thought he was in, but it turned out that sometime in the interim, New London had launched a torpedo that had to travel all the way down the Atlantic coast, go through the Panama Canal, and across the Pacific to get to their mailbox and blow John out of the water. He was so depressed that he took to bed and did not go to the shop that day. Claudia thought it best to leave him alone and went to the market by herself, but by the time she got home, John was up, shaved and showered, dressed, and typing away at another letter.

And thank god for Annette, because after Claudia told her about New London when they had lunch at the French Café on Thursday, she came over with a list of twenty-six more places to try, along with her new electric typewriter with autocorrect. Together, Annette and John banged out twenty-six more letters that night after Claudia went to bed, and two weeks later, a letter came back with a job offer from some place called AEGIS.

Civilian John Calder Ransome was going to be an antimissile radar tracking system engineer, working for the navy. It was something new, and it sounded like part of the reason he got the job was he had stumbled upon AEGIS when no one was supposed to know it existed. A telegram arrived at the same time instructing him not to leave the area, and a special delivery packet followed, full of security clearance papers he had to take over to the navy yard. Pronto.

"I always had a feeling you were going to be responsible for my mysterious disappearance someday," John said.

"So I picked a few folders out of classified," said Annette. "You got a job, didn't you?"

They were having drinks at the Palmetto. It was Claudia's last day at the hospital. The girls threw her a little going-away party after her shift. Then she and John and Edgar Lee had dinner at the Grand Hawaiian. Afterward, Edgar Lee took off in the rattletrap to pick up some girl, and Claudia and John met Annette at the club for a nightcap. John was anxious to see if Annette had been able to find out where AEGIS was.

"They aren't going to blindfold us and put us on a boat, are they, Annette?"

"Anywhere in New England would be fine," said Claudia.

"Well I can't just make it be somewhere, Claudia. You know I'd do anything to make it New England."

"You know where it is then," said John.

"I just found out this morning. It's not New England. I'm sorry Claudia. But it's close. It's New Jersey."

"New Jersey?"

John put his arm around Claudia right away. She was close to tears.

"New Jersey is fine," he said.

"Have you ever been there?"

"No."

"Have you ever been there, Annette?

"No."

"Does anyone we know come from New Jersey?"

They were looking back and forth at each other trying to think, when Mr. Anthony paused at their table while making his rounds of the floor. He had something under his arm.

"I would like to give you this, Mrs. Ransome. It's from all of us at the club." He presented a large, framed photo of the Hula Girls on stage. "It's the same one the Smithsonian selected. The girls all signed it."

It was a publicity photo, a really great shot of the Hulas, and it was framed so tastefully that it looked like the portrait of a champion Olympic team. Claudia gushed over it—sincerely too. Being back in the club, and chatting with the old-hand Hulas as they came over to the table between shows, reminded Claudia of the high purpose to which she had devoted her work in the Hula Girls, her accomplishments on stage and behind the scenes and, most of all, the satisfaction she'd gotten from doing the best she could for her girls. The only trouble was, she didn't want to take the past along.

"When last we spoke, I don't believe your destination had as yet been determined," said Mr. Anthony.

"Oh, that just changed, Mr. Anthony," said John. "Miss Anisinelli says we're going to New Jersey."

"How very fortunate for you both," he said. "And what a coincidence." Mr. Anthony placed a hand over his heart, just under the white carnation. "I'm from Bayonne. I was in business there."

That was all Claudia needed to hear. They were at the hatcheck room getting their wraps. Claudia wasn't teary, just a little down. Her heart was so set on New England, anywhere in New England. It was where she was going to have her baby—in a house in New England. Everything had been going so well.

John draped Annette's jacket over her shoulders, and Claudia heard him whisper in her ear.

"Thank you, Annette. Thank you."

He said it like she had saved his life. Claudia suspected John had been talking to Annette behind her back about you-know-who's psychology. Just because she was so firm about getting into a real house, a home of their own in the real America before she had the baby. Was that so crazy?

CHAPTER FIFTY-FIVE

The wooden marker was split and lying flat on the ground with grass growing through it. There was a square stone in its place, a little thing that was not marble or granite, and Claudia brushed it off and went back to the taxi to get a screwdriver from Takeo. Getting down where she could scratch into the face of the stone was quite a feat because she was eight months pregnant.

"I'm just writing your name down, Mary Ann," she said. "I want Annette to be able to find you. You'll like her. She said she'll bring you things I send you. We're leaving in a few days. On the boat to California, and then Edgar Lee wants to drive across the country. He's a good driver, Mary Ann, so you don't have to worry about him. We're going to buy a station wagon. They have some nice models now. I saw them in *Life*. They're nothing like the cars we used to work on in the shop."

That seemed so long ago, and it was. Almost fourteen years. Cars had changed so much. She wondered what happened to Billings. She would be breaking for lunch right about now sitting on the bench outside the shop with the tomato plants. Mr. Knight would be back in the parts room in the dark, eating his sandwich, and Mary Ann would be alive. Everything would be different. She wouldn't be a registered nurse. She wouldn't be married to John. She might be married to Billings if she could have straightened him out. She wondered what that would have been like. She could have had eight kids by now. He would have shaped up for that. But she wouldn't have Edgar Lee. Maybe it's good only having one life. You can't just walk away from the one that isn't going so great. You have to live with the one you have and make the best of it.

"I'm sorry, Mary Ann," she said. "I don't know what I'm saying."

Claudia tried to shift around to her other side and use her left hand, but that didn't work either. She sat up with the stone between her legs and used both hands on the screwdriver, going at the face sideways. She scraped away, up and down, up and down, until she got tired and had to rest.

"If I have a girl, I'm going to name her Mary Ann so I can say your name a million times every day. And I'm going to teach her how to take care of her hair. I know you never paid any attention to me, but you'll see how nice her hair is, and then you'll know I only bothered you so much about it because I knew you could have such lovely hair. But you know everything now, don't you? I bet you even know what I'm thinking. You must understand everything now. I'm so sorry what happened, Mary Ann, you know I am. And I'm sorry I was so cruel to you and made you be a whore."

Then she bent over and looked at the face of the stone. There were plenty of scratches, but no groove. "This is for the birds, Mary Ann. We're going to do something else."

Claudia got up, dusted off, straightened out her dress, and walked back to the taxi. Takeo took her around to the Palmetto. None of the Hulas was in yet, so she shot the breeze with Max and the new costume designer, and then she went up to talk to Mr. Anthony.

The next morning Claudia picked up some fresh paperwork at the Palmetto, dropped it off at city hall, and was out at the grave in time to meet the man with the digging machine and the undertaker. An old priest and a little retinue from the church arrived in two cars before they got started, and then the carpenters pulled in with a lumber truck. A catering truck came from the club with coffee and donuts. Two girls Claudia didn't know in show bras and grass skirts got out and put up advertising signs for the Palmetto around the truck and served coffee and donuts. The boys loved that. She had to hand it to Mr. Anthony for promotion. The paperwork looked pretty real too.

Claudia did not know if Mary Ann had received extreme unction, so the retinue helped the priest into his vestments, and he presided over the exhumation. Then the undertaker wheeled a new coffin out of the hearse. Claudia had to turn away for that part, but Takeo told her when it was over. After the church contingent left, the carpenters took over and put together a good-looking shipping container around the coffin and forklifted it to the bed of the truck.

Claudia and Takeo followed them through town and down to the docks to see it hoisted onboard. It took all day, but so would scratching Mary Ann's name into the damn stone with a screwdriver. If John and Edgar Lee could have the rattletrap and their FrogDaddy boards, she could have her best friend. She didn't have to say much about it to John. He just raised his eyebrows a little.

On the last day, Claudia went to say goodbye to Jack. All the crosses were the same in the military cemetery, and there were so many of them that she had to go to the office and ask. The navy man there showed her the big chart and looked up the name. "Wyler, Wyler," he said, running one finger down the list in his binder.

This was the last time she would be Claudia Wyler to anybody. She did not belong to Lieutenant Jack Wyler anymore. She belonged to another man. She was Claudia Ransome. Jack was gone, and Claudia Wyler, for that matter, was gone too.

She wondered why she felt so differently about Mary Ann. No one belonged to any one with Mary Ann, they just belonged together. That was different. She was glad she found the hugging ivory polar bears. Mary Ann was probably getting killed at the same time she was paying for the bears in the little shop. Claudia tried not to think about it. She would just look after their bears and try to do a better job than she did looking after Mary Ann.

When she got to Jack's cross, she wanted to say something complimentary about it, but it looked just like all the others. It was distinguished only by his name, Lieutenant Jack Wyler, and dates chiseled into it. Claudia sat down in the grass and looked at the ground in front of the stone. Final resting place. The final resting place of the kiss at cotillion in the Green Room at Sweet Briar. The final resting place of taking showers on the cement patch behind the little white house. The final resting place of leaning over coffee and Chesterfields to concentrate on *Mr. District Attorney*.

How can you ever vow to forsake all others when you remember so much about the first one you belonged to? And what was finally resting there from all that Jack once was? The navy, other girls, the Roadmaster, and what she didn't know when he took every excuse to go back to town at night. His private life was none of her business. He might as well have said that.

Jack tried so hard to live with her. She tried hard too. She could have been the perfect navy wife. What happened? That was a very large question. Maybe she and Jack wouldn't know each other anymore. Claudia tried to put her head down on her knees, but she was too big around the middle, so she just left her legs out straight, leaned back, propped herself up on her elbows, and looked into the empty blue sky, the same color his eyes were, now gone from this earth. No further thought rose up, and no words came to mind. Claudia got to her feet and brushed herself off.

"I wasn't much, was I, Jack?"

Claudia stood in front of Jack's cross, waited a moment for the emptiness to clear, and walked back to Takeo, listening to the silence that denotes consent.

Edgar Lee stayed out all night. Since the rattletrap was dry-docked in the hold of the freighter, some girl in a snazzy sports car dropped him and his SuperJazz FrogDaddy off in the driveway. Claudia heard them come in a little before dawn and got up to look out the second-floor window. It wasn't really spying on Edgar Lee, just checking on him, but it was hard not to notice the little blondie behind the wheel, who was definitely not his girlfriend, Laurie,—and the way Edgar Lee was kissing her. Holy Moses.

He said he had been up to Waimea with his buddies and slept out on the beach. John wasn't up yet, and Claudia was making Edgar Lee his favorite, scrambled eggs, fried spam, and cinnamon buns with lots of butter.

"Were there girls there?"

"A couple," said Edgar Lee.

"They didn't stay after dark, did they?"

"Nah."

"Was Laurie there?"

"Nah."

"Who was the girl who dropped you off? I saw her drive away. She's cute."

"I don't know. Just some girl."

"Does Laurie know about her?"

"How should I know?"

Claudia finished up at the stove, leaned back against it to get the weight off her feet, and watched Edgar Lee wolf down the scrambled eggs, spam, and cinnamon buns all at the same time, never looking up at her. It was the same face she'd seen on a hundred young sailor boys at the club, walking out of the dark corridor in back, keeping their eyes down as they tried to blend back into the crowd. Maybe it was an unfair advantage she had, but she could keep it under wraps.

"I'd better tell you before we get to America, Edgar Lee," she said. "You're going to have less trouble on your hands if you remember something. One girl at a time."

"Yeah, yeah. I know."

"You aren't stringing along two girls, are you?"

"Geez, why am I getting the third degree, Mom?"

"You were out all night, Edgar Lee."

"It was just me and my friends."

"Then where did the cute girl in the red Fiat come from?"

"Ah—"

That wouldn't cut any ice on the stand with Mr. District Attorney. The flimsy alibi. The next questions would shoot it full of holes. Claudia was so pleased that she was finally getting the hang of radio crime drama. But she did not want to let Edgar Lee know she was onto him. He was becoming a real person, and he would have secrets. Someday he would tell them as funny stories or confessions, but it sure as hell wasn't going to be to his mother. Meanwhile, it was just another good reason to skip town.

Takeo pulled up just before noon, and a man from Captain Locarno's office came around to pick up the keys to the apartment house and take a look around. John and Edgar Lee packed the bags in the taxi. Claudia sat in the wicker chair in the driveway and asked if they remembered everything, and then they piled in with a few bags on their laps, including one on Takeo's, and took off for the pier, departure time 4 p.m.

It wasn't exactly the Queen Mary. It was an old prewar freighter that had been used as a troop ship for the boys coming home and God knows what else. It smelled like a barn and was under the flag of some country Claudia never heard of. Nobody spoke English. From way up on deck, a group of scrappy merchant seamen pointed to a rope ladder on the side of the hull but when they saw Claudia get out of the taxi, they all laughed. They made gestures to wait, so John, Edgar Lee, Claudia, and Takeo stood below, looking up at the paint flaking off the hull and down to the water lapping between the ship and the dock, with cigarette butts floating on top.

Annette pulled up in her car and got out with a bottle of champagne.

"I'm not going up that thing in these heels," she said, looking at the rope ladder.

Presently, a boom swung around to their side and lowered a cargo net with a couple of intensely tattooed sea dogs hanging on. So the boys climbed the rope ladder, and the baggage with Claudia and Annette went up in the cargo net. It was fun. It would have been worth having her baby in the cargo net just to tell a good story like that.

Since it wasn't the Queen Mary, Annette was worried about getting stuck on the ship, so she started the goodbyes almost as soon as John popped the cork on the champagne. They could only find two glasses, so they just passed the bottle around, and time got away from them. Suddenly there was a toot, toot on the horn, and everyone ran topside to get Annette and Takeo off the ship. The men on the dock were already taking rope off the cleats and casting off.

John and Edgar Lee shook hands all around. Claudia and Annette kissed each other and hugged, and Claudia hugged Takeo, and kissed him, and promised to put the monkey family in her bedroom for good luck. She kissed Annette one last time through the rope of the cargo net before the boom swung out over the side, and then down went Annette and Takeo, with a little scream from Annette.

The ship swung around and made for the open sea with an enormous prop wash surging up from its broad, rusty stern. Claudia waved and waved until Annette disappeared into the island and the island was swallowed by the horizon and the horizon at last gave way to darkness and stars. Goodbye. Always tears and kisses. Goodbye.

For eight days they looked at the ocean, ate with the crew, and learned a few words in some language. Edgar Lee got to steer the boat every day and said he got a good feel for the rudder and what she could do. Just the same, Claudia wondered why it took eight days to get to San Francisco. A typhoon came out of nowhere one afternoon when the captain and first officer were stuck behind a jammed bulkhead door below. Nobody could get to the bridge. Edgar Lee was at the helm. With his instincts of being a kid on a board going up against big waves, and with John adding his weight to the wheel, the ship came through fine. After that, it was nothing but Annapolis and the navy for Edgar Lee.

Claudia was not worried about having the baby at sea. When she stopped to think about it, she had delivered a good many of the next generation of Honolulu. She was a nurse, and she knew what to do. It was the house, not the boat or the baby, that was on her mind for most of the trip.

The personnel department at AEGIS put John in touch with a Realtor in New Jersey, and they bought a house out of a brochure that came in the mail. They liked the pictures of a big, old stone house on an acre with a carriage house in back. The stone chimney had 1909 carved into the top, and almost out of view in the side yard, they could just see something that looked like a palm tree. The front had stone pillars and a long porch. It was unanimous by secret ballot between the three of them, and John wired the agent $16,000 the day after the brochure came. It was a lot of money, and Claudia didn't want the people in New Jersey to know they were the kind of people who would pay full price for a house, in cash, because she didn't want to get off on the wrong foot. But she did not want to take the chance of losing it. Besides, it was supposed to be a quiet little Quaker town, and you probably had to be pretty bad to get off on the wrong foot with Quakers.

In San Francisco they spent two nights in a hotel while John arranged the transport of Mary Ann, the surfboards, four trunks, and the rattletrap to New Jersey. Then Claudia had to tell John that she'd never make it across country by car. Edgar Lee wasn't happy, but John pulled him aside and explained to him that those are the breaks.

The consolation prize was a TWA Super Constellation to Philadelphia, with stops in Chicago and Atlanta. Claudia and Edgar Lee had never been on an airplane. The takeoffs and landings were exciting, but the hours between were like sitting in the living room on a rainy day if you lived in Tibet and only saw clouds when you looked out the window. Edgar Lee didn't notice because he was trying to make time with the stewardesses.

The TWA stewardesses looked so trim in their little outfits. Edgar Lee was tanned and had that surfer-boy hair in his eyes. They must have thought he was like the wild boy of Borneo, but they weren't much older than he was, so maybe it was alluring to them. It was the first time Claudia caught herself saying, "That's the younger generation for you."

They landed in Philadelphia at seven thirty in the morning with everything planned out. Edgar Lee went to baggage claim, John called the Realtor lady and got her out of bed to meet them at the house with the key in forty minutes, and Claudia held a cab outside of arrivals. It was going to be tight.

The Realtor lady was parked on the street, standing by the car, right on time. When the cab pulled into the driveway, John shouted out the window, "Front door! Front door!"

The poor lady caught on when she saw him help Claudia out of the back seat, and she ran up the sidewalk in her heels and blue satin pleated peg-leg skirt and took the front steps like a mountain goat. John was right behind, bent over with Claudia in a fireman's carry.

"Master bedroom! Master bedroom!" he shouted.

Up the stairs they went. There wasn't a stick of furniture in the place. John put Claudia down in the middle of the floor in the bedroom. It was so empty, there was an echo in the room. Claudia asked the real estate lady if she would be so kind as to go home and bring back some scissors, a pot to boil water, and a couple of towels. That's all a broodmare needed. Claudia got ready to do her stuff.

By the time Edgar Lee's cab pulled in with the suitcases, baby Mary Ann was lying on Claudia's tummy on the floor of the master bedroom. A couple of pushes was all it took. She didn't tear much, so she was lucky. All she had to do was cut the cord and wait for the rest to come out. Mary Ann was a real squawker. She started crying after John gave her the little smack on the bottom, but she wouldn't knock it off, and Claudia realized she had to stop hypnotizing herself with all the love there could possibly be in her eyes, looking at that little thing. So she pulled herself together and got her bosoms going on their first real job. John went to get Claudia her Chesterfields because she really needed a smoke, and that was always something she could do while she was doing something else. He lit one up for her and one for himself and sat down to watch little Mary Ann nursing.

"This would make a great ad for Chesterfield, wouldn't it?" said Claudia.

John started at AEGIS, about two miles away, and Edgar Lee got in on the second half of eleventh grade at the public high school. Mrs. Clark, the real estate lady, turned out to be a gem with getting help to come in, buying furniture, choosing colors, and playing around with decor. The monkey family and the ivory bears went on the top of Claudia's dresser, where she could see them from the bed and talk to them in her thoughts, without John needing to know everything they meant to her.

When it was warm enough, Claudia put little Mary Ann in a big wooden bassinet on the front porch and sat beside her in one of the old cedar chairs that were there when they moved in. She closed her eyes because she wanted to imagine it was the past at its worst parts, and when she opened her eyes, she would be magically transported to where she was now and be so amazed at how things had worked out.

She opened her eyes slowly, first looking down at the gray, freshly painted porch, then rising to little Mary Ann in her bassinet, to the stone columns and the white, wooden railing between them, then to the boxwoods and azaleas showing over the railing, and finally to the grass of the front lawn and the wide, quiet street, overhung by old maples that were not quite leafing out but green at all their ends. When she wrote to her mom, she would try to remember all the things that made her so happy.

It was March. There were robins in the front yard, and it was America.

A SAMPLER

Mary Ann came to rest in the Catholic churchyard in town, and every Sunday Claudia went to sit on her stone and tell her everything that had happened that week. It reminded her of when she and Mary Ann had taken their smoke breaks on the back steps of the Grand Hawaiian and watched the well-heeled pull into the parking lot. Now it was churchyard and Catholics.

When the Catholics came out of their last mass and left, Claudia covered her head with her scarf and went inside to light candles and leave money, just like Mary Ann would have done, and she wasn't resentful about it like she was when Mary Ann was alive. That was because she had her own sins to pay for now. She had killed her own baby. Jack was dead because he came home to give her the gun to defend herself. If Jack didn't count, Joe Johnson certainly did, and Mary Ann did, and maybe there were more, who knows? She prayed that Mary Ann knew how much she loved her and how sorry she was about what happened. Mary Ann would have loved the baby, and it gave Claudia comfort to think Mary Ann could see how well she was taking care of her namesake.

Claudia had two more babies after Mary Ann, each one roughly two years after the last. She named them Annette and Little Claudia. They all had white skin and freckles and lovely red hair.

"It's like they came from Ireland or something," Claudia said to herself as she peered down into the viewer window of her old Kodak box camera. "Annette, stop that," she said. "Claudia, get back in front of Mary Ann. Annette! If I have to come over there, somebody's getting a spanking."

The girls were lined up in their little white dresses, with their little white gloves and shiny black shoes, for a Sunday picture in front of the flowering dogwood tree. It was a pretty spring morning before Easter, which reminded Claudia she had to get them new hats.

"Edgar Lee is making faces at us, Mom," said Mary Ann. "He's behind your back so you can't see."

"Stop making faces, Edgar Lee. You're a grown up. Annette, move in a little. There. All right, everybody, hold still. One, two, three—cheese."

Claudia wanted to try again for a boy. John said it didn't matter so much to him because they had one, Edgar Lee, who was already housebroken and road tested, but he expressed his willingness to take on the job.

"By appointment only," he said with a tired smile after a hard day with the boys at AEGIS.

Claudia made a Tom Collins for John when he came home every night and made an old-fashioned for herself. She always planned a little time to get out of the kitchen before dinner, to sit together in the living room by the stone fireplace while the girls set the table in the dining room. She had fun with John in bed for a few months, but it turned out that her period had flown the coop, this time for good, and that was that. It didn't matter so much, really. When you get married late you take your chances. She had Edgar Lee, and he would always be hers, and she didn't have to think she was about to get killed with a machete to realize how much she loved him. That could happen under ordinary circumstances as well as bad ones, and she liked ordinary better.

That's what she liked about her life, how ordinary it was, doing what everybody else did. The husbands went to work somewhere every day, getting their buffaloes, and the wives stayed home to keep the lid on everything. On Saturday mornings, the dads worked in the yard in their old army khakis or navy bell-bottoms from the war. The moms hung out laundry in the backyards or talked over fences about their new Westinghouse dryers or their new Frigidaires. The neighborhood teemed with kids climbing trees, playing marbles and hopscotch, skipping rope, and roaming all over town on their bikes, getting out to the woods and meadows around town, damming up creeks, and digging tunnels. Everybody knew to be home by dinnertime.

The milkman came very early every day, picked up the empty bottles and dropped off two or four more in the metal rack at the side door. Claudia couldn't wait to pull the paper caps off the bottles and lick the cream at the top off her little finger.

It turned out they had things in the real America that Claudia never would have expected to see in Hawaii. Iron-on blue jean patches! They had glue on one side so all she had to do was iron them on to the worn out knees. Mary Ann and Little Claudia were tomboys, so she used a lot of them for a few years. Another great idea was Green Stamps, which they gave for every purchase at the supermarket. She got the iron for free with her S&H Green Stamps, and—will wonders never cease?—when she went to the market, all she had to do was step on the black mat in front and the door opened all by itself. No one would have thought of that in Hawaii. There weren't enough doors.

Edgar Lee went down to the shore every weekend in the rattletrap and started wowing the girls with his SuperJazz FrogDaddy board. He said there weren't any big waves, so he worked on finesse and got pretty good at amazing moves. Before long, the Wave Weasel became legendary among teenage girls from Manasquan to Cape May. John and Claudia bought a beach house on Long Beach Island. They went down on weekends through September every summer.

Edgar Lee took up snow skiing the first year they were in New Jersey. He went up to the Poconos with his buddies and skied Vermont and New Hampshire, Colorado and Utah. Claudia started noticing letters in girl handwriting coming from everywhere he went. He was senior class president, played all the sports, and kept his grades up. He didn't like being tied down, so he played the field and was nice to the girls who weren't pretty and took them for spins in the rattletrap.

Sometimes he was up late studying, and Claudia made him hot Bosco. They sat at the kitchen table and talked about if God existed or not, and the meaning of life, and morality, and overpopulation. Sometimes the conversation drifted into life in the old days at the Strickland, living in one room together, and Claudia wondered if she should tell him the truth on one of those nights. Thinking about what might happen made her afraid and shaky whenever she was getting up the nerve, and she chain-smoked her Chesterfields so fast that Edgar Lee thought she was cracking up and sent her up to bed.

The summer after junior year, a letter came from Mrs. Preston about Petey. He was fourteen now, so Edgar Lee flew out to Hawaii by himself to see him. He had a good time walking around with Petey and stayed a week with the Prestons in their little white house. He went back and forth to the beach in Takeo's cab and got in some big wave riding.

"Petey's fine," he said when Claudia picked him up at the airport in Philadelphia. "He's just old. They give him a lot of pills wrapped in cheese every day."

Edgar Lee got into Annapolis. John wrote a moving testament to his old classmate, Jack Wyler, class of 1940, killed in action at Pearl Harbor, and Claudia thought that cinched it. Edgar Lee was on cloud nine and surfed his brains out, up and down the Jersey and Carolina coasts for a few weeks, tooling around in the rattletrap and sleeping out on the beaches. In July he reported for Plebe Summer. John and Claudia drove him down in the Rambler. He brought a lot of stuff with him, against John's advice, and sure as shootin', it all came back with John and Claudia. At the gate, the guard, who had a lot of stripes on his sleeves, said Edgar Lee would not need anything from home. Then he looked at Edgar Lee's suit and tie and his surfer-boy hair and said, "Get out of the car, plebe."

It looked kind of ominous to Claudia.

When Edgar Lee came home for Christmas, he was a wreck. He broke down in tears at the kitchen table when he told how bad it was, and he showed Claudia the prescription pills he was taking for a pre-ulcer. He didn't want to go back. Mary Ann lit out for the playroom, and little Annette stood up in the bassinet and stared at Edgar Lee, crying. Then she started crying too. Edgar Lee slept almost twenty hours straight the first night at home.

"Well, he's obviously not going back," said Claudia, "so what are we going to do?" In her mind, it was final.

John was finishing up the dinner dishes at the sink, and Claudia was at the table with her Chesterfields and coffee.

"Are you listening to me?"

"I'm listening," he said.

"It's a shame he's wasted half a year."

"He didn't waste half a year."

"Yes, he did, John. August, September, October, November, December. Okay, five months. I'm sure he tried. You know how hard he tries. I don't want him going back there. You can see what it did to him. Those pills he's taking are pretty strong stuff. I know. I'm a nurse. An eighteen-year-old should not be getting an ulcer."

John came over and sat down across from Claudia and took his pack of Luckys out of the breast pocket, going as slowly as he could, the way he always did when she got excited. It was so annoying.

"I wish you'd take your tie off, John. I don't know how you can stand it all day."

"I just forget it's there," he said, pulling off his tie and opening up the top buttons of his white shirt. "You cut me off, dear."

"Well, what were you going to say, John? I don't think there's anything to discuss."

John lit his Lucky and settled back in the kitchen chair, rolling up his sleeves.

"I was going to say he hasn't wasted five months, he got through five months. And not just anywhere. He got through five months at the Naval Academy. That's a big accomplishment. Now he's got to go back and finish the year."

"Oh, don't be ridiculous, John. He could be a perfectly happy college boy anywhere else. He's bright and hard-working, and he can have girlfriends at college. He's always had girlfriends. He's a fish out of water at the academy, and it's making him sick. It's perfectly clear to me. It was a mistake. He knows it was a mistake too, and we have to accept it."

"Don't get excited."

"I'm not excited," she said, lowering her voice. "I don't even know why we're discussing it. He could go to Penn, or Princeton. They'd take him in a second. He could have a normal college life, and if he still wants the navy, he can join up later."

John was very quiet and looked at his burning Lucky as he tapped it over the ashtray.

"Annapolis was the only place he wanted to go and the only school he applied to. If he drops out now, he won't be the same boy he was before. Even if he goes somewhere else, he'll be a failure in his mind. He can get over an ulcer, but he won't get over thinking he's a failure, maybe for the rest of his life. I know you don't want to see that happen to him. So I'm going to ask you to stay out of it now. I'll talk to him."

Claudia mulled it over quietly. Why did everybody think they had to knock other people down to size? She knew that was going to happen at that damn place the moment they dropped him off at the gate.

"All right. But I want you to ask him what *he* wants to do."

"No point in that," said John. "He wants to go back to high school, and he can't do that."

John looked into her eyes as he said that, and Claudia knew it was time to let go of Edgar Lee. If he had to be talked to, it was not the kind of talk she could do. Edgar Lee needed to be talked to by a man. John had done it before. She trusted his judgment. Everything would be all right.

John talked to Edgar Lee, man-to-man, by the cedar tree in the back yard. Claudia kept Mary Ann away and peeked out the window. John was standing very close to Edgar Lee with his head down, and he was tapping one finger against the flattened palm of his other hand. Edgar Lee stood at attention in front of him. All through Christmas break, Edgar Lee stood at attention, sat at attention at the dinner table, and walked around at attention. It was so drilled into him. His hair was shaved off and everything he said ended with "sir" or "ma'am."

Edgar Lee went back to Annapolis and took his licks. John drove him down in the Rambler, and Claudia stayed home with the girls. When she asked John what he had said to Edgar Lee, it was pretty simple. He said he just told Edgar Lee, one Annapolis man to another, that all he had to do was get through the first year. But it couldn't have been just that. They were out there at the cedar tree a long time. Claudia was beginning to see what a tough, smart man she had. She never would have thought it back in Hawaii. She remembered the only time John and Andrew were side by side, at the Brown Derby, with Annette. She would have put her money on Andrew any day.

At AEGIS, John Ransome ran herd on some brilliant but awkward young men who worked under him. He brought them home for dinner all the time. Claudia didn't know how the work could be so top secret because the installation they worked in was called the battleship in the cornfield by just about everyone in South Jersey. It was a life-size mock-up of the deck and control tower of a battleship, placed right in the middle of a cornfield, with US Navy written all over it. John was always flying to Washington for conferences. He had lunch at the White House with President Eisenhower one time.

They joined the field club and played tennis and went to dances there. John bought a little sailboat and joined a yacht club on the Delaware River, which was only a ten-minute drive, and went out on the water by himself to get away from it all every so often. He mowed the lawn in the summer. In the fall he raked leaves and burned them in little fires on the street or in the backyard like everybody else, and in the winter he shoveled snow. In the spring he sat on the back porch with Little Claudia in his lap while he drank his iced tea, smoked his Luckys, and watched Mary Ann and Annette blow dandelion balls at each other.

Claudia had her routines too. She worked at the hospital in Mount Holly every Thursday on the geriatrics floor. She had coffee with Mrs. Bailey next door on the right or Mrs. Mercer on the left after seeing the men off to work and the kids off to school. One of them always had a baby at home to fuss over. In the fall she put away the summer clothes in the cedar chest in the attic, and in spring she took out the summer clothes and put the winter clothes back in. Mary Ann's hand-me-downs went on to Annette and ended their days on Little Claudia. It was really hard keeping track of whose clothes were whose on wash days. Claudia was very happy with her new Maytag washer. She liked the ads in *Life* and *Good Housekeeping*, where the family of thirteen was lined up beside their Maytag. That poor lady.

The rattletrap blew a head gasket one day in Ship Bottom, so Claudia went down in the station wagon with a tow bar and brought it home. It had a lot of other things wrong with it, and the parts had to come from England, so it took two months to get it out of the garage. Claudia brought little Mary Ann's bassinet into the carriage house when she worked on it, and she explained everything she was doing as she went along. Little Mary Ann didn't understand a thing she said—but neither would John or Edgar Lee. She had never worked on a British car before, but she figured it out in no time. It was just a little lonely when she remembered dreaming of her and Edgar Lee working together on their cars in a barn in New England. Nevertheless, it was such a good father-son project that she let on to the Baileys and the Mercers next door that John and Edgar Lee were the ones making all the noise in the garage every Friday night, working on the famous Austin-Healey.

A few times a year they went down to Alabama to see John's parents, and a few times a year they went to Connecticut to see Claudia's mom and dad. What a relief it was when Little Claudia was big enough, and they didn't have to lug the big wooden bassinet on and off the train. John took it up to the attic and covered it with a sheet to wait for grandchildren. It would probably be Little Claudia who got married first. Mary Ann had a mind of her own, and Annette was persnickety. Little Claudia was just right. She was sweet and pliable. That's what Claudia's mom said about the girls, and Claudia believed it was probably true. They talked on the phone all the time.

Claudia joined the PTA, and when the other moms found out she had experience in show business, they put her in charge of Little Claudia's fourth-grade class play. It was a real challenge because they had to come up with something with singing and dancing, where everyone in the class could play a part. Claudia wound up writing the play by herself because no one else wanted to do it. For the dancing, she was pleased to find a man who had done some dancing during the war as part of the USO, raising money for war bonds. After she found out he was a childless widower and had lunch with him a few times, she wrote a long letter to Annette.

The play was called Hula Girls and Sailor Boys, and everyone had a part as either a Hula Girl or a Sailor Boy, depending on what gender you thought you were. Little Claudia was chubby and would have fit the part of rising to become leader of the Hula Girls, but she was too shy. Instead, Claudia picked a mousey little thing who said she wanted to try, and boy, did she bring the house down. Everyone had fun, and the play was a big success. Little Claudia wore her grass skirt around the house every day until it fell apart and her panties showed. Claudia remembered what that was like.

Edgar Lee stuck it out through thick and thin and graduated from Annapolis. It was a big day for Claudia too because she finally got her picture in *Life* magazine, on the last page of "*Life* Goes to an Annapolis Graduation." It was just after the midshipmen toss their hats in the air. Claudia rushed onto the parade ground before anyone else because she saw exactly where Edgar Lee's hat was, and the photographer from *Life* caught her from behind, bending over the pile of hats, with her slip showing.

She reminded herself that the camera always adds ten pounds, but she didn't really care. She was expecting Little Claudia at the time—so there was ten pounds right off the bat. She didn't even care about getting in *Life* magazine. She was so happy for Edgar Lee. He was going off for his year in the fleet on a destroyer in the Pacific. He said he was going to visit Petey and

Takeo, and look up Pinkie at the Palmetto club when he had shore leave in Honolulu. Edgar Lee was a grown man and a naval officer, and if Mr. Anthony hadn't lost his touch for recruiting gorgeous tomatoes, and Edgar Lee wanted a Hula Girl, well, she didn't have to know about it, did she?

Claudia sat on the beach behind the house on Long Beach Island the night they got back from the Annapolis graduation. It had been a long day. Edgar Lee was on the night train to Vermont for a few days to see a girl named Jenny. Then he was going to San Diego to meet his new ship. Mary Ann and Annette were tucked in and fast asleep. John was out on the deck with his iced tea and last smoke, looking at the stars and ocean. She was eight months pregnant with Little Claudia.

John left her alone for a little while every night when they were on Long Beach Island because she had told him she liked taking time to think about her life. He did not seem to be worried by that. She just liked sitting in sand still warm from the day, looking out at the dark with the waves coming in, the quiet, then the rumbling of a big one, and the whoosh of it running up the sand to her toes, and then quiet again for a few moments before the next one. But sometimes she really did think about her life and how lucky it turned out that she had married so well.

Claudia did not always know what John was thinking these days, but sometimes she saw on his face the same look she had seen on the face of the old man at the French Café years ago when she and Annette were going to meet with Captain Locarno. The way the old man was looking at his old girl. One person who loves you best. It's worth the price of admission, all by itself.

She dug her toes into the sand and felt good and peaceful, and lucky too, to have found a place for herself, taking care of John and the children and the old people at the hospital. She had held up by the ankles so many babies on their first day and whispered into the ears of so many old ones on their last day and made some of them smile.

All those spoonfuls, one at a time, and wiping spills with corners of bibs. All the baths she had given, all the bottoms she had wiped, all the putting to bed and all the numberless stories she had read aloud, and the stories she listened to. John told stories she had heard a hundred times before. That was just part of being an old married couple. Little Mary Ann confided her dreams or brimmed over with tales of what happened at school. The old people at the hospital told stories not so different from her own, of being a kid, coming of age, going off to college, going to war, and living to fight another day. It did not seem to her that anyone was any wiser for the age they were, young or old.

From the old people, the idea she was getting was that the past comes down to what you remember. But she was too young for that, and her past included so much she was trying to forget. It was that awkward stage when you remember everything. Sometimes it feels like standing up to your waist in the ocean, turning around as the waves crash into you. Joy, grief, happiness, sorrow. The big ones can hit you hard and, if you're still standing, you plant your feet and get ready because you know there's another one coming.

The coast of France was out there in the dark, straight across from where Claudia was sitting in the sand, but she felt like imagining everything turned around, as if it were the Pacific before her and she was looking westward toward Hawaii, imagining Edgar Lee's destroyer coming in under the bluffs, where the little white houses were. She remembered hanging laundry on the clothesline and remembered stopping to watch the towers, turrets, and antennas of the navy ships passing, so long ago.

Claudia lit her last Chesterfield for the night and blew the smoke up to the stars. There were so many of them, and the sky was so black. When a wave broke, a white line of surf ran across its entire length as it made its way to shore. She thanked God for Edgar Lee, and John, and her two girls, and the new one coming, the stone house with 1909 carved in the chimney, and her old people at the hospital. The Big Dipper was right over her head. The handle was almost straight up in the sky and the bowl was tipping over. It was exactly the way she felt. Her life had filled up without her knowing it, and the time had come when nothing was left but loving and giving and pouring herself out.

THE END

HONORABLE MENTION

Annette Anisinelli came to New Jersey after receiving Claudia's letter. She returned to Hawaii for her honeymoon and went back every year on vacation. Finally married and freed up from the rigors of dating, Annette devoted herself to exercise. Her series of books on the subject included the popular titles *Exercise with Annette, Slim Down with Annette,* and *Annette's Guide to the Psychology of Weight Loss.* Annette remained best friends with Claudia, and they had lunch together every Tuesday.

Billings Sterrin served fifteen years for the death of his father under a plea agreement of involuntary manslaughter. While in prison in California, he studied ornithology in the prison library. A legal assistant who had worked with his defense attorney fell in love with him, moved to California, and brought him bird books. They got married the day he left prison and moved back to Hawaii, where Billings became the celebrated "Bird Man of Hawaii." He was instrumental in getting protections for the nene and lobbied for its designation as the official bird when Hawaii became a state. He published several books on Asian ornithology and served on the board of the Audubon Society for twenty years.

Mr. Anthony continued to run the Palmetto and became involved in beauty pageant work. He was Master of Ceremonies for the Miss America Pageant in Atlantic City three years in a row and was the first to sing "Here she comes, Miss America." When Claudia saw him on their new television set, she could hardly believe her eyes.

Lawrence "Larry" Alderman left Hawaii shortly after the Grand Hawaiian renovated the kitchen. He returned home to Mississippi, where he married his hometown sweetheart and worked a small farm in the backcountry. He wrote up his dishwashing days for the *New Yorker,* and his first non-fiction book, *Wartime Sketches,* won the National Book Award. His first novel, *Days of Rain,* was on the *New York Times* Best Sellers list for twenty-six weeks. He followed with *The Wounded Passion, Bring Down the Mountain, Leaf of a Severed Branch,* and *Eveline Unwanted.* He won the Pulitzer for his three-volume masterpiece, *Neptune,* a generational saga of a negro sharecropper family. He was lauded by critics everywhere as a leader in the Southern literary renaissance. Claudia read all his books and thought she recognized herself in *Leaf of a Severed Branch* in the character of Helen.

Printed in the USA
CPSIA information can be obtained
at www.ICGtesting.com
LVHW040201260923
759347LV00012B/62